HANS CHRISTIAN ANDERSEN

Fairy Tales

HANS CHRISTIAN ANDERSEN
by George H. Jones

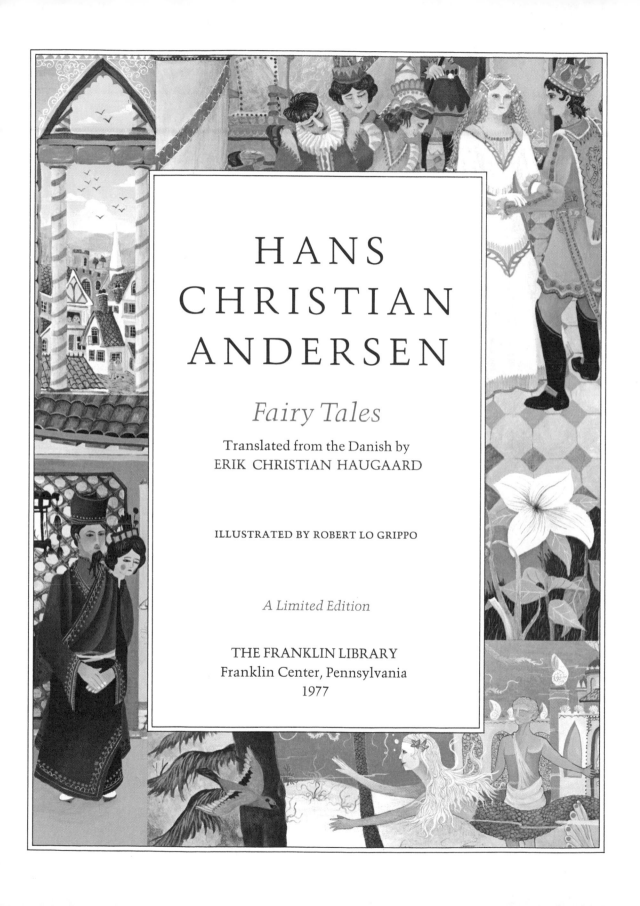

HANS CHRISTIAN ANDERSEN

Fairy Tales

Translated from the Danish by
ERIK CHRISTIAN HAUGAARD

ILLUSTRATED BY ROBERT LO GRIPPO

A Limited Edition

THE FRANKLIN LIBRARY
Franklin Center, Pennsylvania
1977

Copyright © 1974 by Erik Christian Haugaard.

Published by arrangement with Doubleday & Company, Inc.,
and Victor Gollancz Limited.

Special contents © 1977 Franklin Mint Corporation.

Printed in the United States of America

CONTENTS

INCHELINA

Once upon a time there was a woman whose only desire was to have a tiny little child. Now she had no idea where she could get one; so she went to an old witch and asked her: "Please, could you tell me where I could get a tiny little child? I would so love to have one."

"That is not so difficult," said the witch. "Here is a grain of barley; it is not the kind that grows in the farmer's fields or that you can feed to the chickens. Plant it in a flowerpot and watch what happens."

"Thank you," said the woman. She handed the witch twelve pennies, and she went home to plant the grain of barley. No sooner was it in the earth than it started to sprout. A beautiful big flower grew up; it looked like a tulip that was just about to bloom.

"What a lovely flower," said the woman, and kissed the red and yellow petals that were closed so tightly. With a snap they opened and one could see that it was a real tulip. In the center of the flower on the green stigma sat a tiny little girl. She was so beautiful and so delicate, and exactly one inch long. "I will call her Inchelina," thought the woman.

The lacquered shell of a walnut became Inchelina's cradle, the blue petals of violets her mattress, and a rose petal her cover. Here she slept at night; in the daytime she played on the table by the window. The woman had put a bowl of water there with a garland of flowers around it. In this tiny "lake" there floated a tulip petal, on which Inchelina could row from one side of the plate to the other, using two white horsehairs as oars; it was an exquisite sight. And Inchelina could sing, as no one has ever sung before — so clearly and delicately.

One night as she lay sleeping in her beautiful little bed a toad came into the room through a broken windowpane. The toad was big and wet and ugly; she jumped down upon the table where Inchelina was sleeping under her red rose petal.

"She would make a lovely wife for my son," said the toad; and grabbing the walnut shell in which Inchelina slept, she leaped through the broken window and down into the garden.

On the banks of a broad stream, just where it was muddiest, lived the toad with her son. He had taken after his mother and was very ugly. "Croak . . . Croak . . . Croak!" was all he said when he saw the beautiful little girl in the walnut shell.

"Don't talk so loud or you will wake her," scolded the mother. "She could run away and we wouldn't be able to catch her, for she is as light as the down of a swan. I will put her on a water-lily leaf, it will be just like an island to her. In the meantime, we shall get your apartment, down in the mud, ready for your marriage."

Out in the stream grew many water lilies, and all of their leaves looked as if they were floating in the water. The biggest of them was the farthest from shore; on that one the old toad put Inchelina's little bed.

When the poor little girl woke in the morning and saw where she was — on a green leaf with water all around her — she began to cry bitterly. There was no way of getting to shore at all.

The old toad was very busy down in her mud house, decorating the walls with reeds and yellow flowers that grew near the shore. She meant to do her best for her new daughter-in-law. After she had finished, she and her ugly son swam out to the water-lily leaf to fetch Inchelina's bed. It was to be put in the bridal chamber. The old toad curtsied and that is not easy to do while you are swimming; then she said, "Here is my son. He is to be your husband; you two will live happily down in the mud."

"Croak! . . . Croak!" was all the son said. Then they took the bed and swam away with it. Poor Inchelina sat on the green leaf and wept and wept, for she did not want to live with the ugly toad and have her hideous son as a husband. The little fishes that were

INCHELINA

swimming about in the water had heard what the old toad said; they stuck their heads out of the water to take a look at the tiny girl. When they saw how beautiful she was, it hurt them to think that she should have to marry the ugly toad and live in the mud. They decided that they would not let it happen, and gathered around the green stalk that held the leaf anchored to the bottom of the stream. They all nibbled on the stem, and soon the leaf was free. It drifted down the stream, bearing Inchelina far away from the ugly toad.

As Inchelina sailed by, the little birds on the shore saw her and sang, "What a lovely little girl." Farther and farther sailed the leaf with its little passenger, taking her on a journey to foreign lands.

For a long time a lovely white butterfly flew around her, then landed on the leaf. It had taken a fancy to Inchelina. The tiny girl laughed, for she was so happy to have escaped the toad; and the stream was so beautiful, golden in the sunshine. She took the little silk ribbon which she wore around her waist and tied one end of it to the butterfly and the other to the water-lily leaf. Now the leaf raced down the stream — and so did Inchelina, for she was standing on it.

At that moment a big May bug flew by; when it spied Inchelina, it swooped down and with its claws grabbed the poor girl around her tiny waist and flew up into a tree with her. The leaf floated on down the stream, and the butterfly had to follow it.

Oh God, little Inchelina was terrified as the May bug flew away with her, but stronger than her fear was her grief for the poor little white butterfly that she had chained to the leaf with her ribbon. If he did not get loose, he would starve to death.

The May bug didn't care what happened to the butterfly. He placed Inchelina on the biggest leaf on the tree. He gave her honey from the flowers to eat, and told her that she was the loveliest thing he had ever seen, even though she didn't look like a May bug. Soon all the other May bugs that lived in the tree came visiting. Two young lady May bugs — they were still unmarried — wiggled their antennae and said: "She has only two legs, how wretched. No antennae and a thin waist, how disgusting! She looks like a human being: how ugly!"

All the other female May bugs agreed with them. The May bug who had caught Inchelina still thought her lovely; but when all the others kept insisting that she was ugly, he soon was convinced of it

INCHELINA

too. Now he didn't want her any longer, and put her down on a daisy at the foot of the tree and told her she could go wherever she wanted to, for all he cared. Poor Inchelina cried; she thought it terrible to be so ugly that even a May bug would not want her, and that in spite of her being more beautiful than you can imagine, more lovely than the petal of the most beautiful rose.

All summer long poor Inchelina lived all alone in the forest. She wove a hammock out of grass and hung it underneath a dock leaf so that it would not rain on her while she slept. She ate the honey in the flowers and drank the dew that was on their leaves every morning.

Summer and autumn passed. But then came winter: the long, cold winter. All the birds that had sung so beautifully flew away. The flowers withered, the trees lost their leaves; and the dock leaf that had protected her rolled itself up and became a shriveled yellow stalk. She was so terribly cold. Her clothes were in shreds; and she was so thin and delicate.

Poor Inchelina, she was bound to freeze to death. It started to snow and each snowflake that fell on her was like a whole shovelful of snow would be to us, because we are so big, and she was only one inch tall.

She wrapped herself in a wizened leaf, but it gave no warmth and she shivered from the cold.

Not far from the forest was a big field where grain had grown; only a few dry stubbles still rose from the frozen ground, pointing up to the heavens. To Inchelina these straws were like a forest. Trembling, she wandered through them and came to the entrance of a field mouse's house. It was only a little hole in the ground. But deep down below the mouse lived in warmth and comfort, with a full larder and a nice kitchen. Like a beggar child, Inchelina stood outside the door and begged for a single grain of barley. It was several days since she had last eaten.

"Poor little wretch," said the field mouse, for she had a kind heart. "Come down into my warm living room and dine with me."

The field mouse liked Inchelina. "You can stay the winter," she said. "But you must keep the room tidy and tell me a story every day, for I like a good story." Inchelina did what the kind old mouse demanded, and she lived quite happily.

"Soon we shall have a visitor," said the mouse. "Once a week my neighbor comes. He lives even more comfortably than I do. He has a drawing room, and wears the most exquisite black fur coat. If only he would marry you, then you would be well provided for. He can't see you, for he is blind, so you will have to tell him the very best of your stories."

But Inchelina did not want to marry the mouse's neighbor, for he was a mole. The next day he came visiting, dressed in his black velvet fur coat. The field mouse had said that he was both rich and wise. His house was twenty times as big as the mouse's; and learned he was, too; but he did not like the sun and the beautiful flowers, he said they were "abominable," for he had never seen them. Inchelina had to sing for him; and when she sang "*Frère Jacques, dormez vous?*" he fell in love with her because of her beautiful voice; but he didn't show it, for he was sober-minded and never made a spectacle of himself.

He had recently dug a passage from his own house to theirs, and he invited Inchelina and the field mouse to use it as often as they pleased. He told them not to be afraid of the dead bird in the corridor. It had died only a few days before. It was still whole and had all its feathers. By chance it had been buried in his passageway.

The mole took a piece of dry rotten wood in his mouth; it shone as brightly as fire in the darkness; then he led the way down through the long corridor. When they came to the place where the dead bird lay, the mole made a hole with his broad nose, up through the earth, so that light could come through. Almost blocking the passageway was a dead swallow, with its beautiful wings pressed close to its body, its feet almost hidden by feathers, and its head nestled under a wing. The poor bird undoubtedly had frozen to death. Inchelina felt a great sadness; she had loved all the birds that twittered and sang for her that summer. The mole kicked the bird with one of his short legs and said, "Now it has stopped chirping. What a misfortune it is to be born a bird. Thank God, none of my children will be born birds! All they can do is chirp, and then die of starvation when winter comes."

"Yes, that's what all sensible people think," said the field mouse. "What does all that chirping lead to? Starvation and cold when winter comes. But I suppose they think it is romantic."

Inchelina didn't say anything, but when the mouse and mole had their backs turned, she leaned down and kissed the closed eye of the swallow. "Maybe that was one of the birds that sang so beautifully for me this summer," she thought. "How much joy you gave me, beautiful little bird."

The mole closed the hole through which the daylight had entered and then escorted the ladies home. That night Inchelina could not sleep; she rose and wove as large a blanket as she could, out of hay. She carried it down in the dark passage and covered the little bird with it. In the field mouse's living room she had found bits of cotton; she tucked them under the swallow wherever she could, to protect it from the cold earth.

"Good-by, beautiful bird," she said. "Good-by, and thank you for the songs you sang for me when it was summer and all the trees were green and the sun warmed us."

She put her head on the bird's breast; then she jumped up! Something was ticking inside: it was the bird's heart, for the swallow was not really dead, and now the warmth had revived it.

In the fall all the swallows fly to the warm countries. If one tarries too long and is caught by the first frost, he lies down on the ground as if he were dead, and the cold snow covers him.

Inchelina shook with fear. The swallow was huge to a girl so tiny that she only measured an inch. But she gathered her courage and pressed the blanket closer to the bird's body. She even went to fetch the little mint leaf that she herself used as a cover and put it over the bird's head.

The next night she sneaked down to the passageway again; the bird was better although still very weak. He opened his eyes just long enough to see Inchelina standing in the dark with a little piece of dry rotten wood in her hand, as a lamp.

"Thank you, you sweet little child," said the sick swallow, "I feel so much better. I am not cold now. Soon I shall be strong again and can fly out into the sunshine."

"Oh no," she said. "It is cold and snowing outside now and you would freeze. Stay down here in your warm bed, I will nurse you."

She brought the swallow water on a leaf. After he had drunk it, he told her his story. He had torn his wing on a rosebush, and therefore could not fly as swiftly as the other swallows, so he had stayed behind when the others left; then one morning he had fainted from cold. That was all he could remember. He did not know how he came to be in the mole's passageway.

The bird stayed all winter. Inchelina took good care of him, grew very fond of him, and breathed not a word about him to either the

HANS CHRISTIAN ANDERSEN

mole or the field mouse, for she knew that they didn't like the poor swallow.

As soon as spring came and the warmth of the sun could be felt through the earth, the swallow said good-by to Inchelina, who opened the hole that the mole had made. The sun shone down so pleasantly. The swallow asked her if she did not want to come along with him; she could sit on his back and he would fly with her out into the great forest. But Inchelina knew that the field mouse would be sad and lonely if she left.

"I cannot," she said.

The bird thanked her once more. "Farewell. . . . Farewell, lovely girl," he sang, and flew out into the sunshine.

Inchelina's eyes filled with tears as she watched the swallow fly away, for she cared so much for the bird.

"Tweet . . . tweet," he sang, and disappeared in the forest.

Poor Inchelina was miserable. Soon the grain would be so tall that the field would be in shade, and she would no longer be able to enjoy the warm sunshine.

"This summer you must spend getting your trousseau ready," said the field mouse, for the sober mole in the velvet coat had proposed to her. "You must have both woolens and linen to wear and to use in housekeeping when you become Mrs. Mole."

Inchelina had to spin by hand and the field mouse hired four spiders to weave both night and day. Every evening the mole came visiting, but all he talked about was how nice it would be when the summer was over. He didn't like the way the sun baked the earth; it made it so hard to dig in. As soon as autumn came they would get married. But Inchelina was not happy; she thought the mole was dull and she did not love him. Every day, at sunrise and at sunset, she tiptoed to the entrance of the field mouse's house, so that when the wind blew and parted the grain, she could see the blue sky above her. She thought of how light and beautiful it was out there, and she longed for her friend the swallow but he never came back. "He is probably far away in the wonderful green forest!" she thought.

Autumn came and Inchelina's trousseau was finished.

"In four weeks we shall hold your wedding," said the field mouse.

Inchelina cried and said she did not want to marry the boring old mole.

INCHELINA

"Fiddlesticks!" squeaked the field mouse. "Don't be stubborn or I will bite you with my white teeth. You are getting an excellent husband; he has a velvet coat so fine that the queen does not have one that is better. He has both a larder and kitchen, you ought to thank God for giving you such a good husband."

The day of the wedding came; the mole had already arrived. Inchelina grieved. Now she would never see the warm sun again. The mole lived far down under the ground, for he didn't like the sun. While she lived with the field mouse, she at least had been allowed to walk as far as the entrance of the little house and look at the sun.

"Farewell. . . . Farewell, you beautiful sun!" Inchelina lifted her hands up toward the sky and then took a few steps out upon the field. The harvest was over and only the stubbles were left. She saw a little red flower. Embracing it, she said: "Farewell! And give my love to the swallow if you ever see him."

"Tweet . . . Tweet . . ." something said in the air above her.

She looked up. It was the little swallow. As soon as he saw Inchelina he chirped with joy. And she told the bird how she had to marry the awful mole, and live forever down under the ground, and never see the sun again. The very telling of her future brought tears to her eyes.

"Now comes the cold winter," said the swallow, "and I fly far away to the warm countries. Why don't you come with me? You can sit on my back; tie yourself on so you won't fall off and we will fly far away from the ugly mole and his dismal house; across the great mountains, to the countries where the sun shines more beautifully than here and the loveliest flowers grow and it is always summer. Fly with me, Inchelina. You saved my life when I lay freezing in the cold cellar of the earth."

"Yes, I will come," cried Inchelina, and climbed up on the bird's back. She tied herself with a ribbon to one of his feathers, and the swallow flew high up into the air, above the forests and lakes and over the high mountains that are always snow-covered. Inchelina froze in the cold air, but she crawled underneath the warm feathers of the bird and only stuck her little head out to see all the beauty below her.

They came to the warm countries. And it was true what the swallow had said: the sun shone more brightly and the sky seemed twice as high. Along the fences grew the loveliest green and blue grapes. From the trees in the forests hung oranges and lemons. Along the roads the most beautiful children ran, chasing many-colored butterflies. The swallow flew even farther south, and the landscape beneath them became more and more beautiful.

Near a forest, on the shores of a lake, stood the ruins of an ancient temple; ivy wound itself around the white pillars. On top of these were many swallows' nests and one of them belonged to the little swallow that was carrying Inchelina.

"This is my house," he said. "Now choose for yourself one of the beautiful flowers down below and I will set you down on it, it will make a lovely home for you."

"How wonderful!" exclaimed Inchelina, and clapped her hands. Among the broken white marble pillars grew tall, lovely white flowers. The swallow sat her down on the leaves of one of them; and to Inchelina's astonishment, she saw a little man sitting in the center of the flower. He was white and almost transparent, as if he were made of glass. On his head he wore a golden crown. On his back were a pair of wings. He was no taller than Inchelina. In every one of the flowers there lived such a tiny angel; and this one was the king of them all.

"How handsome he is!" whispered Inchelina to the swallow.

The tiny little king was terrified of the bird, who was several times larger than he was. But when he saw Inchelina he forgot his fear. She was the loveliest creature he had ever seen; and so he took the crown off his own head and put it on hers. Then he asked her what her name was and whether she wanted to be queen of the flowers.

Now here was a better husband than old mother toad's ugly son or the mole with the velvet coat. Inchelina said yes; and from every flower came a lovely little angel to pay homage to their queen. How lovely and delicate they all were; and they brought her gifts, and the best of these was a pair of wings, so she would be able to fly, as they all did, from flower to flower.

It was a day of happiness. And the swallow, from his nest in the temple, sang for them as well as he could. But in his heart he was ever so sad, for he, too, loved Inchelina and had hoped never to be parted from her.

"You shall not be called Inchelina any longer," said the king. "It is an ugly name. From now on we shall call you Maja."

"Farewell! Farewell!" called the little swallow. He flew back to the north, away from the warm countries. He came to Denmark; and there he has his nest, above the window of a man who can tell fairy tales.

"Tweet . . . tweet," sang the swallow. And the man heard it and wrote down the whole story.

THE TINDERBOX

A soldier came marching down the road: Left . . . right! Left . . . right! He had a pack on his back and a sword at his side. He had been in the war and he was on his way home. Along the road he met a witch. She was a disgusting sight, with a lower lip that hung all the way down to her chest.

"Good evening, young soldier," she said. "What a handsome sword you have and what a big knapsack. I can see that you are a real soldier! I shall give you all the money that you want."

"Thank you, old witch," he said.

"Do you see that big tree?" asked the witch, and pointed to the one they were standing next to. "The trunk is hollow. You climb up to the top of the tree, crawl into the hole, and slide deep down inside it. I'll tie a rope around your waist, so I can pull you up again when you call me."

"What am I supposed to do down in the tree?" asked the soldier.

"Get money!" answered the witch and laughed. "Now listen to me. When you get down to the very bottom, you'll be in a great passageway where you'll be able to see because there are over a hundred lamps burning. You'll find three doors; and you can open them all because the keys are in the locks. Go into the first one; and there on a chest, in the middle of the room, you'll see a dog with eyes as big as teacups. Don't let that worry you. You will have my blue checkered apron; just spread it out on the floor, put the

THE TINDERBOX

dog down on top of it, and it won't do you any harm. Open the chest and take as many coins as you wish, they are all copper. If it's silver you're after, then go into the next room. There you'll find a dog with eyes as big as millstones; but don't let that worry you, put him on the apron and take the money. If you'd rather have gold, you can have that too; it's in the third room. Wait till you see that dog, he's got eyes as big as the Round Tower in Copenhagen; but don't let that worry you. Put him down on my apron and he won't hurt you; then you can take as much gold as you wish."

"That doesn't sound bad!" said the soldier. "But what am I to do for you, old witch? I can't help thinking that you must want something too."

"No," replied the witch. "I don't want one single coin. Just bring me the old tinderbox that my grandmother forgot the last time she was down there."

"I'm ready, tie the rope around my waist!" ordered the soldier.

"There you are, and here is my blue checkered apron," said the witch.

The soldier climbed the tree, let himself fall into the hole, and found that he was in the passageway, where more than a hundred lights burned.

He opened the first door. Oh! There sat the dog with eyes as big as teacups glaring at him.

"You are a handsome fellow!" he exclaimed as he put the dog down on the witch's apron. He filled his pockets with copper coins, closed the chest, and put the dog back on top of it.

He went into the second room. Aha! There sat the dog with eyes as big as millstones. "Don't keep looking at me like that," said the soldier good-naturedly. "It isn't polite and you'll spoil your eyes." He put the dog down on the witch's apron and opened the chest. When he saw all the silver coins, he emptied the copper out of his pockets and filled both them and his knapsack with silver.

Now he entered the third room. That dog was big enough to frighten anyone, even a soldier. His eyes were as large as the Round Tower in Copenhagen and they turned around like wheels.

"Good evening," said the soldier politely, taking off his cap, for such a dog he had never seen before. For a while he just stood looking at it; but finally he said to himself, "Enough of this!" Then he put the dog down on the witch's apron and opened up the chest.

"God preserve me!" he cried. There was so much gold that there

HANS CHRISTIAN ANDERSEN

was enough to buy the whole city of Copenhagen; and all the gingerbread men, rocking horses, riding whips, and tin soldiers in the whole world.

Quickly the soldier threw away all the silver coins that he had in his pockets and knapsack and put gold in them instead; he even filled his boots and his cap with money. He put the dog back on the chest, closed the door behind him, and called up through the hollow tree.

"Pull me up, you old witch!"

"Have you got the tinderbox?" she called back.

"Right you are, I have forgotten it," he replied honestly, and went back to get it. The witch hoisted him up and again he stood on the road; but now his pockets, knapsack, cap, and boots were filled with gold and he felt quite differently.

"Why do you want the tinderbox?" he asked.

"Mind your own business," answered the witch crossly. "You have got your money, just give me the tinderbox."

"Blah! Blah!" said the soldier. "Tell me what you are going to use it for, right now; or I'll draw my sword and cut off your head."

"No!" replied the witch firmly; but that was a mistake, for the soldier chopped her head off. She lay there dead. The soldier put all his gold in her apron, tied it up into a bundle, and threw it over his shoulder. The tinderbox he dropped into his pocket; and off to town he went.

The town was nice, and the soldier went to the nicest inn, where he asked to be put up in the finest room and ordered all the things he liked to eat best for his supper, because now he had so much money that he was rich.

The servant who polished his boots thought it was very odd that a man so wealthy should have such worn-out boots. But the soldier hadn't had time to buy anything yet; the next day he bought boots and clothes that fitted his purse. And the soldier became a refined gentleman. People were eager to tell him all about their town and their king, and what a lovely princess his daughter was.

"I would like to see her," said the soldier.

"But no one sees her," explained the townfolk. "She lives in a copper castle, surrounded by walls, and towers, and a moat. The king doesn't dare allow anyone to visit her because it has been foretold that she will marry a simple soldier, and the king doesn't want that to happen."

THE TINDERBOX

"If only I could see her," thought the soldier, though it was unthinkable.

The soldier lived merrily, went to the theater, kept a carriage so he could drive in the king's park, and gave lots of money to the poor. He remembered well what it felt like not to have a penny in his purse.

He was rich and well dressed. He had many friends; and they all said that he was kind and a real cavalier; and such things he liked to hear. But since he used money every day and never received any, he soon had only two copper coins left.

He had to move out of the beautiful room downstairs, up to a tiny one in the garret, where he not only polished his boots himself but also mended them with a large needle. None of his friends came to see him, for they said there were too many stairs to climb.

It was a very dark evening and he could not even buy a candle. Suddenly he remembered that he had seen the stub of a candle in the tinderbox that he had brought up from the bottom of the hollow tree. He found the tinderbox and took out the candle. He struck the flint. There was a spark, and in through the door came the dog with eyes as big as teacups.

"What does my master command?" asked the dog.

"What's this all about?" exclaimed the soldier. "That certainly was an interesting tinderbox. Can I have whatever I want? Bring me some money," he ordered. In less time than it takes to say thank you, the dog was gone and back with a big sack of copper coins in his mouth.

Now the soldier understood why the witch had thought the tinderbox so valuable. If he struck it once, the dog appeared who sat on the chest full of copper coins; if he struck it twice, then the dog came who guarded the silver money; and if he struck it three times, then came the one who had the gold.

The soldier moved downstairs again, wore fine clothes again, and had fine friends, for now they all remembered him and cared for him as they had before.

One night, when he was sitting alone after his friends had gone, he thought, "It is a pity that no one can see that beautiful princess. What is the good of her beauty if she must always remain behind the high walls and towers of a copper castle? Will I never see her? . . . Where is my tinderbox?"

He made the sparks fly and the dog with eyes as big as teacups came. "I know it's very late at night," he said, "but I would so like to see the beautiful princess, if only for a minute."

Away went the dog; and faster than thought he returned with the sleeping princess on his back. She was so lovely that anyone would have known that she was a real princess. The soldier could not help kissing her, for he was a true soldier.

The dog brought the princess back to her copper castle; but in the morning while she was having tea with her father and mother, the king and queen, she told them that she had had a very strange dream that night. A large dog had come and carried her away to a soldier who kissed her.

"That's a nice story," said the queen, but she didn't mean it.

The next night one of the older ladies in waiting was sent to watch over the princess while she slept, and find out whether it had only been a dream, and not something worse.

The soldier longed to see the princess so much that he couldn't bear it, so at night he sent the dog to fetch her. The dog ran as fast as he could, but the lady in waiting had her boots on and she kept up with him all the way. When she saw which house he had entered, she took out a piece of chalk and made a big white cross on the door.

"Now we'll be able to find it in the morning," she thought, and went home to get some sleep.

When the dog returned the princess to the castle, he noticed the cross on the door of the house where his master lived; so he took a piece of white chalk and put crosses on all the doors of all the houses in the whole town. It was a very clever thing to do, for now the lady in waiting would never know which was the right door.

The next morning the king and queen, the old lady in waiting, and all the royal officers went out into town to find the house where the princess had been.

"Here it is!" exclaimed the king, when he saw the first door with a cross on it.

"No, my sweet husband, it is here," said his wife, who had seen the second door with a cross on it.

"Here's one!"

"There's one!"

Everyone shouted at once, for it didn't matter where anyone looked: there he would find a door with a cross on it; and so they all gave up.

THE TINDERBOX

Now the queen was so clever, she could do more than ride in a golden carriage. She took out her golden scissors and cut out a large piece of silk and sewed it into a pretty little bag. This she filled with the fine grain of buckwheat, and tied the bag around the princess' waist. When this was done, she cut a little hole in the bag just big enough for the little grains of buckwheat to fall out, one at a time, and show the way to the house where the princess was taken by the dog.

During the night the dog came to fetch the princess and carry her on his back to the soldier, who loved her so much that now he had only one desire, and that was to be a prince so that he could marry her.

The dog neither saw nor felt the grains of buckwheat that made a little trail all the way from the copper castle to the soldier's room at the inn. In the morning the king and queen had no difficulty in finding where the princess had been, and the soldier was thrown into jail.

There he sat in the dark with nothing to do; and what made matters worse was that everyone said, "Tomorrow you are going to be hanged!"

That was not amusing to hear. If only he had had his tinderbox, but he had forgotten it in his room. When the sun rose, he watched the people, through the bars of his window, as they hurried toward the gates of the city, for the hanging was to take place outside the walls. He heard the drums and the royal soldiers marching. Everyone was running. He saw a shoemaker's apprentice, who had not bothered to take off his leather apron and was wearing slippers. The boy lifted his legs so high, it looked as though he were galloping. One of his slippers flew off and landed near the window of the soldier's cell.

"Hey!" shouted the soldier. "Listen, shoemaker, wait a minute, nothing much will happen before I get there. But if you will run to the inn and get the tinderbox I left in my room, you can earn four copper coins. But you'd better use your legs or it will be too late."

The shoemaker's apprentice, who didn't have one copper coin, was eager to earn four; and he ran to get the tinderbox as fast as he could; and gave it to the soldier.

And now you shall hear what happened after that!

Outside the gates of the town, a gallows had been built; around it stood the royal soldiers and many hundreds of thousands of

HANS CHRISTIAN ANDERSEN

people. The king and the queen sat on their lovely throne, and across from them sat the judge and the royal council.

The soldier was standing on the platform, but as the noose was put around his neck, he declared that it was an ancient custom to grant a condemned man his last innocent wish. The only thing he wanted was to be allowed to smoke a pipe of tobacco.

The king couldn't refuse; and the soldier took out his tinderbox and struck it: once, twice, three times! Instantly, the three dogs were before him: the one with eyes as big as teacups, the one with eyes as big as millstones, and the one with eyes as big as the Round Tower in Copenhagen.

"Help me! I don't want to be hanged!" cried the soldier.

The dogs ran toward the judge and the royal council. They took one man by the leg and another by the nose, and threw them up in the air, so high that when they hit the earth again they broke into little pieces.

"Not me!" screamed the king; but the biggest dog took both the king and the queen and sent them flying up as high as all the others had been.

The royal guards got frightened; and the people began to shout: "Little soldier, you shall be our king and marry the princess!"

The soldier rode in the king's golden carriage; and the three dogs danced in front of it and barked: "Hurrah!"

The little boys whistled and the royal guards presented arms. The princess came out of her copper castle and became queen, which she liked very much. The wedding feast lasted a week; and the three dogs sat at the table and made eyes at everyone.

LITTLE CLAUS
AND BIG CLAUS

Once upon a time there lived
in a village two men who had the same name; they were both
called Claus. But one of them owned four horses, while the other
had only one; so to tell them apart the richer man was called Big
Claus and the poorer one Little Claus. Now let's hear what happened to the two of them because that's a real story!

Six days a week Little Claus had to work for Big Claus and loan
him his horse; and in return Big Claus had to let Little Claus
borrow his four horses on Sunday. One day a week Little Claus felt
as if all the horses belonged to him, and he would crack his whip
in the air and shout orders to them merrily.

One morning when the sun was shining brightly and the villag-
ers, all dressed up in their Sunday best, with their prayer books
under their arms, were passing his field, Little Claus cracked his
whip in the air, whistled, and called out very loudly, "Gee up, all
my horses!"

"You may not say that!" exclaimed Big Claus. "Only one of the
horses is yours."

But Little Claus forgot very quickly what Big Claus had said, and
the next time someone went by and nodded kindly in his direction, he shouted, "Gee up, all my horses!"

Big Claus turned around and shouted! "I beg you for the last
time not to call all those horses yours because if you do it once

more I'll take the mallet that I use to drive in the stake for tethering my four horses and hit your one horse so hard that it will drop dead on the spot."

"I promise never to say it again," said Little Claus meekly. But the words were hardly out of his mouth when still another group of churchgoers stopped to watch him plow. They smiled and said good morning in a very friendly way. "What a fine figure I must cut, driving five horses," he thought; and without realizing what he was doing, he cracked the whip and cried, "Gee up, all my horses!"

"I'll give your horse gee up!" screamed Big Claus in a rage; and he took his tethering mallet and hit Little Claus's only horse so hard on the forehead that it fell down quite dead.

"Poor me!" cried Little Claus. "Now I don't have any horse at all!" And he sat down and wept. But as there was nothing else to do he flayed the horse and hung the hide up to dry. When the wind had done its work, Little Claus put the hide in a sack and set off for town to sell it in the market place.

It was a long way and the road led through a forest. The weather turned bad and among the dark shadows Little Claus lost his way. He turned first in one direction and then in another. Finally he did find his way again; but by then it was late afternoon and too late to reach town before nightfall.

Not far from the road he saw a farmhouse. The shutters were closed but above them there shone tiny streams of light. "There I may ask for shelter for the night," Little Claus thought, and made his way to the front door and knocked.

The farmer's wife answered the door, but when she heard what he wanted she shook her head. "You'll have to go away," she ordered. "My husband isn't home and I cannot allow a stranger to come in."

"Then I'll have to sleep outside," said Little Claus. The farmer's wife shut the door without another word; and Little Claus looked about him. Near the house was a haystack, and between that and the dwelling there was a shed with a flat thatched roof.

"I'll stretch out on that," Little Claus mumbled, looking at the roof. "It will make a fine bed and I doubt that the stork will fly down and bite me." The latter was said in jest because there was a stork's nest on the roof of the farmhouse.

Little Claus climbed up on the roof of the shack; and while he

LITTLE CLAUS AND BIG CLAUS

was twisting and turning to make himself comfortable, he realized that from where he lay he could see right into the kitchen of the farmhouse because, at the top, the shutters did not close tightly.

A fine white linen cloth covered the large table and on it were not only a roast and wine but a platter of fish as well. On one side of the table sat the farmer's wife and on the other the deacon; and while she filled his glass with wine, he filled himself with fish because that was his favorite food.

"If only I had been invited too!" Little Claus sighed, and pushed himself as near to the window as he could without touching the shutters. There was a cake on the table too; this was better than a party, it was a feast!

He heard someone galloping on the road; he turned and saw the rider: it was the farmer coming home.

Now this farmer was known for two things: one, that he was a good fellow, and the other, that he suffered from a strange disease; he couldn't bear the sight of a deacon.

One glance and he went into a rage. And that, of course, was the reason why the deacon had come visiting on a day when the farmer wasn't at home; and that too was why the farmer's wife had made the most delicious food she could for her guest.

When they heard the farmer riding up to the door of his house, both the farmer's wife and the deacon were terrified; and she told him to climb into a large empty chest that stood in the corner. The poor man, trembling with fear, obeyed her. Then the woman hid all the food and the wine in the oven, for she knew that if her husband saw all the delicacies he was certain to ask her why she had made them.

"Ow!" groaned Little Claus when he saw the last of the food disappear into the bread oven.

"Is there someone up there?" the farmer called, and when he saw Little Claus lying on the roof of the shed he told him to come down. "What were you doing up there?"

Little Claus explained how he had lost his way in the forest and asked the farmer to be allowed to spend the night in his house.

"You are most welcome," said the farmer, who was the kindest of men, as long as there was no deacon in sight. "But first let's have a bite to eat."

The farmer's wife greeted them both very politely, set the table, and served them a large bowl of porridge. The farmer, who was very hungry, ate with relish; but Little Claus kept thinking of all the delicious food in the oven and couldn't swallow a spoonful.

At his feet under the table lay the sack with the horse hide in it. He stepped on the sack and the horse hide squeaked. "Shhhhhhhh!" whispered Little Claus to the sack; but at the same time he pressed his foot down on it even harder and it squeaked even louder.

"What have you got in the bag?" asked the farmer.

"Oh, it's only a wizard," Little Claus replied. "He was telling me that there's no reason for us to eat porridge when he has just conjured both fish and meat for us, and even a cake. Look in the oven."

"What!" exclaimed the farmer; and he ran to the oven and opened it. There he saw all the good food that his wife had made for the deacon; and she — not daring to tell him the truth — silently served the roast, the fish, and the cake.

After he had taken a few mouthfuls, Little Claus stepped on the sack again so that the hide squeaked.

LITTLE CLAUS AND BIG CLAUS

"What is the wizard saying now?" asked the farmer eagerly.

"He says that he has conjured three bottles of wine for us and that you will find them in the corner next to the oven."

The farmer's poor wife brought out the wine, which she had hidden, and poured it for Little Claus and her husband, who made so many toasts to each other's health that they were soon very merry. Then the farmer began to think about Little Claus's sack and what a wonderful thing it must be to have a wizard.

"Do you think he could conjure the Devil?" the farmer asked. "For now that I have the courage I wouldn't mind seeing what he looks like."

"Why not?" replied Little Claus. "My wizard will do anything I tell him to. . . . Won't you?" he added, stepping on the sack so that it squeaked. Turning to the farmer, Little Claus smiled. "Can't you hear that he said yes? But the Devil has such an ugly face that he's not worth looking at."

"I'm not afraid," said the farmer, and hiccupped. "How terrible can he look?"

"He looks just like a deacon!"

"Pooh!" returned the farmer. "That's worse than I thought! I must confess that I cannot stand the sight of a deacon; but now that I know that it is only the Devil I will be looking at, maybe I can bear it. But don't let him come too near me and let's get it over with before I lose my courage."

"I'll tell my wizard," said Little Claus and stepped on the hide; then he cocked his head as if he were listening to someone.

"What is he saying?" asked the farmer, who could only hear the hide squeak.

"He says that if we go over to the chest in the corner and open it up we shall see the Devil sitting inside. But we must be careful when we lift the lid, not to lift it too high, so the Devil can escape."

"Then you must hold onto the lid while I lift it," whispered the farmer to Little Claus as he tiptoed to the chest in which the deacon was hiding. This poor fellow had heard every word that Little Claus and the farmer had said and was quaking with fear.

The farmer opened the chest no more than an inch or two and peeped inside. "Ah!" he screamed and jumped up, letting the lid fall back into place. "I saw him! He looked exactly like our deacon! It was a dreadful sight!"

After such an experience you need a drink; and Little Claus and the farmer had many, for they drank late into the night.

HANS CHRISTIAN ANDERSEN

"You must sell me that wizard," the farmer finally said. "Ask whatever you want for it. . . . I'll give you a bushel basket full of money, if that's what you'd like."

"I wouldn't think of it," replied Little Claus. "You have seen for yourself all the marvelous things that wizard can do."

"But I want it with all my heart," begged the farmer; and he kept on pleading with Little Claus until at last he agreed.

"I cannot forget that you gave me a night's lodging," Little Claus said. "Take my wizard, but remember to fill the bushel basket to the very top."

"I shall! I shall!" exclaimed the farmer. "But you must take the chest along too. I won't have it in my house. Who knows but that the Devil isn't still inside it?"

And that's how it happened that Little Claus gave the farmer a sack with a horse hide in it and in return was given not only a bushel full of money and a chest but a wheelbarrow to carry them away.

"Good-by!" called Little Claus, and off he went.

On the other side of the forest there was a deep river with a current that flowed so swiftly that you could not swim against it. But the river had to be crossed and so a bridge had been built. When Little Claus reached the middle of that bridge, he said very loudly — so the deacon, who was still inside the chest, could hear him — "What's the point of dragging this chest any farther? It's so heavy, you'd think it was filled with stones. I'm all worn out. I know what I'll do, I'll dump the chest into the stream and if the current carries it home to me, all well and good; and if not, it doesn't matter." Then he took hold of the chest and pushed it, as if he were about to lift it out of the wheelbarrow and let it fall into the water.

"No, stop it!" cried the deacon from inside the chest. "Let me out! Please, let me out!"

"Oh!" shouted Little Claus as if he were frightened. "The Devil is still in there. I'd better throw the chest right into the river and drown him."

"No! No!" screamed the deacon. "I'll give you a bushel of money if you'll let me out!"

"That's a different tune," said Little Claus, and opened the chest. The deacon climbed out and shoved the chest into the river. Together Little Claus and the deacon went to the deacon's home,

LITTLE CLAUS AND BIG CLAUS

where he gave Little Claus the bushel of coins that he had promised him. Now Little Claus had a whole wheelbarrow full of money.

"That wasn't bad payment for my old horse," he said to himself as he dumped all the coins out on the floor of his own living room. "What a big pile it is! It will annoy Big Claus to find out how rich I have become, all because of my horse. I won't tell him but let him find out for himself."

A few minutes later a boy banged on Big Claus's door and asked him if he could borrow his grain measure for Little Claus.

"I wonder what he is going to use that for," thought Big Claus; and in order to find out he dabbed a bit of tar in the bottom of the measuring pail, which was quite clever of him because when it was returned he found a silver coin stuck to the spot.

"Where did that come from?" shouted Big Claus, and ran as fast as he could to Little Claus's house. When he saw Little Claus in the midst of his riches, he shouted even louder, "Where did you get all that money from?"

"Oh, that was for my horse hide, I sold it last night."

"You were certainly well paid!" said Big Claus; and hurried home where he took an ax and killed all four of his horses; then he flayed them and set off for town with their hides.

"Hides for sale! Hides for sale! Who wants to buy hides?" Big Claus shouted from street to street.

All the shoemakers and tanners came out of their workshops to ask him the price of his wares.

"A bushel full of coins for each hide," he replied.

"You must be mad!" they all shouted at once. "Do you think we count money by the bushel?"

"Hides for sale! Hides for sale!" Big Claus repeated. And every time that someone asked him the price he said again, "A bushel full of coins."

"Are you trying to make fools of us?" the shoemakers and the tanners shouted. And while the crowd continued to gather around them, the tanners took their leather aprons and the shoemakers their straps and began to beat Big Claus.

"Hides . . ." screamed one of the tanners. "We'll see to it that your hide spits red!"

"Out of town with him!" they shouted. And certainly Big Claus did his best to get out of town as fast as he could; never in his whole life had he gotten such a beating.

HANS CHRISTIAN ANDERSEN

"Little Claus is going to pay for this!" he decided when he got home. "He is going to pay with his life."

But while Big Claus was in town, something unfortunate had occurred: Little Claus's grandmother had died. And although she had been a very mean and scolding hag, who had never been kind to Little Claus, he felt very sad. Thinking that it might bring her back to life, he put his old grandmother in his own warm bed and decided to let her stay there all night, even though this meant that he would have to sleep in a chair.

It was not the first time that Little Claus had tried sleeping in a chair, but he could not sleep anyway; so he was wide awake when Big Claus came and tiptoed across the room to the bed in which he thought Little Claus was sleeping.

With an ax Big Claus hit the old grandmother on top of the head as hard as he could. "That's what you get for making a fool out of me," he explained. "And now you won't be able to do it again," he added and went home.

"What a wicked man!" thought Little Claus. "If my grandmother hadn't already been dead, he would have killed her."

Very early the next morning he dressed his grandmother in her Sunday best; then he borrowed a horse from his neighbor and harnessed it to his cart. On the small seat in the back of the cart, he put the old woman in a sitting position with bundles on either side of her, so she wouldn't fall out of the cart while he was driving. He went through the forest and just as the sun was rising he reached an inn. "I'd better stop to get something to keep me alive," he said.

It was a large inn, and the innkeeper was very rich. He was also very kind, but he had a ferocious temper, as if he had nothing inside him but pepper and tobacco.

"Good morning," he said to Little Claus. "You're dressed very finely for so early in the morning."

"I'm driving to town with my grandmother," he replied. "She's sitting out in the cart because I couldn't persuade her to come in here with me. I wonder if you would be so kind as to take a glass of mead out to her; but speak a little loudly because she is a bit hard of hearing."

"No sooner said than done," answered the innkeeper; and he poured a large glass of mead which he carried out to the dead woman.

"Here is a glass of mead, which your son ordered for you," said the innkeeper loudly but politely; but the dead woman sat perfectly still and said not a word.

"Can't you hear me?" he shouted. "Here is mead from your son!"

He shouted the same words again as loud as he could, and still the old woman sat staring straight ahead. The more he shouted, the madder the innkeeper got, until finally he lost his temper and threw the mead, glass and all, right into the woman's face. With the mead dripping down her nose, she fell over backward, for Little Claus had not tied her to the seat.

"What have you done?" shouted Little Claus as he flung open the door of the inn. "Why, you have killed my grandmother!" he cried, grabbing the innkeeper by the shirt. "Look at the wound she has on her head!"

"Oh, what a calamity!" the innkeeper exclaimed, and wrung his hands. "It is all because of that temper of mine! Sweet, good Little Claus, I will give you a bushel full of money and bury your grandmother as if she were my own, as long as you'll keep quiet about what really happened, because if you don't they'll chop my head off; and that's so nasty."

And that was how Little Claus got another bushel full of coins; and the innkeeper, true to his word, buried the old woman as well as he would have had she been his own grandmother.

As soon as he got home Little Claus sent his boy to borrow Big Claus's grain measure.

"What, haven't I killed him?" Big Claus exclaimed. "I must find out what's happened. I'll take the measure over there myself."

When he arrived at Little Claus's and saw all the money, his eyes grew wide with wonder and greed. "Where did you get all that from?" he demanded.

"It was my grandmother and not me that you killed, and now I have sold her body for a bushel full of money."

"You were certainly well paid," said Big Claus, and hurried home. When he got there he took an ax and killed his old grandmother; then he dumped the poor old woman's body in his carriage and drove into town. He went at once to the apothecary and asked if he wanted to buy a corpse.

"Who is it and where did you get it from?" the apothecary inquired.

"Oh, it is my grandmother, and I have killed her so I could sell her body for a bushel of money," Big Claus said.

HANS CHRISTIAN ANDERSEN

"God save us!" cried the apothecary. "You don't know what you're saying. . . . If you talk like that you'll lose your head." And the apothecary lectured him, telling him how wicked a crime murder was and that it was committed only by the most evil of men, who deserved the severest punishment. Big Claus was terrified and leaped into his carriage. He set off in the direction of his home, wildly whipping his horses. But no one tried to stop him, for everyone believed that he had gone mad.

"I'll make you pay for this!" Big Claus cried as soon as he was well out of town. "Little Claus is going to pay for this," he repeated when he got home. Then he took a large sack and went to see Little Claus.

"So you fooled me again!" he shouted. "First I killed my horses and then my grandmother; and it's all your fault. But you have fooled me for the last time!" Grabbing Little Claus around the waist, he shoved him into the sack. As he flung the sack over his shoulder he said loudly, "And now I am going to drown you!"

It was quite far to the river, and as he walked the sack with Little Claus in it seemed to grow heavier and heavier. The road went past the church, and Big Claus heard the organ being played and the congregation singing. "It would be nice to hear a hymn or two before I go on," he thought. "Everybody's in church and Little Claus can't get out of the sack." So Big Claus put down the sack near the entrance and went into the church.

"Poor me! Poor me!" sighed Little Claus. He twisted and turned but he could not loosen the cord that had been tied around the opening of the sack.

At that moment an old herdsman happened to pass. He had snow-white hair and walked with a long crook. In front of him he drove a large herd of cows and bulls. One of the bulls bumped into the sack and Little Claus was turned over.

"Poor me! Poor me!" cried Little Claus. "I am so young and am already bound for heaven."

"Think of poor me; I am an old man," said the herdsman, "and am not allowed to enter it."

"Open up the sack!" shouted Little Claus. "You get inside it, instead of me, and then you will get to heaven right away!"

"Nothing could be better," said the old man. He untied the sack and Little Claus crawled out at once.

"Take good care of my cattle," the herdsman begged as he

LITTLE CLAUS AND BIG CLAUS

climbed into the sack. Little Claus promised that he would and tied the sack securely. Then he went on his way, driving the herd before him.

A little later Big Claus came out of the church and lifted the sack onto his back. He was surprised how much lighter it was now, for the old man weighed only half as much as Little Claus.

"How easy it is to carry now; it did do me good to hear a hymn!" he thought.

Big Claus went directly down to the river that was both deep and wide and dumped the sack into the water, shouting after it: "You have made a fool of me for the last time!" For of course he believed that Little Claus was still inside the sack that was disappearing into the river.

On his way home he met Little Claus with all his cattle at the crossroads.

"What!" exclaimed Big Claus. "Haven't I drowned you?"

"Oh yes," answered Little Claus, "You threw me in the river about half an hour ago."

"But where did you get that huge herd of cattle?" Big Claus demanded.

"They are river cattle," replied Little Claus. "I'll tell you every-thing that happened to me. But, by the way, first I want to thank you for drowning me. For now I shall never have anything to worry about again, I am really rich. . . . Believe me, I was frightened when you threw me over the bridge. The wind whistled in my ears as I fell into the cold water. I sank straight to the bottom; but I didn't hurt myself because I landed on the softest, most beautiful green grass you can imagine. Then the sack was opened by the loveliest maiden. She was all dressed in white except for the green wreath in her wet hair. Taking my hand, she asked, 'Aren't you Little Claus?' When I nodded she said, 'Here are some cattle for you and six miles up the road there is an even bigger herd waiting for you.' Then I realized that to the water people the streams and rivers were as roads are to us. They use them to travel on. Far from their homes under the oceans, they follow the streams and the rivers until they finally become too shallow and come to an end. There are the most beautiful flowers growing down there and the finest, freshest grass; the fish swimming around above your head remind you of the birds flying in the air. The people are as nice as they can be; and the cattle fat and friendly."

HANS CHRISTIAN ANDERSEN

"Then tell me why you came up here on land again?" asked Big Claus. "I never would have left a place as wonderful as that."

"Well," said Little Claus, "that is just because I am smart. I told you that the water maiden said that another herd of cattle would be waiting for me six miles up the road. By 'road,' she meant the river; and I am eager to see my cattle. You know how the river twists and turns while the road up here on land is straight; so I thought that if I used the road instead of the river I would get there much faster and save myself at least two miles of walking."

"Oh, you are a lucky man!" exclaimed Big Claus. "Do you think that if I were thrown into the river I would be given cattle too?"

"I don't know why not," replied Little Claus. "But I cannot carry you, as you did me, you're too heavy. But if you'll find a sack and climb into it yourself I'll be glad to go to the bridge with you and push you into the water."

"Thank you very much," said Big Claus. "But if I don't get a herd of cattle when I get down there I'll beat you as you have never been beaten before."

"Oh no! How can you think of being so mean!" whimpered Little Claus as they made their way to the river.

It was a hot day and when the cattle spied the water they started running toward it, for they were very thirsty. "See how eager they are to get to the river," remarked Little Claus. "They are longing for their home under the water."

"Never mind them!" shouted Big Claus. "Or I'll give you a beating right here and now." He grabbed a sack that was lying on one of the bulls' backs and climbed up on the bridge. "Get a rock and put it in with me, I'm afraid that I might float."

"Don't worry about that," said Little Claus. But he found a big stone anyway and rolled it into the sack next to Big Claus before he tied the opening as tightly as he could. Then he pushed the sack off the bridge.

Splash! Plop! Down went Big Claus into the river and straight to the bottom he went.

"I am afraid that he will have trouble finding his cattle," said Little Claus, and drove his own herd home.

THE PRINCESS
AND THE PEA

Once upon a time there was a prince who wanted to marry a princess, but she would have to be a real one. He traveled around the whole world looking for her; but every time he met a princess there was always something amiss. There were plenty of princesses but not one of them was quite to his taste. Something was always the matter: they just weren't real princesses. So he returned home very sad and sorry, for he had set his heart on marrying a real princess.

One evening a storm broke over the kingdom. The lightning flashed, the thunder roared, and the rain came down in bucketfuls. In the midst of this horrible storm, someone knocked on the city gate; and the king himself went down to open it.

On the other side of the gate stood a princess. But goodness, how wet she was! Water ran down her hair and her clothes in streams. It flowed in through the heels of her shoes and out through the toes. But she said that she was a real princess.

"We'll find that out quickly enough," thought the old queen, but she didn't say a word out loud. She hurried to the guest room and took all the bedclothes off the bed; then on the bare bedstead she put a pea. On top of the pea she put twenty mattresses; and on top of the mattresses, twenty eiderdown quilts. That was the bed on which the princess had to sleep.

In the morning, when someone asked her how she had slept, she

HANS CHRISTIAN ANDERSEN

replied, "Oh, just wretchedly! I didn't close my eyes once, the whole night through. God knows what was in that bed; but it was something hard, and I am black and blue all over."

Now they knew that she was a real princess, since she had felt the pea that was lying on the bedstead through twenty mattresses and twenty eiderdown quilts. Only a real princess could be so sensitive!

The prince married her. The pea was exhibited in the royal museum; and you can go there and see it, if it hasn't been stolen.

Now that was a real story!

LITTLE IDA'S FLOWERS

What a pity, all my flowers are dead!" said little Ida. "Last night they were so beautiful, and now all their leaves have withered. Why does that happen?" she asked the student who had come visiting.

The young man was sitting on the sofa. Ida was very fond of him because he knew the most marvelous stories, and with a pair of scissors could cut out of paper the most wonderful pictures: flowers, hearts, little dancing ladies, and castles with doors that could open. He was a happy young man and fond of children.

"Why do my flowers look so sad today?" she asked again, and showed the student her bouquet of dying flowers.

He looked at them a moment before he said, "I know what is wrong with them, they have been dancing all night and that is why they look so tired and hang their heads."

"But flowers can't dance," said little Ida.

"Sure they can," replied the student. "When darkness comes and we go to bed and sleep, then the flowers jump about gaily enough. Nearly every night they hold a grand ball."

"Are children allowed to come to the ball too?" asked little Ida, who was eager to know how flowers brought up their children.

"Oh yes, both the little daisies and the lilies of the valley are allowed to come," smiled the student.

"Where do the most beautiful of the flowers dance?"

HANS CHRISTIAN ANDERSEN

"You have been in the park near the king's summer castle, the one that has the splendid garden. You've been there to feed the swans. Remember how they swim toward you when you throw bread crumbs? That's where the grand ball is held; and very grand it is."

"I was there yesterday with my mother," little Ida said, and looked pensive. "But there wasn't a leaf on any of the trees, and not a flower anywhere. There were a lot this summer. Where are they now?"

"As soon as the king and all his courtiers move into town, then the flowers move up to the castle. There they live a merry life; I wish you could see it. The two most beautiful roses sit on the throne; they are the king and queen. The big red tiger lilies are lords in waiting; they stand behind the throne and bow. Then in come all the most beautiful flowers and the grand ball begins. The blue violets are midshipmen. They dance with the hyacinths and the crocuses, and call them Miss. The tulips and the big yellow lilies are the old ladies, they see to it that everyone behaves and dances in time to the music."

"But," interrupted little Ida, "are the flowers allowed to dance in the king's castle?"

"No one knows they are there," continued the student. "Sometimes the old night watchman, who is supposed to take care of the castle when the king is away, does walk through it. He carries a great bunch of keys, one for every door in the castle; and as soon as the flowers hear the rattle of the keys they hide. The old night watchman can smell them but he has never seen them."

"Oh, how wonderful!" little Ida clapped her hands. "Wouldn't I see the flowers either if I were there?"

"I think you could," said the student. "Next time you are in the park, look in through the windows of the castle and you will probably see them. I was out there today, I saw a long yellow daffodil, she was lying stretched out on a sofa. She was a lady in waiting."

"What about the flowers in the botanical garden; are they allowed to attend the ball too? And how do they get out there? It is a very long way from where they live to the castle."

"Oh sure, they can come!" exclaimed the student. "When flowers want to, they can fly. You have seen butterflies. Don't they look like yellow, red, and white flowers? That is exactly what they were

LITTLE IDA'S FLOWERS

once. They are flowers who have jumped off their stems and have learned to fly with their petals; and when they first get a taste for it, they never return to their stems, and their little petals become real wings.

"But I am not sure that the flowers from the botanical garden know about what goes on beyond their walls. The next time you are there, you can whisper to one of the flowers that there will be a grand ball that night in the castle, and see what happens. Flowers can't keep a secret, so that flower will tell it to the others; and when night comes, they will all fly to the castle. That will certainly surprise the professor who is in charge of the garden. The next day when he takes his morning walk, there won't be a single flower left in the whole botanical garden; and I am sure he will write a paper about it."

"But how will the flower I tell it to talk to the others? I am sure that I have never seen a flower speak," said little Ida.

"They mime. It's a regular pantomime. You have seen how, when the wind blows, all the flowers shake their heads and rustle their leaves; what they are saying to each other is just as plain as what we say with our tongues is to us."

"Does the professor understand what they are saying?" asked little Ida.

"Sure he does. One morning when he came into the garden he saw a large nettle rustle its leaves at a carnation. It was saying, 'You are so beautiful that I love you.' But that kind of talk the professor doesn't like, so he hit the nettle across the fingers — that is, its leaves. But the nettle burned him, and since then the professor has never dared touch a nettle."

"That is very funny!" little Ida laughed.

"I don't think that it's the least bit funny," said the old chancellor, who had just come into the room and had overheard the last part of the conversation; but he never found anything funny. "Such fantastic ideas are nonsense; they are harmful to a child and boring for grownups."

The old chancellor did not like the student, especially when he found him cutting pictures out of paper with a pair of scissors. The student had just finished cutting a hanged man holding a heart; he'd been condemned for stealing hearts. Now the young man had started on another. It was the picture of a witch who was riding on a broom and was carrying her husband on the end of her nose.

HANS CHRISTIAN ANDERSEN

Little Ida thought that everything the student did was amusing; and she thought a great deal about what he had said about her flowers. "My flowers are tired from dancing," she thought, and carried her bouquet over to the little table on which her playthings were. She had a whole drawer full of toys too, and even a doll that lay in its own bed.

The doll's name was Sophie. Little Ida picked her up and explained, "Please, be a good doll and sleep in the drawer tonight. The flowers are sick and have to sleep in your bed, so they can get well."

The doll didn't answer; she was angry because someone else was to sleep in her bed.

Little Ida put the flowers in the bed and pulled the covers up around them. She promised them that if they would be good and lie still she would make them a cup of tea. "You will be well enough to be up and around tomorrow morning," she added. Then she drew the curtains around the bed so the sun wouldn't shine in their eyes.

All that evening she could not think about anything but what the student had told her. When her bedtime came, she ran over to the window and pulled aside the drapes to look at her mother's plants, which were sitting in flowerpots on the window sill. She whispered to both the tulips and the hyacinths, "I know where you are going tonight." The flowers acted as though they hadn't heard her. They moved neither a petal nor a leaf; but little Ida believed what she had been told.

When she got into bed, little Ida lay awake thinking about how beautiful it must have been when all the flowers danced in the royal castle. "I wonder if my flowers have really been there," she muttered; and then she fell asleep.

Late at night she woke; she had dreamed about the flowers and the student, who the chancellor had said was filling her head with nonsense. It was very quiet in the bedroom. On the table beside her parents' bed, the night light burned.

"I wonder if my flowers are still lying in Sophie's bed," she whispered. "Oh, God, how I would love to know!"

She sat up in bed and looked toward the door. It was ajar; in the next room were her flowers and all her playthings. She listened; someone was playing the piano softly and more beautifully than she had ever heard it played before.

LITTLE IDA'S FLOWERS

"Now all the flowers are dancing. Oh, God, how I would love to see it," she whispered. But she didn't dare get up, for she was afraid she would wake her father and mother.

"If only the flowers would come in here," she thought. But the flowers didn't come, and the music kept on playing.

Finally she climbed out of bed, tiptoed over to the door, and looked into the living room.

There was no night light burning in there, but she could see anyway, for the moon shone in through the windows onto the floor. It was so bright that it was almost as light as day. All the tulips and the hyacinths stood in two long rows on the floor; on the window sill stood only their empty flowerpots. The flowers danced so gracefully, holding onto each other's leaves. They formed chains and swung each other around, just as children do when they dance.

A big yellow lily sat at the piano and played. Little Ida remembered that she had seen it in the garden that summer. The student had said, "Why, it looks like Miss Line!" Everybody had laughed at him then; but now little Ida thought that the slender yellow flower really did look like Miss Line; and behaved just as she did when she played. There the flower was, turning its yellow face from side to side and nodding in time to the music.

None of the flowers noticed little Ida. Suddenly a big blue crocus jumped up on the table where her playthings were, went right over to the doll's bed, and drew the curtains. There lay the sick flowers. But they didn't seem sick any more. They leaped out of bed. They wanted to dance too. The little porcelain man, whose chin was chipped, bowed to the flowers. They jumped down onto the floor; and what a good time they had!

Now in Denmark at Shrovetide little children are given a bunch of birch and beech branches tied together with ribbons, and fastened to their twigs are paper flowers, little toys, and candies. It is an old custom for the children to whip their parents out of bed with these switches on Shrove Monday. The switches are pretty and most of the children keep them. Little Ida's had been lying on the table among her other toys. Bump! Down they jumped with their ribbons flying; they thought they were flowers. A handsome little wax doll, with a broad-brimmed hat just like the one the chancellor wore, was tied to the top of the longest branch.

The switches danced the mazurka, for they were stronger than

HANS CHRISTIAN ANDERSEN

the flowers and could stamp their feet. All at once the wax doll began to grow. It became taller and bigger and started screaming at the paper flowers: "What a lot of nonsense to tell a child! What a lot of nonsense!"

Now the wax doll looked exactly like the chancellor; for he, too, wore a broad-brimmed hat and had a yellow complexion and a sour expression. The ribbons started to hit the wax doll across the legs, and he had to pull himself together till he was only a little wax doll again.

It was all so funny that little Ida could not help laughing. The switches kept on dancing, and the chancellor had to dance too — when he was as big and tall as a man and when he was only a little wax doll. He was given no rest, until the flowers begged the switches to stop; the flowers who had lain in the doll's bed felt especially sorry for the little wax doll.

As soon as the switches stopped dancing there came a knocking from the drawer where the doll Sophie lay. The little porcelain man went carefully to the edge of the table, leaned over the side of it, and pulled the drawer open as much as he could—which wasn't very much. Sophie stuck

LITTLE IDA'S FLOWERS

out her head. "I see there is a ball. Why hasn't anyone told me about it?"

"Would you like to dance with me?" asked the porcelain man.

"Pooh! You are chipped," said Sophie, and sat down on the edge of the drawer, with her back to the poor little porcelain man. She thought that one of the flowers would come and ask her to dance, but none of them did. The porcelain man danced by himself and he didn't dance badly at all.

Since none of the flowers seemed to notice her, Sophie jumped down upon the floor. She landed with a crash and all the flowers came running over to ask her whether she had hurt herself; the flowers who had lain in her bed were especially considerate.

But Sophie hadn't hurt herself. Little Ida's flowers thanked her for having been allowed to sleep in her bed, and they told her that they loved her; then they took her out to the middle of the floor,

HANS CHRISTIAN ANDERSEN

where there was a great splash of moonlight, and danced with her. All of the other flowers made a circle around them, and Sophie was so happy that she told the flowers they could keep her bed, even though she didn't like sleeping in the drawer.

"Thank you," the flowers replied. "It is most kind of you, but our life is short. Tomorrow we shall be dead. Tell little Ida to bury us out in the garden where the canary is buried; and next year we shall come to life again and be even more beautiful than we are now."

"You mustn't die!" cried the doll, and kissed the flowers.

At that moment the door of the dining room opened and the most beautiful flowers came dancing in. Little Ida could not imagine where they had come from, unless they were the flowers from the park near the king's castle.

First entered two roses who wore gold crowns. They were the king and the queen. Behind them came the carnations and the lilies, bowing and waving to the other flowers.

There was music. Big poppies and peonies blew on the pods of sweet peas with such vigor that their faces were red. The bluebells tingled. It was a funny orchestra both to watch and to listen to. At last came all the other flowers, dancing: violets, daisies, and lilies of the valley; as they finished their dance, they kissed each other. It was lovely to see.

The flowers said good night to each other, and little Ida climbed back into her little bed and dreamed about everything she had seen.

The next morning when she woke, she ran right over to the doll's bed to see if the flowers were still there. There they were, but now they were all shriveled and dead. Her doll Sophie was in the drawer; she looked awfully sleepy.

"Can you remember what you are supposed to tell me?" little Ida asked. Sophie didn't say a word.

"You are not a good doll," scolded little Ida. "Remember how all the flowers danced with you!" Then she took a paper box that had a lovely picture of a bird on its lid and laid the flowers in it.

"That will be your honorable coffin," she said. "And when my cousins come from Norway, then we'll have a funeral and bury you, so you can come again next summer and be more beautiful than you are now."

The cousins from Norway were two strong boys. Their names

LITTLE IDA'S FLOWERS

were Jonas and Adolph. Their father had given them each a bow and some arrows; and these they had brought along to show little Ida.

She told them about the poor flowers that had died and allowed them to attend the funeral. It was almost a procession. First came the boys with their bows slung over their shoulders, then little Ida, carrying the pretty little paper box. In the corner of the garden they dug a little grave. Ida kissed the flowers before she buried them. Jonas and Adolph shot an arrow above the grave, for they didn't have a gun or a cannon.

THE MAGIC GALOSHES

PART ONE: THE BEGINNING

In one of the houses on East Street, near the King's New Square, which is in the very center of Copenhagen, a big party was being held. It was one of those parties you have to have once in a while, to which you invite everyone who has invited you to a party; then the slate is clean and you can be invited out again. Half of the guests were already playing cards; the other half were sitting in the parlor, waiting for the hostess to entertain them. The conversation lagged, until someone mentioned the Middle Ages; and someone else remarked that he thought that that earlier era was better than our own. Then Councilman Knap held forth ardently on his favorite theory that olden times were far superior to the present. He quite convinced his hostess; and they both agreed to disagree with Oersted's evaluation, to be found in the almanac, which asserts that on the whole modern times are the best. The councilman said that he thought the reign of King Hans was the period in which life had been pleasantest and happiest.

While that discussion is going on, let us go out into the entrance hall, where the wraps, coats, walking canes, umbrellas, and galoshes have been deposited. Here sat two women: one was young, the

42

other old. At first sight you might believe that they were personal maids who had accompanied their mistresses — some ancient dowager or withered old maid — to the party. But on closer examination this thought would be dismissed; they were, in any case, not ordinary servants. Their hands were too delicate, they carried themselves too royally, and their clothes were of a strange, if not daring, fashion. They were fairies. The younger one was only a lady's maid to the lady in waiting of the Fairy of Happiness; and she distributed only lesser blessings. The older one looked very serious and was the Fairy of Sorrow herself; she always delivers her gifts personally to make sure you receive them.

They were telling each other what they had done during that day. The fairy who was only a servant of the lady in waiting to the Fairy of Happiness had very little to tell. She had saved a hat from being drenched; she had obtained a greeting — a slight inclining of the head: a nod — for an honest and decent man from a very elegant nonentity, and small things of that nature. "But I'll let you in on a secret," she added. "Today is my birthday and as a present I have been given the honor of giving humanity a very special pair of galoshes. They are magic galoshes and anyone who has them on is transported instantly to the time in history or the place in the world that he desires to be. And so, at last, some people will have a chance to be happy on earth!"

"Do you believe that?" asked Sorrow. "People will be even more unhappy than they were before and will bless that moment when they get rid of the galoshes."

"Don't be silly," said the younger fairy. "I'll leave the galoshes here by the door; somebody will take them by mistake and obtain happiness!"

So ended the fairies' conversation.

PART TWO: WHAT HAPPENED TO THE COUNCILMAN

It was late and Councilman Knap, who was getting ready to go home, was so engrossed in thinking about the times of King Hans that he put on the magic galoshes instead of his own. As he stepped out onto East Street, he was back in the time of King Hans, which meant that he put his foot down in half a foot of slush and mud because in King Hans's time there was no such thing as a sidewalk.

"It's terribly muddy!" he muttered. "Where is the sidewalk? And what happened to the street lamp?"

The moon had not risen high enough to shed any light on the street; the air was dense and heavy. Everything seemed to be shrouded in darkness. At the corner of the street, below the picture of the Virgin, burned a tiny oil lamp. Its light was so dim that the councilman did not notice it until he was standing right underneath the painting of the Mother and Child.

"I'll bet this is an art gallery," he thought. "And they've forgotten to take down their sign."

Two men, dressed as men did in the time of King Hans, walked past him.

"I wonder why they were wearing those clothes? I'll bet they're coming from a masquerade."

Suddenly he heard pipes and drums. Flares lighted up the street. The councilman stopped to look at the strange procession. First there was a group of drummers, who beat their instruments with great force; they were followed by some soldiers carrying torches and armed with crossbows; finally a man, obviously of great importance and belonging to the church, went by. The councilman was so surprised by the sight that he asked a passer-by who the dignitary was.

"He is the Bishop of Zealand," was the answer.

"My God, what has happened to the bishop?" sighed the councilman, shaking his head. "No," he thought. "That couldn't have been the bishop." And, still in a quandary, he walked the full length of East Street and across High Bridge Square; but he could not find the bridge to the Castle Square. In the darkness he could make out the banks of a stream, where he came upon two young men who were lying in a boat.

"Would you like to be rowed over to the island, sir?" one of them asked.

"Over to the island!" exclaimed the councilman, who still did not realize that he had taken a journey backward in time. "I want to go to Christian's Harbor, I live on Little Beech Road."

Amazed, the two young men just stared at him.

"Just tell me where the bridge is," demanded the councilman. "It is disgraceful that none of the lamps is lighted; and there is mud everywhere, as if one were walking in a swamp."

The more he and the ferrymen talked, the less comprehensible they were to each other.

THE MAGIC GALOSHES

"I can't understand your dialect," he said finally, and turned his back on them.

But where was the bridge? And where was the railing that followed the edge of the stream, to prevent people from falling into it? "It's a scandal that such conditions are allowed." And he had never been as disgusted with his own times as he was now.

"I'll go to the King's New Square where I can get a cab, otherwise I'll never get home."

When he reached the end of East Street, the moon came out. "What is that strange structure?" he muttered to himself when he saw the old eastern gates of the city. He spied a little door and opened it, and expected to be in the King's New Square, but he found himself on a meadow. A channel cut across it; a few bushes were growing; and there were the sheds used for storage by the sea captains from Holland; the whole area was then called the Dutch Meadows.

"Either I have walked into a mirage or I am drunk," whimpered the poor councilman. "Oh, what is this all about? Where am I?"

Convinced that he was very ill, he turned back. When he again stood on East Street, the moonlight had made it possible for him to notice that most of the buildings were half-timbered houses with thatched roofs.

"I am not well," he sighed. "Even though I have had only one glass of punch, it didn't agree with me. It was wrong of them to serve baked salmon and punch, they don't go together. I think I shall return and tell my hostess. They would want to know how wretchedly I feel. . . . But it might be embarrassing; they may have gone to bed already."

He searched for the house where he had attended the party, but he couldn't find it. "Oh, this is horrible! I can't even recognize East Street. Where are all the shops? The houses look as bad as those in the provinces. I am ill. I must not be proud, I need help. This is the house where I dined, I think. . . . It doesn't look the same. But there's a light on. Someone is up. I am terribly sick, I'll have to go in."

The door was ajar and he pushed it open. It was an inn, a tavern of the times. There were several people there: a sea captain, a couple of tradesmen or artisans, and two scholars. They were drinking beer and looking thoughtfully into their tankards. Since they were deep in a discussion, they paid no attention whatever to the new arrival.

HANS CHRISTIAN ANDERSEN

"I am sorry to disturb you," began Councilman Knap to the innkeeper's wife, "but I am not feeling well. Could I trouble you to call a droshky? I have to go to Christian's Harbor and there must still be some cabs at the King's New Square . . ."

The woman stared at him, shook her head, and then spoke to him in German. The councilman thought she could only understand German and therefore repeated his request in that tongue. This, together with his strange dress, confirmed her suspicion that he was a foreigner. She realized, too, that he was ill and she brought him a glass of water. It had been drawn from the well in her garden and was very brackish.

The councilman buried his head in his hands, sighed, and tried to understand what could have happened. He felt that he must say something, and noticing a large sheet of paper lying on a table nearby, he asked, "Is that this evening's newspaper?"

The innkeeper's wife did not understand what he meant; but she handed him the sheet of paper. It was a woodcut of a vision in the sky above the city of Cologne. On seeing such an old print, the councilman got very excited.

"This is very valuable! Where have you found it? It is rare and very interesting! What's written below the woodcut is nonsense, of course. Today we know that what they saw in the sky was the northern lights; and they are probably caused by electricity."

Two of the men who sat near him heard what the councilman had said. One of them rose from his seat, politely doffed his hat, and said in a very serious tone, "You must be a very learned man."

"Oh no!" protested Councilman Knap. "I know just a little about a lot of things, as one is expected to."

"*Modestia* is one of the highest virtues," exclaimed the other man. "Though I must comment: *mihi secus videtur*, to what you have said. But I should be only too glad to suspend my *judicium*."

"May I be so bold as to ask whom I have the pleasure of speaking to?" asked the councilman.

"I hold a *baccalaureus* in the Holy Writ," he replied.

The councilman thought that the man fitted his title. He was convinced that he was talking to an old schoolmaster from darkest Jutland, where one still could encounter such eccentrics.

"Here is not *locus docendi*," continued the old man. "But still I

THE MAGIC GALOSHES

beg you to speak, for I am sure you are well read in ancient literature."

"Of course," the councilman replied, "I like to read the classics, but I like to read modern authors as well. But not these new novels about everyday people; there are so many of them already."

"Everyday people?"

"I mean the new naturalistic novels about the poor; they are filled with such romantic ideas," the councilman explained.

"Oh yes!" the scholar smiled. "They are very well done. The king prefers the romances about Sir Iffven and Sir Gaudian, knights of King Arthur of the Round Table."

"I don't know which novel you are referring to, was it written by Heiberg?" asked the councilman, who was talking of the most popular Danish author of the middle of the nineteenth century.

"No, not Heiberg," the man replied, much surprised. "It was put out by Godfred von Gehmen."

"Von Gehmen, so that's the author, he has a very old name; that's what the first printer in Denmark was called."

"Yes, he is our first and foremost printer of books," agreed the scholar.

The conversation continued quite pleasantly for a while. One of the tradesmen talked about the plague that had harassed Copenhagen a few years before — by which he meant in 1484. The councilman nodded; he thought the man was talking about the cholera epidemic that had taken place when he was a young man. The conversation then turned to the activities of the English privateers, who in 1490 had captured the ships in the very harbor of Copenhagen; and since the councilman believed that the War of 1801 was being discussed, he agreed wholeheartedly when the English were condemned.

But then matters got worse; every few minutes he exchanged an undertaker's smile with one of the other guests. The councilman thought the scholar very ignorant; and that man found him too fantastic and daring. Sometimes they just sat staring at each other in wonder; then the *baccalaureus* would break into Latin, thinking that the councilman understood that language more easily; but it was to no avail.

"How goes it with you, good man?" the innkeeper's wife tugged the councilman's sleeve in order to attract his attention; and the poor man — who while he was talking had forgotten what had happened to him — all at once recalled all his misery.

"Oh, my God! Where am I?" he wailed, and almost fainted.

"We want claret, mead, and Bremer beer!" shouted one of the customers. And you" — he pointed at the councilman — "are going to drink with us."

Two girls, one of them wearing a bonnet of two different colors, curtsied and served them.

The councilman shivered, as if he were freezing. "What is this all about? What is happening to me?" he whimpered. But he had to drink and so he did; and he emptied his tankard as often as the other customers.

One of the tradesmen accused the councilman of being drunk. The councilman said that he did not doubt that he was, and begged the other man to get him a cab so he could go home.

"A what?" the man demanded.

"A cab . . . I want to hire a cab, a droshky."

"He's a Muscovite!" someone shouted angrily.

Never before had Councilman Knap been in such vulgar company. He decided that his country must have returned to heathenism. "This is the most horrible moment of my life," he mumbled. And it was then that he got the idea of escaping by diving under the table and crawling toward the door. But just as he was nearing the portal his newly found friends discovered him and decided that he must not escape. They grabbed him by the legs; and luckily for him, they pulled off the galoshes, and that was the end of the magic.

Councilman Knap was lying on the sidewalk. The street lamp was burning brightly above him. The house before him was familiar. He was back on the East Street he knew. Not far from him sat a night watchman, who was sleeping.

"My God, I must have lain here in the street and dreamed it all. Yes, this is East Street. How horribly that one glass of punch upset me."

A few minutes later he was sitting in a cab, on his way to his home in Christian's Harbor. He thought of the misery and the terror he had just experienced; and he praised with all his heart the reality of his own time, which despite all its faults was superior to the age he had just been in. And that was very sensible of the councilman.

THE MAGIC GALOSHES

PART THREE: THE ADVENTURES OF THE NIGHT WATCHMAN

"Look, there are an old pair of galoshes," said the night watchman. "They must belong to the lieutenant. They are lying right outside his front door."

The night watchman would gladly have rung the bell and delivered the galoshes to their owner, but it was late and he was afraid of waking everyone in the house.

"Such overshoes must keep your feet warm. I wonder what it feels like to have them on?" he remarked as he pulled the galoshes over his shoes. "How soft the leather is." They fitted him perfectly.

"Life is strange," the night watchman philosophized, while he looked up at the lieutenant's windows, where a light was still burning. "He could be in his comfortable bed, sleeping; but he isn't, he's pacing the floor. He is a happy man. He has neither wife nor children, and every evening he is invited to another party. I wish I were the lieutenant, then I should be happy."

No sooner had he said his desire aloud than the galoshes fulfilled it. The night watchman entered the body and the soul of the lieutenant. He was standing in his room and in his hand he had a sheet of pink paper, on which had been written a poem. The lieutenant had composed it himself.

And who has not, at some time or other, felt like writing poetry? You have a thought. You write it down, and there is a poem. This one was called "I Wish I Were Rich!"

"I wish I were rich" — Oh, this I swore
Before my first long pants I wore.
"I wish I were rich" I cried in despair,
For then an officer's uniform I would wear.
The silver spurs, the sword I gained,
But money, alas, I never obtained.

One evening when I was young and gay
A tiny girl kissed me in childish play.
I was rich in fairy tales and clever,
Though, in money, as poor as ever.
She cared only for these tales so old
And then I was wealthy, though not in gold.

HANS CHRISTIAN ANDERSEN

"I wish I were rich," without hope I moan,
The little girl into a woman has grown.
A maiden so perfect, so clever and good,
If she my heart's fairy tale understood,
If she that loved me once, loves me still!
Oh, God! poverty breaks the strongest will.

I wish I were rich in solace and peace
And the pain of hope had long ago ceased.
You, whom I love, shed over this poem no tears.
Read it, as the old read verses from youthful years.
No, better it were if these words of despair
Were writ not on paper but in the night air.

Such are the verses one writes when one is in love; and a sensible man does not have them printed. A lieutenant, love, and poverty: that is an eternal triangle, a broken cupid's arrow. That was the way the lieutenant felt too. He leaned against the window-pane and sighed.

"The poor night watchman, down in the street, is far happier than I am. He has a home, a wife, and children who are sad when he is sad and rejoice when he is gay. Oh, he is far happier than I am. I wish I were he!"

At that very moment the night watchman became the night watchman again; since the galoshes had made him a lieutenant, they could return him to being himself. "That was a terrible dream," he mumbled. "I was the lieutenant, but that was no blessing. I missed my wife and my little ones." He shook his head; the dream stayed with him. A shooting star flew across the heavens.

"There it fell," the night watchman, who was still wearing the magic galoshes, said to himself. "I really wouldn't mind being able to see such things a little closer; especially the moon, for that has a good size and wouldn't slip through your fingers. The student whose clothes my wife washes claims that, when we die, our spirits go visiting the stars. That's not true, I'm sure. But it would be fun to be able to see the moon. I wish my soul would leap up there; then, as far as I am concerned, my body could stay right here on this step."

There are certain wishes that are best left unsaid, especially if you are wearing magic galoshes. Listen to what happened to the poor night watchman.

THE MAGIC GALOSHES

We have all traveled by steam: either by train or across the sea on a steamer. But the speed of steam is a snail's pace compared to the speed of light. It flies nineteen million times quicker than the fastest race horse; and electricity is even faster than light. Death is an electric shock administered to our hearts; and with the wings of electricity our souls leave our bodies. It takes the light of the sun eight minutes and some seconds to travel more than a hundred million miles. But with the speed of electricity it takes the soul even less time to accomplish the same journey. The space between planets is for the soul no greater than the distance between our own home and that of a friend's, even when the latter is very close by. Unfortunately, the electric shock to the heart deprives us of our bodies; unless, like the night watchman, one is lucky enough to be wearing magic galoshes.

Within seconds, the night watchman had traveled more than two hundred thousand miles and landed on the moon. The moon is made of much lighter material than the earth. It is as soft as new-fallen snow. He found himself overlooking one of the many mountain craters that you can see in Dr. Mälder's *Great Atlas of the Moon*. I'm sure you know of it. A good mile down, inside the dead volcano, there was a city. It looked like the whites of eggs poured into a glass of water. Transparent towers, cupolas, and sail-shaped balconies swayed in the thin atmosphere. Our own earth floated like a fiery red globe far above him.

The town was inhabited by very strange-looking creatures, and all of them were, I suppose, what you would call human. One could hardly expect that the night watchman would be able to understand their language, but he could.

Without any difficulty at all, he followed their discussion about our earth and whether it was possible for people to live on it. They concluded that the atmosphere was too heavy to allow for any highly developed, thinking creature like a moonian to survive there. They agreed that only on the moon could be found the conditions necessary for life; and therefore, moonians were the first human beings.

But let's return to East Street and see what happened to the body of the night watchman. Lifeless, he sat on the stairs; his spiked mace had fallen out of his hands, and his eyes were fixed on the moon, as if they were trying to watch his honest soul walking about up there.

"What is the time, night watchman?" asked a passer-by. When

he got no answer, he flicked the good night watchman's nose; and the body lost its balance and lay dead on the sidewalk.

The man who had touched the night watchman was terrified. He looked at the night watchman again: he was dead and dead he remained! It was reported and discussed, and the body taken to the hospital.

Now think what a strange situation it would have been if the soul had suddenly come back to East Street looking for its body and had not found it. Probably it would have gone first to the police station; then to the Lost and Found Office to look among the ownerless objects; and finally, to the hospital. It's comforting to know that the soul is more cunning when it's on its own and doesn't have a body to weigh it down.

As you know, the body was taken to the hospital and put into the bathroom to be washed. But first, of course, it had to be undressed; and the very first article of clothing that was removed were the galoshes. And the soul had to return; straight down from the moon it came and the night watchman came back to life at once. He declared that this had been the worst night in his life and he wouldn't go through another like it, not even for two marks; but now it was over and done with.

The night watchman left the hospital the same day; but the galoshes stayed behind.

PART FOUR: THE TRAPPED HEAD AND A MOST UNUSUAL TRIP

Everyone who lives in Copenhagen knows what the entrance to Frederiks Hospital looks like; but since it is possible that this story will be read as well by people who don't live there we had better describe it.

All around the hospital there's a high fence of heavy iron bars and a gate that is locked at night. They say that very thin medical students have been able to squeeze themselves in and out between the bars, when they were supposed to be on duty. The part of the body which they always found most difficult to get through was the head. In this — as in many other uncomfortable situations in this world — the ones with the smallest heads were the luckiest. Enough, that will have to do as the introduction.

The next night, one of the medical students, whose head could best be described — if we are speaking only physically — as fat,

THE MAGIC GALOSHES

was on duty. It was also raining in torrents outside. But neither of these facts seemed to deter him; he had something to do in town which would only take about a quarter of an hour, and he didn't want to have to explain to the gatekeeper the nature of his errand. He decided to try to squeeze through two of the bars in the fence.

He noticed the galoshes that the night watchman had left behind. "Lucky they're here, I can use them in this rotten weather," he thought, and put them on. "Now all I have to do is squeeze through those bars.

"If only my head were through," he mumbled aloud. And immediately his big round head glided through the bars. Naturally, it was the galoshes that had accomplished this for him. There he was, with his body on one side and his head on the other.

He took a deep breath and tried to squeeze his body through. "I'm too fat!" he cried as he continued to push. "I thought my head would be the most difficult to get through."

Now he tried to pull his head back between the bars, but that was impossible. He could move his neck but that was all. The magic galoshes had placed him in a very difficult position. Unfortunately, he never thought of wishing out loud that his body and his head were both on the same side of the fence; he just pushed and pulled and yanked.

The rain was pouring down and the street was empty. He was too far away to be heard by the gatekeeper, no matter how loudly he shouted. He would have to stay right where he was until morning; then a blacksmith would be called to saw through one of the iron bars. But that would take time. All the boys, in their blue uniforms, from the school across the street would come to watch the blacksmith at his work, and so would half the neighborhood and all the passers-by. And there he would be like a prisoner in the stocks with the street filled with people laughing at him. He felt the blood rush to his head just thinking about it.

"It will drive me mad," he muttered. "I can feel myself going insane. Oh, how I wish my head were free and it were all over and done with."

It was a pity he hadn't said that right away. As soon as his thoughts became words, his head was free. He ran into the hospital as quickly as he could.

The night passed and so did the next day, without anyone coming to the hospital to claim the galoshes.

HANS CHRISTIAN ANDERSEN

There was a performance that evening in a little theater in Canon Street. There was not an empty seat in the theater. Among the recitations there was a new poem. We must hear it:

Grandmother's Glasses

My grandmother's head is cleverly turned;
Two hundred years ago she would have been burned.
She knows every joy and every sorrow
That will happen to people tomorrow.
She knows the future, what next year will bring,
For whom funeral bells will toll or wedding bells ring.
What is my future? Denmark's? or art?
With such secrets my grandmother will not part.
I plagued her; first she was silent, then she got mad.
With downcast eyes I tried to look sorry and sad.
I am her favorite, her sweet little darling,
And so I became happy, as in springtime the starling.
For Grandmother handed me her glasses and said,
"I grant you your wish. Put these on your head.
Then go where people are gathered, to one of these places
Where you do not see one but a thousand faces.
Then look through my glasses and you will be able
To read their futures, like cards on the table."
With joy I ran, feeling bold and free.
But where should I go, where would most people be?
To an amusement park? No, I might catch cold.
To a church? No, there gather only the very old.
To Main Street? Everyone walks there in such a haste.
To the theater? Yes, there people have time to waste.
So here I am, your futures to read and tell.
I will draw truth, like water from a well.
Permit me to put on Grandmother's glasses
And we shall know the future as time passes.
Your silence as agreement I take
And into cards I you now make.

At this point the actor who was reciting put on an old pair of spectacles, then he continued:

THE MAGIC GALOSHES

It is true! How amazing! It makes me smile.
I wish you could see it, too, for a while.
There are no kings, but of knaves aplenty,
In spades and clubs I count more than twenty.
The little Queen of Spades, she has her part;
To the Jack of Diamonds, she has lost her heart.
Her passion is great. Oh, I must look away.
No wonder the Jack looks so happy and gay.
I see money inherited and spent in waste.
I see dark strangers arriving in haste.
Oh, it is all to me quite clear,
But other questions are to be answered here.
What will happen to Denmark next year?
I see it! Oh, my goodness! Oh dear!
If I tell, no newspaper will be sold, I fear.
It is better to wait the news to hear.
The theater, what is its future, its fate?
Silence! I seek the director's friendship, not his hate.
As for my own future, which is nearest to my heart,
I see it clearly, but will not with that secret part.
Do you want me the happiest of all here to find?
It would be easy, but would it be kind?
Do you want me to tell which one will live the longest?
Oh, that kind of news will weaken the strongest.
Should I tell this, or that? With doubt I am filled,
I wish no hope in my neighbor killed.
Maybe it is best that I no one's fortune tell
And leave each to his own heaven or hell,
And show my respect to God and to man
By not trying to do what no one can.

The actor had recited the poem very well and there was enthusiastic applause. Among the audience sat the young student, whom we know from the hospital. He had completely forgotten his misadventure of the night before. As no one had come to claim the galoshes and the weather had not changed, the student was wearing them.

He liked the poem very much, and he thought the idea interesting. He wouldn't mind having such a pair of glasses; but he had no particular desire to see the future through them. What would interest him was to be able to see into other people's hearts. "The future you'll find out about soon enough anyway," he thought. "But what goes on in another man's soul, never. Now take the people who are sitting in the first row; if one could climb into their hearts, as if each one were a different store . . . oh, how my eyes would go shopping! Inside that lady over there" — he bent forward and glanced at a very well-dressed woman — "I'd find a fashion show. . . . The woman next to her has an empty store, in need of being cleaned. . . . Others would sell solider things, there'd be more than one hardware store, I am sure." The student sighed. "I know one little store I'd love to visit; but the owner of that store has already hired a salesman and he's the only bad thing in the whole store. Some owners will stand in their doorways, and, bowing politely, invite one to step in. Oh, how I wish I could!"

That was enough for the galoshes. The student became at once invisible and was sent on the most unusual journey that anyone has ever taken: a trip through the hearts of all the people in the front row of a theater.

The first was the heart of a lady; and the student thought he had entered an orthopedic institute, as the place where doctors remove and straighten bones is called. He was in a room filled with plaster casts of crooked backs, deformed limbs, misshapen bodies. Here the lady preserved all the faults of her friends. She had personally cast them and kept them as a museum, which she visited every day.

He got out as quickly as he could and entered the next person. He seemed to be in a great cathedral; innocent white doves flew above the altar. He would have liked to stay and fall on his knees to worship there, but he had to travel on. Yet even so short a visit had done him good. He could still hear the tones from the organ; he felt as if he were a better person, and not so undeserving to enter the next temple.

This was a garret where a poor, ill mother lay in bed; but God's glorious sun shone in through the windows, and beautiful roses grew in boxes on the roof. Two bluebirds sang in childish joy, while the sick mother blessed her daughter.

Now he was crawling on his hands and knees through a butcher shop. Everywhere there was meat and more meat. He was in the heart of a very rich and highly respected man whose name was well known to all. Then he climbed into the heart of this prominent man's wife. It was an old pigeon coop that was about to fall

THE MAGIC GALOSHES

apart. Her husband's portrait was a weather vane, which was connected to the doors of the coop in such a way that, when he turned, the doors opened or closed.

Now he was in a cabinet of mirrors like the one in Rosenborg Castle. But here the mirrors all greatly enlarged the objects they reflected. On the floor, sitting as still as the Dalai Lama, was this person's tiny personality marveling at its own greatness.

He had entered a sewing box. The place was filled with sharp needles. "I'll bet that this is the heart of an old maid I have gotten into," he thought. But he was wrong. It was the heart of a young officer who had already been decorated several times. He was called a man of esprit!

Very confused, the student tumbled out of the hearts that he had wished to visit. He could not collect his thoughts, and decided that his too lively imagination was playing tricks on him.

"Oh, my God," he sighed. "I think I must have a disposition for madness. Isn't it hot in here? I feel so flushed!" Then he recalled all that had happened to him the night before, how his head had been caught between the iron bars of the fence. "That's where it happened," he muttered. "You have to catch things like that at the outset. What I need is a Russian steam bath. I wish I were lying on the highest shelf in the hot room, right now."

There he was on the top shelf of the steam bath with all his clothes on, including the galoshes. Drops of water dripped from the ceiling down on his face.

"Ow!" he shouted, and jumped down from the shelf and ran to the showers.

An attendant screamed: what was a fully dressed man doing in a steam bath?

The student was quick-witted enough to whisper, "It's a bet." But the first thing he did, when he got back home and into his own room, was to plaster a Spanish fly on his back, in the hope that it would draw out the madness.

The next morning he had a bloody back; and that was all he had got out of wearing the magic galoshes.

PART FIVE: THE COPYIST'S METAMORPHOSIS

The night watchman — have you forgotten him? — well, he had not forgotten the galoshes that he had found in the street. He went

HANS CHRISTIAN ANDERSEN

back to the hospital for them; and when neither the lieutenant nor anyone else in the neighborhood would claim them, he took them to the police station.

"Why, they look just like mine," said one of the copyists who worked there. He put the galoshes down next to his own. "Not even a shoemaker could tell them apart."

"Excuse me . . ." A policeman had entered; he had some papers that he wanted the copyist to make duplicates of. The two men talked for a while. When the policeman left and the copyist looked down once more at the two pairs of galoshes he didn't know which were his. Was it the pair on the right or the one on the left?

"It must be the ones that are wet," he thought. But that was wrong, for the wet pair were the magic galoshes. But why shouldn't someone who works for the police be allowed to make a mistake? The scrivener put them on and stuck the papers he had just been given in his pocket. He had decided to do the rest of his work at home.

It was Sunday morning, and when he stepped outside the weather was so lovely that he changed his mind and set out for Frederiksberg. A walk would do him good. No one was more conscientious or hardworking than he was, and he deserved a little outing: didn't he spend almost all his time behind a desk?

As he walked along, he thought of nothing at all; and therefore the galoshes had no opportunity to show their magic power.

In a park, along a shaded path, he met a friend, a young poet, who told him that on the following day he was going abroad.

"So you're off again," remarked the copyist. "You poets are so happy and free. You can fly wherever you want to; the rest of us have a chain around our ankles."

"True," the poet replied. "But the other end of that chain is fastened to a breadbox. You don't have to worry about tomorrow; and when you grow old you'll have a pension."

"But you lead a better life," said the copyist. "Both of us use the pen, but I only copy unimportant trivialities, while you write poetry and are complimented by the whole world. That must be a pleasure."

The poet shook his head and so did the copyist. They parted, each with his own opinion intact.

"Poets are a queer lot," thought the scrivener. "I wouldn't mind being one. I am sure I shouldn't write such whining verse as most

THE MAGIC GALOSHES

of them do. This is a day for a poet. The spring air is clear; the clouds look newly washed; and there is the smell of greenness everywhere. I haven't felt like this for many years."

He had become a poet already. It wasn't very noticeable; but the idea that poets are different from other human beings is very foolish. There are many people who are more poetic and more sensitive than some of our best poets. What makes the poet unique is that he has a spiritual memory. He can retain his thoughts and his feelings until he has clarified them in words; and this other people cannot do. This was the gift that had now been given to the copyist. But change needs a period of transition, and this was what the copyist had just gone through.

"How lovely the air smells," mumbled the poet. "It reminds me of the smell of violets in my Aunt Lone's apartment. . . . Strange, I haven't thought of her for years. She was a very kind old maid who lived behind the Stock Exchange. No matter how cold the winter was, she always had something — a flower or a branch that was in bloom or just about to sprout — standing in a vase. In midwinter, I have seen violets in her home.

"I remember how I used to put a copper coin on her stove; and then when it was hot, take it off and put it up against the window where it would melt a hole in the ice on the frozen glass pane. Through that peephole I saw the world in a strange perspective! Down by the canals stood the icebound ships, deserted except for the screeching crows.

"When the first breeze of spring began to blow, everything changed. The port was filled with activity. People bustled about, and then they would sing and shout, 'Hurrah!' as the ice was sawn into pieces and the ships were made ready for their journeys to foreign lands.

"And I have sat behind a desk in the police station making out other people's passports, but never my own. That is my fate." He sighed deeply and stood still. "I have never felt like this before. It must be the spring air. I am uneasy and happy at the same time."

From his pocket he took out a sheaf of papers. "These dry pages will give me something else to think about," he said and held them up, so that he could read.

MOTHER SIGBRITH, a tragedy in five acts. That was what was written on the first sheet and it was in his own handwriting. "What's this all about? How can I have written a tragedy?" He started to leaf through the pages.

HANS CHRISTIAN ANDERSEN

THE INTRIGUES ON THE RAMPARTS OF THE CITY, a comedy. "Where did these plays come from? Somebody must have stuck them in my pocket," he reasoned. "Why, there's a letter, too." It was a note from the director of a theater. His plays had been rejected and not very politely.

"Oh . . . hum . . ." grumbled the copyist, who was now a playwright, and sat down on a bench.

His imagination was so alive; and he felt so tenderly toward the world. Without thinking, he bent down and picked a flower. It was only a little daisy that had been growing in the grass, yet it was able to explain to him, in one minute, what it would have taken a botanist long hours to tell. The little flower related the myth of its birth, told of the power of the sun: how it forced its petals to unfurl and give off their lovely scent. This made the poet think of how our lives, too, were a struggle and that it was this that aroused so many of the feelings we have. Sunlight and air, the flower explained, were her suitors, but sunlight was her favorite; and she obeyed it and always held her head up toward it. When it disappeared and night came, she closed her petals and slept in the air's embrace.

"The sunlight makes me beautiful," said the daisy.

"But it is the air that gives you breath, so you can live," whispered the poet.

Nearby a boy was splashing the water in a ditch with a big stick; and green branches were being sprayed with muddy water. The copyist began to think of how each drop of water contained millions of tiny, invisible animals, which were so small, in comparison to himself, that their journey into the air, from the ditch to the bush, must have felt to them as he would feel if he were cast high above the clouds.

The copyist smiled at his own thoughts, and how he seemed to have changed. "I must be asleep and dreaming. How curious it is that I can be in a dream and yet feel so natural. I hope I shall be able to remember all that's happened when I wake up. Now I feel so alive and see everything so clearly. . . . Tomorrow it will all seem like nonsense, I know. All the clever and beautiful things we dream about are like subterranean gold; when brought out into the light of day, they are merely stones. . . . Alas!"

Sadly, the copyist was looking at a little bird that sang as it jumped from branch to branch. "That bird is better off than I am.

THE MAGIC GALOSHES

It is happier. To fly! That is the greatest art. Lucky is he who was born with wings. I wish I were a little lark."

No sooner had he uttered the wish than the sleeves of his jacket became wings; his clothes, feathers; and the magic galoshes, claws. The copyist, feeling the transformation, laughed. "I have never had a dream as foolish as this before." He flew up into a tree and started to sing. But there was no poetry in his song. The magic galoshes were thorough; and like everyone else who does things thoroughly, the galoshes could only do one thing at a time. When the copyist wanted to be a poet, he became one; but when he decided that he would rather be a small bird, then he lost his poetic nature.

"This is a fine state of affairs," he peeped. "In the daytime I work in the police station, copying the most unimaginative reports; and at night I fly as a lark, out here in the Frederiksberg Gardens. One could write a comedy about that."

He flew down on the grass and turned his head in all directions before picking up a piece of straw that, considering his size, appeared as large as a North African palm tree.

Suddenly everything was black as night around him. Some huge thing had enveloped him. It was a boy's cap, which an urchin had thrown over him. A hand creeped in under the hat and grabbed the bird around the back, pressing the wings tightly to its little body.

The lark peeped loudly, "You horrible, naughty little boy. I am a copyist in the Central Police Station!" To the child, it only sounded like the ordinary peeping of a bird. He hit its bill and walked off with it.

Along one of the shady paths he met two upper-class boys coming from school. That is, they were upper class by birth; but as far as their character and intelligence were concerned they belonged to the lowest class. For eight pennies they bought the lark from the poor boy; and that's how the copyist was brought back into the city, to stay in an apartment on the Street of the Goths.

"It's a good thing I'm dreaming, or else I'd be very angry," twittered the copyist. "First I was a poet and now I am a lark. It must have been my poetic nature that transformed me into a bird. It's not so much fun to be a bird, especially when you fall into the hands of boys. I wonder how this will end."

The living room was very expensively furnished. The boys were greeted by a fat woman, who was laughing. But she was not amused by the sight of the lark. "A common little bird," she said. But she would let the boys keep it for today, and pointed to an empty cage that stood near the window.

"It's Polly's birthday," she said in a false, mockingly childish voice, "and the little bird of the field has come to pay its respects."

The parrot didn't say a single word; it swung back and forth very gracefully. But a pretty little canary, who only last summer had been brought from its warm, fragrant native country to cold Denmark, began to sing.

"Crybaby!" said the lady, and threw a white cloth over its cage.

"Peep," cried the canary. "What a terrible snowstorm." It sighed and then was silent.

The cage of the lark — or, as the lady called him, the little common bird — had been put between the canary's and the parrot's.

The only words of human speech that Polly had mastered were: "Let us be human!" This often sounded very comical; but everything else it said was as impossible for human beings to understand as the canary's song. The copyist, however, was now a lark and understood his companions perfectly.

"I flew beneath the palms and flowering almond trees," sang the canary. "I flew with my brothers and sisters above beautiful flowers, and across a sea that was clear as glass; and the seaweed waved to us. I have seen many parrots, too; and they told us many very long and amusing stories."

"They were wild birds," commented the parrot. "They didn't have any education or culture. Let us be human!" it screeched.

"Why don't you laugh when I say that? The lady and her guests always laugh, why shouldn't you? It's a great fault to lack a sense of humor. Let us be human!"

"Don't you remember the lovely girls who danced in the tent that was pitched beneath the flowering trees? Don't you remember the sweet fruits with their succulent juice, and the herbs that grew all over the hillside?"

"Oh yes," yawned the parrot. "But I like it much better here. I get good food and am properly taken care of. I am clever, what more need I ask for? Let us be human! . . . You have a poetic soul, as it is called; but I am educated and witty. You may be a genius, but you are too high-strung. You are always trying to reach higher

THE MAGIC GALOSHES

notes, that is why you are covered up. No one would dare to do that to me. I was so expensive, and I am witty, witty, witty. Let us be human!"

"You — little, gray, Danish bird," began the canary. "You are a prisoner too. I think it is cold now, out in your forest; but, at least, there you are free. They have forgotten to close the door to your cage; and one of the top windows over there is open; fly, little bird, fly!"

In a second the copyist was out of his cage. Just then the cat, with its green, shining eyes, came sneaking into the room through the half-open door and tried to catch the lark. The canary flew around in its cage. Polly flapped her wings and screeched, "Let us be human!"

In mortal fear, the copyist flew toward the open window and escaped. He flew above the roofs of the houses and the streets until he was tired and needed to rest. One of the houses seemed more snug, more cozy, somehow friendlier than the others. A window was open and he flew into his own room, where he perched on the table.

"Let us be human," he said. He hadn't meant anything by it, he was only repeating what Polly had said; but he was immediately transformed into his old shape again.

"God preserve me!" he muttered, climbing down from the table. "How did I ever get up here? I must have walked in my sleep. What a strange dream I had; it was all a lot of nonsense!"

PART SIX: HOW THE GALOSHES BROUGHT LUCK

The next morning a young theological student who had rooms on the same floor knocked on the copyist's door.

"May I borrow your galoshes?" he asked. "I should like to smoke my pipe down in the garden, but the grass is still wet from dew."

The copyist, who was still in bed, told the young man to take his galoshes, which he did. After he had put them on he went down into the garden. It was very small and had only a plum and a pear tree; but tiny as it was, it was a marvel, here in the middle of the city.

The student walked back and forth on the little path. It was only six o'clock in the morning. From far away he could hear the sound of the horn that is blown as the stagecoach departs.

HANS CHRISTIAN ANDERSEN

"Oh, to travel!" he exclaimed. "Nothing in the world would be so wonderful as to be able to travel. It is my greatest wish! The only cure for my restless wanderlust. But I would like to travel far away: to Switzerland or Italy or — "

The galoshes were very prompt in granting wishes, which was fortunate for both him and us, for he might have ended up too far away. As it was, he was journeying through Switzerland. He was in a stagecoach with eight other passengers. He sat squeezed in the middle. He had a headache and a kink in his neck. All his blood seemed to have gone to his legs; in any case, his feet were swollen and his boots pinched.

He slipped back and forth between the waking and the dozing state. In his right-hand pocket he had some letters of credit; in his left, a passport; and on a string around his neck hung a leather purse which contained a few louis d'or. Every time he fell asleep, he dreamed that one of his valuables had been lost; then he would wake with a start and move his hand in a triangle: from left to right and to center, to make sure that everything was there. The umbrellas, canes, and hats hanging from the net above his head made it difficult for him to see out of the window. And when he finally did get a view of the magnificent Swiss mountains, which are so tremendously impressive, he thought exactly what an acquaintance of ours did, who was a poet and wrote his thoughts down in verse, though he hasn't allowed it to be published yet:

> It is so very lovely here.
> I can see Mount Blanc, my dear.
> Oh, this is the land of milk and honey,
> If only I had some more money.

Grand, somber, and dark was the landscape now. The peaks of the mountains were hidden by clouds; and the pine forests looked as scraggy as heather. Now it was beginning to snow and the wind blew; it was very cold.

"Oh!" shivered the student. "I wish I were on the other side of the Alps. There it is already summer; and I would have cashed my letters of credit. The fear that they might not be honored quite spoils my journey. I can't enjoy Switzerland, I wish I were in Italy!"

Instantly, he was there, traveling between Florence and Rome. Trasimeno Lake, reflecting the rays of the setting sun, shone like

THE MAGIC GALOSHES

gold. The mountains surrounding it were dark blue. Here where Hannibal defeated Flaminius grapevines peacefully intertwined their slender fingers. Underneath a laurel tree was a group of beautiful, half-naked children, who were herding black swine. If this scene had been painted on a canvas, everyone would have shouted: "Oh, beautiful Italy!"

Inside the stagecoach, however, neither the student of theology nor any of his companions felt such enthusiasm. The vehicle was filled with mosquitoes and stinging flies. The sprays of myrtle which the passengers waved back and forth to protect themselves were of no avail; the flies stung anyway. No one escaped; every face was swollen and bloody from insect bites. The poor horses looked like carrion flesh. The flies sat on them in mounds, and it helped little that the driver stopped often to scrape them off.

The sun finally set, and the evening air was icy cold. It was very uncomfortable. The mountains and the clouds turned a remarkable green; everything stood out so clearly, almost brilliantly in the light of evening. (Yes, you must go to Italy and see it for yourself; it is impossible to describe it: a hopeless task.) The travelers would have agreed; but they were hungry, tired, and more interested in finding a night's lodging than looking at the beauty of nature.

The road passed through olive orchards. The trees looked like the gnarled willow trees in Denmark. Finally the stagecoach stopped in front of a lonely inn. Half a dozen crippled beggars were waiting outside the entrance. The most respectable of them looked like "Hunger's oldest son, who had reached maturity." All the others were either blind, lame, or had hands without fingers. They were, in truth, "wretchedness dressed in rags."

"Eccellenza, miserabili," they wailed loudly and held out their maimed and deformed limbs for inspection.

The innkeeper's wife came out to receive her guests. She was barefoot, her hair was unkempt, and her blouse was filthy. The doors were fastened with rope and string. Half the tiles on the floor were missing; and bats flew about above them, just below the high ceilings. It stank foully.

"I wish she would set the table out in the stable instead," one of the travelers said. "Then at least we would know where the stink came from."

The windows were opened so that fresh air might enter; but even quicker than the air were the mutilated arms of the beggars and the sound of their whimpering: *"Miserabili. . . . Eccellenza, miserabili. . . ."* The walls were decorated with inscriptions, and half of them had nothing pleasant to say about *bella Italia.*

At last the food arrived: boiled water with a little pepper and rancid oil in it; it was called soup. The same oil had been used in the salad. The main dish was fried cockscomb and rotten eggs. The wine must have been drawn from the vinegar barrel.

During the night, all the baggage was piled up in front of the door as a barricade; and one of the travelers was to remain awake while the others slept. The first one to stand guard was the student of theology. Pooh! The smell in the room was nauseating, and the heat! From outside came the sound of the *miserabili* moaning in their sleep; and inside the mosquitoes hummed, as they flew about in search of their next victim.

"Traveling would be fine if we only didn't have a body," sighed the student. "If one's spirit were free to go by itself. No matter where I am, there is always something that presses against my heart: something I need or want to be rid of. I want something better than moments like this. . . . Something better. . . . The best: but where is it and how do you get it? I know what I really want: the final goal, where I am sure all happiness lies!"

As soon as these words were spoken, he was back in his own room. The long white curtains were drawn. In the middle of the room was a black coffin; and in it lay the body of the student, sleeping death's sleep. His soul had gone on the journey he had desired for it, while his body was still. *"Call no man happy before he is in his grave."* This story strengthens Solon's words.

Every dead body is an immortal sphinx. It answers no questions and neither did the body of the student of theology, despite his having asked the questions himself, only a few days before, in a poem:

> Death, your silence fills with dread my heart;
> Your footprints are the graves and tombs of men.
> When my Jacob's ladder of thought falls apart,
> Shall I only arise as grass in death's garden, then?
> The greatest suffering, unseen we bear,
> He was alone, even to the last.
> Life's injustice our hearts outwear,
> Kind is the earth on the coffin cast.

THE MAGIC GALOSHES

Two figures were in the room: Sorrow herself, and the lady's maid to the lady in waiting of the Fairy of Happiness. They were both looking down at the dead body of the student.

"There, you see," began the Fairy of Sorrow. "How much happiness did your magic galoshes bring humanity?"

The servant of Happiness replied, while she nodded toward the coffin, "At least they brought him who is sleeping there eternal peace."

"Oh no!" Sorrow argued. "He chose to leave life behind him, he was not called! He did not have the strength within his soul to accomplish that which even he himself had set as his goal. I shall do him a favor."

Sorrow pulled the galoshes off the student's feet, and the sleep of death was over; and the resurrected young man rose. Sorrow disappeared, and so did the galoshes; Sorrow thought they belonged to her.

THE WILD SWANS

F ar, far away where the swallows are when we have winter, there lived a king who had eleven sons and one daughter, Elisa. The eleven brothers were all princes; and when they went to school, each wore a star on his chest and a sword at his side. They wrote with diamond pencils on golden tablets, and read aloud so beautifully that everyone knew at once that they were of royal blood. Their sister Elisa sat on a little stool made of mirrors and had a picture book that had cost half the kingdom. How well those children lived; but it did not last.

Their father, who was king of the whole country, married an evil queen, and that boded no good for the poor children. They found this out the first day she came. The whole castle was decorated in honor of the great event, and the children decided to play house. Instead of the cakes and baked apples they usually were given for this game — and which were so easy to provide — the queen handed them a teacup full of sand and said that they should pretend it was something else.

A week later little Elisa was sent to live with some poor peasants; and the evil queen made the king believe such dreadful things about the princes that soon he did not care for them any more.

"Fly away, out into the world with you and fend for yourselves! Fly as voiceless birds!" cursed the queen; but their fate was not as terrible as she would have liked it to be, for her power had its

THE WILD SWANS

limits. They became eleven beautiful, wild swans. With a strange cry, they flew out of the castle window and over the park and the forest.

It was very early in the morning when they flew over the farm where Elisa lived. She was still asleep in her little bed. They circled low above the roof of the farmhouse, turning and twisting their necks, to catch a glimpse of their sister, while their great wings beat the air. But no one was awake, and no one heard or saw them. At last they had to fly away, high up into the clouds, toward the great dark forest that stretched all the way to the ocean.

Poor little Elisa sat on the floor playing with a leaf. She had no toys, so she had made a hole in the leaf and was looking up at the sun through it. She felt as though she were looking into the bright eyes of her brothers; and when the warm sunbeams touched her cheeks, she thought of all the kisses they had given her.

The days passed, one after another, and they all were alike. The wind blew through the rosebush and whispered, "Who can be more lovely than you are?"

The roses shook their heads and replied: "Elisa!"

On Sundays the old woman at the farm would set her chair outside and sit reading her psalmbook. The wind would turn the leaves and whisper, "Who can be more saintly than you?"

The psalmbook would answer as truthfully as the roses had: "Elisa!"

When Elisa turned fifteen she was brought back to the castle. As soon as the evil queen saw how beautiful the girl was, envy and hate filled her evil heart. She would gladly have transformed Elisa into a swan at first sight; but the king had asked to see his daughter, and the queen did not dare to disobey him.

Early the next morning, before Elisa was awake, the queen went into the marble bathroom, where the floors were covered with costly carpets and the softest pillows lay on the benches that lined the walls. She had three toads with her. She kissed the first and said, "Sit on Elisa's head that she may become as lazy as you are." Kissing the second toad, she ordered, "Touch Elisa's forehead that she may become as ugly as you are, so her father will not recognize her." Then she kissed the third toad. "Rest next to Elisa's heart, that her soul may become as evil as yours and give her pain."

She dropped the toads into the clear water and, instantly, it had a greenish tinge. She sent for Elisa, undressed her, and told her to

HANS CHRISTIAN ANDERSEN

step into the bath. As she slipped into the water, the first toad leaped onto Elisa's head, the second touched her forehead, and the third snuggled as close to her heart as it could. But Elisa did not seem to notice them.

When Elisa rose from the bath, there floating on the water were three red poppies. If the toads had not been made poisonous by the kiss of the wicked queen, they would have turned into roses; but they had become flowers when they touched Elisa. She was so good and so innocent that evil magic could not harm her.

When the wicked queen realized this, she took the juice from walnut shells and rubbed Elisa's body till it was streaked black and brown; then she smeared an awful-smelling salve on the girl's face and filtered ashes and dust through her hair. Now it was impossible for anyone to recognize the lovely princess.

Her father got frightened when he saw her, and said, "She is not my daughter." Only the watchdog and the swallows recognized her; but they were only animals and nobody paid any attention to them.

Elisa wept bitterly and thought of her eleven brothers who had disappeared. In despair, she slipped out of the castle. She walked all day across fields and swamps until she came to the great forest. She did not know where she was going; she only knew that she was deeply unhappy and she longed more than ever to see her brothers again. She thought that they had been forced out into the world as she had; and now she would try to find them.

As soon as she entered the forest, night fell. She had come far away from any road or path. She lay down on the soft moss to sleep. She said her prayers and leaned her head against the stump of a tree. The night was silent, warm, and still. Around her shone so many glowworms that, when she touched the branch of a bush, the little insects fell to the ground like shooting stars.

That night she dreamed about her brothers. Again they were children writing on their golden tablets with diamond pens; and once more she looked at the lovely picture book that had cost half the kingdom. But on their tablets her brothers were not only doing their sums, they wrote of all the great deeds they had performed. The pictures in the book became alive: the birds sang, and the men and women walked right out of the book to talk to Elisa. Every time she was about to turn a leaf, they quickly jumped back onto the page, so as not to get in the wrong picture.

THE WILD SWANS

When she awoke, the sun was already high in the heavens; but she couldn't see it, for the forest was so dense that the branches of the tall trees locked out the sky. But the sun rays shone through the leaves and made a shimmering golden haze. The smell of greenness was all around her, and the birds were so tame that they almost seemed willing to perch on her shoulder. She heard the splashing of water; and she found a little brook, and followed it till it led her to a lovely little pool that was so clear, she could see the sand bottom in a glance. It was surrounded by bushes; but at one spot the deer, when they came down to drink, had made a hole. Here Elisa kneeled down.

Had the branches and their leaves not been swayed gently by the wind, she would have believed that they had been painted on the water, so perfectly were they mirrored. Those upon which the sun shone glistened, and those in the shade were a dark green.

Then Elisa saw her own face and was frightened: it was so dirty and ugly. She dipped her hand into the water and rubbed her eyes, her cheeks, and her forehead till she could see her own fresh skin again. She undressed and bathed in the clear pool, and a more beautiful princess than she, could not have been found in the whole world.

When she had dressed, braided her long hair, and drunk from the brook with her cupped hand, she wandered farther and farther into the forest without knowing where she was going. She thought about her brothers and trusted that God would not leave her. There ahead of her was a wild apple tree. Hadn't God let it grow there so that the hungry could eat? Its branches were bent almost to the ground under the weight of the fruit. Here Elisa rested and had her midday meal; before she walked on, she found sticks and propped up the heavily laden branches of the apple tree.

The forest grew darker and darker. It was so still that she could hear her own footsteps: the sound of every little stick and leaf crumbling under her foot. No birds were to be seen or heard, no sunbeams penetrated the foliage. The trees grew so close together that when she looked ahead she felt as if she were imprisoned in a stockade. Oh, here she was more alone than she had ever thought one could be!

Night came and not a single glowworm shone in the darkness. When she lay down to sleep she was hopelessly sad; but then the branches above her seemed to be drawn aside like a curtain, and

HANS CHRISTIAN ANDERSEN

she saw God looking down at her, with angels peeping over His shoulders and out from under His arms. And in the morning when she awoke, she did not know whether she had really seen God or it had merely been a dream.

Elisa met an old woman who was carrying a basket full of berries on her arm, and she offered the girl some berries. Elisa thanked her and then asked if she had seen eleven princes riding through the forest.

"No," the old woman replied. "But I have seen eleven swans with golden crowns on their heads, swimming in a stream not far from here."

She said she would show Elisa the way and led her to a cliff. Below it a little river twisted and turned its way through the forest. It seemed to be flowing in a tunnel, for the trees that grew on either side stretched their leafy branches toward each other and then intertwined. Where the branches were not long enough to span the stream, the trunks had pulled up part of their roots, in order to lean farther out over the water so the branches could meet.

Elisa said good-bye to the old woman and followed the stream until its water ran out into the sea.

Before her lay the beautiful ocean. There was not a sail to be seen nor any boat along the shore. She could not go any farther. How would she ever be able to find her brothers? She looked down. The shore was covered with pebbles: all the little stones were round; they had been made so by the sea. Iron, glass, stones, everything that lay at her feet had been ground into its present shape by water that was softer than her own delicate hand. "The waves roll on untiringly, and grind and polish the hardest stone. I must learn to be as untiring as they. Thank you for the lesson you have taught me, waves; and I am sure that one day you will carry me to my dear brothers."

Among the dried-out seaweed on the beach she found eleven swans' feathers. She picked them up; to each of them clung a drop of water, whether it was dew or a tear she did not know.

Although she was alone, Elisa did not feel lonely for she could watch the ever changing scene before her. The sea transforms itself more in an hour than a lake does in a year. When the clouds above it are dark, then the sea becomes as black as they are; and yet it will put on a dress of white if the wind should suddenly come and

THE WILD SWANS

whip the waves. In the evening when the winds sleep and the clouds have turned pink, the sea will appear like the petal of a giant rose. Blue, white, green, red: the sea contains all colors; and even when it is calm, standing at the shore's edge, you will notice that it is moving like the breast of a sleeping child.

When the sun began to slide down behind the sea, Elisa saw eleven wild swans, with golden crowns on their heads, flying toward the beach. Like a white ribbon being pulled across the sky, they flew one after the other. Elisa hid behind some bushes. The swans landed nearby, still flapping their great white wings.

At the moment when the sun finally sank below the horizon, the swans turned into eleven handsome princes, Elisa's brothers. She shrieked with joy when she saw them. Although they had grown up since she had seen them last, she recognized them immediately and ran out from her hiding place to throw herself in their arms. They were as happy to see her as she was to see them. They laughed and cried, as they told each other of the evil deeds of their wicked stepmother.

"We must fly as wild swans as long as the sun is in the sky," explained the oldest brother. "Only when night has come do we regain our human shape; that is why we must never be in flight at sunset, for should we be up among the clouds, like any other human beings, we would fall and be killed. We do not live here, but in a country on the other side of the ocean. The sea is vast. It is far, far away; and there is no island where we can rest during our long journey. But midway in the ocean, a solitary rock rises above the waves. It is so tiny that we can just stand on it; and when the waves break against it, the water splashes up over us. Yet we thank God for that ragged rock, for if it were not there we should never be able to visit again the country where we were born. As it is, we only dare attempt the flight during the longest days of the year. We stay here eleven summer days and then we must return. Only for such a short time can we fly over the great forest and see our father's castle, and circle above the church where our mother is buried. It is as if every tree, every bush, in our native land were part of us. The wild horses gallop across the plains today as they did yesterday when we were children, and the gypsies still sing the songs we know. That is why we must come back — if only once a year. And now we have found you, our little sister. But we can only stay here two more days; then we must fly across the ocean to that fair land where we live now. How shall we be able to take you along? We have neither ship nor boat!"

"What can I do to break the spell that the queen has cast?" asked Elisa.

They talked almost the whole night through; only for a while did they doze. Elisa was awakened by the sound of wings beating the air. Her brothers had turned into swans again. They flew in circles above her and then disappeared over the forest. But her youngest brother had stayed behind. He rested his white head in her lap, and she stroked his strong white wings. Just before sunset, the others returned; and when twilight came, they were princes once more.

"Tomorrow we must begin the flight back to our new home-land," said the oldest brother. "We dare not stay longer; but how can we leave you behind, Elisa? It will be a whole year before we can return. My arms when I am a man are strong enough to carry you through the forest; wouldn't the wings of all of us be strong enough to carry you over the sea when we are swans?"

"I'll go with you!" exclaimed Elisa.

They worked all night, weaving a net of reeds and willow branches. Just before sunrise, Elisa lay down upon it; and she was so tired that she fell asleep. When the sun rose, and the princes changed into swans again, they picked up the net with their bills and flew up into the clouds with their sleeping sister. The burning rays of the sun fell on her face, so one of the swans flew above her, to shade her with his great wings.

They were far out over the ocean when Elisa awoke. So strange did it feel to be carried through the air that at first she thought she was dreaming. Some berries and roots lay beside her. Her youngest brother had collected this provision for her journey, and it was he who now flew above her and shaded her from the sun.

The whole day they flew as swiftly as arrows through the air; yet their flight would have been even faster had they not been carrying Elisa. Soon the sun would begin to set. Dark clouds on the horizon warned of a coming storm. Elisa looked down; there was only the endless ocean; she saw no lonely rock. It seemed to her that the wings were beating harder now. She would be the cause of her brothers' deaths. When the sun set, they would turn into men again; then they would fall into the sea and be drowned. She prayed to God, but still there was no rocky islet to be seen. Black clouds filled the sky; soon the breath of the storm would be upon them. The waves seemed as heavy as lead, and in the clouds lightning flashed.

The rim of the sun touched the sea. Elisa trembled with fear. Suddenly the swans dove down so fast that she thought that they were falling; but then they spread out their wings again.

Half of the sun had disappeared when Elisa saw the little rock. Looking down from the air, she thought that it looked more like a seal who had raised his head above the water. Just as the sun vanished they landed on the rock; and when the last of its light, like a piece of paper set aflame, flared up and then was gone, her brothers stood around her arm in arm.

The island was so tiny that they had to stand holding onto each other all night. The lightning made the sky bright and the thunder roared. They held each other's hands and sang a psalm, which comforted them and gave them courage.

At dawn the storm was over and the air was fresh and clear. The swans flew away from the rock, carrying Elisa. The sea was still turbulent. The white surf looked like millions of swans swimming on a raging green ocean. When the sun was high in the sky, Elisa saw a strange landscape. There was a mountain range covered with ice and snow. Halfway down the mountainsides was a huge palace, miles long, made of arcades, one on top of the other. And below that was a forest of gently waving palm trees, in which there were flowers with faces as large as millstones. She asked if that were the country where they lived, and the swans shook their heads. What she was seeing was a fata morgana: a mirage, an ever changing castle in the air to which no human being could gain admittance. As Elisa stared at it, the mountains, the castle, and the forest disappeared. It melted together and now there were twenty proud churches, every one alike, with high towers and tall windows. She thought she heard their organs playing, but it was the sound of the sea beating far below. The churches, in turn, changed into ships with towering sails. She was just above them; but when she looked down, she saw only fog driven by wind over the waves. The world of the sea and the air is always changing, ever in motion.

At last she saw the shores of the real country that was their destination. The mountains, which were covered with forests of cedar, were blue in the afternoon light; and she could see castles and towns. Before the sun had set, the swans alighted in front of a cave; its walls were covered with vines and plants that had intertwined and looked like tapestries.

"Tomorrow you must tell us what you have dreamed," said her youngest brother, showing her the part of the cave that was to be her bedchamber.

"May I dream how I can break the spell that the wicked queen cast," she said fervently; and that thought absorbed her so completely that she prayed to God and begged Him to help her; and while she was falling asleep she kept on praying.

Elisa felt as though she were flying into the fata morgana, the castle in the air; and a fairy came to welcome her who was young and beautiful, and yet somehow resembled the old woman whom Elisa had met in the forest and who had told her about the eleven swans with golden crowns on their heads.

"Your brothers can escape their fate," began the fairy, "if you have enough courage and endurance. The waves of the ocean are softer than your hands, yet they can form and shape hard stones; but they cannot feel the pain that your fingers will feel. They have no hearts and therefore they do not know fear: the suffering that you must endure. Look at the nettle that I hold in my hand! Around the cave where you are sleeping grow many of them; only those nettles or the ones to be found in churchyards may you use. You must pick them, even though they blister and burn your hands; then you must stamp on them with your bare feet until they become like flax. And from that you must twine thread with which to knit eleven shirts with long sleeves. If you cast one of these shirts over each of the eleven swans, the spell will be broken. But remember, from the moment you start your work until it is finished, you must be silent and never speak to anyone — even if it takes you years, you must be mute! If you speak one word, that word will send a knife into the hearts of your brothers. Their lives depend on your tongue: remember!"

The fairy touched Elisa's hand with the nettle. It felt like fire and she woke. It was bright daylight. Near her lay a nettle like the one she had seen in her sleep. She fell on her knees and said a prayer of thanks; then she walked outside to begin her work.

Her delicate hands picked the horrible nettles, and it felt as if her hands were burning and big blisters rose on her arms and hands. But she did not mind the pain if she could save her brothers. She broke every nettle and stamped on it with her bare feet

THE WILD SWANS

until it became as fine as flax and could be twined into green thread.

When the sun set, her brothers came. At first they feared that some spell had been cast upon their sister by their evil stepmother, for Elisa was silent and would not answer their questions. But when they saw her hands covered with blisters, they understood the work she was doing was for their sake. The youngest of her brothers cried and his tears fell on her hands; the pain ceased and the burning blisters disappeared.

That night she could not sleep; she worked the whole night through. She felt that she could not rest until her brothers were free. The following day she was alone, but time passed more swiftly. By sunset the first of the nettle shirts was finished.

The next day she heard the sound of hunters' horns coming from the mountains. They came nearer and nearer and soon she could hear dogs barking. Frightened, she bound the nettles she had collected into a bundle with the thread she had already twined and the finished shirt; then she fled into the cave and sat down on the nettle heap.

Out of the thicket sprang a large dog; then came another and another. Barking, they ran back and forth in front of the entrance to the cave. Within a few minutes the hunters followed. The handsomest among them was the king of the country. He entered the cave and found Elisa. Never before had he seen a girl lovelier than she.

"Why are you hiding here, beautiful child?" he asked. Elisa shook her head. She dared not speak because her brothers' lives depended upon her silence. She hid her hands behind her back so that the king might not see how she suffered.

"You cannot stay here," he said. "Follow me, and if you are as good as you are beautiful, then you shall be clad in velvet and silk, wear a golden crown on your head, and call the loveliest of my castles your home."

He lifted her up on his horse. Elisa cried and wrung her hands. The king would not set her down again. "I only want to make you happy," he said. "Someday you will thank me for what I have done." Then he spurred his horse and galloped away with Elisa. The other hunters followed him.

By evening they reached the royal city with its many churches and palaces. The king led her into his castle with its lofty halls, where the waters of the fountains splashed into marble basins, and where the ceilings and the walls were beautifully painted. But none of this did Elisa notice, for she was crying so sorrowfully, so bitterly.

Silently but good-naturedly, she let the maids dress her in regal gowns, braid her hair with pearls, and pull long gloves over her blistered hands. When she entered the great hall, dressed so magnificently, she was so beautiful that the whole court bowed and curtsied. The king declared that she was to be his queen. Only the archbishop shook his head and whispered that he believed the little forest girl to be a witch who had cast a spell over the king.

The king did not listen to him. He ordered the musicians to play and the feast to begin. Dancing girls danced for Elisa; and the king showed her the fragrant gardens and the grand halls of his castle. But neither her lips nor her eyes smiled. Sorrow had printed its eternal mark on her face. Finally the king showed her a little chamber. Its walls and floor were covered by costly green carpets. It looked like the cave where she had been with her brothers. In a corner lay the green thread which she had spun from the nettles, and from the ceiling hung the one shirt that she had already knitted. One of the hunters had taken it all along as a curiosity.

"Here you can dream yourself back to your former home," remarked the king. "Here is the work you used to do; it will amuse you amid present splendor to think of the past."

A sweet smile played for a moment on Elisa's lips when she saw what was nearest and dearest to her heart restored to her. The color returned to her cheeks. She thought of her brothers, and she kissed the king's hand. He pressed her to his breast and ordered that all the church bells be rung and their wedding proclaimed. The silent girl from the woods was to become the queen.

The archbishop whispered evil words in the king's ear, but they did not penetrate his heart. The marriage ceremony was held, and the archbishop himself had to crown the queen. He pressed the golden band down on her head so hard that it hurt. But she did not feel the pain, for sorrow's band squeezed her heart and made her suffer far more.

She must not speak a word or her brothers would die. But her eyes spoke silently of the love she felt for the king, who did everything he could to please her. Every day she loved him more. If only she could tell him of her anguish. But mute she must be until

her task was finished. At night while the king slept, she would leave their bed and go to the chamber with the green carpets, and make the nettle shirts for her brothers. But when she had finished the sixth shirt she had no more green thread with which to knit.

She knew that in the churchyard grew the nettles that she needed. She had to pick them herself. But how was she to go there without anyone seeing her?

"What is the pain in my hands compared to the pain I feel in my heart?" she thought. "I must attempt it and God will help me."

As if it were an evil deed she was about to perform, she sneaked fearfully out of the castle late at night. She crossed the royal park and made her way through the empty streets to the churchyard. The moon was out; and on one of the large tombstones she saw a group of lamias sitting. They are those dreadful monsters with the bodies of snakes and the breasts and heads of women. They dig up the graves of those who have just died, to eat the flesh of the corpses. Elisa had to walk past them. She said her prayers, and though they kept their terrible gaze upon her, they did her no harm. She picked her nettles and returned to the castle.

Only one person had seen her: the archbishop, for he was awake when everyone else was sleeping. Now he thought that what he had said was proven true: the queen was a witch who had cast her spell on the king and all his subjects.

When next the king came to confession, the archbishop told him what he had seen and what he feared. He spoke his condemning words so harshly that the carved sculptures of the saints shook their heads as though they were saying: "It is not true. Elisa is innocent!"

But that was not the way the archbishop interpreted it; he said that the saints were shaking their heads because of their horror at her sins.

Two tears rolled down the king's cheeks, and with a heavy heart he returned to the castle. That night he only pretended to sleep and, when Elisa rose, he followed her. Every night she went on with her work; and every night the king watched her disappear into the little chamber.

The face of the king grew dark and troubled. Elisa noticed it, though she did not know its cause; and this new sorrow was added to her fear for her brothers' fate. On her royal velvet dress fell salt tears, and they looked like diamonds on the purple material,

THE WILD SWANS

making it even more splendid. And all the women of the court wished that they were queens and could wear such magnificent clothes.

Soon Elisa's work would be over. She had to knit only one more shirt; but she had no more nettles from which to twine thread. Once more, for the last time, she would have to go to the churchyard. She shook with fear when she thought of walking alone past the horrible lamias, but she gathered courage when she thought of her brothers and her own faith in God.

Elisa went; and secretly the king and the archbishop followed her. They saw her disappear through the gates of the churchyard. The same terrifying lamias were there, and they were sitting near the place where the nettles grew. The king saw her walk toward them, and he turned away as his heart filled with repulsion, for he thought that Elisa, his queen — who that very night had rested in his arms — had come to seek the company of these monsters.

"Let the people judge her," said he. And the people judged her guilty and condemned her to the stake.

She was taken from the great halls of the castle and thrown into a dungeon, where the wind whistled through the grating that barred the window. Instead of a bed with silken sheets and velvet pillows, they gave her the nettles she had picked as a pillow and the shirts she had knitted as a cover. They could have given her no greater gift. She prayed to God and started work on the last of the shirts. Outside in the streets, the urchins sang songs that mocked and scorned her, while no one said a word of comfort to her.

Just before sunset, she heard the sound of swan's wings beating before her window. It was her youngest brother who had found her. She wept for happiness, even though she knew that this might be the last night of her life. Her work was almost done and her brothers were near her.

The archbishop had promised the king that he would be with Elisa during the last hours of her life. But when he came, she shook her head and pointed toward the door, to tell him to go. Her work must be finished that night or all her suffering, all her tears, all her pain would be in vain. The archbishop spoke some unkind words to her and left.

Poor Elisa, who knew that she was innocent but could not say a word to prove it, set to work knitting the last shirt. Mice ran across the floor and fetched the nettles for her; they wanted to help. And the thrush sang outside the iron bars of the window, as gaily as it could, so that she would not lose her courage.

One hour before sunrise, her brothers came to the castle and demanded to see the king. But they were refused, for it was still night and the guards did not dare wake the king. Elisa's brothers begged and threatened; they made so much noise that the captain of the guard came and, finally, the king himself. But at that moment the sun rose; the brothers were gone but high above the royal castle flew eleven white swans.

A stream of people rushed through the gates of the city. Everyone wanted to see the witch being burned. An old worn-out mare drew the cart in which Elisa sat. She was clad in sackcloth; her hair hung loose and framed her beautiful face, which was deadly pale. Her lips moved; she was mumbling a prayer while she knitted the last shirt. The other ten lay at her feet. Even on the way to her death she did not cease working. The mob that lined the road jeered and mocked her.

"Look at the witch, she is mumbling her spells!" they screamed. "See what she has in her hands! It is no hymnbook; it is witchcraft! Get it away from her and tear it into a thousand pieces!"

And the rabble tried to stop the cart and tear Elisa's knitting out of her hands. But at that moment eleven white swans flew down and perched on the railing of the cart; they beat the air with their strong wings. The people drew back in fear.

"It is a sign from heaven that she is innocent," some of them whispered; but not one of them dared say it aloud.

The executioner took her hand to lead her to the stake, but she freed herself from him, grabbed the eleven shirts, and cast them over the swans. There stood eleven princes, handsome and fair. But the youngest of them had a swan's wing instead of an arm, for Elisa had not been able to finish one of the sleeves of the last shirt.

"Now I dare speak!" she cried. "I am innocent!"

The people, knowing that a miracle had taken place, kneeled down before her as they would have for a saint. But Elisa, worn out by fear, worry, and pain, fainted lifelessly into the arms of one of her brothers.

"Yes, she is innocent!" cried the oldest brother; and he addressed himself to the king and told of all that had happened to himself, his brothers, and their sister Elisa. While he spoke a fragrance of millions of roses spread from the wood that had been

THE WILD SWANS

piled high around the stake. Every stick, every log had taken root and set forth vines. They were a hedge of the loveliest red roses, and on the very top bloomed a single white rose. It shone like a star. The king plucked it and placed it on Elisa's breast. She woke; happiness and peace were within her.

The church bells in the city started to peal, though no bell ringers pulled their ropes, and great flocks of birds flew in the sky. No one has ever seen a gayer procession than the one that now made its way to the royal castle.

THE GARDEN OF EDEN

Once there lived a prince who had a library far greater than anyone else has ever had, either before him or since. All his books were very beautiful; and in them he could read about and see portrayed in pictures, everything that had ever happened in the whole world. There was no country, no people whom he could not learn about; but where the garden of Eden lay was not mentioned in any of his books. This made the prince very sad, for it was paradise that interested him most.

His grandmother had told him, when he was still a little boy just starting school, that in the garden of Eden all the flowers were cakes. On each of them was written, in the finest of sugar: history, geography, addition, subtraction, or the multiplication tables; and all children had to do was to eat the right cakes and they knew their lessons at once. The more cakes they ate, the better educated they became. Then, he had believed his grandmother's story; but as he grew up and became wiser, he understood that the beauty of paradise was far greater and more difficult to conceive:

"Oh, why did Eve pluck the apple and why did Adam eat the forbidden fruit? If I had been Adam, man would never have fallen and sin would not have conquered the world." This he had said to his grandmother when he was a little boy. Now, at seventeen, he felt no differently; and thoughts about the garden of Eden still filled his mind.

His favorite diversion was to take solitary walks in the woods.

THE GARDEN OF EDEN

One day when he had ventured farther than usual a storm overtook him. Though it was not yet evening, the day grew as dark as night and the rain came down in torrents. Soon he lost his way. He slipped in the wet grass and stumbled over the rocks. The poor prince was wet to the skin. Exhausted, he climbed up the side of the cliff, pressing his body against the water-drenched moss. He was about to give up when he heard a strange whistling noise near him; then he came upon a cavern in the cliff wall. Inside the cave was a fire so great that a whole deer could be roasted over it; and that was exactly what was being done. A woman who was so big and strong that she looked like a man, who had put on skirts, was turning a spit on which was a buck, antlers and all.

She put another log on the fire; then she turned and called to the prince, "Come in! Sit down by the fire and dry your clothes."

"It's drafty in here," the prince said. He was shivering as he sat down on the floor near the fire.

"It's going to be a lot draftier when my sons come home," said the woman. "You are in the cave of the winds. The four winds of the world are my sons, do you understand?"

"Where are they now?" asked the prince, who had understood her well enough.

"If a question is stupid, how can one give a clever answer?" grumbled the woman. "My sons are out on their own, playing ball with the clouds, somewhere up there." She pointed upward and toward the entrance to the cave.

"I see," nodded the prince. "You speak more roughly than the women I am used to talking to."

"Well, they are not mothers of sons like mine." The woman grinned. "I have to be tough to keep my sons in tow. But I can take care of them, however stiff-necked they are. See those four leather bags hanging on the wall? They are just as afraid of them as you were of the switch in the corner. I am stronger than they are, and if they don't behave, then I pick any one of them up and put him in a bag, and there he can stay until I let him out again. There is one of them coming now."

It was the north wind. He was clad in bearskin with a sealskin cap pulled down over his ears. He brought hail and snow in with him; and icicles were hanging from his beard.

"You'd better not go near the fire just yet," said the prince, "or you will get frostbite on your hands and your face."

"Frostbite!" laughed the north wind as loud as he could. "Why,

HANS CHRISTIAN ANDERSEN

frost and coldness are what I love. How has such a little weakling as you found your way to the cave of the winds?"

"He is my guest," said the old woman, "and if you are not satisfied with that explanation, then I will put you in your bag. You know that I mean what I say."

That quieted the north wind down, and he began to tell about where he had been and what he had seen during the month that he had been away.

"I have just come from the Arctic Ocean," he began. "I have been visiting the Barents Sea with Russian whalers. I sat sleeping on their tiller when they rounded the North Cape. Fulmars flew around my legs. They are strange birds. They flap their wings once or twice and then hold them out straight, gliding along at a good speed."

"Don't be so long-winded," interrupted his mother. "What was it like on the Barents Sea?"

"Oh, it was beautiful. Flat as a dance floor. The snow was melting and the moss was green. Skeletons of walrus and polar bears lay among the sharp stones. They looked like the limbs of giants and were covered with green mold. One would think that the sun had never shone on them. I blew the fog away so that I could see a little better. Someone had built a shed from the wreckage of stranded ships, with walrus skin stretched over it; it had turned strange green and red colors. A polar bear sat on the roof and growled. I went down to the beach and had a look at the birds' nests there. They were filled with little naked offspring who were screaming with their bills open. I blew down into them; that taught them to keep their mouths shut. Down at the water's edge lay the walruses, looking like giant maggots with pigs' heads and teeth more than a yard long."

"You describe it well," admitted his mother. "My mouth waters, hearing about it."

"The Russians began to hunt the walruses. They thrust their harpoons into the animals, and the blood spouted like geysers high up in the air and spattered the white ice red. It made me think of playing a little game myself. I blew, and brought my own ships, the great icebergs, down to squeeze their boats. You should have heard them whimper and whine; but I whistled higher than they did. I held their ships in my vise of ice; they got so frightened that they started to unload the dead walruses and everything else they had

THE GARDEN OF EDEN

aboard onto the ice. Then I sent them a snowstorm and let them drift south, for a taste of salt water. They will never return to the Barents Sea."

"Then you have done evil," said his mother.

"What good I do, I will let others tell about," said the north wind and grinned. "But there is my brother, the west wind. I like him better than the others, there is a smell of the salt sea about him and he brings some blessed coldness with him."

"Is that the gentle zephyr?" asked the prince.

"It is the zephyr, all right," said the old woman, "but he is not so gentle any more. When he was young he was a sweet-looking boy, but that is all gone now."

The west wind looked like a savage. He wore a helmet on his head. In his hand he held a big club that he had cut from a tree in one of the great mahogany forests of America.

"Where are you coming from?" asked his mother.

"From the great primeval forest," he answered, "where thorny liana stretches itself from tree to tree, where the water snake lives and man has never set foot."

"And what did you do there?"

"I looked at the deep river that fell from the cliffs down into the valley, sounding like thunder, and made a spray great enough to bear a rainbow. I saw a buffalo swim in the river; the currents caught it and carried it, among a flock of ducks, down toward the waterfall. When they came to the rapids, the ducks flew up; but the buffalo couldn't fly, it had to follow the water down the turbulent falls. Oh, I liked that sight so much that I blew a storm great enough to fell trees that have stood a thousand years and break them into kindling."

"Is that all you have done?" asked the old woman.

"I have turned somersaults on the savannah, patted wild horses, and blown down a coconut or two. I have a couple of stories I could tell; but it is best not to tell everything one knows. That you know well enough, old thing." He kissed his mother so that she almost fell over backward. Oh, he was a wild boy!

The south wind arrived; he wore a turban and a Bedouin's cape. "It's cold in here," he said, and threw more wood on the fire. "You can tell that the north wind came home first."

"It is so hot in here that you could fry polar bears," grumbled the north wind.

HANS CHRISTIAN ANDERSEN

"You are a polar bear yourself," retorted the south wind angrily.

"Do you want to be put in the bag?" asked the old woman, and sounded as if she meant it. "Sit down, and tell us about the places you have been."

"In Africa, Mother," began the south wind, crestfallen. "I have been hunting lions with the Hottentots in the land of the Kaffirs; the great plains were olive green; here the antelopes danced, and I ran races with the ostriches, and won every time. I visited the desert, its yellow sand looked like the ocean's floor. There I met a caravan; they had just slaughtered the last of their camels, to get a little to drink. The sun burned down upon them from above, and the hot sand fried them. The great borderless desert stretched all around them. Then I played with the fine dry sand, I whirled it up in pillars, toward the sky. Oh, that was a dance. You should have seen the face of the merchant; he pulled his caftan up over his head to protect himself and then threw himself down in front of me, as if I were Allah, his God. I buried them all in a pyramid of sand. Next time I come I shall blow it away and let their bones be bleached by the sun, so that other travelers can see that which is hard to believe in the loneliness of the desert: the fact that other men have been there before them."

"You have only been evil," scolded his mother; "into the bag you go." She grabbed the south wind around his waist, bent him in half, and stuffed him into one of the leather bags. But the south wind wouldn't keep still and the bag jumped all over the floor; then his mother took it and, using it as a pillow, she sat down upon the bag and he had to lie quietly.

"You have got lively sons," said the prince.

"They are plucky enough; but I can manage them," answered the mother. "Here comes my fourth son."

It was the east wind; he was dressed as a Chinese.

"Oh, that is where you have been," said the mother, and nodded. "I thought you had been in the garden of Eden."

"No, that is where I fly tomorrow," replied the east wind. "Tomorrow it is exactly a hundred years since I was there last. Now I am coming from China. I have danced around the porcelain tower so swiftly that all the little bells rang. Down in the streets the state officials were getting a beating. I didn't count how many bamboo canes were worn out on their backs. All the officers from the first to the ninth grades were being punished. Every time they were hit, they screamed: 'Thank you, thank you, our father protector!' But they didn't mean a word of it, and I rang the bells of the tower, and sang: 'Tsing, tsang, tsu!'"

"You are getting a little too frisky," laughed his mother. "I am glad you are visiting paradise tomorrow; it always improves your manners. Remember to drink from the spring of wisdom, and to bring a bottle full of the water back to your mother."

"I certainly will," said the east wind, "but why have you put my brother from the south in his bag? Let him out. I want him to tell me all about the bird phoenix. The princess in the garden of Eden asks to hear about that bird whenever I visit her. Please let him out, and I shall give you two pocketfuls of tea. I picked it myself and it is fresh and green."

"In appreciation of the tea and because you are my favorite, I will let him out." The old woman untied the bag and the south wind climbed out; he looked embarrassed because the prince had seen his punishment.

"I have a palm leaf." The south wind carefully avoided looking at the prince while he spoke. "You can give it to the princess. On it, the bird phoenix has carefully written, with his bill, his whole life story, all that happened to him during the hundred years he lived. She can read it herself. I saw the bird phoenix set fire to its own nest, as if it were the wife of a Hindu. The dry branches crackled and the smoke had a strange fragrance. At last the bird itself burned with a clear flame and became ashes; and the egg lay red hot among the embers. The shell cracked with a bang like a cannon shot, and the young bird flew up. Now he is king of all the other birds; and the only phoenix in the whole world. He has bitten a mark in the palm leaf; that is his way of sending a greeting to the princess."

"No more talk, let us eat," said the mother of the winds, and started to carve the deer. The prince sat down next to the east wind and they were soon fast friends.

"Tell me," begged the prince, "who is this princess that you are all talking about, and where lies the garden of Eden?"

"Ah! Ha!" laughed the east wind. "Would you like to come along tomorrow? You must remember that no man has been there since Adam and Eve were thrown out. I assume you know about them from the Bible."

"Certainly," said the prince gravely.

HANS CHRISTIAN ANDERSEN

"Well, when they were banished, the garden of Eden sank down underground, but it kept its beauty, its warmth and mild air. The queen of the fairies lives there, and there lies the Island of Bliss, where death can never come. If you will climb up on my back tomorrow, then I shall take you there. That is enough talking for tonight, I am tired."

Soon they all fell asleep. It was still early in the morning when the prince awoke, but to his surprise, he found himself flying high up among the clouds. The east wind was carrying him and had a good grasp on him so that he wouldn't fall. They were up so high that the earth below him with its forests and fields looked like a colored map.

"Good morning," said the east wind. "You could have slept a little longer. There is not much to look at, all the land below us is flat. But if you want to count the churches you can; they look like chalk marks on the green board down there." It was the fields and meadows the east wind referred to as the "green board."

"It wasn't very polite of me not to say good-bye to your mother and your brothers."

"Never mind, a man who is asleep is excused!" grumbled the east wind, and flew even faster. As they passed over the treetops, all the leaves and branches rustled. When they crossed the sea, the waves grew white and the big ships curtsied deeply like swans.

When evening came, they flew in darkness over a great city. The thousands of lights burning below reminded the prince of the sparks that fly from a piece of paper when it has been set on fire. It was so lovely that the prince clapped his hands. But the east wind scolded him and said that he could make better use of his hands by holding on, or he might end up hanging from a church spire.

With grace the great eagles fly over the black forests, but the east wind flies more gracefully. Swift is the horse of the Cossacks, but the east wind is swifter.

"There are the Himalayas," said the east wind. "It is the highest mountain range in Asia; soon we shall be in the garden of Eden."

The wind turned in a southeasterly direction, and soon the prince could smell the fragrance of spices and flowers. Figs and pomegranates grew wild as did a vine that bore both red and blue grapes. Here they rested for a while and stretched themselves out in the soft grass. The flowers nodded to the wind as if they were saying, "Welcome back."

THE GARDEN OF EDEN

"Are we not in the garden of Eden?" asked the prince.

"Not yet," answered the wind, "but it won't be long now before we are there. Can you see the cave up on the side of that cliff? The grapevines almost hide it. We have to fly through it. Wrap your cape tightly around you. Here the sun is burning hot, but in there it is as cold as ice. The birds that fly past the opening of the cave have one wing in the warm summer and the other in the coldest of winters."

"So this is the gate of paradise," thought the prince as he wrapped himself in his cape. In they went, and cold it was; but the distance was short. The east wind spread out his wings, and they burned like fire, lighting the caves through which they flew. There were great blocks of stones, wet from the water endlessly dropping. They had the strangest shapes; some looked like organ pipes and others like banners. Sometimes the room was so large that the ceiling was lost in darkness; other times, the passages were so narrow that they had to crawl on all fours to get through them. The prince thought they looked like burial chambers.

"Are we taking Death's road to paradise?" he asked.

The east wind did not answer. He pointed toward a radiantly blue light ahead of them. The rocks gave way to a mist, which finally looked like a white cloud in the moonlight. It was no longer cold. The air was mild and fresh like mountain air, and yet filled with the fragrance of the roses that grew in the valley.

Below them was a river; its water was as transparent as air. Gold and silver fish swam in it; and so did scarlet eels. Each time they twisted their bodies, blue sparks flew and illuminated the water. The leaves of the water lilies were all the colors of the rainbow, and the flower itself was a flame that drew its substance from the water, as oil lamps draw theirs from oil. A marble bridge carved as intricately as if it had been ivory led to the Island of Bliss, where the garden of Eden lay.

The east wind carried the prince in his arms, across the river to the island, and set him down among the flowers. The leaves and the petals of the flowers sang to him all the songs he had heard as a child, but their voices were far more beautiful than human voices.

The prince could not recognize any of the trees. Were they palm trees or giant water plants? Certainly, he had never before seen any trees so succulent and tall. Long garlands of wonderful vines, like the ones that decorate old holy books and twist themselves around the gilded first letter on their pages, hung between the trees. Around him he saw the strangest mixtures of animals and plants. In the grass stood some peacocks with their great colorful tail feathers spread out. He drew nearer and touched them. They were not animals but giant burdock leaves as splendid as peacocks' tails. Lions and tigers jumped about among the bushes, tame as kittens. Doves as white as pearls beat their wings so near the lions that they touched their manes. Shy antelopes, with dark eyes as deep as pools, nodded their heads as if they, too, wanted to join the game.

There was the fairy, the princess of the garden of Eden. Her clothes were brighter than the sun, and her face as happy as a mother's when she looks at her sleeping child. She was young and beautiful; a train of lovely girls, each with a star in her hair, followed her.

The east wind gave her the palm leaf, the gift from the bird phoenix, and her eyes sparkled with joy. She took the prince by the hand and led him into her castle. The walls had the same transparency that you see when you hold a tulip petal up toward the sun and look through it. The ceiling was a shining flower and the longer you looked at it, the more magnificent it became.

The prince stepped over to one of the windows, looked out through it; and there he saw the tree of knowledge, the snake, and Adam and Eve. Surprised, he turned to the fairy and asked, "Have they not been banished?"

She smiled and explained to him that what he saw were pictures burned into the glass by Time itself. They were not like any painting he had seen, for they were alive: the leaves of the trees moved and the people portrayed in them came and went as in a mirror. He stood before another window and there he saw Jacob's ladder stretching far up into heaven, and he saw the angels, with their great wings, flying around it. Everything that had ever happened still lived inside these glass paintings. Such curious and wonderful works of art only Time could create.

The fairy smiled at his amazement and led the prince into another great hall in the castle, where the walls were transparent paintings of millions and millions of happy faces: all of them laughing and singing; and their laughter merged with the songs into one melodious hymn to happiness. The faces nearest the ceiling were as tiny as rosebuds, or the point you can make with a

THE GARDEN OF EDEN

sharpened pencil on paper. In the middle of the hall grew a large tree and golden apples, the color of oranges, hid among its greenery. It was the tree of knowledge, the tree of good and evil, whose fruits Eve had picked and Adam eaten. From its leaves fell red dewdrops, as though the tree shed tears of blood.

"Come down into my little boat," bade the fairy. "It rocks as though it were floating on the swelling waters, and that is a most delightful feeling; but it never moves, though all the countries of the world will pass by for us to look at."

And they did; first the prince saw the snow-clad mountains of the Alps, with their black forests of fir trees and lace collars of clouds. He heard the melancholy sound of the hunters' horns and the herdsmen yodeling. The scene around them changed; banana palms bent their long leaves down toward them and coal-black swans swam near them; beyond the beach the most fantastic flowers bloomed. They were in the Dutch East Indies, the fifth continent. They heard the priests of the savages chant and saw them dance their wild dances. The islands and their blue mountains disappeared, and in their place rose the great pyramids of Egypt, the endless desert, the sphinx and ancient ruins of temples half buried beneath yellow sand. At last, northern lights burned above them, nature's fireworks, far more splendid than any man could construct. The prince had never been so happy; but then, he had seen a great deal more than I have described.

"Can I stay here forever?" he whispered.

"That depends upon yourself," answered the fairy. "If you do not let that which is forbidden tempt you, as Adam did, then you can live here forever."

"I won't touch the apples of the tree of knowledge," said the prince hastily. "There are so many other fruits as lovely as they."

"Examine your own heart, and if there is courage enough in it, then stay. But if you find doubt and weakness there, then ask the east wind to take you with him. He is leaving now and he will not be back for a hundred years. The years here pass like hours, but even a hundred hours are long enough for both temptation and sin. Every evening I shall leave you; and as I go I shall cry out to you to follow me. I shall wave my hand to beckon you to come. But do not obey me. Every step you take toward me will make it more difficult for you to turn back. If you follow me, you will enter the hall where the tree of knowledge grows; underneath its sweet-smelling branches I sleep. As you bend over me I shall smile, but if you kiss my mouth, then Eden's garden will sink down farther into the earth and will forever be lost for you. The cruel wind of the desert will enfold you and cold rain drip from your hair; and sorrow and care will be your lot."

"I will stay," said the prince.

The east wind kissed him on his forehead and said, "Be strong! And I shall see you again when a hundred years have passed. Farewell, farewell!" The east wind spread out his great wings that shone like the lightning of summer or the northern lights of winter.

"Farewell, farewell!" shouted all the flowers and the bushes; and the birds of the air followed him as far as the gate of the garden.

"Now begins our dance," whispered the fairy. "When it is over and the sun begins to set, I shall cry out, begging you to follow me. But do not do it. Every night for a hundred years this will happen; but each time you refuse me makes it easier for you to do it the next time, until at last it will give you no pain. This is the first night and I have warned you."

The fairy led him into a chamber made of white, transparent lilies; their yellow stamens were little golden harps and from them came the most delightful music. The loveliest young maidens, light and slender, danced around him; their gauzelike clothes, like mist, half concealed their beautiful bodies. They sang while they danced a hymn to life: to their own eternal life in paradise.

The sun was setting; the heavens became like gold and the lilies turned the color of roses. The maidens handed the prince a cup of wine; he drank it and felt even more intensely happy than he had before. The back wall of the chamber disappeared and he looked into the great hall where the tree of knowledge grew. Its beauty blinded him. The song coming from the countless faces on the wall sounded like his mother's voice singing to him: "My child, my dearest child."

The fairy waved to him, beckoned to him, and cried lovingly, "Follow me, follow me." He forgot all his promises and ran toward her, on this his very first evening in the garden of Eden. The fragrance of all the strange spices of the world that came from the garden grew stronger, and the music of the harps even more beautiful. In the hall of the tree, it seemed to him that all the millions of happy faces nodded yes, and sang, "One must know and experi-

THE GARDEN OF EDEN

ence everything; man is the master of the world." The dewdrops falling from the leaves of the tree of good and evil no longer looked like tears but like red shining stars.

"Follow me, follow me," whispered a voice, and for each step the prince took, his cheeks grew redder and his blood pulsed even faster through his veins.

"I must," he breathed, "it is no sin to follow beauty and happiness. I just want to see where she sleeps, I shall not kiss her. Nothing is lost unless I do that, and I shall not. I am strong, I am not weak!"

The fairy threw off her beautiful robes and disappeared in among the branches.

"I have not sinned yet," muttered the prince, "and I shall not do it." But he pulled the branches apart to look. There she lay sleeping, as beautiful as only the fairy in the garden of Eden can be. She smiled in her sleep; he bent over her and saw a tear hanging from her long eyelashes.

"Are you crying because of me?" he whispered. "Do not cry, fairest, most beautiful woman! Now I understand the happiness of paradise. It flows with my blood through my veins into by brain, my thoughts. I feel the strength of the angels' eternal life within my mortal body. Let everlasting night come, the riches of one moment like this are enough for me." He kissed away her tear, he kissed her eyes, and his mouth touched hers.

A fearful clap of thunder was heard, deeper, more frightening than any ever heard before. The fairy vanished and the garden of Eden sank into the earth: deep, deep down. The prince saw it disappear into the dark night like a far distant star. He felt a deathly coldness touch his limbs; his eyes closed, and he fell down as though he were dead.

The sharp lashes of the wind whipped his face and the cold rain drenched him, then he awoke. "What have I done?" he sighed. "I have sinned as Adam did. Sinned and caused paradise to sink deeper into the earth." He opened his eyes and saw a star blinking far away, sparkling as the garden of Eden had when it disappeared. It was the morning star.

He rose. He was in the forest near the cave of the winds; their mother was sitting on a tree stump. She looked at him with anger and disgust.

"Already the first evening," she scolded. "I thought so. If you were my boy, then I would put you in a bag."

HANS CHRISTIAN ANDERSEN

"That is exactly what will happen to him," said Death, who was standing in the shadow of one of the big trees. He was a strong old man with a scythe in his hands and large black wings on his back. "In a coffin I shall put him, but not now. Let him first wander about on earth, atoning for his sins, becoming good if he can. Then I shall come, when he least expects it, and put him in a black coffin. I shall carry him on my head to the stars, for there, too, blooms the garden of Eden; and if he has learned to be kind and good, then he shall live there forever. But if his heart and thoughts are filled with sin, then he shall sink in his coffin deeper into the earth than the garden of Eden sank. Only once every thousand years shall I come to fetch him, to find out whether he must be sent even deeper into the earth or be taken to the bright and sparkling star."

THE FLYING TRUNK

Once there was a merchant who was so rich that he could easily have paved a whole street with silver coins and still have had enough left over to pave a little alley as well. But he didn't do anything so foolish, he made better use of his money than that. He didn't give out a copper coin without getting a silver one in return; that's how good a merchant he was, but he couldn't live forever.

His son inherited all his money, and he was better at spending than at saving it. Every night he attended a party or a masquerade. He made kites out of bank notes; and when he went to the beach, he didn't skim stones; no, he skimmed gold coins. In that way, the money was soon gone, and finally he had nothing but four pennies, a pair of worn-out slippers, and an old dressing gown. He lost all his friends; they didn't like to be seen with a person so curiously dressed. But one of them was kind enough to give him an old trunk and say to him, "Pack and get out." That was all very well, but he had nothing to pack, so he sat down inside the trunk himself.

It was a strange trunk; if you pressed on the lock, then it could fly. That is what the merchant's son did, and away it carried him. Up through the chimney, up above the clouds and far, far away. The trunk creaked and groaned; its passenger was afraid that the bottom would fall out, for then he would have a nasty fall. But it didn't, the trunk flew him directly to the land of the Turks and landed.

The merchant's son hid the trunk beneath some leaves in a forest and started to walk into town. No one took any notice of him, for in Turkey everyone wears a dressing gown and slippers.

He met a nurse carrying a babe in her arms. "Hey, you Turkish nurse," he said, "what kind of a castle is that one, right outside the city, with windows placed so high up the walls that no one but a giant could look through them?"

"That is where the princess lives," replied the nurse. "It has been prophesied that a lover will cause her great suffering and sorrow, that is why no one can visit her unless the king and the queen are present."

"Thank you," said the merchant's son. He ran back into the forest where he had hidden the trunk, climbed into it, and flew up to the roof of the palace; then he climbed through a window, in to the princess.

She was sleeping on a sofa and looked so beautiful that the merchant's son had to kiss her. She woke up and was terrified at the sight of the strange man, but he told her that he was the God of the Turks and that he had come flying through the air to visit her. That story didn't displease her.

They sat next to each other on the settee and he told her stories. He made up one about her eyes being the loveliest dark forest pools in which thoughts swam like mermaids. He told her that her forehead was a snow mountain filled with grand halls, whose walls were covered with beautiful paintings. And he told her about the storks that bring such sweet little children. Oh, they were delightful stories; then he proposed and she said yes.

"Come back on Saturday," she said, "then the king and queen come for afternoon tea. They will be proud that I am going to marry the God of the Turks. But make sure, sir, that you have some good fairy tales to tell them. My mother likes noble and moral stories, and my father lively ones that can make him laugh."

"Stories are the only wedding gift I shall bring," said the merchant's son, and smiled most pleasingly. Before they parted, the princess gave him a sword with a whole lot of gold coins attached to the hilt; and these he was in need of.

The merchant's son flew away and bought himself a new dressing gown. When he returned to the forest he started to compose

THE FLYING TRUNK

the fairy tale that he would tell on Saturday. And that wasn't so easy. But finally he was finished and Saturday came.

The king, the queen, and the whole court were having tea with the princess. They greeted him most kindly.

"Now you must tell us a fairy tale," said the queen, "and I want it to be both profound and instructive."

"But at the same time funny," added the king.

"I will try," said the merchant's son.

Here is his story; if you listen carefully, you will understand it: "Once upon a time there were some sulphur matches who were extremely proud because they came of such good family. Their family tree, of which each of them was a tiny splinter, had been the largest pine tree in the forest. The matches lay on a shelf between a tinderbox and an old iron pot; and to them they told the story of their childhood and youth:

"'Then we lived high, so to speak. We were served diamond tea every morning and evening; it is called dew. Whenever the sun was out it shone upon us, and all the little birds had to tell us stories. We knew that we were rich, for we could afford to wear our green clothes all year round, whereas the poor beeches and oaks had to stand quite naked in the winter and freeze. Then the woodcutter came, it was a revolution! The whole family was split. The trunk of our family tree got a job as the mainmast on a full-rigged ship; he can sail around the whole world if he feels like it. We are not sure what happened to the branches, but we got the job of lighting fires for the mean and base multitudes; that is how such noble and aristocratic things as we are ended up in the kitchen.'

"'My life has been quite different,' said the iron pot that stood on the shelf beside the matches. 'From my very birth I have been scrubbed and set over the fire to boil. I have lost count of how many times that has happened. I do the solid, the most important work here, and should be counted first among you all. My only diversion is to stand properly cleaned on the shelf and engage in a dignified conversation with my friends. We are all proper stay-at-homes here, except for the water bucket, which does run down to the well every so often, and the market basket. She brings us news from the town, but as far as I am concerned it is all disagreeable. All she can talk about are the people and the government. Why, the other day an old earthen pot got so frightened that it fell down and broke in pieces. The market basket is a radical!'

HANS CHRISTIAN ANDERSEN

"'You talk too much!' grumbled the tinderbox. 'Let us have a pleasant evening.' And the steel struck the flint so that sparks flew.

"'Yes, let us discuss who is the most important person here,' suggested the matches.

"'I don't like to talk about myself,' said an earthenware pot. 'Let's tell stories instead. I will begin with an everyday story, the kind that could have happened to any of us. I think that kind of story is the most amusing: *By the Baltic Sea where the Danish beeches mirror their — "'*

"'That is a beautiful beginning,' exclaimed the plates. 'We are sure we will love that story.'

"'There I spent my youth in a quiet home,' continued the earthenware pot. 'The furniture was polished each week, the floors washed every second day, and the curtains were washed and ironed every fortnight.'

"'How interestingly you describe it,' interrupted the feather duster. 'One can hear that a woman is talking, there is an air of cleanliness about it all.'

"'How true, how true!' said the water bucket, and jumped, out of pure joy, several inches into the air.

"The earthenware pot told its story; and both the middle and the end were just as interesting as the beginning had been.

"All the plates clattered in unison as applause; and the feather duster took some parsley and made it into a garland with which to crown the pot. She knew it would irritate the others; besides, she thought, 'If I honor her today, she will honor me tomorrow.'

"'We will dance,' said the big black pair of tongs; and so they did! Goodness, how they could stretch their legs. The cover on the old chair, over in the corner, split right down the middle just trying to follow them with his eyes. 'Where are our laurel leaves?' demanded the tongs when they had finished; and they were crowned with a garland too.

"'Vulgar rabble,' thought the matches; but they didn't say it out loud.

"The samovar was going to sing; but it had caught cold — at least so it claimed, but it wasn't true. She was too proud; she would only sing in the dining room, when the master and mistress were present.

"Over on the window sill was an old pen that the maid used to write with. There was nothing special about it except that it had been dipped a little too deeply in the inkwell. The pen thought

THE FLYING TRUNK

that this was a distinction and was proud of it. 'If the samovar won't sing,' remarked the pen, 'we shouldn't beg it to. Outside the window hangs a bird cage with a nightingale in it; why not let him sing? True, his voice is untrained and he is quite uneducated; but his song has a pleasing naive simplicity about it.'

"'I object. I think it is most improper,' complained the tea-kettle, who was a half sister of the samovar. 'Why should we listen to a foreign bird? Is that patriotic? Let the market basket judge between us.'

"'I am annoyed and irritated,' shouted the market basket. 'It is most aggravating; what a way to spend an evening! Let's put everything back in its right place, then I'll rule the roost, as I ought to. And you'll see what a difference that will make.'

"'Let's make noise! Let's make noise!' screamed all the others.

"At that moment the door opened and the maid entered. Instantly, they stood still and kept quiet, every one of them. But even the smallest earthenware pot thought to herself, 'I am really the most important person here in the kitchen and, if I had wanted to, I could have made it into a most amusing evening.'

"The maid took a match, struck it, and lighted the fire. 'Now everyone can see,' thought the match, 'that we are the true aristocrats here. What a flame we make. What glorious light!' And that was the end of the match, it burned out."

"That was a lovely fairy tale," said the queen. "I feel just as if I had been in the kitchen with the matches. You shall have our daughter."

"Certainly," said the king. "We will hold the wedding on Monday," and he patted the merchant's son on the back, for now he was part of the family.

On Sunday evening the whole town was illuminated in honor of the impending marriage. Buns and pretzels were given away to everyone; and the street urchins whistled through their fingers. It was a moving sight.

"I'd better add to the festivities," thought the merchant's son. He went out and bought all the fireworks he could, put them in the trunk, and flew up in the air.

Ah! how high he flew and the fireworks sputtered, glittered, and banged. Such a spectacle no one had seen before. All the Turks jumped a foot up into the air and lost their slippers. Now they knew it was the God of the Turks who would be marrying their princess.

HANS CHRISTIAN ANDERSEN

When the merchant's son had returned in his trunk to the forest, he decided to go back into town in order to hear what everyone was saying about his performance — and it's quite understandable that he should want to.

And the things that people said! Everyone had seen something different, but they all agreed that it was marvelous.

"I saw the God himself," said one man. "He had eyes like stars and a beard like the foaming ocean."

"He flew wearing a cloak of fire," said another, "and the prettiest cherubs were peeping out from under its folds."

It was all very pleasing to hear; and tomorrow was his wedding day!

He hurried back to the forest to sleep the night away in his trunk. But where was it?

It had burned to ashes. A little spark from one of the fireworks had ignited it; and that was the end of the trunk, and the merchant's son too! Now he could not fly to his bride.

She waited for him on the roof all day. She is still waiting for him, while he is wandering around the world, telling fairy tales; but they are not so lighthearted as the one he told about the sulphur matches.

THE STORKS

On the roof of the last house at the edge of the town, storks had built their home. The mother stork was sitting in the nest. Her four little ones stuck their heads up and peeped out over the edge. Their bills were still black, for they were so young that they had not yet turned red. A few feet away on the ridge of the roof stood their father, as rigidly as a soldier on guard. He was standing on one leg, as still as a wooden statue.

"It looks very distinguished to have a sentry at the nest," he thought. "No one knows that it is my own family; people passing by will believe that I am here on duty. It looks most noble." So he stayed where he was without blinking an eyelid.

Some children were playing down in the street. They looked up at the storks, and the boldest boy among them began singing the old nursery rhyme about the storks. Soon the others joined him:

> Stork, stork, with legs so long,
> And wings so broad and strong,
> Fly home to your wife and your nest.
> The four young ones you love best:
> The first shall be hanged from the gallow,
> The second shall be dipped in tallow,
> The third shall be plucked and burned,
> The fourth upside down shall be turned.

HANS CHRISTIAN ANDERSEN

"Listen to what the boys are singing," said the young storks. "They say we are going to be hanged and burned."

"Don't listen to them," advised their mother. "What one does not hear cannot hurt one."

But the little boys kept singing and pointing their fingers at the storks. Only one of them — his name was Peter — said it was a shame to make fun of the birds, and he wouldn't join the others in their naughty game.

The mother tried to comfort her young ones. "Don't pay any attention to them," she said. "Look how calmly your father is standing guard on one leg."

"We are still afraid," squeaked the young storks, and hid beneath their mother.

The next day the children were playing in the street again, and when they saw the storks they began to sing the song once more:

> The first shall be hanged from the gallow,
> The second shall be dipped in tallow,
> The third shall be plucked and burned,
> The fourth upside down shall be turned.

"Are we really to be hanged and burned?" asked the young storks again.

"Nonsense!" said their mother. "You are going to learn to fly, then we will visit the meadow and the lake. The frogs will give us a concert, Croak . . . Croak! Afterward we eat them, it is a marvelous amusement!"

"What happens after that?" asked her young ones.

"Then comes the harvest maneuvers, when all the storks in the whole district gather together. It is of great importance to be able to fly well then, for if you can't the general kills you. He sticks his bill right into your heart. So pay attention and learn your lessons."

"So we are going to be killed after all," exclaimed the young storks. "Listen, the boys are singing that song again."

"Listen to me and not to those bad boys," grumbled their mother. "After the great maneuvers, we fly to the hot countries. They are far from here. We have to fly over forests and mountains. We travel to Egypt, where they have triangular stone houses so high that their tops reach the clouds; they are called pyramids. They are so ancient that no stork can remember when they were built. Near

THE STORKS

them flows a river with muddy banks; one walks in mud and eats frogs all day."

"Oh," sighed her young ones.

"Yes," continued their mother, "one does nothing else but eat all day. While we are living in comfort, it is so cold up here that there is not a green leaf left, and all the clouds freeze to pieces and fall down as little white flakes."

"Do the naughty children freeze to pieces too?" asked the young storks.

"Not quite, but almost. They have to stay inside, in little dark rooms, while you are free to fly about among the flowers in the warm sunshine."

Time passed and the young storks were old enough to stand up in the nest and look about them. Their father came every day with frogs, little snakes, and other goodies that he found. He was fond of his children and did his best to amuse them. He twisted his long neck and made noise with his bill and told them stories about the swamp.

"Now I will have to teach you to

HANS CHRISTIAN ANDERSEN

fly," said their mother one day, and commanded all four of them up on the ridge of the roof. There they stood, and none too steadily; they used their wings to balance themselves, but they almost fell down.

"Now look at me," commanded their mother. "This is the way you must hold your head, and this the way to keep your legs. One . . . two, one . . . two. You flap your wings; they will bring you ahead in this world."

The mother stork flew in a little circle around the house and landed again. The young ones made some clumsy hops and one of them almost fell off the roof.

"I don't want to learn to fly," said the one that had almost fallen, and climbed back into the nest. "I don't care about the warm countries."

"Do you want to freeze to death when winter comes? Shall I call the boys, so that they can come and hang or burn you?"

"Oh no," said the little stork, and jumped out on the roof again.

By the third day of their training they could really fly. One of them thought that he could sit down in the air as in the nest; but then he fell and learned that to stay in the air you have to use your wings. The boys down in the street were still singing their stupid song.

"Shouldn't we fly down and prick out their eyes?" suggested one of the young storks.

"No nonsense here!" called the mother. "Listen to me, that is more important than anything else. One . . . two . . . three. First we circle to the left around the chimney, then we turn and fly the opposite way around. . . . That was fine! You have been so good that tomorrow I am going to take you all down to the swamp. You will meet some other distinguished families of storks there. Now make sure you behave yourselves better than all the other children there. Remember to hold your heads high and walk straight. It not only looks fine but makes the others respect you."

"But aren't we to avenge ourselves on the naughty children?" asked the young storks.

"Let them scream as loudly as they wish. You will fly high above the clouds, and see the pyramids, while they will stay and freeze here, where there is not a green leaf anywhere or a sweet apple for them to eat."

"We want our revenge anyway," the young ones whispered, though not so loud that their mother could hear them.

THE STORKS

The child who had started singing the song and mocked the storks most was only six years old and small for his age at that. But the young storks thought he was a hundred, for he was much bigger than their father and mother. They had no real idea of the difference between children and grownups, and all their hate and wish for revenge were directed toward this particular little boy. He had started it and was the worst child, as far as they were concerned. As the storks grew their anger against the children grew too; and at last their mother had to promise them that they would have their vengeance, but she wanted them to wait until one of the days just before they left.

"I have to see first how you get along on the great harvest maneuver. If your flying is too poor, then the general will put his bill right through you and pierce your heart, and then, after all, the boys will be proven right and you can't blame them."

"We will do our best," said the young storks, and they did. They trained every day, and soon flew so well in formation that it was a pleasure to watch them.

The harvest began and all the storks gathered in preparation for the long flight down to Africa. It was a grand maneuver; in great flocks, they flew over the forests and the towns, and the general observed each one's flight closely. The young storks in this story did particularly well; they were given the grade: A plus frogs and snakes! That was the best grade one could get, and they were allowed to eat the frogs and snakes and that they quickly did.

"Now is the time for our revenge," they demanded.

"Yes," said their mother. "I have thought about it and now I know how it shall be done. There is a pond where all the little children lie until the stork comes and gets them for delivery to their parents. There they lie dreaming far more pleasantly than they ever will later in their lives. All parents love and desire such little sweet babes and all children want a little sister or little brother. Now we will fly to that pond and bring all the good children who didn't sing the ugly song a little brother or sister; but the bad ones shan't ever get any."

"But the one who started it all, that ugly, horrible little boy," screamed all the young storks, "what shall we do to him?"

"In the pond there is a dead child," said the mother. "He has dreamed himself to death. We will bring that baby to the boy and he will cry because we have brought him a dead little brother. But in all your anger, have you forgotten the good little boy who

HANS CHRISTIAN ANDERSEN

shamed the others when they made fun of you? Him we will bring both a brother and a sister; and since his name is Peter, you shall all be called Peter."

All that the mother said came true, and the storks in Denmark are still called Peter, even to this day.

THE SWINEHERD

There once was a poor prince.
He had a kingdom and, though it wasn't very big, it was large
enough to marry on, and married he wanted to be.

Now it was rather bold of him to say to the emperor's daughter:
"Do you want me?" But he was a young man of spirit who was
quite famous, and there were at least a hundred princesses who
would have said thank you very much to his proposal. But the
emperor's daughter didn't. Let me tell you the story.

On the grave of the prince's father there grew a rose tree. It was a
beautiful tree that only flowered every fifth year; and then it bore
only one rose. That rose had such a sweet fragrance that anyone
who smelled it forgot immediately all his sorrow and troubles. The
prince also owned a nightingale which sang as though all the
melodies ever composed lived in its throat — so beautiful was its
song. The prince decided to send the rose and the nightingale to
the emperor's daughter, and had two little silver chests made to put
them in.

The emperor ordered the gifts to be carried into the grand
assembly room where the princess was playing house with her
ladies in waiting. That was their favorite game and they never
played any other. When the princess saw the pretty little silver
chests she clapped her hands and jumped for joy.

HANS CHRISTIAN ANDERSEN

"Oh, I hope one of them contains a pretty little kitten," she said; but when she opened the chest, she found a rose.

"It is very prettily made," said one of the ladies in waiting.

"It is more than pretty; it is nice," remarked the emperor. Then the princess touched the rose and she almost wept with disappointment.

"Oh, Papa," she shrieked. "It is not glass, it's real!"

"Oh, oh!" shrieked all the ladies in waiting. "How revolting! It is real!"

"Let's see what is in the other chest first, before we get angry," admonished the emperor. There was the nightingale, who sang so beautifully that it was difficult to find anything wrong with it.

"*Superbe! Charmant!*" said the ladies in waiting. They all spoke French, one worse than the other.

"That bird reminds me of the late empress' music box," said an old courtier. "It has the same tone, the same sense of rhythm."

"You are right," said the emperor, and cried like a baby.

"I would like to know if that is real too," demanded the princess.

"Oh yes, it is a real bird," said one of the pages who had brought the gifts.

"In that case we will let the bird fly away," said the princess; and she sent a messenger to say that she would not even permit the prince to come inside her father's kingdom.

But the prince was not easily discouraged. He smeared his face with both black and brown shoe polish, put a cap on his head, then he walked up to the emperor's castle and knocked.

"Good morning, Emperor," said the young man, for it was the emperor himself who had opened the door. "Can I get a job in the castle?"

"Oh, there are so many people who want to work here," answered the emperor, and shook his head. "But I do need someone to tend the pigs, we have such an awful lot of them."

And so the prince was hired as the emperor's swineherd. There was a tiny, dirty room next to the pigpen, and that was where he was expected to live.

The young man spent the rest of the day making a very pretty little pot. By evening it was finished. The pot had little bells all around it, and when it boiled, they played, ever so sweetly:

Ach, du lieber Augustin,
Alles ist weg, weg, weg.

THE SWINEHERD

But the strangest and most wonderful thing about the pot was that, if you held your finger in the steam above it, then you could smell what was cooking on any stove in town. Now there was something a little different from the rose.

The princess was out walking with her ladies in waiting, and when she heard the musical pot she stopped immediately. She listened and smiled, for *"Ach, du lieber Augustin"* she knew. She could play the melody herself on the piano with one finger.

"It is a song I know!" she exclaimed. "That swineherd must be cultured. Please go in and ask him what the instrument costs."

One of the ladies in waiting was ordered to run over to the pigpen, but she put wooden shoes on first.

"What do you want for the pot?" she asked.

"Ten kisses from the princess," said the swineherd.

"God save us!" cried the lady in waiting.

"I won't settle for less," said the swineherd.

"Well, what did he want?" asked the princess.

"I can't say it," blushed the lady in waiting.

"Then you can whisper it," said the princess; and the lady in waiting whispered.

"He is very naughty," said the princess, and walked on. But she had gone only a few steps when she heard the little bells play again, and they sounded even sweeter to her than they had before.

Ach, du lieber Augustin,
Alles ist weg, weg, weg.

"Listen," she said, "ask him if he will be satisfied with ten kisses from one of my ladies in waiting."

"No, thank you!" replied the swineherd to that proposal. "Ten kisses from the princess or I keep my pot."

"This is most embarrassing," declared the princess. "You will all have to stand around me so no one can see it."

And the ladies in waiting formed a circle and held out their skirts so no one could peep. The swineherd got his kisses and the princess the pot.

Oh, what a grand time they had! All day and all evening they made the little pot boil. There wasn't a stove in the whole town that had anything cooking on it that they didn't know about. They knew what was served for dinner on every table: both the count's and the cowherd's. The ladies in waiting were so delighted that they clapped their little hands.

"We know who is going to have soup and pancakes and who is eating porridge and rib roast! Oh, it is most interesting."

"Very!" said the imperial housekeeper.

"Keep your mouth shut. Remember, I am the princess," said the emperor's daughter.

And all the ladies in waiting and the imperial housekeeper said: "God preserve us, we won't say a word."

The swineherd — that is to say, the prince whom everyone thought was a swineherd — did not like to waste his time, so he constructed a rattle which was so ingenious that, when you swung it around, it played all the waltzes, polkas, and dance melodies ever composed since the creation of the world.

"It is superb!" exclaimed the princess as she was walking past the pigsty. "I have never heard a more exquisite composition. Do go in and ask what he wants for the instrument, but I won't kiss him!"

"He wants a hundred kisses from the princess," said the lady in waiting who had been sent to speak to the swineherd.

"He must be mad," declared the princess. She walked on a few steps and then she stood still. "One ought to encourage art," she said. "I am the emperor's daughter. Tell him he can have ten kisses from me just as he got yesterday. The rest he can get from my ladies in waiting."

"But we don't want to kiss him," they all cried.

"Stuff and nonsense!" replied the princess, for she was angry. "If I can kiss him, you can too. Besides, what do you think I give you room and board for?"

And one of the ladies in waiting went to talk with the swineherd. "One hundred kisses from the princess or I keep the rattle," was the message she came back with.

"Then gather around me!" commanded the princess. The ladies in waiting took their positions and the kissing began.

"I wonder what is going on down there by the pigsty," said the emperor, who was standing out on the balcony. He rubbed his eyes and put his glasses on. "It is the ladies in waiting. What devilment are they up to? I'd better go down and see." Then he pulled up the backs of his slippers, for they were really only a comfortable old pair of shoes with broken backs. Oh, how he ran! But as soon as he came near the pigsty he walked on tiptoe.

THE SWINEHERD

The ladies in waiting were so busy counting kisses — to make sure that the bargain was justly carried out and that the swineherd did not get one kiss too many or one too few — that they didn't hear or see the emperor, who was standing on tiptoe outside the circle.

"What's going on here?" he shouted. When he saw the kissing he took off one of his slippers and started hitting the ladies in waiting on the tops of their heads, just as the swineherd was getting his eighty-sixth kiss.

"*Heraus!* Get out!" he screamed, for he was really angry; and both the swineherd and the princess were thrown out of his empire.

There they stood: the princess was crying, the swineherd was grumbling, and the rain was streaming down.

"Oh, poor me!" wailed the princess. "If only I had married the prince. Oh, I am so unhappy!"

The swineherd stepped behind a tree, rubbed all the black and brown shoe polish off his face, and put on his splendid royal robes. He looked so impressive that the princess curtsied when she saw him.

"I have come to despise you," said the prince. "You did not want an honest prince. You did not appreciate the rose or the nightingale, but you could kiss a swineherd for the sake of a toy. Farewell!"

The prince entered his own kingdom and locked the door behind him; and there the princess could stand and sing:

> *Ach, du lieber Augustin,*
> *Alles ist weg, weg, weg.*

For, indeed, everything was "all gone"!

THE PINE TREE

Out in the forest grew a very nice looking little pine tree. It had plenty of space around it, so that it got both fresh air and all the sunshine it could want. Near it grew some larger pine and other evergreen trees; but the little pine was so busy growing that it took no notice of them, or of the children who came to the forest to pick wild strawberries and raspberries, not even when they sat down near it and said so loudly that anyone could have heard them: "Goodness, what a beautiful little tree!" No, the tree heard nothing, for it was not listening.

The following year it was a little taller and had a new ring of branches; and the next year it had one more. That is the way you can tell the age of a pine tree — by the rings of branches it has.

"Oh, how I wish I were as big as the big trees," moaned the little pine tree. "Then I could spread my branches out, and with my top, I could see far out into the wide world! The birds would come and nest in me; and when the wind blew, then I would bend and sway as elegantly as the other trees."

The warm sunshine gave it no pleasure, nor did the songs of the little birds or the sight of the red clouds that drifted across the sky at sunset.

Winter came. The snow lay white and sparkling. Rabbits came running, and jumped over the little pine tree. "Oh, how mortifying!" it cried every time. But two years passed before the little tree

114

THE PINE TREE

had grown so tall that the rabbits could no longer jump over it but had to run around it instead.

"To grow, to grow," thought the pine tree, "to become tall and old; there's nothing in the world so marvelous!"

In the autumn the woodcutter came to chop down some of the older trees. He came every year and the young tree, now that it was growing up, shook inside itself when the tall, mighty trees fell with a thunderous crash to the ground. Their branches were shorn and there they lay: naked, thin, and long. One could hardly recognize them. They were loaded onto a horse-drawn wagon and carried out of the forest.

Where were they being taken? What would happen to them?

In spring, when the swallows and the storks returned, the young pine put the question to them: "Do any of you know where the trees go and what happens to them?"

The swallows didn't know, but the storks looked thoughtful for a moment. Then one of them said, "I think I know. I have met many tall ships on my way to Egypt. The ships have lofty masts and they smell of pine, so I'm sure they must be pine. I tell you, they stood proudly."

"If only I were old enough to become a mast and sail across the ocean," said the pine tree. "Tell me about the ocean. What does it look like?"

"It's too big for me to try to tell about it," replied the stork, and walked away.

"Be glad that you are young," whispered the sun's rays. "Enjoy your strength and the pleasure of being alive."

The wind kissed the young tree and the dew shed tears over it; but the pine tree noticed neither.

Just before Christmas, some of the trees that were cut down weren't any older or taller than the one who was so dissatisfied. These trees did not have their branches shorn; but they were loaded onto wagons and driven out of the forest just as the other, larger trees had been.

"Where are they going?" asked the pine tree. "None of them was any taller than I am; and I saw one that was at least a foot shorter. Why were they allowed to keep their branches? And where were they going?"

"We know! We know! We know!" chirped the sparrows. "We have been in the town and looked through the windows. We know where they are. They have come to glory. They have been given the greatest honor a tree could wish for. They have been planted right in the middle of the warm living rooms of people's houses. They are decorated with silver and gold tinsel. There are apples and toys and heart-shaped cookies and hundreds of candles on their branches."

The pine tree was so excited that its boughs trembled. "And what else happened to them?"

"We don't know," chirped the sparrows. "We've told you everything we saw."

"Have I been created to become like that?" thought the tree jubilantly. "Will that glory be mine? Why, that is much better than sailing across the oceans. Oh, how I long for it to happen! I wish it soon would be Christmas again. I am as tall and as good looking as the trees that were chosen last year. I wish I were on the wagon already. I wish I were in the warm room being decorated. I wonder what will happen after that? Something even better, even grander will happen, why else should they put gold and silver on me? But what will it be? How I long for it to happen! How I suffer from anticipation. I can hardly understand myself. . . . Oh, how difficult it is to be me!"

"Be happy with us," said the wind and the sunshine. "Be glad that you are young; enjoy your youth and your freedom, here in nature."

But the tree was not happy. It grew and grew; and now it was dark green both in winter and summer, and people who passed by often remarked, "What a lovely tree!"

Then one Christmas, it was the first tree to be cut down. It felt the ax sever it from its roots; and it fell with a sigh to the ground. A feeling of pain, of helplessness, came over it, and never for a moment did it think of the glory that was to come. It only felt the sadness of leaving the place where it had grown. It knew that it would never see again the little bushes and flowers that had grown around it, or hear the songs of the little birds that had sat on its branches. No, parting was no pleasure.

The tree didn't recover before it was being unloaded in town and heard someone say, "What a beautiful tree! We shall have that one and no other."

Two servants in livery carried the tree up to a magnificent hall. Portraits were hanging on the walls, and next to the big tile stove

THE PINE TREE

stood two Chinese vases with lions on their lids. There were rocking chairs, and sofas covered with silk; and on a table lay picture books and toys worth more than a hundred times a hundred crowns — so at least the children claimed. The tree was planted in a bucket filled with sand, but nobody could see that it was an old one, for it was covered by a green cloth and stood on a many-colored rug.

The tree shook with expectation. What was about to happen? The servants and the young ladies of the family started to decorate it. On the branches they hung little colored nets that were filled with sweets; and golden apples and walnuts were tied to the tree so that they looked as if they were growing there. A hundred little red, blue, and white candles were fastened on the branches; and among them, on the green needles, sat little dolls that looked exactly like human beings. At last, on the very top of the tree was placed a golden star. It was magnificent, unbelievably magnificent!

"Tonight . . . tonight," everyone said. "Tonight it will be glorious!"

"Oh," thought the tree, "why doesn't night come! The candles will be lit — I wonder what will happen then! Will the other trees come from the forest and look at me? Will the sparrows peep in through the windows? Will I grow roots and stand here both summer and winter?"

The poor tree had a bark-ache from anticipation, which for a tree is as annoying as headache is to a human being.

Finally evening did come, and the candles were lit. Oh, how beautiful it looked. The poor tree trembled with emotion. In fact, it shook so much that one of its branches caught on fire, which smarted and hurt.

"God preserve us!" cried the ladies, and put out the fire.

Now the poor tree didn't even dare tremble; it was horrible! There it stood, rigid and still, and fearing every moment that it might lose some of its decorations. How bewildering everything was! The big doors opened and the children came running in. They were so wild, especially the older ones, they looked as if they wanted to overturn the tree. The little children were so overawed by the tree that they just stood and stared silently. But that didn't last long; soon they were making as much noise as the older ones. The grownups came last; but they had seen the sight many times before. Soon they all were dancing and singing around the tree;

then the presents, which had been hung on the tree, were given out.

"What are they doing?" thought the tree. "What is going to happen now?"

The candles burned down and were extinguished, and the children were allowed to plunder the tree. They grabbed the little nets with sweets in them and pulled at the candied fruit and the nuts. They were so rough that they almost broke off the branches; and they would certainly have upset the tree, had it not been for the string with which its top was attached to the ceiling.

Now the children danced and played, and no one but the old nurse paid any attention to the tree; she kept walking around and around it, looking among the branches to see if she could find an apple or a fig which the youngsters might have overlooked.

"A story! A story!" screamed all the children, and pushed a fat man toward the Christmas tree.

He sat down beneath it, for, as he said, he liked sitting among the "greenery," and it wouldn't harm the tree to hear a story. "But I shall tell only one," he declared. "You can choose between 'Willowy, Wollowy' and 'How Humpty-dumpty Fell Down the Stairs but Won the Princess Anyway.'"

"'Willowy, Wollowy'!" screamed several of the children.

"'Humpty-dumpty'!" screamed the others; and the room was filled with their shouting.

"Isn't there something that I am supposed to do?" thought the tree, not knowing that it had already done everything that it was supposed to do.

The man told the story of "How Humpty-dumpty Fell Down the Stairs but Won the Princess Anyway." When he had finished all the children screamed that they wanted more, for they hoped to be able to persuade him to tell the story of "Willowy, Wollowy" too; but they couldn't. They had to be satisfied with the story about Humpty-dumpty.

The pine tree stood still, deep in its own thoughts. The birds out in the forest had never told a story like that. "No, that's the way of the world," it said to itself. "Humpty-dumpty falls down the stairs but he wins the princess anyway." The tree believed that the story it had heard was true because the man who had told it looked so trustworthy. "Yes, who knows?" it whispered to itself. "Maybe I, too, will fall down the stairs and win the princess." And the tree looked forward to the next day, when it would again be decorated with lights and hung with toys.

"Tomorrow," it thought, "tomorrow I shan't tremble as I did today. I shall really enjoy myself, and hear the story of Humpty-dumpty again; and maybe the one about 'Willowy, Wollowy' too." All night long the tree silently thought of the glory that was to come on the following day.

The next morning the servants came.

"Now it all starts all over again," thought the tree.

But it didn't. The servants dragged the tree up two flights of stairs into the attic, where they threw it in a dark corner which the daylight never reached.

"What is the meaning of this?" the tree asked itself. "Why have I been put here? What will happen now?"

The tree leaned itself up against the wall and thought and thought. It had plenty of time for thinking, because days and nights went by without anyone coming into the attic to disturb it. When finally someone did come, it was only to put some old boxes up there. The tree was hidden in the corner and quite forgotten.

"Now it is winter outside," thought the tree. "The earth is so hard and covered with snow that they cannot plant me. They are sheltering me here till spring. How considerate man is! I just wish it weren't so dark and so terribly lonely! There isn't even a rabbit here. It was so nice out in the forest when the ground was covered with snow and the rabbits darted about. Though I didn't like it when I was very small and they could jump over me. But here it is so quiet and I am terribly lonely."

"Twick . . . twick," said a little mouse, and nipped its way out of the wall.

"Twick . . . twick . . ." And another, even smaller mouse appeared.

The two little mice sniffed at the tree and then climbed up among the branches.

"It is cold," remarked the mice. "But otherwise it is a quite nice attic. Don't you think so, old pine tree?"

"I am not old," protested the pine tree. "There are lots of trees in the forest much older than I am."

"Where do you come from?" asked one of the little mice. Those little creatures were very curious and they asked the tree one question after another. "What do you know? What can you tell us?

HANS CHRISTIAN ANDERSEN

Tell us about the most beautiful place in the world. Have you been there? . . . Have you ever been in the larder, by the way? In the larder where there are cheeses lying on shelves, hams hanging from the ceiling, and where you can dance on tallow candles; and where you can come in thin and go out fat?"

"I don't know of any such place," replied the tree. "But I know the forest where the sun shines and the birds sing." And the pine tree told them of its youth in the woods.

The little mice listened quietly, for they had never heard of such a place; and when the tree was finished they said, "Think how much you have seen! How happy you must have been!"

"Happy?" repeated the pine tree, and thought about what it had told the little mice. "Yes, I suppose I had a quite good time," it confessed. Then the tree told about Christmas Eve and how it had been decorated with candles and sweets.

"Oh," sighed the mice, "how fortunate you have been, old pine tree."

"I am not old!" protested the tree. "I have come this very winter from the forest. I am in my prime. I just appear a little stunted because I have been cut down."

"You tell about everything so marvelously," exclaimed the little mice; and the next night they brought along four of their friends.

The pine tree again told the story of its youth in the forest and what had happened to it on Christmas Eve; and the more it told, the more clearly it could remember everything.

"Yes, they were good times; and they can come again. They will come again! Humpty-dumpty fell down the stairs but he won the princess anyway." And the pine tree remembered a little birch tree that had grown nearby it in the forest, for to the pine tree the little birch was a real princess.

"Who was Humpty-dumpty?" asked the little mice.

The pine tree told them the fairy tale it had heard. It could remember every word of it. The little mice were so pleased that they climbed to the very top of the tree to show their appreciation. The next night more mice came; and on Sunday two rats arrived. But they criticized the story and said it wasn't amusing at all. This made the poor little mice sad, for now they thought less of the story too.

"Don't you know any other stories?" asked one of the rats.

"No, I only know that one," admitted the pine tree. "I heard it

THE PINE TREE

on the happiest night of my life; but then I didn't know that it was the happiest."

"It is a particularly uninteresting story. Don't you know any about bacon or candle stumps? No stories that take place in a larder?"

"No," the tree answered.

"Well, in that case you're not worth listening to," said the rats, and left.

The mice stayed away too; and the pine tree sighed in its loneliness. "It was nice when the quick little animals came visiting and listened to what I had to tell. But now that is over too. I must remember to be happy when I am taken out again," the tree muttered. "I wonder when that will be."

Finally, one morning it happened. The servants came up to the attic and started moving boxes about; they were cleaning up. When they found the tree in the corner they handled it roughly and threw it about. At last a young man carried it down the many flights of stairs out into the yard.

"Now life begins again," it thought. There was fresh air and it felt the sun's rays. Everything was happening so fast, and it was so excited at being outside, that the tree looked at the world about it but not at itself. The yard was bordered by a garden where all the bushes and trees were in flower. The roses covered the little fence and smelled so sweetly. The linden tree was in bloom. The swallows flew about singing, "Tweet, tweet. . . . My lover has come." But they didn't mean the pine tree.

"Now I am going to live!" shouted the tree joyously, and spread out its branches. But all its needles were yellow and dead. It was thrown into a corner of the yard where the nettles prospered. The golden star from Christmas Eve was still on its top and the sun reflected in it.

Playing in the yard were two of the children who had danced around the tree on Christmas Eve and had loved it so much then. The younger child now ran over and tore the golden star from the tree.

"Look what I found on this horrid old Christmas tree," he said. He was wearing boots and he kicked the tree's branches so that many of them broke.

The pine tree saw all the greenness about it; then it looked at itself and wished it had been left in the dark corner of the attic. It

HANS CHRISTIAN ANDERSEN

remembered its youth in the forest, the glory of Christmas Eve, and the little mice who had listened so contentedly to the story about Humpty-dumpty.

"Gone! Gone!" sighed the poor tree. "If I only could have been happy while I had a chance to be. Now it is all over and gone! Everything!"

One of the servants came and cut the tree up for kindling. It became a little pile of wood. The cook used it to light the kitchen range. It flared up instantly and the tree sighed so deeply that it sounded like a shot. The children who were playing in the yard heard it, and they ran in and sat down in front of the stove.

"Bang! Bang!" they cried.

Every time the tree sighed, it thought of a summer day in the forest, or a winter night when the stars are brightest, and it remembered Christmas Eve and Humpty-dumpty: the only fairy tale it had ever heard and knew how to tell. Then it became ashes.

The children returned to the yard to play. The little boy had fastened the golden star to his chest. The star the pine tree had worn on the happiest evening of its life. But that was a long time ago; now the pine tree is no more, just as this story is over; for all stories — no matter how long they are — must eventually come to an end.

MOTHER ELDERBERRY

Once upon a time there was a little boy who had caught cold. He had got his feet wet, and no one could imagine how, for the weather had been dry for days. His mother undressed him and put him to bed; then she took out the teapot to make elderberry tea, for that is such a good remedy for colds. Just at that moment the pleasant old man who had his lodgings on the top floor entered. He lived completely alone, for he had neither wife nor children of his own, but he was very fond of other people's children and knew how to tell the most amusing fairy tales and stories.

"Now drink your tea like a good boy," said the mother, "and maybe you will be told a story."

"If I only knew one that he hasn't heard already," said the old man, and nodded kindly. "But tell me, how did the little fellow get his feet wet?"

"Where, indeed!" The mother shook her head. "That is a mystery."

"Are you going to tell me a story?" asked the boy.

"Maybe, if you can tell me exactly how deep the ditch is that runs along the lane next to your school; I would rather like to know that."

"In the deepest place, the water is halfway up to the top of my boots," answered the boy.

HANS CHRISTIAN ANDERSEN

"That solves the mystery of the wet feet," said the old gentleman. "Now I should tell you a story, but I can't remember any that you haven't heard."

"You can make one up. Mother says that anything you touch becomes a fairy tale."

"No, that kind of story or fairy tale is not worth much; it is not like the real ones who come knocking on my forehead and say: 'Here I am, let me in.'"

"Won't one come knocking soon?" asked the boy. And his mother laughed as she put the elderberries in the teapot and poured boiling water on them.

"Please tell me a story! Please!" begged the boy.

"A fairy tale only comes when it wants to, for fairy tales and stories are so highborn that they won't obey anyone, not even kings . . . Stop!" he cried suddenly, and held up his forefinger. "There it is! Be careful. It is in the teapot."

The boy looked at the teapot. Slowly the lid lifted; up out of the top of the pot came fresh elderberry branches and from them hung clusters of white flowers. Now they were coming out of the spout as well. They grew and grew until they became a full-grown elderberry tree whose limbs crossed his bed and pushed aside the curtains. It was a grand tree! And how beautifully it smelled!

In the middle of the tree sat an old woman. She wore a dress that was as green as the elder leaves and had a pattern of white elder flowers. It was hard to tell whether her dress was made of cloth or out of real flowers and leaves. The old woman smiled kindly down at the boy.

"What is her name?" the lad asked.

"The Greeks and the Romans thought she was a wood nymph and called her dryad. Down in the 'new cottages' — which aren't very new, being three hundred years old — the old sailors who live there call her Mother Elderberry," the old man explained. "Now keep an eye on her. I shall tell you a story, while you look at the beautiful elder tree.

"It takes place in the 'new cottages.' Down in one of those tiny, narrow yards that the old sailors call their gardens, there grew a lovely elder tree, just like the one you are looking at. One sunny afternoon an old couple were sitting in its shade. He was an old, retired sailor, and she was a very old woman, who was his wife. They were so old that they had great-grandchildren and soon

MOTHER ELDERBERRY

would celebrate their fiftieth wedding anniversary. But, alas! they could not remember the date. Mother Elderberry sat up in her tree looking very pleased with herself. 'I know which day it is,' she said.

"The old couple hadn't heard her. They were talking about the old times, when they had been young.

"'Can you remember,' began the old seaman, 'when we were children and played in this very yard, how we used to stick twigs in the earth and make believe we were making a garden?'

"'Yes, I remember,' said his wife. 'We watered them and one of them was an elder branch and it struck roots and began to grow. And now it is such a big tree that we two old souls can sit in its shade.'

"'Yes,' agreed the old sailor. 'Over there in the corner of the yard there used to stand an old tub, filled with water; that was the ocean my ships sailed on. I had carved them myself with my own knife. But it didn't take long before I walked the deck of a real ship, did it?'

"'No, but first we went to school,' the old woman smiled. 'And then we were confirmed and we both cried in church that day. In the afternoon we walked hand in hand up to the top of the Round Tower and looked out over the world. Later, we trudged all the way out to the Royal Gardens in Frederiksberg; there we saw the king and queen being rowed in their beautiful boat through the canals of the park.'

"'Rougher voyages than that were to be my lot. Remember how long I was to be away; it was not months but years.'

"'And I cried.' Again the old woman smiled. 'I thought for sure that you were dead and I would never see you again. I thought you were drowned and were lying deep down, under the dark waves. Many a night I got out of my warm bed to look at the weather vane to see if the wind had changed; it changed often enough but still you didn't come home. I remember one day — oh, what terrible weather we had; it was pouring! — I had heard the garbage wagon rumbling down the street and I came running down from the kitchen with the garbage pail. I was a servant then. I stood for a moment in the open door to look at the rain, and the mailman came and gave me a letter. It was from you. I tore it open and read it right through. I was so happy that I both laughed and cried. You wrote that you were in the warm countries where coffee grows. — How lovely it must be there! — You described it all so well that I feel as if I had been there. . . . There I stood with the garbage pail in my hand, while the rain streamed down, when all at once I felt an arm around my waist — '

"'Yes, and you gave that poor fellow such a box on the ears that it could be heard all the way down the street.'

"'How could I have known it was you! You had come home as fast as your letter. Oh, how handsome you were, and that you are still! You had a long yellow silk handkerchief sticking out of your pocket and a shiny hat on your head. You looked so fine. But what a day it was, the street looked like a river.'

"'And then we got married,' laughed the old man. 'Do you remember? Then came the children: first the boy, then Marie, Niels, Peter, and Hans Christian.'

"'And they all turned out so well. They are liked and respected by everyone.'

"'And their children, in turn, have got little ones now,' said the old sailor, and nodded. 'We have great-grandchildren who have spirit. You know, I think it was about this time of the year that we got married.'

"'Yes, this very day is your golden wedding day,' said Mother Elderberry, and put her head between the old man and his wife. They thought she was a neighbor who had stuck her head in over the fence.

"They looked at each other; and each reached out for the other's hand. A few minutes later their children and grandchildren came to congratulate them, for they knew that it was the old couple's fiftieth wedding anniversary and had been there earlier that day; but the old couple had forgotten their visit, while they could recall everything that had happened half of a century ago.

"The scent of the elder flowers was heavy; the sun was just setting, and its glow gave the old man and his wife red cheeks. Their youngest grandchild danced around them happily. 'Tonight we are going to have a feast and eat roast potatoes.' That was his favorite food.

"Old Mother Elderberry nodded and shouted, 'Hurrah!' with everyone else."

"But that was no fairy tale," complained the little boy.

"That is your opinion," said the kind old man who had told the story. "Let us ask Mother Elderberry."

"The child is right, it was no fairy tale," said Mother Elderberry. "But now it comes, for out of reality are our tales of imagination

MOTHER ELDERBERRY

fashioned. If this were not true, then my elder tree could not have grown out of the teapot."

Mother Elderberry lifted the boy in her arms and pressed him to her breast. The flowering branches of the elder tree enfolded them. Now they were in an arbor and it was flying through the air with them inside it. It was a most delightful feeling. All at once Mother Elderberry changed into a young girl. She still had on her green dress with the pattern of white elder flowers, but there was a live flower pinned to her breast and around her curly golden hair there was a wreath of elder flowers. She and the boy kissed each other; and then they were one in age and desires.

Hand in hand, they left the arbor. On the green lawn lay his father's cane, tethered to a stick; for, to the children the cane was a horse. And when they mounted it to gallop around the garden, it had both a head and a flowing black mane.

"Now we shall ride for miles and miles!" shouted the boy. "We shall ride all the way to the castle we visited last year."

They rode round and round the garden. The little girl, who we know was none other than Mother Elderberry, said to the boy, "Now we are out in the country. Look, that's a farmer's house. See that wall with the big lump, protruding from it, like a giant egg, that's the oven for baking bread. In the shade of the elder tree nearby, you can see a flock of hens scratching the earth for worms. Look at the cock. See how he swaggers! . . . Now we are passing the church. It is built on a hill; near it are two ancient oak trees; one of them is wizened. . . . Now we are at the blacksmith's shop. The red fire glows. The man is naked to the waist. See his muscles as he lifts his hammer. . . . The sparks are flying all about him. . . . Away we go to the castle!"

Everything the little girl, who was riding behind him on the stick, described, the little boy saw; and yet they had only ridden around the lawn. Later they played on the gravel path and made a little garden of their own, and the girl took the elder flowers from the wreath in her hair and planted them. They grew just as the branch had, which the old seaman and his wife had planted; and they walked, hand in hand, just as the old people had done when they were children. But they didn't climb up the Round Tower or go out to the Royal Gardens of Frederiksberg. No, the little girl put her arm around the boy's waist and away they flew all around Denmark.

Spring changed into summer; soon it was harvest; and then the

HANS CHRISTIAN ANDERSEN

white winter came. A thousand pictures were mirrored in the little boy's eyes and heart, while the little girl repeated: "This you shall never forget!"

During their flight the sweet scent of elder flowers was all about them. The boy smelled only faintly the perfume of the roses and the fragrance of the fresh beech branches, for the elder flower bloomed in the girl's heart, and the boy never strayed from her.

"How beautiful spring is here!" she said; and they were standing in the midst of the tender green beech forest. At their feet grew the woodruff like a green carpet; and the fragile anemones, with their pale pink petals, were everywhere.

"Oh, I wish it were always spring!" exclaimed the little boy.

"How beautiful summer is here!" she said. Now they were flying past an old castle. Its red brick walls reflected in the water of the moat, where white swans made ripples in the mirror-like surface. The great white birds were looking at the long cool avenue of trees. The wind made waves in the field of grain as if it were a sea. In the ditches along the roads, yellow and red flowers bloomed; and the stone hedges were covered with wild hops and flowering bindweed. In the evening the pale moon rose. Down in the meadow the scent of newly cut hay filled the air. "This you will never forget."

"How beautiful autumn is here!" said the little girl; and the sky suddenly seemed twice as high and twice as blue. The woods had turned yellow, brown, and red, and they heard the barking of the hunting dogs. Flocks of screeching birds flew above the blackberry-covered stones of the Viking graves. The sea had turned almost black, and the sails appeared whiter against the dark color of the water. Down in the barn old women and young girls and children were busy picking the hops, dumping them into large vats. The young people sang the songs of the day, but the old women told stories of trolls and gnomes. What could be pleasanter?

"How beautiful winter is here!" said the little girl; and the trees were decked in hoarfrost and looked like a coral forest. Snow crunched under the children's boots and sounded as if they were wearing new shoes. At night shooting stars fell from the dark heavens. Christmas trees were lit and gifts exchanged. Someone was playing the violin; there was dancing in the farmer's living room, and from the kitchen came platters full of apple fritters that were refilled as soon as they were eaten. Then even the poorest child could say: "It is lovely in winter!"

MOTHER ELDERBERRY

Yes, it was truly beautiful. The little girl showed him the whole country of Denmark; and everywhere they went there was the smell of elder flowers; and there flew the flag with a white cross on the red background, the same one that flew from the mast of the ship on which the old sailor had sailed.

The boy became a young man. Now he was ready to journey out into the wide world: far, far away to the warm countries, where coffee grows. When they parted the little girl took the elder flower from her bosom and gave it to him. He put it between two of the pages of his hymnbook, and far from home, when he took down the book, it would always open to the pages where the elder flower was. The more he gazed at the dry, pressed flower, the more alive and fresh it became. He smelled the perfume of the Danish forest, and among the green branches he saw the face of the little girl peeking out at him and whispering: "Oh, it is beautiful here in spring, in summer, in autumn, and in winter." And his mind would paint a hundred pictures of all that he had seen.

Many years went by, the young man became an old man who sat underneath the elder tree with his wife. They held each other's hands, as the great-grandfather and great-grandmother from the "new cottages" had. They talked of bygone times and how it soon would be their golden anniversary.

The little girl with the big blue eyes and the wreath of elder blossoms in her hair sat up in the tree and nodded kindly down at them. "Today is your golden wedding day," she declared, and took two elderberry flowers from her wreath and kissed them. First they shone like silver and then like gold; she put one on each of the old couple's heads and they became golden crowns. The old man and the old woman sat like a king and queen under the fragrant elder tree. The old man told his wife the story of Mother Elderberry as it had been told to him when he was a little boy. And they both realized that much of the story could have been about themselves, and that was the part they liked best.

"Well," said the little girl in the tree, "some people call me Mother Elderberry; others call me the dryad; but my real name is memory. I sit in the tree that grows and grows; I can remember everything and therefore I can tell stories. Now let me see, do you still have your flower?"

The old man opened his hymnbook and there lay the elder flower, as fresh as if it had just been put there. Memory nodded

HANS CHRISTIAN ANDERSEN

and the setting sun shone on the heads of the two old people who were wearing golden crowns. They closed their eyes and then . . . Well, then the fairy tale is over.

The little boy lay in his bed; he didn't quite know whether he had dreamed the last part of the story or whether it had been told to him. The teapot stood on the table, but no elder tree was growing out of it. And the old man who had told him the story was about to go out through the door; it closed, and he was gone.

"Mother, it was wonderful," said the little boy. "I have been in the warm countries."

"I will believe that," laughed his mother. "If one drinks two big cups of elder tea, it is no wonder!" Then she tucked the blankets around him so he wouldn't be cold. "I think you fell asleep while we were arguing about whether the story was a proper fairy tale or not."

"And where is Mother Elderberry?" asked the boy.

"She is in the teapot," answered the mother, "and there she can stay."

THE DARNING NEEDLE

Once upon a time there was a darning needle who was so refined that she was convinced she was a sewing needle.

"Be careful! Watch what you are holding!" she shouted to the fingers who had picked her up. "I am so fine and thin that if I fall on the floor you will never be able to find me again."

"Don't overdo it," snarled the fingers, and squeezed her around the waist.

"Look, I am traveling with a retinue," said the needle. She was referring to the thread that trailed behind her but wasn't knotted. The fingers steered the needle toward the cook's slippers; the leather had split and had to be sewn.

"This is vulgar work," complained the darning needle. "I can't get through it. I shall break! I shall break!" And then she broke. "Didn't I tell you I was too fine?" she whined.

Had it been up to the fingers, then the darning needle would have been thrown away; but they had to mind the cook, so they dipped the needle in hot sealing wax and stuck it into the cook's blouse.

"Now I have become a brooch," exclaimed the darning needle. "I have always felt that I was born to be something better. When you are something, you always become something." Then she laughed inside herself; for you cannot see from the outside when a needle is laughing. There she sat as proudly as if she were looking out at the world from a seat in a golden carriage.

"May I take the liberty of asking you whether you are made of gold?" The darning needle was talking to her neighbor, a pin. "You look very handsome, and you have a head, even though it is small. Take my advice and let it grow a little bigger; not everyone can be so fortunate as to be dipped in sealing wax." The darning needle drew herself up a little too proudly; for she fell out of the blouse and down into the sink, at exactly the moment when the cook was rinsing it out.

"Here we go, traveling!" exclaimed the darning needle. "I hope I won't get lost." But she did get lost.

"I am too fine for this world," she remarked when she finally came to rest at the bottom of a gutter. "But I know who I am and where I come from, and that is always something." And the darning needle kept her back straight and remained cheerful.

All sorts of garbage were floating by above her: twigs, straw, pieces of newspaper. "Look how they sail on," mumbled the needle. "They have no idea what is sticking up right beneath them; and I can stick! Look at that old twig; it does not think about anything else in the whole world but twigs, because it is one. There goes a straw. . . . Look how it turns first one way and then the other. . . . Don't think so much of yourself, or you may get hurt on the curbstone. . . . There comes a newspaper; everything written in it is already forgotten, and yet it spreads itself out as if it were of great importance. . . . I sit patiently and wait. I know who I am and that I shall never change."

One day something shiny came to rest near the needle. It was a glass splinter from a broken bottle, but the darning needle thought it was a diamond. Since it glittered so nicely, she decided to converse with it. She introduced herself as a brooch. "I presume you are a diamond," she said. And the glass splinter hastily agreed that he was "something of that nature." Each of them believed that the other was valuable, and so they began to discuss how proud and haughty the rest of the world was.

"I have lived in a box belonging to a young lady," began the darning needle. "She was a cook, and she had five fingers on each hand. There never existed creatures so conceited as those fingers; and yet they were only there to take me out of the box and put me back."

THE DARNING NEEDLE

"Did they shine?" asked the glass splinter.

"Shine!" sneered the needle. "Oh, they were haughty. They were five brothers: all born fingers; and they stood in a row next to each other, in spite of there being so much difference in their sizes. The one who resembled the others the least was the thumb. He was short and fat and had only one joint in his back, so he could only bend once. He always kept to himself, and said that if he were ever chopped off a man's hand that man could not become a soldier. The other four fingers stuck together. The first one was always pointing at everything, and if the cook wanted to find out whether a sauce was too sour or too sweet, that finger was stuck into the dish or the pot; and it guided the pen when she wrote. The next finger was the tallest and he looked down on the others. The third one wore a gold ring around his stomach; and the fourth one never did anything, and that's what he was proud of. They bragged and boasted day and night! That was all they could do well. And I dived into the sink."

"And here we sit and glitter," said the glass splinter. At that moment the water in the gutter suddenly rose and went over its sides, taking the glass splinter with it.

"Well, he got his advancement," said the darning needle. "I was left behind, but I am too refined to complain. That, too, is a form of pride but it is respectable." And the needle kept her back straight and went on thinking.

"I am almost convinced that a sun ray must have given birth to me. When I think of it, the sun is always searching for me underneath the water; but I am so fine that my own mother cannot find me. If I had my old eye — the one that was broken off — I think I would cry. No, I wouldn't anyway, crying is so vulgar."

One day some street urchins were rummaging in the gutter. They found nails, coins, and the like. They made themselves filthy and they enjoyed doing it.

"Ow!" cried one of the boys. The needle had pricked him. "What kind of a fellow are you?"

"Fellow! I am a lady!" protested the darning needle. The sealing wax had long since worn off and she was black; but black things look thinner, so she thought that now she was even finer than before.

"Here comes an eggshell!" shouted another boy, and stuck the pin into it.

HANS CHRISTIAN ANDERSEN

"How well it becomes a black needle to stand before a white sail! Everyone can see me. I hope I shan't get seasick and throw up, that is so undignified.

"There is no remedy against seasickness better than an iron stomach, and the awareness of being just a bit above the common herd. I feel much better. The more refined one is, the more one can bear."

"Crash!" said the eggshell. A wagon wheel had rolled over it.

"Ow!" cried the darning needle. "Something is pressing against me. I think I am going to be seasick after all. I fear I will break!"

But it didn't break, even though a loaded wagon drove over it. There it lay, lengthwise in the gutter; and there we'll leave it.

THE BELL

In the narrow streets of the
city, at dusk, just as the sun was setting and painting the clouds
above the chimney pots a fiery red, people would sometimes hear
a strange sound like the knell of a great churchbell. Only for a
moment could it be heard, then the noise of the city — the rumbling of the carts and the shouting of the peddlers — would drown
it out. "It is the vesper bell, calling folk to evening prayers; the sun
must be setting," was the usual explanation.

To those who lived on the outskirts of the town, where the
houses were farther away from each other and had gardens around
them — some places were even separated by a field — the sunset
was much more beautiful and the sound of the bell much louder.
It seemed to come from a church in the depth of a fragrant forest,
and it made the people who heard it feel quite solemn as they
looked toward the darkening woods.

As time passed people began to ask each other whether there
wasn't a church in the woods. And it was not far from that thought
to the next: "The bell sounds so beautiful, why don't we go out
and try to find it?"

Now the rich people got into their carriages and the poor people
walked; but to all of them the road to the forest seemed very long.
When they finally reached some weeping willows that grew on the
edge of the woods they sat down under the trees to rest; and,

135

looking up into the branches, believed that they were sitting in the middle of the forest. One of the bakers from town pitched a tent there and sold cakes. Business was good, and soon there were two bakers. The second one to arrive hung above his tent a bell, which was tarred on the outside to protect it from the rain, but it had no tongue.

When the people came back to town they said that their outing had been very romantic; and that word is not as tepid as a teaparty. Three persons claimed to have penetrated the forest and come out on the other side. They had heard a bell, but they said that the sound seemed to come not from the woods but from the town. One of them had written a sonnet about the bell, in which he compared its sound to that of a mother's voice when she speaks to her lovely, beloved child; the last line declared that no melody could be sweeter than that bell's song.

At last the emperor heard about it, and he promised that whoever found out where the sound came from would be given the title of "Bell Ringer of the World," even if he discovered that it wasn't a bell that made it.

Now many people went out in search of the bell; they did it for the title and for the wages that went with it. But only one returned with an answer: an explanation of a sort. He had been no farther in the forest than the rest — and that hadn't been very far — but he claimed that the bell-like sound came from a great owl who was sitting inside a hollow tree. It was the bird of wisdom and it was incessantly knocking its head against the trunk; but whether the ringing was caused by the bird's head or the tree trunk he had not yet decided. The emperor bestowed upon him the title of "Bell Ringer of the World," and every year he published a paper on the subject, without anyone becoming any wiser.

One Sunday in May, when the children who had reached the age of fourteen were confirmed, the minister preached so movingly that all the young people present had tears in their eyes. It was a solemn occasion; after all, it was expected that they should become grownups; and that as soon as the ceremony was over, their child-souls would enter the bodies of reasonable adults. It was a beautiful day, and after the service all the children who had been confirmed walked, in a flock, to the forest. The sound of the unknown bell was particularly strong that day; and all of them had a great desire to go and search for it. That is, all of them except three: One girl

THE BELL

had to hurry home for the final fitting of her new dress, which had been especially sewn for a ball she was to attend that night. The dress and the ball had been her real reasons for being confirmed. Another was a poor boy who had had to borrow both shoes and suit from the son of his parents' landlord; and they were to be delivered back as soon as the ceremony was over. The third was a boy who declared that he never went anywhere without his parents' permission. He had always been a good boy and would continue to be one even after he was confirmed; that is nothing to poke fun at — but all the other children did.

So three of them stayed behind but all the rest went on. The sun was shining, the birds were singing, and the young people who had just been confirmed were singing too. They walked hand in hand, for they hadn't become anything in the world yet, and they could afford to be friendly.

Soon two of the smallest became tired and turned back toward the town; and a couple of girls sat down in a meadow to braid wreaths of wild flowers; so they were four fewer. When the rest of the group reached the weeping willow trees, where the baker's tent was pitched, most of them said, "Well, here we are; you can see that the bell doesn't really exist. It is just something one imagines."

But from deeper in the woods came the sound of the bell: sweet and solemn; and five of the children decided to go on, just a little farther. It was not easy to make one's way through the forest; the trees grew close together, blackberry brambles and other thorny bushes were everywhere. But it was beautiful; the sun rays played and they heard the nightingale sing. It was glorious, but it was no place for girls; their dresses would be torn.

They came to great boulders covered with different kinds of moss. They heard the gurgling of a spring: "Gluck, gluck."

"I wonder if that isn't the bell," said one of the five, and lay down on the ground in order to hear the bubbling of the water better. "I think I ought to investigate this some more," he added, and let the other four go on without him.

They came to a house made of branches and bark. A huge wild apple tree towered above it and roses grew in such abundance up its walls that they covered the roof of the little cottage. On one of the ramblers hung a little silver bell. Was that the bell that they had heard? All but one of the boys agreed that it was. He claimed that this bell was too small and delicate to be heard so far away; besides, it did not produce the kind of music that could touch a man's heart. "No," he said. "It is an entirely different bell that we heard before."

But the youth who had spoken was a king's son, and one of his comrades remarked, "Oh, his kind always wants to think themselves cleverer than the rest of us."

They let him go on alone. When the cottage and his friends were lost from sight, the great loneliness of the forest engulfed the prince. He could still hear the little bell, which had pleased his friends, tingle merrily; and from farther away — borne on the wind's back — came the sound of the people at the baker's tent singing as they drank their tea. But the knell of the great bell of the forest grew stronger and stronger; then it seemed to be accompanied by an organ; he thought the sound of it came from the left where the heart is.

Leaves rustled, twigs snapped; someone else was making his way through the woods. The prince turned; in front of him stood another boy. He had wooden shoes on his feet, and the sleeves of his tunic were too short because he had outgrown it. He was the youth who had had to return the clothes he had worn at confirmation, as soon as the ceremony was over. The landlord's son had got his finery back, and the poor lad had put on his own old clothes, stuck his feet into his clogs, and set off in search of the great bell whose deep clang had called on him so powerfully that he had had to follow it.

"Let us go on together," proposed the prince. But the poor boy looked down at his wooden shoes and pulled at the sleeves of his tunic to make them a little longer. His poverty made him shy, and he excused himself by saying that he feared he could not walk as fast as the prince. Besides, he thought that the bell was to be found on the other side of the forest; on the right, where everything great and marvelous is.

"Then I suppose we shall not meet again," said the prince, and nodded to the poor boy, who walked into the densest part of the forest, where brambles and thorns would tear his worn-out clothes to shreds and scratch his face, legs, and hands till blood streamed down them. The prince did not escape being scratched, but the sun did shine on the path he took, and we shall follow him, for he was a good and courageous boy.

"I will find the bell," he declared, "if I have to go to the end of the world to do it."

THE BELL

On the limbs of a tree sat ugly monkeys; they grinned and screamed to each other: "Throw something at him! Throw something at him. He is a royal child!"

But the prince did not even notice them; he walked on deeper and deeper into the forest. Here grew the strangest flowers: lilies shaped like white stars, with blood-red stamens; tulips as blue as the sky; and apple trees, whose fruit looked like soap bubbles. — How such a tree would have glittered in the sunlight! — He passed green meadows where deer played in the grass underneath solitary oak trees. In every crack and crevice of their trunks grew grass and moss.

There were many lakes in which white swans swam; he could hear the beating of their great wings. He lingered and listened. More than once he wondered whether the knell might not come from somewhere deep inside one of the lakes; but then, when he strained his ears, he understood that the sound came from far away, from the very depth of the forest.

The sun was setting and the sky turned red as fire. The forest became so still that the prince sank down on his knees and said, "I shall never find what I seek! The sun is setting; soon the night will come — the dark, dark night. . . . But maybe I can still get another glimpse of the sun, see it once more before it disappears, by climbing that cliff over there, which is higher than the tallest trees."

His hands grabbed the brambles that grew among the wet stones, and he pulled himself upward. So eager was he to reach the top of the cliff that he noticed neither the slimy snakes nor the toads who barked like dogs.

Just before the sun set he reached the summit. Oh, what splendor! Below him stretched the ocean, that great sea that was flinging its long waves toward the shore. Like a shining red altar the sun stood where sea and sky met. All nature became one in the golden sunset: the song of the forest and the song of the sea blended and his heart seemed to be part of their harmony. All nature was a great cathedral: the flowers and the grass were the mosaic floors, the tall trees and swaying clouds were its pillars and heaven itself was the dome. High above the red color was disappearing for the sun had set. The millions of stars were lighted: the millions of little diamond lamps. The prince spread out his arms toward it all: the forest, the ocean, and the sky. But just at that moment, from the right side of the cliff came the poor boy with his ragged tunic and

HANS CHRISTIAN ANDERSEN

his wooden shoes. He had arrived there almost as quickly by going his own way.

The two boys ran to meet each other. There they stood, hand in hand, in the midst of nature's and poetry's great cathedral; and far above the great invisible holy bell was heard in loud hosanna.

THE HILL OF THE ELVES

Some lizards were darting in and out of the cracks and crevices of an old oak tree. All of them could speak lizard language, so they understood each other.

"Have you heard all the rumbling and grumbling inside the old hill where the elves live?" asked one of the lizards. "I haven't been able to sleep a wink these last two nights. I might as well have had a toothache."

"Oh yes, something is going on up there, for sure," began another lizard. "Last night they put the hill on four red pillars and let it stand like that until it was almost time for the cock to crow. They certainly gave their home a good airing. The elfin maidens have to learn a new dance in which they stamp their feet. There is no doubt about it, something is up."

"I have talked with an acquaintance of mine, an earthworm," declared a third lizard. "I met him as he was coming out of the hill, where he has been digging for the last two days. He has heard a good deal. — The poor creature can't see but he's a master at both hearing and feeling. — The elves are expecting very important guests. The earthworm wouldn't tell me who they were, but that's probably because he didn't know. The will-o'-the-wisps have all been hired to make a torchlight procession, as it's called. All the gold and silver in the whole hill — and there's enough of it — is to be polished and set out in the moonlight."

HANS CHRISTIAN ANDERSEN

"Who can the visitors be?" cried all the lizards. "What is going to happen? Listen to the humming! Listen to the buzzing!"

Just at that moment the hill of the elves opened and an old elfin lady came tripping out. She had the same hollow back that all elves have, and she was very respectably dressed. She was the elfin king's housekeeper, and distantly related to him; that was why she wore an amber heart on her forehead. Goodness, how she could run. Away she went down to the marsh where the night raven lived.

"You are invited to the Mount of the Elves this very night," she said. "But you will have to do us the favor of delivering the invitations. Since you have no home of your own and cannot return our hospitality, you will have to make yourself useful instead. We are expecting distinguished guests, trolls of the greatest importance, and the elfin king wants to impress them."

"Whom am I to invite?" asked the night raven.

"Well, to the grand ball, anyone can come," began the old elfin lady. "Even human beings are invited; that is, those who have some small talent akin to ours: such as being able to talk in their sleep. But the party tonight is to be more select; only those of the highest rank are to attend. I argued with the elfin king about the guest list, for in my opinion neither ghosts nor spooks should be on it. . . . The old merman and his daughters, the mermaids, must be the first ones you invite. They don't like to be where it's dry, so tell them that they can count on having a wet stone each to sit on, if not something better. Remember to say that that's a promise; and I don't think they'll refuse. After that call on all the older trolls of the highest rank who have tails, the river spirit, and the gnomes. Then there are the graveyard sow, the Hell horse, and the three-legged church monster; it wouldn't do to forget them. They belong to the clergy; but that is their profession, so I shan't hold it against them. Besides, we are all related, and they visit us regularly."

"Caw!" said the night raven, and flew away to deliver the invitations.

The elfin maidens were already dancing on top of the hill. Over their shoulders were long shawls woven from mist and moonlight. They looked very pretty, if you like that sort of thing.

The great hall in the middle of the mount had certainly been done up. The floors had been washed in moonlight, and all the walls had been waxed with witches' grease till they shone like tulip petals.

THE HILL OF THE ELVES

Out in the kitchen frogs were being roasted on spits, and snakes stuffed with children's fingers were baking. The salads were made of toadstool seeds, garnished with moist snouts of mice; and for dressing there was hemlock juice. Saltpeter wine that had been aged in tombs and beer from the bog-witch brewery had been poured into decanters. Altogether a festive — though a bit conservative — menu. Rusty nails and bits of colored glass from a church window were the desserts.

The old elfin king's crown had been polished with powder ground from slate pencils. For this purpose only pencils that have belonged to especially studious boys may be used; and those are hard to find. In the bedchambers the newly washed curtains were being made to stick to the walls with the help of snakes' spit. Everywhere, everybody was busy. There were bustle and commotion throughout the hill.

"Now I'll burn some horsehair and swine bristles, and then I shall have done my share," remarked the old elfin lady who was the elfin king's housekeeper.

"Dear . . . dear Father," pestered the youngest of the elfin king's daughters, "won't you tell us who the distinguished guests are?"

"Well, I suppose I have to," began the king. "Two of you had better be prepared to get married because two of you are going to get married. The old troll king of Norway is coming. Dovre — his castle — is made of granite, and it is large and so high that on the roof of the great hall there is always snow. He has a gold mine, too; and that is nothing to sneeze at, even though some people do. He is bringing his sons along, and they are thinking of getting married. The old troll is a real Norwegian: honest, full of life, and straightforward. I have known him a long, long time. We became friends at his wedding. He had come to Denmark for a wife. She was the daughter of the king of the chalk cliffs of Möen; but she's been dead a long time now.

"How I look forward to seeing the old fellow again. I have been told that his sons are a spoiled couple of cubs: cocky and badmannered. But who knows, such talk may all be slander. Time will rub the nonsense off them, anyway. Let me see you show them how they ought to behave."

"When are they coming?" asked his oldest daughter.

"That depends upon the wind and the weather," sighed the king. "They are traveling by ship. I wanted them to journey

HANS CHRISTIAN ANDERSEN

through Sweden, but the old troll is conservative. He doesn't keep up with the changing times, which in my opinion is very wrong of him."

At that moment two will-o'-the-wisps came running into the hall. One ran faster than the other and that was why he came first.

"They are coming! They are coming!" they both shouted.

"Hand me my crown and I shall go out and stand in the moonlight," said the king of the elves and, followed by the elfin maidens, he went to meet the guests.

His daughters lifted their shawls and curtsied all the way to the ground.

There he was: the troll king from Dovre! His crown was made of ice and polished pine cones. He was wearing a bearskin coat and heavy boots. His sons, on the other hand, were lightly dressed: their collars were open and they weren't wearing suspenders. They were two big strapping fellows.

"Is this a hill?" laughed the younger one. "In Norway we would call it a hole in the ground."

"Don't be silly," said the old troll king. "Holes go inward and hills go upward. Don't you have eyes in your head?"

The thing that surprised the two young men most was that they could understand the language; and they said so.

"Don't make fools of yourselves," scolded their father, "or everybody will think that you were born yesterday and put on the stove to dry overnight."

They entered the great hall where all the guests were gathered; they had arrived so fast you would think that the wind had blown them there. The old merman and his daughters were sitting in tubs full of water and feeling right at home. Except for the sons of the troll king, everyone exhibited his or her best table manners, while the two young men put their feet on the table. But they thought that anything they did was becoming.

"Take your feet out of the dishes!" bellowed the old troll king.

His sons obeyed him, but not right away. They tickled their dinner partners — two young elfin maidens — with pine cones that they had brought in their pockets from Norway. In the middle of the dinner they took off their boots to make themselves more comfortable and handed them to the elfin maidens to take care of.

But the old troll king was a different sort than his sons. He

THE HILL OF THE ELVES

described so well the proud mountains of Norway, the rivers and streams that leaped down the cliffs, white and bubbling, and sounded like both a thunderclap and an organ playing, when they plunged into the valleys far below. He told about the salmon that could leap up the swiftest waterfall, while the river nymphs played on their golden harps. He made them imagine a still winter night, when you can hear the sound of sleigh bells and see the young people skate, carrying burning torches, across the glasslike surface of the lakes, where the ice is so transparent that the skaters can watch the fish fleeing, in terror, below them. Yes, he knew how to tell a story well; it seemed to all the other guests that they could hear the buzz of the great sawmills and the singing of the young men and women as they danced the Halling dance.

"Hurrah!" the troll king suddenly cried; and in the midst of his storytelling kissed the old elfin lady so that it could be heard throughout the hall. "That was a brotherly kiss," he explained, in spite of their not being related at all.

Now the young elfin maidens danced. First the simple dances and then the new one in which they stamped their feet. The final one was the most difficult and was called "Stepping Outside the Dance." How they twirled and twisted. One could hardly make out which were legs and which were arms, or which end was up and which was down. The poor Hell horse got so dizzy watching it that he began to feel sick and had to leave the table.

"Whoa!" shouted the old troll king. "They have got legs, and they can dance; but what else can they do?"

"Judge for yourself," said the elfin king, and called his youngest daughter to him. She was as fair as moonlight and the most delicate of the sisters.

She stuck a white wand in her mouth and vanished — that was her accomplishment.

The old troll king said that this was not the kind of talent he would want his wife to have, and he was sure that his sons agreed with him.

The second sister could walk beside herself, so that she looked as if she had a shadow; something that neither elves nor trolls possess.

The third sister's talent lay in an entirely different direction. She had been apprenticed to the bog witch and knew both how to brew beer and how to garnish elder stumps with glowworms.

"She will make a good housewife," said the troll king, and

winked at her. He would have drunk a toast in her honor but he thought he had drunk enough already.

Now came the fourth sister. She had a golden harp. When she struck the first string, they all lifted their left legs — for trolls and elves are left-legged — and when she struck the second string they all had to do exactly what she commanded.

"She is a dangerous woman," said the troll king. His two sons sneaked out of the hall; they were bored.

"And what can the next one do?" asked the troll.

"I have learned to love Norway," she said softly. "And I will only marry a Norwegian."

But the youngest of the elfin king's daughters whispered to the old troll king, "She says that because she once heard a Norwegian verse in which it was prophesied that, when the world went under, the mountains of Norway would stand as a tombstone over it; and she is terribly afraid of dying."

"Ha-ha!" laughed the old troll king. "And you let the cat out of the bag. . . . And what can the seventh and last of them do?"

"The sixth comes before the seventh," said the elfin king, who knew how to count.

The sixth daughter was so shy that she did not want to step forward. "I can only tell people the truth," she finally whispered, "and that no one likes to hear, so I am busy sewing on my shroud."

Now came the seventh; and she was the last of the sisters. What could she do? She could tell fairy tales, as many as anyone wanted to hear.

"Here are my five fingers, tell me a fairy tale for each of them," demanded the troll king.

The elfin maiden took his hand in hers and began. The king of the trolls laughed so hard that he almost split his sides. When she came to the finger that was encircled by a gold ring — it looked as if it knew that there was an engagement in the air — the troll cried, "Hold onto what you have got! My hand is yours. You I shall marry myself!"

But the elfin maiden protested that she still had two stories to tell: one for the ring finger and one for the little finger, which would be short.

"They can wait," said the king of the trolls. "We can hear them next winter. And you shall tell us about the pine trees, the birches, the crinkling frost, and about the gifts that the river nymphs bring;

THE HILL OF THE ELVES

for we do so love a well-told tale in Norway, and no one there knows how to tell them. We shall sit in my granite hall that is lighted by pine pitch torches and drink mead out of golden horns that once belonged to Viking kings. The river nymph has given me a couple of them. The echo — he is a tall, thin fellow — will come and sing for us. He knows all the songs that the milkmaids sing when they drive their herds into the meadows. Oh, we'll have a good time! The salmon will leap and knock on our granite walls, but we won't let him in. Oh, believe me! Norway is a dear old place! . . . But where are my sons?"

Where were his sons? They were racing about on the field blowing out the poor will-o'-the-wisps, who had been peacefully assembling for the torchlight parade.

"What do you mean by running about like this?" scolded their father. "I have chosen a mother for you. Now you can find wives for yourselves among your aunts."

But the boys said they would rather drink toasts and make speeches, for they had no desire to get married. So they made speeches and they toasted each other, and when they were finished they turned their glasses upside down so that everyone could see that they were empty. Then they took off their shirts and lay down on the table to sleep, for, as they said, they didn't "stand on ceremony."

The old troll king danced with his young bride and exchanged boots with her, for that is more refined than exchanging rings.

"Now the cock crows!" shouted the old elfin lady who was the housekeeper and kept an eye on everything. "We have to close the shutters or the sun will burn us all."

And the hill of the elves closed. But outside the lizards were running up and down the old oak tree.

"Oh, I did like that old Norwegian troll king," said one of the lizards.

"I liked his sons best," said the earthworm, but the wretched little creature couldn't see.

THE JUMPING COMPETITION

The flea, the grasshopper, and the jumping jack decided to hold a competition to see which of them could jump the highest. They invited the whole world, and anyone else who wanted to come, to look at it. Each of them felt sure that he would become the champion.

"I will give my daughter to the one who jumps the highest," declared the king. "Honor is too paltry a reward."

The flea was the first to introduce himself. He had excellent manners; but then he had the blood of young maidens in him and was accustomed to human society, and that had left its mark on him.

Then came the grasshopper. He was stout but not without grace and dressed in a green uniform, which he had acquired at birth. He said he was of ancient family and that his ancestors came from Egypt. He claimed that he was so highly esteemed in this country that he had been brought directly from the fields and given a card house. It was three stories high and all made of picture cards. It had both doors and windows.

"I sing so well," he boasted, "that sixteen native crickets, who have been cheeping since birth — but never have been honored with a card house — grew so thin from envy, when they heard me sing, that they almost disappeared."

Both the flea and the grasshopper gave a full account of their

THE JUMPING COMPETITION

merits. Each of them thought it only fitting that he should marry a princess.

Now came the jumping jack. He was made from the wishbone of a goose, two rubber bands, some sealing wax, and a little stick that was mahogany. He didn't say a word, which made the whole court certain that he was a genius. The royal dog sniffed at him and said that he came of good family. The old councilor, who had received three decorations as a reward for keeping his mouth shut, declared that the jumping jack was endowed with the gift of prophecy. One could tell from looking at its back whether we would have a mild winter or not; and that was more than one could tell from the back of the fellow who wrote the almanac.

The old king merely said, "I don't talk much, but I have my own opinion about everything."

The competition began. The flea jumped so high that one could not see him; and then everyone said he hadn't jumped at all, which was most unfair! The grasshopper only jumped half as high as the flea but landed right in the face of the king and that did not please His Majesty, who said it was repulsive.

Now it was the jumping jack's turn; he sat so still and appeared so pensive that everyone decided that he wouldn't jump at all.

"I hope he hasn't got sick," said the royal hound, and sniffed at him; but just at that moment he jumped. It was a little, slanted jump, but high enough so that he landed in the lap of the princess, who was sitting on a golden stool.

"The highest jump is into my daughter's lap," declared the king. "The jumping jack has shown both intelligence and taste; she shall marry him." And the jumping jack got the princess.

HANS CHRISTIAN ANDERSEN

"I jumped highest," said the flea. "But it is of no importance; she can keep him: wishbone, rubber bands, sealing wax, mahogany stick, and all! I don't care! I know I jumped the highest, but in this world it's only appearance that counts."

The flea enlisted in a foreign army and it was rumored that he was killed in battle.

The grasshopper sat down in the ditch and thought about the injustice of the world. "It's appearance that counts! It's appearance that counts!" he said. And then he sang his own sad song. It's from him that we have the story, which, even though it has been printed, may still be a lie.

THE SHEPHERDESS
AND THE CHIMNEY SWEEP

Have you ever seen a really old cabinet, the kind whose wood is dark from age and that doesn't have a spot on it that isn't carved, so that it looks like a mass of vines and twirls? Once there stood in a parlor just such an heirloom that had been in the family for four generations. From the bottom to the top there were roses and tulips; everywhere there were curlicues, and little deer heads with numerous antlers peered out from among them. But the most amazing figure was in the center panel. It was a man with a long beard, who had little horns sticking out of his forehead and the legs of a goat. He had a grin on his face — for you could hardly call it a smile. He looked so funny that the children who lived in the house gave him a name. They called him Mr. Goat-legged Commanding-General-Private-War-Sergeant because it was so difficult to say, even for a grownup; and they knew of no one — either living or carved — who could boast of such a fine title.

From his cabinet he was always looking straight across the room at a little table that stood beneath a mirror, for on the table was the loveliest little porcelain shepherdess. She had her skirt pinned up with a red rose; on her feet were golden shoes, on her head she had a golden hat, and in her hand was a shepherd's crook. Oh, she was beautiful! Next to her stood a little chimney sweep, and he was black as coal, except for his face, which was as pink and white as

151

hers. Somehow this seemed wrong; he ought to have had at least a dab of soot on his nose or his cheek. But he was of porcelain too, and his profession was make-believe; he might just as well have been a prince. There he stood with his ladder in his hands looking as delicate as the shepherdess. They were standing close together, for that was the way they had always been placed; and so they thought it was natural that they be engaged. They had much in common: both were young, both were made from the same clay, both were breakable.

Near them on the table there was another figure; he was three times as big as either of them. He was a Chinese mandarin and he knew how to nod. He was of porcelain too, and insisted that he was the shepherdess' grandfather. Although he couldn't really prove that he was related to her at all, he behaved as if he had as much right over her as her parents and demanded that she obey him. Now Mr. Goat-legged Commanding-General-Private-War-Sergeant had asked for the shepherdess' hand in marriage, and the Chinese mandarin had nodded.

"You will have a husband who I am almost certain is made of mahogany," said the old mandarin. "You will be called Mrs. Goat-legged Commanding-General-Private-War-Sergeant. He has a whole cabinetful of silverware, plus all that he has hidden in the secret compartments."

"I don't want to live in a dark closet!" wailed the shepherdess. "They say that he has eleven porcelain wives in there already."

"Then you shall be number twelve!" declared the Chinese mandarin. "And tonight! As soon as the cabinet creaks, there shall be a wedding, my dear, and that is as certain as it is that I am Chinese!" And he nodded his head back and forth until he fell asleep.

The little shepherdess cried and cried; then she looked up at her beloved, the chimney sweep. "I beg you to go with me out into the world, for we cannot stay here," she sobbed.

"I will do anything that you ask," he replied. "Let's go at once. I must be able to earn a living at my profession."

"If only we were down on the floor already," she said anxiously. "I won't feel safe before we are out in the wide world."

The chimney sweep did his best to console her. He showed her where she should set her little feet along the carved edges of the table and on the leaves of the gilded vines that wound themselves around its legs. He made use of his ladder and soon they had

THE SHEPHERDESS AND THE CHIMNEY SWEEP

reached the floor. But then they looked up at the cabinet, where there was an uproar. All the carved deer were shaking their antlers in fury; and Mr. Goat-legged Commanding-General-Private-War-Sergeant was jumping up and down. "They're eloping! They're eloping!" he cried as loud as he could over to the Chinese mandarin.

A drawer in the wall, just a little above the floor, was luckily open and the frightened lovers jumped inside it. Here lay three or four incomplete decks of cards and a little puppet theater. The puppets were performing a play. In the front row of the audience sat all the queens: hearts, diamonds, spades, and clubs, fanning themselves with their tulips; behind them sat the knaves and looked both above and below the ladies in the front row, just to show that they had heads at both ends, exactly as they always do in a deck of cards. The play was about two lovers who weren't allowed to be together and reminded the poor shepherdess so much of her own situation that she wept and wept.

"I can't bear it!" she said. "We must get out of here."

By the time they were back down on the floor again, the old Chinese mandarin was awake. He was nodding his head and rocking back and forth with his whole body, which was rounded at the bottom, for he had no legs.

"Here comes the old mandarin!" screamed the little shepherdess, and fell down on her porcelain knees because she was so upset.

"I have an idea," said the chimney sweep. "We could climb down into the potpourri jar, over there in the corner. There we shall be among roses and lavender and we can throw salt in the eyes of anyone who comes."

"It won't do!" cried the shepherdess. "The potpourri jar and the mandarin were once engaged. It's a long time ago but a certain amount of affection always remains for the lovers of one's youth. . . . No, we have no choice, we must go out into the wide world."

"But do you realize what that means?" asked the chimney sweep. "Have you thought about how wide the world is and that we can never come back?"

"I have!" she said determinedly.

The chimney sweep looked steadfastly into her eyes. "The only way I know how to get out is through the chimney. Have you the courage to climb into the belly of the stove and up through the flue into the chimney? From there on, it's upward, ever upward, where no one can reach us, till we come to the opening; and then we shall be out in the wide world."

He led her over to the stove and opened the door. "Oh, how dark it looks," she said. But she followed him into the belly of the stove and crawled with him up the flue, though it was pitch dark.

"Now we are in the chimney. Look up and you will see a star!"

It was true, there was a star shining through the darkness, as if it wished to guide them on their way. They climbed, they crawled; it was a terrible journey: up, up they went. The chimney sweep hoisted and held onto the shepherdess, showing her where to put her little porcelain feet. Finally they reached the top of the chimney and sat down on the edge of it. They were exhausted and they had every right to be.

The star-filled sky was above them and all the roofs of the city were below them. They could see far and wide, out into the world. The poor little shepherdess had never imagined that the wide world would be so big. She leaned her head on the chimney sweep's shoulder and cried so hard that the gold in her waistband began to chip.

"It's far too much!" she sobbed. "I cannot bear it! The world is much too big. I wish I were back on the table beneath the mirror. I shall never be happy again until I am! I followed you out into the wide world; now you must take me home, if you care for me at all."

The chimney sweep tried to reason with her. He talked about the Chinese mandarin and Mr. Goat-legged Commanding-General-Private-War-Sergeant; but that just made her cry all the more. Finally she kissed him, and then he could only obey her.

And they climbed back down the chimney with great difficulty, crawled through the flue, and entered the belly of the stove; there they peeped out through the door to see what was going on in the parlor.

Not a sound came from the room. In the middle of the floor lay the old Chinese mandarin. He had fallen off the table when he tried to follow them. Now he was in three pieces and his head had rolled over in a corner. Mr. Goat-legged Commanding-General-Private-War-Sergeant stood where he always had been, deep in thought.

THE SHEPHERDESS AND THE CHIMNEY SWEEP

"How horrible!" exclaimed the little shepherdess. "Old Grandfather is broken and it's all our fault! I shan't live through it!"

"He can be glued," said the chimney sweep. "He can be put together again. . . . Don't carry on so! . . . All he needs is to be glued and have a rivet put in his neck, and he'll be able to say as many nasty things as he ever did."

"Do you think so?" she asked. They climbed up onto the table and stood where they had before.

"Well, this is as far as we got!" the chimney sweep said. "We could have saved ourselves a whole lot of trouble."

"Do you think it will be expensive to have Grandfather put together again?" asked the shepherdess. "Oh, how I wish it were already done!"

And Grandfather was glued and a rivet was put in his neck; and then he was as good as new, except for one thing: he couldn't nod any more.

"You seem to think so much more highly of yourself since you have been broken," said Mr. Goat-legged Commanding-General-Private-War-Sergeant. "I can't understand why anyone should be proud of being glued. Am I to have her or not?"

The chimney sweep and the little shepherdess looked pitifully at the Chinese mandarin; they were so terrified that he would nod. But he couldn't nod; and he didn't want to admit to a stranger that he had a rivet in his neck and would never be able to nod again. So the two young porcelain lovers stayed together. They blessed the rivet in Grandfather's neck and loved each other until they broke.

THE SHADOW

On the shores of the Mediterranean the sun really knows how to shine. It is so powerful that it tans the people a mahogany brown; and the young scholar who came from the north, where all the people are as white as bakers' apprentices, soon learned to regard his old friend with suspicion. In the south one stays inside during most of the day with the doors and shutters closed. The houses look as if everyone was asleep or no one was at home. The young foreigner felt as if he were in prison, and his shadow rolled itself up until it was smaller than it had ever been before. But as soon as the sun set and a candle lighted the room, out came the shadow again. It was truly a pleasure to watch it grow; up the wall it would stretch itself until its head almost reached the ceiling.

"The stars seem so much brighter here," thought the scholar, and he walked out onto his balcony where he stretched himself just as his shadow had done. And on all the balconies throughout the city people came out to enjoy the cool evening. Had the town appeared dead and deserted at noon, certainly now it was alive! People were flocking into the streets. The tailors and the shoemakers moved their workbenches outside; the women came with their straight-backed chairs to sit and gossip. Donkeys heavily laden with wares tripped along like little maids. Children were everywhere. They laughed, played, and sometimes cried as children will

156

THE SHADOW

do, for children can run so fast that they are not certain whether it is a tragedy or a comedy they are enacting. And the lights! Thousands of lamps burned like so many falling stars. A funeral procession, led by little choir boys in black and white, passed with mournful but not sad-looking people following the black-draped horse and wagon. The church bells were ringing. "This is life!" thought the young foreigner, and he tried to take it all in.

Only the house directly across from his own was as quiet now as it had been at midday. The street was very narrow and the opposite balcony was only a few yards away. Often he stood and stared at it, but no one ever came out. Yet there were flowers there and they seemed to be flourishing, which meant that they were cared for or else the sun would long since have withered them. "Yes," he concluded, "they must be watered by someone." Besides, the shutters were opened, and while he never saw any light, he sometimes heard music. The scholar thought this music "exquisite," but that may be only because all young northerners think everything "exquisite" the first time they are in the south.

He asked his landlord if he knew who lived across the street, but the old man replied that he did not and, in fact, had never seen anyone enter or leave. As for the music, he could hardly express how terrible he thought it. "It's as if someone were practicing," he said. "The same piece, over and over and over again! And it's never played all the way through! It's unbearable!"

One night the young foreigner, who slept with his balcony door open, awakened with a start. A breeze had lifted his drapes so that he caught a glimpse of the opposite balcony. The flowers were ablaze with the most beautiful colors and in their midst stood a lovely maiden. For an instant the scholar closed his eyes to make sure that he had had them open. In a single leap he was standing in front of the drapes. Cautiously, he parted them; but the girl had vanished, the light had disappeared, and the flowers looked as they always did. The door, however, had been left open, and from far inside he could hear music; its gentle strains seemed to cast a spell over him, for never before had he taken such delight in his own thoughts. How does one get into that apartment? he wondered; and he perused the street below. There was no private entrance whatever, only a group of small shops; surely one could not enter a home through a store.

The next evening the scholar was sitting as usual on his balcony.

HANS CHRISTIAN ANDERSEN

From his room the lamp burned brightly, and since his shadow was very shy of light, it had stretched itself until it reached the opposite balcony. When the young man moved, his shadow moved. "I believe my shadow is the only living thing over there," he muttered. "See how it has sat down among the flowers. The balcony door is ajar. Now if my shadow were clever, it would go inside and take a look around; then it would come back and tell me what it had seen. Yes, you ought to earn your keep," he said jokingly. "Now go inside. Did you hear me? Go!" And he nodded to his shadow and his shadow nodded back at him. "Yes, go! But remember to come back again." There the scholar's conversation with his shadow ended. The young man rose, and the shadow on the opposite balcony rose; the young man turned around and the shadow also turned around; but then there happened something that no one saw. The shadow went through the half-open door of the other balcony, while the scholar went into his own room and closed the drapes behind him.

The next morning on his way to the café where he had his breakfast and read the newspapers, the scholar discovered that he had no shadow. "So it really went away last night!" he marveled. More than anything else, the young man was embarrassed; people were certain to notice, and might demand that he explain or, worse than that, might make up explanations of their own. He returned at once to his room and there he remained for the rest of the day. That evening he walked out onto his balcony for a bit of fresh air. The light streamed from behind him as it had on the evening before. He sat down, stood up, stretched himself; still there was no shadow, and though it was doubtful that anyone could see him, he hurried inside again almost immediately.

But in the warm countries everything grows much faster than it does in the north, and less than a week had passed before a shadow began to sprout from the scholar's feet. "The old one must have left its roots behind, what a pleasant surprise!" he thought happily. Within a month he walked the streets unconcerned; his shadow, though a little small, was quite respectable. During the long trip, for the scholar was going home, it continued to grow until even a very big man, which the scholar was not, would not have complained about its size.

Settled once more in his own country, the scholar wrote books about all that is true and beautiful and good. The days became

THE SHADOW

years. The scholar was now a philosopher, and the years became many. One evening when he was sitting alone in his room there was a very gentle knock at the door.

"Come in," he called. But no one came, so the philosopher opened the door himself. Before him stood the thinnest man that he had ever seen but, judging from his clothes, a person of some importance. "Whom do I have the honor of addressing?" the philosopher asked.

"I thought as much," replied the stranger. "You don't recognize me, now that I have a body of my own and clothes to boot. You never would have believed that you would meet your old shadow again. Things have gone well for me since we parted. If need be, I can buy my freedom!" The shadow jiggled its purse, which was filled with gold pieces, and touched the heavy gold chain that it wore around its neck. On all of its fingers were diamond rings, and every one was genuine.

"I must be dreaming!" exclaimed the philosopher. "What is happening?"

"Well, it isn't something that happens every day," said the shadow, "but then, you're not an ordinary person. Nobody knows that better than I do, didn't I walk in your first footsteps? . . . As soon as you found that I could stand alone in the world, you let me go. The results are obvious. Without bragging, I can say few could have done better. . . . Of late, a longing has come over me to talk with you before you die — you must die, you know. Besides, I wanted to see this country again, only a rogue does not love his native land. . . . I know that you have a new shadow. If I owe you or it anything, you will be so kind as to tell me."

"Is it really you?" cried the philosopher. "It's so incredible! I wouldn't have believed that one's shadow could come back to one as a human being!"

"Tell me how much I owe you," insisted the shadow. "I hate to be in debt."

"How can you talk like that?" replied the philosopher. "What debt could there be to pay? Be as free as you wish! I am only happy to see you again. And I rejoice in your good luck. Sit down, old friend," he invited most cordially. "Tell me how all this came about, and what you saw that night in the house across the street."

"Yes, I will tell you about it," agreed the shadow, and sat down. "But first you must promise me that you will never tell anyone that I once was your shadow. I've been thinking of becoming engaged; after all I am quite rich enough to support a large family."

"Don't give it another moment's thought," the philosopher said. "I will never tell anyone who you really are. Here is my hand on it. A man is no better than his word."

"And a word is a shadow," remarked the shadow, because it could not speak otherwise.

It was really amazing, how human the shadow appeared. It was dressed completely in black, but everything was of the finest quality from its patent leather boots to its hat of the softest felt. The gold chain and the rings have already been described, but one's eye fell upon them so often that one cannot help mentioning them again. Yes, the shadow was well dressed, and clothes make the man.

"Now I shall begin," announced the shadow, and it stamped its boots as hard as it could on the philosopher's new shadow, which was curled up like a poodle at the feet of the man. Perhaps it did this because it hoped to attach the philosopher's shadow to itself, or maybe just because it was arrogant; but the new shadow did not appear ruffled. It lay perfectly still and listened, for it too wanted to know how one could be free and become one's own master.

"Do you know who lived in the house across the street?" asked the shadow. "That's the best of all, it was Poetry! I was there for three weeks, and that is just as edifying as having lived three thousand years and read everything that's ever been composed or written. This I say, and what I say is true! I have seen all and I know all!"

"Poetry!" cried the philosopher. "Yes . . . yes. She is often a hermit in the big cities. I saw her myself once, but only for a short moment and my eyes were drowsy from sleep. She was standing on the balcony and it was as if the northern lights were shining around her. . . . Go on, go on! There you were on the balcony; then you walked through the doorway and . . . and . . ."

"I was in the entrance hall. That's what you sat looking at all the time, the vestibule. There was no lamp in there, and that's why from the outside the apartment appeared dark. But there was a door. It opened onto another room, which opened onto another, which opened onto another. There was a long row of rooms and anterooms before one reached the innermost where Poetry lived. And these were ablaze with more than enough light to kill a shadow, so I never saw the maiden up close. I was cautious and patient, and that is the same as being virtuous."

"Come, come," commanded the philosopher curtly. "Tell me what you saw."

"Everything! And I'll tell you about it, but first . . . It has nothing whatever to do with pride, but out of respect to my accomplishments, not to speak of my social position, I wish you wouldn't address me so familiarly."

"Forgive me!" exclaimed the philosopher. "It is an old habit, and they are the hardest to get rid of. But you are quite right, and I'll try to remember. . . . Please do continue, for I am immensely interested."

"Everything! I have seen all, and I know all!"

"I beg you to tell me about the innermost room where Poetry dwelled. Was it like the beech forest in spring? Was it like the interior of a great cathedral? Or was it like the heavens when one stands on a mountaintop?"

"Everything was there!" replied the shadow. "Of course, I never went all the way in. The twilight of the vestibule suited me better, and from there I had an excellent view. I saw everything and I know all. I was at the court of Poetry, in the entrance hall."

"But what did you see?" urged the philosopher. "Did Thor and Odin walk those halls? Did Achilles and Hector fight their battles again? Or did innocent children play there and tell of their dreams?"

"I am telling you that I was there. And you understand, I saw everything that there was to see. You could not have stayed there and remained a human being, but it made a human being of me! I quickly came to understand my innermost nature, that part of me which from birth can claim kinship to Poetry. When I lived with you, I didn't even think about such things. You'll remember that I was always larger at sunrise and at sunset, and that I was more noticeable in the moonlight than you were. Still, I had no understanding of my nature; that did not come until I was in the vestibule, and then I became a human being.

"I was fully mature when I came out; by then you had already left the south. Being human made me ashamed to go around as I was; I needed boots, clothes, and all the other trimmings that make a man what he is. So there was nothing else for me to do but hide. . . . I wouldn't say this to anyone but you, and you mustn't

HANS CHRISTIAN ANDERSEN

mention it in any of your books. . . . I hid under the skirts of the woman who sold gingerbread men in the market. Luckily, she never found out how much her petticoats concealed. I came out only in the evening; then I would walk around in the moonlight, stretching myself up the walls to get the kinks out of my back. Up and down the streets I went, peeping through the windows of the attics as well as the drawing rooms. And I saw what no one ever sees, what no one ever should see! It's really a horrible world, and I wouldn't be human if it weren't so desirable. I saw things that ought to be unthinkable; and these were not only done by husbands and wives, but by parents and the sweet, innocent children! I saw," said the shadow, "I saw everything that man must not know, but what he most ardently wishes to know — his neighbor's evil! If I had written a newspaper, everyone would have read it; but instead I wrote directly to the persons themselves, and I wreaked havoc in every city that I came to. People feared me so much and were so fond of me! The universities gave me honorary degrees, the tailors gave me clothes, and the women said that I was handsome. In a word, each donated what he could, and so I became the man that I am. . . . But it is getting late, and I must say good-by. Here is my card. I live on the sunnier side of the street and am always home when it rains."

"How strange!" remarked the philosopher after the shadow had left.

The years and the days passed, and the shadow came again. "How are things going?" it asked.

"Oh," replied the philosopher, "I have been writing about all that is true and beautiful and good, but no one cares to hear about anything like that, and I am terribly disappointed because those are the things that are dear to me."

"Well, they aren't to me," said the shadow. "I've been concentrating on gaining weight, and that there's some point in. You don't understand the world, that's what's the matter with you. You ought to travel. I am going on a trip this summer, would you like to join me? If you would like to travel as my shadow it would be a pleasure to have you along. I'll pay for your trip!"

"You go too far!" retorted the philosopher.

"It all depends how you look at it. The trip will do you good and, traveling as my shadow, you'll have all your expenses paid by me."

"Monstrous!" shouted the philosopher.

THE SHADOW

"But that's the way of the world, and it isn't going to change," said the shadow, and left.

Matters did not improve for the philosopher; on the contrary, sorrow and misery had attached themselves to his coattails. For the most part, whenever he spoke of the true and the beautiful and the good, it was like setting roses before a cow. Finally he became seriously ill. "You look like a shadow of your former self," people would say, and when he heard these words a shiver went down his spine.

"You ought to go to a health resort," suggested the shadow when it came to visit him again. "There's no other alternative. I will take you along for old time's sake. I'll pay the expenses, and you'll talk and try to amuse me along the journey. I'm going to a spa, myself, because my beard won't grow. That's a disease too, you know, because beards are a necessity. If you're sensible, you'll accept. We'll travel as friends."

And so they traveled, the shadow as master and the master as shadow, for whether they were being driven in a coach, riding horseback, or simply walking, they were always side by side and the shadow kept itself a little in the fore or in the rear, according to the direction of the sun. It knew how to create the impression that it was the superior. The philosopher, however, was not aware of any of this. He had a kind heart, which did not even have a guest room reserved for envy. The journey was not yet over when the philosopher suggested to the shadow, "Now that we're traveling companions — and when you consider the fact that we've grown up together, shouldn't we call each other by first names? It makes for a much pleasanter atmosphere."

"There's something in what you say," began the shadow, who now was the real master. "You have spoken frankly, and what you have said was well meant; therefore, I ought to be honest with you. As a philosopher, you know how strange nature can be. Some people cannot bear to have a rough piece of material next to their bodies, and others can't hear a nail scratching on glass without it upsetting their nervous systems. Well, I would have the same feeling if you were to call me by my first name. I would have the feeling that I was being pressed to the ground, as if my relationship to you had never changed. You understand it's merely a feeling, it has nothing whatever to do with pride. But I could call you by your first name and satisfy half of your request."

From then on, the shadow always spoke and referred to the

HANS CHRISTIAN ANDERSEN

philosopher by his first name. "He goes too far," thought the man. "He's hardly civil to me." But when one is poor, one does more thinking than speaking.

At last they arrived at the famous resort where people came from all over the world to be cured. Among the guests was a beautiful princess who suffered from seeing too clearly, which is a very painful disease. She noticed at once that one of the new arrivals was very different from everyone else. He had come to make his beard grow, she was told. "But that's not the real reason," she muttered to herself. And to satisfy her curiosity, she went right up and spoke to the stranger, for the daughter of a king need not stand on ceremony with anyone.

"Your trouble is that you cannot cast a shadow," the princess announced.

"Your Royal Highness is getting well!" exclaimed the shadow. "I know that you suffered from seeing too clearly, but you must be getting over it. You show signs of perfect health. . . . I grant you that it is a very unusual one, but I do have a shadow. Other people have just ordinary shadows, but I despise the ordinary. You know how one dresses one's servants so that their livery is finer than one's own clothes; well, I let my shadow pretend that he is human. As you can see, I have even bought him a shadow. It was very expensive, but I am fond of doing the original."

"What!" thought the princess. "Have I really been cured? This is the finest spa there is. How fortunate I am to be born in the time when these marvelous waters were discovered. . . . But just because I am well is no reason to leave. I'm enjoying myself here. That stranger interests me, I hope his beard won't grow too quickly."

That night there was a grand ball that everyone attended, and the shadow danced with the princess. The princess was light on her toes, but the shadow was even lighter; such a graceful partner she had never had before. They discovered that he had once visited her country while she was abroad. There, too, the shadow had peeped through all of the windows, those that faced the street and those that did not. He had seen both this and that; and he knew how to tell about some of what he had seen and how to hint at the rest, which was even more impressive. The princess was astounded. She had never spoken to anyone who was so worldly wise, and out of respect for what he knew, she danced with him again.

THE SHADOW

The next time they danced together the princess fell in love. The shadow noticed the sudden change with relief. "She's finally been cured of seeing too clearly," he thought.

The princess would have confessed her feelings immediately if she hadn't been so prudent. She thought of her realm and of the people she ruled. "He knows well the ways of the world, that's a good sign," she commented silently. "He dances well, that is also a virtue. But is he really educated, for that is very important? I'd better test him." Then she began to ask the shadow questions so difficult that she herself did not know the answers.

An expression of confusion came over the shadow's face. "You cannot answer!" exclaimed the princess.

"I learned the answers to questions like that in childhood," said the shadow. "I believe that even my shadow, who is sitting over there by the door, could respond correctly."

"Your shadow! That really would be remarkable!"

"I can't say for certain," continued the shadow. "I just wouldn't be surprised if he could. After all, he's never done anything but follow me around and listen to what I say. Yes," he cried in a sudden burst of enthusiasm, "I believe he will be able to answer you! . . . But, Your Royal Highness, if you will allow me to make a suggestion. My shadow is so proud of being thought to be human, if Your Royal Highness wishes to create the right atmosphere, so that the shadow will be able to do his best, please treat him as if he were a man."

"I'd prefer it that way," said the king's daughter, and she joined the philosopher, who was alongside the door. She questioned him about the sun and the moon, and about the human race, both inside and out; and he answered every query both cleverly and politely.

"What must the man be worth, if his shadow is so wise!" thought the princess. "It would be a blessing for my people if I chose him for my husband. I shall do it!"

The shadow was very amenable. It agreed without hesitation that their plans must not be revealed until the princess had returned home. "I will not even tell my shadow," he said, while he thought how admirably the world had been created.

Not long after they came to the land which the princess ruled whenever she was there.

"My good friend," the shadow began to the philosopher. "Now that I am as happy and as powerful as anyone can hope to be, I'd

HANS CHRISTIAN ANDERSEN

like to share my good fortune with you. You may live with me always, here in the castle; you may drive with me in the royal coach; and you will be paid one hundred thousand gold pieces a year. In return, all I ask is that you let everyone call you a shadow; that you never admit to anyone that you have ever been a human being; and that once a year, when I sit on the balcony so that the people can pay me homage, you lie at my feet as a shadow should. . . . I might as well tell you that I am marrying the princess, and the wedding is tonight."

"No, this cannot happen!" cried the philosopher. "I don't want to do it, and I won't! You are a fraud! I will tell everything! You've fooled both the people and the princess; but now I will tell them that I am a human being and that you are only my shadow, who's been masquerading as a man!"

"No one will believe you," warned the shadow. "Now be reasonable or I'll call the guard."

"I intend to ask for an audience with the princess," replied the philosopher.

"But I will speak with her first," said the shadow, "and you will be imprisoned."

The shadow's threat very quickly became a reality, for the royal sentry knew whom the princess had chosen to be her husband.

"You are shivering," remarked the princess as soon as he entered her chambers. "You must not get sick this evening, not for the wedding!"

"I've just had the most horrible experience that one can have," replied the shadow. "Imagine! . . . Oh, how fragile a shadow's brain must be! . . . Imagine, my shadow has gone mad. He believes he is a man. And that I . . . that I am his shadow!"

"How dreadful!" she exclaimed. "He isn't running around loose, I hope."

"No, no, he's not," he said softly. "I am so afraid he will never get well."

"Poor shadow," continued the princess. "He must be suffering terribly. It would really be kinder to free him from that particle of life he has. Yes, the more I think about it, the more convinced I am that it's necessary for him to be done away with. . . . Quietly, of course."

"It seems so cruel," said the shadow, "when I think of how loyal

THE SHADOW

a servant it was," and a sound resembling a sigh escaped from the shadow's lips.

"How noble you are!" exclaimed the princess.

That night the whole city was brilliantly lighted. The cannons were shot off. Bum! Bum! Bum! The soldiers presented arms. Oh, what a wedding it was! The shadow and the princess came out onto the balcony, and the people screamed, "Hurrah!"

The philosopher heard nothing of all of this, for they had already taken his life.

THE OLD HOUSE

Once upon a time there stood
in a street a very old house; it was nearly three hundred years old.
You could tell what year it had been built by reading the date cut
into one of the beams; all around it tulips and curling hop vines
had been carved. Right above the entrance a whole verse had been
inscribed, and above each window appeared a grinning face. The
second story protruded out over the first. The lead gutters, which
hung under the roof, were shaped like dragons, with the monster's
head at either end. The water was supposed to spout out of their
mouths, but it didn't; the gutter was filled with holes and the
water ran out of the dragons' stomachs.

All the other houses in the street were new and well kept, their
walls were straight and smooth, and they had large windows. It was
quite reasonable that they should feel themselves superior to the
old house. Had they been able to speak they probably would have
said: "How long are we to tolerate that old ruin? Bow windows are
out of fashion and, besides, they obstruct our view. It must believe
itself to be a castle, judging from the size of the steps leading up to
the entrance, and that iron railing makes one think of funerals;
not to speak of the brass knobs. It's embarrassing!"

Right across from the old house stood a new house; it was of the
same opinion as all the other houses in the street. But behind one
of its windows sat a little boy, a little red-cheeked child with

168

THE OLD HOUSE

bright, shining eyes who preferred the old house, and that both in the daytime when the sun shone and at night in the moonlight. When he looked at the walls of the old house, with its cracks and bare spots where the mortar had fallen off, then he could imagine how the street once had looked: in olden times, when all the houses had had broad steps leading up to their doors, and bay windows, and gables with tall pointed roofs. He could see the soldiers marching through the streets armed with halberds. Oh, he found the old house worth looking at and dreaming about.

Its owner was an old man who wore the strangest old-fashioned pants, a coat with brass buttons, and a wig that you could see was a wig. Every morning an old servant arrived to clean and run errands for the old gentleman; otherwise, he was all alone. Sometimes he came to the window and looked out into the street; then the little boy nodded to him and the old man nodded back. In this manner they became acquainted; no, more than that, they were friends, although they had never spoken to each other.

The little boy heard his parents say, "Our neighbor, across the street, must be terribly lonely."

Next Sunday the boy made a little package and, when he saw the servant going by in the street, he hurried down and gave it to him. "Would you please give this to your master?" he asked. "I have two tin soldiers, and I would like your master to have one of them, for I have heard that he is so terribly lonely."

The old servant smiled and nodded and took the little package, with the tin soldier inside it, to his master. Later that day a message arrived, inviting the boy to come and visit the old man. The child's parents gave their permission; and thus he finally entered the old house.

The brass knobs on the iron railing seemed to shine so brightly that one might believe that they had been newly polished in honor of the boy's visit. The little carved trumpeters in the oak doorway seemed to be blowing especially hard on their instruments, for their cheeks were all puffed up. It was a fanfare! "Tra . . . tra . . . trattalala! The boy is coming! Tra . . . tra . . . trattalala!" The door was opened and he stood in the hall. All the walls were covered with paintings portraying ladies in long silk gowns and knights in armor. The boy thought that he could hear the silk gowns rustle and the armor clang. Then there were the stairs; first they went up a goodish way, and then down a little bit, and ended in a balcony.

HANS CHRISTIAN ANDERSEN

It was wooden and a bit rickety, grass and weeds grew out of every crack, making it look more like a garden than a balcony. Antique flowerpots with human faces and donkey ears stood ranged in a row; the plants grew to suit themselves. One of them was filled with carnations that spread out over the rim in all directions; that is, the green leaves and the stems, the flowers hadn't come yet. One could almost hear the plant saying: "The breeze has caressed me and the sun has kissed me and promised me a flower next Sunday, a little flower next Sunday."

The old servant led the boy into a chamber where the walls did not have paper on them; no, they were covered with leather, which had gilded flowers stamped upon it.

> Gilding fades all too fast.
> Leather, that is meant to last,

said the walls.

In the room were high-backed armchairs with carvings all over them. "Sit down, sit down!" they cried. And when you sat down in them they mumbled. "Ugh, how it cracks inside me! I think I got rheumatism like the old cabinet. Ugh, how it creaks and cracks."

At last the little boy entered the room with the bow windows. Here the old master of the house greeted him. "Thank you for the tin soldier, my little friend," said he. "And thank you for coming."

"Thanks, thanks," said all the furniture, although it sounded a little more like: "Crack . . . crack." There were so many chairs, tables, and cabinets in the room that they stood in each other's way, for they all wanted to see the little boy at once.

In the center of one of the walls hung a picture of a beautiful young girl. She was laughing and dressed in clothes from a bygone time. She did not say "thank you" or "crack" as the furniture had, but she looked down so kindly at the little boy that he could not help asking, "Where did you get her?"

"From the pawnbroker's," replied the old gentleman. "His shop is filled with pictures that no one cares about any more. The people they portray have been dead so long that no one remembers them. But though she has been dead and gone for fifty years, I knew her once."

Under the portrait hung a bouquet of faded flowers, carefully preserved behind glass. They looked old enough to have been

THE OLD HOUSE

picked half a century ago. The pendulum of the grandfather clock swung back and forth, and the hands moved slowly around, telling everything in the room that time was passing and that they were getting older; but that did not disturb the furniture.

"My parents say that you are terribly lonely," said the little boy.

"Oh," the old man smiled, "that is not altogether true. Old thoughts, old dreams, old memories come and visit me and now you are here. I am not unhappy."

Then from a shelf he took down a book that was filled with wonderful pictures. There were processions in which there were golden carriages, knights, and kings who looked like the ones in a deck of cards; and then came the citizens carrying the banners of their trades: the tailors' emblem was a pair of scissors held by a lion; the shoemakers had an eagle with two heads above their banner — for, as you know, shoemakers do everything in pairs. What a picture book that was!

The old man left for a moment to fetch some comfits, apples, and nuts; it was certainly nice to be visiting in the old house.

"But I can't stand it here!" wailed the tin soldier, who was standing on the lid of a chest. "It is so lonely and sad here; once you have lived with a family one cannot get accustomed to being alone. I can't stand it! The days are ever so long and the evenings feel even longer. It is not the same here as in your home, where your parents talked so pleasantly and you sweet children made such a lot of lovely noise. No, that poor old man really is lonely. Do you think anybody ever gives him a kiss? Or looks kindly at him? Here there is no Christmas tree ever, or gifts! The only thing he will ever get will be a funeral! . . . I can't stand it!"

"You mustn't take it so to heart," said the little boy. "I think it is very nice here. All the old thoughts and dreams come to visit, so he said."

"I see none of them and I don't want to either," screamed the tin soldier. "I can't stand it!"

"You will have to," said the little boy just as the old man returned with the comfits, apples, and nuts; and at the sight of them the boy forgot all about the soldier.

Happy and content, the little boy returned home. Days and weeks went by. The boy nodded to the old man from his window, and from the funny bow window of the old house the greeting was returned. Finally the little boy was asked to come visiting again.

HANS CHRISTIAN ANDERSEN

The carved trumpeters blew, "Tra . . . tra . . . trattalala. . . . The boy is here! . . . Tra tra!" The knights in armor clanged with their swords and the silk gowns of the ladies rustled, the leather on the wall said its little verse, and the old chairs that had rheumatism creaked. Nothing had changed, for in the old house every day and hour were exactly alike.

"I can't stand it!" screamed the tin soldier as soon as he saw the boy. "I have wept tin tears! It is much too mournful and sad here. Please, let me go to the wars and lose my arms and legs, that at least will be a change. I can't stand it, for I know what it is like to have old thoughts and old memories come visiting. Mine have been here and that is not amusing. Why, I almost jumped right off the lid of the chest. I saw all of you and my own home as plainly as if I had been there. It was Sunday morning and all you children were standing around the big table singing hymns, as you always do on Sunday. Your parents were nearby, looking solemn. Suddenly the door opened and little Maria, who is only two years old, entered. She always dances whenever she hears music, and she tried to dance to the tune you were singing, but hymns are not made for dancing—they are too slow. She stood first on one leg and flung her head forward, and then on the other and flung her head forward, but it didn't work out. You looked grave, all of you, but I found it too difficult not to laugh — at least inside myself. I laughed so hard that I fell off the table and hit my head so hard that I got a lump on it. I know it was wrong of me to laugh and the lump was punishment for it. That is what the old man meant by old thoughts and memories: everything that has ever happened to you comes back inside you. . . . Tell me, do you still sing your hymns on Sunday? Tell me something about little Maria and about my comrade, the other tin soldier. He must be happy. Oh, I can't stand it!"

"I have given you away," said the little boy. "You will have to stay, can't you understand that?"

The old man brought him a drawer in which lay many wonderful things. There were old playing cards with gilded edges, a little silver piggy bank, and a fish with a wiggly tail. Other drawers were opened and all the curiosities were looked at and examined. Finally the old man opened the harpsichord; on the inside of the lid was a painting of a landscape. The instrument was out of tune but the old man played on it anyway, and hummed a melody.

"Ah yes, she used to sing that," he sighed, and looked up toward

THE OLD HOUSE

the painting he had bought from the pawnbroker and his eyes shone like a young man's.

"I am going to the wars! I am going to the wars!" screamed the tin soldier as loudly as he could, and fell off the chest.

"What could have happened to him?" said the old man. Together he and the boy were searching for the little soldier on the floor. "Never mind, I will find him later," said the old man, but he never did. There were so many cracks in the floor and the tin soldier had fallen right down through one of them; there he lay buried alive.

The day passed and the little boy returned home. Many weeks went by, winter had come. All the windows were frozen over. The little boy had to breathe on the glass until he could thaw a little hole so that he could see out. Across the street the old house looked quite deserted; the snow lay in drifts on the steps. They had not been swept; one would think no one was at home. And no one was. The kind old man had died.

That evening a hearse drew up in front of the old house and a coffin was carried down the steps. The old man was not to be buried in the town cemetery but somewhere out in the country, where he had been born. The hearse drove away. No one followed it, for all his friends and family had died long ago. The little boy kissed his fingers and threw a kiss after the hearse as it disappeared down the street.

A few days afterward an auction was held; the furniture in the old house was sold. The boy watched from the window. He saw the knights in armor and the ladies with their silken gowns being carried out of the house. The old high-backed chairs, the funny flowerpots with faces and donkey ears were bought by strangers. Only the portrait of the lady found no buyer; it was returned to the pawnbroker. There it hung; no one remembered her and no one cared for the old picture.

Next spring the house itself was torn down, "It was a monstrosity," said the people as they went by. One could see right into the room with the leather-covered walls; the leather was torn and hung flapping like banners in the wind. The grass and weeds on the balcony clung tenaciously to the broken beams. But at last all was cleared away.

"That was good," said the neighboring houses.

A new house was built, with straight walls and big windows but not quite where the old house had stood; it was a little farther back

HANS CHRISTIAN ANDERSEN

from the street. On the site of the old house a little garden was planted, and up the walls of the houses on either side grew vines. A fine iron fence with a gate enclosed it, and people would stop in the street to look in, for it was most attractive. The sparrows would sit in the vines and talk and talk as sparrows do, but not about the old house, for they were too young to remember it.

Years went by and the little boy had become a grown man, a good and clever man of whom his parents could be justly proud. He had just got married and had moved into the new house. His young wife was planting a little wild flower in the front garden. He was watching her with a smile. Just as she finished, and was patting the earth around the little plant, she pricked her little hand. Something sharp was sticking out of the soft earth. What could it be?

It was — imagine it! — the tin soldier! The one that had fallen off the chest and down through a crack in the flooring. It had survived the wrecking of the old house, falling hither and thither as beams and floors disappeared, until at last it had been buried in the earth and there it had lain for many years.

The young woman cleaned the soldier off with a green leaf and then with her own handkerchief. It had perfume on it and smelled so delicious that the soldier felt as though he were awakening from a deep sleep.

"Let me have a look at him," said the young man; then he laughed and shook his head. "I don't believe it can be him, but he reminds me of a tin soldier that I once had." Then he told his wife about the old house and its old master and about the tin soldier that he had sent over to keep the old man company, when he had been a boy, because he had known that the old man was so terribly alone.

He told the story so well that his young wife's eyes filled with tears as she heard about the old house and the old man. "It could be the same soldier," she said. "I will keep it so that I shall not forget the story you have told me. But you must show me the old man's grave."

"I do not know where it is," her husband replied. "No one does; all those who knew him were dead. You must remember that I was a very small boy then."

"How terribly lonesome he must have been," sighed the young woman.

THE OLD HOUSE

"Yes, terribly lonesome," echoed the tin soldier. "But it is truly good to find that one is not forgotten."

"Good," screamed something nearby in a so weak a voice that only the tin soldier heard it. It was a little piece of leather from the walls of the old house. The gilding had gone long ago, and it looked like a little clod of wet earth. But it still had an opinion, and it expressed it.

> Gilding fades all too fast,
> But leather, that is meant to last.

But the tin soldier did not believe that.

THE HAPPY FAMILY

$\mathbb{T}$he largest leaves here in Denmark are the burdock leaves. If a little girl holds one in front of her tummy, then it will serve as an apron. If it should rain, one can use one as an umbrella; it is big enough. The burdock plant never grows alone; it is fond of company. Where you find one you will find more, and sometimes a whole forest of them. They look beautiful; and all this beauty is snail food. Those large white snails that the aristocrats and other grand people used to make into fricassee in the old times, and exclaim enthusiastically about how delicious they were — "What a flavor!" they used to cry — well, those white snails live on burdock leaves. And, as a matter of fact, it was for their sake that the burdock was originally planted.

Now there once was an old manor house where no one ate the snails; the custom had died there long ago, as had most of the snails; but the burdock, it thrived. They spread out all over the paths, and some of the lawns, for burdocks are not easy to get rid of. A good part of the park was a jungle of burdock leaves; and if a solitary plum or apple tree had not survived, no one would ever have believed that there once had been a garden there. In the very center of this forest lived the last survivors of the white snails. They were a couple and very, very old.

Exactly how old they were they didn't know, but they could remember that once their family had been numerous, and that

176

THE HAPPY FAMILY

their ancestors had come from some foreign land. That the burdock forest had been planted for their sake they knew too; and that they were proud of it. They had never been outside, but they knew vaguely that there was a world outside; it was called the manor house. There snails were cooked until they turned black and then they were served on a silver dish. What happened afterward was not clear to them. They didn't have any idea either what it was like to be "cooked" or "served on a silver dish." But that the whole ceremony was extremely elegant and distinguished they had no doubt. Neither the toad, nor the dung beetle, nor the earthworm — all of whom had been asked — could tell them anything about it, since none of their family had ever been "cooked" or "served on a silver dish."

The old white snails knew that they were the most distinguished beings in the whole world, that the forest of burdocks had been planted for their sake, and that the manor house stood merely so that they someday could be brought there, to be cooked and put on a silver dish.

They lived a lonely yet happy life; as they had no children of their own, they had adopted an ordinary garden snail. They had brought him up carefully, as though he were their own; their only disappointment had been that he wouldn't grow. However, the mother snail was always imagining that he was becoming fatter — in spite of his being just an ordinary snail — and she would beg her husband, who hadn't noticed it, to just feel their son's house. This the father snail would do, and then he would agree with her.

One day the rain was pouring down!

"Listen to how it is drumming on the burdock leaves," said the father snail.

"It is raining through," cried his wife. "Look how the water is running down the stalks. Everything will be soaked down here. But we have our houses and even the little one has his. Certainly, we were created superior to all other creatures in the world. We are the true aristocrats, born with houses on our backs, and with a whole forest of burdock leaves especially sprouting and growing for our sake. I wonder how far our forest stretches and what is beyond it?"

"Nothing," replied her husband. "There can be no better place than this, and what is beyond does not interest me."

"Oh, I am not sure of that," argued his wife. "I wouldn't mind being taken up to the manor house to be boiled and served on a silver plate. All our ancestors have been; I am sure it is something very special, to have that happen to one."

"I believe it possible that the manor house has fallen apart and become a ruin," said the father snail. "Or possibly the burdocks have grown so large around it that the people inside it can't get out. But all that is of no importance! You are always fretting. I am afraid our son takes after you, he is so restless. For the last three days he has been crawling up that stalk there, it gives me a headache just to look at him."

"Don't scold him!" said the mother snail. "He keeps a dignified pace, I am sure he will be a credit to us. After all, what have we old people to live for but our children? Have you thought about where we are going to find a wife for him? I wonder if anywhere in this forest there lives anyone of our own kind."

"Black slugs there are enough of; but they are not real snails, they have no houses of their own. Although they are common they think a lot of themselves. But we could ask the ants, they are always running about as if they had something important to do; they may have come across a snail that would make a wife for our little son."

"Oh yes! We know of the sweetest one," said the ants. "But it may be difficult to arrange; you see, she is a queen."

"That is of no importance," said the old snails. "Does she have a house of her own?"

"She has a castle," replied the ants proudly. "The loveliest ant castle with seven hundred corridors."

"Thank you," said the snail mother but she didn't mean it. "Our son is not going to live in an anthill. If you have nothing better to suggest, then we will ask the mosquitoes, they fly about everywhere."

"We have found a wife for him," buzzed the mosquitoes. "About a hundred yards from here there lives, on a gooseberry bush, a little snail. She has a house of her own; she lives all alone and is old enough to get married."

"I think she should come to him," said the father snail. "It is more fitting, since she only has a gooseberry bush; whereas, our son has a whole burdock forest."

The mosquitoes flew to make the proposal; it took her a whole week to come; but that only proved that she was a proper snail.

THE HAPPY FAMILY

A wedding was held. Six glowworms shone as brightly as they could, but otherwise the affair passed off very quietly, for the old folks could not endure riotous merriment. The mother of the bridegroom made the speech, for her husband was much too overcome by emotion to say a word. The young people were given the burdock forest as their inheritance; and both of the old snails declared that it was the best place in the whole world. The old snail mother promised them that if they lived a decent and upright life, and multiplied, then they and their children would be taken to the manor house to be cooked and served on a silver dish.

After the speech, the two old snails crept inside their houses and slept; and that so deeply that they never came out again.

The young couple reigned over the burdock forest and had a very, very large family. But none of them was ever boiled or served on a silver dish, which made them believe that the manor house had fallen into ruin and that all the human beings in the world had died. Since no one ever contradicted them, it was true. The rain drummed down on the burdock leaves to make music for them, and the sun shone on the forest for their sake; and every little snail in the whole family was very, very happy.

THE NIGHTINGALE

In China, as you know, the emperor is Chinese, and so are his court and all his people. This story happened a long, long time ago; and that is just the reason why you should hear it now, before it is forgotten. The emperor's palace was the most beautiful in the whole world. It was made of porcelain and had been most costly to build. It was so fragile that you had to be careful not to touch anything, and that can be difficult. The gardens were filled with the loveliest flowers; the most beautiful of them had little silver bells that tinkled so you wouldn't pass by without noticing them.

Everything in the emperor's garden was most cunningly arranged. The gardens were so large that even the head gardener did not know exactly how big they were. If you kept walking you finally came to the most beautiful forest, with tall trees that mirrored themselves in deep lakes. The forest stretched all the way to the sea, which was blue and so deep that even large boats could sail so close to the shore that they were shaded by the trees. Here lived a nightingale who sang so sweetly that even the fisherman, who came every night to set his nets, would stop to rest when he heard it, and say: "Blessed God, how beautifully it sings!" But he couldn't listen too long, for he had work to do, and soon he would forget the bird. Yet the next night when he heard it again, he would repeat what he had said the night before: "Blessed God, how beautifully it sings!"

180

THE NIGHTINGALE

From all over the world travelers came to the emperor's city to admire his palace and gardens; but when they heard the nightingale sing, they all declared that it was the loveliest of all. When they returned to their own countries, they would write long and learned books about the city, the palace, and the garden; but they didn't forget the nightingale. No, that was always mentioned in the very first chapter. Those who could write poetry wrote long odes about the nightingale who lived in the forest, on the shores of the deep blue sea.

These books were read the whole world over; and finally one was also sent to the emperor. He sat down in his golden chair and started to read it. Every once in a while he would nod his head because it pleased him to read how his own city and his own palace and gardens were praised; but then he came to the sentence: "But the song of the nightingale is the loveliest of all."

"What!" said the emperor. "The nightingale? I don't know it, I have never heard of it; and yet it lives not only in my empire but in my very garden. That is the sort of thing one can only find out by reading books."

He called his chief courtier, who was so very noble that if anyone of a rank lower than his own, either talked to him, or dared ask him a question, he only answered, "P." And that didn't mean anything at all.

"There is a strange and famous bird called the nightingale," began the emperor. "It is thought to be the most marvelous thing in my empire. Why have I never heard of it?"

"I have never heard of it," answered the courtier. "It has never been presented at court."

"I want it to come this evening and sing for me," demanded the emperor. "The whole world knows of it but I do not."

"I have never heard it mentioned before," said the courtier, and bowed. "But I shall search for it and find it."

But that was more easily said than done. The courtier ran all through the palace, up the stairs and down the stairs, and through the long corridors, but none of the people whom he asked had ever heard of the nightingale. He returned to the emperor and declared that the whole story was nothing but a fable, invented by those people who had written the books. "Your Imperial Majesty should not believe everything that is written. A discovery is one thing and artistic imagination something quite different; it is fiction."

HANS CHRISTIAN ANDERSEN

"The book I have just read," replied the emperor, "was sent to me by the great Emperor of Japan; and therefore, every word in it must be the truth. I want to hear the nightingale! And that tonight! If it does not come, then the whole court shall have their stomachs thumped, and that right after they have eaten."

"*Tsing-pe!*" said the courtier. He ran again up and down the stairs and through the corridors; and half the court ran with him, because they didn't want their stomachs thumped. Everywhere they asked about the nightingale that the whole world knew about, and yet no one at court had heard of.

At last they came to the kitchen, where a poor little girl worked, scrubbing the pots and pans. "Oh, I know the nightingale," she said, "I know it well, it sings so beautifully. Every evening I am allowed to bring some leftovers to my poor sick mother who lives down by the sea. Now it is far away, and as I return I often rest in the forest and listen to the nightingale. I get tears in my eyes from it, as though my mother were kissing me."

"Little kitchenmaid," said the courtier, "I will arrange for a permanent position in the kitchen for you, and permission to see the emperor eat, if you will take us to the nightingale; it is summoned to court tonight."

Half the court went to the forest to find the nightingale. As they were walking along a cow began to bellow.

"Oh!" shouted all the courtiers. "There it is. What a marvelously powerful voice the little animal has; we have heard it before."

"That is only a cow," said the little kitchenmaid. "We are still far from where the nightingale lives."

They passed a little pond; the frogs were croaking.

"Lovely," sighed the Chinese imperial dean. "I can hear her, she sounds like little church bells ringing."

"No, that is only the frogs," said the little kitchenmaid, "but any time now we may hear it."

Just then the nightingale began singing.

"There it is!" said the little girl. "Listen. Listen. It is up there on that branch." And she pointed to a little gray bird sitting amid the greenery.

"Is that possible?" exclaimed the chief courtier. "I had not imagined it would look like that. It looks so common! I think it has lost its color from shyness and out of embarrassment at seeing so many noble people at one time."

THE NIGHTINGALE

"Little nightingale," called the kitchenmaid, "our emperor wants you to sing for him."

"With pleasure," replied the nightingale, and sang as lovely as he could.

"It sounds like little glass bells," sighed the chief courtier. "Look at its little throat, how it throbs. It is strange that we have never heard of it before; it will be a great success at court."

"Shall I sing another song for the emperor?" asked the nightingale, who thought that the emperor was there.

"Most excellent little nightingale," began the chief courtier, "I have the pleasure to invite you to attend the court tonight, where His Imperial Majesty, the Emperor of China, wishes you to enchant him with your most charming art."

"It sounds best in the green woods," said the nightingale; but when he heard that the emperor insisted, he followed them readily back to the palace.

There every room had been polished and thousands of little golden lamps reflected themselves in the shiny porcelain walls and floors. In the corridors stood all the most beautiful flowers, the ones with silver bells on them; and there was such a draft from all the servants running in and out, and opening and closing doors, that all the bells were tinkling and you couldn't hear what anyone said.

In the grand banquet hall, where the emperor's throne stood, a little golden perch had been hung for the nightingale to sit on. The whole court was there and the little kitchenmaid, who now had the title of Imperial Kitchenmaid, was allowed to stand behind one of the doors and listen. Everyone was dressed in their finest clothes and they all were looking at the little gray bird, toward which the emperor nodded very kindly.

The nightingale's song was so sweet that tears came into the emperor's eyes; and when they ran down his cheeks, the little nightingale sang even more beautifully than it had before. His song spoke to one's heart, and the emperor was so pleased that he ordered his golden slipper to be hung around the little bird's neck. There was no higher honor. But the nightingale thanked him and said that he had been honored enough already.

"I have seen tears in the eyes of an emperor, and that is a great enough treasure for me. There is a strange power in an emperor's tears and God knows that is reward enough." Then he sang yet another song.

HANS CHRISTIAN ANDERSEN

"That was the most charming and elegant song we have ever heard," said all the ladies of the court. And from that time onward they filled their mouths with water, so they could make a clucking noise, whenever anyone spoke to them, because they thought that then they sounded like the nightingale. Even the chambermaids and the lackeys were satisfied; and that really meant something, for servants are the most difficult to please. Yes, the nightingale was a success.

He was to have his own cage at court, and permission to take a walk twice a day and once during the night. Twelve servants were to accompany him; each held on tightly to a silk ribbon that was attached to the poor bird's legs. There wasn't any pleasure in such an outing.

The whole town talked about the marvelous bird. Whenever two people met in the street they would sigh; one would say, "night," and the other, "gale"; and then they would understand each other perfectly. Twelve delicatessen shop owners named their children "Nightingale," but not one of them could sing.

One day a package arrived for the emperor; on it was written: "Nightingale."

"It is probably another book about our famous bird," said the emperor. But he was wrong; it was a mechanical nightingale. It lay in a little box and was supposed to look like the real one, though it was made of silver and gold and studded with sapphires, diamonds, and rubies. When you wound it up, it could sing one of the songs the real nightingale sang; and while it performed its little silver tail would go up and down. Around its neck hung a ribbon on which was written: "The Emperor of Japan's nightingale is inferior to the Emperor of China's."

"It is beautiful!" exclaimed the whole court. And the messenger who had brought it had the title of Supreme Imperial Nightingale Deliverer bestowed upon him at once.

"They ought to sing together, it will be a duet," said everyone, and they did. But that didn't work out well at all; for the real bird sang in his own manner and the mechanical one had a cylinder inside its chest instead of a heart. "It is not its fault," said the imperial music master. "It keeps perfect time, it belongs to my school of music." Then the mechanical nightingale had to sing solo. Everyone agreed that its song was just as beautiful as the real nightingale's; and besides, the artificial bird was much pleasanter

HANS CHRISTIAN ANDERSEN

to look at, with its sapphires, rubies, and diamonds that glittered like bracelets and brooches.

The mechanical nightingale sang its song thirty-three times and did not grow tired. The court would have liked to hear it the thirty-fourth time, but the emperor thought that the real nightingale ought to sing now. But where was it? Nobody had noticed that he had flown out through an open window, to his beloved green forest.

"What is the meaning of this!" said the emperor angrily, and the whole court blamed the nightingale and called him an ungrateful creature.

"But the best bird remains," they said, and the mechanical bird sang its song once more. It was the same song, for it knew no other; but it was very intricate, so the courtiers didn't know it by heart yet. The imperial music master praised the bird and declared that it was better than the real nightingale, not only on the outside where the diamonds were, but also inside.

"Your Imperial Majesty and gentlemen: you understand that the real nightingale cannot be depended upon. One never knows what he will sing; whereas, in the mechanical bird, everything is determined. There is one song and no other! One can explain everything. We can open it up to examine and appreciate how human thought has fashioned the wheels and the cylinder, and put them where they are, to turn just as they should."

"Precisely what I was thinking!" said the whole court in a chorus. And the imperial music master was given permission to show the new nightingale to the people on the following Sunday.

The emperor thought that they, too, should hear the bird. They did and they were as delighted as if they had gotten drunk on too much tea. It was all very Chinese. They pointed with their licking fingers toward heaven, nodded, and said: "Oh!"

But the poor fisherman, who had heard the real nightingale, mumbled, "It sounds beautiful and like the bird's song, but something is missing, though I don't know what it is."

The real nightingale was banished from the empire.

The mechanical bird was given a silk pillow to rest upon, close to the emperor's bed; and all the presents it had received were piled around it. Among them were both gold and precious stones. Its title was Supreme Imperial Night-table Singer and its rank was Number One to the Left. (The emperor thought the left side was more distinguished because that is the side where the heart is, even in an emperor.)

The imperial music master wrote a work in twenty-five volumes about the mechanical nightingale. It was not only long and learned but filled with the most difficult Chinese words, so everyone bought it and said they had read and understood it, for otherwise they would have been considered stupid and had to have their stomachs poked.

A whole year went by. The emperor, the court, and all the Chinese in China knew every note of the supreme imperial night-table singer's song by heart; but that was the very reason why they liked it so much: they could sing it themselves, and they did. The street urchins sang: "Zi-zi-zizzi, cluck-cluck-cluck-cluck." And so did the emperor. Oh, it was delightful!

But one evening, when the bird was singing its very best and the emperor was lying in bed listening to it, something said: "Clang," inside it. It was broken! All the wheels whirred around and then the bird was still.

The emperor jumped out of bed and called his physician but he couldn't do anything, so the imperial watchmaker was fetched. After a great deal of talking and tinkering, he repaired the bird, but he declared that the cylinders were worn and new ones could not be fitted. The bird would have to be spared; it could not be played so often.

It was a catastrophe. Only once a year was the mechanical bird allowed to sing, and then it had difficulty finishing its song. But the imperial music master made a speech wherein he explained, using the most difficult words, that the bird was as good as ever; and then it was.

Five years passed and a great misfortune happened. Although everyone loved the old emperor, he had fallen ill; and they all agreed that he would not get well again. It was said that a new emperor had already been chosen; and when people in the street asked the chief courtier how the emperor was, he would shake his head and say: "P."

Pale and cold, the emperor lay in his golden bed. The whole court believed him to be already dead and they were busy visiting and paying their respects to the new emperor. The lackeys were all out in the street gossiping, and the chambermaids were drinking coffee. All the floors in the whole palace were covered with black carpets so that no one's steps would disturb the dying emperor; and that's why it was as quiet as quiet could be in the whole palace.

But the emperor was not dead yet. Pale and motionless he lay in his great golden bed; the long velvet drapes were drawn, and the golden tassels moved slowly in the wind, for one of the windows was open. The moon shone down upon the emperor, and its light reflected in the diamonds of the mechanical bird.

The emperor could hardly breathe; he felt as though someone were sitting on his chest. He opened his eyes. Death was sitting there. He was wearing the emperor's golden crown and held his gold saber in one hand and his imperial banner in the other. From the folds of the curtains that hung around his bed, strange faces looked down at the emperor. Some of them were frighteningly ugly, and others mild and kind. They were the evil and good deeds that the emperor had done. Now, while Death was sitting on his heart, they were looking down at him.

"Do you remember?" whispered first one and then another. And they told him things that made the cold sweat of fear appear on his forehead.

"No, no, I don't remember! It is not true!" shouted the emperor. "Music, music, play the great Chinese gong," he begged, "so that I will not be able to hear what they are saying."

But the faces kept talking and Death, like a real Chinese, nodded his head to every word that was said.

"Little golden nightingale, sing!" demanded the emperor. "I have given you gold and precious jewels and with my own hands have I hung my golden slipper around your neck. Sing! Please sing!"

But the mechanical nightingale stood as still as ever, for there was no one to wind it up; and then, it couldn't sing.

Death kept staring at the emperor out of the empty sockets in his skull; and the palace was still, so terrifyingly still.

All at once the most beautiful song broke the silence. It was the nightingale, who had heard of the emperor's illness and torment. He sat on a branch outside his window and sang to bring him comfort and hope. As he sang, the faces in the folds of the curtains faded and the blood pulsed with greater force through the emperor's weak body. Death himself listened and said, "Please, little nightingale, sing on!"

THE NIGHTINGALE

"Will you give me the golden saber? Will you give me the imperial banner? Will you give me the golden crown?"

Death gave each of his trophies for a song; and then the nightingale sang about the quiet churchyard, where white roses grow, where fragrant elderberry trees are, and where the grass is green from the tears of those who come to mourn. Death longed so much for his garden that he flew out of the window, like a white cold mist.

"Thank you, thank you," whispered the emperor, "you heavenly little bird, I remember you. You have I banished from my empire and yet you came to sing for me; and when you sang the evil phantoms that taunted me disappeared, and Death himself left my heart. How shall I reward you?"

"You have rewarded me already," said the nightingale. "I shall never forget that, the first time I sang for you, you gave me the tears from your eyes; and to a poet's heart, those are jewels. But sleep so you can become well and strong; I shall sing for you."

The little gray bird sang; and the emperor slept, so blessedly, so peacefully.

The sun was shining in through the window when he woke; he did not feel ill any more. None of his servants had come, for they thought that he was already dead; but the nightingale was still there and he was singing.

"Don't ever leave me," begged the emperor. "I shall only ask you to sing when you want to. And the mechanical bird I shall break in a thousand pieces."

"Don't do that," replied the nightingale. "The mechanical bird sang as well as it could, keep it. I can't build my nest in the palace; let me come to visit you when I want to, and I shall sit on the branch outside your window and sing for you. And my song shall make you happy and make you thoughtful. I shall sing not only of those who are happy but also of those who suffer. I shall sing of the good and of the evil that happen around you, and yet are hidden from you. For a little songbird flies far. I visit the poor fishermen's cottages and the peasant's hut, far away from your palace and your court. I love your heart more than your crown, and yet I feel that the crown has a fragrance of something holy about it. I will come! I will sing for you! Only one thing must you promise me."

"I will promise you anything," said the emperor, who had

HANS CHRISTIAN ANDERSEN

dressed himself in his imperial clothes and was holding his golden saber and pressing it against his heart.

"I beg of you never tell anyone that you have a little bird that tells you everything, for then you will fare even better." And with those words the nightingale flew away.

The servants entered the room to look at their dead master. There they stood gaping when the emperor said: "Good morning."

THE STEADFAST
TIN SOLDIER

Once there were five and twenty
tin soldiers. They were all brothers because they had been made
from the same old tin spoon. With their rifles sticking up over
their shoulders, they stood at attention, looking straight ahead,
in their handsome red and blue uniforms.

"Tin soldiers!" were the first words they heard in this world;
and they had been shouted happily by a little boy who was clapping his hands because he had received them as a birthday gift. He
took them immediately out of the box they had come in and set
them on the table. They were all exactly alike except one, who was
different from the others because he was missing a leg. He had
been the last one to be cast and there had not been enough tin. But
he stood as firm and steadfast on his one leg as the others did on
their two. He is the hero of our story.

Of all the many toys on the table, the one you noticed first was a
pasteboard castle. It was a little replica of a real castle, and through
its windows you could see right into its handsomely painted halls.
In front of the castle was a little lake surrounded by trees; in it
swans swam and looked at their own reflections because the lake
was a glass mirror. It was all very lovely; but the most charming
part of the castle was its mistress. She was a little paper doll and she
was standing in the entrance dressed like a ballerina. She had a
skirt of white muslin and a blue ribbon draped over her shoulder,

HANS CHRISTIAN ANDERSEN

which was fastened with a spangle that was almost as large as her face. The little lady had her arms stretched out, as if she were going to embrace someone. She stood on one leg, and at that on her toes, for she was a ballet dancer; the other, she held up behind her, in such a way that it disappeared under her skirt; and therefore the soldier thought that she was one-legged like himself.

"She would be a perfect wife for me," he thought. "But I am afraid she is above me. She has a castle and I have only a box that I must share with twenty-four soldiers; that wouldn't do for her. Still, I would like to make her acquaintance." And the soldier lay down full length behind a snuffbox; from there he could look at the young lady, who was able to stand on the toes of only one leg without losing her balance.

Later in the evening, when it was the children's bedtime, all the other tin soldiers were put back in the box. When the house was quiet and everyone had gone to bed, the toys began to play. They played house, and hide-and-seek, and held a ball. The four and twenty tin soldiers rattled inside their box; they wanted to play too, but they couldn't get the lid open. The nutcracker turned somersaults, and the slate pencil wrote on the blackboard. They made so much noise that the canary woke up and recited his opinion of them all in verse. The only ones who didn't move were the ballerina and the soldier. She stood as steadfast on the toes of her one leg as the soldier did on his. His eyes never left her, not even for a moment did he blink or turn away.

The clock struck twelve. Pop! The lid of the snuffbox opened and out jumped a troll. It was a jack-in-the-box.

"Tin soldier," screamed the little black troll, "keep your eyes to yourself."

The tin soldier acted as if he hadn't heard the remark.

"You wait till tomorrow!" threatened the troll, and disappeared back into its box.

The next morning when the children were up and dressed, the little boy put the one-legged soldier on the window sill. It's hard to tell whether it was the troll or just the wind that caused the window to open suddenly and the soldier to fall out of it. He dropped down three stories to the street and his bayonet stuck in the earth between two cobblestones.

The boy and the maid came down to look for him and, though they almost stepped on him, they didn't see him. If only the tin soldier had shouted, "Here I am!" they would have found him; but he thought it improper to shout when in uniform.

It began to rain; first one drop fell and then another and soon it was pouring. When the shower was over two urchins came by. "Look," said one of them, "there is a tin soldier. He will do as a sailor."

The boys made a boat out of a newspaper, put the tin soldier on board, and let it sail in the gutter. Away it went, for it had rained so hard that the gutter was a raging torrent. The boys ran along on the sidewalk, clapping their hands. The boat dipped and turned in the waves. The tin soldier trembled and quaked inside himself; but outside, he stood as steadfast as ever, shouldering his gun and looking straight ahead.

Now the gutter was covered by a board. It was as dark as it had been inside the box, but there he had had four and twenty comrades. "I wonder how it will all end," thought the soldier. "I am sure it's all the troll's doing. If only the ballerina were here, then I wouldn't care if it were twice as dark as pitch."

A big water rat that lived in the gutter came up behind the boat and shouted, "Have you got a passport? Give me your passport!"

The tin soldier didn't answer but held more firmly onto his rifle. The current became stronger, and the boat gathered speed. The rat swam after him; it was so angry that it gnashed its teeth. "Stop him! Stop him!" the rat shouted to two pieces of straw and a little twig. "Stop him! He hasn't got a passport and he won't pay duty!"

The current ran swifter and swifter. The tin soldier could see light ahead; he was coming out of the tunnel. But at the same moment he heard a strange roaring sound. It was frightening enough to make the bravest man cringe. At the end of the tunnel the gutter emptied into one of the canals of the harbor. If you can imagine it, it would be the same as for a human being to be thrown down a great waterfall into the sea.

There was no hope of stopping the boat. The poor tin soldier stood as steady as ever, he did not flinch. The boat spun around four times and became filled to the brim with water. It was doomed, the paper began to fall apart; the tin soldier was standing in water up to his neck. He thought of the ballerina, whom he would never see again, and two lines from a poem ran through his mind.

HANS CHRISTIAN ANDERSEN

Fare thee well, my warrior bold,
Death comes so swift and cold.

The paper fell apart and the tin soldier would have sunk down into the mud at the bottom of the canal had not a greedy fish swallowed him just at that moment.

Here it was even darker than it had been in the sewer; the fish's stomach was terribly narrow, but the soldier lay there as steadfast as he had stood in the boat, without letting go of his rifle.

The fish darted and dashed in the wildest manner; then suddenly it was still. A while later, a ray of light appeared and someone said, "Why, there is a tin soldier." The fish had been caught, taken to the market, and sold. The kitchen maid had found the soldier when she opened the fish up with a big knife, in order to clean it. With her thumb and her index finger she picked the tin soldier up by the waist and carried him into the living room, so that everyone could admire the strange traveler who had journeyed inside the belly of a fish. But the tin soldier was not proud of his adventures.

How strange the world is! He was back in the same room that he had left in the morning; and he had been put down on the table among the toys he knew. There stood the cardboard castle and the little ballerina. She was still standing on one leg, the other she had lifted high into the air. She was as steadfast as he was. It touched the soldier's heart and he almost cried tin tears — and would have, had it not been so undignified. He looked at her and she at him, but never a word passed between them.

Suddenly one of the little boys grabbed the soldier, opened the stove, and threw him in. The child couldn't explain why he had done it; there's no question but that the jack-in-the-box had had something to do with it.

The tin soldier stood illuminated by the flames that leaped around him. He did not know whether the great heat he felt was caused by his love or the fire. The colors of his uniform had disappeared, and he could not tell whether it was from sorrow or his trip through the water. He looked at the ballerina, and she looked at him. He could feel that he was melting; but he held on as steadfastly as ever to his gun and kept his gaze on the little ballerina in front of the castle.

The door of the room was opened, a breeze caught the little

THE STEADFAST TIN SOLDIER

dancer and like a sylph she flew right into the stove. She flared up and was gone. The soldier melted. The next day when the maid emptied the stove, she found a little tin heart, which was all that was left of him. Among the ashes lay the metal spangle from the ballerina's dress; it had been burned as black as coal.

THE COLLAR

Once upon a time there was a fine gentleman whose only worldly possessions were a bootjack, a comb, and a loose collar; but that was such a fine one that it would have enhanced the best shirt in the world; and this story is about the collar. He was old enough to begin thinking about marriage when, by chance, he found himself being washed in the same tub as a lady's garter.

"Ah," sighed the collar. "Never have I met anyone so soft and dainty, with so slender and lovely a figure. May I ask your name?"

"I won't tell you," snapped the garter.

"Where exactly do you . . . belong?" asked the collar.

The garter, who was by nature shy, found the question indiscreet and didn't answer.

"I think you must be a kind of waistband," continued the collar. "Something that is worn on the inside. I see that you are both useful and decorative, Miss . . . Miss . . ."

"Please don't talk to me!" said the garter. "I have given you neither cause nor permission to do so."

"Your beauty is cause enough and gives its own permission," replied the collar, who thought himself not only gallant but also witty.

"Don't come near me!" screamed the garter. "There is something . . . something masculine about you."

THE COLLAR

"I am a gentleman. I own both a bootjack and a comb," boasted the collar, but he was lying: the comb and bootjack belonged to his master.

"Don't come near me!" moaned the garter. "I am not used to such treatment."

"Prude!" snapped the collar. Just at that moment he was taken out of the tub; then he was starched and hung over a chair out in the sunshine. A little bit later he was taken in and put on an ironing board.

"Madam," began the collar as soon as he saw the warm iron, "I assume that you are a widow. The very sight of you makes me warm, and all my wrinkles disappear. Be careful not to burn a hole in me. . . . Please, will you marry me?"

"Rag!" snarled the iron as it passed proudly over the collar, imagining that it was a steam engine drawing a whole string of railway cars behind it. "Rag!" repeated the iron on its return journey.

The collar was found to be just a little frayed on the edges and the maid took a pair of scissors to cut off the few loose threads.

"Oh!" exclaimed the collar when he saw the scissors. "You must be a prima ballerina. What leg movement! Never have I seen anything so elegant; no human being could surpass you!"

"I know that," said the scissors.

"You deserve to be a countess!" declared the collar. "All I have is a bootjack, a comb, and a gentleman to wait upon me; I wish I were a count!"

"Is he proposing?" screamed the scissors; she was angry, so she really cut the collar and then it was spoiled.

"I suppose I'd better propose to the comb!" thought the collar, and said, "How pretty your teeth look, miss, and you have not lost one of them. Tell me, have you never thought of marriage?"

"Didn't you know," said the comb, and blushed, "that I am engaged to the bootjack?"

"Engaged indeed!" sneered the collar. Now that there was no one else to propose to, he decided to become a cynic.

Time passed and finally the collar ended in the rag pile of the paper mill. There was a big rag party, and the fine linen stayed in one bunch and the coarse in another, as is the custom in this world. All the rags liked to talk and had a lot to tell, but the collar talked more than anyone else because he so loved to brag.

HANS CHRISTIAN ANDERSEN

"I have had so many sweethearts! Women couldn't leave me alone! But then, I was a gentleman and so well starched. I had both a comb and a bootjack though I never used either of them. You should have seen me then, when I was buttoned and lying on my side. I shall never forget my first fiancée. She was a waistband: so soft, so refined and beautiful, I was the cause of her death; she drowned herself in a washtub for my sake. Then there was the widow, she was red hot with passion but I abandoned her. My wound, which you can still see, was given me by a prima ballerina; she was infatuated and fierce. My own comb loved me. She lost all of her teeth because of it — I believe she cried them out. Oh yes, I have lived! And I have a great deal on my conscience. But what troubles me most is to think of the garter — I mean the waistband — and her unhappy end in the washtub. I deserve to be made into paper, that will atone for it."

All the rags were made into paper, but the collar became the particular piece of paper that this story is printed on. This was his punishment for having bragged so much and told so many lies. The collar's fate is worth remembering. How can you be sure that you won't end in the rag pile, be made into paper, and have your whole life's story — even the most intimate and secret parts — printed on you; and then, like the rag, have to run around the world telling everyone about it?

THE YEAR'S STORY

It was one of the last days in January; there was a horrible snowstorm. The wind was whirling the snow through the streets and lanes of the town. The windows of the houses were so covered with snow that you could not see through them, and from the roofs little avalanches fell down into the streets. People could hardly walk against the wind; and if they had it behind them, it was almost worse, for then they had to run. When two people met they held onto each other in order not to fall. All the carriages and horses were covered with snow, it looked as if they had been powdered; and the servants who stood on the backs of the carriages bent their knees, in order not to be so tall that their faces got whipped by the wind. The pedestrians walked as close to the carriages as they could, to get a bit of protection from the wind; they could easily keep up with them, for the vehicles could not drive very fast. When the storm finally died down, a narrow path was shoveled along the sidewalks. Every time two people met, they paused, for the path was too narrow for them to pass each other. Which one was to be polite and step into the snowbank, that was the question. Usually neither of them was willing to get his feet wet in order that the other man could keep his dry. Silently, they faced each other, until by some unspoken agreement both of them would sacrifice one foot by putting it into the deep snow.

HANS CHRISTIAN ANDERSEN

Toward evening the wind disappeared completely; the heavens looked as if they had been swept, and the stars shone as if they had been newly minted. Some of them had a blue tinge to them. And it froze. In the morning the snow had formed a crust strong enough to bear the weight of a sparrow. There were enough of them; they hopped around on the snow and on the shoveled path, but they couldn't find much to eat, and all of them were freezing.

"Peep!" said one sparrow to another. "So that is what they call the New Year! Why, it is worse than the old one; we might as well have kept it. I am very dissatisfied and I have good reasons for being so."

"Yes, all the human beings were lighting firecrackers to celebrate the New Year," piped a particularly cold little sparrow. "They were so happy to get rid of the Old Year that I expected that the weather would get warm. But what happened! It is colder now than ever. I think the calendar is not working."

"You are so right," said a third sparrow. He was old and had a tuft of white on top of his head. "It is their own invention, the calendar; they believe that everything obeys it. But they are wrong. I go by nature's calendar and, according to that, the New Year starts when Spring comes."

"But when does Spring come?" asked all the other sparrows.

"Spring comes when the stork comes back. But he is not very dependable. Here in the city he never shows himself, he prefers the country. Let us fly out there and wait for him; Spring is always a little closer out there."

"That is all very well," said a little sparrow that had been peeping all the time without really saying anything. "But in the city one has certain conveniences that I am afraid I shall miss in the country. The family who live in a house near here have hung little wooden boxes on the walls for us to nest in. My husband and I have made our home in one, and there we have brought up our children. I know the family have done it in order to have the pleasure of seeing us fly about; I am sure they wouldn't have done it otherwise. They throw bread crumbs out, too. It amuses them and gives us a living. We feel we are being taken care of. That is why my husband and I will stay here; not that we are satisfied, mind you, we certainly are not! But we will stay."

"And we shall fly out to the country and see if Spring isn't coming soon," said the others; and away they flew.

THE YEAR'S STORY

It certainly was colder out in the country than it had been in the city; at least, a couple of degrees. The wind was as sharp as a knife when it blew across the snow-covered fields. The farmer, driving in his sleigh, would slap his hands on his back to keep them warm, and that even though he had woolen mittens on. The whip lay in his lap and his lean horses ran so fast that steam rose from their sweaty flanks.

The sparrows jumped about in the sleigh track and froze. "Tweet . . . peep!" they said. "When does Spring come? Why does it take so long?"

"So long, so long." The words seemed to echo across the fields. Where did the voice come from? Were the words spoken by that strange old man who was sitting in the middle of the big snowdrift over there? A long white beard, he had, and frosty silver hair; he was dressed in a white cloak like the ones the peasants used to wear. His cheeks were pale but his eyes were clear.

"Who is that old fellow?" asked the sparrows.

"I know who he is," answered an old raven who was sitting on a fence post. Since we are all small birds in the eyes of God — and the raven knew it — he condescended to answer the sparrows' question. "I know the old man! It is Winter: the old fellow from last year. He didn't die on the first of January, just because the calendar said so. No, he is the guardian of the little prince, Spring. He is the governor. Oh, it is so cold! You little birds must be freezing."

"That is what I said," piped the smallest of the sparrows. "That calendar is only a human invention. It doesn't fit nature. They should have let us figure it out, we are more delicately created."

A week went by and then another. The forest was black and the little lake was frozen. It looked as if it were not water but lead. The clouds were not real clouds but more like frozen bits of fog hanging over the landscape. The crows flew in flocks but did not scream. It was as if the world slept. Suddenly a ray of sunlight fell upon the ice of the frozen lake and the surface looked like melting tin. The snow on the fields and the hills looked a little different; it didn't sparkle any more. But the white figure, the old man, still sat on top of the snowdrift and looked toward the south. He did not seem to be aware that the blanket of snow that covered the ground was slowly melting and seeping into the earth. A little patch of green appeared and here all the sparrows gathered.

HANS CHRISTIAN ANDERSEN

"Tweet . . . peep! Spring is coming!" they shouted.

"Spring, Spring!" The word traveled across the fields and meadows, through the black-brownish woods, where the moss that grew on the tree trunks already was green. From the south, flying through the air, came the first two storks of the year. On the back of each rode a little child: a girl and a boy. They kissed the earth and, wherever they walked, snowdrops bloomed in the snow. Hand in hand, they went over to old man Winter, greeted him and embraced him; at that moment they were all three hidden in a heavy fog. It spread and covered the whole landscape: everything! Then the wind began to blow; first weakly, making the fog dance like a curtain, then more strongly, until it had swept the fog and mist away. Warmly the sun shone. Winter, the old man, had gone; the children of Spring now sat on the throne of the year.

"That is what I call a proper New Year," said the sparrows. "Now we will have our rights back and compensation for all we have suffered this winter."

Wherever the two children went, green buds appeared on the bushes and trees. The grass in the meadows grew taller and taller. The little girl carried flowers in her apron, and these she threw all about her as

she walked; but no matter how many she cast, her little apron was as full as ever. In her eagerness she shook her apron over the apple trees, so that they were filled with flowers long before they had green leaves; they looked almost as if they had been covered by snow.

She clapped her hands and the boy clapped his, and birds came, no one knew from where, and they all sang and twittered: "Spring has come!"

It was lovely to watch! Many an old granny came outside in the sunshine; how nice and warm it was. Down in the meadow all the yellow flowers bloomed just as they had when she was a girl. "The world is young again," she thought; and said, "What a blessed day it is!"

The woods were still a brownish green, though every branch was covered with buds, and down among the roots the fragrant woodruff grew, and violets and tender anemones. Each blade of grass was filled with power. Oh yes, the earth was covered by the most elegant carpet, and on it sat Spring's young couple and held hands. They sang and laughed; and grew and grew.

A mild rain fell, but the young ones did not notice it, for who can distinguish between raindrops and the tears of happiness? The bride and the bridegroom kissed each other; and at the moment the buds on the trees burst, and when the sun rose all the woods were green.

Hand in hand, Spring's children walked beneath the new green roof of the forest, where the fleeting shadows caused shadings in the greenness. Each leaf had a maiden's innocence. The river and the brooks sang as their clear water rushed across stones, coloring the gravel. All nature seemed to shout of its own eternity, and the cuckoo and the lark sang. It was a beautiful spring, only the willow tree was cautious; it was wearing woolen mittens on its flowers.

Days passed and weeks passed; great waves of heat came rolling from the south and turned the wheat yellow. In the little lakes in the woods, the big leaves of the northern lotus spread themselves out over the still waters; and the fishes would swim underneath them, enjoying their shade. Ripe, juicy, almost black cherries hung from the trees and all the rosebushes were blooming. The sun baked the cottage walls. There on the south side, on a bench, sat the wife of Summer. She was a beautiful woman; maybe even lovelier than she had been, when last we saw her, as the young bride of Spring. She is looking toward the horizon where black clouds are building a mountain range all the way up to the sun. Like a petrified black-blue ocean, the clouds swallow up the sky. In the forest, not a bird is singing. Nature is silent. No breezes blow, everything is still, locked in expectancy. But along roads and paths everyone is hurrying, and that whether they are walking, riding, or driving in a carriage. They have one thought, all of them, and that is to seek shelter.

Suddenly a great light bursts forth, blinding and sharper than the sun's. Then again darkness, followed by the noise of a great thunderclap. The rain pours down. Light and darkness, silence and thunder alternate. In the marshes the young reeds, with their brown feather-like tops, sway and roll like waves on an ocean. The branches of the trees are hidden behind sheets of water, and the grain on the field lies prostrate flat on the ground. It looks as though it could never raise itself up again.

But as suddenly as the thunderstorm came it is gone. A few single drops of rain fall, and then the sun breaks through the clouds. To every straw and leaf pearly drops of water cling. Again the birds are singing, and in the pools in the woods the fishes are leaping, while mosquitoes fly in swarms above the water. On a boulder on the beach sits Summer. He is a powerful man; his arms and legs are muscular. His hair is wet from the shower. He stretches himself; he and all the nature around him seem rejuvenated by the bath. Summer is strength and fertility, the crowning of hopes.

Sweet was the fragrance of the field of flowering clover. The bees flew across it; in the center lay some stones. In Viking times it had been a holy place. Blackberry brambles now covered the altar stone. Here the queen bee and her court built a castle of wax and filled it with honey. Only Summer and his wife saw it; and truly, it was for their sake that the offering was laid on the altar stone.

When the sun set, the evening sky shone more golden than any church cupola, and from the pale darkness of the summer night the moon looked down.

Weeks went by, and days. The farmers began to harvest, and their sharp scythes glistened in the sunlight as they reaped the grain. The branches of the apple trees bent toward the ground, heavy with red and yellow fruit. The hops smelled sweetly. Under the hazelnut bushes, filled with nuts, rested a man and a woman: Summer and his grave and beautiful wife.

THE YEAR'S STORY

"What richness," she sighed, "a blessed homely wealth, and yet I long for something else, I do not know what it is. Rest? Peace? No, it is neither, and more than both, that I wish for! Look, they are plowing again. Man always wants more; he is never satisfied. The storks are flying in flocks now, following the plowman. The bird from Egypt that carried us through the air. Do you remember when we, as children, came here to the north? We brought sunshine and flowers and the green woods. The wind is turning them yellow and brown now, like southern trees; but here they do not bear golden fruits."

"You shall see them," said Summer. "Be happy!" And he spread out his arms toward the woods, and its leaves turned red and golden. The fruit of the wild rose shone red on its brambles and the elderberries hung like black grapes from the trees. The wild chestnuts fell out of their blackish-green shells; and deep in the forest the violets flowered once again.

The queen of the year grew more and more silent and thoughtful. "The evening air is cold," she said, and her cheeks grew pale. "The night mist is damp! I long for the land of my childhood."

She watched the storks fly south, following each one with her eyes until it disappeared. She looked up at the empty nest; a cornflower grew in one of them, as though the nest were there for its protection; then the sparrows came visiting.

"The noble owners have left," they mocked as they searched the nest for something eatable. "I guess they couldn't take a bit of wind; it was too much for them, and so they left. Well, a pleasant journey is all I can wish them. Tweet!"

The leaves turned more and more yellow, and soon the trees would stand naked again. The harvest was over and the fall storms had begun. On a bed of yellow leaves lay the queen of the year; she looked toward the twinkling stars; the sun had set. Her husband stood near her. The wind rustled the leaves and she was gone. A butterfly, the last of the year, flew through the cold air.

From the sea drifted the wet and cold autumn fogs; the long nights of winter had begun. The king of the year stood with snow-white hair, and the first snow of the year covered the fields. The church bell rang the joyous message of Christmas.

"The bells are ringing to celebrate the birth of the New Year," said the king of the year. "Soon they will come, the new king and queen, and I shall be allowed to rest, as she does now. Rest and find peace in the stars."

HANS CHRISTIAN ANDERSEN

Out in the forest, among the pine and spruce trees, walked the Christmas angel; she consecrated those trees that were to take part in the feast.

"May you bring happiness and joy," said the king of the Old Year. The last few weeks had made an ancient man of him; his hair was no longer white but silver, like the frost. "Soon I shall rest. The new rulers are now receiving their scepter and their crown."

"But still the power is yours, not theirs," said the angel of Christmas. "You must rule, not rest. Let the snow lay like a warm blanket over the young grain. Learn to bear the burden it is to rule, while others are praised and honored; and yet you are still master. Learn to be forgotten while you live! The hour of your freedom will come when Spring comes."

"And when does Spring come?" asked Winter.

"When the first storks arrive," answered the angel.

With silver hair and snow-white beard, Winter sat and waited; old but not decrepit, strong as the winter storms and the all-powerful ice. He sat on his snowbank and looked toward the south, as Winter had done the year before.

The ice on lakes and fjords groaned and the snow creaked when you walked on it. The children were skating. The ravens and crows looked very decorative on the white background. Everything was still, not a wind stirred. Winter clenched his hands, and the thickness of the ice grew by inches, every night.

The sparrows came flying out from town and asked, "Who is that old man over there?"

And the raven who sat on the fence post — it was either the same one as last year or his son — answered, "It is Winter. The old fellow is not dead as the calendar says. He is the guardian for the New Year, for Spring, who will soon be here."

"When does Spring come?" asked the sparrows. "Then we will get a decent government, the last one was no good!"

Deep in thought, Winter nodded toward the naked, leafless forest, where every branch, every trunk, showed its graceful forms. An ice-cold mist covered all. Winter, the master of the world, was dreaming of his youth, his manhood. When the sun rose, the forest was clad in ice, the white frost decked each branch, each twig. It was Winter's dream of Summer. The sunlight melted the ice, and it fell from the branches, down onto the snow.

"When is Spring coming?" asked the sparrows.

THE YEAR'S STORY

"Spring, Spring!" came the echo from the drifts of snow; and the sun grew warmer and warmer.

The snow was melting and the birds sang, "Spring is coming!"

The storks flew high in the air: the first of the year. On their backs rode two lovely children; the birds landed on a field. The children kissed the earth and embraced old man Winter, and like a mist he disappeared. The year's story had ended!

"It is all very true," said the sparrows. "And it is a pretty story, but that's not what the calendar says, and that is what counts in this world."

IT IS PERFECTLY TRUE!

It is a monstrous story!" said a hen. She lived in a part of the town far away from where the event had taken place. "It is a horrible story and it has happened in a henhouse. I am glad that I am not sleeping alone on the perch tonight. I would not dare close my eyes!"

And then she told the story. The other hens were so shocked that their feathers stood up, and the rooster's comb fell down. It is perfectly true!

But we will start at the beginning and that took place in another corner of the town in a henhouse. The sun had just set and all the hens had flown up on their roost. Among them was a white-feathered hen with stumpy legs; she laid an egg every day and was very respectable. Now as she sat down on her perch she picked at her feathers a bit, and one little feather fell out.

"There it went," she said. "The more I pick myself, the more beautiful I will become." This was said for fun, for she was a cheerful soul, though otherwise — as I have already said — very respectable.

It was dark on the perch; the hens sat roosting side by side, but the hen that sat nearest to the one who had lost a feather wasn't asleep. She had heard what had been said and she hadn't; and that is a very wise thing to do if you want to live in peace with your neighbors. But still she could not help telling the hen next to her what she had heard.

IT IS PERFECTLY TRUE!

"Did you hear what was said? I won't mention names, but there is a hen among us who is going to pluck her feathers off just to look more attractive. If I were a rooster I would despise her!"

Right above the henhouse lived an owl family; and they have sharp ears. They heard every word that the hen had said and the mother owl rolled her eyes and beat her wings. "Don't listen, but I suppose you couldn't help but hear it. I heard it with my own ears and one has to hear a lot before they fall off. There is one of the hens in the henhouse that has so forgotten all decency and propriety that she is sitting on the perch and picking off all her feathers, while the rooster is looking at her."

"*Prenez garde aux enfants!*" said the father owl. "It is not fit for the children to hear!"

"But I will tell our neighbor about it," said the mother. "She is such a courteous owl. I hold her in the highest esteem." And away she flew.

"Tu-whit! Tu-whoo!" both the owls hooted, and so loudly that the pigeons could not help hearing it. "Have you heard, have you heard! Tu-whoo! There is a hen that has plucked all her feathers off for the rooster's sake. She will freeze to death, if she hasn't already, tu-whoo!"

"Where? Where?" cooed the pigeons.

"In the neighboring yard! I have almost seen it with my own eyes. It is a most indecent story, but it is perfectly true."

"True, true, every word," cooed the pigeons, and repeated the story in their own henhouse. "There is a hen — some say that there are two — that have plucked all their feathers off in order to look different and in that way gain the attention of the rooster. They have played a dangerous game, for one can catch a cold that way and die of fever; and they are dead, both of them!"

"Wake up! Wake up!" crowed the cock, and flew up on the fence. Sleep was still in his eyes, but he crowed anyway. "Three hens have died of unrequited love for a rooster! They have plucked all their feathers off. It is a nasty story. I won't keep it, pass it on!"

"Pass it on, pass it on," piped the bats. And the hens clucked and the roosters crowed: "Pass it on, pass it on." And in this manner the story went from henhouse to henhouse until it arrived back at the very place where it had started.

"There are five hens, so it is said, that have all plucked their feathers off to prove which one of them had become thinnest

HANS CHRISTIAN ANDERSEN

because of unhappy love for the rooster. Then they pecked each other until blood flowed and they all fell down dead! It's a shame for their families and a great loss to their owner."

The hen who had lost the first little feather naturally did not recognize the story; and as she was a decent and respectable hen, she said, "I despise those hens! But there are more of that kind! Such things must not be kept secret! I will do whatever I can to have it printed in the newspaper, then the whole country will hear about it. And that is what those hens and their families deserve."

And it was published in the newspaper and it is perfectly true that one little feather can become five hens!

THE PIXY
AND THE GROCER

There once was a proper student; he lived in a garret and didn't own a thing. There once was a proper grocer; he lived on the first floor and owned the whole house. Now the pixy stayed with the grocer, for there on Christmas Eve he was given a whole bowlful of porridge with a lump of butter in it. That the grocer could afford, therefore the pixy lived in his store, and from that a moral can be drawn.

One evening the student came knocking on the grocer's back door. He needed a candle and a piece of cheese for his supper; and he was, as usual, his own errand boy. He was given his wares and paid for them. The grocer wished him good evening and the grocer's wife gave him a friendly nod, though she was a woman who could do more than nod her head: she could talk anyone's ear off. The student nodded back and would have gone, had he not started reading what was written on the paper that the cheese had been wrapped in. It was a page torn from an old book of poetry that deserved a better fate than to be used as wrapping paper.

"Most of the pages of that book are still here," said the grocer. "I gave an old woman some coffee beans for it; you can have the rest for eight pennies."

"Thank you," replied the student. "Let me have what is left of the book instead of the cheese, I can eat plain bread for supper. It would be a pity if all of it were torn to pieces. You are a splendid

211

person, a practical man, but you have no more idea of what poetry is than that old barrel over there."

Now that was not a very nice thing to say, especially about the barrel. But both the grocer and the student laughed; it had been said in fun. It annoyed the pixy though. He had overheard the remark and thought it was an insult to the grocer, who owned the whole house and sold the very best quality butter.

Night fell; the store was closed and everyone had gone to sleep except the student and the pixy. He sneaked into the grocer's bedroom. The grocer's wife was sleeping with her mouth open and the pixy stole her sharp tongue: she didn't use it while she slept. Everything in the whole house that he put the tongue on was given the power of speech. Each of them could express its feelings and formulate its thoughts just as well as the grocer's wife could. But since there was only one tongue, they could only speak one at a time, which was a blessing, I am sure, or they all would have talked at once.

The first thing that was allowed to borrow the tongue was the barrel; it was filled with old newspapers. "Is it really true," asked the pixy, "that you don't know what poetry is?"

"Certainly I know what poetry is," said the barrel. "It's something printed on the back page of a newspaper that people cut out sometimes. I think that I have more poetry inside me than the student has. And what am I compared to the grocer, just a poor old barrel."

Then the pixy put the tongue on the coffee grinder and there it certainly wagged. He also put it on the tub of butter and the cash drawer just to hear their opinions. They agreed unanimously with the barrel, and the opinion of the majority must be respected.

"I will fix that student!" muttered the pixy, and sneaked up the back stairs to the garret where the young man lived. The student was still up, a light was burning in his room. The pixy looked through the keyhole. The young man was sitting reading the old book he had bought for eight pennies.

How bright the room seemed! It was as if a ray of light came from the book, a luminous tree whose branches spread out across the ceiling. The leaves were fresh and green and on each branch flowers bloomed and fruit hung. The flowers were faces of young maidens, some with radiant dark eyes and other with clear blue ones. The fruits were sparkling stars. All the while the most beautiful music could be heard.

THE PIXY AND THE GROCER

Such splendor the little pixy had never seen or even thought possible. He stood on his toes and looked and looked until the light was put out. Even when the student had blown out his candle and gone to bed, the pixy tarried. He could still hear the music, a song so soft and comforting; a lovely lullaby for the student, who was falling asleep.

"But that was fantastic!" mumbled the pixy. "That I had not expected! I think I will move in with the student!" Then he thought — and he thought very sensibly — "But the student does not have any porridge." And he sighed.

Down the stairs he went, down to the grocer. And that was lucky, for the barrel had almost worn out the grocer's wife's tongue. It had lectured, giving all the opinions that were written in the old newspapers inside it. When the pixy came it had just begun to repeat them. He took the tongue and gave it back to its owner. But from that time on the whole store, from the cash drawer to the firewood that lay by the stove, all had the same opinions as the barrel, whom they so honored and respected that when the grocer, in the evening, would read aloud the theater column to his wife, they thought that the barrel had written it.

But the pixy no longer stayed downstairs in the evening to listen to the grocer and his wife. No, as soon as the student had lit his candle, it was as if the light from the garret were an anchor cable that drew him up. He had to go and peek through the keyhole. He experienced greatness. He saw what we see when God, disguised as the storm, walks across the turbulent ocean. He cried without knowing why he cried, but found that in those tears happiness was hidden. "How wonderful it must be," he thought, "to sit under the magic tree together with the student." But that was not possible; he had to be satisfied with looking through the keyhole.

The autumn winds blew; the cold air whistled through the loft and down the corridor where the little pixy was standing, his eyes glued to the keyhole of the student's door. It was cold, wretchedly cold; but the pixy did not feel it before the student had put out his light and the sound of the music that came from the garret had ceased. But then he froze! He hurried down into his own little warm corner that was so cozy and comfortable.

At Christmas when the porridge with the lump of butter in it was served, the pixy acknowledged no other master than the grocer.

One night the pixy was awakened by a terrible noise. People

were banging on the shutters of the store, the whole street was as light as day from a fire. Everyone wanted to know whose house was burning. Was it his own or the neighbor's? It was terrible! The grocer's wife got so disconcerted that she took off her gold earrings and put them in her pocket, in order to save something.

The grocer hurriedly collected his bonds and the maid her silk shawl: that was her luxury, the one she could afford. All the people wanted to save what was dearest to them, and so did the pixy. He ran up the stairs and into the student's room. The young man was standing calmly at the window looking at the fire in the house across the street. The little pixy grabbed the book that was lying on the table, put it into his red cap, and ran. He had saved the most valuable thing in the house.

He climbed out on the roof and up on the chimney stack; there, illuminated by the burning house, he sat holding his treasure tightly with both his hands.

Now he finally understood his heart's desire, where his loyalty belonged! But when the fire in the house across the street had been put out, then he thought about it again. "I will share myself between them," he said, "for I cannot leave the grocer altogether. I must stay there for the sake of the porridge."

That was quite human! After all, we, too, go to the grocer for the porridge's sake.

THE MILLENNIUM

They will come on wings of steam, the young citizens of America will fly through the air, across the great ocean, to visit old Europe. They will come to see the monuments of bygone ages, the ruins of the great cities, just as we today visit Southeast Asia to stare at the crumbling glories of the past.

Thousands of years hence, they will come.

The Thames, the Danube, and the Rhine will still be flowing; Mount Blanc will stand with its snow-covered peak. The northern lights will be shining above the Scandinavian countries, though generations upon generations will have become dust. Many of those men, who to us seem so mighty, will be as nameless as the Vikings who rest in their grave chambers inside the hills, on top of which the farmers today like to place a bench, so that they can watch the wind make waves in the flat fields of grain.

"To Europe!" cry the young Americans. "To the land of our forefathers! To the wonders of an earlier civilization. To beautiful Europe!"

The airships will be crowded, for it is much faster to fly than to sail. The passengers will have already made their hotel reservations by telegraphing ahead. The first European coast to come into view will be Ireland's, but the passengers will still be sleeping; they will have given orders not to be awakened before the airship is over

England. The airship will land in Shakespeare's country, as the more cultured of the passengers call it — others call England the "land of the machine" or the "land of politics."

A whole day will these busy travelers give to England and Scotland; then they will be off via the tunnel under the Channel to France: the country of Charlemagne and Napoleon. The learned among them will discuss the Classicist and Romantic movements that so interested the Frenchmen of the distant past. Molière's name will be mentioned. Heroes, scientists, and poets whom we have never heard of — they have yet to be born in that crater of Europe, Paris! — will be on the lips of these young people.

Then the airship will fly over that country from which Columbus sailed and where Cortes was born: Spain, the home of Calderón, who composed his dramas in perfect verse. Beautiful dark-eyed women will still inhabit its fertile dales; one will hear the names of *el Cid* and the Alhambra in the old songs that people will still be singing.

Through the air, across the sea to Italy, where the Eternal City of Rome once was. It will be gone; the Campagna will be a desert. Only one wall of St. Peter's will still be standing, and there will be doubt as to its authenticity.

To Greece, to sleep one night in a luxury hotel on the top of Mount Olympus, so one will be able to say that one has been there; and then onward to the Bosporus, to rest for a few hours on the site of Byzantium. They will watch poor fishermen repairing their nets, while they listen to tales about Turkish harems of an all but forgotten age.

They will fly above ruins of great cities along the Danube, which in our times are still unknown. They will land to look at impressive monuments — accomplishments that lie in the future, but which will be admired as achievements of the fruitful past.

They will come to Germany, which once was crisscrossed by railroads and canals: the land where Luther spoke, Goethe sang, and Mozart once held the scepter of music. When they speak of science and the arts, they will mention other names that we do not know. One day will be the time they allot to Germany and one for all of Scandinavia: for the fatherlands of Oersted and Linnaeus, and for Norway, the young country of old heroes. Iceland will be visited on the homeward journey; the geyser will spout no longer, and the volcano Hekla will have died; but the cliff-bound island will stand in the turbulent sea as a memorial tablet to the sagas.

"There's so much to see in Europe," the young Americans will say. "And we have seen it all in a week, just as the famous guide-book promised we could." Then they will discuss the author of the book which they all will have read: *Europe Seen in Seven Days.*

THE PIGGY BANK

The children's room was filled with toys; on top of the cabinet stood a piggy bank. It was a fat clay pig with a slit in back that had been enlarged with a knife, so that silver crowns could slide through it. Two of those heavy coins had made that journey, besides innumerable pennies. The piggy bank was so filled that it didn't rattle when you shook it; and higher no piggy bank can rise. He stood on top of the cabinet and looked down upon everything in the room; he knew he could buy it all with the money he had in his stomach, and that was a very comfortable feeling.

Everything else in the room knew it, too, though they didn't talk about it. One of the drawers in the chest was open; in it lay a doll. She was old and had once broken her neck, but it had been repaired. Now she sat up and suggested, "Let us play human beings, it is amusing." At once everything started to jump about. The paintings on the wall turned around, in order to show that they had backs as well as fronts. That irritated the doll, who thought they had done it just to be contrary.

It was the middle of the night, but the moon was shining in through the window, giving free illumination. All the toys were invited to join the game, even the old baby carriage, though it didn't really belong. "Everyone has his own good points," it said. "We can't all be aristocrats; some have to work for a living."

THE PIGGY BANK

The piggy bank was the only one that had received a written invitation; the others feared that he was so far above them that he couldn't hear a spoken one, even if they shouted. He didn't answer. If he were going to watch the game, then he would only do it from his own home. He felt that everyone should comply with his wishes, even when he hadn't expressed them; and everyone did.

The little doll theater was erected in such a place that the piggy bank could watch the performance. They would start the evening by giving a play; later on there would be tea and intelligent conversation. But the rocking horse began talking immediately about the breeding and the breaking of horses; and the baby carriage talked about railroads and steam engines; they were always so professional. The clock on the wall talked politics; it declared that it knew the time, but the other toys said it was slow. The walking cane just stood about admiring its own silver knob, and the two embroidered pillows on the sofa, who were pretty but stupid, giggled.

Finally the play could begin. Everyone had been told that they could applaud or make any noise they wished, such as banging, rumpling, or whistling. The riding whip said it would "crack" for the young people in the play but not for the old: they were so boring.

"I will bang away for anyone," said the firecracker.

The spittoon stood humbly in the corner and mumbled, "One has to be somewhere."

The play was terrible but the acting was marvelous. All the players played in the center of the stage, to make sure their performances were seen.

The doll who once had broken her neck almost lost her head, she was so moved. The piggy bank was touched too, but in his own way; he thought of doing "something" for one of them, such as leaving him a small sum in his will.

All enjoyed themselves so much that they decided to skip the tea and just have the "intelligent conversation." They all felt "just like human beings," and that was not meant satirically. All of them thought their own opinions cleverer than their neighbors', and they all wondered what the piggy bank was thinking about. He was thinking very seriously about wills and funerals: long, slow-moving thoughts. But death and funerals have a habit of coming before one wishes them to come. . . .

HANS CHRISTIAN ANDERSEN

"Crash!" Down fell the piggy bank and broke into hundreds of pieces, while the money rolled all over the floor. One of the silver crowns rolled all the way to the door; it wanted to get out into the world and it did, and so did the pennies. The broken pieces of the piggy bank were thrown in the trash can. It wasn't the kind of funeral he had expected.

The next day a new piggy bank stood on the cabinet. He looked just like the other one; and he too couldn't rattle but that was because he was empty. He had just started his career; and with those words we will end our story.

THE LITTLE MATCH GIRL

It was dreadfully cold, snowing, and turning dark. It was the last evening of the year, New Year's Eve. In this cold and darkness walked a little girl. She was poor and both her head and feet were bare. Oh, she had had a pair of slippers when she left home; but they had been too big for her — in truth, they had belonged to her mother. The little one had lost them while hurrying across the street to get out of the way of two carriages that had been driving along awfully fast. One of the slippers she could not find, and the other had been snatched by a boy who, laughingly, shouted that he would use it as a cradle when he had a child of his own.

Now the little girl walked barefoot through the streets. Her feet were swollen and red from the cold. She was carrying a little bundle of matches in her hand and had more in her apron pocket. No one had bought any all day, or given her so much as a penny. Cold and hungry, she walked through the city; cowed by life, the poor thing!

The snowflakes fell on her long yellow hair that curled so prettily at the neck, but to such things she never gave a thought. From every window of every house, light shone, and one could smell the geese roasting all the way out in the street. It was, after all, New Year's Eve; and this she did think about.

In a little recess between two houses she sat down and tucked her feet under her. But now she was even colder. She didn't dare go home because she had sold no matches and was frightened that her father might beat her. Besides, her home was almost as cold as the street. She lived in an attic, right under a tile roof. The wind whistled through it, even though they had tried to close the worst of the holes and cracks with straw and old rags.

Her little hands were numb from cold. If only she dared strike a match, she could warm them a little. She took one and struck it against the brick wall of the house; it lighted! Oh, how warm it was and how clearly it burned like a little candle. She held her hand around it. How strange! It seemed that the match had become a big iron stove with brass fixtures. Oh, how blessedly warm it was! She stretched out her legs so that they, too, could get warm, but at that moment the stove disappeared and she was sitting alone with a burned-out match in her hand.

She struck another match. Its flame illuminated the wall and it became as transparent as a veil: she could see right into the house. She saw the table spread with a damask cloth and set with the finest porcelain. In the center, on a dish, lay a roasted goose stuffed with apples and prunes! But what was even more wonderful: the goose — although a fork and knife were stuck in its back — had jumped off the table and was waddling toward her. The little girl stretched out her arms and the match burned out. Her hands touched the cold, solid walls of the house.

She lit a third match. The flame flared up and she was sitting under a Christmas tree that was much larger and more beautifully decorated than the one she had seen through the glass doors at the rich merchant's on Christmas Eve. Thousands of candles burned on its green branches, and colorful pictures like the ones you can see in store windows were looking down at her. She smiled up at them; but then the match burned itself out, and the candles of the Christmas tree became the stars in the sky. A shooting star drew a line of fire across the dark heavens.

"Someone is dying," whispered the little girl. Her grandmother, who was dead, was the only person who had ever loved or been kind to the child; and she had told her that a shooting star was the soul of a human being traveling to God.

She struck yet another match against the wall and in its blaze she saw her grandmother, so sweet, so blessedly kind.

"Grandmother!" shouted the little one. "Take me with you! I

THE LITTLE MATCH GIRL

know you will disappear when the match goes out, just like the warm stove, the goose, and the beautiful Christmas· tree." Quickly, she lighted all the matches she had left in her hand, so that her grandmother could not leave. And the matches burned with such a clear, strong flame that the night became as light as day. Never had her grandmother looked so beautiful. She lifted the little girl in her arms and flew with her to where there is neither cold nor hunger nor fear: up to God.

In the cold morning the little girl was found. Her cheeks were red and she was smiling. She was dead. She had frozen to death on the last evening of the old year. The sun on New Year's Day shone down on the little corpse; her lap was filled with burned-out matches. "She had been trying to warm herself," people said. And no one knew the sweet visions she had seen, or in what glory she and her grandmother had passed into a truly new year.

IB AND LITTLE CHRISTINA

There is a river in Denmark called the River of the Gods, the Gudenaa; and not far from its shores, as it flows through the forest of Silkeborg, rises a ridge, on the west side of which was situated a small farm — in fact, it is still there. Even when the rye and barley stand high in the fields, you can see the sandy soil beneath the grain; and the harvest is always meager. This story takes place some years ago; and the farmer who tilled it then had three sheep, a pig, and two oxen. He could have kept a couple of horses but he felt as most farmers in that area did: "Horses eat up their profits themselves." Jeppe was the farmer's name. He farmed in the summer and carved wooden shoes in the winter. He was a skillful carver; but he had a younger helper who was even better than he was, and understood how to make clogs so that they were strong; and yet not heavy and shapeless. They also made other household wares which fetched a good price. Although Jeppe and his family were not rich, no one in that district would have called them poor.

Little Ib was seven years old. He was an only child, and he liked to sit by his father and watch him carve. The boy whittled sticks and sometimes he cut his fingers. One day he did manage to carve two little objects that looked like a pair of tiny wooden shoes. These he wanted to give to Christina, the daughter of the barge-man, who lived in a cottage on the heath. The little girl was very

IB AND LITTLE CHRISTINA

beautiful, and so delicate that she did not look at all like a barge-man's daughter. Had she had clothes to match the loveliness that God had given her, then no one would have guessed that she had been born in a poor cottage on the lonely heath. Her father was a widower who made his living by transporting lumber from the woods down to the locks at Silkeborg. Sometimes he would even sail as far as Randers with his barge. As there was no one at home to take care of little Christina—she was a year younger than Ib—she was always with her father, except on his journeys to Randers. Then her father would bring her to Jeppe's house to stay.

Ib and little Christina never fought, neither when they played nor at table. They would play in the sand, pretend they were making a little garden, or just tumble about. One day they ventured as far as the top of the ridge beyond which was the forest. They found the nest of a snipe with eggs in it; that had been a very exciting adventure.

Ib had never been on the heath, nor had he ever sailed with a barge down the river and through the lakes. But one day Christina's father invited him on a trip, and his parents gave their consent. The evening before they were to set out, the bargeman came to fetch him, and he spent the night in the little cottage on the heath.

Early the next morning the children were sitting on top of the woodpile, in the barge, eating bread and raspberries. Christina's father and his helper were poling the barge down the river; they were following the current, so they sailed along at a good speed. One after another they sailed through the lakes. Every time they entered one, Ib was sure that the river had ended, for bulrushes, reeds, and trees seemed to enclose the lake; but finally a narrow opening would appear that they could sail through. Sometimes the trees leaning out over the narrow river would almost hinder their passing, but always the barge sailed on. Some of the oak trees had naked branches that had lost all their bark and looked as if they had rolled up their sleeves to show their withered old arms. Many of the old alder trees had loosened themselves from the banks and now stood like little islets in the river. White and yellow water lilies floated amid their big green leaves. It certainly was a lovely trip. At last they came to the locks where eels were caught and shipped as far away as Copenhagen. The water rushed over the lock and fell as a waterfall on the other side; and that was something for Ib and little Christina to look at.

At that time no factory or town had been built there yet; there was only the old farm on which not many people lived. The water rushing over the lock and the cry of the wild ducks were the only sounds to be heard. The lumber was loaded onto a bigger barge; and Christina's father bought a little newly slaughtered pig and some eels. Then they were ready for the homeward journey. The pig and the eels were put into a basket. Now they had the current against them, but not the wind; so they hoisted a sail and that was as good as having two horses pull the barge.

When they reached the part of the forest where the bargeman's helper lived, they moored the barge at the bank. Christina's father told the children to stay on board and not to touch anything, while he accompanied his young helper to his home. The bargeman said that he would be back very soon.

The children obeyed him at first, but not for long. They had to peep into the basket that contained the eels and the pig. They took the little pig out; and when they both tried to hold it at once, it fell overboard; and the little dead animal floated away with the current.

It was a terrible calamity! Ib leaped to the shore and soon Christina followed him. "Take me with you!" she cried. They ran in among the trees; and within a few minutes the barge and the river disappeared from their view. Christina fell and began to cry, but Ib calmed her.

"The house is right over there. Come along," he said; but the house was not "right over there," and soon the two children were lost. They walked on and on; the dried leaves rustled and dead branches broke with cracking sound as they stepped on them.

Someone was shouting far away. The children stopped to listen, but then they heard the hoarse frightening cry of an eagle; and they ran. A little while later they came upon a blueberry patch covered with the most delicious large, ripe berries. They were so tempting that they had to sit down and eat them. Their cheeks and lips were stained deep blue. Again they heard someone shouting.

"We will get spanked because of the pig," observed little Christina.

"Let us go home to my parents," said Ib, who was certain that Christina was right. "It is not far from here." The children walked

IB AND LITTLE CHRISTINA

on and finally they came to a road, but it did not lead home. It began to grow dark, and they were very frightened. The terrible stillness of the forest was broken by the terrifying hooting of owls and the cries of other birds that they did not know. Christina cried and Ib cried. They wept for an hour or more before they both lay down under some bushes and fell asleep.

The sun was already high in the sky when they awoke, but they were very cold. They could see the sun shining on top of a nearby hill. Up there they would be able to get warm, and Ib hoped that he would be able to see his home. But they were in another part of the forest, far away from the little farm. When they climbed the hill they found a little pool, and where the sun's rays fell on the water, they could see the fishes swimming. Such a sight they had never seen before. A few minutes later they found some hazelnut bushes and their fears were forgotten. They cracked the nuts and ate them. Although they were far from ripe, they already had little kernels. Then something terribly frightening happened!

A tall woman stepped out from behind the bushes. Her face was brown and her hair was black. She carried a bundle on her back and a big strong cane in her hands; she was a gypsy. At first the children could not understand what she said. She took three nuts out of her apron pocket and told them that they were "wishing nuts," and that each of them contained something marvelous.

Ib looked at the woman for a long time; her expression seemed kind. He asked her if he could have her "wishing nuts," and she gave them to him. Then she picked a whole pocketful of nuts from the bushes for herself.

The two children stared wide-eyed at the "wishing nuts."

"Is there a carriage and horses in one of them?" asked Ib.

"In that one there is a golden carriage with golden horses," answered the woman, and pointed to one of the nuts in the boy's hand.

"Give it to me then," begged little Christina; and Ib gave it to her.

"Is there a pretty little necklace like the one Christina is wearing in this one?" demanded Ib.

"There are ten necklaces," said the woman, "and dresses, stockings, and hats."

"Then I want that one too," shouted little Christina, and Ib gave it to her. The third nut was a little black one. "That one you can keep," said Christina. "It is a pretty one, too."

"And what is in that?" asked Ib.

"What is best for you," said the gypsy.

Ib kept the nut. The gypsy woman said that she would show them the way home; but she led them astray, sending them in the opposite direction from the one they should have gone. But one cannot accuse her of trying to steal the children, and she might have acted in good faith.

In the middle of the forest they met Chris the forester. He knew Ib and he took the children home. Both the bargeman and Ib's parents had been so upset that the children were forgiven, though they deserved a spanking, not only for having let the pig fall in the water but also for running away.

That evening after Christina and her father had returned to their home on the heath, Ib took out the nut that contained what was "best for him." He placed it between the door and its casing and cracked it by closing the door. There was no kernel in it, just some black dirt; it was worm-eaten.

"I thought so!" Ib was not surprised. "How could there be room in a little nut for what was 'best'? Christina will get no carriage or dresses out of her nuts either," Ib muttered.

Winter came; and the years passed by. Finally Ib was old enough to be confirmed. Every Sunday that spring he walked the many miles to the church to receive religious instruction. One day the bargeman came by. He had news to tell: little Christina was old enough to earn her own keep and he had found her a good position in the family of a wealthy innkeeper near Herning. She was to help in the house and they would see to it that she was confirmed.

Ib and little Christina said good-by to each other. "The little sweethearts," they were called. Christina showed Ib the two little "wishing nuts" he had given her, and which he had received from the gypsy that day in the forest; and she told him that the little pair of wooden shoes that he had cut for her were in the bottom of the chest in which she had packed her clothes. Then they parted.

Ib was confirmed but continued living at home, for his father had died and he had to help his mother. He had become as good a carver of wooden shoes as his father had been; and in the summer he took good care of their little farm. Not often did they hear from Christina, but the news that they did get was always good. She

IB AND LITTLE CHRISTINA

wrote to her father about her confirmation and the letter was filled with descriptions of the new clothes she had received from her mistress.

The next spring, on a particularly beautiful day, someone knocked on the door of the little farm. It was the bargeman and Christina; she had been offered a ride in a carriage as far as Tem and back. This had been an opportunity to come home for a visit. Beautiful she was and her clothes were as elegant as any lady's. Ib, who was wearing his work clothes, could hardly utter a word. He took her hand and held it tightly, but his tongue was all tied up in knots. Christina's wasn't: she talked and talked, there was so much to tell, and she kissed Ib boldly on the mouth.

"Don't you know me any more?" she asked.

All he could manage to reply, even though they were alone together, was: "You have become a fine lady and I am so . . . so coarse! But oh, Christina, how I have thought about you and of the time when we were children together!"

Arm in arm, they walked up to the top of the ridge; from there they could see the river and as far as the heath, where Christina's father lived. Ib did not say a word; but as they were returning — and Ib was to go to his home and Christina to her father's — Ib realized how very much he wanted Christina to be his wife. Hadn't they been called "sweethearts" since they were little children? Now he knew that he had always expected that one day they would marry; and he felt as though they were engaged though neither of them had ever spoken a word about it.

Christina could only stay a few hours because she had to be in Tem early the following morning, when the carriage departed that would take her back to the inn at Herning.

Ib and the bargeman accompanied her to Tem. It was a lovely night; the moon was full. All the way, Ib held Christina's hand, and when they finally arrived at their destination he did not want to let go of it. He had great difficulty saying what anyone could have read in his eyes. He spoke only a few words but every one of them came from his heart. "If you have not become used to finer things than I can give you, and if you will be satisfied with living in my mother's house with me as your husband, then I think the two of us should become man and wife. . . . But I will not hurry you."

"Yes, let us wait a little while, Ib," replied Christina, and pressed his hand; then he kissed her on the mouth. "I trust you, Ib," she said. "And I think that I love you! But I would like to have time to think about it."

They parted and Ib told the bargeman that he and Christina were as good as engaged. Christina's father was pleased and not surprised. Although he spent the night at Ib's home, they did not talk any more about it.

A year went by. Two letters had passed between Ib and Christina, and both of them had been signed: "Yours unto death." Then one day the bargeman arrived; he had greetings from Christina. That was easy enough to say. What followed was more difficult and he took his time saying it. Everything went well for Christina; more than well, but then she was a good girl. The innkeeper's son had been home on a visit, he had a good job in an office in Copenhagen. He had taken a liking to Christina and she to him. His parents were not against them marrying, but Christina felt that she had given Ib her word; and therefore she was going to say no. "Even though such a marriage would be fortunate for a poor girl like herself," concluded the bargeman.

At first, Ib did not say a word, but his face turned as white as a newly washed sheet. He shook his head and then mumbled, "I would not wish Christina to say no to good fortune for my sake."

"Write her a few words about it," urged the bargeman.

Ib wrote, but every time he had written a sentence he crossed it out again. All the words seemed wrong to him. Many pages he tore up, but by morning the letter to little Christina was finished. Here it is:

I have read the letter that you wrote to your father. In it you say that everything goes well for you and that you have an opportunity for bettering yourself. Ask your own heart, Christina! If you want to marry me, then remember that I am poor. Do not consider me or my feelings, but only yourself. You are not bound to me; should you feel that you have given me your "promise," then I release you from it. May all the happiness in the world be yours, Christina. God may console my heart.

Ever your devoted friend,
Ib

IB AND LITTLE CHRISTINA

The letter was sent and Christina received it.

A few months later, the banns were read in the little church on the heath and in the big church in Copenhagen. The bridegroom was too busy with his affairs to be able to travel to Jutland. Christina journeyed with her future mother-in-law to the capital, where the young people were to live. Christina had arranged to meet her father in the little village of Funder, which was on the main highway to the south; there they said good-by to each other.

Every once in a while someone would speak about Christina when Ib was present; but Ib himself never mentioned her. He had become so silent, so pensive. He often thought about the nuts that the gypsy woman had given them. Now Christina had got her carriage and all the dresses she could wish for, over across the water in the king's city, Copenhagen. The "wishing nuts" had proven themselves. His nut had been filled with black earth, and the gypsy had said that that was best for him. Now he understood what she had meant: the dark grave was best for him.

Years went by; not many, but to Ib they seemed long. The old innkeeper and his wife died and their son inherited their wealth: several thousand silver crowns. Now certainly Christina could have her golden carriage and even more dresses than she ever could wear.

Then two years passed during which not even the bargeman received any letters from Christina. Finally one came; it was not a happy one. Poor Christina, neither she nor her husband had been able to handle the sudden richness; it had not been a blessing, for they had not earned it themselves.

The heather bloomed and withered; and many a snowstorm swept across the heath and up over the ridge that protected Ib's little farmhouse. Spring came and Ib was plowing his meager fields. Suddenly he felt the plow shake as if it had hit a stone. Something black, shaped like a wood shaving, stuck up from the earth. Ib picked it up; it was metal and, where the plowshare had cut into it, it shone. It was a heavy arm ring of gold from heathen times.

The Viking grave had long ago been leveled. Now its treasure had been found. Ib showed it to the minister, who admired it and told him to take it to the district commissioner.

The official sent a report to Copenhagen and advised Ib to deliver the golden arm ring to the museum himself. "You have found in the earth the finest treasure, the best that could be found," he said.

"The best!" thought Ib. "The best for me, and found in the earth. The gypsy woman was right, my wishing nut, too, has proven true."

Ib sailed from Aarhus to the capital; and since he had never sailed before except with the bargeman up and down the river Gudenaa, it felt like an ocean journey.

In Copenhagen he received the gold value of the arm ring: six hundred silver crowns! Now Ib — who knew so well the forest and the heath — took a walk along the endless streets, lined with stone buildings.

The evening before he was to sail home, he lost his way, when he was out walking, and ended in one of the poorest quarters of the city, called Christian's Harbor. It was late and the street was deserted. He noticed a little child coming out of one of the most dilapidated of the houses, and he asked her for directions. The little girl looked up at him; she was crying, and said nothing. He asked her what was the matter; and she answered, but he could not understand her.

They were standing under a street lamp. Ib looked down at the child; the light was shining in her face. How strange! He saw with wonder that she looked exactly as Christina had, when she was a child.

He followed the little girl into a miserable house and up the worn, rickety stairs to the garret. They entered a little room right under the roof. The air was foul and it was dark. Ib struck a match. Over in a corner stood a bed; in it lay a woman: the little girl's mother.

"Can I help you?" asked Ib. "This little girl found me down in the street but I am a stranger to the city, myself. Can I call the neighbors?" He stepped closer to the bed and looked down at the woman: it was Christina!

At home, he had not heard her name mentioned in years, because everyone knew that Ib did not like to be reminded of her. Besides, all the rumors had been unpleasant. It was said that the inherited money had made her husband lose his common sense. He had given up his good position and they had traveled in foreign countries. When they returned, they had lived high and got into debt, rather than curtail the luxuriousness of their way of life. It

IB AND LITTLE CHRISTINA

was the old story of the cart going down the hill so fast that it finally overturned. The many merry friends who had dined at their table when wealth decked it now felt no pity. They said he deserved his fate, he had acted like a madman. One morning the body of Christina's husband had been found in a canal near the harbor.

Christina had been pregnant then; her child conceived in wealth was born in poverty. The baby had only lived a few weeks. Now Christina lay ill to death in a garret as dismal and bare as the room she had slept in as a child on the heath. But now, when she had known luxury, she could not bear her poverty, her wretchedness. The little girl, who had brought Ib to her, was her daughter, her older and only living child. Her name, too, was Christina.

"I am afraid that I am dying," she mumbled. "What will happen to my child? Where in the world can she find a home?"

Ib lit another match and found a stump of candle; its little flame lighted up the dismal chamber.

Ib looked at the little girl and was again reminded of Christina as she had looked as a child. For her sake he would take the little girl, bring her up, and be kind to her. The dying woman looked up at him; the pupils of her eyes grew larger and larger. Did she recognize him? Ib never knew, for she never spoke again.

We are back in the forest near the River of the Gods as it is called, not far from the heath. It is fall, the western storms have started. The wind is blowing the leaves off the trees. In the bargeman's hut strangers are living. Inside the little farmhouse, so snugly protected from the wind by the ridge, the stove is burning. It is as warm and comfortable as if it were summer; sunshine is here, the kind that shines from a child's eyes. Though it is October, the lark still sings in the little girl's laughter. Here lives gaiety and winter is far away. Little Christina is sitting on Ib's knee; he is both father and mother to her. Her real parents have disappeared, as dreams do to a grownup. The little farmhouse is cozy and neat. The girl's mother sleeps in the churchyard for the poor in Copenhagen.

They say that Ib has a tidy sum put away, gold from the earth; he is rich and he has his little Christina.

THE EMPEROR'S
NEW CLOTHES

Many, many years ago there was an emperor who was so terribly fond of beautiful new clothes that he spent all his money on his attire. He did not care about his soldiers, or attending the theater, or even going for a drive in the park, unless it was to show off his new clothes. He had an outfit for every hour of the day. And just as we say, "The king is in his council chamber," his subjects used to say, "The emperor is in his clothes closet."

In the large town where the emperor's palace was, life was gay and happy; and every day new visitors arrived. One day two swindlers came. They told everybody that they were weavers and that they could weave the most marvelous cloth. Not only were the colors and the patterns of their material extraordinarily beautiful, but the cloth had the strange quality of being invisible to anyone who was unfit for his office or unforgivably stupid.

"This is truly marvelous," thought the emperor. "Now if I had robes cut from that material, I should know which of my councilors was unfit for his office, and I would be able to pick out my clever subjects myself. They must weave some material for me!" And he gave the swindlers a lot of money so they could start working at once.

They set up a loom and acted as if they were weaving, but the loom was empty. The fine silk and gold threads they demanded

THE EMPEROR'S NEW CLOTHES

from the emperor they never used, but hid them in their own knapsacks. Late into the night they would sit before their empty loom, pretending to weave.

"I would like to know how they are getting along," thought the emperor; but his heart beat strangely when he remembered that those who were stupid or unfit for their office would not be able to see the material. Not that he was really worried that this would happen to him. Still, it might be better to send someone else the first time and see how he fared. Everybody in town had heard about the cloth's magic quality and most of them could hardly wait to find out how stupid or unworthy their neighbors were.

"I shall send my faithful prime minister over to see how the weavers are getting along," thought the emperor. "He will know how to judge the material, for he is both clever and fit for his office, if any man is."

The good-natured old man stepped into the room where the weavers were working and saw the empty loom. He closed his eyes, and opened them again. "God preserve me!" he thought. "I cannot see a thing!" But he didn't say it out loud.

The swindlers asked him to step a little closer to the loom so that he could admire the intricate patterns and marvelous colors of the material they were weaving. They both pointed to the empty loom, and the poor old prime minister opened his eyes as wide as he could; but it didn't help, he still couldn't see anything.

"Am I stupid?" he thought. "I can't believe it, but if it is so, it is best no one finds out about it. But maybe I am not fit for my office. No, that is worse, I'd better not admit that I can't see what they are weaving."

"Tell us what you think of it," demanded one of the swindlers.

"It is beautiful. It is very lovely," mumbled the old prime minister, adjusting his glasses. "What patterns! What colors! I shall tell the emperor that it pleases me ever so much."

"That is a compliment," both the weavers said; and now they described the patterns and told which shades of color they had used. The prime minister listened attentively, so that he could repeat their words to the emperor; and that is exactly what he did.

The two swindlers demanded more money, and more silk and gold thread. They said they had to use it for their weaving, but their loom remained as empty as ever.

Soon the emperor sent another of his trusted councilors to see how the work was progressing. He looked and looked just as the prime minister had, but since there was nothing to be seen, he didn't see anything.

"Isn't it a marvelous piece of material?" asked one of the swindlers; and they both began to describe the beauty of their cloth again.

"I am not stupid," thought the emperor's councilor. "I must be unfit for my office. That is strange; but I'd better not admit it to anyone." And he started to praise the material, which he could not see, for the loveliness of its patterns and colors.

"I think it is the most charming piece of material I have ever seen," declared the councilor to the emperor.

Everyone in town was talking about the marvelous cloth that the swindlers were weaving.

At last the emperor himself decided to see it before it was removed from the loom. Attended by the most important people in the empire, among them the prime minister and the councilor who had been there before, the emperor entered the room where the weavers were weaving furiously on their empty loom.

"Isn't it *magnifique?*" asked the prime minister.

"Your Majesty, look at the colors and the patterns," said the councilor.

And the two old gentlemen pointed to the empty loom, believing that all the rest of the company could see the cloth.

"What!" thought the emperor. "I can't see a thing! Why, this is a disaster! Am I stupid? Am I unfit to be emperor? Oh, it is too horrible!" Aloud he said, "It is very lovely. It has my approval," while he nodded his head and looked at the empty loom.

All the councilors, ministers, and men of great importance who had come with him stared and stared; but they saw no more than the emperor had seen, and they said the same thing that he had said, "It is lovely." And they advised him to have clothes cut and sewn, so that he could wear them in the procession at the next great celebration.

"It is magnificent! Beautiful! Excellent!" All of their mouths agreed, though none of their eyes had seen anything. The two swindlers were decorated and given the title "Royal Knight of the Loom."

The night before the procession, the two swindlers didn't sleep at all. They had sixteen candles lighting up the room where they worked. Everyone could see how busy they were, getting the emperor's new clothes finished. They pretended to take the cloth from the loom; they cut the air with their big scissors, and sewed with needles without thread. At last they announced: "The emperor's clothes are ready!"

Together with his courtiers, the emperor came. The swindlers lifted their arms as if they were holding something in their hands, and said, "These are the trousers. This is the robe, and here is the train. They are all as light as if they were made of spider webs! It will be as if Your Majesty had almost nothing on, but that is their special virtue."

"Oh yes," breathed all the courtiers; but they saw nothing, for there was nothing to be seen.

"Will Your Imperial Majesty be so gracious as to take off your clothes?" asked the swindlers. "Over there by the big mirror, we shall help you put your new ones on."

The emperor did as he was told; and the swindlers acted as if they were dressing him in the clothes they should have made. Finally they tied around his waist the long train which two of his most noble courtiers were to carry.

The emperor stood in front of the mirror admiring the clothes he couldn't see.

"Oh, how they suit you! A perfect fit!" everyone exclaimed. "What colors! What patterns! The new clothes are magnificent!"

"The crimson canopy, under which Your Imperial Majesty is to walk, is waiting outside," said the imperial master of court ceremony.

"Well, I am dressed. Aren't my clothes becoming?" The emperor turned around once more in front of the mirror, pretending to study his finery.

The two gentlemen of the imperial bedchamber fumbled on the floor, trying to find the train which they were supposed to carry. They didn't dare admit that they didn't see anything, so they pretended to pick up the train and held their hands as if they were carrying it.

The emperor walked in the procession under his crimson canopy. And all the people of the town, who had lined the streets or were looking down from the windows, said that the emperor's clothes were beautiful. "What a magnificent robe! And the train! How well the emperor's clothes suit him!"

HANS CHRISTIAN ANDERSEN

None of them were willing to admit that they hadn't seen a thing; for if anyone did, then he was either stupid or unfit for the job he held. Never before had the emperor's clothes been such a success.

"But he doesn't have anything on!" cried a little child.

"Listen to the innocent one," said the proud father. And the people whispered among each other and repeated what the child had said.

"He doesn't have anything on. There's a little child who says that he has nothing on."

"He has nothing on!" shouted all the people at last.

The emperor shivered, for he was certain that they were right; but he thought, "I must bear it until the procession is over." And he walked even more proudly, and the two gentlemen of the imperial bedchamber went on carrying the train that wasn't there.

CLOD HANS

AN OLD TALE RETOLD

$\mathbf{F}$ar out in the country there
was an ancient manor house. The squire who lived in it had two
sons. Both of them were so clever that they could answer more
questions than anyone would care to ask them. They decided to
propose to the princess; this they dared do because the princess
had officially proclaimed that she would marry the man in her
kingdom who spoke most wittily.

They had only a week to prepare themselves, but that was
enough, for they were well educated and that is an advantage. One
of them knew by heart the Latin dictionary and the town newspaper for the last three years, and that backward as well as forward.
The other one had memorized all the guild laws and regulations,
even the ones that most guild masters had never heard about. He
felt that this enabled him to discourse on politics; besides that, he
could embroider suspenders, for he was artistic.

"I will win the princess!" said both of them.

Their father gave them each a horse; the son who knew the
dictionary and the newspapers by heart was given a black one; the
embroiderer and expert on guild laws, one as white as milk. Now
they greased their jaws with cod liver oil in order to be able to
speak even faster than usually; and then they were ready to depart.
All the servants were lined up to wave good-by. Just as the two
brothers were mounting their horses, their younger brother came

239

running out of the house. I haven't mentioned him before because no one thought anything of him, and he wasn't really considered part of the family. He was not a scholar like the other two, and that is why they called him Clod Hans.

"You are all dressed up, where are you going?" shouted Clod Hans.

"To the king's castle, to win the princess by our wit. Haven't you heard what the drums have announced and the herald proclaimed?" one of them asked; and the other brother told Hans of the princess' decision to marry the man who could speak most wittily.

"Goodness me! I am going too!" declared Clod Hans while his brothers laughed and rode off.

"Father, let me have a horse!" he shouted. "I have just decided to get married. If she takes me, well and good. If she doesn't, then I will take her."

"Nonsense!" said the father. "I will not give you a horse; you can't speak well; you have no wit. You're not even presentable!"

"Well, if I can't have a horse," laughed Clod Hans, "then I will take the billy goat; that is mine and I can ride it." Up he jumped on the billy goat, dug his heels into its sides, and away he rode. The goat ran as fast as it could and Clod Hans sang and shouted as loud as he could: "Here am I, here am I!"

His two brothers did not say a word to each other. They were too busy getting witty ideas. They rode so sedately you might think they were attending a funeral.

"Hello! Hello!" shouted Hans as soon as he caught up with them. "Here am I! And look what I found in the middle of the road!" He held up a dead crow for them to look at.

"Clod!" they said. "And what are you going to do with that?"

"Give it to the princess!"

"You do just that!" they laughed, and rode on a little bit faster, for they didn't want to be seen in company with their brother.

"Hello, hello, here I am again. Look what I have found! It is not every day that one stumbles across such a treasure!"

The two brothers turned around in their saddles to see what their younger brother had now. "Clod!" they said. "It is only an old wooden shoe and broken at that. Are you going to give that to the princess too?"

"I certainly will!" declared Hans, while his brothers laughed and spurred their horses.

CLOD HANS

"Hello, hello! Here am I!" screamed Clod Hans a little while later. "It is too marvelous, just look!"

"What have you found now?" asked the brothers.

"Oh!" sighed Hans. "Can you imagine how pleased the princess will be?"

"Ugh!" exclaimed his brothers. "Why, it is only mud from a ditch."

"Yes, that is exactly what it is," agreed Hans, "but of the very best quality, the kind that slips right through your fingers. I have filled my pockets with it."

This time the brothers did not laugh, they just rode as fast as they could and arrived at the city gate a whole hour before Clod Hans. Everyone who had come to propose to the princess was given a number and had to line up in a row. They stood so close together that they couldn't move their arms; and that was fortunate, for otherwise they would have torn each other's eyes out, just because one had got there ahead of the other.

All the other citizens of the town crowded around the castle and tried to look through the windows; they wanted to watch the princess receiving her suitors. But as each of them entered the royal hall, he seemed to lose his tongue, for all of them could only stammer and stutter.

"No good!" said the princess every time. "Out!"

The first of the brothers entered, the one who knew the Latin dictionary and the newspapers by heart; but he had forgotten every word of them while he stood in the row with the other suitors. The floor creaked as he walked across it, and the ceiling of the room was an enormous mirror that reflected everything upside down. At one of the windows stood three scribes and an alderman, who wrote down all that was said, so that it could be printed in the newspaper, which would be sold in the streets that very afternoon for twopence. And if that was not frightening enough, the heat would have made anyone uncomfortable; the stoves had red-hot potbellies.

"It is hot in here!" said the unhappy suitor.

"That is because my father is roasting roosters today," said the princess.

"Bah!" That wasn't what he had expected and there he stood with his mouth open. He wanted to say something witty, but he couldn't.

"No good!" said the princess. "Out!"

And outside he had to go. Now came the second brother.

"It is terribly hot," he said.

"Yes, we are roasting roosters," said the princess.

"What did — What?" mumbled the poor man; and all the scribes wrote: "What did — what?"

"No good!" said the princess. "Out!"

Now came Clod Hans. He rode on his billy goat right into the royal hall. "Goodness me, it is hot in here," he said.

"That is because I am roasting roosters today," said the princess.

"That is fine," said Clod Hans, "maybe I can get my crow fried as well."

"That might be possible," laughed the princess. "But do you have anything to fry it in? All our pots and pans are in use."

"Sure, I have," said Clod Hans, and held up the old wooden shoe. "Here is a pot to put it in," and he dropped the crow into the broken shoe.

"Why, it is enough for a meal," said the princess, "but where are you going to get the gravy?"

"I've got pockets full of it! So much that I have some to spare." And Clod Hans showed her the mud.

"That is what I like!" exclaimed the princess. "Somebody who can speak up for himself. I will marry you! But do you know that every word we have said has been written down and will be printed in the newspaper? At one of the windows stand three scribes and an old alderman, and he is the worst, because he does not understand a word of what anyone says." The princess said this to frighten Clod Hans, and the scribes neighed like horses and shook their pens, so blots of ink sprayed onto the floor.

"Well, if the alderman is the most important, then he deserves the best!" shouted Clod Hans, and took all the mud out of his pockets and threw it in the old man's face.

"That was nobly done!" laughed the princess. "I couldn't have done it, but I am sure I will learn how!"

Clod Hans married the princess and became king. He sat on a throne with a crown on his head. I got the story straight out of the alderman's newspaper and that cannot be trusted.

THE BOTTLE

$\mathbf{I}$n a crooked alley, among other ill-repaired houses, stood one that was particularly narrow and tall. It was a half-timbered house, and many of the beams were rotten. Only very poor people lived there. Outside the garret window hung a bird cage; it was as decrepit as the house, and its inhabitant did not even have a proper bath: the neck of a broken bottle, corked and hung upside down, had to suffice. The old maid who lived in the garret was standing by the open window, enjoying the warm sunshine. She had just fed the little linnet, and the songbird was hopping back and forth in the cage, singing merrily.

"Yes, you may sing," said the bottleneck. It didn't really speak, for bottlenecks can't talk, but it thought all this inside itself, as we all do sometimes. "Yes, you can sing. You are healthy and well, not an invalid like me. You don't know what it's like to lose your whole lower parts and be left with only a neck and mouth; and then, on top of it, to have a cork stuffed into you. Then you wouldn't sing so loud! But it is good that someone is happy. I have nothing to sing about, and I can't sing. But I have lived an exciting life! I remember when the tanner took me along on a picnic and his daughter got engaged. I was a whole and proper bottle then. Goodness me, it seems just like yesterday. . . . Oh yes, I have experienced a lot. I was created in fire and heat, have sailed across the ocean, lain in the dark earth, and been higher up in the sky

243

than most people. Now I am perched above the street in the sunshine; yes, my story bears repeating. But I am not going to tell it out loud, because I can't."

But the bottleneck could reminisce and it did. The bird sang, and the passers-by down in the alley thought about their own problems or didn't think at all, while the bottleneck reflected upon its life.

It remembered the great oven in the factory, where it had been blown into life. As soon as it had been formed, while it was still burning hot, it had been able to look into the burning red oven. It had felt a desire to jump back into it and be melted down again, but as it cooled that fancy had disappeared. The bottle had stood in a row together with all his sisters and brothers; there had been a whole regiment of them. They had all come from the same oven, but some had been blown into champagne bottles and others into beer bottles, and that makes a difference. Although later on, after they have come out into the world and the beer or the champagne has been drunk, then a beer bottle can be refilled with the costly wine from Vesuvius, Lachryma Christi, and the champagne bottle with boot blacking. But birth still counts and that you can tell from the shape. Nobility remains nobility, even when it contains only boot blacking.

All the bottles were put into cases, and so was the bottle that this story is about. It never occurred to him then that he would end as a useless bottleneck, and then have to work his way up to becoming a birdbath — for that is better than being nothing at all.

He saw daylight again when the cases of bottles were unpacked in the wine merchant's cellar. Now he was rinsed for the first time, that was a strange experience; then he was put on a shelf. There he lay empty and without a cork, he felt awkward; something was missing but he did not know quite what it was. Then the bottle was filled with wine, corked, and sealed. A label was pasted on it which said, "very fine quality." The bottle felt as though he had passed an examination and received the highest grade. The wine was young and the bottle was young; and the young tend to be lyrical. All sorts of songs about things, that the bottle couldn't possibly know a thing about, seemed to be humming inside him. He saw clearly the green sunlit mountains, where the grapes had grown, as well as the maidens and young men who had kissed each other while they picked the fruit. Oh yes, it is lovely to live! The

THE BOTTLE

bottle was filled with passion and love, just as young poets are before they know much about either.

One morning the bottle was sold. The tanner's apprentice had been sent down to buy a flask of the "very best wine." It was put into the picnic basket together with ham, cheese, sausage, the best-quality butter, and the finest bread. It was the tanner's daughter who packed the basket. She was young and lovely, with a smile in her brown eyes and laughter on her lips. Her hands were soft and white, but the skin on her neck was even whiter. She was one of the most beautiful girls in the town and not yet engaged.

She had the picnic basket on her lap, while they drove out into the forest. The bottle peeped out through the snowy white tablecloth that covered the basket; his cork was covered by red sealing wax. He could look right into the face of the young girl and he saw, too, the young seaman who was sitting beside her. They had been friends since childhood. He was the son of a portrait painter. He had just received his mate's license and was to sail the following day on a long voyage to foreign lands. While preparing the basket for the picnic they had talked about the voyage; and there had been no joy or laughter to be seen in the young girl's face.

When they arrived in the forest the young couple went for a walk alone, and what did they talk about? Well, the bottle never knew, for he had stayed in the picnic basket. A very long time seemed to pass before he was taken out. But when it finally happened, something very pleasant seemed to have taken place. Everyone was smiling and laughing, the tanner's daughter too. She didn't say much, but two red roses were blooming on her cheeks.

The tanner took out his corkscrew and grabbed the bottle! It was a strange experience to be opened for the first time. The bottleneck had never forgotten that solemn moment when the cork was drawn and the wine streamed into the glasses.

"To the engaged couple!" toasted the tanner. They all emptied their glasses, and the young mate kissed his bride-to-be.

"Happiness and contentment!" exclaimed the old couple to the young.

The glasses were filled once more. "A happy homecoming and a wedding, a year from now!" shouted the young man. When they had drunk this toast, he grasped the now empty bottle. "You have been part of the happiest day of my life, you shall serve no one after that!"

HANS CHRISTIAN ANDERSEN

The young mate threw the bottle high into the air. The tanner's daughter followed it with her eyes; she could not know then that she would see the very same bottle fly through the air once more during her life. The bottle landed in a little pond in the woods. The bottleneck remembered it all very clearly; he could even recall what he had thought when he lay in the water! "I gave them wine, and they gave me swamp water in return, but they meant well." The poor bottle could no longer see the picnic party, but heard them laughing and singing. Finally two little peasant boys came by, looked in among the reeds, noticed the bottle, picked it up; and now he had an owner again.

In the house in the woods, the oldest son had been home the day before; he was a seaman and was about to set out on a long voyage. His mother was making a package of one thing and another that she thought might be useful on so long a journey. His father would take it to the ship and give it to the lad together with his parents' blessings. A little bottle of homemade liquor had already been filled; but when the boys entered with the larger and stronger bottle, the woman decided to put the liquor in that one instead. It was brewed from herbs and was especially good for the stomach. So the bottle was filled once more, this time not with red wine but with bitter medicine, and that was of the "very best" quality too.

Lying between a sausage and a cheese, it was delivered to Peter Jensen, who was the older brother of the two boys who had found the bottle. Now the ship's mate was the very young man who had just become engaged to the tanner's daughter. He did not see the bottle; and if he had, he would not have recognized it, or imagined that the very bottle that had contained the wine with which he had toasted to a happy homecoming could be on board his ship.

True, the bottle was no longer filled with wine, but what it contained was just as desirable to Peter Jensen and his friends. They called Peter the "apothecary," for it was he who doled out the medicine that cured stomachaches so pleasantly. Yes, that was a good period in the bottle's life; but at last it was empty.

It had stood forgotten in a corner a long time; then the terrible tragedy occurred. Whether it happened on the journey out or on the return voyage was never clear to the bottle, since he had not gone ashore. The ship was caught in the midst of a storm; great heavy black waves broke over the railing and lifted and tossed the vessel; the mast broke; and a plank in the hull was pressed loose.

THE BOTTLE

The water poured in so fast that it was useless to try to pump it out. It was a dark night. In the last few minutes before the ship sank, the young mate wrote on a piece of paper, "In Jesus' name, we are lost." Then he added the name of the ship, his own name, and that of his sweetheart. He put the sheet of paper into an empty bottle he had found, corked it, and threw it into the raging sea. He did not know that he had once before held that bottle in his hands, on the day of his engagement.

The ship sank, the crew was lost, but the bottle floated like a gull on the waves. Now that he had a sad love letter inside him, he had a heart. The bottle watched the sun rise and set, thought that the red disk was like the opening of the oven in which he had been born; he longed to float right into it. Days of calm were followed by a storm. The bottle was not broken against a cliff-bound shore, nor was it swallowed by a shark.

For years it drifted, following the currents of the ocean toward the north and then toward the south. He was his own master, but that, too, can become tiresome in the long run.

The note, the last farewell from a bridegroom to his bride, would only bring pain if ever it were held by the hand it had been meant for. Where were they now, those little white hands that had spread the tablecloth on the green moss the day of the picnic? Where was the tanner's daughter? Where was the country where it had happened? The bottle didn't know, he just drifted with the waves and the wind. Although he was thoroughly tired of it; after all, that wasn't what he was meant for. He had no choice in the matter, even when he finally floated to shore. It was a foreign country, the bottle didn't understand a word of what was said; and that was most irritating. You miss so much when you don't understand the language.

The bottle was picked up, opened, and the note was taken out to be read. But the finder did not understand what was written on it; he turned the note both upside down and right side up, but he could not read it. He realized that the bottle had been thrown overboard and that the note was a message from a ship, but what it said remained a mystery to him. The note was put back in the bottle and the bottle put away in a closet.

Every time there were visitors the note was shown in the hope that someone could read it, but no one who came ever could. The note that had been written with pencil was made less and less

HANS CHRISTIAN ANDERSEN

legible by the many hands that held it. Finally the letters could no longer be seen and the bottle was put up in the attic. Spider webs and dust covered him, while he dreamed about the past: the good old days when he had been filled with wine and had been taken on a picnic. Even the days on the ocean seemed pleasant now; the years when he had floated on the sea and had had a secret inside him: a letter, a sigh of farewell.

It remained in the attic twenty years and would have stayed there even longer had not the owner decided to enlarge his house. The whole roof was torn down. The bottle was brought out and the story of how it was found told once more. The bottle did not understand what was being said, for you don't learn a language by standing twenty years in an attic. "If only they had allowed me to stay in the closet downstairs, then I would probably have learned it," thought the bottle.

Once more he was washed and rinsed — and he certainly needed it. The bottle was so clean and transparent that he felt young in his old age; but the note had been lost in the process.

Now the bottle was filled up with seeds: what kind they were the bottle didn't know. Again he was corked, and then wrapped in paper so tightly that not a bit of light came through. He could see neither the sun nor the moon; and the bottle felt that this was a great shame, for what is the point of traveling if you don't see anything? But travel it did; and it arrived safely at its destination and was unpacked.

"They certainly have been careful" — the bottle heard someone say — "but I suppose it has broken anyway." But the bottle was whole, and he understood every word that was said. They spoke his own language, the first one he had heard when he came red hot out of the melting pot: the language that had been spoken at the wine merchant's, at the picnic, and on the ship — his native tongue, the one he understood! The bottle had come home! Oh, what a lovely welcome sound! The bottle nearly jumped for pure joy out of the hands that had picked him up. He hardly felt the cork being drawn and the seeds being shaken out, so happy was he!

He was put down in a cellar, again to be hidden and forgotten by the world. But it's good to be home even when one has to stay in the cellar. The bottle did not even count the years and days he stayed there. Finally somebody came and removed all the bottles, himself included.

THE BOTTLE

The garden outside the house had been decorated. Colored lamps hung from all the trees and bushes; they looked like shining tulips. It was a lovely evening, perfectly still, and the sky was filled with stars. There was a new moon, a tiny sliver of silver surrounding a pale disk; it was a beautiful sight for those who look at beauty.

The paths at the edges of the garden were illuminated too — at least, enough so you could find your way. In the spaces between the bushes of the hedge, bottles with candles in them had been placed. Here, too, stood the bottle that was fated to end as a birdbath. He found the whole affair marvelously to his taste; here he stood, among the greenery, attending a party; he could hear laughter and music and all the sounds of gaiety. True, it came mostly from another part of the garden, where the colored lamps were hung. He had been placed in the more lonesome area; but that gave the bottle more time for reflection. He felt that he stood there not only for amusement and beauty but also because he was useful. Such a combination is superior and can make one forget the twenty years one has spent in the attic — and that sort of thing it is best to forget.

A young couple came walking by, arm in arm, just as the other young couple, on the day of the picnic, had: the tanner's daughter and the mate from the ship. The bottle felt that he was reliving something that had happened once before. Among the guests were some who had not been really invited but were allowed to come and look at the festivities. One of these was an old maid; she had no kin but she had friends. She was having exactly the same thoughts as the bottle; she was also recalling an afternoon spent in the woods, and a young couple walking arm in arm. She had been half of that sight and those had been the happiest moments of her life, and they are not forgotten, regardless of how old one becomes. She did not recognize the bottle nor he her.

That is the way of the world, we can pass each other unnoticed until we are introduced to each other again. And those two were to meet once more, now that they lived in the same town.

From the garden, the bottle was taken to the wine merchant, rinsed, and then once more filled with wine. It was sold to a balloonist, who, on the following Sunday, was to ascend into the sky in a balloon. A great crowd of people gathered to see the event and the regimental band played. The bottle saw all the preparations for the air voyage from a basket, where he lay together with a rabbit who was to be dropped down with a parachute on. The poor bunny, who knew its fate, looked anything but happy. The balloon grew and grew and finally rose from the ground when it couldn't grow any fatter; then the ropes that held it down were cut and it slowly ascended into the sky, carrying the basket with the balloonist, the bottle, and the frightened rabbit up into the air. The crowd below cheered and screamed: "Hurrah!"

"It is a strange feeling," thought the bottle. "It is another way of sailing but, at least, up here you can't run aground."

Many thousands of people were watching the balloon and the old maid in the garret was looking at it too. She was standing at her window, where the bird cage with the little songbird hung; at that time it did not have a glass birdbath but only a cracked cup that had lost its handle. On the window sill was a myrtle bush; the flowerpot had been moved a little out of the way so that the woman could lean out of the window and get a better view of the balloon.

She could see everything clearly: how the balloonist threw the rabbit out and its tiny parachute unfolded.

Now he was taking the bottle and uncorking it. He drank a toast to all the spectators. But he did not put the bottle back; instead he cast it high into the air. The old maid saw that too, but she did not know that this was the very bottle she had seen fly once before: in the springtime of her life, on that happy day in the green forest.

The bottle had hardly the time to think half a thought, not to talk of a whole one. The high point of his life had come and so unexpectedly! Far below him were the towers and roofs of the city; the people looked so tiny.

The bottle descended with quite a different speed than the rabbit had. The bottle performed somersaults as he fell; he had been half filled with wine, but soon that was gone. He felt so young, so joyful and gay. What a journey! The sun reflected in him and every person below was following him with their eyes.

The balloon was soon out of sight and so was the bottle; it fell on a roof and splintered. It hit with such force that all the little pieces danced and jumped, and did not rest before they had fallen all the way down into a yard. The neck of the bottle was whole; it looked as if it had been cut from the rest of the bottle with a diamond.

THE BOTTLE

"It would do as a birdbath," said the man who found it. He lived in a cellar. But since he had neither cage nor bird, he thought it a little expensive to buy them just because he had an old bottleneck that could be used as a birdbath. He remembered the old maid who lived up under the roof, she might find it useful.

A cork was put in the bottleneck, and it was hung upside down in the cage of the little bird that sang so beautifully. Now it was filled with fresh water instead of wine; and what used to be "up" was "down," but that is the sort of change that sometimes does happen in this world.

"Yes, you can sing," sighed the bottleneck, who had had so many adventures. The bird and the old maid knew only of the most recent one when he had been up in a balloon.

Now the bottle had become a birdbath; he could hear the rumble of the traffic down in the street and the voice of the mistress talking to an old friend. They were not talking about the bottleneck but about the myrtle bush in the window.

"There is no reason for you to spend two crowns on a bridal bouquet for your daughter," the old maid was saying. "I will cut you a beautiful one from my bush. You remember the myrtle bush you gave me the day after I had become engaged? Well, the little bush over in the window is a cutting from that one. You hoped that I would cut my bridal bouquet from it, but that day never came. Those eyes are closed that should have shone for me and been the happiness of my life. On the bottom of the sea he sleeps now, my beloved. The bush you gave me became old, but I became even older. When it was just about to die, I cut a branch from it and planted it. Look how it has thrived; finally, it will attend a wedding: your daughter's."

There were tears in the old woman's eyes as she talked about the young man who had loved her when she was young. She recalled his toast and the first kiss he had given her; but that she did not tell about, for she was truly an old maid. No matter how much she thought about the past, it never occurred to her that just outside the window, in the bird cage, hung a witness to those times: the neck of the very bottle that had contained the wine with which her engagement had been celebrated. The bottleneck did not recognize her either, nor did he listen to what she was saying, but that was mostly because the bottleneck never thought about anyone but himself.

THE PHILOSOPHER'S STONE

You remember the story about Holger the Dane? I don't want to tell it to you; I am only asking to find out whether you remember how Holger won great India, which stretches east as far as the end of the world, where grows a tree called the Tree of the Sun. As Christian Pedersen says — you don't know who Christian Pedersen is? Well, that doesn't matter, it is of no importance whether you know him or not. Holger the Dane made the priest Jon ruler over all of Indialand. You have never heard of priest Jon? Well, never mind, he is not really important either; he is not in the story at all. What I want to tell you about is the Tree of the Sun, that stands in Indialand, which stretches east to the end of the world. Once anyone would have understood immediately what I was talking about; but that was before one was taught geography in the manner that we are now — and that, too, is of no importance.

The Tree of the Sun was magnificent; I have never seen it and neither will you. Its crown was the size of a whole forest and was miles and miles around. Its limbs were so gigantic that their crooked shapes were like dales and hills; they were covered with moss as soft as velvet, in which the most beautiful flowers grew. Every branch and twig that protruded from the main boughs was a tree, and each was different from all the others: one was a palm tree, another a beech tree, a third a plane tree; all the kinds of trees

HANS CHRISTIAN ANDERSEN

in the whole world were there. The sun was always shining on it, for truly it was the Tree of the Sun. Birds from all corners of the world visited it. They came from the forests of America, the rose gardens of Denmark, and the jungles of Africa, where elephants and lions believe that they are the rulers. Birds from both the poles came; and naturally, the swallows and the storks were there as well. Not only birds lived in the Tree of the Sun; deer, antelope, squirrels, and thousands of other animals made their home there.

The crown of the tree was like a fragrant garden, and in the very center of it, where the great limbs were high hills, there was a crystal palace; and from its towers you could see all the countries of the world. The towers were shaped like lilies. Their huge stems were hollow and you could climb them because there were staircases inside. Every leaf was a balcony; you could step out on it and admire the view. And in the tallest flower was a round hall that had no other roof than the blue sky with its sun and stars. The lower chambers of the castle were magnificent, too, though in a different manner. On their polished walls the whole world was mirrored, and you could see what was happening everywhere. You did not have to read a newspaper, which was lucky because there wasn't any. The pictures on the walls were alive and moving; they showed everything that was taking place, no matter where it was happening; all one had to have were the time and the desire to look. But too much is too much, even for the wisest of men; and it was he who lived in that castle: the wisest of all mankind. His name was so difficult to pronounce that you wouldn't be able to say it, so there's no point in my mentioning it: it is of no importance.

He knew everything that a man can hope to know while on earth. He knew about every invention that had already been made and all those that ever would be; but no more than that, for everything has its limits. He was twice as wise as old King Solomon, who was known for his wisdom. He understood the powers of nature and ruled over them; Death himself had to bring him a list of those who were to die. One thought, however, disquieted the mighty ruler of the castle in the Tree of the Sun, and this was that King Solomon had died. In his fate, he saw his own; and although he had raised himself even higher than Solomon had above the rest of humanity, through knowledge and wisdom, he would someday die too; and so would his children. Like leaves on the trees, they

THE PHILOSOPHER'S STONE

would wizen, fall to earth, and become dust. The generations of man were like leaves, he thought: new leaves always unfolded to take the place of the old, but those that withered never lived again; they became fertilizer for other plants.

What happened to the human being after the angel of death visited him? What did it mean, to die? The body disintegrated, but the soul — yes, what was the soul? What happened to it? Where did it go?

Religion, man's solace, said: "To an everlasting life." But how was the transition possible? Where and how did the soul live? The pious answered: "We are going to heaven above."

"Above," repeated the wisest of men, and looked toward the sun and the stars. But he knew that the world was a globe; and above and below depended upon where you stood on it. He knew, too, that if he climbed the highest mountain on earth, then the "clear blue sky," which we see, would appear black below him. The sun would be a glowing ball without its rays, and the earth itself seem to be in a shroud of orange mist. Limited is the power of our sight and so much knowledge is denied our souls. How little we know, even the wisest of us. How few of the questions that most concern us can we find answers to.

In a small chamber of the castle lay the greatest treasure on earth, the Book of Truth. Everyone may read it, but only a short section at a time. For many eyes the letters quiver and move so much on the page that they cannot make out the words. In some places the print is so faded that the pages appear blank. The wiser one is, the more one can read. And the wisest of all men, who lived in the middle of the Tree of the Sun, could read more than anyone else. He knew how to collect the light of the sun, of stars, and of the hidden powers of the spirit and make them illuminate the pages, so that even the most difficult parts became easy to read. But the chapter titled, "Life after Death," remained a perfect blank, even to him. This made the wisest of men very sad. He speculated and speculated as to how he could find, here on earth, a light strong enough to bring forth the letters, so that he could read what was written in the Book of Truth on that subject.

Just like the wise King Solomon, he understood the language of the animals, but that did not help in this matter. He found herbs and metals, medicines that could cure sickness, remove death for a while; but in none did he find anything that could destroy death

HANS CHRISTIAN ANDERSEN

itself. In everything and everywhere did he search for a light that could make it possible for him to read the chapter about "Life after Death." But he did not find it; the Book of Truth lay open in front of him with its blank page. The Bible of Christianity promises in words of consolation an everlasting life, but he was not satisfied with that. He wanted to read it in his own book and he couldn't.

He had five children: four sons, brought up as only the wisest father could do it, and one daughter. She was beautiful, gentle, and clever, but blind. This affliction did not seem to trouble her; her father and her brothers were her eyes and her own pure nature the judge of everything she heard.

The sons had never been farther away from the castle than the great branches reached. The sister had not even been that far; they were happy being children in the land of childhood, in the fragrant magic world of the Tree of the Sun. Like all other children, they loved to be told stories, and their father told them many tales and strange things, which ordinary children might not have understood; but they were as wise as the most mature people among us are. He helped them to understand the living, moving pictures on the wall of the castle, which showed the ways of men and the events that were happening in the whole world.

Many times his young sons expressed a wish to take part in the struggles they were seeing on the walls and to perform great deeds of valor. Then their father would sigh and say: "The ways of the world are bitter and filled with grief. What you see is not reality, for you watch it from the safe world of childhood and that makes all the difference." He spoke to them about beauty, goodness, and truth: the three concepts that kept the world from falling apart; and how the pressure that the world inflicted on goodness, beauty, and truth transformed them into a precious stone that was far more beautiful than any diamond. This gem was, in truth, the philosopher's stone. Their father explained that, just as you became more certain of God's existence by studying nature, so by studying man did you become assured that this jewel called the philosopher's stone, existed too. He could not tell any more about it, for he knew no more. Now this would have been very difficult for other children to understand, but these children could; and we may hope that, later on, others will understand it as well.

The children asked their father to tell them what beauty, goodness, and truth were and he did. He told them, too, how God had

THE PHILOSOPHER'S STONE

created the first human being out of clay and then had kissed His creation five times: five kisses of fire, five kisses from the heart. These kisses from God gave us our five senses; with them and through them we understand, feel, and protect beauty, goodness, and truth. The five senses are our sensitivity both outward toward the world and inward into our souls; they are the root and the flower of the human plant.

The children thought and thought about what their father had told them; indeed, it was never out of their minds. One night the oldest brother had a marvelous dream, and the strangest part of it was that his three brothers dreamed the same dream. Each of them had dreamed that he had journeyed out into the world, found the philosopher's stone, and returned bearing it as a living flame on his forehead. Each one had come home riding on his horse, over the velvet boughs of the Tree of the Sun to his father's castle, just as the sun was rising. The light that shone from the jewel had clearly illuminated the pages of the Book of Truth, so that they could read what was written there about life beyond the grave. Their sister had not had the dream; she had no thought of going out into the wide world, her world was her father's house.

"I will ride out into the wide world," declared the wise man's oldest son. "That is a journey I must make. I want to take part in the affairs of men. Goodness and truth shall I serve, and they will guard beauty. Much will be different once I am part of the world." Yes, these were courageous words: the kind that are easy to say in front of the fireplace in your father's house, before you have been in a storm or felt the bramble's thorns.

The four brothers had five senses just as everyone else has, and they were excellent in all of them, but each brother had especially developed one of his senses. The oldest brother had a sense of sight that was far stronger than is usual. He could see the past as well as the present. He could see all the countries of the world at once, and under the earth, where its treasures are hidden. He could see into other human beings as if their chests were windows, so he knew more than the rest of us, who have to be satisfied with being able to guess what a blush on the cheek or a tear in the eye means. The deer and the antelope accompanied him as far as the western border; from there he followed the flight of the wild swans toward the northwest; and soon he was far away from his father's realm that stretched east to the end of the world.

HANS CHRISTIAN ANDERSEN

How wide he opened his eyes! There was a lot to look at. And it is very different to see things with your own eyes than to look at them in pictures, regardless of how marvelous the pictures are, and the ones he had seen in his father's castle had been excellent. So surprised was he when he saw the trash, the cheap tinsel that mankind considered beautiful, that his eyes almost popped out of his head; but he held onto them, for he needed his eyes for the deeds he wanted to do.

Wholeheartedly and steadfastly he went to work for the cause of beauty, truth, and goodness. But all too often he saw ugliness receive the praise that should have been given to beauty. The good was hardly noticed, while mediocrity was applauded instead of being criticized. People looked at a man's name, not at his deeds; his appearance and not his character; his position and not how he fulfilled it. But that is the way of the world and it cannot be different.

"There is work enough for me," he said, and began at once. He sought truth; but when he found it, the Devil — the Father of all Lies — was there too. The Devil would have liked to put out the seer's eyes at once, but he thought that too crude. The Devil prefers to do things in a refined way. He let the young man look at truth and beauty, and goodness as well; but while he was looking at them, the Devil blew motes into his eyes: one into each of them. Then he blew on the motes until they became beams, and his sight was no more. The seer was blind! There he stood in the middle of the wide world, not trusting it and not trusting himself; and once you have given up both the world and yourself, then it is all over.

"All over," sang the wild swans that flew across the ocean toward the east.

"All over," chirped the swallows on their way toward the Tree of the Sun; and the tidings they brought were not good.

"The seer did not succeed," said the second brother. "Maybe he who hears will fare better." The second brother had developed his sense of hearing so much that he could hear the grass grow.

He said good-by to his father, his two brothers, and his sister, mounted his horse, and rode away filled with the very best intentions. The swallows followed him, and he followed the swans, and soon he was far from home, out in the wide world.

But one can get too much of a good thing, and that the second brother found only too true. For he heard not only the grass grow,

THE PHILOSOPHER'S STONE

but every human heartbeat, both in joy and in sorrow. The world was like a watchmaker's shop and all the watches were going tick-tock and the great clocks were striking ding-dong. It was more than anyone could bear! He kept listening as long as he could, but at last all the noise and din were too much for him. Street urchins screamed and shouted. Some of them were sixty years old, for it is not age but behavior that makes a guttersnipe, though they were really more amusing than annoying. He heard gossip whistling through all the streets and alleys, and lies shouting that they were the masters of the world. The bells on the fool's cap claimed that they were church bells. Oh, it was all too much for the young man!

He put his fingers into both his ears but that didn't help. He could still hear the singer who sang out of tune, the clamor of evil, the voices of slander and pompous chatter, the stubborn shouting of worthless ideas till they were recited in a chorus like thunder. Everywhere there was sound: marching, crying, clattering, screeching, wailing, banging. It was too frightening, too horrible! Deeper and deeper he dug his fingers into his ears; and finally the eardrums burst. Now he could hear nothing at all. Beauty, truth, and goodness were silenced too. His hearing, which was the bridge for his thoughts, was gone. He grew silent and suspicious and trusted no one, not even himself. That was a great misfortune. He would never find the philosopher's stone and take it back to his father's castle. He abandoned his search and he abandoned himself; and the second was worse than the first. The birds that flew east to the Tree of the Sun brought the message. He wrote no letter, for there was no mail service.

"Now it is my turn," said the third brother. "I have a nose for the work." That was not the most elegant way to express oneself, but that was the manner in which he usually spoke, and one had to take him as he was. He had a cheerful disposition and he was a poet, a real one who could say in verse what couldn't be said in prose. He perceived many things long before other people could.

"I can smell a rat," he would boast; and in truth, it was sense of smell that he had especially developed. This made him an expert on beauty, he felt. "Some love the smell of apples, others the odor in a stable," he said. "Each region of smell in beauty's realm has its adherents. Some feel most at home in the smoke-filled atmosphere of cheap cafés, where tallow candles smoke rather than burn, and the odor of stale beer mixes with the stink from cheap tobacco.

HANS CHRISTIAN ANDERSEN

Others like the pungent perfume of the jasmine flowers, or they rub their bodies with oil of cloves and that smell is not easy to get rid of. Some seek the clean air of the seashore and others climb mountains to be able to look down upon the trivial life below!" This he said before he had left his father's house; one would think he already knew the world of man, but he didn't. It was the poetical part of him that had spoken: the gift of imagination that God had given him while he lay in his cradle.

He bade good-by to his father's house in the Tree of the Sun. He did not ride away on a horse; no, he mounted an ostrich, for that could run faster. But as soon as he saw the wild swans he picked out the strongest among them and rode on that instead, for he liked a change. He flew across the ocean to foreign lands, where great forests surrounded deep lakes, and there were huge mountains and proud cities. Wherever he flew, the sun broke forth from behind dark clouds. Every flower, every bush smelled more fragrant, as if they wanted to do their very best, while such a friend and protector of odors was near them. Yes, even an ill-tended rose hedge, that was half dead, unfolded new leaves and bloomed. Its single flower was particularly lovely, even the black slug saw the beauty of the little rose.

"I will put my mark on it," the slug said. "I will spit on it, for more I cannot do for anyone."

"That is the fate of beauty in this world," said the poet. He composed a little song about it, and he sang it himself; but no one listened to it. So he gave the town crier two silver coins and a peacock feather as payment; and he shouted the song, accompanied by his drum, through all the streets and squares. Then people listened and said that they understood it — it was so profound. Now the poet composed other songs about beauty, goodness, and truth. They were listened to in the cafés, where the tallow candles smoked; and they were heard in the fragrant meadow, the forest, and on the boundless sea. It seemed he would be more successful than his two other brothers.

This did not please the Devil. He came at once, bringing with him large portions of incense. There were all kinds: royal and ecclesiastical, and the very strongest that the Devil distills, which is brewed from honor, glory, and fame. It is potent enough to make even an angel dizzy, not to speak of a poet. The Devil knows how to catch everyone; and the youngest brother was caught with

THE PHILOSOPHER'S STONE

incense. He couldn't get enough of it and soon he had forgotten his quest and his home as well as himself; he went up in smoke, the smoke of incense.

When the little birds heard it they became ever so sorrowful; they mourned so deeply that they did not sing for three whole days. The slug became even blacker than he was before, but that was because he was envious, not because he mourned.

"It was I that gave him the idea," he claimed, "they should have burned incense for me. I inspired his famous song for drums about the ways of the world. It was I who spat on the rose; and I have witnesses to prove it."

But back in Indialand, which stretches east to the end of the world, they heard no news. All the little birds had mourned for three days and not sung a note. They had felt their sorrow so intensely that by the time the three days were over they had forgotten what it was they had been mourning over; that happens in this world.

"Maybe I'd better go out into the world and get lost too," said the fourth brother. He had a sense of humor, although he wasn't a poet, which was a good enough reason for his feeling happy. The two younger brothers had brought gaiety and laughter to the castle, and now they both would be gone.

Sight and hearing have always been considered the most important of the senses, the ones it is a virtue to develop. The others are considered lesser; but that was not the opinion of the fourth brother. He had developed his taste, in the widest sense of the word, and he thought that taste was the real governor of everything. It ruled over not only what went through the mouth but what went into the soul as well. He stuck a finger into every pot and pan, and every barrel and bottle, to taste what was in them; but that was the coarser part of his duties. To him every human being was a pot in which a dinner was cooking and every country in the world a kitchen — in a spiritual sense, of course. Now this he considered the finer duty of taste and he was eager to try it.

"Maybe I will have more luck than my brothers," he said. "But what means of transportation should I choose? Is the balloon invented?" he asked his father, who knew about all the inventions that had been made or were ever going to be made; but he was told that no one had thought of a balloon yet; nor had steamships or railways been invented.

HANS CHRISTIAN ANDERSEN

"I will take a balloon anyway," he declared. "My father knows how to make one; and I will learn how to steer it as I fly. Everyone who sees me will think that he is seeing a mirage. As soon as I get to my destination I will burn the balloon; therefore, I'd better have a few of those future inventions called sulphur matches, too."

He received all he had asked for, and away he flew. The birds followed him farther than they had his brothers; they wanted to see how that flight would end. Other birds joined them. They, too, were curious; they thought the balloon was a new kind of bird. He certainly had company. The air was black with birds; they looked like a cloud, a locust swarm from Egypt. Soon he was far out in the wide world.

"The east wind is certainly a true friend and a great help to me," he said.

"You mean the east and the west," said the winds. "If we both hadn't helped you, you couldn't have sailed northwest."

He didn't hear what the winds said; and it really doesn't matter whether he did or not for our story. The birds got tired of following him. When the flock was largest, two of the birds had declared that too much was being made of the balloonist; he would get a swollen head from it.

"It is nothing to follow, after all it is only air, we find it degrading," one said to the other.

They stayed behind; and so did all the other birds. "A balloon is nothing," they all agreed.

Finally the balloon descended above a big city. The balloonist searched for the highest place in the town; it was a tall church spire. There he sat down so that he could observe what was going on; the balloon flew away, which was not according to plan. What happened to it I don't know — and it doesn't matter; after all, it hadn't been invented yet.

He sat on the very top of the spire all alone; the birds were tired of him and he of them. Out of all of the city's chimneys came smoke and smell.

"They are altars raised for your sake," said the wind, who wanted to pay him a compliment.

The fourth brother looked down in the street below him and watched the passers-by: one was proud of his money; the next of his keys, though they opened nothing; a third of his clothes, though moths would eat them; a fourth of his body, though worms would eat that.

THE PHILOSOPHER'S STONE

"Vanity! I think I will have to stir this soup a little and taste it," he said. "But not right away; I will stay here for a while. The wind blows so nicely on my back; it is very enjoyable. I think I will stay as long as it comes from the same direction. I need a little peace in order to think. 'It is best to sleep late in the morning if one has a hard day's work ahead,' say the lazy. Laziness is the root of all evil, but there is no evil in me or in my family. That's what I say and the world agrees with me. I will stay as long as that wind blows, it is just to my taste."

The fourth brother, the one who had developed taste, stayed right where he was. He was sitting on top of the weather vane, and when it turned, he turned with it, so the wind always blew on his back. We will leave him there, he can sit there forever and taste.

But the castle in the center of the Tree of the Sun seemed empty now that all the brothers had gone, one after the other.

"I am afraid that they have fared badly," said their father. "They will never bring back the brilliant stone. It will never be found. They are gone! They are dead!" He bent over the Book of Truth and stared at the page on which he should have been able to read about the life after death, but he could see nothing.

His blind daughter was his only consolation, his only joy, and she loved him dearly. For his happiness' sake she wished that the jewel would be found and brought home to the castle. She longed for her brothers, and thought sadly about where they could be and whether they were still alive. She wished fervently that she would dream about them; but even in her dreams she never saw them. Finally one night she dreamed that she heard their voices; they called to her from the wide world. She had had to follow them. She was far, far away and at the same time in her father's house, as is possible in dreams. She did not meet her brothers, but she felt something in her hand. It burned like fire but did not pain her; it was the philosopher's stone, the gem that her father desired so much, and she took it to him.

When she woke she thought that she still held the jewel in her hand, but it was a spindle from her spinning wheel. Through the night she had spun a thread finer than that which spiders make. It was so thin that the human eye could not see it, and yet because it had been moistened by her tears it was as strong as the anchor tow of a ship.

She rose from her bed. She felt that the dream had to be realized. It was still night and her father was sleeping. She kissed his hand

and, taking the spindle, she fastened one end of the thread to her father's house — for otherwise, being blind, she would not be able to find her way back — and set out into the wide world. She trusted that the thread would guide her home. From the Tree of the Sun she picked four leaves. These she would give to the wind that it might take one to each of her brothers as a greeting if she did not meet them.

How would she fare, this poor blind child? She had the invisible thread and she had one quality that her brothers had not had, which would serve her well: devotion. It gave her eyes on each of her fingers and made it possible for her to hear with her heart.

Out into the strange, turbulent world she walked; and wherever she went, the sun would shine so she could feel its warmth and a rainbow would span from the dark clouds to the clear blue sky. She heard the birds sing and smelled the orange groves and apple orchards so intensely that she could almost taste the fruits. She heard soft and lovely music, sweet songs of joy, but also discordant screams. It was a strange duet; the verses were at war with each other; it was humanity's thoughts and judgments she was listening to.

> Life is a dungeon dark and deep,
> A night in which we weep.

Then another voice sang:

> Life is the rose on the vine
> And every day the sun does shine.

Then a more bitter voice was heard:

> Man's life in self-interest is spent,
> That truth is evident.

But still another voice argued:

> Love's river winds its way,
> Changing November into May.

Then a whining voice mocked:

> Everything is small and mean
> And truth on lies will lean.

THE PHILOSOPHER'S STONE

A moment later another sang:

> Truth and goodness are strong.
> Right always outlives wrong.

Then many voices in a great chorus sang:

> Make fun of all, sneer and attack,
> Bark with the dogs in the pack.

This was not answered by the world but by a voice that came from the blind girl's heart:

> Trust yourself and trust your God,
> And let His will be done. Amen.

Wherever the girl came, among young or old, women or men, her devotion brought forth truth, goodness, and beauty. She brought a ray of light — a ray of hope — into the artist's workshop, the salons of the rich, and even into the dismal factories where great wheels clattered and turned. She was like the drop of dew that falls on a thirsting plant.

That was more than the Devil could allow. He has more brains than ten thousand men. He found a way to put a stop to it. He took the bubbles that form in the rotten waters of a swamp and caused the sevenfold echoes of lies to pass over them in order to make them stronger. Then he made a powder of false obituaries, verses of homage for which the poets had been paid, and sermons for which the preacher expected to be paid. This he dissolved and cooked in tears that envy had shed; at last he sprinkled a little powder from a vain old maid's cheek into it. Out of this brew he constructed a girl who in appearance and movement was a perfect copy of the blind girl, whom humanity had given the name "The Angel of Devotion." The Devil had begun his game, for the world did not know which of the two girls was the true one. And how should humanity know? After all, they looked alike.

The poor blind girl repeated to herself the words she had sung before:

> Trust yourself and trust your God,
> And let His will be done. Amen.

Then she gave the four leaves that she had plucked from the Tree of the Sun to the winds that they might deliver them to her

HANS CHRISTIAN ANDERSEN

brothers. She felt certain that they would receive them, just as she had been sure that jewel that was more precious than all others would be found and brought to her father's house.

"My father's house." The girl said the words out loud. "Yes, here on earth the gem is to be found, here is its hiding place. I am bringing back something more than my mere certainty of its existence: I feel within my closed hand the glow of the jewel. I can feel it pulse and swell. Every little grain of truth that the wind carried have I caught and kept. I have let them absorb the odor of beauty — and I took the sound of the human heart beating for the good, and added that. It is nothing but dust; but from these grains the jewel is formed. Look, my hand is filled with it!"

With the speed of thought she had returned to father's house following the invisible thread. Now she held out her hand to him.

The evil one brewed a storm and whipped the Tree of the Sun; the doors to the castle sprang open and the wings of the wind rushed through the chambers.

"It will blow away!" shouted the father, and grabbed his daughter's hand.

"No," she shouted back at him. "It cannot be blown away, for I feel that its warmth and power have entered my soul."

The shining dust was blown from her hand. Like a flame, it flew across the page of the Book of Truth on which one could read about the eternal life. The page was no longer blank. One word in illuminated letters was written there, one single word:

FAITH!

The four brothers had returned; they had felt a longing for their home when the leaves from the tree fell on their chests, and they had obeyed it. The birds, the deer, and antelope, yes, all the animals of the forest had come to join in their gladness. And why shouldn't they, when they were allowed to?

As you have often seen when a single ray of light shines through a keyhole into a dark room, a shiny column of dust appears. Much more splendid than this — even more colorful than the rainbow — glittered and sparkled the word "FAITH" on the page, made as it was from grains of truth mixed with beauty and goodness. It shone more powerfully than the column of fire did that night when Moses and the people of Israel left for the Land of Canaan. From the word "FAITH" begins the bridge of hope that leads to the All-loving, to eternity.

HOW TO COOK SOUP
UPON A SAUSAGE PIN

In all countries there are old sayings that everyone knows, even the school children, and it is hard to understand that the rest of the world does not know them too. Such a familiar expression in Danish is "to cook soup upon a sausage pin." It means to make a lot out of nothing; gossips and journalists are experts at preparing this dish. But what is a sausage pin? It is a small wooden peg used for closing the sausage skin after the meat has been stuffed into it; you can imagine how strong a soup one could cook on that. Well, that was the introduction; it contained information and that is always useful. Now I can begin the story.

"It was a delightful dinner last night!" exclaimed an old female mouse to an acquaintance, who had not been invited to the party. "I was seated number twenty-one from the right of the old mouse king, and that is a respectable place. Shall I tell you what we ate? It was a very well-composed dinner. Moldy bread, pork crackling, tallow candles, and sausages; and everyone was served everything twice; it was as good as getting two meals. The atmosphere was most congenial, everyone spoke the most charming nonsense just as they would have at home. Everything was eaten; the only things left were the sausage pins. And that is the reason why we talked about them and the saying 'to cook soup upon a sausage pin.' Everybody had heard the expression but no one had ever tasted the soup or knew how it was made. We drank a toast to its inventor;

267

HANS CHRISTIAN ANDERSEN

he deserved to be made director of a poorhouse! Now wasn't that witty? The old mouse king stood up and made a promise that he would marry the young mouse who could make the best-tasting soup cooked upon a sausage pin. She would become his queen; and he gave the female mice a year and a day to find out how it was done."

"That is fair enough!" said the second mouse. "But tell me, how do you make it?"

"Yes, how does one cook soup upon a sausage pin? That is what everybody asked, both the young and the old. They all wanted to be queen; but no one knew how and few wanted to trouble themselves by going out into the wide world to find out, and that seemed necessary. It is not so easy to leave one's family — the old familiar nooks and corners where one might stumble over a cheese rind or smell pork crackling — to go out in the world and risk starvation — or an even worse fate: to be eaten alive by a cat!"

It was probably thoughts like these that kept most of the young female mice from leaving their homes in order to find the recipe. But four young and very poor mice declared that they would try their luck; they would each go to one of the corners of the world and see whom fortune smiled upon. They were each given a sausage pin so that they wouldn't forget why they were traveling; they could use them as walking canes.

It was in the beginning of May when they left; and a year later on the first of May they were back. But only three of them; the fourth one did not arrive, though the day of trial and decision had come!

"Why must there always be sadness mixed with joy?" said the mouse king, while he sent out invitations to all the mice within miles. They were to meet in the royal kitchen, for that was the most appropriate place to hold the contest. The three mice who had been out traveling were lined up in a row; where the fourth should have stood was placed a sausage pin with black crepe around it. No one dared say anything before the three mice had spoken and the king had given his judgment. Now we shall hear what happened!

WHAT THE FIRST LITTLE MOUSE HAD HEARD AND LEARNED ON HER JOURNEY

"When I started on my journey out into the wide world," began the little mouse, "I thought, as most young mice do, that I knew

HOW TO COOK SOUP UPON A SAUSAGE PIN

just about everything there is to know; but in that I was mistaken; it takes years and days to grow wise. I found a ship that was sailing north and sailed on it, for I had heard that a cook on board a boat has to learn to make much out of nothing. But the pantry was filled with bacon and barrels full of salt pork. We lived well; and it was no place to learn how to cook soup upon a sausage pin. We sailed many days and nights. The ship rolled and tossed, and the place was too damp for my taste. When we arrived at our destination I disembarked; that was far up north!

"It is strange to come from one's own nook, sail on a ship that is also a kind of nook, and then come out into the wide world. The ship had become a little like home; and once I left it I realized that I was more than a hundred miles away in a foreign country! Great forests stretched farther than the eye could see, all of them were pine and birch; they smelled so fresh and strong, I found it very unpleasant. The wild flowers had such a spicy odor that they made me sneeze. I was thinking of sausages all the time. The water in the lakes looked clear enough at the shore, but when you looked at them from a distance they were black as ink. There was something white floating on the surface; at first I thought it was foam, but I found out that it was swans. I saw them fly and walk, too. When you have seen a swan walk, then you know that it is a cousin of a goose: it waddles; there is no way of hiding the family that one belongs to. I stayed with my own kind, the field mice; they were, however, ignorant of finer culinary art, and that, after all, was the purpose of my journey. That it was possible to cook soup upon a sausage pin was to them such an absurd idea that soon the whole forest knew about it. They all deemed it impossible; and at that moment I would never have guessed that that very night I was to learn how it is done.

"It was midsummer, that was why the forest smelled so strong and the flowers so spicy, and the lakes where the swans swam looked so black. At the edge of the forest near a little cluster of houses, a pole as tall as the mast of a ship had been raised. On its very top hung a wreath and colored ribbons: it was a maypole. Young people were dancing around it and singing, while the violins played. Oh, it was a gay sight, as the sun set; and later on, too, as the moon rose, but I didn't join them; after all, a little mouse does not belong at a dance. I sat in the soft moss and held onto my sausage pin.

"The moonlight fell especially on a spot beneath a big tree where the moss was particularly soft and delicate — if I dared I would say that it was as exquisite as the mouse king's fur! It was green and healthy for the eyes to look at. Suddenly a band of little creatures came; they were so small that they only reached my knees. They looked like human beings, but their proportions made them far lovelier. They called themselves elves. Their clothes were made from the petals of flowers, embroidered with the wings of flies and mosquitoes, which looked very fetching indeed. They appeared to be looking for something; I couldn't make out what it was.

"Two of them came over to me; the most distinguished of them pointed at my sausage pin and said, 'This is exactly what we need! It had been cut to the right size.' The more he looked at my walking cane, the happier he became.

"'You may borrow it but not keep it,' said I.

"'Not keep it,' repeated all the little creatures who now had gathered around my pin. I let go of it and they carried it over to the spot where the moss was so particularly soft; and there in the center they raised the sausage pin. They wanted a maypole too; and I must admit, the pin was just the right size for them. Then they decorated it and that was a beautiful sight!

"Tiny little spiders spun golden threads all around it; and on these veils and banners were hung; they were so white that they hurt one's eyes to look upon. They had been bleached in moonlight. Colors gathered from butterflies' wings were sprinkled on the white linen; and then the banners and veils looked like flowers and glittered like diamonds. I could hardly recognize my old sausage pin. Such a maypole as it became you could not match in the whole world. Not until now did the main party of the elves arrive. They had no clothes on at all, because among elves that is considered most elegant. I was invited to attend the party, but at a distance, because I was too big.

"Now began the music! It was as if a thousand glass bells were being struck. At first I thought that swans were singing; then I believed that I recognized the voices of the thrush and the cuckoo. 'All the forest is singing,' I thought. I seemed to hear children's voices and birds' songs and glass bells all merging in the most beautiful melodies. And all that lovely music came from the elves' maypole, which was nothing but my sausage pin! I couldn't believe that so much could be made out of a wooden peg, but I suppose that everything depends not upon the material but upon whose hands form it. I was so touched that I cried for joy as only a little mouse can.

"The night was all too short, but that far north it isn't very long at that time of the year. As day broke, there came a breeze; ripples appeared upon the surface of the lake, and all the banners and veils disappeared into the air, as did the bridges and balconies the spiders had strung from leaf to leaf in the trees. Six elves brought the sausage pin back and asked me if I had any wish that they could grant me. I begged them to tell me how one cooked soup on a sausage pin.

" 'How we do it you have already seen,' laughed their leader. 'I am sure even you did not recognize your old sausage pin.'

" 'But that was not cooking soup,' I said, and explained why I had set out on my travels and what I was expected to find out. 'What use is it to our king, or to our great kingdom, that I have seen this wonderful sight? I can't shake it out of the pin while I declare: "Here comes the soup!" Though I suppose it would do as a dish for the mind after one's stomach was filled.'

"The elf dipped his finger in a blue violet and said to me, 'Watch, now I will stroke your walking cane, and when you have returned to the mouse king's palace, then touch the warm, royal chest of the king with the cane and immediately violets will be growing all the way up the stick; and that even if it is the middle of the winter. That is a gift worth bringing home and I will give you something more. . . .' "

But before the little mouse told what else the elf had given her, she touched the chest of the king and immediately the loveliest bouquet of flowers sprang forth. It smelled so strongly that the mouse king ordered the mice who stood nearest the fire to put their tails into it so that the smell of singeing hair could clear the air. The odor of violets was not a favorite; everyone found it nauseating.

"Yes," said the little mouse, "that, I believe, is what is called the first course." She turned; the sausage pin and the flowers were gone and she stood with the bare stick in her hand. Now she lifted it as if it were a conductor's baton.

" 'Violets are for sight, smell, and feeling,' said the elf to me, 'but I will give you something, too, to please hearing and taste.' "

Now the little mouse swung her baton and the music began — not the kind she had heard in the forest when the elves held their ball; no, it was the kind fit for a kitchen. What a lot of noise! It was as though the wind suddenly were whirling down the chimney and through all the stovepipes. Pots and kettles boiled over. The big frying pan clattered as if it were going to jump down on the floor; then suddenly all was silent and you could hear the little tea-kettle's solitary song. It sounded so strange; it had neither a beginning nor an end. Then the pots and pans began again; they did not care for harmony but sang each its own song. The little mouse swung her baton more and more wildly. Again the pots boiled over and the wind shot down the chimney. Ugh! it was a frightening racket; and at last the little mouse got so scared herself that she dropped the baton: her sausage pin.

"That was strong soup," said the old mouse king. "Are you going to serve it now?"

"That was all," declared the little mouse, and curtsied.

"Was that all?" said the mouse king. "Well, let us hear what the next one has to tell us."

WHAT THE SECOND LITTLE MOUSE HAD TO TELL

"I was born in the royal library," began the second mouse. "Neither my family nor I had ever had the pleasure of being in a dining room, not to speak of a larder. Not before I had traveled did I see a kitchen like the one we are gathered in. Frankly, we starved in the library; but we did acquire knowledge. The rumor reached us about the royal reward that had been promised the one who could cook soup upon a sausage pin. My old grandmother drew forth a manuscript wherein it was written — she couldn't read herself, but had heard it once read aloud — that poets could cook soup upon a sausage pin. Now she asked me if I was a poet. I told her no, whereupon she told me to become one.

" 'But how does one do that?' I asked, for that seemed to me as difficult as cooking soup. But my grandmother, who had listened to a lot of books being read out loud, said that three ingredients were necessary, namely: intelligence, fantasy, and feeling! If I could manage to get those things inside me, then I would be a poet, and the problem of the sausage pin would be easily solved.

"I walked west, out into the wide world, to become a poet.

"I knew that intelligence was the most important, the other two parts were not nearly as respected. Therefore I set out to acquire

HOW TO COOK SOUP UPON A SAUSAGE PIN

intelligence first; but where was it to be found? Go to the ant to become wise, an old king of the Jews had once said. This I knew from the library, so I went straight for the nearest anthill and hid near it, in order to become wise.

"They are a very respectable nation, the ants; they are pure intelligence. Everything in their world is solved as though it were an arithmetic problem; it is all figured out. To work and lay eggs, they say, is living: both in your own time and in the future; and that is what they do. They are divided into the clean ants and the dirty. All ranks are numbered: the queen ant is number one, and her opinions are the only ones that count, for she has swallowed all the wisdom there is.

"Now that was very important for me to know. She said so much that was so clever that I found it stupid. She said that the top of her anthill was the highest point in the world; it was built right next to an old oak tree, and that the oak tree was much higher than the anthill could not be disputed; so the ants never talked about the tree. One day one of the ants, having lost its way, climbed up the trunk of the tree. It didn't get to the top but just a bit of the way up. When it returned home to the hill, it told everyone of the discovery it had made: that there existed in the world outside something much taller than their hill. The ants found this an insult to them, to their nation, and to society. The ant who had made the discovery was condemned to wear a muzzle and to spend the rest of its life in solitary confinement. A short time later, another ant made the same journey and came to the same conclusion. He, too, spoke about his discovery but in a learned and vague manner. Since he was a very respectable ant and belonged to the faction called 'clean,' the other ants believed him. When he died an eggshell was put up as a monument to him, for all the ants agreed that they respected science.

"I noticed," continued the little mouse, "that the ants carried their eggs on their backs. One of them lost hers and in spite of her strenuous efforts could not get them up on her back again. . . . Two other female ants came running over to help her. They pushed and they shoved until they were almost about to lose their own eggs in the process; but then they stopped trying to assist the other poor ant, for they believe that one has to think of oneself first. The queen ant said they showed both heart and brain: 'These are the two attributes that place us first among respectable creatures! But intelligence must be the master, it is far more important, and I have more brains than any other ant.' She stood up on her two hind legs, you couldn't mistake any of the lesser ants for her, and I ate her.

"'Go to the ant and become wise.' Now I had swallowed the queen.

"I walked over to the oak tree. It was very ancient; it had a massive trunk and a great spreading crown. I knew from my time in the library that within each tree lives a woman called a dryad; she is born with the tree and dies when it does. When this oak girl saw me she screamed, for she was as afraid of mice as all women are. But in truth she had more reason to be; after all, I could have gnawed the tree in two, and then she would have died. But I spoke to her in a friendly and warm manner to put her at her ease, and she allowed me to climb right up on her fine little hand. I told her why I had gone out into the wide world and she promised me that that very evening she would help me to obtain another of the treasures I was searching for. She told me that Fantasy was a very dear friend of hers and that he often came to rest under the boughs of the tree. She told me that he was as beautiful as the God of Love and that he called her 'his dryad.'

"'This great rugged, craggy, beautiful old oak tree is just to his taste, with its roots deep down under the ground and its crown high up in the sky. This oak has experienced drifts of cold snow, sharp and bitter winds, and the sweet sunshine: to know them all is a blessing.' Yes, that is the way the dryad talked.

"'The birds in my branches sing about foreign lands, on one of my dead limbs a stork has built its nest; it looks nice and I like to hear about the land of the pyramids,' the dryad explained. 'Fantasy likes all this too, but it is not enough for him, I have to tell him tales of life in the woods as well; about my own childhood when I was a little sapling — so small that the nettles grew taller than I — and all that I have experienced since then. Hide over there among the woodruff, and when Fantasy comes I shall tear a little feather from his wings. You can have it; no poet has ever had a better one.'

"Fantasy came and the dryad tore a little feather from one of his wings and I caught it," said the little female mouse. "I put it in water to soften it a bit, for it was very difficult to digest; but I finally managed to get it down. It is not so easy to become a poet by

HOW TO COOK SOUP UPON A SAUSAGE PIN

the way of the stomach, one has to swallow an awful lot. But now I had both intelligence and fantasy; and the third ingredient necessary for a poet, I knew, could be found in the library. I had heard a critic of much importance say that novels exist to free humanity from superfluous tears; in other words, they are a kind of sponge that absorbs feelings. I recalled a couple of these books, and they had always looked very appetizing to me; they had been read so often and were so filled with greasy fingerprints that I felt sure they had a wealth of feeling within them.

"I hurried home to the library and ate almost a whole novel that very first day. I only ate the soft part, which is the most important; the crust or the binding, as it is called, I didn't touch. When I had digested two novels I could already feel things moving inside me. I ate a little of a third and then I had become a poet — that is what I said to myself and everybody agreed with me — I had headaches, stomachaches, and . . . I can hardly list all the aches I had.

"I began to think of all the stories that one could make up about a sausage pin. My thoughts were full of pins — the queen ant must have had an extraordinary brain. I thought of the man who became invisible when he put a white pin in his mouth; and the pin people used to pin their hopes with; and the pins and needles that people sat on; not to speak of the length of the pin needed to pin one down. All my thoughts became pins. And for every pin a story could be told, for I am a poet and I have worked hard to become one. I can serve you a pin, a story each day of the week, that is my soup!"

"Let us hear the third mouse," said the mouse king.

"Pip, pip," someone said at the kitchen door. That was the fourth mouse: the one they had all believed to be dead. She came running in so fast that she overturned the sausage pin with the black crepe around it. She had been running both day and night, and even though she had been able to ride on a freight train for part of the way, she had almost come too late. She pushed her way through the crowd until she stood before the king. She looked awfully rumpled. She had lost her sausage pin but not her tongue. She began to talk at once. She must have thought that everyone had just been waiting to hear her, and that nothing in the world was as important as what she had to say. She took them all by surprise and gave no one time to object while she talked. This is what she had to say.

HANS CHRISTIAN ANDERSEN

WHAT THE FOURTH MOUSE, WHO SPOKE BEFORE THE THIRD MOUSE, HAD TO RECOUNT

"I set out for the big city immediately," she began. "The name of it I don't recall; I have such difficulty remembering names. I had traveled by rail and was taken from the station, among some confiscated goods, to the courthouse. There I happened to overhear a prison warden who was talking about his prisoners. He was especially talking about one of them; this prisoner had said some rash words that had been printed and commented upon all over the city. 'It is all soup upon a sausage pin,' said the warden, 'but that soup may cost him his head.'

"This naturally made me very interested in that prisoner and I managed to get into his cell, for behind every locked door there is usually a mousehole. He looked very pale. He had a long beard and two shining eyes. The lamp smoked but the walls and the ceiling were used to it, they couldn't have got any blacker than they were. The prisoner scratched pictures and verses on the wall, white on black. I did not read them. I think he was lonely; I was a welcome guest. He tempted me with little pieces of bread and whistled softly to make me come nearer. He was so happy to see me that I gained confidence and we became friends. He shared his bread and water with me and gave me sausage and cheese to eat.

"I lived well but it was especially the company that kept me there. He let me run up and down his arms, even inside his sleeve. I climbed into his beard and he called me his little friend; I grew very fond of him and he of me. I forgot my errand out in the wide world; I forgot my sausage pin. It fell into a crack in the floor and is lying there still. I wanted to stay where I was, for, if I left, the poor prisoner would have no one, and that is too little to possess in this world.

"I stayed but he didn't! He talked ever so sorrowfully to me that last night we were together, and gave me a double ration of bread and cheese; then he threw me a finger kiss and was gone. I never saw him again. I do not know his story.

"'Soup on a sausage pin,' the warden had said, and I moved in with him; but I should never have trusted him. He took me in his hands but only to put me in a cage, in a treadmill. You can run and run in that as long as you want to; you will still stay in the same place. The only thing that happens is that you make a fool of yourself.

HOW TO COOK SOUP UPON A SAUSAGE PIN

"But the warden's little grandchild was a sweet little girl with golden curly hair, happy eyes, and a mouth made for laughing. 'Poor little mouse,' she said, while she looked into my ugly cage; then she pulled out the iron pin and let me go. I jumped down upon the window sill, and from there out on the roof and down in the gutter. I was free, free! That was my only thought, not the purpose of my journey.

"It was dark, the middle of the night; I had found shelter in an old tower where there lived a watchman and an owl. I didn't trust either of them, least of all the owl. It looks like a cat and has one great fault: it eats mice. But one can make a mistake, and I had, for the owl was a very respectable old bird, terribly well educated; she knew more than the night watchman and almost as much as I.

"The little owlets made a fuss over everything. 'Don't make soup on a sausage stick,' their mother would say, and that was just about the strongest reprimand she ever gave them, for she loved her young ones dearly. I felt so confident, so trusting toward her, that I said aloud, 'Pip,' from where I was hiding. My faith in her made her very pleased and she assured me that she would protect and keep all other animals from harming me; she wouldn't eat me before winter, when it was hard to find food.

"She was very intelligent and wise. She proved to me that the night watchman could not hoot unless he used the horn that hung from his shoulder. 'He thinks so much of himself. He believes that he is as wise as an owl. They are supposed to be so great, and they are so little. Soup on a sausage stick!'

"I asked her then for the recipe and she explained to me. 'Soup on a sausage stick is a phrase human beings have constructed; it can be interpreted in many ways, and every person thinks his own is the best. But the truth of the matter is that it is nothing.'

" 'It is nothing!' I repeated, and then the truth dawned on me. The truth is often unpleasant, yet nothing is above it, and to this the owl agreed. I thought long about it; finally I decided that when I brought back the truth with me, then I was bringing more than soup on a sausage pin. I hurried in order to get home in time." She took a deep breath and then announced: "The mice are an enlightened nation, and the king of the mice is above everyone else. He will make me his queen, for truth's sake!"

"But your truth is a lie," shouted the little mouse who had not been allowed to speak yet. "I can cook the soup and I will do it!"

HANS CHRISTIAN ANDERSEN

HOW THE SOUP WAS COOKED

"I have not traveled," declared the fourth mouse. "I have stayed in our country and that, I think, was the most sensible thing to do. One does not have to make a journey, everything can be got here just as well. I stayed at home! I have not learned anything from supernatural beings, or eaten my way to being a poet, or held conversations with owls. What I know I have taught myself! Now put the pot on the fire and fill it with water, all the way up to the brim. Make the fire burn well, for I want the water to be really boiling, then throw in the sausage pin. Now will Your Majesty be so kind as to stick his tail down in the soup and stir it? The longer Your Majesty does it the stronger the soup will be. No more is needed, no other ingredients, it needs only to be stirred."

"Couldn't someone else do it as well?" asked the mouse king.

"No!" said the little female mouse. "That kind of power can only be found in a royal tail."

The water in the pot was boiling furiously. The mouse king stood as close to it as he dared, then he stuck out his tail, in the same manner as mice do when they take the cream off the top of the milk with their tails. But here was no cream to lick afterward, only steam from the boiling water. Quickly, he jumped away!

"Yes, naturally, that must be the way it is made. You are to be my queen!" he declared. "But I think we will wait to make the soup until our golden wedding. Then the poor in my country will have something to look forward to."

The wedding was held, but some of the mice said — not at the castle but when they came home later — that that could not be called cooking soup upon a sausage pin, it was more like cooking soup upon a mouse tail.

They found a few of the other things that had been said quite clever; but most of it could have been said somewhat differently and better.

"Now I would have explained it this way or that way. . . ." That was the critique; it is always clever; and it comes last.

The story went around the world; people's reactions to it were divided, but the story remained whole. And that is the most important in great things as well as in small — in cooking soup upon a sausage pin. Just remember, don't expect to be thanked for it.

THE RED SHOES

Once there was a little girl who was pretty and delicate but very poor. In the summer she had to go barefoot and in the winter she had to wear wooden shoes that rubbed against her poor little ankles and made them red and sore.

In the same village there lived an old widow whose husband had been a shoemaker; and she sat sewing a pair of shoes from scraps of red material. She did her very best, but the shoes looked a bit clumsy, though they were sewn with kindness. They were meant for the poor little girl, whose name was Karen.

Now on that very day that her mother was to be buried, Karen was given the red shoes. Though they weren't the proper color for mourning, she had no others, so she put them on. Raggedly dressed, bare-legged, with red shoes on her feet, she walked behind the pauper's coffin.

A big old-fashioned carriage drove by; in it sat an old lady. She noticed the little girl and felt so sorry for her that she went at once to the minister and spoke to him. "Let me have that little girl, and I shall be good to her and bring her up."

Karen thought it was because of her new red shoes that the old lady had taken a fancy to her. But the old lady declared that the shoes looked frightful and had them thrown into the stove and burned. Karen was dressed in nice clean clothes and taught to

279

HANS CHRISTIAN ANDERSEN

read and to sew. Everyone agreed that she was a very pretty child; but the mirror said, "You are more than pretty, you are beautiful."

It happened that the queen was making a journey throughout the country, and she had her daughter, the little princess, with her. Everywhere people streamed to see them. When they arrived at a castle near Karen's village, the little girl followed the crowd out there. Looking out of one of the great windows of the castle was the little princess. So that people could see her, she was standing on a little stool. She had no crown on her head but she wore a very pretty white dress and the loveliest red shoes, made from morocco. They were certainly much prettier than the ones the old shoemaker's widow had made for Karen. But even they had been red shoes, and to Karen nothing else in the world was so desirable.

Karen became old enough to be confirmed. She was to have a new dress and new shoes for this solemn occasion. The old lady took her to the finest shoemaker in the nearby town and he measured her little foot. Glass cabinets filled with the most elegant shoes and boots covered the walls of his shop. But the old lady's eyesight was so poor that she didn't get much out of looking at the display. Karen did; between two pairs of boots stood a pair of red shoes just like the ones the princess had worn. Oh, how beautiful they were! The shoemaker said that they had been made for the daughter of a count but that they hadn't fit her.

"I think they are patent leather," remarked the old lady. "They shine."

"Yes, they shine!" sighed Karen as she tried them on. They fit the child and the old woman bought them. Had she known that they were red, she wouldn't have because it was not proper to wear red shoes when you were being confirmed. But her eyesight was failing — poor woman! — and she had not seen the color.

Everyone in the church looked at Karen's feet, as she walked toward the altar. On the walls of the church hung paintings of the former ministers and their wives who were buried there; they were portrayed wearing black with white ruffs around their necks. Karen felt that even they were staring at her red shoes.

When the old bishop laid his hands on her head and spoke of the solemn promise she was about to make — of her covenant with God to be a good Christian — her mind was not on his words. The ritual music was played on the organ; the old cantor sang, and the

THE RED SHOES

sweet voices of the children could be heard, but Karen was thinking of her red shoes.

By afternoon, everyone had told the old lady about the color of Karen's shoes. She was very angry and scolded the girl, telling her how improper it was to have worn red shoes in church, and that she must remember always to wear black ones, even if she had to put on an old pair.

Next Sunday Karen was to attend communion. She looked at her black shoes and she looked at her red shoes; then she looked at her red shoes once more and put them on.

The sun was shining, it was a beautiful day. The old lady and Karen took the path across the fields and their shoes got a bit dirty.

At the entrance to the church stood an old invalid soldier leaning on a crutch. He had a marvelously long beard that was red with touches of white in it. He bowed low toward the old lady and asked her permission to wipe the dust off her feet. Karen put her little foot forward too.

"What pretty little dancing shoes!" said the soldier and, tapping them on the soles, he added, "Remember to stay on her feet for the dance."

The old lady gave the soldier a penny, and she and Karen entered the church.

Again everyone looked at Karen's feet, even the people in the paintings on the wall. When she knelt in front of the altar and the golden cup was lifted to her lips, she thought only of the red shoes and saw them reflected in the wine. She did not join in the singing of the psalm and she forgot to say the Lord's Prayer.

The coachman had come with the carriage to drive them home from church. The old lady climbed in and Karen was about to follow her when the old soldier, who was standing nearby, remarked, "Look at those pretty dancing shoes."

His words made her take a few dancing steps. Once she had begun, her feet would not stop. It was as if the shoes had taken command of them. She danced around the corner of the church; her will was not her own.

The coachman jumped off the carriage and ran after her. When he finally caught up with her, he grabbed her and lifted her up from the ground, but her feet kept on dancing in the air, even after he managed to get her into the carriage. The poor old woman was

HANS CHRISTIAN ANDERSEN

kicked nastily while she and the coachman took Karen's shoes off her feet, so she could stop dancing.

When they got home, the red shoes were put away in a closet, but Karen could not help sneaking in to look at them.

The old lady was very ill. The doctors had come and said that she would not live much longer. She needed careful nursing and constant care, and who else but Karen ought to give it to her? In the town there was to be a great ball and Karen had been invited to go. She looked at the old lady, who was going to die anyway, and then she glanced at her red shoes. To glance was no sin. Then she put them on; that too did no great harm. But she went to the ball!

She danced! But when she wanted to dance to the left, the shoes danced to the right; and when she wanted to dance up the ballroom floor, the shoes danced right down the stairs and out into the street. Dance she did, out through the city gates and into the dark forest.

Something shone through the trees. She thought it was the moon because it had a face. But it was not; it was the old soldier with the red beard. He nodded to her and exclaimed, "Look what beautiful dancing shoes!"

Terrified, she tried to pull off her shoes. She tore her stockings but the shoes stayed on. They had grown fast to her feet. Dance she did! And dance she must! Over the fields and meadows, in the rain and sunshine, by night and by day. But it was more horrible and frightening at night when the world was dark.

She danced through the gates of the churchyard; but the dead did not dance with her, they had better things to do. She wanted to sit down on the pauper's grave, where the bitter herbs grew, but for her there was no rest. The church door was open and she danced toward it, but an angel, dressed in white, who had on his back great wings that reached almost to the ground, barred her entrance.

His face was stern and grave, and in his hand he held a broad, shining sword.

"You shall dance," he said, "dance in your red shoes until you become pale and thin. Dance till the skin on your face turns yellow and clings to your bones as if you were a skeleton. Dance you shall from door to door, and when you pass a house where proud and vain children live, there you shall knock on the door so that they will see you and fear your fate. Dance, you shall dance. . . . Dance!"

THE RED SHOES

"Mercy!" screamed Karen, but heard not what the angel answered, for her red shoes carried her away, down through the churchyard, over the meadows, along the highways, through the lanes: always dancing.

One morning she danced past a house that she knew well. From inside she heard psalms being sung. The door opened and a coffin decked with flowers was carried out. The old lady who had been so kind to her was dead. Now she felt that she was forsaken by all of mankind and cursed by God's angel.

Dance she must, and dance she did. The shoes carried her across fields and meadows, through nettles and briars that tore her feet so they bled.

One morning she danced across the lonely heath until she came to a solitary cottage. Here, she knew, the executioner lived. With her fingers she tapped on his window.

"Come out! Come out!" she called. "I cannot come inside, for I must dance."

The executioner opened his door and came outside. When he saw Karen he said, "Do you know who I am? I am the one who cuts off the heads of evil men; and I can feel my ax beginning to quiver now."

"Do not cut off my head," begged Karen, "for then I should not be able to repent. But cut off my feet!"

She confessed her sins and the executioner cut off her feet, and the red shoes danced away with them into the dark forest. The executioner carved a pair of wooden feet for her and made her a pair of crutches. He taught her the psalm that a penitent sings. She kissed the hand that had guided the ax and went on her way.

"Now I have suffered enough because of those red shoes," thought Karen. "I shall go to church now and be among other people."

But when she walked up to the door of the church, the red shoes danced in front of her, and in horror she fled.

All during that week she felt sad and cried many a bitter tear. When Sunday came she thought, "Now I have suffered and struggled long enough. I am just as good as many of those who are sitting and praying in church right now, and who dare to throw their heads back with pride." This reasoning gave her courage, but she came no farther than the gate of the churchyard. There were the shoes dancing in front of her. In terror she fled, but this time she really repented in the depth of her heart.

She went to the minister's house and begged to be given work. She said that she did not care about wages but only wanted a roof over her head and enough to eat. The minister's wife hired the poor cripple because she felt sorry for her. Karen was grateful that she had been given a place to live and she worked hard. In the evening when the minister read from the Bible, she sat and listened thoughtfully. The children were fond of her and she played with them, but when they talked of finery and being beautiful like a princess, she would sadly shake her head.

When Sunday came, everyone in the household got ready for church, and they asked her to go with them. Poor Karen's eyes filled with tears. She sighed and glanced toward her crutches.

When the others had gone, she went into her little room that was so small that a bed and a chair were all it could hold. She sat down and began to read from her psalmbook. The wind carried the music from the church organ down to her, and she lifted her tear-stained face and whispered, "Oh, God, help me!"

Suddenly the sunlight seemed doubly bright and an angel of God stood before her. He was the same angel who with his sword had barred her entrance to the church, but now he held a rose branch covered with flowers. With this he touched the low ceiling of the room and it rose high into the air and, where he had touched it, a golden star shone. He touched the walls and they widened.

Karen saw the organ. She saw the old paintings of the ministers and their wives; and there were the congregation holding their psalmbooks in front of them and singing. The church had come to the poor girl in her little narrow chamber; or maybe she had come to the church. Now she sat among the others, and when they finished singing the psalm they looked up and saw her.

Someone whispered to her: "It is good that you came, Karen."

"This is His mercy," she replied.

The great organ played and the voices of the children in the choir mingled sweetly with it. The clear, warm sunshine streamed through the window. The sunshine filled Karen's heart till it so swelled with peace and happiness that it broke. Her soul flew on a sunbeam up to God; and up there no one asked her about the red shoes.

THE LITTLE MERMAID

Far, far from land, where the waters are as blue as the petals of the cornflower and as clear as glass, there, where no anchor can reach the bottom, live the mer-people. So deep is this part of the sea that you would have to pile many church towers on top of each other before one of them emerged above the surface.

Now you must not think that at the bottom of the sea there is only white sand. No, here grow the strangest plants and trees; their stems and leaves are so subtle that the slightest current in the water makes them move, as if they were alive. Big and small fishes flit in and out among their branches, just as the birds do up on earth. At the very deepest place, the mer-king has built his castle. Its walls are made of coral and its long pointed windows of amber. The roof is oyster shells that are continually opening and closing. It looks very beautiful, for in each shell lies a pearl, so lustrous that it would be fit for a queen's crown.

The mer-king had been a widower for many years; his mother kept house for him. She was a very intelligent woman but a little too proud of her rank: she wore twelve oysters on her tail; the nobility were only allowed six. Otherwise, she was a most praise-worthy woman, and she took excellent care of her grandchildren, the little princesses. They were six lovely mermaids; the youngest was the most beautiful. Her complexion was as fine as the petal of

HANS CHRISTIAN ANDERSEN

a rose and her eyes as blue as the deepest lake but, just like everyone else down there, she had no feet; her body ended in a fishtail.

The mermaids were allowed to play all day in the great hall of the castle, where flowers grew on the walls. The big amber windows were kept open and the fishes swam in and out, just as the swallows up on earth fly in through our windows if they are open. But unlike the birds of the air, the fishes were not frightened, they swam right up to the little princesses and ate out of their hands and let themselves be petted.

Around the castle was a great park where there grew fiery-red and deep-blue trees. Their fruits shone as though they were the purest gold, their flowers were like flames, and their branches and leaves were ever in motion. The earth was the finest sand, not white but blue, the color of burning sulphur. There was a blue tinge to everything, down on the bottom of the sea. You could almost believe that you were suspended in mid-air and had the blue sky both above and below you. When the sea was calm, the sun appeared like a crimson flower, from which all light flowed.

Each little princess had her own garden, where she could plant the flowers she liked. One of them had shaped her flower bed so it resembled a whale; and another, as a mermaid. The youngest had planted red flowers in hers: she wanted it to look like the sun; it was round and the crimson flowers did glow as though they were so many little suns. She was a strange little child: quiet and thoughtful. Her sisters' gardens were filled with all sorts of things that they had collected from shipwrecks, but she had only a marble statue of a boy in hers. It had been cut out of stone that was almost transparently clear and had sunk to the bottom of the sea when the ship that had carried it was lost. Close to the statue she had planted a pink tree; it looked like a weeping willow. The tree was taller than the sculpture. Its long soft branches bent toward the sand; it looked as if the top of the tree and its root wanted to kiss each other.

The princesses liked nothing better than to listen to their old grandmother tell about the world above. She had to recount countless times all she knew about ships, towns, human beings, and the animals that lived up on land. The youngest of the mermaids thought it particularly wonderful that the flowers up there had fragrance, for that they did not have on the bottom of the sea. She

also liked to hear about the green forest, where the fishes that swam among the branches could sing most beautifully. Grandmother called the birds "fishes"; otherwise, her little grandchildren would not have understood her, since they had never seen a bird.

"But when you are fifteen, then you will be allowed to swim to the surface," she promised. "Then you can climb up on a rock and sit and watch the big ships sail by. If you dare, you can swim close enough to the shore to see the towns and the forest."

The following year, the oldest of the princesses would be fifteen. From one sister to the next, there was a difference in age of about a year, which meant that the youngest would have to wait more than five whole years before she would be allowed to swim up from the bottom of the sea and take a look at us. But each promised the others that she would return after her first day above, and tell about the things she had seen and describe what she thought was loveliest of all. For the old grandmother could not satisfy their curiosity.

None of the sisters longed so much to see the world above as the youngest, the one who had to wait the longest before she could leave her home. Many a night this quiet, thoughtful little mermaid would stand by the open window, looking up through the dark blue waters where the fishes swam. She could see the moon and the stars; they looked paler but larger down here under the sea. Sometimes a great shadow passed by like a cloud and then she knew that it was either a whale or a ship, with its crew and passengers, that was sailing high above her. None on board could have imagined that a little beautiful mermaid stood in the depths below them and stretched her little white hands up toward the keel of their ship.

The oldest of the sisters had her fifteenth birthday and swam up to the surface of the sea. When she returned she had hundreds of things to tell. But of everything that had happened to her, the loveliest experience by far, she claimed, had been to lie on a sandbank, when the sea was calm and the moon was out, and look at a great city. The lights from the windows and streets had shone like hundreds of stars; and she had been able to hear the rumbling of the carriages and the voices of human beings and, best of all, the sound of music. She had seen all the church towers and steeples and heard their bells ring. And just because she would never be

THE LITTLE MERMAID

able to enter the city, she longed to be able to do that more than anything else.

How carefully her youngest sister listened to every word and remembered everything that she had been told. When, late in the evening, the little mermaid would stand dreaming by the window and look up through the blue water, then she imagined that she could see the city and hear the bells of the churches ringing.

The next year the second of the sisters was allowed to swim away from home. Her little head had emerged above the water just at the moment when the sun was setting. This sight had been so beautiful that she could hardly describe it. The whole heaven had been covered in gold and the clouds that had sailed above her had been purple and crimson. A flight of wild swans, like a white veil just above the water, had flown by. She had swum toward the sun, but it had set, taking the colors of the clouds, sea, and sky with it.

The third of the sisters, who came of age the following year, was the most daring among them. She had swum way up a broad river! There she had seen green hills covered with vineyards, castles, and farms that peeped out through the great forests. She had heard the birds sing and the sun had been so hot that she had had to swim under the water, some of the time, just to cool off. In a little bay, she had come upon some naked children who were playing and splashing in the water. She had wanted to join them, but when they saw her they got frightened and ran away. A little black animal had come: it was a dog. But she had never seen one before. It had barked so loudly and fiercely that she became terrified and swam right back to the sea. What she never would forget as long as she lived were the beautiful forest, the green hills, and the sweet little children who had been able to swim even though they had no fishtails as she had.

The fourth of the sisters was timid. She stayed far away from shore, out in the middle of the ocean. But that was the most beautiful place of all, she asserted. You could see ever so far and the sky above was like a clear glass bell. The ships she had seen had been so far away that they had looked no bigger than gulls. But the little dolphins had turned somersaults for her and the great whales had sprayed water high up into the air, so that it looked as though there were more than a hundred fountains.

The fifth sister's birthday was in the winter and, therefore, she saw something none of her sisters had seen. The ocean had been

HANS CHRISTIAN ANDERSEN

green, and huge icebergs had been floating on it. Each of them had been as lovely as a pearl and yet larger than the church towers that human beings built. They had the most fantastic shapes and their surface glittered like diamonds. She had climbed up on the largest one of them all; the wind had played with her long hair, and all the ships had fearfully kept away. Toward evening a storm had begun to blow; dark clouds had gathered and bolts of lightning had flashed while the thunder rolled. The waves had lifted the iceberg high up on their shoulders, and the lightning had colored the ice red. The ships had taken down their sails; and on board, fear and terror had reigned. But the mermaid had just sat on her iceberg and watched the bolts of lightning zigzag across the sky.

The first time that any of the sisters had been allowed to swim to the surface, each had been delighted with her freedom and all she had seen. But now that they were grownups and could swim anywhere they wished, they lost interest in wandering far away; after a month or two the world above lost its attraction. When they were away, they longed for their father's castle, declaring it the most beautiful place of all and the only spot where one really felt at home.

Still, many evenings the five sisters would take each other's hands and rise up through the waters. They had voices far lovelier than any human being. When a storm began to rage and a ship was in danger of being wrecked, then the five sisters would swim in front of it and sing about how beautiful it was down at the bottom of the sea. They begged the sailors not to be frightened but to come down to them. The men could not understand the mermaids' songs; they thought it was the wind that was singing. Besides, they would never see the beauty of the world below them, for if a ship sinks the seamen drown, and when they arrive at the mer-king's castle they are dead.

On such evenings, while her sisters swam, hand in hand, up through the water, the youngest princess had to stay below. She would look sadly up after them and feel like crying; but mermaids can't weep and that makes their suffering even deeper and greater.

"Oh, if only I were fifteen," she would sigh. "I know that I shall love the world above, and the human beings who live up there!"

At last she, too, was fifteen!

"Now you are off our hands," said the old dowager queen. "Let me dress you, just as I dressed your sisters." She put a wreath of

---

THE LITTLE MERMAID

white lilies around her hair; each of the petals of every flower was half a pearl. She let eight oysters clip themselves onto the little mermaid's tail, so that everyone could see that she was a princess.

"It hurts," said the little mermaid.

"One has to suffer for position," said her old grandmother. The little mermaid would gladly have exchanged her heavy pearl wreath for one of the red flowers from her garden (she thought they suited her much better) but she didn't dare.

"Farewell," she said and rose, light as a bubble, up through the water.

The sun had just set when she lifted her head above the surface. The clouds still had the color of roses and in the horizon was a fine line of gold; in the pale pink sky the first star of evening sparkled, clearly and beautifully. The air was warm and the sea was calm. She saw a three-masted ship; only one of its sails was unfurled, and it hung motionless in the still air. Up on the yards the sailors sat, looking down upon the deck from which music could be heard. As the evening grew darker, hundreds of little colored lamps were hung from the rigging; they looked like the flags of all the nations of the world. The little mermaid swam close to a porthole and the swells lifted her gently so that she could look in through it. The great cabin was filled with gaily dressed people; the handsomest among them was a young prince with large, dark eyes. He looked no older than sixteen, and that was, in truth, his age; that very day was his birthday. All the festivities were for him. The sailors danced on the deck, and as the young prince came up to watch them, a hundred rockets flew into the sky.

The night became as bright as day and the little mermaid got so frightened that she ducked down under the water. But she soon stuck her head up again; and then it looked as if all the stars of the heavens were falling down on top of her. She had never seen fireworks before. Pinwheels turned; rockets shot into the air, and their lights reflected in the dark mirror of the sea. The deck of the ship was so illuminated that every rope could clearly be seen. Oh, how handsome the young prince was! He laughed and smiled and shook hands with everyone, while music was played in the still night.

It grew late, but the little mermaid could not turn her eyes away from the ship and the handsome prince. The colored lamps were put out. No more rockets shot into the air and no more cannons were fired. From the depth of the ocean came a rumbling noise. The little mermaid let the waves be her rocking horse, and they lifted her so that she could look in through the portholes. The ship started to sail faster and faster, as one sail after another was unfurled. Now the waves grew in size and black clouds could be seen on the horizon and far away lightning flashed.

A storm was brewing. The sailors took down the sails. The great ship tossed and rolled in the huge waves that rose as though they were mountains that wanted to bury the ship and break its proud mast. But the ship, like a swan, rode on top of the waves and let them lift her high into the sky. The little mermaid thought it was very amusing to watch the ship sailing so fast, but the sailors didn't. The ship creaked and groaned; the great planks seemed to bulge as the waves hit them. Suddenly the mast snapped as if it were a reed. It tumbled into the water. The ship heeled over, and the sea broke over it.

Only now did the little mermaid understand that the ship was in danger. She had to be careful herself and keep away from the spars and broken pieces of timber that were being flung by the waves. For a moment it grew so dark that she could see nothing, then a bolt of lightning illuminated the sinking ship. She looked for the young prince among the terrified men on board who were trying to save themselves, but not until that very moment, when the ship finally sank, did she see him.

At first, she thought joyfully, "Now he will come down to me!" But then she remembered that man could not live in the sea and the young prince would be dead when he came to her father's castle.

"He must not die," she thought, and dived in among the wreckage, forgetting the danger that she herself was in, for any one of the great beams that were floating in the turbulent sea could have crushed her.

She found him! He was too tired to swim any farther; he had no more strength in his arms and legs to fight the storm-whipped waves. He closed his eyes, waiting for death, and he would have drowned, had the little mermaid not saved him. She held his head above water and let the waves carry them where they would.

By morning the storm was over. Of the wrecked ship not a splinter was to be found. The sun rose, glowing red, and its rays gave color to the young prince's cheeks but his eyes remained

THE LITTLE MERMAID

closed. The little mermaid kissed his forehead and stroked his wet hair. She thought that he looked like the statue in her garden. She kissed him again and wished passionately that he would live.

In the far distance she saw land; the mountains rose blue in the morning air. The snow on their peaks was as glittering white as swan's feathers. At the shore there was a green forest, and in its midst lay a cloister or a church, the little mermaid did not know which. Lemon and orange trees grew in the garden, and by the entrance gate stood a tall palm tree. There was a little bay nearby, where the water was calm and deep. The mermaid swam with her prince toward the beach. She laid him in the fine white sand, taking care to place his head in the warm sunshine far from the water.

In the big white buildings bells were ringing, and a group of young girls was coming out to walk in the garden. The little mermaid swam out to some rocks and hid behind them. She covered her head with seaweed so that she could not be seen and then peeped toward land, to see who would find the poor prince.

Soon one of the young girls discovered him. At first she seemed frightened, and she called the others. A lot of people came. The prince opened his eyes and smiled up at those who stood around him — not out at the sea, where the little mermaid was hiding. But then he could not possibly have known that she was there and that it was she who had saved him. The little mermaid felt so terribly sad; the prince was carried into the big white building, and the little mermaid dived sorrowfully down into the sea and swam home to her father's castle.

She had always been quiet and thoughtful. Now she grew even more silent. Her sisters asked her what she had seen on her first visit up above, but she did not answer.

Many mornings and evenings she would swim back to the place where she had last seen the prince. She watched the fruits in the orchard ripen and be picked, and saw the snow on the high mountains melt, but she never saw the prince. She would return from each of these visits a little sadder. She would seek comfort by embracing the statue in her garden, which looked like the prince. She no longer tended her flowers, and they grew into a wilderness, covering the paths and weaving their long stalks and leaves into the branches of the trees, so that it became quite dark down in her garden.

At last she could bear her sorrow no longer and told one of her sisters about it; and almost at once the others knew as well. But no one else was told; that is, except for a couple of other mermaids, but they didn't tell it to anyone except their nearest and dearest friends. It was one of these friends who knew who the prince was. She, too, had seen the birthday party on the ship, and she could tell where he came from and where his kingdom was.

"Come, little sister," the other princesses called, and with their arms around each other's shoulders they swam.

All in a row they rose to the surface when they came to the shore where the prince's castle stood. It was built of glazed yellow stones and had many flights of marble stairs leading up to it. The steps of one of them went all the way down to the sea. Golden domes rose above the roofs, and pillars bore an arcade that went all the way around the palace. Between the pillars stood marble statues; they looked almost as if they were alive. Through the clear glass of the tall windows, one could look into the most beautiful chambers and halls, where silken curtains and tapestries hung on the walls; and there were large paintings that were a real pleasure to look at. In the largest hall was a fountain. The water shot high up toward the glass cupola in the roof, through which the sunbeams fell on the water and the beautiful flowers that grew in the basin of the fountain.

Now that she knew where the prince lived, the little mermaid spent many evenings and nights looking at the splendid palace. She swam nearer to the land than any of her sisters had ever dared. There was a marble balcony that cast its shadow across a narrow canal, and beneath it she hid and watched the young prince, who thought that he was all alone in the moonlight.

Many an evening she saw the prince sail with his musicians in his beautiful boat. She peeped from behind the tall reeds; and if someone noticed her silver-white veil, they probably thought that they had only seen a swan stretching its wings.

Many a night she heard the fishermen talking to each other and telling about how kind and good the prince was; and she was so glad that she had saved his life when she had found him, half dead, drifting on the waves. She remembered how his head had rested on her chest and with what passion she had kissed him. But he knew nothing about his rescue; he could not even dream about her.

More and more she grew to love human beings and wished that

THE LITTLE MERMAID

she could leave the sea and live among them. It seemed to her that their world was far larger than hers; on ships, they could sail across the oceans and they could climb the mountains high up above the clouds. Their countries seemed ever so large, covered with fields and forests; she knew that they stretched much farther than she could see. There was so much that she wanted to know; there were many questions that her sisters could not answer. Therefore she asked her old grandmother, since she knew much about the "higher world," as she called the lands above the sea.

"If men are not so unlucky as to drown," asked the little mermaid, "then do they live forever? Don't they die as we do, down here in the sea?"

"Yes, they do," answered her grandmother. "Men must also die and their life span is shorter than ours. We can live until we are three hundred years old; but when we die, we become the foam on the ocean. We cannot even bury our loved ones. We do not have immortal souls. When we die, we shall never rise again. We are like the green reeds: once they are cut they will never be green again. But men have souls that live eternally, even after their bodies have become dust. They rise high up into the clear sky where the stars are. As we rise up through the water to look at the world of man, they rise up to the unknown, the beautiful world, that we shall never see."

"Why do I not have an immortal soul!" sighed the little mermaid unhappily. "I would give all my three hundred years of life for only one day as a human being if, afterward, I should be allowed to live in the heavenly world."

"You shouldn't think about things like that," said her old grandmother. "We live far happier down here than man does up there."

"I am going to die, become foam on the ocean, and never again hear the music of the waves or see the flowers and the burning red sun. Can't I do anything to win an immortal soul?"

"No," said the old merwoman. "Only if a man should fall so much in love with you that you were dearer to him than his mother and father; and he cared so much for you that all his thoughts were of his love for you; and he let a priest take his right hand and put it in yours, while he promised to be eternally true to you, then his soul would flow into your body and you would be able to partake of human happiness. He can give you a soul and yet keep his own. But it will never happen. For that which we consider

HANS CHRISTIAN ANDERSEN

beautiful down here in the ocean, your fishtail, they find ugly up above, on earth. They have no sense; up there, you have to have two clumsy props, which they call legs, in order to be called beautiful."

The little mermaid sighed and glanced sadly down at her fishtail.

"Let us be happy," said her old grandmother. "We can swim and jump through the waves for three hundred years, that is time enough. Tonight we are going to give a court ball in the castle."

Such a splendor did not exist up above on the earth. The walls and the ceilings of the great hall were made of clear glass; four hundred giant green and pink oyster shells stood in rows along the walls. Blue flames rose from them and not only lighted the hall but also illuminated the sea outside. Numberless fishes — both big and small — swam close to the glass walls; some of them had purple scales, others seemed to be of silver and gold. Through the great hall flowed a swiftly moving current, and on that the mermen and mermaids danced, while they sang their own beautiful songs. Such lovely voices are never heard up on earth; and the little mermaid sang most beautifully of them all. The others clapped their hands when she had finished, and for a moment she felt happy, knowing that she had the most beautiful voice both on earth and in the sea.

But soon she started thinking again of the world above. She could not forget the handsome prince, and mourned because she did not have an immortal soul like his. She sneaked out of her father's palace, away from the ball, from the gaiety, down into her little garden.

From afar the sound of music, of horns being played, came down to her through the water; and she thought: "Now he is sailing up there, the prince whom I love more than I love my father and mother: he who is ever in my thoughts and in whose hands I would gladly place all my hope of happiness. I would dare to do anything to win him and an immortal soul! While my sisters are dancing in the palace, I will go to the sea witch, though I have always feared her, and ask her to help me."

The little mermaid swam toward the turbulent maelstrom; beyond it the sea witch lived. In this part of the great ocean the little mermaid had never been before; here no flowers or seaweeds grew, only the gray naked sea bed stretched toward the center of the maelstrom, that great whirlpool where the water, as if it had been set in motion by gigantic mill wheels, twisted and turned: grind-

THE LITTLE MERMAID

ing, tearing, and sucking anything that came within its reach down into its depths. Through this turbulence the little mermaid had to swim, for beyond it lay the bubbling mud flats that the sea witch called her bog and that had to be crossed to come to the place where she lived.

The sea witch's house was in the midst of the strangest forest. The bushes and trees were gigantic polyps that were half plant and half animal. They looked like snakes with hundreds of heads, but they grew out of the ground. Their branches were long slimy arms, and they had fingers as supple as worms; every limb was in constant motion from the root to the utmost point. Everything they could reach they grasped, and never let go of it again. With dread the little mermaid stood at the entrance to the forest; her heart was beating with fear, she almost turned back. But then she remembered her prince and the soul she wanted to gain and her courage returned.

She braided her long hair and bound it around her head, so the polyps could not catch her by it. She held her arms folded tightly across her breast and then she flew through the water as fast as the swiftest fish. The ugly polyps stretched out their arms and their fingers tried to grasp her. She noticed that every one of them was holding, as tightly as iron bands, onto something it had caught. Drowned human beings peeped out as white skeletons among the polyps' arms. There were sea chests, rudders of ships, skeletons of land animals; and then she saw a poor little mermaid who had been caught and strangled; and this sight was to her the most horrible.

At last she came to a great, slimy, open place in the middle of the forest. Big fat eels played in the mud, showing their ugly yellow stomachs. Here the witch had built her house out of the bones of drowned sailors, and there she sat letting a big ugly toad eat out of her mouth, as human beings sometimes let a canary eat sugar candy out of theirs. The ugly eels she called her little chickens, and held them close to her spongy chest.

"I know what you want," she cackled. "And it is stupid of you. But you shall have your wish, for it will bring you misery, little princess. You want to get rid of your fishtail, and instead have two stumps to walk on as human beings have, so that the prince will fall in love with you; and you will gain both him and an immortal soul." The witch laughed so loudly and evilly that the toad and eels she had had on her lap jumped down into the mud.

HANS CHRISTIAN ANDERSEN

"You came at the right time," she said. "Tomorrow I could not have helped you; you would have had to wait a year. I will mix you a potion. Drink it tomorrow morning before the sun rises, while you are sitting on the beach. Your tail will divide and shrink, until it becomes what human beings call 'pretty legs.' It will hurt; it will feel as if a sword were going through your body. All who see you will say that you are the most beautiful human child they have ever seen. You will walk more gracefully than any dancer; but every time your foot touches the ground it will feel as though you were walking on knives so sharp that your blood must flow. If you are willing to suffer all this, then I can help you."

"I will," whispered the little mermaid, and thought of her prince and how she would win an immortal soul.

"But remember," screeched the witch, "that once you have a human body you can never become a mermaid again. Never again shall you swim through the waters with your sisters to your father's castle. If you cannot make the prince fall so much in love with you that he forgets both his father and mother, because his every thought concerns only you, and he orders the priest to take his right hand and place it in yours, so that you become man and wife; then, the first morning after he has married another, your heart will break and you will become foam on the ocean."

"I still want to try," said the little mermaid, and her face was as white as a corpse.

"But you will have to pay me, too," grinned the witch. "And I want no small payment. You have the most beautiful voice of all those who live in the ocean. I suppose you have thought of using that to charm your prince; but that voice you will have to give to me. I want the most precious thing you have to pay for my potion. It contains my own blood, so that it can be as sharp as a double-edged sword."

"But if you take my voice," said the little mermaid, "what will I have left?"

"Your beautiful body," said the witch. "Your graceful walk and your lovely eyes. Speak with them and you will be able to capture a human heart. Have you lost your courage? Stick out your little tongue, and let me cut it off in payment, and you shall have the potion."

"Let it happen," whispered the little mermaid.

The witch took out a caldron in which to make the magic

THE LITTLE MERMAID

potion. "Cleanliness is a virtue," she said. And before she put the pot over the fire, she scrubbed it with eels, which she had made into a whisk.

She cut her chest and let her blood drip into the vessel. The steam that rose became strange figures that were terrifying to see. Every minute, the witch put something different into the caldron. When the brew reached a rolling boil, it sounded as though a crocodile were crying. At last the potion was finished. It looked as clear and pure as water.

"Here it is," said the witch, and cut out the little mermaid's tongue. Now she was mute, she could neither speak nor sing.

"If any of the polyps should try to grab you, on your way back through my forest," said the witch, "you need only spill one drop of the potion on it and its arms and fingers will splinter into a thousand pieces."

But the little mermaid didn't have to do that. Fearfully, the polyps drew away when they saw what she was carrying in her hands; the potion sparkled as though it were a star. Safely, she returned through the forest, the bog, and the maelstrom.

She could see her father's palace. The lights were extinguished in the great hall. Everyone was asleep; and yet she did not dare to seek out her sisters; now that she was mute and was going away from them forever. She felt as if her heart would break with sorrow. She sneaked down into the garden and picked a flower from each of her sisters' gardens; then she threw a thousand finger kisses toward the palace and swam upward through the deep blue sea.

The sun had not yet risen when she reached the prince's castle and sat down on the lowest step of the great marble stairs. The moon was still shining clearly. The little mermaid drank the potion and it felt as if a sword were piercing her little body. She fainted and lay as though she were dead.

When the sun's rays touched the sea she woke and felt a burning pain; but the young prince stood in front of her and looked at her with his coal-black eyes. She looked downward and saw then that she no longer had a fishtail but the most beautiful, little, slender legs that any girl could wish for. She was naked; and therefore she took her long hair and covered herself with it.

The prince asked her who she was and how she had got there. She looked gently and yet ever so sadly up at him with her deep blue eyes, for she could not speak. He took her by the hand and led

HANS CHRISTIAN ANDERSEN

her up to his castle. And just as the witch had warned, every step felt as though she were walking on sharp knives. But she suffered it gladly. Gracefully as a bubble rising in the water, she walked beside the prince; and everyone who saw her wondered how she could walk so lightly.

In the castle, she was clad in royal clothes of silk and muslin. She was the most beautiful of all, but she was mute and could neither sing nor speak. Beautiful slave girls, clad in silken clothes embroidered with gold, sang for the prince and his royal parents. One sang more beautifully than the rest, and the prince clapped his hands and smiled to her; then the little mermaid was filled with sorrow, for she knew that she had once sung far more beautifully. And she thought, "Oh, if he only knew that to be with him I have given away my voice for all eternity."

Now the slave girls danced, gracefully they moved to the beautiful music. Suddenly the little mermaid lifted her hands and rose on the tips of her toes. She floated more than danced across the floor. No one had ever seen anyone dance as she did. Her every movement revealed her loveliness and her eyes spoke far more eloquently than the slave's song.

Everyone was delighted, especially the prince. He called her his little foundling. She danced again and again, even though each time her little foot touched the floor she felt as if she had stepped on a knife. The prince declared that she should never leave him, and she was given permission to sleep in front of his door on a velvet pillow.

The prince had men's clothes made for her, so that she could accompany him when he went horseback riding. Through the sweet-smelling forest they rode, where green branches touched their shoulders and little birds sang among the leaves. Together they climbed the high mountains and her feet bled so much that others noticed it; but she smiled and followed her prince up ever higher until they could see the clouds sail below them, like flocks of birds migrating to foreign lands.

At night in the castle, while the others slept, she would walk down the broad marble stairs to the sea and cool her poor burning feet in the cold water. Then she would think of her sisters, down in the deep sea.

One night they came; arm in arm they rose above the surface of the water, singing ever so sadly. She waved to them, and they recognized her, and they told her how much sorrow she had brought them. After that they visited her every night; and once she saw, far out to sea, her old grandmother. It had been years since she had stuck her head up into the air; and there, too, was her father the mer-king with his crown on his head. They stretched their hands toward her but did not dare come as near to the land as her sisters.

Day by day the prince grew fonder and fonder of her; but he loved her as he would have loved a good child, and had no thought of making her his queen. And she had to become his wife or she would never have an immortal soul, but on the morning after his marriage would become foam on the great ocean.

"Don't you love me more than you do all others?" was the message in the little mermaid's eyes when the prince kissed her lovely forehead.

"Yes, you are the dearest to me," said the prince, "for you have the kindest heart of them all. You are devoted to me and you look like a young girl I once saw, and will probably never see again. I was in a shipwreck. The waves carried me ashore, where a holy temple lay. Many young girls were in service there; one of them, the youngest of them all, found me on the beach and saved my life. I saw her only twice, but she is the only one I can love in this world; and you look like her. You almost make her picture disappear from my soul. She belongs to the holy temple and, therefore, good fortune has sent you to me instead, and we shall never part."

"Oh, he does not know that it was I who saved his life," thought the little mermaid. "I carried him across the sea to the forest where the temple stood. I hid behind the rocks and watched over him until he was found. I saw that beautiful girl whom he loves more than me!" And the little mermaid sighed deeply, for cry she couldn't. "He has said that the girl belongs to the holy temple and will never come out into the world, and they will never meet again. But I am with him and see him every day. I will take care of him, love him, and devote my life to him."

Everyone said that the young prince was to be married; he was to have the neighboring king's daughter, a beautiful princess. A magnificent ship was built and made ready. It was announced that the prince was traveling to see the neighboring kingdom, but that no one believed. "It is not the country but the princess he is to inspect," they all agreed.

HANS CHRISTIAN ANDERSEN

The little mermaid shook her head and smiled; she knew what the prince thought, and they didn't.

"I must go," he had told her, "I must look at the beautiful princess, my parents demand it. But they won't force me to carry her home as my bride. I can't love her. She does not look like the girl from the temple as you do. If I ever marry, I shall most likely choose you, my little foundling with the eloquent eyes." And he kissed her on her red lips and played with her long hair, and let his head rest so near her heart that it dreamed of human happiness and an immortal soul.

"Are you afraid of the ocean, my little silent child?" asked the prince as they stood on the deck of the splendid ship that was to sail them to the neighboring kingdom. He told the little mermaid how the sea can be still or stormy, and about the fishes that live in it, and what the divers had seen underneath the water. She smiled as he talked, for who knew better than she about the world on the bottom of the ocean?

In the moonlit night, when everyone slept but the sailor at the rudder and the lookout in the bow, she sat on the bulwark and looked down into the clear water. She thought she saw her father's palace; and on the top of its tower her old grandmother was standing with her silver crown on her head, looking up through the currents of the sea, toward the keel of the ship. Her sisters came; they looked at her so sorrowfully and wrung their white hands in despair; she waved to them and smiled. She wanted them to know that she was happy, but just at that moment the little cabin boy came and her sisters dived down under the water; he saw nothing but some white foam on the ocean.

The next morning the ship sailed into the harbor of the great town that belonged to the neighboring king. All the church bells were ringing, and from the tall towers trumpets blew, while the soldiers stood at attention, with banners flying and bayonets on their rifles.

Every day another banquet was held, and balls and parties followed one after the other. But the princess attended none of them, for she did not live in the palace; she was being educated in the holy temple, where she was to learn all the royal virtues. But at last she came.

The little mermaid wanted ever so much to see her; and when she finally did, she had to admit that a more beautiful girl she had never seen before. Her skin was so delicate and fine, and beneath her long dark lashes smiled a pair of faithful, dark blue eyes.

"It is you!" exclaimed the prince. "You are the one who saved me, when I lay half dead on the beach!" And he embraced his blushing bride.

"Oh, now I am too happy," he said to the little mermaid. "That which I never dared hope has now happened! You will share my joy, for I know that you love me more than any of the others do."

The little mermaid kissed his hand; she felt as if her heart were breaking. His wedding morning would bring her death and she would be changed into foam of the ocean.

All the churchbells rang and heralds rode through the streets and announced the wedding to the people. On all the altars costly silver lamps burned with fragrant oils. The priests swung censers with burning incense in them, while the prince and the princess gave each other their hands, and the bishop blessed them. The little mermaid, dressed in silk and gold, held the train of the bride's dress, but her ears did not hear the music, nor did her eyes see the holy ceremony, for this night would bring her death, and she was thinking of all she had lost in this world.

The bride and bridegroom embarked upon the prince's ship; cannons saluted and banners flew. On the main deck, a tent of gold and scarlet cloth had been raised; there on the softest of pillows the bridal couple would sleep.

The sails were unfurled, and they swelled in the wind and the ship glided across the transparent sea.

When it darkened and evening came, colored lamps were lit and the sailors danced on the deck. The little mermaid could not help remembering the first time she had emerged above the waves, when she had seen the almost identical sight. She whirled in the dance, glided as the swallow does in the air when it is pursued. Everyone cheered and applauded her. Never had she danced so beautifully; the sharp knives cut her feet, but she did not feel it, for the pain in her heart was far greater. She knew that this was the last evening that she would see him for whose sake she had given away her lovely voice and left her home and her family; and he would never know of her sacrifice. It was the last night that she would breathe the same air as he, or look out over the deep sea and up into the star-blue heaven. A dreamless, eternal night awaited her, for she had no soul and had not been able to win one.

Until midnight all was gaiety aboard the ship, and the mermaid danced and laughed with the thought of death in her heart. Then the prince kissed his bride and she fondled his long black hair and, arm in arm, they walked into their splendorous tent, to sleep.

The ship grew quiet. Only the sailor at the helm and the little mermaid were awake. She stood with her white arms resting on the railing and looked toward the east. She searched the horizon for the pink of dawn; she knew that the first sunbeams would kill her.

Out of the sea rose her sisters, but the wind could no longer play with their long beautiful hair, for their heads had been shorn.

"We have given our hair to the sea witch, so that she would help you and you would not have to die this night. Here is a knife that the witch has given us. Look how sharp it is! Before the sun rises, you must plunge it into the heart of the prince; when his warm blood sprays on your feet, they will turn into a fishtail and you will be a mermaid again. You will be able to live your three hundred years down in the sea with us, before you die and become foam on the ocean. Hurry! He or you must die before the sun rises. Our grandmother mourns; she, too, has no hair; hers has fallen out from grief. Kill the prince and come back to us! Hurry! See, there is a pink haze on the horizon. Soon the sun will rise and you will die."

The little mermaid heard the sound of her sisters' deep and strange sighing before they disappeared beneath the waves.

She pulled aside the crimson cloth of the tent and saw the beautiful bride sleeping peacefully, with her head resting on the prince's chest. The little mermaid bent down and kissed his handsome forehead. She turned and looked at the sky; more and more, it was turning red. She glanced at the sharp knife; and once more she looked down at the prince. He moved a little in his sleep and whispered the name of his bride. Only she was in his thoughts, in his dreams! The little mermaid's hand trembled as it squeezed the handle of the knife, then she threw the weapon out into the sea. The waves turned red where it fell, as if drops of blood were seeping up through the water.

Again she looked at the prince; her eyes were already glazed in death. She threw herself into the sea and felt her body changing into foam.

The sun rose out of the sea, its rays felt warm and soft on the deathly cold foam. But the little mermaid did not feel death, she saw the sun, and up above her floated hundreds of airy, transparent forms. She could see right through them, see the sails of the

THE LITTLE MERMAID

ship and the blood-red clouds. Their voices were melodious, so spiritual and tender that no human ear could hear them, just as their forms were so fragile and fine that no human eye could see them. So light were they that they glided through the air, though they had no wings. The little mermaid looked down and saw that she had an ethereal body like theirs.

"Where am I?" she asked; and her voice sounded like theirs — so lovely and so melodious that no human music could reproduce it.

"We are the daughters of the air," they answered. "Mermaids have no immortal soul and can never have one, unless they can obtain the love of a human being. Their chance of obtaining eternal life depends upon others. We, daughters of the air, have not received an eternal soul either; but we can win one by good deeds. We fly to the warm countries, where the heavy air of the plague rests, and blow cool winds to clear it. We carry the smell of flowers that refresh and heal the sick. If for three hundred years we earnestly try to do what is good, we obtain an immortal soul and can take part in the eternal happiness of man. You, little mermaid, have tried with all your heart to do the same. You have suffered and borne your suffering bravely; and that is why you are now among us, the spirits of the air. Do your good deeds and in three hundred years an immortal soul will be yours."

The little mermaid lifted her arms up toward God's sun, and for the first time she felt a tear.

She heard noise coming from the ship. She saw the prince and the princess searching for her. Sadly they looked at the sea, as if they knew that she had thrown herself into the waves. Without being seen, she kissed the bride's forehead and smiled at the prince; then she rose together with the other children of the air, up into a pink cloud that was sailing by.

"In three hundred years I shall rise like this into God's kingdom," she said.

"You may be able to go there before that," whispered one of the others to her. "Invisibly, we fly through the homes of human beings. They can't see us, so they don't know when we are there; but if we find a good child, who makes his parents happy and deserves their love, we smile and God takes a year away from the time of our trial. But if there is a naughty and mean child in the house we come to, we cry; and for every tear we shed, God adds a day to the three hundred years we already must serve."

THE OLD OAK TREE'S
LAST DREAM

A CHRISTMAS STORY

On the outskirts of the forest, on a bank above the beach, grew an old oak tree. It was three hundred and sixty-five years old, but to the tree those years did not seem longer than as many days and nights would to a human being. We are awake during the day and sleep at night, and it is then we have our dreams. But the oak tree is awake three seasons of the year and only sleeps during the fourth. It is only in the winter that it rests; that is its night after that long day that is called spring, summer, and autumn.

Many a warm day the mayflies danced around its leaves and branches, soared on their fragile wings to the very crown of the tree. Ever happy were the little insects and, when they grew tired, they rested on a broad green oak leaf. Then the tree could not help saying, "Poor little you, one day is your whole life. How short, how sad is your fate!"

"Sad," the mayfly always replied. "What do you mean by that? Everything is so beautiful, so warm, and so lovely; and I am so happy."

"But only one day and then all is over."

"Over," said the mayfly. "What is over? Are you over too?"

"No, I live many thousands of your days, and my days are so long that they last almost a year, which is so long that you cannot even figure it out."

THE OLD OAK TREE'S LAST DREAM

"I do not understand you. You live thousands of my days, but I have thousands of moments to be happy in. Do you think that all the beauty in the world will die when you do?"

"No," answered the tree. "That will last much longer than even I can imagine."

"Well there, you see, we live equally long; it is just our ways of figuring that are different."

And the little mayfly flew away again, up into the air, and rejoiced that it had been given such lovely fine wings. The air was filled with the scent of flowering clover from the fields, wild roses from the hedges, elder trees, honeysuckle, woodruff, primroses, and wild mint. The fragrance was so strong that the mayfly felt quite drunk from it. The day was long and beautiful, so filled with happiness, so full of joy. When finally the sun did set, the little fly felt tired from all it had experienced so intensely. The wings were no longer strong enough to carry it. Ever so gently it sank down among the soft grass, nodding its head as if it were saying yes. It slept so peacefully, so happily, and that was death.

"Poor little mayfly," said the oak tree, "its life was much too short."

Every summer the mayflies repeated their dance and the oak held the same conversation with them. Generations upon generations of mayflies died, and yet each new insect born was just as happy, just as carefree, as all those that had gone before it. The oak tree was awake through its spring morning, its summer noon, and its fall evening. It felt that soon it was time to sleep; the oak tree's night, winter, was coming.

Already the storms were singing: "Good night, good night! We pluck your leaves. See, there one fell. We pluck, we pluck! We sing you to sleep. We undress you and shake your old branches; they creak but it does them good. Sleep now, sleep, it is your three hundred and sixty-fifth night, which means you are young yet. Sleep. From the clouds snow is falling, it is a warm blanket around your feet. Sleep and dream sweet dreams!"

The oak tree stood nude with its bare branches against the sky, ready to sleep through its long night, ready to dream many a dream just as human beings do.

It, too, had been tiny once: an acorn had been its cradle. By human reckoning it was now in the fourth century of its life. It was the biggest tree in the forest, and its crown rose up high above the others. Sailors used it as a landmark to navigate by, and the wood pigeons built their nests in it. In the fall the migrating birds would rest among its bronze leaves before they flew south. But now in the winter its branches were naked, and only crows and jack-daws used them; they sat there discussing hard times and com-plaining about how difficult it was to find food, now that winter was here.

It was at the holy Christmastime that the oak tree dreamed the most beautiful dream it had ever dreamed. We shall hear it:

The tree felt that something holy, something solemn and yet joyful, was happening. From every direction it heard church bells ringing. In its dream, it was not winter but the loveliest warm summer day. The branches in its great crown spread themselves out green and fresh, the sun rays played upon its leaves, and the air was filled with the fragrance of flowering trees and bushes. Color-ful butterflies played hide-and-seek and the mayflies danced as if the whole world had been created just for their enjoyment. Every-thing the tree had seen and experienced through its long life passed by in an endless parade. It saw knights with their ladies; they were riding out to hunt, with feathers in their caps and falcons on their hands. And the tree heard the dogs bark and the sound of the hunters' horns. Then strange soldiers camped beneath its branches; they pitched their tents and made fires. The sun re-flected in their shining weapons; they ate and drank and sang as if they had conquered time as well as the country. Two shy lovers came and cut their names in its bark; they were the first to do it but others would follow. Once an aeolian harp had been hung in the oak's branches by a happy youth. That had happened so many years ago, yet it hung there again in the dream; and the wind blew through it and made music. The wood pigeons cooed, and the cuckoo called out once for each year that the oak tree had left of its life; but the cuckoo is not to be trusted.

The tree felt as if a great wave of strength, of life, were passing through it. From its tiniest root, deep down in the ground, to its topmost little twigs, it experienced an awareness of life and warmth. It felt its strength increase, it was growing taller and taller. Its great crown was now enormous. As it grew, its feeling of happi-ness became more and more intense, and it had such a great longing for the sun that it wanted to grow right up into that golden warm sphere.

In its dream, the tree had grown so tall that its top branches were

THE OLD OAK TREE'S LAST DREAM

above the clouds; flocks of birds were flying below them; even the swans could not fly above its crown.

Every leaf had become an eye that could see. All the stars were out, even though it was day, and they looked so clear, so bright, and shone as brilliantly as the eyes of children or of the lovers who met beneath the old oak tree.

What a wonderful moment, so full of joy! Yet in the midst of all its happiness the tree felt a longing for other trees and the bushes that grew far below it. It wished that they, too — and even the little flowers and herbs — could lift themselves high up in the sky as it was doing, and experience its joy. The great oak tree wanted to share its godlike ecstasy. It felt that unless everyone took part in this great dream of happiness it would not be complete. This wish ran through it from root to leaves and was as strong as a human being's desires.

The crown of the tree swayed as its branches turned to look downward. It smelled the odor of woodruff and the stronger fragrance of violets and honeysuckle, and thought that it could hear the cuckoo call.

The top branches of the other trees of the forest now peeped through the clouds; they, too, were growing, lifting themselves up to the sky, toward the sun. Bushes and flowers followed; some of them had freed themselves from the earth and were flying. The birch, like a bolt of white lightning, passed the old oak. The whole forest was flying up toward the sky, even the brown reeds from the swamp were coming. The birds had followed the plants. On a blade of grass sat a grasshopper and played with his wings on his hind legs. Beetles and bees and all the other insects had come, and all of them shared the old oak tree's joyous ecstasy.

"But where are the little blue flowers from the pond?" shouted the oak tree. "And the red harebell and the little primrose?" The old oak did not want anyone to be forgotten.

"We are here, we are here!" sang voices all around it.

"But the woodruff from last summer and all the lilies of the valley from the summer before that, where are they? I remember the year when the wild apples bloomed so beautifully. Oh, so much beauty do I recall through all the years of my life! If it only were all alive now and could be with us!"

"We are, we are," came cries from somewhere higher up; they must have flown there earlier.

"That is the most marvelous of all," rejoiced the old oak tree.

"Everything that I have known is here. Nothing has been forgotten, not the tiniest flower or the smallest bird. How is such joy possible? Where is such happiness conceivable?"

"In heaven it is possible," sang the voices.

And the tree felt its roots loosen their grasp on the earth.

"Yes, that is best!" the oak cried. "Now no bands hold me down. I can fly up into the everlasting light, the eternal glory! And all that I held dear is with me. None has been forgotten, all are here with me, all!"

That was the oak tree's dream; and while it was dreaming a great storm blew across the sea and the land. The waves rushed toward the shore and were crushed on the beach, and the wind tore at the old oak tree's branches. Just at the moment when it dreamed that its roots gave way, in its flight toward heaven, it was torn from the ground by the wind and fell. Its three hundred and sixty-five years of life were now as a day is for the mayfly.

Christmas morning the sea had calmed and the storm was over. The church bells were gaily ringing, and above each house, even the smallest and poorest cottages, a blue ribbon of smoke rose from the chimney, like the smoke at a Druid feast of thanksgiving. The sea grew calmer and calmer, and on board the big ships, which the night before had been so hard pressed by the storm, the sailors hoisted gay colorful flags in the rigging to celebrate the holy day.

"The big tree is gone! The old oak tree we used as a landmark!" the sailors shouted, amazed. "It fell in the storm. What shall we use now? There is none that can replace it."

That was the old oak tree's funeral sermon; it was short but well meant. The tree itself lay stretched out on the snow-covered beach. From the ship came the sound of the sailors singing a carol about the joyful season, when Christ was born to save mankind and give us eternal life. The sailors were singing of the same dream, the beautiful dream that the old oak tree had dreamed Christmas Eve: the last night of its life.

THE TALISMAN

$\mathbb{T}$here once were a prince and
a princess who had just gotten married. They were so very happy
that they had only one worry: the thought that they might not
always be as happy as they were now. Therefore, they wanted a
talisman that could protect them against discontent in their marriage. They had heard of a wise hermit who lived out in the forest,
of whom it was said that he had remedies for all the griefs of this
world. The prince and the princess went to seek his advice and
told him about what troubled their hearts.

The wise man listened to them and said, "Travel through all the
countries of the world and, when you meet a couple who are truly
contented in their married life, ask them to give you a small piece
of the linen that they are wearing next to their bodies. Once you
have that, keep it always with you. A little piece of such linen is,
indeed, a very powerful charm!"

The prince and the princess set out on their journey. They had
not ridden far when they heard of a knight who was supposed to be
most happily married. They rode up to his castle and asked him
and his noble wife if it were true, as it had been rumored, that they
were perfectly content in their marriage.

"Yes," answered the knight, "it is true, except for one thing. We
have no children." Here the talisman was not to be found, so the
young royal couple continued their journey.

HANS CHRISTIAN ANDERSEN

They came to a large city where lived an honorable citizen of whom it was said that he had lived a long life in perfect union with his wife. To his home they made their way to ask the couple if their marriage was as happy as everyone said it was.

"Yes, it is!" answered the good man. "My wife and I have lived in perfect harmony; if only we had not had so many children, for they have caused us so much trouble and grief." Here, too, they need not ask for any talisman.

And the prince and princess traveled on, asking everywhere if anyone knew a couple whose marriage had brought them only joy, but nowhere were they told of any.

One day as they were riding through a meadow they saw a shepherd sitting and playing on his flute. Just at that moment his wife, carrying an infant in her arms, with a little boy beside her, came walking out to her husband. As soon as the shepherd spied his wife he jumped up and ran to meet her. He greeted her and took the babe from her arms and fondled and kissed it. The shepherd's dog had come too; it jumped for joy around the boy and licked his hand. The wife put down a pot that she had brought with her and said, "Come, my husband, and eat." The shepherd was hungry but the first bite he gave the baby, and the second he shared between his son and the dog.

All this the prince and princess heard and saw. They dismounted, walked up to the little family, and asked: "You seem to us to be what we would call a happily married couple, aren't you?"

"Yes, truly we are happy," answered the shepherd. "I think no prince or princess could be happier than we are."

"Then listen to me," said the prince. "Be so kind as to give us a tiny piece of the linen you are wearing under your clothes. You shall be well paid for it."

The shepherd and his wife blushed and looked embarrassed. Finally he said, "God knows that we would gladly give you not only a tiny piece of our linen but our shirts and shifts as well, if we only had any, but we don't."

The prince and princess had to travel on without the talisman they sought. Finally they grew tired of this endless journey and set their course for home. As their road went through the forest and past the wise hermit's cottage, they stopped to tell him how poorly he had advised them.

The wise man smiled and said, "Has your journey really been in

THE TALISMAN

vain? Have you not returned enriched from your experiences?"

"Yes," admitted the prince, "I have learned that contentment is the rarest blessing on this earth."

"And I have learned," said the princess, "that for contentment all that is needed is to be content!"

The prince took the princess' hand in his, and with expressions of the deepest love they looked at each other.

The wise man blessed them and said, "In your hearts you have found the true talisman. Guard it carefully, and the evil spirit of discontent will never — no matter how long you live — have any power over you."

THE BOG KING'S DAUGHTER

he storks tell their young
ones many stories and fairy tales. All of them take place in the
swamps and bogs where storks like to live. They usually choose
stories that fit the ages of their children. The smallest are satisfied
if their parents say: "Muddle, duddle . . . cribble, crabble"; that is
plot and morality enough for their taste. But the older ones are not
so easily satisfied; they demand something with a deeper meaning
or at least a story about their own family. The storks know two
stories that are very ancient and very long: one of them is the story
of Moses, who was set sailing out upon the waters of the Nile by
his mother and was found by a princess. He was carefully brought
up and well educated and became a great man. Where he is buried
no one knows. That story every child has heard. The other tale is
not well known, possibly because it is a bit provincial. It is a fairy
tale that has been told by stork mothers for a thousand years; each
one of them has told it a little better than her mother, and we shall
tell it best of all.

The first storks who told it had experienced it themselves, they
had been part of it. They had their summer residence on top of the
roof of the wooden house of a Viking chieftain who lived near the
great bog in the north of Jutland, which is called Vendsyssel. If one
were to describe it learnedly — as it is described in a Danish
geography book — then one must explain that once this was an

314

THE BOG KING'S DAUGHTER

ocean bed, but the waters departed and the land rose. Today the bog is very large, but once it was even larger; there were miles and miles of swamp, marshland, and stretches of peat. There were no trees worth talking about, and over the bog hovered, almost always, a dense fog. At the turn of the eighteenth century there were still wolves there; and it was even wilder a thousand years ago. Yet the landscape was the same; the reeds were no taller, and they had the same feathery flowers and slender leaves. The birch tree's bark was as white as it is now, and the branches with their fine green leaves hung toward the earth as gracefully. The animal life, too, has not changed. The flies, then, were as troublesome as they are now; and the storks wore the same black and white livery with red stockings. But the human beings were dressed differently, though their fate was the same, if they stepped out upon the surface of the great bog: a thousand years ago — as today — they would slowly sink into the muddy ooze down to the bog king. That was the name given to the ruler of the great bog. Some called him the swamp king, but we prefer the bog king and the storks agree with us, for that is what they called him. Very little is known about his rule, which may be just as well.

Near the bog, on the shores of the fjord, a Viking chief had built a big house. It had a stone cellar, three floors and a tower, constructed of logs. On top of the roof a pair of storks had built their nest. The mother stork, who was brooding, was convinced that every one of her eggs would hatch.

One evening the father stork was away from the nest longer than usual, and when he finally returned he looked upset and unhappy. "I have something horrible to tell you," he said.

"Don't!" exclaimed his wife. "Remember I am brooding. If you upset me, it might harm the eggs!"

"You must know what has happened!" insisted the male stork. "She has come, the daughter of our landlord in Egypt, and now she has disappeared!"

"The girl who is related to the fairies? Tell me, tell me! Don't keep me in suspense, that is not good for me when I am sitting on eggs!"

"You know, my dear, that she believed the doctors who said that the water lilies, here in the north, would cure her father. She has flown up here. She was wearing a swanskin and came together with the two other princesses who fly up here every year to bathe —

HANS CHRISTIAN ANDERSEN

they believe the waters make them retain their youth. The young princess was here and now she is gone!"

"You are so long-winded, get to the point!" complained his wife. "The eggs may catch cold; I can't stand being kept in suspense."

"You know I keep an eye on everything," the male stork continued. "Last night I was down in the reeds, where the mud is solid enough for me to stand, and I saw three swans. There was something about their flight that said: 'Look out, they are not swans, they are something else wearing swanskins.' You know as well as I, how one can feel that a thing just isn't right."

"Yes, yes!" His wife was getting very impatient. "Tell me about the princess and never mind the swanskins, they bore me!"

"You know that right in the center of the bog there is a lake — you can see part of it from here if you stand up. Near the reeds at the shore, there lay the trunk of an old alder tree, and the three swans landed on it. They flapped their wings and looked around. Then one of them cast off her swanskin and I recognized her. She was the princess from the palace in Egypt. She had nothing to cover herself with but her long black hair. She asked the other two to guard her swanskin, while she dived down into the water to pluck the flower that she thought she had spied underneath the water. The other two swans flew up, taking the princess' swanskin with them in their bills. I wondered what they wanted to do with it; and I am sure the princess would have liked to ask the same question. We were answered soon enough.

" 'Dive down into the dark water!' cried the swans. 'Never again shall you see Egypt, you shall stay here in the wild bog forever!' Then, with their beaks, they tore her swanskin into hundreds of pieces. The feathers flew around them; it looked like a snowstorm. Then the two evil princesses flew away."

"It is horrible!" exclaimed the mother stork. "I can't bear hearing stories like that. I am sure it is not good for me. . . . But tell me what happened afterward, please tell me!"

"The princess cried and her tears fell on the trunk of the old alder tree. It began to move! It wasn't an alder tree, it was the bog king himself! The one who lives in the bog and rules it. I saw the tree trunk turn in the water, and then it no longer looked like a tree trunk. Its long branches were not branches but arms! The poor girl got frightened. She tried to jump up onto the shore, but she was too heavy to stand in the muddy bog. At that place the ooze can't

THE BOG KING'S DAUGHTER

even bear me. She sank down into the bog and at the same moment the bog king disappeared. I think he pulled her down. Some big black bubbles rose to the surface, burst, and were gone. Now she is buried in the bog and she will never return to Egypt and bring her father the flower. You couldn't have borne seeing it, I am sure!"

"I don't think you should even have told me about it now; it may spoil the eggs! The princess will take care of herself, I am sure; there is always someone who is ready to help her kind. Now if it had been you or I who had been sucked down into the mud, then everything would have been over."

"Still, I will keep an eye on the place," said the male stork, and he did.

A long time passed; then one day a green stalk shot up through the water. When it reached the surface a leaf unfolded, and in the center of it was a bud. The leaf grew bigger and bigger, and so did the bud. One morning when the stork flew above it he saw that the bud was opening in the warm sunshine. In the flower lay a little girl, a beautiful child; she looked so much like the princess from Egypt that the stork thought it might be she, grown smaller. But on second thought he found it more reasonable that the child was her daughter with the bog king, and that was why she was lying in a water lily.

"She can't stay there," thought the stork. "There is no room in my nest, we are already crowded. But the Viking chief's wife has no child, and I know she wants one badly. I have heard her sighing. Since they claim that I bring children I might as well do it for once. I will give it to our landlady; it will make her happy."

The stork took the little girl in his bill and flew up to the house. There he pecked a hole in the window — that was easy, for it was only covered by a pig's bladder. He lay the baby beside the sleeping woman, then he flew back up to his wife to tell her all about it. The children were allowed to listen; after all, they were almost grown up.

"You see, the princess isn't dead, she must have sent the little girl up with the water lily. And I found a home for her."

"I told you all the time that, if she couldn't take care of herself, then someone else would take care of her," said the mother stork. "But you should think a little more about your own family and less about others. It will soon be time to leave; my wings are itching.

HANS CHRISTIAN ANDERSEN

The cuckoo and the nightingale have already left, and the quails are saying that the wind will soon blow just right for flying south. I am sure our children will do well on the maneuver; I know them, I am their mother."

The Viking chieftain's wife was overjoyed when she awoke and found the little girl. She kissed and fondled the little baby, but the child did not seem to like it, she kicked and screamed and cried. Finally she fell asleep and no child has ever looked lovelier than she did then. The Viking woman felt so happy and lighthearted that she was sure that her husband and his men would soon be home; they would come just as unexpectedly as the child had. She got busy putting the house in order. She ordered the slaves to polish the old shields that hung on the walls and told her maid to bring out the tapestries that had pictures of their gods woven in them: of Odin, Thor, and Freya. Skins were placed on the wooden benches and dry firewood on the great central fireplace, so that it could be lit as soon as the voyagers returned. The mistress worked along with the others; by evening she was very tired, and she slept well throughout the night.

Just before the sun rose she awoke. The child was gone! She got terribly frightened and jumped out of bed to look for it. She lit a bit of kindling and then she saw at the foot of her bed not the child but a big ugly frog. She felt sick at the sight of it and grabbed a large piece of firewood to kill it. But the toad looked up at her with such infinitely sad eyes that she couldn't. She looked around the room. The frog gave a pathetic little croak, and the woman shivered at the sound. Then she ran and opened up the shutters. Just at that moment the sun rose. Its first rays came in through the opening and fell on the bed, where the big frog was sitting. Its broad mouth became small; its ugly limbs straightened and took on the lovely shape of her little child. The ugly frog was gone.

"What has happened!" she cried. "I must have had an evil dream. There is my lovely fairy child!" She picked up the little girl, kissed her, and pressed her to her heart. But the baby acted more like an angry kitten; she scratched and bit.

The Viking chief did not return that day or the next. He was on his way home but had the wind against him. It blew toward the south for the storks' sake. Fair winds for one are foul for another.

The next night the Viking woman realized how things were with her little child; she was bewitched. By day she was as beautiful as a

THE BOG KING'S DAUGHTER

fairy but her character was wild and evil; at night she was an ugly frog with sad sorrowful eyes and sat whimpering quietly. These transformations in the girl, whom the stork had brought, were caused by the two natures within her. In the daytime she had the shape and appearance of her lovely mother but the soul of her father. At night her kinship with the bog king could be seen in her body, but then she had the sweet character and heart of her mother.

The chieftain's wife was frightened and sorrowful: who could break such a curse? Yet she loved the unfortunate creature that fate had brought to her. She was determined not to tell her husband about the child being bewitched, for she feared that he would set her out in the wilderness to be eaten by wolves, as this was the Viking custom with babies that were deformed. She vowed — poor woman — that her husband would never see the child except by day.

One morning the sound of the wings of storks could be heard. They were resting after the big maneuver and were now ready for the flight south. There were more than two hundred of them.

"Everybody ready!" was the command. "Children and wives stay with your husbands!"

"I feel so light," said one of the stork children. "It creeps and crawls inside me right down into my legs, as if I were filled with living frogs. How wonderful it is to travel!"

"Keep in your places," admonished their mother and father, "and don't talk too much, it is bad for the breathing."

And away they flew!

Right at that moment a horn was blown. The Vikings had landed. Their ships were loaded with rich booty. They had come from the coasts of Gaul, where the people — just as they did in England — prayed: "Free us from the wild Norsemen."

A great celebration took place in the Viking hall near the great bog. A vat of mead was carried in and the great fire was lit. Horses were butchered, and the warm horse blood was sprayed on the new slaves, in honor of Odin: a heathen baptism. The smoke drifted from the fire up to the roof, soot dripped from the great beams; but no one took any notice.

The house was filled with guests and everyone received a costly present. All old disagreements and broken promises were forgotten. They drank and they ate, and they threw the gnawed bones in each other's faces — that was considered amusing. The poet of the time, who was called a *skjald*, was a warrior too; he had been on the voyage, so he knew what he was composing verses about. He sang ballads about their adventures, recalling every battle each Viking had fought in. His verses always ended with the same words! "Richness vanishes and friends die, as one must die oneself; only the fame of greatness never dies." Then they would all bang with their knives or hit their shields with their gnawed bones, so the noise could be heard far away.

The chieftain's wife sat on the women's bench, dressed in a silken gown; she wore gold bracelets and an amber necklace. The *skjald* did not forget to mention her in his verses; he sang about the golden treasure she had brought her rich and famous husband. In truth, the chieftain was pleased with his child, whom he had only seen while the sun was in the sky. She was beautiful, and as for her temper, he liked it. "She will become a valkyrie, who will fight as well as any man and not be frightened by the sound of a sword as it cleaves the air," he said proudly.

The vat of mead was empty and another one was carried into the hall. Oh yes, these were people who could drink. The Vikings had a proverb: "Cattle know when it is best to stop grazing, but a fool never realizes the size of his own stomach." Although all of them knew these words, they seemed to have forgotten them. Just as they did not remember another proverb from that time: "A good friend becomes a bore if he stays too long in another man's house." For weeks the guests stayed, for the sake of the meat and the mead.

Once more that year the Vikings went on a raid, but only across the waters to England. The Viking woman was again alone with her little girl. By now she loved more deeply the sighing frog with the sad lovely eyes than the beautiful girl who bit and tore at her.

The raw and cold autumn fog, which, although it has no mouth, gnaws the leaves of the trees, now covered the landscape. The first snowflakes had followed each other down from the clouds. Winter was not far away. The sparrows had moved into the storks' nest and were criticizing endlessly the departed owners. But where were the father and mother stork and all their children?

They were in Egypt, where the sun in winter shines as warmly as it does in Denmark in the summer. Tamarisks and acacias were in bloom there, and above the temple dome shone Mohammed's

THE BOG KING'S DAUGHTER

moon. On the tops of the tall, slender towers many stork couples sat resting from their long journey. Whole flocks of them had built their nests in the ruins of the other temples; those once busy places that were forgotten now. The date palms lift their leaves high up in the air like gigantic parasols. The whitish-gray pyramids look as if they had been drawn on the clear air of the desert. There the ostrich demonstrates that, although it cannot fly, it at least can run; and the lion, with its sad and knowing eyes, contemplates the marble sphinx that stands half buried in the sand. The waters of the Nile were low and the muddy riverbed was alive with frogs. For a stork that was the most pleasant sight of all. The young ones, who had not been in Egypt before, thought it was all an optical illusion, so marvelous was it.

"No, it is real, and that is the way it always is here in our winter residence!" said the stork mother.

"Aren't we going any farther?" asked the young ones. "Aren't we going to see even more?"

"There isn't much more to see," answered their mother. "The part that is fertile is a little too wild. The trees grow too close together in the jungle, and among their branches are thorny vines; only the elephants with their thick skins and broad feet can make their way through there. The snakes are too big to eat and the lizards too agile to catch. And if you go in the other direction, toward the desert, you will get sand in your eyes, and that is not pleasant. No, it is best to stay here, where there are plenty of frogs and grasshoppers. I will stay here, and so will you!"

And they stayed. The old ones had a nest on top of a minaret; there they rested, while they smoothed down their feathers and polished their bills on their long red legs. They would lift their heads and nod gravely toward other storks, as they looked out over the landscape with their brown eyes that seemed to shine with intelligence. The young female storks would wander about in the swamp, making friends and eating a frog for every third step they took. Often they would walk around with a little snake dangling in their bills; they thought it looked attractive, and besides, it tasted good. The young males fought with each other; they would flap their wings and fight such duels with their beaks that sometimes blood would flow.

After a while they all got engaged, which was only natural; then they built nests of their own, and argued and fought some more. In the hot countries everyone has a hot temper, but it was all very entertaining. The older storks, found it amusing to watch; they thought anything their own offspring did most marvelous and unique. Every day the sun shone, and every day there was enough to eat; the only thing left to do was to enjoy oneself.

But inside the great castle life was not amusing at all. The great powerful ruler of the country lay as still as a mummy on his couch in the great hall of the castle. The walls were all covered with murals; it looked as if he were lying in the center of an enormous tulip. Servants and relations flocked around him. He wasn't dead, but he wasn't alive either. The water lily from the north that could have saved him would never be found. His young and beautiful daughter who had flown in a swanskin over the ocean and the great mountains, far to the north, to fetch it would never return. "She is dead and gone," said the two princesses who had accompanied her on the journey. Listen to the pretty story they told:

"We were flying, all three of us, high up in the air when a hunter saw us; he shot an arrow and it hit our friend. She sank down toward a little lake, while she sang her good-by: her swan song. By

THE BOG KING'S DAUGHTER

the shore of the lake, under a birch tree, we buried her! We took revenge. We tied burning tinder under the wings of the swallow that lived underneath the hunter's roof. It flew home to its nest and set fire to his house. The hunter died in the fire and the flames could be seen as far as the birch tree under which the princess rests, where she has become dust in the dust. She will never come back to Egypt."

Then they cried, both of them; and the father stork, who heard it all, clattered with his bill, he was so angry.

"Lies and more lies," he said. "I felt like running my beak right through them!"

"And breaking it!" replied his wife. "You would be a sight then! Think a little more about yourself and your family. What is outside it shouldn't concern you."

"I will fly over to the great dome and listen tomorrow, when all the wise men assemble to discuss the king's illness. Maybe they will get a little nearer to the truth."

The learned and the wise gathered, and talked and talked; but the stork couldn't understand their chatter. It did not help the sick man either, or his daughter who was lost in the great bog. We could listen a little to what was said; one has to hear an awful lot of that kind of talk before one dies. But since this is a story and we are free to travel in time as well as space, let's hear about the first assembly of the wise and learn what happened when the king became ill, a year before. We ought to know at least as much as the stork could understand.

"Love breeds life, and the highest form of love breeds the highest form of life. Only through love can our sick king be brought back to life." This had been said at the first assembly, and the learned and the wise had all agreed that it was true.

"It is a beautiful thought," the stork had explained as soon as he came home to the nest.

"I don't quite understand it," his wife had said, "and I don't believe the fault is mine. It is unclear! But it doesn't matter, I have enough to think about already."

The learned and the wise had then gone on to discuss the different forms of love: the one between lovers, and the one that parents feel for their children, besides the more complicated forms, such as the one between light and the plants — how the sun rays kiss the black earth, making the seeds sprout. That part of the discussion was so learned and so filled with long and difficult words that the stork could understand almost none of it, let alone be able to repeat it when he got home. He became very morose, half closed his eyes, and stood on one leg for a whole day. Excessive learning is very hard to bear.

But one thing he did know, for he had heard it said often enough, both by the courtiers and the ordinary people — and they had talked from their hearts: it was a disaster to the whole country that the king was sick, and it would be a great blessing to the people if he got well.

"But where grows the flower that can give him back his health?" That was the question everyone had asked last year. They had studied old learned books, the stars, the weather, and the clouds, and used every possible detour to get at the truth. The wise and the learned — as we know — had agreed upon the maxim, "Love breeds life, life to our father." They repeated it over and over again and wrote it down as a prescription: "Love breeds life." But how the prescription was to be filled, that no one knew. At last they had agreed that the princess, who loved her father so much, must be the one to find the answer. And the wise men even decided how she was to go about it. At night, when the new moon had disappeared from the sky, she was to go out in the desert to the marble sphinx. There she should cast away the sand from the half-buried door at its base and walk through the long corridors that led to the center of one of the great pyramids. Here lay buried one of the great kings from ancient times. The princess was to enter this chamber of death and splendor, and lean her head against the decorated casing that contained the mummy. The dead king would then reveal to her how her father could be saved.

She had done what had been demanded of her, and in a dream she had learned that in the wild bog in the north — the place had been very accurately described — there grew a lotus flower that would bring back her father's health. She was to dive into the black water and pick the first flower that touched her breast.

This had all happened a year and a day before, and that was why the princess had flown in a swanskin from Egypt north to Denmark. The storks knew all about this; and now we know it, which makes the whole story easier to understand. We know, too, that the bog king took her down to his castle and that everyone in Egypt thought she was lost forever — that is, everyone but the wisest of

THE BOG KING'S DAUGHTER

all the wise; he was of the same opinion as the mother stork: "The princess will take care of herself."

"I think I will steal the swanskins from the two evil princesses," proposed the father stork, "then they won't be able to fly north and do more harm. I will hide the swanskins up there until there will be a use for them."

"What do you mean by up there?" asked his wife.

"In our nest up by the bog, in Denmark. Our children can help me carry them. Should they be too heavy, then we can find a hiding place along the way and carry them the rest of the way next year. One swanskin is enough for the princess, but you know how it is when you travel in the north, you can never have clothes enough along."

"Nobody is going to thank you for it," grumbled his wife. "But you are the master; no one listens to me except when I am laying eggs."

In the Viking hall by the great bog, the young girl had been given a name. She was called Helga. A name too soft to fit her character. Years passed; each spring the storks traveled north and each fall they returned to Egypt. Helga grew, became a big girl, and then a maiden sixteen summers old. Beautiful was the shell, but the kernel was hard and cruel; she was wilder and more ferocious than most people in those grim and brutal times.

She found pleasure in seeing the red blood of the horses that were offered to Odin stain her white hands. And once, in a fit of temper, she had bitten the head off a black cock that was to be offered to Thor. To her father she said — and she meant it — "Should your enemies come and tear the roof off the hall while you slept, I should not wake you. I would not warn you, for my cheeks are still burning from the time, years ago, when you slapped my face."

But the Viking chieftain did not believe her; his daughter's beauty blinded him to all her faults. He did not know how Helga's soul and body changed when night fell. When she rode, she sat on the horse as if she and the animal were one; and if sometimes the horse got into a fight with another horse, she stayed on its back, laughing while the animals kicked and bit each other. When the Vikings returned from a raid, she would throw herself into the waters of the fjord and swim out to the boat to greet them. From her beautiful long hair she cut strands and with them she made bowstrings.

"Self-made is well made," she would say, and laugh.

Her foster mother — the Viking woman — according to the times and habits of the country, was a strong-willed and capable woman; but toward her daughter she was soft and frightened, for she knew the curse that rested on the poor child.

To make her mother miserable — as if she enjoyed seeing the poor woman's terror — Helga would throw herself over the side of the well when her mother was nearby. The wretched woman would watch while, froglike, she swam in the freezing well water; then, more agilely than a cat, she would climb the steep stone sides of the well and rush into the hall, while her clothes were still dripping wet, so that she dampened the fresh leaves that had been strewn on the floor.

But at twilight, just before the sun set, Helga changed; she became quiet and thoughtful. Then she was obedient and would listen to what was said to her. She would draw close to her mother and, when the sun went down and her appearance and nature were transformed, she would sit still and sorrowful in her frog shape. Her body was much larger than any frog's, and therefore she was all the uglier; she looked like a horrible dwarf with a frog's head and webbed hands and feet. Her eyes alone were lovely with their infinite sadness. Of voice she had none. All she could manage was a hollow croak that sounded like a child sobbing in its dreams. Then her foster mother would take her on her lap and, disregarding her ugly body, she would look into her sad eyes and say, "I could almost wish that you always would be my silent frog child, for you are far more frightening to look at when your outside is beautiful and your inside ugly."

And the poor woman wrote magic runic letters on birch bark and put them on her frog child to break the spell, but none of them worked.

"One wouldn't think she had ever been so small that she could lie in a water lily," said the father stork. "She is a real woman now and the image of her mother, the Egyptian princess. We have never seen her again. And you, my dear, and the Egyptian wise man were wrong, she couldn't take care of herself. Through all these years, ever since she disappeared, I have flown back and forth across the

THE BOG KING'S DAUGHTER

bog but I have seen no sign of her. Once, when I came up here a few days before you and the young ones, in order to repair the nest and put things in order, I flew all night — as if I were an owl or a bat — above the place where she disappeared, but I didn't see a thing. The swanskins that it took us three years to bring up here will never be used. Now they have lain on the bottom of the nest these many years; and if this log house burns down, they will be lost."

"And so will our good nest!" said his wife angrily. "You are less concerned about that than those toys made of feathers, and that precious bog princess of yours. Why don't you dive down and stay with her! You are neither a good father nor a good husband; that I said the very first time that I laid eggs. We will be lucky if that Viking hussy doesn't send an arrow through one of our children. She is a madwoman and doesn't know what she is doing. But she ought to remember that we are of an ancient family and have lived here a lot longer than she has. We pay our taxes — and that is only right — one feather, one egg, and a young one, every year. When she is around, then I stay in the nest. Don't think that I fly down in the yard as I used to, and still do in Egypt, where I am friends with almost everyone and even take a look into the pots and pans. No, here I stay at home, and grow more and more irritated over that wench and over you, too! You should have let her stay in the water lily, then we would have been rid of her."

"You are more respectable than your speech shows," said her husband. "I know you even better than you know yourself."

He made a little jump, beat the air twice with his wings, and sailed upward on the breeze. When he had risen, he again flapped his wings as he turned and made a circle. The sunlight shone upon his white feathers; his long neck and bill were stretched straight forward, it was a lovely sight.

"He is the handsomest of the lot of them," said his wife, "but that I will never tell him."

The Vikings returned from their raids abroad early that autumn. Among the prisoners was a Christian priest, one of those who were enemies of Odin and Thor. This new religion, which had already won so many converts in the south, was often discussed among the warriors, as well as among the women of the house. A man called the holy Ansgarius was preaching it, no farther away than Hedeby near Slien. Even Helga had heard about Christ, who for love of humanity gave up his life. But it had gone in one ear and out the other. The word "love" did not seem to have any meaning to her, except at night when, in the wretched shape of a frog, she sat silently in a tiny locked room. But her foster mother had been deeply moved when she listened to the legends told about this strange man who was the Son of God.

The Vikings, who had been abroad, described the great temples built of costly stones for this God whose message was love. Once they had brought back with them two big vessels made of gold; they were richly decorated and had smelled of strange spices. They were censers, which the Christian priests swung in front of their altars, where blood never flowed, although bread and wine were changed into the blood of Him who had sacrificed Himself for the sake of generations yet unborn.

Down into the deep stone cellar of the house the young Christian was carried. His hands and feet were bound. He was handsome. "As handsome as the God Balder," the chieftain's wife claimed.

His plight did not move Helga. She suggested that his legs should be pierced, a rope pulled through them and tied to the tail of a bull. "Then let the dogs loose, and the bull will run as fast it can across the meadows toward the heath, dragging him behind it. That would be an amusing sight and it would be fun to follow on horseback!" she suggested.

Such a horrible death the Vikings would not make him suffer, but because he had offended the gods, he would be offered to them. In the little copse where the stone altar to Odin stood, he was to be killed; and this would be the first time a human being had been sacrificed there.

Young Helga begged to have the privilege of spraying the warm blood on the statues to the gods. She sharpened her knife and when a dog — of which there were so many around the house — ran by her she stuck her knife into it and said with a laugh, "That was to test it."

With horror her mother looked at the evil girl. When night came, and Helga's body and soul changed, then she spoke to her of her sorrow and misery. The ugly frog with the troll-like body stood in front of her and looked up at her with sad eyes and seemed to understand what she was saying.

"Never, even to my husband, have I admitted how doubly you

THE BOG KING'S DAUGHTER

have made me suffer," said the Viking chieftain's wife. "I have more pity for you than I even knew I had. Great is a mother's love; but you, you have never felt love for anything. Your heart is made from the black cold mud of the bog! Why did you ever come to my house!"

The pathetic creature shook, it was as if the words had touched the invisible cord that connects soul and body; great tears formed in its eyes.

"But dark times will come for you," her foster mother continued, "and they will be hard for me too. Better would it have been if you had been set out as a babe on the heath and the cold night air had lulled you to sleep." The woman cried bitterly, then she rose and walked to her bed, which stood on the other side of the leather curtain that divided the room. She was angry and in despair.

The miserable frog sat forlorn in its corner. Every once in a while a sound like a stifled sigh was heard; full of pain was this muffled cry that came from the heart of the poor creature. She seemed to be listening as if she were waiting for someone; then she waddled over to the door and with great difficulty she removed the bar that locked it. Her webbed hand grabbed the tallow lamp, then she drew the iron bar that closed the trap door that led to the cellar. Noiselessly she descended the stairs. In a corner of the underground room she found the helpless prisoner sleeping. She touched him with her cold and slimy hand. He awoke and, seeing the horrible creature in front of him, he shivered with fright, for he thought that she was an evil spirit. The frog took a knife and cut the ropes that bound the man, then she waved her hand to make him understand that he was to follow her.

He mumbled all the holy names that he could remember and crossed himself, but still the creature in front of him stood unchanged. Then he quoted a line from the psalms: "'Blessed is he that considereth the poor, the Lord will deliver him in time of trouble.' . . . Who are you? Why have you, who are so filled with mercy, the shape of an animal?"

The frog beckoned and led the priest through a corridor out into the stable. She pointed to a horse; he led it outside and swung himself onto its back. With surprising agility, the big frog mounted the animal too; she sat in front of the priest and held onto the horse's mane. The priest understood that his strange companion wanted to guide him, and followed the directions that the frog indicated by a nod or a movement with its webbed hands. Soon they were out on the heath, far away from the Vikings' hall.

The priest felt that the grace and mercy of Our Lord manifested themselves through the strange creature who had saved him. He prayed and sang a hymn. The frog trembled. Was it the prayer that touched the monster's soul? Or did she shiver because it soon would be morning? What did she feel? Suddenly the frog straightened itself and grabbed the bridle to stop the horse; she wanted to dismount. But the priest would not let go of his strange companion. He held onto it while he sang another hymn, hoping that this might break the magic spell that the poor creature so obviously was suffering under.

The horse galloped on. The horizon turned pink, and soon the first ray of the sun broke through the low clouds of morning. With it came the transformation of soul and body: the frog with the sad eyes became the beautiful girl with the evil heart. The priest was horrified when he realized that he held not a giant frog but a beautiful girl in his arms. He jumped down from the horse; he was convinced that the powers of evil were playing some terrible trick upon him. Helga dismounted as quickly as he had and, drawing the knife that hung from her belt, she attacked the shocked and confused young priest.

"Let the blade of my knife reach you," she screamed. "Let it draw blood! You look pale, slave! Beardless fool!"

The two of them wrestled, but it was as if unseen powers gave the young priest strength. The roots of an old tree that grew on the bank of the tiny stream helped him, for Helga's feet got caught in one of them and she fell. The priest dipped his hand in the clear water and, spraying it on her forehead and chest, he bade the unclean spirit leave her and baptized her in the name of Our Lord Jesus Christ. But the water of baptism only has strength when those it falls upon have faith.

Yet had she not the faith herself, it was that very attribute in the young priest that gave him power over her. His strength fascinated her, and she let her arms fall to her sides and stopped fighting with him. To her he seemed a mighty magician: pale and amazed, she looked at this man who knew so many enchantments and charms. To her, his prayers and psalms sounded like magic and the sign of the Cross looked like witchcraft. Had the young man swung a knife or a sharp ax in front of her face, she would not have

THE BOG KING'S DAUGHTER

blinked; but, when he drew with his finger the sign of the Cross on her forehead, she shuddered and closed her eyes. There she sat like a tame bird, with her head bowed.

He spoke to her gently about that deed of love she had performed herself when, in her frog shape, she had come and cut the ropes that held him and led him back to freedom and to life. She was still bound by bands far stronger than those a knife could cut. But also she could gain her freedom and learn to love the eternal light of God. He would take her to Hedeby, the town where the holy Ansgarius lived and worked. He would be able to break the spell.

Although she was willing to ride in front of him, he would not allow her to. "You must sit behind me on the horse, for your magic beauty comes from the Evil One, I fear it!" said the young priest, paused and then added: "But the victory was mine, in Christ!"

He fell on his knees and prayed most piously. The whole forest became a holy church; the birds sang as if they belonged to the congregation, and the wild mint smelled so fragrantly that one could believe it was trying its best to pretend that it was incense. The young priest said aloud the words from the Gospel: "'To give light to them that sit in the darkness and in the shadow of death, to guide our feet into the way of peace.'"

Then he preached about the nature of God and His love for all; and while he spoke the horse stood still as if it, too, were listening.

Patiently, Helga let the young priest help her up on the animal's back and there she sat like a sleepwalker. The young man tied two twigs together in the form of a cross and, holding the sign before him, they rode deeper and deeper into the forest. The trees grew close together, the road became narrower and narrower; soon it was hardly a path. Sharp brambles grew everywhere and scratched the travelers as they forced their way through them. They followed a stream that soon became a swamp and they had difficulty finding their way around it.

The young priest talked while they rode. His words were not without power, for his faith in the mild God of love, Whom he followed, was great, and he was earnest in his wish to save this young girl's soul. Drops of water will hollow out the hardest stone and the surf of the ocean will wear down the sharpest reefs. Now the dew of God's grace was wearing down the hardness in Helga's soul. She did not know it, any more than the seed in the earth knows that the warm sun and the rain are bringing forth its green sprouts and its flower.

As the mother's lullaby enters the baby's mind and the child can repeat the sounds without understanding their meaning, so did the young priest's words enter Helga's soul.

The forest gave way to open country but not for long; the green woods soon closed around them again. Just before sunset they met a band of robbers.

"Where have you stolen that beautiful maid!" one of them cried as he grabbed the bridle, while the others forced the riders down from their horse.

They were many and the priest had no other weapon than the knife he had taken from Helga. He defended himself well with it; one of the robbers flung an ax at him but he sprang aside and the ax made a deep wound in the neck of the horse. The blood spouted out of the gash and the animal fell to the ground. Then Helga, who had seemed to be in a trance, suddenly awoke and threw herself upon the dying beast. The young priest stood in front of her to protect her, but one of the robbers swung his heavy iron hammer and hit the young man's head so hard that his skull was split. Blood and brain spattered all around him as he fell to the ground, dead.

The robbers grabbed Helga's white arms, but just at that moment the sun set; the last ray of its light disappeared and she changed into an ugly frog. A whitish-green mouth covered her whole face, her arms became thin and slimy, her fine hands became broad with webs between the fingers. The robbers let go of her in horror; there she stood as an ugly monster in their midst. True to her frog nature, she jumped high above the robbers' heads and disappeared in the greenery. The robbers thought that what they had seen was the secret magic of the evil demigod Loke, and they hurried away.

The full moon had risen in the sky when Helga in her pitiful frog shape climbed out of the thicket. She stopped by the bodies of the priest and the dead horse and looked down at them with eyes in which there almost were tears. She made the same sobbing sound a child makes just before starting to cry, and threw herself down over one and then the other of the still bodies. She carried water from a nearby stream and sprayed it on them in the hope of reviving them. But dead they were and dead they would remain. The thought that the wild animals of the woods would eat them was too horrible to bear. She began to dig in the earth, but she had no spade, only a stick: a thick branch of a tree. The webs between her fingers burst and bled.

Soon she realized that she would never be able to dig a hole deep enough. She washed the blood from the dead priest's face and covered it with fresh leaves; then she took the biggest branches she could find and piled them over the bodies of the man and the horse. She knew that even this would not keep the wolves or foxes away, and therefore she looked for the biggest stones that she could carry, and placed them on top of the branches. When the mound was finished she stuffed moss between the stones, and only then did she believe that the grave would be undisturbed.

It had taken her the whole night to finish her work. Now the sun rose, and in its first rays Helga stood as beautiful as ever, but her fine hands were bleeding and for the first time tears ran down her blushing, youthful cheeks.

Now the two natures within her fought. She trembled as if she had had a fever. She looked about with fear and wonder in her eyes. She appeared like a person that had just awakened from a nightmare. She rushed over to a birch tree and held onto it to support herself; then suddenly she climbed up the tree agilely as a squirrel. There in the top of the tree she remained all day sitting perfectly motionless.

All around her reigned the stillness of the forest — thus it is often described, although if one listens carefully and looks closely enough, nature is never still. Two butterflies flew in circles around each other: were they fighting or playing? At the foot of the tree in which the frightened Helga sat were some anthills, and hundreds of tiny creatures moved unceasingly in and out of their homes. In the air danced clouds of little flies and mosquitoes, and big dragon-flies flew about on their golden wings. Earthworms crawled out of the wet ground, and moles emptied the earth from their burrows, making little hills. But no one saw little Helga or paid any attention to her, except for a couple of magpies. They landed on the branch on which Helga was sitting. She did not move and the birds, as filled with curiosity as only magpies can be, hopped a little closer to her. The girl blinked and that was enough to frighten the birds. They flew away no wiser than they had come.

When the sun was near setting, Helga felt herself beginning to transform and she slid down the trunk of the tree. When the sun

HANS CHRISTIAN ANDERSEN

disappeared beneath the horizon, she stood as an ugly frog once more, her webbed hands still torn from the work of the night before. But her eyes had changed, they were not a frog's but the lovely eyes of a young girl, the mirror of a human soul.

Near the grave lay the cross that the young priest had made, the last work of his own hands. Helga picked it up and planted it among the stones that covered the dead priest and the horse. The act brought back the memory of the day before, and she burst into tears. In grief, she decided to make a border of crosses around the graves to decorate them. As she drew the crosses the webs between her fingers fell off: like a torn glove, they lay in the dust. She walked down to the stream and washed; with wonder she looked at her fine white hands. She made the sign of the Cross in the air in the direction of the grave. Her broad frog mouth quivered; her tongue tried to form a word, and that name she had heard so often on that ride through the forest came from her lips. Clearly and distinctly she spoke: "Jesus Christ."

The frog skin fell from her body and there she stood in all her youthful, girlish beauty. But her head was bent; she was tired and she lay down on the moss by the stream and slept.

Toward midnight she awoke. In front of her stood the dead horse; little flames played in the wound on its neck and its eyes glowed. Close by the horse stood the young priest. "More beautiful than Balder," would the Viking woman have said, if she had seen him. Like the horse, he was strangely luminous.

He looked at Helga with eyes so sad and serious and yet so gentle, she felt that she was being judged justly and that there was no corner of her heart that he did not see. With that sharpness of memory that the souls will have on the Day of Judgment, Helga remembered her life. Every kindness performed toward her, every loving word spoken to her, became terribly real. She understood that it was love that had fought and been victorious in the struggle within her, between her soul and the mire from the bog. She realized that she had followed a will greater than her own and that she herself had not been the maker of her own fate. She had been guided and led. She bent her head humbly in front of Him who can see into the most secret compartment of our hearts. And in that moment she felt a flame that purified her, the flame of the Holy Ghost.

"You, daughter of the bog," said the ghost of the priest, "of earth were you made and from the earth you shall be resurrected. The sunbeam within you shall return to its Maker, not to the sun but to God. No soul is doomed, but earthly life can be long and the flight into eternity can seem endless. I come from the land of the dead, where the radiant mountains are, and where all perfection lives. You, too, shall one day travel through the dark valleys to that land. I cannot lead you to Hedeby and a Christian baptism now, for you have a duty to perform back in the bog. You must return and break the shield of water that covers and hides the living root from which you grew."

He lifted her up on the horse and gave her a golden censer to hold like the ones she had seen in the Vikings' hall. A strong, sweet fragrance came from it. The wound in the young priest's head shone like a jewel as he picked up the cross and, holding it high, mounted the horse. The horse galloped but not along the paths — no, they flew through the air, high above the forest. Far down below them, Helga could see the mounds where Viking chiefs had been buried mounted on their horses. Now they rose, these giant specters of man and horse, and stood on top of their grave-hills. In the moonlight the golden bands around their foreheads shone, while their capes fluttered in the wind. The monstrous lind-worm that guards buried treasure stuck its ugly head out of its cave and looked about. Tiny dwarfs ran back and forth carrying lanterns; they looked like sparks from the ashes of burned paper.

Above the heath, the forest, the lakes, and streams they flew, toward the great bog. They circled it and the priest held high the cross, and in the moonlight the two sticks looked like gold. He chanted the mass, and when he sang a hymn, Helga sang too, like a child copying her mother. She swung the censer, and the fragrance of incense spread across the bog and became so strong that the reeds in the swamp shot forth blossoms, and from the muddy depth water lilies sprouted and grew. Everything alive responded, and the dark waters of the bog became covered by a colorful tapestry of water lilies. In the center of it lay a sleeping woman, young and beautiful. Helga thought that she was seeing her own reflection in the water; but it was the bog king's wife, the princess from Egypt.

The dead priest ordered that the sleeping woman be lifted up on the horse, but the burden was too great, the body of the horse was now like a shroud in the wind. The priest made the sign of the

Cross and the phantom horse gained strength enough to carry all three of them onto the shore.

Just as they reached solid ground the cock crowed. The priest and the horse became a mist that was borne away by the wind. Helga and her mother stood facing each other, alone.

"Is this my own image I see, reflected in the deep waters?" asked the mother.

"Is that myself I see mirrored in the lake's shiny shield?" exclaimed the daughter.

The two drew near to each other and embraced. The mother understood who it was she held in her arms. "My daughter, the flower of my heart! The lotus of the deep waters," she said, and cried. Her tears were like a baptism of love for Helga.

"In a swanskin I came here and I shed it by the dark lake," the mother explained. "Then I sank down into the deep mire of the bog and it closed around me like a dark wall. Something drew me down, ever downward. I felt a pressure on my eyes, as if sleep were closing them. And I did sleep, I dreamed. I was back in Egypt in the stone chamber of the pyramid. In front of me stood the trunk of the alder tree that had frightened me so, when I stood on the shores of this lake. I looked closely at the cracks and clefts in its bark, and they gained color and became the hieroglyphic writing on a casket such as mummies are laid in. As I stared at it, it opened and out stepped the ancient king: a mummy, black as pitch, glittering like the black slugs that creep in the forest. Whether it was the bog king or the mummy from the pyramids, I did not know. He flung his arms around me, and I felt that now I would die. But life did not desert me. I felt a warmth in my chest. The bog king was gone and a little bird was singing and flapping its wings. It flew from my chest up toward the dark ceiling: a long green string connected the bird to me. I heard its song and understood its message: 'Freedom! Sunshine!' A longing for the father of things! I thought of my own father, far away in the sun-drenched land of Egypt. I loosened the string and freed the bird, let it fly home to my father. A deep, heavy sleep came over me and I dreamed no more, until a fragrance and chanting voices woke me and drew me up from the dark."

The green string from the mother's heart to the bird's wing, where was it now? Thrown away among other useless things. Only the stork had seen it. It was the green stalk that had shot up

THE BOG KING'S DAUGHTER

through the water to form the flower that had made a cradle for the child who now stood beside her mother.

While they stood there embracing, the stork saw them and flew in circles above them. Then he flew back to the nest to get the swanskins he had kept there so faithfully. He threw one to each of the women. The feathery skins covered them, and they rose from the ground as two white swans.

"Now we can talk together," said the stork, flying beside them. "True, we have not the same shaped bills, but we will understand each other. It was lucky that you came this morning. If you had waited a day longer we would have been gone. My wife and I and the young ones will be going south today. . . . Yes, look at me, I am an old friend of yours from the Nile. So is my wife. Her heart is softer than her bill; she was always of the opinion that the princess would take care of herself. My children and I have carried the swanskins up here. . . . Oh, it makes me happy to see you! It is so lucky that we are still here. As soon as the sun is high in the sky we will be gone. We are not flying alone, there is a whole party of storks going. We will fly ahead and you can follow, then you won't lose your way; but don't worry, my youngsters and I will keep an eye on you."

"The lotus flower that I was to bring will fly beside me," said the Egyptian princess. "The flower of my heart I bring and the riddle has been solved. Homeward! Homeward!"

But Helga insisted that she could not leave before she had bade good-by to her foster mother, the Viking chieftain's wife. She remembered every kind word, every tear her foster mother had shed because of her; and at that moment she loved her more than she loved her real mother.

"Yes," said the stork. "Let us fly to the Vikings' hall. There my wife and children are waiting. They will open their eyes wide and clatter their bills when they see you. Not that my wife is one for idle clatter; she talks in short sentences, but her heart is kinder than her tongue. I will make a clatter so they know we are coming."

And the stork clattered loudly with his long bill, and away they flew to the Viking hall.

There everybody was still asleep. Helga's foster mother had lain awake until late, worrying about what could have happened to her daughter who had disappeared together with the Christian priest three days before. She realized that Helga must have helped him to escape, for it was her horse that was missing in the stable. What strange powers had been the cause of this? The Viking woman had pondered long about it. She had heard that Christ had performed miracles for those who followed him. These thoughts stayed with her in her sleep and became real in her dreams. She dreamed that she was awake, sitting up in her bed; outside the world was dark and a horrible storm was brewing. Now the winds gathered, she could hear the surf breaking on the beaches; the great Midgard-worm which encircles the earth was racked by convulsions. The days of the old gods were over, their night had come: Ragnarok, the last battle of the gods, was being fought. The end of the world was near; now the gods would die. The horns blew, and over the rainbow rode the gods, clad in armor, on their way to fight their last battle. In front of them flew the valkyries and behind them walked the Viking chiefs, whom fame had brought to Odin's hall. The northern lights glittered as they illuminated the sky and yet darkness was victorious. It was a fearful sight.

Close to the frightened woman sat little Helga in her frog shape; she also seemed filled with fear, she drew closer to her foster mother. And the Viking woman dreamed that she took the frog on her lap and held it close; in spite of its horrible shape she pressed it with love to her heart. Outside the hall the sound of a furious battle could be heard. The arrows flew like hailstones. The time had come when the earth and the heavens would burst and the stars fall from the sky. All would be destroyed in the great fire, but from its ashes a new earth and heaven would rise. She knew it would come, and that grain would grow where now the waves of the salt sea rolled over the desolate sand. Balder, the gentle loving God, would be released from the Kingdom of the Shadows and rise into the heavens. He came! In her dream the Viking woman saw him, and she recognized him. Balder the God was the Christian priest.

"Jesus Christ!" she cried to him, and kissed the frog-child on her lap. At that moment the frog disappeared and Helga stood before her, as beautiful as ever; but kind and gentle as she had never been before. Helga kissed the hands of her foster mother and thanked her for all the love and care that she had given her. She blessed her for the thoughts that she had sown in her heart, which now bore fruit. The Viking woman said aloud, once

THE BOG KING'S DAUGHTER

more, the name of the "New God," as people called him in the north: "Jesus Christ." Helga became a great swan. She spread out her wings and flew away and the beat of her wings woke the sleeping woman.

As she opened her eyes, she heard still the sound of the feathered blows from her dream. She knew that now was the time that the storks flew south. She rose from her bed and walked outside to see them fly and wish them farewell. The air was filled with storks, flying in great circles; but in the yard by the well, where Helga had frightened her so often with her wild tricks, stood two swans. They looked at her and the dream was still real within her; she recalled how she had seen Helga change into a swan. Then she remembered the face of the young priest as she had seen it in her dream, and she felt a sudden joy that she could not explain.

The swans flapped their big wings and bent their slender necks as if they were greeting her. The Viking woman spread out her arms toward them and smiled, though tears ran from her eyes.

At that moment the last of the storks flew up. The whole sky resounded with the noise of their wings beating and the clatter of their bills.

"We won't wait for the swans," declared the mother stork. "If they want to come along it has to be now. We can't wait any longer. I think it is very cozy to fly together in a family. The way the finches fly, males and females separately, is, in my eyes, indecent! And I don't like the way the swans flap their wings. What formation do they fly in?"

"Everyone flies in his own manner," said her husband patiently. "The swans fly in a slanted line, the cranes in a triangle, and the plover in a winding line, like a snake."

"Don't mention the word 'snake' while we are in the air," admonished his wife. "It will awaken desires in the young ones that can't be satisfied!"

"Are those the high mountains that I have heard about?" asked Helga, who was flying in her swanskin.

"They are thunder clouds drifting by underneath us," answered the mother.

"What are those tall white clouds ahead?" Helga asked a little while later.

"They are the tops of the great mountains where the snow never

HANS CHRISTIAN ANDERSEN

melts," said her mother; and they flew over the Alps and across the blue Mediterranean.

"Africa, Egypt!" Jubilantly the daughter of the Nile said the words as she, in the feathered dress of a swan, saw below her the yellow-white sandy coast of her home. The storks, too, flew faster when they saw it.

"I can smell the mud of the Nile and the frogs!" said the mother stork to her young ones who were seeing Egypt for the first time. "It tickles my stomach! Oh! You'll see how good everything is going to taste! You will meet the marabou, cranes, and the ibis. They all belong to our family, but they are not nearly as handsome or beautiful as we are. They believe that they are something, especially the ibis, who has been spoiled by the Egyptians. They make a mummy out of him when he dies, and stuff him full of spices, so he won't smell. I prefer stuffing myself with live frogs, and so will you, my children. Better a full stomach while one is alive than a lot of glory after one is dead. That is my opinion and I am always right!"

"Now the stork has come," the servants said in the palace by the Nile.

On a couch covered by leopard skins their royal master lay, neither dead nor alive, waiting, hoping for the lotus flower from the north that would bring his health back to him. Into the great hall flew two white swans; they had come with the storks. They cast off their shiny feathers and there stood instead two beautiful women, as alike as two drops of dew. They bent over the withered shape of the old man on the couch, and as Helga touched her grandfather, blood flowed to his cheeks, his eyes gained luster again, and his lifeless limbs moved. He stood up, well and rejuvenated, and embraced his daughter and his grandchild, like a man happily greeting the dawn after a long dark dream.

There was great joy in the palace and in the storks' nest, too; but in the latter it was mostly over the food: the place was swarming with frogs. While the learned and wise men quickly wrote down the story of the two princesses and the flower of health, which was such a blessing for the royal house and the whole country, the two storks told the story in their own way to their family and friends. But not before everyone had eaten their fill; after all, that was more important than listening to stories.

"Now you must become something," whispered the mother stork to her husband. "You deserve a reward!"

THE BOG KING'S DAUGHTER

"What should I become?" said her husband. "And what have I really done? It was nothing!"

"You have done more than anyone else. Without you and our youngsters, the princesses would never have seen Egypt again. I am sure you will become something! I think they will give you a doctor's degree, and our children will inherit it, as will their children in turn. You already look like a doctor of philosophy — in my eyes!"

The learned and wise men developed the fundamental idea and moral that ran through the story: "Love breeds life!" It could be explained in several ways: "The warm sunlight was the Egyptian princess and she entered the darkness of the bog; in the meeting between light and dark — the latter being the bog king — the flower sprang . . ."

"I can't remember it word for word," said the father stork, who had been listening from the top of the roof to the learned and wise men discuss the matter, and now was telling about it at home in his nest. "Everything that was said was very complicated and so intelligent that they all were decorated immediately by the king. Even the cook got a medal, but I think that was because of the soup."

"And what did you get?" asked his wife. "Don't tell me they have forgotten the most important person of all, namely, you? The learned ones have only clattered their bills. But maybe they will remember you later?"

When night fell and the peace of sleep reigned over the house there was one who was still awake. It was not the stork who stood guard on one leg at his nest, for he was sleeping soundly. No, it was Helga who was not asleep; she was standing on the balcony of her room, looking up at the stars. They seemed so much clearer and brighter here than in the north, and yet they were the same. She thought about her foster mother, the Viking woman, who lived near the great bog. She remembered her sweet, gentle eyes and the tears they had shed over the wretched frog-child who had now become a princess and was standing in the warm night by the waters of the Nile and dreaming. She thought about how full of love that woman's heart must have been, for her to be able to feel affection for a creature so miserable that when she wore a human shape she was an evil beast, and when she became an animal was ugly to look at and repulsive to touch. A bright star reminded her of how the wound in the dead priest's head had glittered when

they rode through the night. She thought of the words he had
spoken on their first ride together, how he had talked of the origin
of love and its greatest expression, which is the love of all living
things.

So much had been given her, so much had she won, so much
had she accomplished. Helga's thoughts dwelled both day and
night upon this great sum of her good fortune. She was like a child
who quickly turns from the giver to the gift. She felt certain that
even greater happiness would come, gifts even more splendid than
the ones she had already received. Was she not fortune's child for
whom miracles had been performed? One day these feelings of
exuberance became so overwhelming that she forgot the giver
completely. The arrogance of youth possessed her, and her eyes
sparkled with a wild courage. Suddenly she heard a great noise
from the courtyard below her. She saw two ostriches running in
circles around each other. She had never seen this animal before,
this great bird, so plump and heavy with its short wings that looked
as though they had been clipped. She wondered whether some
misfortune might have happened to it and asked someone why it
looked like that. And she heard, for the first time, the old Egyptian
legend about the ostrich.

Once he had been a very beautiful bird with big strong wings.
One evening the other big birds of the forest had said to him:
"Brother, should we not tomorrow — if God wills — fly down to
the river to bathe and drink?"

And the ostrich had answered, "Yes, I will it!"

Next morning they flew high up in the sky toward the sun,
which is the eye of God. Higher and higher they went. The ostrich
flew faster and higher than all the others. Arrogantly he flew
toward the light, trusting his own strength and not the Superior
Being who had given it to him. He would not say "if God wills."
The chastising angel drew the veil from the fiery sun and the hot
flames burned the wings of the ostrich. The wretched bird sank
down to the earth. Never again would his wings carry him high up
in the air. He and his kind were condemned to stay forever on the
ground. Frightened, the ostrich runs in meaningless circles to
remind us human beings to say, as we set out on a journey: "If God
wills."

Helga bent her head thoughtfully; then she looked down at the
running bird. She sensed its fear and foolish joy in seeing its own

shadow cast on the sunlit white wall. In her mind — in her soul — grave, serious thoughts struck root. A life so rich, so happy, had been won, what would the future bring? The best — "if God wills."

In the early spring, when the storks got ready to fly north, Helga took a golden ring and scratched her name in it. She beckoned to the stork and he came. She asked the stork to take it to her foster mother, that the Viking woman might know that the child she had cared for was still alive and well, and had not forgotten her.

"It is uncomfortable," said the stork who was wearing the ring around his neck, "but gold and honor one does not throw in the ditch. Now they will know, up there in the north, that the stork brings good luck."

"You lay gold and I lay eggs," said his wife, "but see if we get any thanks for it. I think it is humiliating!"

"But one has one's good conscience, my dear!" answered her husband.

"You can't hang that around your neck," replied his wife. "And no one has ever grown fat on it."

And away they flew!

The little nightingale that sang among the tamarisk bushes would soon be leaving for the north too. Near the wild bog, Helga had often heard it sing. She would send a message with it; the language of the birds she knew because she had once flown in a swanskin. She had kept in practice by talking to the storks and the swallows. The nightingale would surely understand her. She asked him to fly to the place in the forest in Jutland where the grave of branches and stones was, and there to sing a song and ask the other little birds to do the same.

And the nightingale flew; and so did time!

At harvest the eagle, from the top of a pyramid, saw a caravan of richly loaded camels traveling across the desert. Magnificently clad soldiers, on white Arabian horses, with pink soft muzzles and nostrils, and long manes and tails, guarded it. Important guests were coming. A royal prince from Arabia, who was as handsome as princes ought to be, was making his way to the royal palace.

The stork nests were empty, for the owners had not returned yet, but they were expected. And by chance and good fortune, they did arrive later that day. It was a day of festivity and joy. A wedding was to take place, and Helga was the bride. Clad in silk and jewels, she sat at the head of the table with her bridegroom, the young prince of Arabia. On one side of them sat Helga's mother, and on the other her grandfather.

Helga was not looking at her bridegroom's brown handsome face, nor did she notice his passionate glances. She was looking through the big window out at the night sky where the bright stars sparkled in the heavens.

Suddenly the air was filled with the sound of the beating of storks' wings. Although the old stork couple were tired from their long flight and certainly deserved to rest, they flew first to the balcony of Helga's room and perched there on the railing. They had already heard about the feast and knew in whose honor it was being held. They had also been told, as soon as they entered the country, that they had been depicted in a mural that told the story of Helga's life.

"That was very thoughtful of them," said the male stork.

"I don't think it was so much," disagreed his wife. "They could hardly have done less."

Helga rose from the table and went to her balcony. She knew the storks would be there. Affectionately, she stroked their backs, and the old storks bent their necks. Their young children, who had come with them, felt themselves greatly honored.

Helga looked again up at the clear, star-filled sky. She saw a figure floating near her. It was the dead young priest. He had also wanted to see her on this her wedding day; he had come from paradise.

"The splendor, the glory, is far greater than anything found on this earth," he said.

Helga pleaded so sweetly and so fervently — as she never before had begged for anything — to be allowed to look into paradise — if only for a moment, to see the face of God.

The young priest lifted her up into the glory which cannot be described, to see that which cannot be imagined. And she herself felt transformed so that the splendor which she saw before her was also within her.

"Now we must return," said the young priest.

"Just one more glance," begged Helga. "One short minute more."

"We must return to the earth, all the guests are leaving," he warned.

THE BOG KING'S DAUGHTER

"One last glance, the very last!"

Helga was back on the balcony, but all the lights had been put out. The great hall was empty and the storks were gone. Where was her bridegroom? In three short minutes, everything had disappeared.

Frightened, Helga walked through the great hall into the smaller room next to it. There she found some strange foreign soldiers sleeping. She opened another door, which should have led to her own room, but now it led out into the garden. The sun was just rising. Three minutes and a whole night was gone!

She saw some storks and called to them in their own language. A male stork looked at her and came nearer.

"You speak our language," he said, "but who are you and where do you come from?"

"It is me, it is Helga! Don't you know me? We spoke together three minutes ago up on the balcony."

"You are mistaken," said the stork. "It must have been something you dreamed."

"No! No!" protested Helga, and reminded him of the Viking hall near the great bog, and how he had brought her the swanskins.

The stork blinked its eyes. "That is an old, old story. It happened so long ago that my great-great-great-grandmother was alive then. It is true that such a princess once lived here in Egypt, but she disappeared on her wedding night and never returned. It happened hundreds of years ago. You can read the story on the monument in the garden. There are pictures of swans and storks, and on top stands a statue of the princess herself." Finally Helga understood what had happened and she fell on her knees.

The sun was ascending in the sky and its strong rays fell on the kneeling girl; and just as the rays of the sun in time past had changed the ugly frog into the beautiful princess, so did they now change Helga into one single beautiful ray of light, that shot upward to God.

Her body disappeared, became dust; and where she had knelt lay a withered lotus flower.

"That was a new ending to an old story," said the male stork. "I hadn't expected it, but I rather liked it."

"I wonder what the children will think of it?" asked his wife.

"Yes, that is most important," agreed her husband.

THE WINNERS

The winner of the annual prize was to be announced; as a matter of fact, there were two prizes: a big one and a little one. They were awarded to those who ran the fastest, not in a single race, but for general, all-year-round running.

"I won the first prize," declared the hare. "And it is only just; after all, I have both family and friends on the committee. But that the snail should be given the second prize, I think, is an insult."

"No!" argued the fence post, who had witnessed the awards being presented. "One has to consider diligence, industry, and perseverance as well; several very sensible people have said that and I agree with them. It took the snail half a year to get across the threshold, and he broke his hipbone in the rush. He has lived for and thought about nothing else but his running and this race. Besides, he ran with his house on his back, which is very praiseworthy. That is why he was given second prize."

"They might have thought of me," interrupted the swallow. "No one is faster than I, and that both in forward flight and in turns. If there is someone, I have never seen him, and I have traveled far and wide."

"Yes, that is what is the matter with you," answered the fence post. "Always traveling, always ready to leave your country. You are not a patriot, you can't be considered."

341

THE WINNERS

"What if I stayed in the swamp all winter?" asked the swallow. "If I slept half the year, would I qualify then?"

"Get a signed certificate from the bog witch that you have slept half the year in your native land, and I promise you that you will be eligible next year."

"I really think I deserved first prize, not second," mumbled the snail. "Everyone knows that the hare only runs because he is such a coward. He is afraid of his own shadow! But I have made running into my occupation, my life's work! And I have become an invalid in its service. If anyone should have won first prize, it should have been me! But I don't make a fuss, I despise people who do."

And the snail spat.

"I can explain and defend the choosing of the winners — my votes, in any case, were justly cast," said the old pole that the surveyor had dug down to mark the boundary between two farms; the pole had been a member of the committee. "I believe in order, regularity, and calculation. Seven times before have I had the honor of being a member of the committee that has awarded the prizes, but this is the first time that it has been done according to my system. Each time I have looked for something solid, a certain fixed point to start from; therefore I have always begun with the beginning of the alphabet for the first prize, and from the end for the second prize. Now you will notice that the eighth letter after *A* is *H*, and that is why I voted for the *hare* for the first prize. Now the eighth letter, counting from the end of the alphabet, is *S* and that is why I voted that the *snail* should receive the second prize. Next time, *I* ought to be given the first prize and *R* the second. There must always be order in everything, one has to know where one stands!"

"I would have voted for myself if I hadn't been on the committee," said the mule, who had been one of the judges. "Mere speed is not the only consideration; how much one can pull is of importance too. But I didn't let that influence my judgment, nor did I pay any particular attention to how cleverly the hare behaves in flight, how he jumps first to one side, then to the other in order to fool his pursuer. No, I was particularly concerned about another point, which should not be passed over lightly: beauty! It was this I took into consideration. I saw the hare's lovely long ears, they were a pleasure to look at! They reminded me of my own when I was young; and therefore I cast my vote for the hare!"

HANS CHRISTIAN ANDERSEN

"Hush," said the fly, "I don't want to make a speech, I just want to say something. I have run faster than many a hare. The other day I broke the hind leg of one of them. I was sitting on the front of the engine that pulls the train. I often travel by rail, it is the best place I know of to contemplate one's own speed. A young hare was running in front, I am sure it wasn't aware that I was there. In the end, it either had to get off the track or be run over. It didn't make it, my engine drove over its leg. I was there. The hare stayed behind and I rushed on. If that is not called winning a race, I would like to know what is. But I don't need any prize."

"I think," began the wild rose, but it didn't say anything out loud, for that was against its nature, although in this case it would have been a good thing if it had. "I think the sunbeam should have received the first prize, and the second too. In no time at all it flies the long way from the sun down to us and yet arrives with strength enough left to waken all of nature. It has a beauty within it that makes us roses blush and gives us our scent. The honorable committee seem not to have noticed the sunbeam at all. If I were a sunbeam I would give them all a sunstroke; but that would only make them mad, and mad they are already. I shan't mention it," thought the wild rose. "Peace in the forest! How lovely it is to bloom, to spread one's fragrance, please those that love one, and to live in legend and song. The sunbeam will survive us all."

"What was the first prize?" asked the earthworm who, having overslept, had just arrived.

"Free admittance to a cabbage garden," answered the mule. "I was the one that suggested the prize. Since the hare was to win it, I — as a rational member of the committee — decided it might as well be something useful. Now the hare is provided for. The snail got permission to sit on a stone fence and bask in the sunshine, besides being given the first permanent appointment as a judge for all future races. It is always a good thing to have an expert on the committee. I must say that I am expecting great things in the future, since we have had such a promising start."

THE BELL DEEP

$\mathbb{D}$ing, dong! Ding, dong!"

The ringing comes from the bell deep in Odense River.

What river is that?

Don't you know? Well, all the children in the town of Odense do. They may not be able to tell you where it comes from — its source, that is too far away — but the part from the lock, past the gardens and down to the water mill, where the wooden bridges are, all the children have explored.

Little yellow water lilies grow in the water — the ones that are called "river buttons." Along the shore there are reeds with featherlike tufts and sturdy, big, black bulrushes. Where the river passes through the "monk's meadow" and the field on which linen used to be laid out to bleach, the bank of the river is lined with willow trees; they are so old and crooked that they lean far out over the water. Nearer the town there are gardens on both sides of the river. No two of these are alike. Some of the plots are all but covered with flowers and have pretty little bowers that look like big dollhouses. Other gardens are more practical, and here cabbages grow in straight lines like soldiers on parade. Some places the river is so deep, an oar can't reach the bottom. The deepest place is near where the cloister used to be; here the old man of the river lives. During the day when the sun rays shine down through the water, he sleeps. But at night, especially when the moon is full, he some-

349

times shows himself. He is ancient. Grandmother says that she heard about him from her grandmother. He is a very lonesome old man and has no one to talk to except an old church bell. The bell once hung in the tower of St. Alban's Church, and of that building not a trace is left today.

"Ding, dong! Ding, dong!" pealed the bell one evening when the church and the tower were still standing. Just as the sun set and the bell was at the highest point in its swing, it tore itself loose and flew out of the tower and through the air. In the light from the setting sun it looked fiery red.

"Ding, dong! Ding, dong! I am going to bed," tolled the bell, and disappeared in the river at its very deepest point. And that is how that place got its name: the bell deep. But the bell was mistaken about one thing, it wasn't going to get much sleep down there. The old man of the river likes to ring the bell. Sometimes he rings it so loudly that it can be heard through the water, up on the shore. Some people say that this is a warning that someone is about to die, but that is not true. It rings in order to tell the river man stories; since the bell came, he is not so alone any more.

What kind of stories can the old bell tell? It is terribly old. It existed long before Grandmother's grandmother was born, although it is a child compared to the old man of the river, for he is as ancient as the river itself. He is a quite funny old man. His pants are made of eelskins, his jacket of fish scales, and it is buttoned with the little yellow water lilies. His hair is filled with reeds and his long beard with duckweed, which is not really very attractive.

It would take more than a year to tell all of the stories the bell knows. Some of them are short, others are long, and the bell tells them as it likes — often it repeats itself. All the stories are about earlier times: the dark and cruel ages.

"There used to be a monk who often climbed up in the tower of the church. He was young and handsome, but also more pensive than the other monks. He would look across the river — which was broader then — toward the cloister on the other side. He used to come in the evening just as the nuns were lighting the candles in their cells; he knew which one was hers. He had known 'her' well once.

"And when he thought about those days, his heart would beat like a bell: Ding, dong!"

Yes, this was the manner in which the bell used to talk.

THE BELL DEEP

"I remember the bishop's fool, he used to sit right under me while I was pealing. He didn't seem to worry, although I might have hit him, and if I had, I would have crushed his skull. He would play with two little sticks and sing or maybe, one should say, shout:

"'Here I can sing loudly what I do not dare to whisper below. I can sing about all that is hidden behind lock and key, where it is cold and wet and the rats eat the living. No one knows it. No one hears it! Not even now, for the bells are tolling so loud! Ding! Dong!'

"Oh yes, he was mad, that fool!"

Here is another story: "There was a king called Knud. The monks and the bishops bowed to him, but when he taxed the peasants of Jutland too heavily and spoke ill of them, they took weapons in hand and drove him out. They hunted him down as though he were a stag. He fled to the church and locked its doors. Outside a great mob gathered — I heard all about it, for the crows, the ravens, and the jackdaws were so frightened from the noise of the screaming and the shouting that they sought refuge with me, up in the bell tower. Although the jackdaw was frightened, it was as nosy as ever, and it flew down to look through the church windows. King Knud lay in front of the altar praying, and his two brothers, Erik and Benedict, stood near him with their drawn swords, ready to defend him. But the king's servant, Blake, had betrayed his master, and the crowd outside knew where the king was. Soon stones flew through the windows; the king and his men were killed. There were screams and cries of birds and men, and I shouted too. I sang and I rang. Ding, dong! Ding, dong!

"A church bell is hung up high so it can see far and wide. The birds visit it and the bell understands their language. But the bell's best friend is the wind who knows everything. For the wind and the air are brothers, and all that is living the air surrounds; it can even come inside our lungs. No word is spoken, no sigh is made, without the air having heard it. The wind tells what the air knows, and the church bells understand and ring it out for the whole world to know: Ding, dong! Ding, dong!

"But I heard too much, I learned too much, and my knowledge became too great, too heavy a weight to carry. The beam that I was fastened to broke, and I flew out into the air and fell down into the Odense River, into the deep hole where the river man lives. He is

HANS CHRISTIAN ANDERSEN

terribly lonesome; and so I tell him all the stories I know: Ding, dong! Ding, dong!"

This is the story Grandmother heard when she listened to the sound coming from the bell deep in Odense River.

But the schoolteacher does not agree with her. He says, "There is no bell down in the river, and even if there was, it couldn't ring under water. And there is no old man of the river, either, that is only an old wives' tale!" The schoolteacher also claims that, when the church bells peal so merrily, it is not the bells as much as the air that rings, for without the air the sound would not carry. But that is what Grandmother said the bell had told her; and if Grandmother and the schoolteacher agree, then I am sure that it is true. Be careful, be cautious, take good care of yourself. That is the motto of both of them.

The air knows everything! It is around us and inside us. It tells about our deeds and thoughts; its song can be heard farther than the pealing of the bell in Odense River — the one that is living with the old river man. The air delivers its message far up in the heavens. It exists eternally, or at least till the bells of paradise will ring: "Ding, dong! Ding, dong!"

THE EVIL KING

There once lived an evil and arrogant king whose ambition was to conquer all the countries of the world and make every man alive fear his name. With sword and fire he scourged the world; his soldiers tramped down the grain and set fire to the farms. Even the apple trees in the gardens did not escape. They stood black and leafless, and their fruits hung roasted on the branches. Many a poor mother, carrying her naked babe in her arms, would try to hide behind the crumbling, soot-smeared walls that had once been her home. If the soldiers found her and her child, then they would laugh like fiends: evil spirits from hell itself could not have behaved worse. But the king found that everything was going just as he wanted it to. Day by day his power increased and his name became more fearful to all. Luck seemed to smile on whatever he did. The plunder from the conquered towns, their gold and treasures, he had brought to his own capital, and soon it was rich beyond belief. Now he built beautiful palaces, churches, and arcades, and everyone who saw them exclaimed, "Oh, what a great king!" None gave a thought to the suffering he had caused the world, none heard the sighs and cries of lament that came from the ruins of the towns he had destroyed.

The king looked at his golden treasures and at his palaces and he thought as the man in the crowd did: "What a great king!" But he also thought, "I must have even more, more! No power must

353

be mentioned as equal to mine!" And the king made wars upon all his neighbors and he conquered them all. When the king drove through the streets of his city, the vanquished kings were bound to his carriage with golden chains. In the evening, when he dined, they had to lie like dogs at his and his courtiers' feet, and they would throw them scraps from their table.

The king had statues of himself placed on all the squares of the cities and in the royal castles. He wanted them in the churches too, up at the altar, but the priests refused, saying, "King, you are great, but God is greater, we do not dare!"

"Well," said the evil king, "then I must conquer God too."

In foolish arrogance he had an artificial ship built with which he could sail through the air. It was as colorful as a peacock's tail and seemed to contain a thousand eyes. But every eye was the muzzle of a gun. The king himself sat in the middle of the ship and when he pressed a button a thousand bullets would fly and the guns would then reload themselves. A hundred strong eagles were harnessed to the ship and he flew up toward the sun. The earth was below him. At first, with its forests and mountains, it looked like a plowed field, where the grass peeped up through the overturned turf. Later, as he flew higher, it appeared like a flat map; until, at last, it was hidden by clouds and mist.

The eagles flew higher and higher. At last God sent one of his countless angels, and the evil king fired a thousand bullets at him. Like hailstones hitting the earth, the bullets sprang in all directions when they touched the angel's shining wings. One, only one, drop of blood dripped from the white feathers of his wings. That drop fell on the ship of the evil king. It burned itself into it and it was as heavy as a thousand hundredweights of lead. The ship fell down toward the earth so fast that the strong wings of the eagles were broken. The wind rushed past the king's head, and the great clouds around him, which had been formed by the smoke from the burning cities he had destroyed, took on the strangest menacing shapes. One was like a gigantic crab reaching out its great pincers toward him, and another looked like a dragon. When at last his ship came to rest in the top of some trees, he lay half dead among the ruins.

"I will conquer God!" he screamed. "I have sworn to do it and I shall!"

For seven years he set all his workmen to building ships that

THE EVIL KING

could fly through the air; and he ordered his blacksmith to form thunderbolts of the strongest steel, with which he planned to destroy the fortress of God's heaven. Then, from all the countries he ruled, he gathered an army greater than any seen before. When they stood in formation, shoulder to shoulder, they covered many square miles.

They all embarked in the marvelously constructed airships; and the king himself was ready to enter his, when God let a swarm of mosquitoes loose. Like a little cloud, they flew around the king and stung his face and hands. In fury, he drew his sword and slashed the air but harmed not a single insect. He ordered that costly blankets be brought and that he be wrapped in them, so that no mosquito could reach him. His command was obeyed, but one mosquito had hidden in the innermost blanket; it crept into the king's ear and stung him there. The sting burned like fire and the poison entered his brain. He threw off the blankets and tore his clothes in rage from the pain. Naked and screaming, he danced in front of his brutish soldiers. They laughed and mocked the mad king who would conquer God and was himself vanquished by one tiny mosquito.

THE GIRL WHO
STEPPED ON BREAD

I suppose you have heard about
the girl who stepped on the bread in order not to get her shoes
dirty, and how badly she fared. The story has been both written
down and printed.

She was a poor child, but proud and arrogant; she had what is
commonly called a bad character. When she was very little it had
given her pleasure to tear the wings off flies, so they forever after
would have to crawl. If she caught a dung beetle, she would stick a
pin through its body; then place a tiny piece of paper where the
poor creature's legs could grab hold of it; and watch the insect
twist and turn the paper, round and round, in the vain hope that,
with its help, it could pull itself free of the pin.

"Look, the dung beetle is reading," little Inger — that was her
name — would scream and laugh. "Look, it is turning over the
page."

She did not improve as she grew up; in fact, she became worse.
She was pretty, and that was probably her misfortune; otherwise,
the world would have treated her rougher.

"A strong brine is needed to scrub that head," her own mother
said about her. "You stepped on my apron when you were small, I
am afraid you will step on my heart when you grow older."

And she did!

A job was found for her as a maid in a house out in the country.

THE GIRL WHO STEPPED ON BREAD

The family she worked for was very distinguished and wealthy. Both her master and mistress treated her kindly, more as if she were their daughter than their servant. Pretty she was and prettily was she dressed, and prouder and prouder she became.

After she had been in service for a year her mistress said to her, "You should go and visit your parents, little Inger."

She went, but it was because she wanted to show off her fine dresses. When she came to the entrance of her village, near the little pond where the young men and girls were gossiping, she saw her mother sitting on a stone. The woman was resting, for she had been in the forest gathering wood, and a whole bundle of faggots lay beside her.

Inger was ashamed that she — who was so finely dressed — should have a mother who wore rags and had to collect sticks for her fire. The girl turned around and walked away, with irritation but no regret.

Half a year passed and her mistress said again, "You should go home for the day and visit your old parents. Here is a big loaf of white bread you can take along. I am sure they will be very happy to see you."

Inger dressed in her very best clothes and put on her new shoes. She lifted her skirt a little as she walked and was very careful where she trod, so that she would not dirty or spoil her finery. That one must not hold against her; but when the path became muddy, and finally a big puddle blocked her way, she threw the bread into it rather than get her shoes wet. As she stepped on the bread, it sank deeper and deeper into the mud, carrying her with it, until she disappeared. At last, all that could be seen were a few dark bubbles on the surface of the puddle.

This is the manner in which the story is most often told. But what happened to the girl? Where did she disappear to? She came down to the bog witch! The bog witch is an aunt of the elves, on their father's side. The elves everyone knows. Poems have been written about them and they have been painted, too. But about the bog witch most people don't know very much.

When the mist lies over the swamps and bogs, one says, "Look, the bog witch is brewing!" It was into this very brewery that Inger sank, and that is not a place where it is pleasant to stay. A cesspool is a splendidly light and airy room in comparison to the bog witch's brewery. The smell that comes from every one of the vats is

HANS CHRISTIAN ANDERSEN

so horrible that a human being would faint if he got even a whiff of it. The vats stand so close together that there is hardly room to walk between them, and if you do find a little space to squeeze through, then it is all filled with toads and slimy snakes. This is the place that Inger came to. The snakes and toads felt so cold against her body that she shivered and shook. But not for long. Inger felt her body grow stiffer and stiffer, until at last she was as rigid as a statue. The bread still stuck to her foot, there was no getting rid of it.

The bog witch was at home that day; the brewery was being inspected by the Devil's great-grandmother. She is an ancient and very venomous old lady who never wastes her time. When she leaves home, she always takes some needlework with her. That day she was embroidering lies and crocheting thoughtless words that she had picked up as they fell. Everything she does is harmful and destructive. She knows how to sew, embroider, and crochet well, that old great-grandmother!

She looked at Inger, and then took out her glasses and looked at her a second time. "That girl has talent!" she declared. "I would like to have her as a souvenir of my visit. She is worthy of a pedestal in the entrance hall of my great-grandson's palace."

The bog witch gave Inger to the Devil's great-grandmother. And that is the way she went to hell. Most people go straight down there, but if

THE GIRL WHO STEPPED ON BREAD

you are as talented as Inger, then you can get there via a detour.

The Devil's entrance hall was an endless corridor that made you dizzy if you looked down it. Inger was not the only one to decorate this grand hall; the place was crowded with figures all waiting for the door of mercy to open for them, and they had long to wait. Around their feet, big fat spiders spun webs that felt like fetters and were as strong as copper chains, and they would last at least a thousand years. Every one of these immovable statues had a soul within it that was as restless as its body was rigid and stiff. The miser knew that he had forgotten the key to his money box in its lock and he could do nothing about it. Oh, it would take me much too long to explain and describe all the torments and tortures that they went through. Inger felt how horrible it was to stand there as a statue, her foot locked to the bread.

"That is what one gets for trying to keep one's feet clean," she said to herself. "Look how they are all staring at me!" That was true, they were all looking at the latest arrival, and their evil desires were mirrored in their eyes and spoken without sound by their horrible lips. It was a monstrous sight!

"I, at least, am a pleasure to look at," thought little Inger. "I have a pretty face and pretty clothes on." She moved her eyes; her neck was too stiff to turn. Goodness me, how dirty she was! She had forgotten all the filth and slime she had been through in the bog witch's brewery. All her clothes were so covered with mire that she looked as if she were dressed in mud. A snake had got into her hair and hung down her neck. And from the folds of her dress big toads looked up at her and barked like Pekinese dogs. It was all very unpleasant. But she comforted herself with the thought that the others didn't look any better than she did.

But far worse than all this was the terrible hunger she felt. She couldn't bend down and break off a piece of the bread she was stepping on. Her back was stiff and her arms and legs were stiff, her whole body was like a stone statue; only her eyes could move. They could turn all the way around, so that she looked inside herself and that, too, was an unpleasant sight. Then the flies came; they climbed all over her face, stepped back and forth across her eyes. She blinked to scare them away, but they couldn't fly; their wings had been torn off. That was painful too, but the hunger was worse. Inger felt as if her stomach had eaten itself. She became more and more empty inside, horribly empty.

"If this is going to last long, then I won't endure it!" she said to herself. But it didn't stop, it kept on; and she had to endure it.

A tear fell on her head, rolled down her face and chest, and landed on the bread; and many more tears followed. Who was weeping because of little Inger? She had a mother up on earth, it was she who was weeping. Those tears that mothers shed in sorrow over their bad children always reach the children, but they do not help them, they only make their pain and misery greater. Oh, that terrible hunger did not cease. If only she could reach the bread she was stepping on. She felt as if everything inside her had eaten itself up, and she was a hollow shell in which echoed everything that was said about her up on earth. She could hear it all, and none of it was pleasant, every word was hard and condemning. Her mother wept over her, but she also said: "Pride goes before a fall! That was your misfortune, Inger! How you have grieved your poor mother!"

Everyone up on earth — her mother, too — knew about the sin she had committed, how she had stepped on the bread and disappeared into the mire. A shepherd had seen it happen, and he had told everyone about it.

"You have made me so miserable, Inger!" sighed her mother. "But that is what I expected would happen."

"I wish I had never been born," thought Inger. "That would have been much better. But it doesn't help now that my mother cries."

She heard her master and mistress, who had been like parents to her, talking. "She was a sinful child," they said. "She did not appreciate God's gifts but stepped on them; it will not be easy for her to find grace."

"They should have been stricter," thought Inger, "and shaken the nonsense out of me."

She heard that a song had been made up about her, "The haughty girl who stepped on the bread to keep her pretty shoes dry." It was very popular, everyone in the country sang it.

"Imagine that, one has to have it thrown in one's face so often, and suffer so much for such a little sin," thought Inger. "The others should also be punished for their sins. Then there would be a lot to punish! Uh! How I suffer!"

And her soul became as hard as or even harder than her shell. "How can one improve in such company as there is down here?" she thought. "But I don't want to be good! Look how they stare!" And her soul was filled with hatred against all other human beings.

THE GIRL WHO STEPPED ON BREAD

"Now they have something to talk about up there. Oh, how I suffer!"

Every time that her story was told to some little child, Inger could hear it; and she never heard a kind word about herself, for children judge harshly. They would call her the "ungodly Inger" and say that she was disgusting, and even declare that they were glad that she was punished.

But one day, as hunger and anger were tearing at her insides, she heard her story being told to a sweet, innocent little girl, and the child burst out crying. She wept for the haughty, finery-loving Inger. "But won't she ever come up to earth again?" she asked.

And the grownup who had told her the story said, "No, she will never come up on earth again."

"But if she said she was sorry and she would never do it again?"

"But she won't say she is sorry," answered the grownup.

"I wish she would," cried the little girl. "I would give my dollhouse, if she only could come back up on earth again. I think it must be so terrible for poor Inger."

Those words did reach Inger's heart and, for a moment, relieved her suffering. For this was the first time someone had said "poor Inger" and not added something about her sin. A little innocent child had cried for her sake and begged that she should be saved. She felt strange and would have liked to cry herself, but she could not weep, and that, too, was a torment.

As the years passed she heard little from the earth above her; she was talked about less and less. Down in hell's entrance hall nothing ever changed. But one day she did hear a sigh and someone saying, "Inger! Inger! How you have made me suffer, but I thought you would." That was her mother, she was dying.

Sometimes she heard her name mentioned by her old master and mistress; but they spoke kindly, especially her mistress. "I wonder if I will ever see you again, Inger! After all, one cannot be certain where one will go."

But Inger was pretty certain that her kind old mistress would not end where she herself was.

Time passed: long and bitter years. When Inger, finally, again heard her name, she seemed to see above her, in the darkness of the endless hall, two bright stars shining; they were two kind eyes up on earth that now were closing. So many years had gone by that the little child who once had wept so bitterly because of "poor

Inger" now was an old woman whom God had called up to Him. At that last moment when all her memories and thoughts of a long life passed through her mind, she remembered, too, that as a little child she had cried bitterly when she heard the story of Inger. In the moment before death, that which had happened so long ago was reexperienced so vividly by the old woman that she said aloud, "Oh, my Lord, have I not, like Inger, often stepped on Your gifts, and not even been aware that I have done it? Have I not, too, felt pride within me, and yet You have not deserted me. Do not leave me now!"

As the old woman's eyes closed, the eyes of her soul opened for all that before had been hidden. Since Inger had been in her thoughts as she died, she now could see her in all her misery. At that sight, she burst into tears just as she had done as a child; in paradise she stood weeping because of Inger. Her tears and prayers echoed in the shell of the girl who stood as a statue in the Devil's entrance hall. Inger's tortured soul was overwhelmed by this unexpected love from above: one of God's angels was crying for her. Why had this been granted her? Her tortured soul thought back upon its life on earth and remembered every deed it had done. The soul trembled and wept the tears that Inger had never shed. The girl understood that her folly had been her own; and in this moment of realization she thought, "Never can I be saved!"

No sooner had she had this thought than a light far stronger than that of a sunbeam shone from heaven down upon her. Far faster than the sun rays melt the snowman, or the snowflake disappears when it lands on a child's warm mouth, did the statue of Inger melt and vanish. Where it had stood, a little bird flew up toward the world above.

Fear-ridden and full of shame, the bird hid in the darkest place it could find, a hole in an old crumbling wall. Its little body shivered. The bird was afraid of every living thing. It could not even chirp, for it was voiceless. It sat in the dark for a long time before it dared peek out and see the glory around it — for the world is, indeed, gloriously beautiful.

It was night; the moon was sailing in the sky and the air was fresh and mild. The bird could smell the fragrance of the trees and bushes. It glanced at its own feather dress and realized how lovely it was; everything in nature had been created with loving care. The bird would have liked to be able to express her thoughts in song;

THE GIRL WHO STEPPED ON BREAD

gladly would she have lifted her voice as the nightingale or the cuckoo does in spring, but she couldn't. But God, who hears the silent worm's hymn of praise, heard and understood hers, as He had David's when they only existed in the poet's heart and had not yet become words and melody.

Through days and weeks these soundless songs grew within the little bird; although they could not be expressed in words or music, they could be asserted in deeds.

Autumn passed and winter came, and the blessed Christmas feast drew near. The farmers hung a sheaf of oats on a pole in the yard so that the birds of the air should not go hungry on this day of Our Saviour's birth.

When the sun rose Christmas morning, it shone on the sheaf of oats and all the twittering little birds that flew around it. At that moment the little lonesome bird that did not dare go near the others, but hid so much of the time in the little hole she had found in the old wall, uttered a single "Peep." A thought, an idea, had come to her! She flew from her hiding place, and her weak little peep was a whole song of joy. On earth she was just another sparrow but up in heaven they knew who the bird was.

The winter was hard and harsh. The lakes were covered with ice, and the animals in the forest and the birds knew lean times; it was difficult to find food. The little bird flew along the highway. In the tracks made by the sleds she sometimes found a few grains of oats. At the places where the travelers had rested, she would sometimes find little pieces of bread and crumbs. She ate very little herself but called the other starving sparrows, so that they could eat. In town, she looked for the yards where a kind hand had thrown bread and grain for the hungry birds, and when she found such a place she would eat only a few grains and give all the rest away.

Through the winter, the little bird had collected and given away so many crumbs that they weighed as much as the bread that Inger had stepped on, in order not to dirty her shoes. As the last little tiny piece of bread was found and given away, the wings of the little bird grew larger and their color changed from gray to white.

"Look! There's a sea gull flying out over the lake," said the children as they followed the flight of the white bird that dived down toward the water and then swung itself up high into the sky. The white wings glittered in the sunshine and then it was gone. "It has flown right into the sun," the children said.

ANNE LISBETH

Anne Lisbeth was like milk and blood: young, gay, and lovely to look at. Her eyes were bright and her teeth shiny white. She stepped lightly in the dance; she was thoughtless and frivolous. And what did all this beauty and lightheartedness gain her?

"That disgusting little brat!" True, he was no beauty. An unwanted child can be got rid of, and Anne Lisbeth's was given to the ditchdigger's wife to take care of, for she asked the smallest payment. Then Anne Lisbeth moved up to the count's castle; there she sat dressed in her Sunday best every day of the week. Not a wind was allowed to blow on her, nor was an angry word ever spoken to her, because that might harm her! She was the wet nurse of the infant count; he had been born at the same time as her own child. Oh, how she loved this noble little baby! He was as delicate as a prince and as handsome as an angel!

Her own child? Well, he was down in the ditchdigger's hut, where the tempers boiled more often than the pots, and hard words stood on the menu every day. Often no one was home. The little boy cried, but unheard tears can't touch anyone. He would cry himself to sleep; and sleep is marvelous, for while you are asleep you can't feel either hunger or thirst. As time passes the weeds shoot up, as people say; and Anne Lisbeth's boy did grow, though he was always smaller than the other boys his age. He

ANNE LISBETH

belonged in the ditchdigger's family; after all, they had been paid to take him in. Anne Lisbeth was rid of him; she moved to the city and married well.

In her home it was always nice and warm, and should she walk outside, then she had both hat and coat to put on. She never went to the ditchdigger's hut, it was much too far away. Besides, the boy was theirs. He had too hearty an appetite, they claimed, so they set him to work to earn his keep. He could take care of the neighbor's cow and see to it that it didn't stray into the wheat fields.

The watchdog of the castle stood outside in the sunshine and barked at anyone who came by, but if it rained it had a doghouse that was warm and dry. Anne Lisbeth's boy sat in the ditch when the sun shone and whittled a stick. One spring day he found three wild strawberry plants. He was sure they would have berries and the thought made him happy, but the flowers fell off and no strawberries came. If it rained he had to stay where he was, for he was tending the cow; he was wet to the skin and he had to wait for the wind to dry him. Whenever he came to the farm, the servant girls and the other hired hands played tricks on him and hit him.

"You are ugly, disgusting!" they cried. He was used to hearing those words.

Well, what happened to Anne Lisbeth's boy? What do you suppose? What does happen to those whose lot is never to be loved?

Since the land had no use for him, he took to the sea. He sailed on a broken-down old tub, stood at the tiller while the captain drank. Dirty and disgusting he looked, always cold and always hungry; one would think he had never got enough to eat: and that was true, he hadn't.

It was late in the year. The weather was raw and cold, the wind cut right through his clothes. It was blowing hard and they had only one sail up. It was a rotten little sloop, with only two men as crew. To be more accurate, only one and a half: the skipper and his boy. The clouds had made twilight of the day, but now it was growing really dark and bitterly cold it was. The skipper poured himself a drink to get some warmth inside him. The glass he drank from was old; its foot had been broken off, and the skipper had made a new one of a piece of wood that was painted blue. If one drink helped, then two ought to help twice as much, thought the skipper, and poured himself another. The ditchdigger's boy, as he was called — though in the church register it was written that he was Anne Lisbeth's — held onto the tiller with hands that were dirty from pitch and filth. He was ugly, his hair stuck out in all directions, and he was cowed and had squinty eyes.

The wind blew from the stern, the sail filled out. The wind caught it fully and the old ship raced ahead. The top of a wave broke over the railing and drenched the boy. The wind was raw and wet. Something happened! What was it? What burst?

The boat lurched and turned broadside on to the waves. With a loud crack, the mast broke, and sail and rigging came falling down. The boy at the tiller screamed: "Jesus Christ save me!"

The boat had hit a rock and now it sank like an old shoe in the village pond. It went down with mice and men, as the saying goes. There were plenty of mice on board, but of men only one and a half: the skipper and the ditch digger's boy. No one saw it happen, except the screaming gulls and the fishes; and they didn't see it, really, for they fled as the water roared in through the hole in the hull. The boat sank in about ten feet of water, just deep enough to hide both ship and crew. Gone and forgotten they were. Only the glass with the blue-painted wooden foot remained afloat; it drifted toward shore and was finally broken in the surf. It had done good service and it had been loved, which was more than Anne Lisbeth's boy ever had been. Only in heaven are there no souls that can say, "I have never been loved."

Anne Lisbeth had lived for many years in the town and was used to being spoken to respectfully. She liked to boast about the time when she had lived in a castle, driven in a carriage, and conversed with baronesses and countesses. She would fall into ecstasy about her little count, who had looked like an angel and who had loved her as much as she had loved him. He had kissed her and put his arms about her neck. Why, he was all her joy, and half her life!

Now he was almost a grownup: fourteen years old and as clever and learned as anyone and handsomer than everyone. Of this she was certain, although she had not seen him since she had carried him in her arms; it was, after all, quite far to the castle, almost a journey.

"But I must go there soon," said Anne Lisbeth. "I must see my joy once more, my sweet little count. I am sure he longs for me too, and still cares for me and remembers the time when he put his little angelic arms around my neck and whispered, 'Anne Lis.' Oh!

that sounded as lovely as a violin. Yes, I must go and visit him!"

She drove with a freight wagon as far as the village near the castle; the rest of the way she had to walk.

The castle looked as large and impressive as it had the first time she had seen it. The park around it had not changed either; but all the servants were strangers, not one of them remembered an "Anne Lisbeth." They did not seem to appreciate her importance, but surely the countess would tell them who she was — and so would her own little count, whom she was at long last to see.

Anne Lisbeth had to wait a long time — and time is always long when you have to wait. Just before dinner she was called in to the countess, who spoke very kindly to her. She would be able to see her little sweet boy after dinner; she would be called in again then.

How tall and thin he had become, but he had the same eyes and the same angelic mouth. He looked at her but didn't say a word. Maybe he had not recognized her. He turned as if he were going to leave, and Anne Lisbeth grabbed his hand and pressed it to her mouth.

"That is enough," he said, and left the room. — He whom all her loving thoughts had dwelled upon; he whom she had loved above all else; he who had been all her earthly pride.

Anne Lisbeth walked back along the road toward the village. She was so unhappy. He had acted toward her as though she were a stranger. He had not given her a thought or said a kind word, although she once had carried him in her arms through long nights; and since that time, not one day had passed without her thinking about him.

A big black raven landed on the road in front of her and screeched again and again. "My God!" she cried. "What bird of ill omen are you?"

She was passing the ditchdigger's house, and his wife was standing in the doorway. Anne Lisbeth stopped to talk to her.

"You have done well," said the ditch digger's wife. "You look healthy and plump. One can see you have prospered."

"Oh yes, I can't complain," answered Anne Lisbeth.

"The boat went down. Both Lars the skipper and the boy drowned. Well, that was the end of it. I had hoped that the boy might help me in my old age with a few coppers. He won't cost you any more money, Anne Lisbeth."

"Are they drowned!" exclaimed Anne Lisbeth, and then they talked no more about it.

Anne Lisbeth was still feeling miserable because her little count whom she loved so much had not even talked to her. It had cost her money to take that journey and what had she gained from it? Not much, but that she was not going to tell the ditchdigger's wife. After all, she did not want her to think that Anne Lisbeth was not welcome in the castle any more. At that moment the raven screeched again.

"You black monster!" shouted Anne Lisbeth. "Why are you trying to scare me?"

She had brought some coffee and chicory with her; it was an act of kindness to give them to the ditchdigger's wife so that she could make some coffee. While the ditchdigger's wife was in the kitchen, Anne Lisbeth sat down in a chair and fell asleep.

She had a strange dream in which appeared a person she had never seen in a dream before. She dreamed about her son: the child who had starved and frozen in this very hut, and now lay at the bottom of the sea — only God knows where. She dreamed that she was sitting right where she was and that the ditchdigger's wife had gone out to make coffee — even in her dream she could smell it brewing. Suddenly a boy, as beautiful as the young count, stood in the door of the hut and said to her: "Now the end of the world is coming, hold onto me, for in spite of everything you are my mother. You have an angel in heaven to guard you, hold onto me!"

He grabbed her by the sleeve, and at that moment she heard a great noise; and Anne Lisbeth guessed that that was the end of the world. The angel lifted her up, but something heavy held onto her shoulders and her legs. It felt as though a hundred women had grabbed hold of her and they were shouting: "If you are to be saved we have a right to be saved too. Hang on! Hang on!"

And they did hold onto her, and that was too much for Anne Lisbeth's sleeve. "Ritch," it said, and was torn to pieces; and she fell back down on the ground. So real and so frightening was the dream that she woke and almost fell off the chair. Afterward she felt so dizzy and confused that she couldn't remember exactly what it was she had dreamed, only that it had been unpleasant.

The coffee was served and drunk. The two women talked and then it was time for Anne Lisbeth to leave. She walked to the nearest village, where she was to meet the freightman and drive in

ANNE LISBETH

his wagon back to the town where she lived. Unfortunately his wagon had broken and he would not be able to leave before the following evening. Anne Lisbeth speculated upon the cost of a night's lodging at the inn and then decided that, if she did not walk along the road but followed the beach instead, she would save many a mile and could be home by morning.

The sun had set, but the church bells seemed still to be ringing — no, it wasn't bells, it was the big frogs down in the lake that were croaking. But at last they grew silent too. And now the whole world was still, not a bird was heard; they had gone to sleep, and the owl, who is usually up at this time, was not home. So still was the mirror of the sea that not even the tiniest ripples lapped on the shore. The only sound that Anne Lisbeth heard was that of her own footsteps in the sand. No splash from leaping fish broke the silence, everything under the water, both living and dead, was mute.

Anne Lisbeth did not think about anything while she walked, but that did not mean that no thoughts were in her mind. They lie asleep within our heads and never leave us, old thoughts that we have had before, as well as new ones that we have still to encounter.

"Virtue is its own reward," so it is written; and it is also written, "The wages of sin is death." So much has been written, so much has been said, and one does not remember it all. So it was with Anne Lisbeth, but one can be made to remember!

Within our hearts are all virtues and vices — in yours and in mine! They lie there like grains, so small that they are invisible; then, from outside a sun ray or an evil hand touches them. You turn a corner, whether to the right or to the left may be of supreme importance. And the little seed grows till it suddenly bursts and enters your blood. From then on it directs where you will go. When you are walking along drowsily, such fearful thoughts do not come to your mind, but that does not mean that they are not there.

Anne Lisbeth was tired. She felt as if she were about to doze, but her thoughts were aroused. From one midsummer to the next, our hearts have a whole year to account for: How many sinful thoughts have we had? How many words have we spoken against God, our neighbors, and our own conscience? But we forget, we do not think about them, and neither did Anne Lisbeth. She had not broken any laws of the land; she knew that others considered her a decent, upright woman.

As she walked along the beach she saw something lying in the sand. What was it? She stopped. It was a man's hat that the waves had thrown up on land. She wondered when and from what ship it had fallen overboard. She took a few steps toward it. But what was that lying over there? She got very frightened, but there was nothing to be frightened of. What had scared her was merely a large stone covered by broken reeds and seaweed. It looked like the body of a human being, but it was only a stone and some seaweed. Yet her fear stayed with her as she walked on; and now so many thoughts came to her. She remembered all the old tales and superstitions she had heard, when she was a child, about the ghosts of those who had drowned. How these specters attacked the lonesome wanderer and demanded that they carry them to the churchyard and bury them there.

"Hang on, hang on!" the ghosts had cried in the stories she had heard. And as Anne Lisbeth repeated these words to herself, she suddenly remembered the dream she had had in the ditchdigger's cottage. So real did it become to her that again she felt the weight of the other mothers clinging to her, while they screamed: "Hang on! Hang on!"

And she remembered how the world had come to an end, and how the sleeves of her blouse had ripped, so that her child, who on the Day of Judgment had tried to save her, could no longer hold onto her. Her own child, the one she had borne but never loved, and had never even given a thought to. Now that child rested on the bottom of the sea, and his ghost could come and demand of her, "Bury me in Christian soil. Hang on! Hang on!"

As these thoughts passed through her mind, fear bit her heels and she hurried on. Dread like a cold hand squeezed her heart so that it hurt. She looked out over the sea. A mist came rolling in; it obscured and changed the shapes of bushes and trees. She looked up at the moon. It appeared as a pale, pale disk. Her body felt heavy, as if she were carrying a great weight. "Hang on! hang on!" the words echoed in her mind.

Again she turned to look at the moon, and now its white face seemed very close to her and the fog hung like a winding sheet from her shoulders. "Hang on, hang on, bring me to my grave!" She expected to hear those words any moment.

ANNE LISBETH

There was a sound! What was it? It could not be frogs or the cry of a raven or a crow. A hollow voice said, "Bury me, bury me." She had heard it plainly. It was the voice of her child, the one who now rested on the bottom of the sea. He would never find peace until he was carried to the churchyard and there buried in hallowed ground. She would dig his grave. She walked in the direction where she thought a church stood, and now it seemed to her that her body felt lighter, that the burden was gone.

Hurriedly she turned and walked instead toward her home, but then the weight returned. "Hang on, hang on!" The cry sounded again like the deep voice of some monstrous frog or frightened bird.

"Bury me, bury me."

The fog was cold and wet, and her face and hands were cold and damp from fear. The world outside was pressing on her and she herself had become an empty void in which thoughts she had never had before were free to fly.

In the north, in one warm spring night, the whole beech forest can put forth leaves, and when the sun rises it stands in all its tender green glory. In one second within us, when our conscience awakes, all the evil, all the sins committed throughout a lifetime, can unfold before us. At this moment no excuses, no mitigating circumstances, help; our deeds bear witness against us and our thoughts are formed into words that shout the truth to the world. We are horrified at what we see, at the evil that has been inside us, which we have not even tried to destroy — the harm we have done in arrogance and thoughtlessness. Inside our hearts are all virtues and all vices; but vices thrive in the poorest soil.

What we have said in words, Anne Lisbeth felt, and her feelings so overpowered her that she fell to the ground and crawled on all fours like an animal.

"Bury me, bury me," whispered the voice, and gladly would she have buried herself, if that would have meant the end of all memories.

It was her day of reckoning, and it brought her only fear and dread. All the superstitions she knew mixed as heat and icy coldness with her blood, and tales she had not remembered for years came back to her. As soundlessly as the clouds that pass by the pale moon, a specter rushed by her. Four dark horses with fire coming from their nostrils drew a carriage in which sat the evil count who, more than a hundred years before, had lived and ruled in this district. Now at midnight he drove from the churchyard to his castle and back again. He was not pale as ghosts usually are described. No, his face was as black as burned-out coals. He nodded to Anne Lisbeth and waved.

"Hang on, hang on!" he shouted. "Then you can again drive in a count's carriage and forget your own child!"

She ran and at last she reached the churchyard. The black crosses on the graves and the black ravens that lived in the church tower became one. All the crosses became ravens that cried and screamed at her. She remembered that unnatural mothers are called "raven mothers," for that bird is known, to its shame, for not taking good care of its young. Would she become a black bird when she died: a raven?

She threw herself down on the ground and with her fingers dug in the hard earth until blood ran from her nails. And all the time she heard the voice saying, "Bury me, bury me!" She feared that the cock would crow and the eastern sky grow red before she had finished her work; and then all would be lost.

The cock crowed and the sun rose. The grave was but half finished! A cold hand caressed her face and a voice sighed, "Only half a grave." It was the spirit of her son, who now had to return to the bottom of the sea. Anne Lisbeth sank to the ground and all thoughts and feelings left her.

It was almost noon when she awoke. Two young men had found her. She was not lying in the churchyard but on the beach. In front of her was the big hole she had dug. She had cut her hands on a broken glass, the stem of which had been forced down into a little square piece of wood that was painted blue.

Anne Lisbeth was sick. Her conscience had dealt the cards of superstition, and she had read them. She now believed that she had only half a soul; the ghost of her son had taken the other half with him, down to the bottom of the sea. She would not be able to enter heaven unless she could get back that part of her soul that lay beneath the deep waters of the ocean.

Anne Lisbeth was brought home, but she was no longer the woman she had been. Her thoughts were like threads, all tangled up in knots; only one idea was clear to her: that she must find again the ghost of her child, carry him to the churchyard, and bury him there, so that she could win back her soul.

ANNE LISBETH

Many a night she was missed at home, but they knew where they could find her: down on the beach, waiting for the ghost of her son to come. A year went by and then one night she disappeared, and this time they could not find her; all day they searched in vain.

Toward evening the bell ringer who had come to ring the bells for vespers saw her. In front of the altar lay Anne Lisbeth. She had been there since morning. She had no strength left but the light in her eyes was one of joy. The last of the sun's rays fell on her face and gave it the pink color of health. The sun rays were reflected in the brass clasps of the old Bible that lay upon the altar. It had been opened upon the page of the prophet Joel, where it is written: "Rend your heart and not your garments, and turn unto the Lord your God." This, they said, was quite by chance, as so much is in this world.

In Anne Lisbeth's sun-filled face one could see that she had found peace. She whispered that she was well, that she was not afraid any more. The ghost had come at last. Her son had been with her and said: "You dug only a half a grave for me, but for a whole year and a day you have buried me in your heart, and that is the right place for a mother to keep her child." Then he had given her back the half of her soul that he had taken with him and led her up here to the church.

"Now I am in God's house," she said, "and here one is blessed."

When the sun finally went down, Anne Lisbeth's soul went up to where fear is unknown and all struggles cease. And Anne Lisbeth had striven.

THE PEN
AND THE INKWELL

It was once remarked by someone who was looking at the inkwell on an author's desk: "Isn't it strange, all that can come out of an inkwell? I wonder what will come from it next? Oh, it is a wonder!"

"That it is," agreed the inkwell. "It is very hard to understand. And that has always been my opinion." The inkwell was talking to the pen and everything else that happened to be on the desk. "It is, indeed, strange and wonderful what can come out of me! Why, I would call it almost unbelievable! Sometimes I don't even know myself what will come next — what will happen when human beings dip into me. One drop of me is enough to cover half a page of paper, and what cannot be written on that! I am someone quite extraordinary. From me springs all poetry; descriptions of people who have never lived, and yet are more alive than those who walk around on two legs; the deepest feelings; the greatest wit; and the loveliest word paintings of nature. How can all that be inside me — I who do not even know nature — but nonetheless it is! All of these gallant knights on their magnificent horses and all the beautiful young girls who live in books have, in fact, been born in me. Yes, I cannot even understand it myself."

"There you spoke the truth!" said the quill pen. "You do not understand because you cannot think; if you could, you would realize that you contain merely liquid. You exist so that I can

THE PEN AND THE INKWELL

express upon paper the thoughts that are within me, so that I can write them down. It is the pen that writes! This no man doubts, and I can assure you that most human beings have a great deal more insight into poetry than an old inkwell."

"You have not had much experience yet," said the inkwell. "You are young in the service, though already half used up, I am afraid. Do you really believe that you are the poet? You are only a servant, and I have had many of them before you arrived. Both English steel pens and those who can claim geese as their family. I have known all kinds of pens. I cannot even count the number that have been in my service; and more will come, I am sure. He wears them out, the human being who does the manual labor, he who writes down what is inside me. I wonder what he will lift out of me next."

"Ink tub!" sneered the pen.

Later in the evening the poet came home. He had attended a concert where he had heard an excellent violinist play. He was still very excited about what he had heard. The musician had enticed such marvelous sounds out of his instrument. At one moment it sounded like drops of water falling from the trees, one pearly drop after another; and the next, like a storm riding through a pine forest. The poet had thought he had heard his own heart weeping, so captured had he been by the music. It was not only the strings that had sung but the whole instrument, wood and all. And all the while it had looked so easy: the bow had danced so lightly across the strings. One was almost convinced that anyone could have done it, so effortless had the performance appeared. The violin sang by itself and the bow moved by itself; the two were one. One almost forgot their master: the musician who played upon them and gave to these two dead objects a soul. But the poet had not forgotten him; he pondered over it and wrote down his thoughts.

"How absurd it would seem if the bow and the violin should be proud and haughty about their accomplishments. Yet we, human beings, often are; the poets, the artists, the scientists, and even the generals often boast in vain pride. Yet they are all but instruments that God plays upon. To Him alone belongs all honor. We have nothing to pride ourselves upon!"

Later the poet wrote a parable and called it "The Genius and His Instrument."

"Well, madam, that put you in your place," said the pen to the

HANS CHRISTIAN ANDERSEN

inkwell when the two of them again were alone. "I suppose you heard him read aloud what I had written down?"

"You wrote what I ordered you to write," retorted the inkwell. "It was especially your silly arrogance and pride that made me think of it, I am sure. But I suppose you can't even understand when you are being made fun of! That whole thing was meant for you and it came from the very depth of me. Don't you think I can recognize my own sarcasm?"

"Ink skirt!" screamed the pen.

"Scribble pin!" shouted the inkwell.

Each of them thought his own repartee the cleverer, and there is nothing so satisfying as the feeling that one has had the last word. It makes for pleasant slumber, and both the inkwell and the pen went to sleep. But the poet was not asleep; like tones from a violin, thoughts upon thoughts came to him. They fell like pearls and rode through the forest like the storm; he felt the cry of his own heart and the spark of the Eternal Master.

To Him alone belongs the honor and the glory!

THE COCK
AND THE WEATHERCOCK

There were two cocks on the farm, one on the roof and one on the manure heap. They were vain and proud, both of them. But which one had the greater right to be? Tell us your opinion — it won't make any difference, we will stick to our own anyway.

The henyard was divided from the manure heap by a wooden fence and in the manure grew a cucumber; it knew that it was a vegetable and it was proud of being one.

"That is something one is by birth," the cucumber mumbled to herself. "We can't all be born cucumbers; there must be other species as well. Hens and ducks and the other animals on the farm had to be created too. The cock I look up to; he is always sitting on the fence crowing. He is of a great deal more importance than the weathercock, who is placed a little too high up and can't even say, 'Peep,' not to speak of crowing. He has no hens or chickens of his own, and when he sweats, it is green. He never thinks about anyone but himself. Now the cock on the farm, he is something else! When he struts about, it is a dance, a ballet. When he crows, it is music! Wherever he goes, people know how important a trumpeter is! If he came in here and ate me up, leaves and stalk and all, I would call it a blessed death. My body would become his!" said the cucumber.

Toward night there was a horrible storm. The hens, the chick-

HANS CHRISTIAN ANDERSEN

ens, and the cock sought shelter. The wooden fence fell, which made a frightening noise. Several tiles flew off the roof, but the weathercock stayed where he was, he did not even turn. He couldn't, which was really strange since he was quite new and had been cast recently. But he was the kind that was born old; steady and sober-minded from birth. He resembled in no way the fluttering birds of the air, the swallows or the sparrows; as a matter of fact, he despised them. "Small birds, common and ordinary," he called them. As for shape and coloring, he found the pigeons more to his taste; their feathers shone like mother-of-pearl, they could almost pass for weathercocks. But he declared that they were fat and stupid and never thought about anything except filling their stomachs. They were uninteresting company. Most of the migrating birds had visited the weathercock and told him fantastic stories about foreign lands, where there were eagles and great birds of prey. The tales had been amusing and interesting the first time he heard them, but the birds always repeated themselves and that the weathercock found tedious. They were tiresome, and life was boring. There was no one worth associating with, everything was flat and dull!

"The world is no good!" he declared. "Twaddle and nonsense: all of it!"

The weathercock was oversophisticated. The cucumber would have found him very interesting and attractive, but she didn't know him, so she admired the cock from the henyard; and now that the fence had blown down, he came visiting.

"What did you all think of that cock's crow?" he asked the hens and the chickens — he was referring to the storm. "I found it a bit raw, it lacked elegance."

Then he stepped up on the manure pile with the determined step of a hussar — he was wearing spurs. All the hens and chickens followed him.

"Vegetable," he said to the cucumber; and in that one word she found such breeding and refinement that she did not even notice that the cock pecked at her and ate her up.

"A blessed death!"

The hens gathered around and the chickens came too, for where one ran the others followed. They clucked and they peeped and they all looked at the cock and admired him, for he was one of their own kind.

THE COCK AND THE WEATHERCOCK

"Cock-a-doodle-doo," he crowed. "All the chickens become hens in the henyards of the world, if and when I say so!"

The hens and the chickens clucked and peeped in agreement, all of them. Then the cock crowed some news to the world: "A cock can lay eggs! And do you know what is in such an egg? In it lies a basilisk! No one dares or can stand to look at such a monster. Human beings know it and now you know it too. Now you understand what I am capable of! What a fantastic creature I am!"

The cock flapped his wings, raised his red cockscomb, and crowed once more. All the hens and chickens were a little scared, and very thrilled that someone they knew so well should be such an incredibly important creature. They clucked and peeped so loud that the weathercock could hear them.

And he did; but he pretended that he hadn't, and didn't move. "Nonsense, all of it!" he said to himself. "Henyard roosters cannot lay eggs; and I can't be bothered to lay one. If I wanted to, I am sure I could, but the world is not worthy of an egg. Everything is tiresome, life is a bore! I can't even be bothered to sit here any longer!"

And at that moment the weathercock broke and fell down into the yard. It didn't hit the rooster and kill it. "Though that was its intention," declared all the hens.

Here is the moral of the story: "It is better to boast and crow than to be blasé and break."

THE TWELVE PASSENGERS

It was freezing cold. The night was clear, the wind was still, and the sky was filled with stars. "Bang! Bang!" That was a firecracker. They were being shot off because it was New Year's Eve and the clock was just striking twelve.

"Trat tra . . . Trat tra!" the coachman's bugle was heard as the stagecoach arrived at the city gate. There were twelve passengers; exactly the number that there was room for: every seat was occupied.

"Hurrah! Hurrah!" In all the houses people were shouting, "Hurrah!" for the New Year. They were standing glass in hand, ready to toast: "Health and prosperity in the New Year!" they said. Or they made other wishes for each other; such as: "May you find a nice wife," or "May you earn lots of money," or "May all this unpleasant nonsense come to an end." This latter, of course, was rather too much to ask.

While everyone was welcoming in the New Year, the stagecoach waited outside the city gate with its passengers.

Who were these strangers? They had their passports and luggage, and in it there were gifts for you and me, for everyone in the whole city. But what did they want and what did they bring?

"Good morning," they said to the sentry at the gate.

"Good morning," he answered; and it was, after all, past

midnight. "Your name and profession," the sentry asked the first man who descended from the coach.

"Look in the passport," he grumbled. "I am I!" He was big and gruff. He was wearing a bearskin coat and sled boots. "I am the man a lot of people pin their hopes on. Come around tomorrow and I will tell you what New Year is like. I throw away pennies and silver coins as well; you can scramble for them. And I give grand balls: thirty-one of them, that is all the nights I have to give away. I am a merchant, my ships are all icebound, but it is warm in my office. My name is January; my luggage is filled with unpaid bills."

The next passenger was more amusing. He was a theater director who only played comedies and held masquerades. He traveled with an empty barrel as luggage.

"I live for the pleasure of others and for myself because I have such a short life, only twenty-eight days. Sometimes a collection is made among the family and I am given an extra day, but I don't care one way or the other. Hurrah!"

"Don't shout so loud!" said the soldier on guard.

"Certainly I may!" said the traveler. "I am Prince of the Carnival, though I travel under the name of Februarius."

Now the third of the strangers came out of the coach. He was thin and tall. One would think that he had never got enough to eat. He was always fasting and proud of it. They say that he can tell the weather for the rest of the year, but that is not a profession one can grow fat on. He wore a black suit with a few violets in his buttonhole; they were very small.

"March, March!" screamed the fourth, and pushed him out of the way with a laugh. "March, March, right inside with you. I can smell they are brewing punch in there." But that wasn't true at all. He was just playing an April fool's prank on the thin man. Now this fourth traveler looked like a lively fellow; he did not work hard and kept a lot of holidays. But he was subject to moods.

"With me it is always rain or sunshine," he declared. "I can both laugh and cry at the same time. My suitcase is filled with summer clothes, but it is not wise to put them on. You will have to accept me as I am. When I am dressed up I wear a silk shirt and a woolen muffler."

Now a lady got out of the coach.

"Miss May," she said. She was wearing summer clothes but had overshoes on her feet. Her light green dress was made of silk. She had put anemones in her hair and she smelled so strongly of woodruff that the poor guard sneezed.

"God bless you," she said, and meant it. She was very pretty indeed, and she sang — not in the theaters, but out in the forest, among the fresh green trees. She sang for her own pleasure and not for applause. In her sewing bag she kept a book of poetry.

"Here comes our young mistress!" they cried from inside the stagecoach. Out stepped a young woman, beautiful and proud. She was born to wealth, one could see that. She waited for the longest day of the year to throw a party; she wanted her guests to have time enough to eat all the courses. She could afford to drive in her own carriage, but she had sat in the coach along with the others because she didn't want them to think that she was too proud to join them. As traveling companion she had her younger brother, Julius.

He also was well to do and was wearing a white suit and a Panama hat. He carried so little luggage that it could hardly have been less: a pair of bathing trunks.

Now came Madame August. She was a wholesale dealer in apples and other fruits. She owned farms, too; she looked big and fat and comfortable. She took part in all the work and could carry the beer barrel herself out to her workers at harvest time. "In the sweat of thy brow shalt thou eat thy bread." That is written in the Bible, but afterward one can hold a feast and dance. Yes indeed, she was a straightforward person.

Next a man came out. He was a painter by profession. The trees in the forest were his canvas. He changed their color and made them even more beautiful. Red, yellow, and brown were his favorites. He could whistle like a starling and had decorated his beer mug with a garland of hops; it was very pretty and he had an eye for the pretty. He traveled light, a pot of paint and some brushes were all his baggage.

Now came the farmer; he was concerned about plowing and getting the soil ready for the coming year, though he had time to think of hunting. He carried a gun and a dog ran at his side; he had his hunting bag filled with nuts. Goodness me, he carried a lot of goods with him, among other things, an English plow. He talked incessantly about economics, but one had a hard time hearing what he said, for the next passenger, who had already got out of the coach, had a bad cold and was sniffing and coughing.

383

THE TWELVE PASSENGERS

He was November! His cold was so bad that he used a sheet as a handkerchief. But he thought he might get rid of it as soon as he had found some lumber to cut, for that was his profession.

Now came the last of the passengers, a little old lady carrying a brazier. She was freezing, but her eyes shone like two stars. In her other hand she had a little potted pine tree. "I will tend it so well that it will grow big enough by Christmas to reach all the way up to the ceiling. Then it shall have lighted candles, apples, and sugar pigs on it. My little brazier gives as much warmth as a stove. I shall take my fairy-tale book out of my pocket and read aloud. And the children will sit perfectly still, while the dolls on the tree come alive, and the little wax angel on the top of the tree will flutter his golden wings and fly down and kiss every person in the room, both grownups and children. Yes, he will kiss the poor children, too, who are standing outside, singing Christmas carols, singing about the star that once shone over Bethlehem."

"The coach is leaving," shouted the guard, "now that the passengers have got out."

"Let the twelve of them enter the city one at a time," said the captain of the guard. "I will keep your passports, they are only good for one month each When that is over, then I shall write a report on your behavior. Mr. January, you may enter first."

And Mr. January entered.

When the year is over I shall tell you what the twelve passengers brought me and you and all of us. I don't know now, nor do I think they even know themselves — for surely we live in a strange time.

THE DUNG BEETLE

The emperor's horse had been awarded golden shoes, one for each hoof. It was such a beautiful animal, with strong legs and a mane that fell like a veil of silk over its neck. Its eyes were sad, and when you looked into them you felt certain that if the horse could speak it would be able to answer more questions than you could ask. On the battlefield it had carried its master through a rain of bullets and a cloud of gun smoke. It was a true war horse, and once when the emperor was surrounded by the enemy, it had bit and kicked their horses and then, when all seemed lost, it had leaped over the carcass of an enemy steed to carry the emperor to safety. The horse had saved his master's golden crown and his life, which was worth a great deal more to the emperor than all the crown jewels. And that was why the blacksmith had been given orders to fasten a golden shoe on each of its hoofs.

The dung beetle climbed to the top of the manure pile to watch. "First the big and then the small," he said. "Not that size is important," he added as he lifted one of his thin legs and stretched it up toward the blacksmith.

"What do you want?" the man asked.

"Golden shoes," replied the dung beetle while balancing on five legs.

"You must be out of your mind to think that you should have

golden shoes," the blacksmith exclaimed, and scratched himself behind his right ear.

"Golden shoes!" repeated the dung beetle crossly. "Am I not as good as that big clumsy beast that needs to have a servant to groom it, and even to see to it that it doesn't starve? Do I not belong to the emperor's stable too?"

"But why does the horse deserve golden shoes, have you any idea about that?"

"Idea!" cried the dung beetle. "I have a very good idea of how I deserve to be treated and how I am treated. Now I have been insulted enough; there is nothing left for me to do but go out into the wide world."

"Good riddance," said the smith.

"Brute!" returned the dung beetle, but the blacksmith, who had already returned to his work, did not hear him.

The dung beetle flew from the stable to the flower garden; it was a lovely place that smelled of roses and lavender.

"Isn't it beautiful here?" a ladybug called to him. She had just come for a visit and was busy folding her fragile wings beneath her black-spotted armor. "The flowers smell so sweet that I think I shall stay here forever."

The dung beetle sniffed. "I am used to something better. Why, there isn't even a decent pile of dung here."

The dung beetle sat down to rest in the shadow of a tiger lily. Climbing up the flower's stem was a caterpillar. "The world is beautiful," the caterpillar said. "The sun is very warm and I am getting quite sleepy. When I fall asleep — or die as some call it — I am sure that I shall wake up as a butterfly."

"Butterfly, indeed! Don't give yourself airs. I come from the emperor's stable, and no one there — not even the emperor's horse — has any notions like that. Those who can fly, fly. . . . And those who can crawl, crawl." And then the dung beetle flew away.

"I try not to let things annoy me; but they annoy me anyway," the dung beetle thought as it landed with a thud in the middle of a great lawn, where it lay quietly for a moment before falling asleep.

Goodness, it was raining. It poured! The dung beetle woke with a splash and tried to dig himself down into the earth but he couldn't. The rain had formed little rivers, and the dung beetle swam first on his stomach and then on his back. There was no

HANS CHRISTIAN ANDERSEN

hope of being able to fly. "I shan't live through it," he muttered, and sighed so deeply that his mouth filled with water. There was nothing to do but lie still where he was, and so he lay still.

When the rain let up for a moment the dung beetle blinked the water out of his eyes and looked about. He saw something white and crawled through the wet grass toward it. It was a piece of linen that had been stretched out on the grass to bleach. "I am used to better but it will have to do," he thought. "Though it's neither as warm nor as comfortable as a heap of dung; but when you travel you have to take things as they come."

And he stayed under the linen a whole day and a whole night; and it rained all the time. Finally, the following morning, the dung beetle stuck his head out from the fold of the linen and, seeing the gray sky, he was very annoyed.

Two frogs sat down on the linen. "What glorious weather," said one to the other. "It's so refreshing and this linen is soaking wet; to sit here is almost as pleasant as to swim."

"I would like to know," began the other frog, "if the swallow, who travels a good deal in foreign countries, ever has been in a land that has a better climate than ours. As much rain as you need; and a bit of wind, too — not to talk of the mist and the dew. Why, it is as good as living in a ditch. If you don't love this climate, then you don't love your country."

"Have you ever been in the emperor's stable?" the dung beetle asked. "There the wetness is spicy and warm. I prefer that kind of climate because I am used to it; but when you travel you can't take it along, that's the way things are. . . . Could you tell me if there is a hothouse in this garden, where a person of my rank and sensitivity would feel at home?"

The frogs either couldn't or wouldn't understand him.

"I never ask a question more than once," said the dung beetle after he had repeated his query the third time without getting an answer.

He walked along until he came upon a piece of a broken flowerpot. It shouldn't have been lying there but the gardener hadn't seen it, so it provided a good home for several families of earwigs. Earwigs do not need very much room, only company, especially lady earwigs, who are very motherly. Underneath the piece of pottery there lived several lady earwigs; and each of them thought that her children were the handsomest and most intelligent in the whole world.

THE DUNG BEETLE

"My son is engaged," one of them announced. "That innocent joy of my life. . . . His most cherished ambition is to climb into the ear of a minister. He is charmingly childish, and being engaged will keep him from running about, and that is a great comfort to a mother."

"Our son," began another mother earwig, "came straight out of the egg. He is full of life and that is a joy. He is busy sowing his wild oats, and that, too, can make a mother proud. Don't you agree with me, Mr. Dung Beetle?" She had recognized him by his shape.

"You are both right," remarked the dung beetle; and the earwigs invited him to come into their home and make himself comfortable.

"Now you must meet my children," said a third mother earwig.

"And mine!" cried a fourth. "They are so lovable and so amusing, and they only misbehave when they have stomachaches and it's not their fault that you get one so easily at their age."

All the mothers talked and their children talked; and when the little ones weren't talking, they were pulling at the dung beetle's mustache with the little tweezers that each of them had in his tail.

"Always up to something! Aren't they darling?" the mothers said in a chorus, and oozed mother love. But the dung beetle was bored and asked for directions to the nearest hothouse.

"It is far, far away, nearly at the end of the world, on the other side of the ditch," explained one of the lady earwigs. "If one of my children ever should think of traveling so far away I would die. I am sure of it."

"Well, that is where I am going," said the dung beetle, and to show that he was really gallant, he left without saying good-by.

In the ditch he met many relatives: all of them dung beetles. "This is our home," they said. "It is quite comfortable: warm and wet. Please step down into the land of plenty. You must be tired after all your travels."

"I am!" replied the dung beetle. "I have lain a whole day and a whole night on linen. Cleanliness wears you out so. Then I stood under a drafty flowerpot until I got arthritis in my wings. It is a blessing to be with my own kind again."

"Do you come from the hothouse?" one of the older dung beetles asked.

"Higher still. I was born in the emperor's stable with golden shoes on. I am traveling incognito on a secret mission. And no matter how much you coaxed, I wouldn't tell you about it." With these words the dung beetle crept into the mud and made himself comfortable.

Nearby sat three young lady dung beetles. They were tittering because they didn't know what to say.

"They are not engaged, though they are beautiful," remarked their mother. The young ladies tittered again, this time because they were shy.

"Even in the emperor's stable I have never seen anyone more beautiful," agreed the dung beetle, who had traveled far and wide.

"They are young and virtuous. Don't ruin them! Don't speak to them unless you have honorable intentions. But I see you are a gentleman, and therefore I give you my blessings!"

"Hurrah!" cried all the other dung beetles, and congratulated the foreigner on his engagement. First engaged, then married; there was no reason to put it off.

The first day of married life was good, and the second was pleasant enough, but on the third began all the responsibilities of providing food for his wives, and soon there would probably be offspring.

"They took me by surprise," thought the dung beetle. "Now I shall surprise them."

And so he did. He ran away. All day the wives waited, and all night too; then they declared themselves widows. The other dung beetles were angry and called him a ne'er-do-well, because they feared that now they would have to support the deserted wives.

"Just behave as if you were virgins again," said their mother. "Come, you are still my innocent girls. But shame on the tramp who abandoned you."

In the meantime, the dung beetle was sailing across the ditch on a cabbage leaf. It was morning and two human beings who happened to be passing noticed him and picked him up. They turned the dung beetle over and looked at him from all sides, for these two men were scholars.

The younger of the two, who was the most learned, said, "'Allah sees the black scarab in the black stone that is part of the black mountain.' Isn't it written thus in the Koran?" Then he translated the dung beetle's name into Latin and gave a lecture in which he explained its genealogy and history. The older scholar remarked that there was no reason to take the dung beetle home with them,

THE DUNG BEETLE

because he already had a much more beautiful scarab in his collection.

The dung beetle's feelings were hurt and he flew right out of the scholar's hand, high up into the sky. Now that his wings were dry he was able to make the long journey to the hothouse in one stretch. Luckily, a window was open and he flew straight in and landed on a pile of manure that had been delivered that morning.

"This is sumptuous," he said as he dug himself down into the dung, where he soon was asleep. He dreamed that the emperor's horse was dead and that he — the dung beetle — had not only been given its four golden shoes but had been promised two more. It was a pleasant dream and when the dung beetle awoke he climbed out of the manure to look about him. How magnificent everything was!

There were slender palm trees, whose green leaves appeared transparent when the sun shone on them; and below the trees were flowers of all colors. Some were red as fire, and some were yellow as amber, and some were as pure white as new-fallen snow. "What a marvelous display!" exclaimed the dung beetle. "And think how delicious it all will taste as soon as it is rotten. It is a glorious larder. I must go visiting and see if I can find any of my family living here. I cannot associate with just anybody. I have my pride, and that I am proud of." Then he crawled on, recalling as he did so, his dream and how the horse had died and he was given its gold shoes.

Suddenly a little hand picked him up, and again he was pinched and turned over. The gardener's son and one of his playmates had been exploring in the hothouse and, when they saw the dung beetle, they decided it would be fun to keep it. They wrapped it in a leaf from a grapevine, and the gardener's son stuck it in his pocket.

The dung beetle tried to creep and to crawl, and the boy closed his hand around him and that was most uncomfortable.

The boys ran to the big pond at the other end of the garden. A worn-out wooden shoe with a missing instep became a ship. With a stick for a mast and the dung beetle, who was tied to the stick with a piece of woolen thread, as the captain, the ship was launched.

The pool was large and the dung beetle thought he was adrift on an ocean. He got so frightened that he fell over on his back and there he lay with all his legs pointing up toward the sky.

There were currents in the water and they carried the wooden shoe along. When it got out too far, one of the boys would roll up his trousers — both boys were barefooted — and wade out to bring the shoe nearer the shore. Suddenly, while the shoe was quite far out, almost in the center of the pond, someone called the boys, called them in so stern a voice that they forgot all about the shoe and ran home as fast as they could. The wooden shoe drifted on and on. The dung beetle shuddered with fear, for he couldn't fly away, tethered as he was to the mast.

A fly came to keep him company. "Lovely weather, don't you agree? I think I'll rest here for a moment in the sun. A very comfortable place you have here."

"Nonsense!" cried the dung beetle. "How can I be comfortable when I am tied to the mast? You talk like an idiot, so I'm sure you must be one."

"I'm not tied to anything," said the fly, and flew away.

"Now I know the world," muttered the dung beetle. "It is cruel and I am the only decent one in it. First they refused to give me golden shoes, then they made me lie on wet linen and stand for hours in a draft. Finally, I am tricked into marriage; and when I show my courage by going out into the world to find out what that's like and see how I will be treated there, I am captured by a human puppy who ties me to a mast and sets me adrift on a great ocean. And all the while the emperor's horse runs about with golden shoes on; and that's almost the most annoying part of it all. In this world you must not ask for sympathy. My life has been most interesting. . . . But what difference does that make if no one ever hears about it? . . . But does the world deserve to hear my story? . . . If it did, I would have been given the golden shoes. Had I got them, it would have brought honor to the stable. The stable missed its chance, so did the world, for everything is over."

But everything was not over; some young girls who were out rowing on the pond saw the little ship.

"Look, there is a wooden shoe," one of them said.

"Someone has tied a beetle to the mast," said another; and she leaned over the side of the boat and grabbed the wooden shoe. With a tiny pair of scissors she carefully cut the woolen thread, so that no harm came to the dung beetle. When they returned to

THE DUNG BEETLE

shore the girl let him go in the grass. "Crawl or fly, whichever you can, for freedom is a precious gift," she said.

The dung beetle flew straight in through an open window of a large building and landed in the long, soft, silken mane of the emperor's horse, who was standing in the stable where they both belonged. He held on tightly to the mane, then he relaxed and began to think about life.

"Here I am, sitting on the emperor's horse. I am the rider. . . . What am I saying?" The dung beetle was talking out loud. "Now everything is clear to me! And I know it is true! Didn't the blacksmith ask me if I didn't have some idea why the emperor's horse was being shod with golden shoes? Now I understand that it was for my sake that the horse was given golden shoes."

The dung beetle was in the best of humors. "It is traveling that did it!" he thought. "It broadens your horizon and makes everything clear to you."

The sun shone through the window. Its rays fell upon the horse and the dung beetle. "The world is not so bad," remarked the dung beetle. "It all depends on how you look at it." And the world, indeed, was beautiful, when the emperor's horse was awarded golden shoes because the dung beetle was to ride it.

"I must dismount," he thought, "and go and tell the other dung beetles how I have been honored. I will tell them of my wonderful adventures and how I enjoyed traveling abroad. And I'll tell them, too, that I have decided to stay at home until the horse wears out his golden shoes."

WHAT FATHER DOES
IS ALWAYS RIGHT

Now I want to tell you a story that I heard myself when I was a very little boy, and every time that I have thought of it since, it has seemed to me to be more beautiful. For stories are like people: some — though not all — improve with age, and that is a blessing.

Have you ever been in Denmark and seen the countryside? If you have, then you must have seen one of those really old cottages that has a thatched roof that is overgrown with moss and a stork's nest perched on its ridge. The walls are crooked. The windows are small, and only one of them has a hasp and hinges so that it can be opened. The oven for baking bread juts out of the wall like a well-filled stomach. There are a hedge of elderberries and a tiny pond surrounded by willow trees, where a duck and some ducklings swim. In the yard there is an old dog that barks at everyone who goes by.

In such a cottage, far out in the country, there once lived a farmer and his wife. They had little that they could get along without, but they did have something, and that was a horse that had to graze at the edge of the road because they didn't have a paddock. Sometimes the farmer rode on the horse when he went to town; and sometimes his neighbor borrowed it, and that was to the farmer's advantage, for country people believe that one good turn deserves another. But one day the farmer realized that he'd be

WHAT FATHER DOES IS ALWAYS RIGHT

doing himself a better turn if he sold the horse or traded it for something which he had more use for, though he didn't know what it could be.

"That you'll find out soon enough," said his wife. "You know best, Father. There's a market in town today. Why don't you ride in on the horse, and there you can sell it or trade it for something else. Whatever you do, I am sure it will be right."

She tied his cravat, which she knew how to do better than anybody else. She made a double bow because that made him look more gallant. She brushed his hat with the palm of her hand, and then she kissed him warmly on the lips. Off he rode on the horse that was to be sold or traded, just as he saw fit; for striking a bargain was something he knew how to do.

The sun was shining and there wasn't a cloud in the sky. The dusty road was filled with folk on their way to market; some in wagons, others on horses, and many on their own poor legs. It was terribly hot and there was not a scrap of shade along the road.

The farmer noticed a man who was leading a cow that was as beautiful as any cow could be; and he thought, "I'll bet that cow gives a lot of good milk." Then he called to the man, "Listen — you with the cow — I'd like to talk with you!" And when the other man turned around, he continued: "I know that a horse is worth more than a cow. But a cow would be more useful to me. Shall we trade?"

"Why not?" said the man.

Now here is where the story should have ended but then it wouldn't have been worth telling. The farmer had done what he had set out to do, and so he should have turned around and gone back home with his new cow. But he thought that, since he had meant to go to the market, it was a pity to miss seeing it.

He walked quickly and the cow walked quickly, and pretty soon they had caught up with a man who was leading a sheep. It was a fine animal with a heavy coat of wool. "A sheep like that I wouldn't mind owning," he thought. "In the winter when it gets too cold you can always take a sheep inside with you. Besides, I don't have enough grazing for a cow, and a sheep is satisfied with what it can find on the side of the road." And the more he looked at the sheep, the better he liked it.

"How would you like to trade your sheep for my cow?" he finally asked. And that bargain was made.

He hadn't gone far with his sheep when he spied a man who was sitting and resting on a big stone. He had good reason for wanting to rest: he was carrying a goose that was bigger than most ganders.

"A fine fat goose!" the farmer cried as he lifted his hat. "How pretty it would look in our pond and then Mother would have someone to give the potato peelings to. How often has she said that we ought to have a goose. And now she can have one! What about trading? I'll give you a sheep for a goose and throw a thank you into the bargain."

"A sheep for my goose?" said the stranger. "Why not? And you can keep your thank you, for I don't like to drive too hard a bargain."

The farmer tucked the goose under his arm and walked on. As he came nearer the town the traffic became greater and greater. All about him were people and animals. There wasn't space for them all on the road; they walked in the gutters and the embankments, and even on the fields. The town's gatekeeper had tethered his hen in his potato patch for fear that she might get frightened by all the confusion and run away. The hen's tail was as finely feathered as a cock's, and as she said, "Cluck! Cluck . . ." she winked. What that meant I cannot tell you, but I do know what the farmer thought: "That hen is as good as the minister's best hen, the one that won the prize at the fair. I wish it were mine. A hen can always find a grain of corn by itself; besides, it can lay eggs. I think I will strike a bargain."

From thought to action is no further than the tongue can travel in a few seconds. The gatekeeper got the goose and the farmer the white hen.

The farmer had done a lot that morning and traveled far. He was thirsty and hungry. The sun was baking hot, as if it had been hired by the innkeeper.

As he was entering the inn, the farmer collided with one of the servants, who was carrying a sack over his shoulder. "What have you got in the sack?" the farmer asked.

"Rotten apples," the other man replied, "and I am on my way to the pigpen with them."

"A whole sackful, what an awful lot that is! I wish Mother could see it. Last year, on our old apple tree next to the woodshed, there was only one single apple. Mother put it in the cupboard and there it lay till it was all dried up and no bigger than a walnut. 'It makes me feel rich just to look at it,' she used to say. Think how she would feel if she had a sackful."

WHAT FATHER DOES IS ALWAYS RIGHT

"What will you give me for it?" asked the servant.

"My hen," the farmer replied; and the words were no sooner said than he found he had a sack of rotten apples in his hands instead of a hen.

He went into the taproom, which was crowded with people. There were butchers, farmers, merchants, horse dealers, and even a couple of Englishmen, who were so rich that their pockets were bursting with gold coins. All Englishmen like to gamble, that's a tradition in their country. Now just listen to what happened.

The taproom was next to the kitchen, and the stove that was used for cooking extended right through the kitchen wall into the taproom. Innkeepers are economical and this kind of stove is a great saving in winter. The farmer, without giving it a thought, put his sack of apples down on the stove, and soon they began to simmer and sputter.

"Suss! Suss!" the apples said, and aroused the curiosity of one of the Englishmen.

"What's that?" he asked.

And the farmer told him the whole story of how he had traded his horse for a cow, his cow for a sheep, his sheep for a goose, his goose for a hen, and finally the hen for a sack of rotten apples.

"Your wife will beat you with a rolling pin when you get home. She'll raise the roof," the Englishman commented.

"Beat me?" exclaimed the farmer. "She'll kiss me and say that what Father does is always right."

"I'll make you a wager," said the two Englishmen both at once. "A barrel of gold and a sackful of silver."

"The barrel of gold is enough and, if I lose, I'll fill a barrel with rotten apples and you can have Mother and me for good measure."

"Done! Done!" cried the Englishmen, for betting is in their blood.

They hired the innkeeper's horses and his carriage, and off they went, rotten apples and all. When they came to the farmer's house they drove right up to the door; the old dog barked, and the farmer's wife came out to greet them.

"Good evening, Mother," said the farmer.

"Thank God you arrived home safely," his wife replied.

"Well, I traded the horse."

"Trading is a man's business," she said and, in spite of the strangers, she threw her arms around him.

"I traded it for a cow."

"Thank God for the milk," she exclaimed. "Now we'll have both butter and cheese. That was a good bargain."

"But I traded the cow for a sheep."

"How clever of you," she said happily. "We have just enough grass for a sheep; and sheep's milk is good and the cheese is good, too. I can knit socks and a nightshirt from the wool; and I wouldn't have been able to do anything with cow's hair. A cow just sheds her hair and that's all. What a wise and thoughtful husband you are!"

"But I traded the sheep for a fat goose."

"Oh, my good husband, are we really going to have goose on St. Martin's Eve? You are always thinking of ways to please me. We will tether the goose in the ditch and by November she'll be even fatter."

"I traded the goose for a hen," he said proudly, for now he realized how very well he had done that day.

"That was a good exchange," said the wife. "Hens lay eggs and from eggs come little chicks. Soon we shall have a real henyard and that is something I have always wanted."

"I traded the hen for a sackful of rotten apples."

"Now I must kiss you, my dear husband! While you were away I thought that I should like to make a fine supper for you to eat when you got home; and I decided to make an omelet with chives. I had eggs but no chives. Our neighbor, the schoolmaster, has chives; but, as all the world knows, his wife is a stingy old crow, and when I asked her whether I could borrow some chives, 'Borrow!' she squawked. 'Nothing grows in your garden, not even a rotten apple.' Now I can lend her ten rotten apples, or even a whole sackful, if she wants them. That was the best bargain of all; and now I must give you a kiss." And she kissed him full on the mouth.

"I like that!" cried one of the Englishmen, while the other laughed. "From bad to worse, and they do not even know it! Always happy, always contented. That was worth the money!" And they gave a barrel full of gold coins to the farmer whose wife gave him kisses instead of blows.

Yes, it pays for a wife to admit that her husband is cleverer than she is.

Well, that was that story. I heard it when I was a boy and now you have heard it too; and now you know that what Father does is always right.

THE UGLY DUCKLING

It was so beautiful out in the country. It was summer. The oats were still green, but the wheat was turning yellow. Down in the meadow the grass had been cut and made into haystacks; and there the storks walked on their long red legs talking Egyptian, because that was the language they had been taught by their mothers. The fields were enclosed by woods, and hidden among them were little lakes and pools. Yes, it certainly was lovely out there in the country!

The old castle, with its deep moat surrounding it, lay bathed in sunshine. Between the heavy walls and the edge of the moat there was a narrow strip of land covered by a whole forest of burdock plants. Their leaves were large and some of the stalks were so tall that a child could stand upright under them and imagine that he was in the middle of the wild and lonesome woods. Here a duck had built her nest. While she sat waiting for the eggs to hatch, she felt a little sorry for herself because it was taking so long and hardly anybody came to visit her. The other ducks preferred swimming in the moat to sitting under a dock leaf and gossiping.

Finally the eggs began to crack. "Peep . . . Peep," they said one after another. The egg yolks had become alive and were sticking out their heads.

"Quack . . . Quack . . ." said their mother. "Look around you." And the ducklings did; they glanced at the green world about them, and that was what their mother wanted them to do, for green was good for their eyes.

HANS CHRISTIAN ANDERSEN

"How big the world is!" piped the little ones, for they had much more space to move around in now than they had had inside the egg.

"Do you think that this is the whole world?" quacked their mother. "The world is much larger than this. It stretches as far as the minister's wheat fields, though I have not been there. . . . Are you all here?" The duck got up and turned around to look at her nest. "Oh no, the biggest egg hasn't hatched yet; and I'm so tired of sitting here! I wonder how long it will take?" she wailed, and sat down again.

"What's new?" asked an old duck who had come visiting.

"One of the eggs is taking so long," complained the mother duck. "It won't crack. But take a look at the others. They are the sweetest little ducklings you have ever seen; and every one of them looks exactly like their father. That scoundrel hasn't come to visit me once."

"Let me look at the egg that won't hatch," demanded the old duck. "I am sure that it's a turkey egg! I was fooled that way once. You can't imagine what it's like. Turkeys are afraid of the water. I couldn't get them to go into it. I quacked and I nipped them, but nothing helped. Let me see that egg! . . . Yes, it's a turkey egg. Just let it lie there. You go and teach your young ones how to swim, that's my advice."

"I have sat on it so long that I guess I can sit a little longer, at least until they get the hay in," replied the mother duck.

"Suit yourself," said the older duck, and went on.

At last the big egg cracked too. "Peep . . . Peep," said the young one, and tumbled out. He was big and very ugly.

The mother duck looked at him. "He's awfully big for his age," she said. "He doesn't look like any of the others. I wonder if he could be a turkey? Well, we shall soon see. Into the water he will go, even if I have to kick him to make him do it."

The next day the weather was gloriously beautiful. The sun shone on the forest of burdock plants. The mother duck took her whole brood to the moat. "Quack . . . Quack . . ." she ordered.

One after another, the little ducklings plunged into the water. For a moment their heads disappeared, but then they popped up again and the little ones floated like so many corks. Their legs knew what to do without being told. All of the new brood swam very nicely, even the ugly one.

THE UGLY DUCKLING

"He is no turkey," mumbled the mother. "See how beautifully he uses his legs and how straight he holds his neck. He is my own child and, when you look closely at him, he's quite handsome. . . . Quack! Quack! Follow me and I'll take you to the henyard and introduce you to everyone. But stay close to me, so that no one steps on you, and look out for the cat."

They heard an awful noise when they arrived at the henyard. Two families of ducks had got into a fight over the head of an eel. Neither of them got it, for it was swiped by the cat.

"That is the way of the world," said the mother duck, and licked her bill. She would have liked to have the eel's head herself. "Walk nicely," she admonished them. "And remember to bow to the old duck over there. She has Spanish blood in her veins and is the most aristocratic fowl here. That is why she is so fat and has a red rag tied around one of her legs. That is the highest mark of distinction a duck can be given. It means so much that she will never be done away with; and all the other fowl and the human beings know who she is. Quack! Quack! . . . Don't walk, waddle like well-brought-up ducklings. Keep your legs far apart, just as your mother and father have always done. Bow your heads and say, 'Quack!'" And that was what the little ducklings did.

Other ducks gathered about them and said loudly, "What do we want that gang here for? Aren't there enough of us already? Pooh! Look how ugly one of them is! He's the last straw!" And one of the ducks flew over and bit the ugly duckling on the neck.

"Leave him alone!" shouted the mother. "He hasn't done anyone any harm."

"He's big and he doesn't look like everybody else!" replied the duck who had bitten him. "And that's reason enough to beat him."

"Very good-looking children you have," remarked the duck with the red rag around one of her legs. "All of them are beautiful except one. He didn't turn out very well. I wish you could make him over again."

"That's not possible, Your Grace," answered the mother duck. "He may not be handsome, but he has a good character and swims as well as the others, if not a little better. Perhaps he will grow handsomer as he grows older and becomes a bit smaller. He was in the egg too long, and that is why he doesn't have the right shape." She smoothed his neck for a moment and then added, "Besides, he's a drake; and it doesn't matter so much what he looks like. He is strong and I am sure he will be able to take care of himself."

"Well, the others are nice," said the old duck. "Make yourself at home, and if you should find an eel's head, you may bring it to me."

And they were "at home."

The poor little duckling, who had been the last to hatch and was so ugly, was bitten and pushed and made fun of both by the hens and by the other ducks. The turkey cock (who had been born with spurs on, and therefore thought he was an emperor) rustled his feathers as if he were a full-rigged ship under sail, and strutted up to the duckling. He gobbled so loudly at him that his own face got all red.

The poor little duckling did not know where to turn. How he grieved over his own ugliness, and how sad he was! The poor creature was mocked and laughed at by the whole henyard.

That was the first day; and each day that followed was worse than the one before. The poor duckling was chased and mistreated by everyone, even his own sisters and brothers, who quacked again and again, "If only the cat would get you, you ugly thing!"

Even his mother said, "I wish you were far away." The other ducks bit him and the hens pecked at him. The little girl who came to feed the fowls kicked him.

At last the duckling ran away. It flew over the tops of the bushes, frightening all the little birds so that they flew up into the air. "They, too, think I am ugly," thought the duckling, and closed his eyes — but he kept on running.

Finally he came to a great swamp where wild ducks lived; and here he stayed for the night, for he was too tired to go any farther.

In the morning he was discovered by the wild ducks. They looked at him and one of them asked, "What kind of bird are you?"

The ugly duckling bowed in all directions, for he was trying to be as polite as he knew how.

"You are ugly," said the wild ducks, "but that is no concern of ours, as long as you don't try to marry into our family."

The poor duckling wasn't thinking of marriage. All he wanted was to be allowed to swim among the reeds and drink a little water when he was thirsty.

He spent two days in the swamp; then two wild geese came — or

THE UGLY DUCKLING

rather, two wild ganders, for they were males. They had been hatched not long ago; therefore they were both frank and bold.

"Listen, comrade," they said. "You are so ugly that we like you. Do you want to migrate with us? Not far from here there is a marsh where some beautiful wild geese live. They are all lovely maidens, and you are so ugly that you may seek your fortune among them. Come along."

"Bang! Bang!" Two shots were heard and both the ganders fell down dead among the reeds, and the water turned red from their blood.

"Bang! Bang!" Again came the sound of shots, and a flock of wild geese flew up.

The whole swamp was surrounded by hunters; from every direction came the awful noise. Some of the hunters had hidden behind bushes or among the reeds but others, screened from sight by the leaves, sat on the long, low branches of the trees that stretched out over the swamp. The blue smoke from the guns lay like a fog over the water and among the trees. Dogs came splashing through the marsh, and they bent and broke the reeds.

The poor little duckling was terrified. He was about to tuck his head under his wing, in order to hide, when he saw a big dog peering at him through the reeds. The dog's tongue hung out of its mouth and its eyes glistened evilly. It bared its teeth. Splash! It turned away without touching the duckling.

"Oh, thank God!" he sighed. "I am so ugly that even the dog doesn't want to bite me."

The little duckling lay as still as he could while the shots whistled through the reeds. Not until the middle of the afternoon did the shooting stop; but the poor little duckling was still so frightened that he waited several hours longer before taking his head out from under his wing. Then he ran as quickly as he could out of the swamp. Across the fields and the meadows he went, but a wind had come up and he found it hard to make his way against it.

Toward evening he came upon a poor little hut. It was so wretchedly crooked that it looked as if it couldn't make up its mind which way to fall and that was why it was still standing. The wind was blowing so hard that the poor little duckling had to sit down in order not to be blown away. Suddenly he noticed that the door was off its hinges, making a crack; and he squeezed himself through it and was inside.

HANS CHRISTIAN ANDERSEN

An old woman lived in the hut with her cat and her hen. The cat was called Sonny and could both arch his back and purr. Oh yes, it could also make sparks if you rubbed its fur the wrong way. The hen had very short legs and that was why she was called Cluck Lowlegs. But she was good at laying eggs, and the old woman loved her as if she were her own child.

In the morning the hen and the cat discovered the duckling. The cat meowed and the hen clucked.

"What is going on?" asked the old woman, and looked around. She couldn't see very well, and when she found the duckling she thought it was a fat, full-grown duck. "What a fine catch!" she exclaimed. "Now we shall have duck eggs, unless it's a drake. We'll give it a try."

So the duckling was allowed to stay for three weeks on probation, but he laid no eggs. The cat was the master of the house and the hen the mistress. They always referred to themselves as "we and the world," for they thought that they were half the world — and the better half at that. The duckling thought that he should be allowed to have a different opinion, but the hen did not agree.

"Can you lay eggs?" she demanded.

"No," answered the duckling.

"Then keep your mouth shut."

And the cat asked, "Can you arch your back? Can you purr? Can you make sparks?"

"No."

"Well, in that case, you have no right to have an opinion when sensible people are talking."

The duckling was sitting in a corner and was in a bad mood. Suddenly he recalled how lovely it could be outside in the fresh air when the sun shone: a great longing to be floating in the water came over the duckling, and he could not help talking about it.

"What is the matter with you?" asked the hen as soon as she had heard what he had to say. "You have nothing to do, that's why you get ideas like that. Lay eggs or purr, and such notions will disappear."

"You have no idea how delightful it is to float in the water, and to dive down to the bottom of a lake and get your head wet," said the duckling.

"Yes, that certainly does sound amusing," said the hen. "You must have gone mad. Ask the cat — he is the most intelligent being I know — ask him whether he likes to swim or dive down to the bottom of a lake. Don't take my word for anything. . . . Ask the old woman, who is the cleverest person in the world; ask her whether she likes to float and to get her head all wet."

"You don't understand me!" wailed the duckling.

"And if I don't understand you, who will? I hope you don't think that you are wiser than the cat or the old woman — not to mention myself. Don't give yourself airs! Thank your Creator for all He has done for you. Aren't you sitting in a warm room among intelligent people whom you could learn something from? While you, yourself, do nothing but say a lot of nonsense and aren't the least bit amusing! Believe me, that's the truth, and I am only telling it to you for your own good. That's how you recognize a true friend: it's someone who is willing to tell you the truth, no matter how unpleasant it is. Now get to work: lay some eggs, or learn to purr and arch your back."

"I think I'll go out into the wide world," replied the duckling.

"Go right ahead!" said the hen.

And the duckling left. He found a lake where he could float in the water and dive to the bottom. There were other ducks, but they ignored him because he was so ugly.

Autumn came and the leaves turned yellow and brown, then they fell from the trees. The wind caught them and made them dance. The clouds were heavy with hail and snow. A raven sat on a fence and screeched, "Ach! Ach!" because it was so cold. When just thinking of how cold it was is enough to make one shiver, what a terrible time the duckling must have had.

One evening just as the sun was setting gloriously, a flock of beautiful birds came out from among the rushes. Their feathers were so white that they glistened; and they had long, graceful necks. They were swans. They made a very loud cry, then they spread their powerful wings. They were flying south to a warmer climate, where the lakes were not frozen in the winter. Higher and higher they circled. The ugly duckling turned round and round in the water like a wheel and stretched his neck up toward the sky; he felt a strange longing. He screeched so piercingly that he frightened himself.

Oh, he would never forget those beautiful birds, those happy birds. When they were out of sight the duckling dove down under the water to the bottom of the lake; and when he came up again he

THE UGLY DUCKLING

was beside himself. He did not know the name of those birds or where they were going, and yet he felt that he loved them as he had never loved any other creatures. He did not envy them. It did not even occur to him to wish that he were so handsome himself. He would have been happy if the other ducks had let him stay in the henyard: that poor, ugly bird!

The weather grew colder and colder. The duckling had to swim round and round in the water, to keep just a little space for himself that wasn't frozen. Each night his hole became smaller and smaller. On all sides of him the ice creaked and groaned. The little duckling had to keep his feet constantly in motion so that the last bit of open water wouldn't become ice. At last he was too tired to swim any more. He sat still. The ice closed in around him and he was frozen fast.

Early the next morning a farmer saw him and with his clogs broke the ice to free the duckling. The man put the bird under his arm and took it home to his wife, who brought the duckling back to life.

The children wanted to play with him. But the duckling was afraid that they were going to hurt him, so he flapped his wings and flew right into the milk pail. From there he flew into a big bowl of butter and then into a barrel of flour. What a sight he was!

The farmer's wife yelled and chased him with a poker. The children laughed and almost fell on top of each other, trying to catch him; and how they screamed! Luckily for the duckling, the door was open. He got out of the house and found a hiding place beneath some bushes, in the newly fallen snow; and there he lay so still, as though there were hardly any life left in him.

It would be too horrible to tell of all the hardship and suffering the duckling experienced that long winter. It is enough to know that he did survive. When again the sun shone warmly and the larks began to sing, the duckling was lying among the reeds in the swamp. Spring had come!

He spread out his wings to fly. How strong and powerful they were! Before he knew it, he was far from the swamp and flying above a beautiful garden. The apple trees were blooming and the lilac bushes stretched their flower-covered branches over the water of a winding canal. Everything was so beautiful: so fresh and green. Out of a forest of rushes came three swans. They ruffled their feathers and floated so lightly on the water. The ugly duckling recognized the birds and felt again that strange sadness come over him.

"I shall fly over to them, those royal birds! And they can hack me to death because I, who am so ugly, dare to approach them! What difference does it make? It is better to be killed by them than to be bitten by the other ducks, and pecked by the hens, and kicked by the girl who tends the henyard; or to suffer through the winter."

And he lighted on the water and swam toward the magnificent swans. When they saw him they ruffled their feathers and started to swim in his direction. They were coming to meet him.

"Kill me," whispered the poor creature, and bent his head humbly while he waited for death. But what was that he saw in the water? It was his own reflection; and he was no longer an awkward, clumsy, gray bird, so ungainly and so ugly. He was a swan!

It does not matter that one has been born in the henyard as long as one has lain in a swan's egg.

He was thankful that he had known so much want, and gone through so much suffering, for it made him appreciate his present happiness and the loveliness of everything about him all the more. The swans made a circle around him and caressed him with their beaks.

Some children came out into the garden. They had brought bread with them to feed the swans. The youngest child shouted, "Look, there's a new one!" All the children joyfully clapped their hands, and they ran to tell their parents.

Cake and bread were cast on the water for the swans. Everyone agreed that the new swan was the most beautiful of them all. The older swans bowed toward him.

He felt so shy that he hid his head beneath his wing. He was too happy, but not proud, for a kind heart can never be proud. He thought of the time when he had been mocked and persecuted. And now everyone said that he was the most beautiful of the most beautiful birds. And the lilac bushes stretched their branches right down to the water for him. The sun shone so warm and brightly. He ruffled his feathers and raised his slender neck, while out of the joy in his heart, he thought, "Such happiness I did not dream of when I was the ugly duckling."

THE SNOWMAN

Ｉt crackles and creaks inside of me. It is so cold that it is a pleasure," said the snowman. "When the wind bites you, then you know you're alive. Look how the burning one gapes and stares." By "the burning one" he meant the sun, which was just about to set. "But she can't make me blink; I'll stare right back at her."

The snowman had two triangular pieces of tile for eyes, and a children's rake for a mouth, which meant that he had teeth. His birth had been greeted by the boys with shouts of joy, to the sound of sleigh bells and the cracking of whips.

The sun set and the moon rose, full and round, beautiful in the blue evening sky.

"There she is again, just in another place. She couldn't stay away." The snowman thought that the sun had returned. "I guess that I have cooled her off. But now she's welcome to stay up there, for it is pleasant with a bit of light, so that I can see. If only I knew how to move and get about, then I would go down to the lake and slide on the ice as the boys do. But I don't know how to run."

"Out! Out! Out!" barked the old watchdog, who was chained to his doghouse. He was hoarse and had been so ever since he had been refused entrance to the house. That was a long time ago now; but when the dog lived inside, it had lain next to the stove. "The sun will teach you to run. I saw what happened to last year's

407

snowman and to the one the year before last. . . . Out! Out! Out! . . . They are all gone."

"What do you mean by that, comrade?" asked the snowman. "How can that round one up there teach me to run?" By "that round one," he meant the moon. "She ran when I looked straight into her eyes. Now she is trying to sneak back from another direction."

"You are ignorant," said the watchdog. "But you have only just been put together. The round one up there is called the moon. The other one is the sun and she will be back tomorrow. She will teach you how to run, right down to the lake. I've got a pain in my left hind leg and that means the weather is about to change."

"I don't understand him," thought the snowman, "but I have a feeling that he was saying something unpleasant. The hot one — the one that was here a moment ago and then went away, the one he called the sun — is no friend of mine. Not that she's done me any harm; it's just a feeling I have."

The weather did change. In the morning there was a heavy fog. During the day it lifted, the wind started to blow, and there was frost. The sun came out and what a beautiful sight it was! The hoarfrost made the forest appear like a coral reef; every tree and bush looked as if it were decked with white flowers. In the summer when they have leaves, you cannot see what intricate and lovely patterns the branches make. But now they looked like lace and were so brilliantly white that they seemed to radiate light. The weeping birch tree swayed in the wind as it did in summer. Oh, it was marvelous to see. As the sun rose higher in the sky its light grew sharper and its rays made everything appear as if it were covered with diamond dust. In the blanket of snow that lay upon the ground were large diamonds, blinking like a thousand small candles, whose light was whiter than snow.

"Isn't it unbelievably beautiful?" said a young girl who was taking a walk in the garden with a young man. "I think it's even lovelier now than it is in summer." And her eyes shone, as if the beauty of the garden were reflected in them.

They stopped near the snowman to admire the forest. "And a handsome fellow like that you won't see in the summer either," remarked the young man, pointing to the snowman.

The girl laughed and curtsied before the snowman, then she took the young man's hand in hers and the two of them danced across the snow, which crunched beneath their feet as if they were walking on grain.

"Who were they?" the snowman asked the dog. "You've been here on the farm longer than I have. Do you know them?"

"Certainly," answered the old dog. "She has patted me and he has given me bones. I would never bite either of them."

"Why do they walk hand in hand? I have never seen boys walk like that."

"They are engaged," the old dog sniffed. "Soon they will be moving into the same doghouse and will share each other's bones."

"Are they as important as you and I?" asked the snowman.

"They belong to the house and are our masters," replied the dog. "You certainly know precious little, even if you were only born yesterday. I wouldn't have believed such ignorance existed if I hadn't heard it with my own ears. But I have both age and knowledge, and from them you acquire wisdom. I know everyone on the farm; and I have known better times, when I didn't have to stand here, chained up and frozen to the bone. . . . Out! Out! Get out!"

"I love to freeze," said the snowman. "Tell me about the time when you were young, but stop rattling your chain like that, it makes me shudder inside."

"Out! Out!" barked the old dog. "I was a puppy once. 'See that lovely little fellow,' they used to say, and I slept on a velvet chair. I lay in the lap of the master of the house and had my paws wiped with embroidered handkerchiefs. They kissed me and called me a sweetheart, and their little doggy-woggy. When I grew too big to lie in a lap they gave me to the housekeeper. She had a room in the cellar. — You can look right into her window from where you are standing. — Down there I was the master. It wasn't as nicely furnished as upstairs, but it was much more comfortable. I had my own pillow to lie on, and the housekeeper gave me just as good food and more of it. Besides, upstairs there were children and they are a plague, always picking you up, squeezing you, and hugging you, and carrying you about as if you had no legs of your own to walk on. . . . Then there was the stove. In winter there is nothing as lovely as a stove. When it was really cold I used to crawl all the way under it. I still dream of being there, though it's a long time since I was there last. . . . Out! Out! Out!"

"Is a stove a thing of beauty?" asked the snowman. "Does it look like me?"

"You're as much alike as day and night. The stove's as black as coal; it has a long black neck with a brass collar around it. The fire's in the bottom. The stove lives on wood, which it eats so fast that it breathes fire out of its mouth. Ah! To lie near it or, better still, underneath it; until you have tried that you have no idea what comfort is. . . . You must be able to see it from where you are. That window, there, just look in."

And the snowman did and he saw the stove: a black, polished metal figure with brass fixtures. The little door at the bottom, through which ashes could be removed, had a window in it; and the snowman could see the light from the fire. A strange feeling of sadness and joy came over him. A feeling he had never experienced before. A feeling that all human beings know, except those who are made of snow.

"Why did you leave her?" The snowman somehow felt certain that the stove was of the female sex. "How could you bear to go away from such a lovely place?"

"I had to," answered the old watchdog. "They threw me out, put a chain around my neck, and here I am. And all I had done was to bite the youngest of the children from upstairs. I was gnawing on a bone and he took it away. A bone for a bone, I thought, and bit him in the leg. But the master and the mistress put all the blame on me. And ever since then I have been chained. The dampness has spoiled my voice. Can't you hear how hoarse I am? . . . Out! Out! Get out! . . . And that is the end of my story."

The snowman, who had stopped listening to the watchdog, was staring with longing through the cellar window into the house-keeper's room, where the stove stood on its four black legs. "She is exactly the same height as I am," he thought.

"It creaks so strangely inside of me," the snowman muttered. "Shall I never be able to go down into the cellar and be in the same room with her? Isn't it an innocent wish, and shouldn't innocent wishes be granted? It is my greatest, my most earnest, my only wish! And it would be a terrible injustice if it were never fulfilled! I shall get in, even if I have to break the window to do it."

"You will never get down into the cellar," the old dog said. "And if you did manage it, then the stove would make sure that you were out in a minute. . . . Out! Out!"

"I am almost out already!" cried the snowman. "I feel as if I were about to break in two."

All day long the snowman gazed through the window. In the

evening the housekeeper's room seemed even more inviting. The light from the stove was so soft. It was not like the moonlight or the sunlight. "Only a stove can glow like that," he thought. Every so often, when the top door of the stove was opened to put more wood in, the bright flames would shoot out, and the blaze would reflect through the window and make the snowman blush from the neck up.

"It's more than I can bear!" he exclaimed. "See how beautiful she is when she sticks out her tongue."

The night was long, but not for the snowman, who was daydreaming happily. Besides, it was so cold that everything seemed to tingle.

In the morning the cellar window was frozen; the most beautiful white flowers decorated the glass, which the snowman did not appreciate because they hid the stove from his view. It was so cold that the windows couldn't thaw and the running nose on the water pump in the yard grew an icicle. It was just the kind of weather to put a snowman in the best of moods, but it didn't. Why, it was almost a duty to be content with weather like that; but he wasn't. He was miserable. He was suffering from "stove-yearning."

"That is a very serious disease, especially for a snowman to get." The old watchdog shook his head. "I have suffered from it myself, but I got over it. . . . Out! Out! Get out! . . . I have a feeling that the weather is going to change."

And it did. It became warmer and the snowman became smaller. He didn't say a word, not even one of complaint, and that's a very telling sign.

One morning he fell apart. His head rolled off and something that looked like the handle of a broom stuck up from where he had stood. It was what the boys had used to help hold the snowman together and make him stand upright.

"Now I understand why he longed for the stove," said the old watchdog. "That's the old poker he had inside him. No wonder. Well, now that's over. . . . Out! Out! Out!"

And soon the winter was over, and the little girls sang:

> Come, anemones, so pure and white,
> Come, pussy willows, so soft and light,
> Come, lark and cuckoo, and sing
> That in February we have spring.

And no one thought about the snowman.

IN THE DUCKYARD

In the duckyard . . . The hens called it the henyard, for there were hens there too, but this story is about a duck, so we shall call it the duckyard since that is the name the ducks prefer. . . . In the duckyard there once was a duck who came from Portugal. She had laid eggs, been slaughtered, and then been eaten; and that was her biography. But all the little ducklings who had crawled out of her eggs had been called Portuguese and that name they were very proud of. When our story takes place there was only one member of the family left, and she was very fat, which is considered beautiful among ducks.

"Cock-a-doodle-doo," cried the cock, who had twelve wives and was very haughty.

"Ugh, how his crowing hurts my ears," the Portuguese said. "I wish he would learn to modulate his voice. But he is beautiful. I won't deny it, even though he isn't a drake. But to be able to modulate your voice is a sign of culture. Now the little songbirds who nest in the linden tree, they know the art. They sing so beautifully. . . . There's something in their songs that touches me indescribably. . . . I call it something Portuguese. If I had such a little songbird I would be a mother to it — kind and loving! It is part of my nature to be loving. It is in my blood: my Portuguese blood."

She had no sooner finished speaking than a little songbird fell,

412

IN THE DUCKYARD

headfirst, from the roof of the house into the duckyard. The cat had caught the poor little fellow, and somehow he had managed to escape but not without a broken wing.

"Isn't that exactly what you would expect from a cat — brutality!" exclaimed the Portuguese. "I know that cat, hasn't he eaten two of my ducklings? That such a creature should be allowed to walk about freely, especially on roofs, is more than I can understand. It would never be allowed in Portugal."

She felt very sorry for the little songbird, and so did all the other ducks, even though they weren't Portuguese. As they stood in a circle around him, they said, "Poor unfortunate creature. We cannot sing, but we appreciate music and are sensitive to art, though we don't talk about it."

"And why not?" said the Portuguese. "Just to show my appreciation, I will do something for the poor little thing, for that is a duty." Then she climbed into the water trough and splashed with her wings.

The water streamed down over the little songbird and he nearly drowned, but he knew he had been drenched out of kindness.

"That was a good deed!" said the Portuguese to the other ducks. "I hope it will be a good example to all of you."

"Pip," said the little songbird. His broken wing made it very difficult for him to shake himself dry. "You have a good heart, madam." He wanted to show his appreciation for the shower, though he hoped he would never get another.

"I have never thought about being good-hearted," the Portuguese began, and spread her wings. "But this I know: I love all my fellow creatures, all except the cat. And to demand that I should love the cat would be quite unreasonable. You can make yourself at home. I am from a foreign land, and you can see it by the beauty of my feathers and my posture. All the other ducks are natives. They don't have my blood. But it hasn't gone to my head. Only this I must say: if anyone here understands you, then it is I."

"She has a *wortugal* stuck in her gizzard," cried one of the ordinary ducklings, who was known to be wittier than all the others.

The other ordinary ducks nudged each other and snickered. "Wortugal . . . Quack . . . Quack . . . Wortugal, Portugal . . . Quack . . . Quack . . ." They all agreed that their companion's joke was one of the funniest they had ever heard "Wortugal, Portugal." But now it was time that they, too, befriended the little songbird.

"We don't waddle around with long and difficult words in our bills, but that doesn't mean that we are not kind or sensitive. We care about you too, but when we do you a favor we won't shout about it. Kind acts are best done quietly."

"You have a beautiful voice," one of the older drakes began as he stepped closer to the songbird. "It must be very gratifying for you to know how much pleasure you give to others. Not that I understand art; and that is why I keep my bill shut about it. After all, it is better to be silent than to say a lot of stupidities, as some people do."

"Don't pester him," the Portuguese ordered. "He needs lots of rest and proper attention." Turning to the little bird, she suggested, "Would you like another shower?"

"Oh no. Please let me stay dry," whispered the songbird.

"Water is the best cure for everything. It has never done me any harm," the Portuguese argued. "Amusing company helps too. Look who's coming. It's the Chinese hens. They have feathers on their legs, but they are quite respectable anyway. They have foreign blood in their veins, but they were born here, and that in my opinion is a virtue."

The Chinese hens came and before them walked the cock. "You are a songbird," he said politely, and this was very unusual, for he considered courtesy unmasculine. "You do what you can with the little voice you have and I appreciate it. But in order really to be heard one needs a chest," he asserted while he took a deep breath and held it as long as he could.

"Isn't he sweet?" remarked one of the Chinese hens. The songbird looked up at her; his feathers were still wet and ruffled from his shower. "He looks almost as beautiful as a newly hatched Chinese chick."

The Chinese hens spoke kindly to the songbird — very softly and in the most educated Chinese. Every word had a *ph* sound. "We belong to the same race as you do. The ducks, even the Portuguese, are web-footed. You don't know us yet, but then, who does? Who has taken the trouble to find out who we are? No one! And yet we are members of an aristocratic family, born to position above the others. We don't make a fuss about it. We try to see everyone else's good points and only talk about their virtues — though this can be difficult when so few of the creatures here have

IN THE DUCKYARD

any. Excluding ourselves and the cock, there isn't an intelligent fowl in the henhouse, but at least they are all respectable, that's more than you can say about any of the ducks. Don't trust that duck with the curled tail, she is false. As for the one with the green feathers in her wings, she is too talkative. She won't let you get a word in edgewise, and she has never held an opinion worth listening to. The fat one is a gossip, always telling malicious tales. We couldn't talk that way if we wanted to, because it would be against our nature; we say nice things about others or we don't say anything at all. The Portuguese is the only one of the whole lot of them who is the least bit educated, and she is too passionate and talks too much about Portugal."

"Goodness, how those Chinese hens whisper," said one ordinary duck to another ordinary duck. "But what a bore they are, and that's why we've never talked to them."

The drake joined the little group around the songbird. He was a little surprised at all the attention it was receiving, for he thought it was a sparrow. "I can't see the difference," he explained. "They all belong to the artistic crowd and they are all the same size. Since they exist, we shall have to put up with them."

"Don't mind him," the Portuguese whispered to the little songbird. "He is all business and business is all to him. . . . Now I think I had better take a nap. One owes it to oneself to take good care of oneself. I must grow fat, otherwise I shall never be stuffed and roasted, and this, after all, is the purpose of life."

The Portuguese blinked. She was a good duck; she found a good place to lie down, and there she slept soundly. The little songbird plucked at his broken wing, then he nestled as close as he could to his protector. "The duckyard is a pleasant place to be," he thought.

The hens walked about among the ducks only while they were looking for food; now that there was nothing more to be found, they went back to their own part of the yard, led by the Chinese hens.

The witty duckling remarked to the other ducklings that the Portuguese was waddling about in her second "ducklinghood."

"Ducklinghood . . . Ducklinghood!" screamed all the other young ducks. "My, how clever he is. . . ." Then they eagerly repeated his previous joke over and over again: "Wortugal . . . Portugal . . ." they cried until they grew tired and fell asleep.

For a while all was quiet, then a maid came from the kitchen of the farmhouse and emptied a bucketful of garbage into the duck-yard. Splash!

At once all the ducks were up and about with their wings spread. The Portuguese woke too, and as she rose she stepped right on top of the little songbird.

"*Peep,*" he cried. "You are so heavy, madam."

"It was your own fault, weren't you in the way? Don't be so thin-skinned. I am nervous too, but you will never hear me say '*Peep.*'"

"Don't be angry," said the little bird, "the *peep* just escaped me by mistake."

The Portuguese was not listening. She was too busy eating, gobbling down garbage as quickly as she could. In the meantime the songbird composed a song for her, and when she had finished eating and again lay down, he began to sing:

> Tweet . . . Tweet . . .
> Of your good heart I sing
> And its message bring,
> Tweet . . . Tweet . . .
> To the sky
> Oh, so high.
> Tweet . . . Tweet . . .

"I always rest after meals," the Portuguese complained. "When you live in a duckyard you must learn to behave like a duck. Now it is time to sleep."

The poor little songbird was amazed and unhappy; he had only meant to please the Portuguese. While she slept he found a grain of wheat and placed it in front of her. But when the duck woke up she was irritable because she had slept badly.

"That's something for a chicken, not for me; and please don't bother me all the time."

"Why are you mad at me, when all I want to do is to make you happy?" the songbird cried.

"Mad!" she exclaimed. "How dare you call me mad? Don't ever make such a mistake again."

"Yesterday," sniffed the little songbird, "yesterday there was only sunshine. Today everything is dark and gray. It makes me so sad."

"Hum. . . . You can't tell time," replied the Portuguese crossly.

IN THE DUCKYARD

"The day isn't done yet. Don't stand there with such a long, sad face."

"Please don't look at me like that," the little bird begged. "That's the way those two evil eyes looked at me just before I fell down from the roof into the duckyard."

"Of all the nerve!" screamed the Portuguese. "Imagine anyone comparing me to a cat, to a carnivorous animal! I who haven't a mean bone in my body! I who have taken such good care of you! I'll teach you better manners, I will!" And she bit off the songbird's head and left his body dead and still.

"Now what have I done?" the Portuguese asked herself. "Was I too severe? Well, if he couldn't take that, then he wasn't meant for this world. Didn't I try to be a mother to him? How could I have done otherwise, when I have such a kind heart?"

The neighbor's cock stuck his head over the fence and crowed so that he could be heard in the next county.

"You'll be the death of us all, with your crowing," the Portuguese cried. "The little songbird lost his head because of it, and I almost lost mine."

"He doesn't look like much now," the cock admitted as he glanced at the headless songbird.

"Speak with respect of him," snapped the Portuguese. "His breast was small but he sang with true artistry. And he had that loving nature and tender soul which all animals and so-called human beings ought to have."

All the ducks gathered around the body of the little songbird. Ducks have a passionate nature and their passions are most deeply aroused by envy and pity. And as there was no reason to envy the songbird, they were filled with pity.

They were joined by the Chinese hens. "We shall never see another songbird like him. . . . He was almost Chinese," they said. And then they clucked and cried. And all the other hens clucked and cried. But the ducks had the reddest eyes.

"We have soft hearts," the ducks exclaimed. "No one can deny it."

"It is true," cried the Portuguese. "Ducks are almost as soft-hearted here as they are in Portugal."

But the drake, who hadn't cried, grunted, "What about something to eat! Is there anything more important than eating? A dead musician more or less doesn't matter. There are plenty more where he came from."

THE BUTTERFLY

The butterfly wanted a sweet-heart, and naturally it had to be a flower. He inspected them. Every one sat as properly and quietly on her stalk as a young maiden should. The trouble was that there were too many of them to choose from, and the butterfly didn't want to be bothered by anything so fatiguing. That is why he flew over to the camomile flower. She is called by some the French daisy and she knows how to tell the future. Young people who are in love ask her questions, and then answer them by tearing off her petals, one at a time. This is the rhyme they usually recite:

> With all her [or his] heart . . .
> With only a part . . .
> Not lost forever . . .
> She'll love me never.

Or something like that. You can ask the camomile flower any questions you want to. When the butterfly came, he did not tear off any of the petals; he kissed them instead, for he was of the opinion that you get furthest with compliments.

"Sweet daisy, dear camomile flower, matron of all the flowers, you who are so clever that you can see the future, answer me: which of the flowers will be my sweetheart? This one or that one?

418

THE BUTTERFLY

Please tell me so that I can fly directly over to her and propose at once."

The camomile flower did not answer. The butterfly had insulted her by calling her a matron. She was a virgin and hadn't been proposed to yet. The butterfly asked the same question a second time and a third, then he got bored and flew away to go courting on his own.

It was early spring. Snowdrops and crocuses were still in bloom. "How sweet they are," he remarked. "Just confirmed, but they have no personalities." Like so many young men, he preferred older girls. He flew to the anemones but he found them too caustic. The violets were a little too romantic and the tulips a little too gaudy.

Soon the Easter lilies came, but they were a little too bourgeois. The linden blossoms were too small and had too large a family. The apple blossoms were so beautiful that they could be mistaken for roses, but they were here today and gone tomorrow. "Our marriage would be too short," the butterfly muttered.

He was most attracted by one of the sweet peas. She was red and white, pure and delicate; and was one of those rare beauties who also knows what a kitchen looks like. He was just about to propose when he happened to notice a pea pod with the withered flower at its tip. "Who is that?" he asked with alarm.

"That is my sister," replied the sweet pea.

"So that is what she will look like later," thought the butterfly. "How frightening!" And he flew away.

The honeysuckle had climbed over the fence. What a lot of girls there were, and all of them with long faces and yellow skins. The butterfly didn't care for them. But whom did he like? To find out, you must ask him.

Spring passed, summer passed, and then autumn came. Still the butterfly had no wife. The flowers were dressed in their finery, but they had lost their fresh innocence and scent of youth. As the heart grows older it needs scent, odor, perfume to arouse it; and the dahlias and the hollyhocks have none.

The butterfly lighted on a little mint plant with curly leaves. "She has no flowers, but she is a flower from her roots to the tip of her tiny leaves. She smells like a flower. I shall marry her." And the butterfly proposed.

The mint plant stood stiff and silent. At last she replied:

HANS CHRISTIAN ANDERSEN

"Friendship, but no more! I am old and you are old. We can live for each other, but marriage, no! It would be ridiculous at our age."

And that is how it happened that the butterfly never got married. He had searched too long for a wife, and now he had to remain a bachelor.

It was late in the autumn. The rains had come and the wind blew down the backs of the willow trees. It was not the weather to be out flying in, especially in summer clothes. But the butterfly was not outside, he was in a room that was kept summer-warm by a stove, where he could keep himself alive.

"But to live is not enough," declared the butterfly. "One must have sunshine, freedom, and a little flower." He flew to the windowpane. There he was seen, admired, and a pin was stuck through him. He was "collected" and that is as much as a human being can do for a butterfly.

"Now I sit on a stalk just like the flowers," he said. "It isn't very comfortable, probably just like being married: you are stuck." And with that he consoled himself.

"Not much of a consolation," said the potted plants who lined the window sill.

"But you cannot trust potted plants," thought the butterfly, "they have associated too much with human beings."

THE SNAIL
AND THE ROSEBUSH

A round the garden ran a hedge of hazelnuts, beyond it there were fields and meadows, where cows and sheep grazed; but in the center of the garden there was a rosebush in full bloom. Under it lay a snail who was very satisfied with the company he kept: his own.

"Wait till my time comes," he would say, "and see what I shall accomplish. I am not going to be satisfied with merely blossoming into flowers, or bearing nuts, or giving milk as the cows and sheep do."

"Oh, I do expect a lot of you. Won't you tell me when it's going to happen?" asked the rosebush very humbly.

"I must take my time," replied the snail. "Do you think anyone would expect very much of me if I hurried the way you do?"

The following year the snail lay in the same sunny place, under the rosebush. The plant was full of buds and flowers; there were always fresh roses on it, and each and every one was a tiny bit different from all the others. The snail crept halfway out of his house and stretched his horns upward; then he pulled them back in again.

"Everything looks exactly as it did last year. No change and no advancement. The rosebush is still producing roses; it will never be able to do anything else."

Summer was past and autumn was past. Until the first snow, the

421

HANS CHRISTIAN ANDERSEN

rosebush continued to bloom. The weather became raw and cold. The rosebush bent its branches toward the ground and the snail crawled down into the earth.

Another spring came. The rosebush blossomed and the snail stuck its head out of its house. "You are getting old," he said to the rosebush. "It is about time you withered and died. You have given the world everything you could. Whether what you gave was worth anything or not is another question, and I don't have time to think about it. But one thing is certain and that is that you have never developed your inner self, or something more would have become of you. Soon you will be only a wizened stick. What have you got to say for yourself? . . . Aren't you listening? . . . Can you understand what I am saying?"

"You frighten me so." The rosebush trembled. "You have asked me about things I have never thought about."

"I don't think you've ever thought about anything. Have you ever contemplated your own existence? Have you ever asked yourself why you are here? Why you blossom? Why you are what you are, and not something else?"

THE SNAIL AND THE ROSEBUSH

"No," the rosebush said. "My flowers spring forth out of joy. I cannot stop them from coming. The sun is warm, the air refreshing. I drink the dew and the rain. From the soil and the air I draw my strength. I feel so happy that I have to flower. I cannot do anything else."

"You have lived a very comfortable and a very indolent life," said the snail severely.

"How true! I have never lacked anything. But you have been given much more than I. You are a thinker. You can think deeply and clearly. You are gifted. You will astound the world."

"Astound the world! Not I!" The snail drew in his horns and then stretched them out again. "The world means nothing to me. Why should I care about the world? I have enough within myself. I don't need anything from the outside."

"But isn't it the duty of all of us here on earth to do our best for each other, to give what we can? I know I have only given roses. But you who have received so much, what have you given? What will you give?"

"What have I given! What shall I give!" snarled the snail. "I spit on the whole world. It is not worth anything and means nothing to me. Go on creating your roses, since you cannot stop anyway. Let the bushes go on bearing their nuts, and the cows and the sheep giving their milk. Each of them has their own public; and I have mine in myself. I am going to withdraw from the world; nothing that happens there is any concern of mine." And the snail went into his house and puttied up the entrance.

"It is so sad," said the rosebush. "No matter how much I wanted to, I couldn't withdraw into myself. My branches are always stretching outward, my leaves unfolding, my flowers blooming. My petals fall off and are carried away by the wind. But one of my roses was pressed in a mother's psalmbook, another was pinned on a young girl's breast, and one was kissed by a child to show his joy in being alive. Those are my remembrances: my life."

The rosebush went on blooming innocently, and the snail withdrew from the world, which meant nothing to him, by hibernating in his house.

The years passed. The rosebush had become earth and the snail had become earth; even the rose that had been pressed in the psalmbook was no more. But in the garden rosebushes bloomed and there were snails, who spat and retreated into their houses: the world meant nothing to them.

Should I tell the story from the beginning again? I could but it would be no different.

"THE WILL-O'-THE-WISPS
ARE IN TOWN,"
SAID THE BOG WITCH

Once there was a man who was well acquainted with fairy tales. They used to come knocking at his door. But lately he had not had any such visitors, and he wondered why the fairy tales didn't come any more. True, he had not thought of the fairy tales during the last few years and had not been expecting them to just come to his door, for outside there was war and inside — in the houses — there were the sorrow and despair that war brings.

Without thinking of the dangers, the stork and the swallow had made their long journey home, only to find their nests destroyed, the houses in the villages burned, and the fences around the fields broken. In the churchyards the enemy horses grazed among the tombstones. These were hard times, dark times, but even periods of unhappiness must end. "Now it is over," he said, but still the fairy tales did not come and knock at his door.

A whole year went by, and he missed them sorely. "Maybe they'll never come again," he thought. He recalled vividly the many forms that they had taken in the past. One had been a lovely young girl with a wreath of flowers in her hair and a birch branch in her hand. She had been as beautiful and fresh as spring itself, with eyes as deep and clear as the little lakes in the forest. Often the fairy tale had been a peddler, who would take his pack from his back and open it right there in the living room; and out would

"THE WILL-O'-THE-WISPS"

come the loveliest silk ribbons and every one had a verse on it. Best of all had it been when the fairy tale came as a little old woman with silver-white hair, and eyes large with age and filled with knowledge. For she could tell tales from the really ancient times: from the era before the one in which the princesses spun on golden spinning wheels and were guarded by dragons. And she could make the stories seem so alive that you saw spots in front of your eyes and the floor became black with human blood. Oh, she told gruesome tales, dreadful to hear and see, and yet such a pleasure, for they had happened so very long ago.

"I wonder whether she will ever come again," said the man, and looked so intently at the door that he saw black spots in front of his eyes and on the floor. "But maybe it is not blood," he muttered, "maybe it is bits from the mourning bands of the dark days that are only just past."

Suddenly it occurred to him that the fairy tales might be in hiding like the princesses in the old tales: that, like the princesses, they wanted to be found, and when, finally, they were discovered they would be more brilliant and more beautiful than they had ever been before.

"Who knows where a fairy tale can hide? It can be under a piece of straw that has been carelessly dropped at the edge of a well. I must be careful . . . ever so careful. It can be hidden in a withered flower that has been pressed between the leaves of one of the big, heavy books on my bookshelves."

The man walked over to his bookcase and took down the latest book; it was very serious and he thought it would help to clear his mind. There was no flower pressed between any of its leaves, but only a learned discourse concerning the national hero of his country: Holger the Dane. It seems that this very courageous man had never existed but had been invented by a French monk, who wrote a novel that was "translated into and widely printed in the Danish language." So Holger the Dane could never have taken part in any battle, nor was he liable to come to save his native land, if and when the nation were in mortal danger. Danish children could sing of his exploits, and even the grownups could hope it was not only a legend that he would return; but Holger the Dane was no different from William Tell. Both of them were no more than hot air, not worth wasting one's time on, according to the author of this very scholarly book.

"I believe what I believe," said the man, and put the book back. "No path is made where no foot has trod."

He went to the window sill and looked at the plants and flowers. Maybe the fairy tale had hidden in the red tulip with the golden-edged petals, or in the rose, or in the colorful camellia. But he did not find any fairy tale; only the sunshine playing among the leaves.

"The flowers that bloomed in our days of sorrow were more beautiful than these. But those we cut and made into wreaths to decorate the coffins that were draped in flags. Maybe the fairy tale was buried with the flowers. But would not the flowers have known, and the earth? Yes, even the coffin would have sensed it; and the new flowers as they bloomed — and even each blade of grass — would have told us that fairy tales do not die.

"Maybe it has been here and knocked at my door, but I did not hear it. Then life seemed so hard to bear, and all our thoughts were dark. Spring seemed an intrusion then, and the songs of the birds and the fresh green leaves on the trees, that should have made us happy, instead almost made us angry. Even the old songs that we loved were put aside with all the other things that were so dear to us, because our hearts were too heavy to bear them. Yes, then the fairy tale could have knocked on our doors and it would not have been heard; and no one would have bade it welcome. It probably just knocked and when no one answered it walked away.

"I shall go out and search for it, out in the country, in the forest, by the open sea."

Far away from any city there stood an old castle with red brick walls, corbie gables, and towers, one of which had a banner flying above it. Here the nightingale sits singing on the branch of a beech tree, gazing at the apple blossoms and believing them to be roses. In summer the bees swarm around their queen, singing their own songs. In the autumn storms raid the forest, whip the leaves from the branches, to tell of man's fate. At Christmas, from the open sea, one hears the song of the wild swan, while up at the castle everyone moves closer to the stove and is in a mood to hear the old ballads and sagas.

In the older part of the garden there was an avenue of chestnut trees, and there, attracted by their shade, walked the man who had set out to find a fairy tale. For here the wind had once sung to him

"THE WILL-O'-THE-WISPS"

the story of "Valdemar Daae and His Daughters." Here, too, a druid, who lived in an old oak tree — she is the mother of all the fairy tales — had told him the tale of the old oak tree's last dream. When his grandmother on his mother's side had been alive, there had been hedges here that had been carefully trimmed; but now there were only ferns and nettles that grew as they pleased and concealed almost all the sculpture. The mosses grew right up into the old stone figures' eyes. For all of that they could see just as well as they always had been able to, but the man who was searching for the fairy tale could not. He could not see the fairy tales any more. Where could they be?

From the tops of the old trees crows by hundreds cried, "Here! Here! Here!"

He left the garden by crossing the bridge over the moat, and entered the little copse of alder trees. Here were the henyard and the duckpond, and the little hexagonal house where the old woman who ruled over this little world lived. She knew exactly how many eggs had been laid and how many chickens had been hatched; but she was not a fairy tale, for she had been both baptized and vaccinated, and lying in the top drawer of her chest, she had certificates to prove it.

Not far from the old woman's house was a hillock covered with red hawthorn and lovely yellow laburnum bushes. Here there was an old tombstone. It had been brought there many years before from the churchyard in the market town, where it had been chiseled to honor the memory of a former member of the town council. There he was surrounded by his wife and five daughters, all wearing ruff collars and with their hands folded. If you look long enough at such a stone it becomes part of your thoughts; then it is as if your mind has entered the stone until both are one, and it will tell you about bygone times. In any case, that was what happened to the man who was looking for the fairy tale.

This particular day, he found a living butterfly resting on the stone head of the councilor. It fluttered its wings and flew a little distance away, as if it meant to show the man what was growing there. He bent down. The butterfly had alighted on a four-leaf clover. Four-leaf clovers bring good luck, and here there was not only one but seven of them.

"Luck comes in crowds," said the man, and picked them all and put them in his pockets. "They say that good luck is like ready cash, but I would have preferred to find a fairy tale," he added with disappointment.

The large red sun went down, and from the meadows vapors rose. The bog witch was brewing something.

It was late in the evening. The man stood alone by the window in his room and looked out over the garden, the fields, the meadows, and beyond them to the seacoast. The moon was almost full and its rays played upon the mist and made the meadow appear like a silver lake, as if the moon wished to prove the old legend true that told how there once had been a lake there. The man thought about the book he had read explaining that William Tell and Holger the Dane were merely folklore. "As the moonlight can make the lake that is no longer there reappear, so can the beliefs of the ordinary people make the legends of old live. Oh yes, Holger the Dane is not dead! And when his country is in mortal danger he will come back!" the man concluded.

There was a noise at the window. Perhaps it was a bird: an owl or a bat; the kind of guests one does not open the window for, no matter how often they knock. Suddenly the window opened by itself and there stood an old woman looking in at him.

"I beg your pardon!" exclaimed the man, very surprised. "Who are you? You must be standing on a ladder because my room is on the second story."

"You have four-leaf clovers in your pocket, seven of them, and one is a six-leaf clover." The old woman sniffed and looked about the room.

"Who are you?" demanded the man.

"I am the bog witch," she replied at last. "The bog witch who brews, that's me. And I am brewing beer right now, but one of the bog children, in a fit of temper, pulled the tap out of the barrel and cast it up here, at the castle, where it hit your window; and now all the beer is running out, which is really to no one's advantage."

"Please," began the man, who was looking for a fairy tale, "could you tell me —"

"Maybe I could," she interrupted, "but now I have something more important to attend to." And she was gone.

Just as the man was about to close the window she was back again.

"Well, that's done," she said. "Half of the beer has run out, and

"THE WILL-O'-THE-WISPS"

I'll have to brew again tomorrow, if the weather keeps. What did you want to ask me? I've come back again because I always keep my word. Besides, you have seven four-leaf clovers in your pocket, one of which is a six-leaf clover, and that I respect. A six-leaf clover is one of nature's medals. It can be found growing along the side of the road but not by just anyone. What do you want? Don't stand on ceremony, I have to get back to my barrels and my brewing."

The man asked the bog witch whether she had seen a fairy tale.

"By the eternal brewing vat!" said the bog witch, and laughed. "Haven't you known enough fairy tales? I am sure most people have. In our times, we have more important things to think about. Why, even the children don't care about them any more. The little girls would rather have a new dress; and as for the boys, I think they'd prefer a cigar. To listen to fairy tales! You are behind the times! Today we don't listen, we do things!"

"What do you mean?" asked the man. "How can you know so much about the world when you only associate with frogs and will-o'-the-wisps?"

"Yes, you be careful of the will-o'-the-wisps; they've got loose. Come down to the meadow and I'll tell you about it. I haven't the time to stand here any longer. But hurry, while your four-leaf clovers are still fresh and the moon is up." And away she went.

The bell in the tower clock struck twelve. Before the quarter chimes were heard, the man had run through the garden and was approaching the meadow. The fog was gone. The bog witch had finished her brewing.

"What a time it took you," said the bog witch. "Troll beings are faster than human beings. I am glad I was born a troll."

"What can you tell me?" The man was quite out of breath because he had hurried so much. "Is it something about a fairy tale?"

"Can't you talk about anything else?" The bog witch sounded irritated.

"Can you tell me what the poetry of the future will be like?"

"Don't be so high-flown. Come down to earth and maybe I'll answer you," replied the bog witch. "You only think about poetry and the fairy tale — as if she were the madam who ruled the roost. She is probably older than I am though she looks younger. I know her quite well. . . . I was young once myself — and that's not a disease that only children suffer from. I was quite a beautiful elf maiden then. And, like the others, I danced by the light of the moon and listened to the song of the nightingale; and I went for walks in the forest where I sometimes met the fairy tale. She was always running about. She would sleep one night in a tulip and the next in a rose; and then she used to like to dress herself up in the mourning crepe that was draped around the candles in the church."

"You know a lot of lovely things," said the man quite humbly.

"I know as much as you do, anyway," said the bog witch, and wrinkled her nose, which wasn't as pretty as it had been when she was an elf maiden. "Poetry and the fairy tales are cut from the same cloth; and as far as I am concerned, they can go and lie down wherever they please. All their work and all their talk — the same stuff can be brewed both cheaper and faster than they do it. I'll give you some for nothing. I have a chestful of bottled poetry. There you will find the essence of poetry, the very best of it, brewed from both bitter and sweet herbs: all the poetry that a man needs, and he can put a drop or two on his handkerchief for Sundays and holidays."

"How amazing!" exclaimed the man. "You mean you actually have poetry in bottles?"

"More than you could bear to sniff," answered the bog witch. "Have you heard the story about the girl who stepped on a loaf of bread to avoid getting her shoes dirty? I believe someone wrote it down and it has since been printed."

"I am the one who wrote it," said the man.

"Well, in that case you must be familiar with it. Do you remember what happened to the girl, how she sank down into the ground? Well, she landed right in my brewery, on the very day when the Devil's great-grandmother was paying me a visit. 'Give me that creature who's just sunk down here as a memento,' begged the Devil's great-grandmother, 'and I'll put her on a pedestal to remind me of my visit with you.'

"So I gave her the girl and the Devil's great-grandmother in return gave me her portable medicine chest — not that I have any use for it, it's filled with poetry in bottles. Look around! You have your seven four-leaf clovers in your pocket and one of them is a six-leaf clover, so you ought to be able to see it."

There in the middle of the meadow was something that looked

"THE WILL-O'-THE-WISPS"

like the stump of an alder tree, but it was the cabinet that had belonged to the Devil's great-grandmother. "Anyone in the whole world could come and make use of it, the problem is to be able to find it," said the bog witch.

The cabinet could be opened in front and in back, on all four sides, and at the corners. It was a work of art and yet it resembled an ordinary tree stump. Poets from all over the world, but especially from our own Denmark, were to be found here in imitation. The best of their work had been selected, criticized, improved upon, and finally brought up to date. With great talent — that is the word generally used when one does not want to say "genius" — the Devil's great-grandmother had taken from nature the smell or the taste that seemed most like this or that poet, added a bit of witchcraft to it, and presto! she had poetry in bottles, preserved for eternity.

"Let me have a look inside!" begged the man.

"I have more important things than that to talk with you about," the bog witch insisted.

"But now that we are here," mumbled the man as he opened the chest. "There are bottles of all different sizes," he said excitedly. "What's in this one? . . . And in that?"

"That one is called 'Aroma of May.'" The bog witch stared at the small green bottle. "I haven't tried it, but they say that, if you spill a little on the floor, where it falls a beautiful pond appears, the kind you find in the forest in which water lilies and mint are growing. A drop or two in a notebook, even one from the first grade, and you have a comedy of fragrance strong enough to be produced and long enough to make you fall asleep. I am sure that it is meant as a compliment to me that the label reads: 'Brewed by the Bog Witch.'"

Another bottle was called "Scandal." It looked as if it contained only dirty water, and that was what was in it; but a powder of town gossip, made up of two grains of truth and two barrels of lies, had been added to make it fizz. The mixture had been carefully stirred with a birch branch — not one that had been used on a criminal's back or by a schoolmaster on naughty children, but a branch that had been taken from a broom with which the gutters were swept.

There was also a bottle of devotional poetry, ready to be set to music like the psalms. Every drop in the bottle had been inspired by the portals of hell, and penned with the sweat and blood of

penance. Some say that this bottle contains only the gall of doves;
but others, who know nothing about zoology, claim that doves are
so good and gentle that they don't have any gall.

There stood the bottle of all bottles: the largest of them all, and it
took up half the space in the cabinet. It was filled with true-to-life
everyday stories. It had been doubly sealed with skin from both the
hide and the bladder of a pig, because it lost its flavor so easily.
From this bottle, every nation could make its own soup, all depending on how you turned and tipped the bottle. There was old
German blood soup with robber dumplings; tasteless English gov-
erness soup; a French *potage à la Coque*, made from the legs of
cock and sparrows' eggs — in Danish, it is called cancan soup.
There was also a soup for those who like high society, with counts
and courtiers in the bottom of the plate and a greasy glob of
philosophy floating on top. Oh, there was an endless variety in that
bottle; but the best soup of all was Copenhagen soup, at least that
was what everybody in Denmark said.

Tragedy had been put into champagne bottles because it must
begin with a bang. Light comedy was nothing but a bottleful of
sand to throw into the eyes of the audience. There were bottles of
the more vulgar kind of comedy but they were empty except for
the playbills, on which the titles were in the boldest type: "Do You
Dare to Spit in the Machine?" "A Right to the Jaw." "The Sweet
Donkey."

The man looked thoughtfully at all the bottles, but the bog witch
had no patience with them, she had more important matters to
think about.

"You have looked long enough at that junk shop," she said.
"Now you know what's to be found there, but what it is really
important for you to know I haven't told you yet. The will-o'-the-
wisps are in town; and some people, who have more sense in their
legs than in their heads, have already fallen into the bog chasing
them. This is more important than talking about poetry or fairy
tales. Maybe I should keep quiet about it, but something — I don't
know what it is, maybe fate — bids me speak. It is stuck in my
throat and has to come out: the will-o'-the-wisps are in town! They
are on the loose. Beware, all human beings!"

"I don't understand a word you're saying," said the man, who
looked as confused as he was.

"Make yourself comfortable. Sit down on the cabinet, but be

careful not to fall in and break the bottles; after all, you know what's inside them. I shall tell you all about the great event. It happened only yesterday. It has happened once or twice before in history, but that doesn't make it any less important. There are three hundred and sixty-four days left. . . . You know how many days there are in a year, I suppose."

With that as an introduction the bog witch finally began her tale: "Yesterday a great event took place out in the swamp. A will-o'-the-wisp was born; that is, twelve will-o'-the-wisps were born, for that is the number there is in a litter. And it was a very special event, for these will-o'-the-wisps, if they want to, can change themselves into human beings, and live and rule among you as if they had been born of women. It caused great excitement; and all the will-o'-the-wisps — both the male and the female — were dancing in the fields. There are female will-o'-the-wisps, but there is none in that litter.

"I was sitting on the cabinet, right where you are now, and had all twelve of the little ones in my lap. They were shining like glowworms and had already begun to hop about. They grew by the minute; and within a quarter of an hour they were as big as their father or their uncles. Now it is an old law — a boon granted long ago to the will-o'-the-wisps — that when the moon is in the particular position that it was last night, and the wind is blowing from the particular direction that it did last night; then all of the will-o'-the-wisps born during that hour and that minute can become human beings. For a whole year they have a chance to show what use they can make of their powers. A will-o'-the-wisp can move so quickly that he can travel around the whole world. The only things he needs to be careful of are sea and storm, which could put out his light. They can enter any human being — man or woman — they choose to and imitate his talk and behavior to perfection. If during one year the will-o'-the-wisp can make three hundred and sixty-five people err in a grand, not a small way, leaving the road of truth and decency, then he will be rewarded by being appointed to the greatest position that a will-o'-the-wisp can hope for; namely, to become a runner in front of the Devil's carriage of state. He will be given a bright orange uniform and taught how to breathe fire.

"Now that is something to make any will-o'-the-wisp lick his chops. But there are also dangers for such an ambitious will-o'-the-wisp. If a human being sees through his disguise, he can blow out the light and back into the swamp the will-o'-the-wisp must go. If he gets sick with longing for his family and the bog, his light will flicker and finally go out; and that is the end of him, he can never be relighted. And even if he does manage to remain a whole year among men, he still runs a risk; for if he fails to turn three hundred and sixty-five people from searching for truth and beauty, and doing good, then he must lie forever in a rotten tree and just glow, without being able to move about. And no punishment could be worse for a will-o'-the-wisp because they do so like to gallivant about.

"While they sat in my lap I told them of the honor they could achieve, but also of the risks they would have to run. I warned them that it would be more comfortable and secure to remain in the marsh, instead of running after fame and glory. But they were already imagining themselves dressed in bright orange and breathing fire out of their mouths. Some of the old will-o'-the-wisps said, 'Stay with us.' But there were others who encouraged them.

"'Go and play all the tricks you can on human beings,' they cried. 'Man has drained our swamps and dried up the meadows, what will become of our descendants?'

"'We want to breathe fire! We want to breathe fire!' shouted the newly born will-o'-the-wisps; and there was nothing more to discuss.

"To celebrate the decision there was a minute-long dance; it couldn't have been shorter. The elf maidens joined in the dance, but that was in order not to appear too proud, for in truth they preferred dancing by themselves. Then came the time for the giving of gifts to the twelve will-o'-the-wisps. Down in the swamp we call it playing ducks and drakes because the presents are skimmed across the water like stones.

"Each of the elf maidens gave a will-o'-the-wisp a piece of her veil. 'Take it,' the elf maidens explained, 'for as soon as you have it in your hands, you'll know all the difficult dance steps; you'll be able to do all the swings and turns, exactly when and as you should; and you'll have a bearing that will make you respected in the proudest company.'

"The raven taught every will-o'-the-wisp to say, 'Braaaa . . . Braaaa . . . Braaaaa.' And that is well worth knowing how to say, especially at the right moment.

"THE WILL-O'-THE-WISPS"

"The stork and the owl presented their gifts, but they said that they weren't worth mentioning, so I won't tell what they were.

"While these festivities were going on, King Valdemar and his men came riding by. And when the old king, who has been condemned to hunt until Judgment Day, heard of the event he gave away two of his hounds as a gift. These dogs are as swift as the wind and can carry as many as three will-o'-the-wisps at a time on each of their backs.

"Two old nightmares, who earn their living by hauling wares for those who live in the swamp, taught the will-o'-the-wisps the art of slipping through keyholes, which means that every door will be open to them.

"Two witches — but no relations of mine — offered to show the will-o'-the-wisps the way to town. Usually they ride on their own long hair, which they tie into knots to have something hard to sit on; but this time they rode on King Valdemar's dogs and had on their laps the young will-o'-the-wisps, who were setting out on their travels to bewilder and mislead human beings. Whoosh! And away they went!

"Now you know everything that happened last night. The will-o'-the-wisps are in town and they've already started their work. Exactly how or what they are doing I cannot say. But I have had a pain in the big toe of my left foot most of the day and there's always a reason for that."

"What a fairy tale!" exclaimed the man, who had not said a word while the bog witch was talking, but who had felt like interrupting a couple of times.

"No, it is only the beginning of the adventure," the bog witch corrected him. "Do you know what shapes the will-o'-the-wisps have taken or whose bodies they may enter, in order to lead the poor human creatures astray?"

"It is a whole novel about will-o'-the-wisps, and in twelve volumes: one for each will-o'-the-wisp. . . . Or better still, a musical comedy," the man said excitedly.

"Why don't you write it?" the bog witch asked. A moment later she added, "But maybe you shouldn't."

"It is a great deal easier and pleasanter not to." The man sighed. "If I write anything, then I shall be at the mercy of the newspapers, and that is as horrible for an author, as it is for a will-o'-the-wisp to lie in a rotten tree stump and glow, without being able to move or say a word."

"That's for you to decide," said the bog witch. "Let those write who can; and those who can't, they can write too. They need only come to me and I'll let them take anything they want from the cabinet filled with bottled poetry. . . . But as for you, my good man, it seems to me that you have had enough ink on your fingers already. You have reached an age when you ought to be old enough not to chase fairy tales. Have you understood my tale? Do you realize what is going on?"

"I know that the will-o'-the-wisps are in town. You have told me so. I have heard it and, what is more, I have understood what it means," the man replied sadly. "But what do you want me to do? If I start saying that certain honorable men are only will-o'-the-wisps in disguise, I'll be stoned."

"They can wear skirts as well," said the bog witch, looking at him thoughtfully. "They can enter a woman, too. They don't mind going to church, but they prefer to creep inside the minister and hold the sermon. On election day they are busy; they are speaking not for their country's sake but for their own. They become artists, too. But when they have taken over art, then there is no art. . . . I talk on and on. . . . Whatever it was that got stuck in my throat is almost gone now. I have spoken against my own family — for, though distant, the will-o'-the-wisps are cousins of mine — and now I am the savior of humanity! I don't know why I have done it, it is certainly not to get a medal. It's the maddest thing I could do: to tell everything to a poet and now the whole town will know about it."

"But no one will care," said the man. "Not one person will pay any attention to anything I say. They will all believe that I am telling a fairy tale when I say: '"Beware! The will-o'-the-wisps are in town!" said the bog witch!'"

THE SILVER SHILLING

Hurray! Here I go out into the wide world," exclaimed the newly minted silver shilling. It clinked and rolled and out into the world it came.

It passed through the warm, moist hands of children; felt the cold, clammy palm of the miser; and was kept a whole week by a poor old couple before they dared to spend it. Whenever it got into the purse of a young person it was soon out again. As I have said, it was a silver shilling; and it was made of quite pure silver, with only a very little copper in it. Now it happened that after it had traveled about in its native country for a whole year it went for a trip abroad. By chance it was overlooked in the bottom of a purse, and its owner did not even know that he had it along.

"Why, there is a shilling from home," he said when he finally noticed it. "Well, since it's come this far, it might as well do the trip with me as a tourist." The shilling almost jumped for joy. It was dropped back into the purse, which now was filled with foreign coins, but they came and went, while the silver shilling remained: and this, it felt, was an important distinction.

Several weeks went by. The coin had traveled far, without knowing exactly where it was. The other coins explained that they were in France or in Italy, and mentioned the names of towns, but how could the little shilling have any idea what the place looked like? One really cannot see the world from the bottom of a purse.

HANS CHRISTIAN ANDERSEN

One morning the shilling noticed that the opening of the purse wasn't completely closed; and so it moved up there in order to get a glance outside.

This it never should have done, for now it would have to pay the penalty for being curious. The shilling slid out of the purse and into its owner's trousers' pocket. That evening, after the purse was put aside for safekeeping, the traveler's clothes were brushed; and the coin fell out of the pocket and down onto the floor. No one heard it and no one saw it.

In the morning the man dressed and traveled on, but without his silver shilling. It was found by someone else, who put it in his purse where there were three other coins, all ready to do service.

"It is lovely to travel," said the shilling, "to see different people and learn their customs."

But at that very moment someone shouted: "That coin is false! It is counterfeit!" And it is at this point that the silver shilling's real adventures began; at least, so the coin itself seemed to think, for it would always start its story here:

"'False! Counterfeit!' A shiver went through me. After all, hadn't I been made at the Royal Mint of almost pure silver? Couldn't I clink as a silver coin ought to? Wasn't my stamp genuine? I felt sure that there must be some mistake. The voice couldn't be talking about me; but it was! I was called false and said to be worth nothing. Then I heard another voice say, 'I'll spend it tonight, when it's dark.' And that was to be my future. I was to be spent in the dark, and discovered and cursed in the daylight. 'Counterfeit! Worthless! I must get rid of it,' were the words that always greeted me."

Every time the coin was picked up, it would tremble and quake, for it knew that it was being passed on dishonestly, as a coin of the realm.

"Oh, poor me!" it lamented. "What good did it do me that I was made of silver, and bore a picture of our king, when he wasn't respected there? In this world you only have the value that the world gives you. How horrible it must be to really be counterfeit, to sneak through life knowing that one deserves no better fate. It must be monstrous, for even though I was innocent, I had a bad conscience. Every time I was taken out of a purse I dreaded the moment when I would be looked at. I knew what would happen. I would be rejected, thrown across the counter, as if I were the personification of deceit.

THE SILVER SHILLING

"Once I was given to a poor working woman as payment after a long day of toil. But she didn't know how to get rid of me. No one would accept me. Oh, I was a disaster for the poor woman.

"'I will have to fool someone,' she said, 'even though it is a sin and a shame, for I am too poor to keep a false coin. I can try to pass it off on the rich baker. It won't hurt him because he can afford it.'

"Now I was to give that poor woman a bad conscience," sighed the shilling. "And I thought to myself, 'Could I really have changed so much with age?'

"And the woman took me to the rich baker, but he knew his currency. I had hardly been put down on his counter before I was flung right back into the poor woman's face. I felt a great sadness come over me. I, who had had such a happy youth, confident of my value and my genuineness, now was the cause of grief to others. I became melancholy, as melancholy as a silver coin can be when it is unwanted. The woman picked me up and took me home with her. 'I won't try to fool anyone with you again,' she said, gazing at me with kindness and generosity. 'I shall drill a hole in you so everyone can see that you are counterfeit. . . . And yet, it suddenly struck me that you might be a lucky coin! Just like that, out of nowhere the thought came to me that you were a lucky coin. I'll make a hole in you anyway, but then I will put a string through it and give you to the neighbor's little girl to wear as a good-luck charm.'

"And that was what she did. It isn't very pleasant to have a hole drilled through you, but you can bear an awful lot when you know that the intentions are good. A string was drawn through me and that's how I became a medal and was hung around a little girl's neck. The child smiled at me and kissed me; and I spent one whole night sleeping on her innocent, warm breast.

"In the morning the girl's mother took me between her thumb and her forefinger and looked at me intently; she had her own ideas about what ought to be done with me. She took a pair of scissors and cut the string.

"'A good-luck charm, let's see how much your luck amounts to.' She put me in vinegar, so that I became green; and then she puttied up my hole and rubbed me so that no one would notice that I had a hole. When it grew dark, she took me to the office of the state lottery, to find out how much luck I would bring.

"How horrible I felt! I had a pain in the middle of myself, as if I were about to break in two. At the state lottery office there would

HANS CHRISTIAN ANDERSEN

be a whole till full of coins both large and small, and every one of them proud of their faces and inscriptions; and there in front of them all, I knew I would be called counterfeit and thrown back at the woman. But it didn't happen. There were so many people buying tickets that I was thrown unnoticed in among the other coins. Whether or not she ever won anything on that lottery ticket, I cannot tell you. All I know is that the next morning I was discovered and humiliated again. Once more I was put aside and then sent on my way to deceive someone else. And it is unbearable to have to play the fraud when you are honest; and I see no reason to deny that I am honest.

"A year and a day went by. I passed from one hand to another, from one house to another. Always cursed, always unwelcome. No one had any faith in me and finally I had no faith in myself, or in the world. It was a difficult time.

"One day I was given to a tourist. He looked so ignorant and innocent that, naturally, he was cheated. He took me for good currency without a glance but, when he wanted to use me, he heard the hue and cry, 'Counterfeit! Valueless!'

"'I was given it as change,' he said, looking at me carefully. Then he smiled broadly and that was the first time that a face had smiled when it was examining me. 'What are you doing here?' he asked. 'It is a coin from my own country. A good honest silver shilling that has had a hole drilled through it, as if it were counterfeit. That's really funny! I'll take good care of you and see to it that you come home again.'

"Happiness rushed through me when I heard myself being called 'good' and 'honest.' And now I was to go home. Back to my native country again, to that land where everyone knew that I was made of pure silver — almost pure silver, that is — and that the face on my head was that of our king. I would have sparkled with joy if nature had meant for me to sparkle, but only steel can sparkle, not silver.

"I was wrapped in a piece of fine white paper so that I would not have to associate with the other coins and get lost again. I was only brought out on special occasions when my owner met people from his own country, and they spoke well of me and said that I was very interesting. Isn't it funny that you can be called interesting when you haven't said a single word?

"Finally, I was home and my trials and tribulations were over.

THE SILVER SHILLING

Life was pleasant again. I was silver and my inscription was authentic. It didn't matter that a hole had been drilled through me to proclaim me as false, because I wasn't and that is all that is important. Don't give up, eventually justice will triumph. That's my philosophy," said the silver shilling.

IN THE CHILDREN'S ROOM

Father and Mother and all the other children had gone to the theater. Only Anna and her grandfather were at home.

"We want to go to the theater too," announced Grandfather, "and the performance might as well begin at once."

"But we have no theater," sighed little Anna. "And no actors, for my old doll can't act because she is too dirty; and my new doll may not, because I don't want her clothes to get wrinkled."

"You can always find actors as long as you aren't too choosy. Now let's build the theater," Grandfather said, and took down some books from the bookcase. "We stand them up: three on one side and three on the other, in slanting rows; and here, we'll put this old box in the middle as a backdrop. The scene is a living room, as anyone can plainly see. And now for the actors. Let's take a look in this chest here. . . . As soon as we have the characters and know their personalities, the play will write itself. Here is a pipe; it has a bowl but no stem; and here is a glove that has lost its mate. They could be father and daughter."

"But two characters are not enough," complained little Anna. "What about my brother's vest — he has grown too big to wear it — couldn't that be in the play too?"

"It is big enough for a part," agreed Grandfather, examining the vest. "It can be a suitor. Its pockets are empty, how interesting.

442

IN THE CHILDREN'S ROOM

Empty pockets are often the cause of an unhappy love affair. . . .
Look what we have here: a high-heeled boot with spurs. He can
dance the waltz and the mazurka, for he can both swagger and
stamp. He is made for the part of the troublesome suitor whom the
heroine doesn't care for. Now tell me what kind of play you would
like: a tragedy or the kind of comedy that the whole family can
attend?"

"A family play!" cried the little girl. "Both Mother and Father
say that those are the best."

"I know at least a hundred of them. Those that are translated
from French are the most popular, but that wouldn't quite do for a
little girl. We can take the nicest of them, though the stories are
almost all alike. Here, I'll put all the plots in a bag and shake it well,
and then you pick one. . . . That's right. Here it is: age-old and
brand-new. Now for the playbill." Grandfather held up the newspaper and pretended that he was reading it:

The Pipe Bowl
OR
Love's Labors Are Never Lost
A family play in one act.

LIST OF CHARACTERS:

Mr. Pipe Bowl . . . . Father
Miss Glove . . . . Daughter
Mr. Vest . . . . Sweetheart
Mr. Boot . . . . A Suitor.

"Now the play can begin. The curtain slowly goes up. . . . True,
we have no curtain, but only very narrow-minded people make a
fuss about trifles. All the characters are on stage. The first one to
speak is the pipe bowl. He is very angry. If there had been any
tobacco in him, he would have fumed.

" 'No back talk here. I am master in my own house. I am father
of my own daughter. Is no one going to listen to what I say? Von
Boot has a shining personality. He is so well polished that you can
mirror yourself in him. He is made of morocco and wears spurs.
No more talk! He shall have my daughter!'

"Now listen carefully, little Anna," Grandfather warned. "Now
the vest is going to speak. He has a silk lining but that hasn't made

him smug. He is modest and yet he knows his own value. He has a right to say what he is going to say:

" 'I am spotless and of quality, so I should be taken into consideration. I am lined with genuine silk and have braiding.'

" 'Your spotlessness won't last till the day after the wedding; then you'll have to be washed and your colors aren't fast.' That was the pipe bowl who was speaking; and he goes on, 'Now Von Boot is waterproof and his skin is strong, yet he is finely made. He can creak and his spurs can jingle. He is of the latest fashion.' "

Suddenly little Anna interrupted. "Why don't they speak in verse? Mother says that it's so charming."

"What the public demands the actors must do," replied her grandfather with a smile. "Now watch little Miss Glove and how she stretches her fingers toward Mr. Vest and sings!

> " 'To be without a mate
> That fate I should hate.
> But all the owls can hoot,
> I'll not marry Von Boot.
> I would rather die,
> Or forever in a drawer lie.'

" 'Nonsense!' says the pipe bowl. Now Mr. Vest speaks to Miss Glove:

> " 'Beloved glove, beloved dove,
> My heart beats all for love.
> You shall be mine
> And I'll be thine.
> Love!
> Glove!'

"In the meantime Von Boot begins to stamp on the floor. He is terribly angry. His spurs are jingling."

"Oh, what a wonderful play!" Anna applauded with both her little hands.

"Quiet, please," said her grandfather. "During a play the best applause is silence. You must show that you are well brought up and deserve to sit in the orchestra. Now Miss Glove is going to sing her aria:

IN THE CHILDREN'S ROOM

> " 'I cannot speak,
> I am so weak.
> Yet I must sing
> Of love's broken wing.'

"Now we come to the intrigue. That is the most important part of the plot and the whole originality of the play depends on it. Mr. Vest steps upstage. Watch him! He is approaching old Mr. Pipe Bowl. There! He took old Pipe Bowl and put him in his pocket. Don't applaud him, that is so plebeian; though he would probably like you to do it. Actors can't get enough applause. Now Mr. Vest speaks directly to the audience.

" 'You are in my pocket, my deepest pocket, and you shall never get out again until you have agreed to our marriage. I hold out my right hand to the left-hand glove.' "

"It's awfully exciting!" exclaimed little Anna.

"From inside the pocket of Mr. Vest we hear the voice of Mr. Pipe Bowl:

> " 'I am so sick.
> What a terrible trick!
> Here I am in the dark,
> There's no light, not a spark.
> I cannot move about.
> Let me out! Let me out!
> If you set me free,
> I promise to agree
> To your future marriage
> If you let me out of this carriage!' "

"Is that the end already?" asked little Anna, a bit disappointed.

"Oh no," answered Grandfather. "Only for Von Boot; the others have a long play ahead of them still. Now the lovers kneel before Mr. Pipe Bowl, and Miss Glove sings:

> " 'Father!'

"And Mr. Vest sings:

> " 'Bless your son and daughter!'

HANS CHRISTIAN ANDERSEN

"Then Mr. Pipe Bowl gives his blessings and there is a wedding. Everyone joins in the chorus:

> " 'The play is over
> The moral taught,
> Please applaud
> As you ought.'

"Now we clap and call everyone out to take a bow; even the furniture, for though they only sang in the chorus, they are made of mahogany."

"Tell me," said little Anna, "was our play just as good as the one the others are seeing in the real theater?"

"Oh, our comedy was much better," replied Grandfather. "It was shorter and inspired. And now I am sure the water for tea must be boiling."

THE TEAPOT

Once there was a teapot who was very proud. She was proud of being porcelain. She was proud of her spout and she was proud of her broad handle, for they gave her something to boast about both in front and in back. She didn't talk about her lid, which had been broken and then glued together. There is no point in talking about your shortcomings; others willingly do that for you. The cups, the cream pitcher, the sugar bowl — the whole tea service preferred discussing the mended lid to talking about the fine spout and the strong handle. And this the teapot knew.

"I know what they think," she said to herself. "And I know my own faults, too, and admit them; and that I call modesty and humility. We all have faults, and we all have our talents, too. The cups have a handle and the sugar bowl has a lid, but I have both. And one thing more that neither one of them will ever have: a spout. That is what makes me queen of the tea table. The sugar bowl and the cream pitcher are servants of taste, but I am its mistress. I disseminate my blessings among a thirsting humanity. In my interior, fragrant Chinese leaves are mixed with insipid boiling water."

This was the way the teapot had talked when she was still a youngster. One day while she was standing on the tea table, she was lifted by a very refined and delicate hand. Unfortunately, the refined and delicate hand was also careless. The teapot fell to the floor, and both her spout and her handle were broken off. — We shan't talk about the lid, for that has been mentioned enough already. — The teapot had fainted: there she lay with boiling water running out of her. But the worst was yet to come: they laughed at her — the teapot! — not at the careless hand that had dropped her.

"I shall never forget it! Never . . ." she would mutter to herself when she thought about her youth. "They said I was an invalid and put me in a corner of the closet. But I didn't stay there long; the next day I was given to a beggar woman, who had come to ask for leftovers from the table. I was to know poverty, and the thought made me quite speechless. Yet then and there began what I would call a better life. One is one thing and becomes another.

"I was filled up with earth, which for a teapot is the same as being buried. But inside the earth a bulb was placed. I don't know who put it there, but there it was. I am sure it was meant as a substitute for the Chinese leaves and the boiling water, and to console me for my broken spout and lost handle. The bulb lay in the earth inside me, and it became my heart: my living heart. And I was alive, something I had never been before. Within me were power and strength, and my pulse beat. The bulb sprouted. It was so filled with thoughts and feelings that it almost burst; then it flowered. I could see it. I carried it within me and I forgot myself when I looked at its beauty.

"Oh, that is the greatest blessing, to be able to forget yourself in caring for others. The flower didn't say thank you; I don't think it even noticed me. But everyone admired the flower, and if that made me happy, think of how much happier it must have made the flower.

"One day I heard someone say that the flower was so lovely that it deserved a better flowerpot. They cracked me in two, and that hurt terribly. My plant was placed in a finer flowerpot, and I was thrown out into the yard, and here I lie, an old broken piece of pottery. But I have my memories and they cannot be taken from me."

PEITER, PETER, AND PEER

It is unbelievable how much children in our age know. Why, one hardly knows what they don't know. That the stork has brought them from the well or the millpond and delivered them to their father and mother is such an old story that they don't believe it; and that is too bad, for it is the truth.

But how do the little babies get in the millpond or the well? That is something not everybody knows, yet there are some who do. Have you ever looked at the heavens on a clear night when all the stars are out? Then you will have noticed the shooting stars. They look as if they were falling and then suddenly they disappear. The most learned cannot explain what they don't understand themselves; but if you know, then you can, even if you are not learned. What looks like a little Christmas-tree candle falling from the heavens is the spark of a soul coming from God. It flies down toward the earth. As it comes into our heavy atmosphere, its glow becomes so faint that our eyes can no longer see it. It is so fine and fragile, it is a little child of the heavens, a little angel; but without wings, for it is going to be a human being. Slowly, it glides through the air, and the wind carries it and puts it down inside a flower. It may be a violet, a rose, or a dandelion. There it lies for a while. It is so tiny and airy that a fly — or, in any case, a bee — could fly away with it.

HANS CHRISTIAN ANDERSEN

When the insects come to search for honey, the little air-child is in the way; but they don't kick it out, they are too kind for that; no, they carry it to a water-lily leaf and leave it there. The air-children climb down into the water, where they sleep and grow until they have reached the right size. Then, when the stork thinks one of them is big enough, he picks it up and flies with it to a family who want a sweet little child. But whether the children are sweet or not, depends upon what they have drunk while they lay in the millpond; whether they have drunk clear water, or water filled with mud and duckweed, for that makes them very earthy.

The stork never tries to do any matching up, he thinks that the first place is the best. One baby comes to wonderful parents, another to a mother and father so hard and mean that it would have been better to stay in the millpond.

The little ones cannot remember what they have dreamed while they lay under the water lilies and the frogs sang for them, "Croak . . . croak . . . croak!" That, in human language, means: "Come, sleep and dream." They have no memory either of which flower they have lain in, though sometimes when they grow up, one of them will say, "I like that flower best." And that is the flower they slept in when they were air-children.

The stork lives to be very old, and he always takes an interest in the children he has brought and how they fare in this world. He can't do anything for them, he can't change their circumstances, for he has his own family to look after. But he doesn't forget them; on the contrary, he thinks about them often.

I know an old stork, a very honest bird, who is very learned. He has delivered a lot of children and knows all their stories. There isn't a one that doesn't have a bit of duckweed and mud in it. I asked him to tell the biography of just one child, and he gave me three for the one I asked for. They all had the same family name: Peitersen.

Now the family Peitersen was very respectable. The husband was one of the town's two-and-thirty councilors, and that was a great distinction, so he devoted his whole life to being a councilor, and that was what he lived for. Now first the stork brought them a little Peiter; that was the name they gave the child. And the next year he came with another boy, and they called him Peter. And the third year Peer was brought. Peiter, Peter, and Peer — all variations of the same name: Peitersen.

PEITER, PETER, AND PEER

They were three brothers, three shooting stars. Each had lain in a flower and slept beneath the leaf of a water lily in the millpond, and from there they had been brought by the stork to the family Peitersen who lived in the house on the corner; and everyone in town knew whose house it was.

They grew in body and spirit, and all three wanted to be something finer than one of the town's two-and-thirty men.

Peiter said he wanted to be a robber, but that was because he had seen the comedy, *Fra Diavolo*, which had convinced him that a robber's trade was the best in the world. Peter wanted to be a trumpet player. And Peer, that sweet little well-behaved child, so plump and round, whose only fault was that he bit his nails, he wanted to be a "daddy." These were the answers they gave when anyone asked them what they wanted to be when they grew up.

They were sent to school, and one was the head of the class; another in the middle; and the third was the dunce, which doesn't mean that they weren't equally intelligent and good. Their parents, who had insight, swore that they were. The boys attended their first children's ball, smoked cigars when no one was looking, and generally became cleverer and more and more educated.

Peiter was the most difficult, which is not unusual for a robber. He was, in truth, a very naughty child; but that was caused, according to his mother, by worms. Naughty children always suffer from worms, they have mud in their stomachs. Once his stubbornness and obstinacy brought about the ruin of his mother's new silk dress.

"Don't shake the coffee table, my little lamb," she had said. "You might upset the cream pitcher and splash my new silk dress."

The little "lamb" grabbed the handle of the cream pitcher and poured its contents right down in Mama's lap. The poor woman could not help saying, "My lamb, my little lamb, how could you do such a thing?" That the child had a will of his own she had no doubt. A will of one's own is the same as character; and that to a mother is a sign of great promise.

He could have become a robber but he didn't; he only dressed like one. He wore an old hat and let his hair grow. He was going to be an artist, but he never got any further than dressing like one. More than anything else, he looked like a bedraggled hollyhock. As a matter of fact, he drew all his models so terribly tall that they looked like hollyhocks. It was the flower he loved best of all; the stork said that he had once lain in one.

Peter had lain in a buttercup, and he looked greasy around the corner of his mouth. His skin was so yellow that, if the barber had cut his cheek, I am sure butter would have oozed out instead of blood. He was born to sell butter, and could have had his own shop with a sign about it, except that, deep inside himself, he was a trumpet player. He was the musical member of the Peitersen family, and that single one was noisy enough for them all, said the neighbors. He composed seventeen polkas in one week and then transcribed them into an opera for trumpet and drums. Ugh! Was it lovely!

Peer was white and pink, little and ordinary; he had lain in a daisy. He didn't fight back when the older boys hit him; he was sensible, and the sensible person always gives up. When he was very small he collected slate pencils; later he collected stamps; and finally he was given a little cabinet to keep a zoological collection in. He had a dried fish, three newborn blind rats in alcohol, and a stuffed mole. Peer was a scientist and a naturalist. His parents were very proud of him and Peer was very proud of himself. He preferred a walk in the forest to going to school. Nature attracted him more than education.

Both his brothers were engaged, while Peer was still dedicating his life to completing his collection of the eggs of web-footed birds. He knew a great deal more about animals than he did about human beings. As for the highest feeling, love, he was of the opinion that man was inferior to the animal. He knew that the male nightingale would serenade his wife the whole night through, while she was sitting on the eggs. He — Peer — could never have done that; nor could he, like the stork, have stood on one leg on top of the roof all night, just to guard his wife and family; he couldn't have stood there an hour.

One day, as he was studying a spider and its web, he gave up the idea of marrying altogether. Mr. Spider weaves his nets to catch thoughtless flies, young or old, fat or thin; he exists only to weave nets and support his family. But Mrs. Spider has only one thought in her mind: her husband. She eats him up, out of love. She eats his head, his heart, and his body; only the long thin legs are left dangling in the web, where he used to sit worrying about the family. This is the truth, taken right out of a zoology book. Peer

PEITER, PETER, AND PEER

saw it, and thought about it. "To be so adored by one's wife that she eats one up — no human being can love like that, and maybe it's just as well."

Peer decided never to get married and never to give any girl a kiss, for that is the first step toward marriage. But he got a kiss, the kiss none of us escapes, the final kiss of death. When we have lived long enough, the order is given to Death: "Kiss away!" and away we go. A light comes from God, so bright that it blinds us and everything grows dark. The human soul that came as a falling star flies away again, but not to rest in a flower or dream beneath the water-lily leaf. Now its journey is more important; it flies into eternity and what that is like, no one knows. No one has seen that far, not even the stork, however good his eyesight is, and however much he knows.

He didn't know any more about Peer, but a great deal more about Peiter and Peter. I had heard enough about them, and I am sure you have too. I said thank you to the bird. And imagine, for such an ordinary story, the stork wanted payment. He wanted it in kind: three frogs and grass snakes. Will you pay him? I won't! I have neither frogs nor grass snakes on me.

THE TOAD

The well was deep, and therefore the rope that held the bucket was long and the winch difficult to turn. Although the water was clear, the sun had never mirrored itself in it; but as far as its rays reached, green plants grew among the stones.

In the well lived a family of toads. They were immigrants and had arrived there — or rather the old mother toad, who was still alive, had arrived there — head over heels. The green frogs, who had been the earliest inhabitants and swam in the water, acknowledged the toads as part of the family and called them guests. The toads, however, had no thought of leaving. They lived in the "dry part" of the well; that is what they called the wet stones.

The mother frog had once been on a journey; she had traveled in the water bucket on its way up. The light had been too much for her, it had hurt her eyes; and happily, she had escaped. With a huge splash she had landed in the well again. She had survived the jump, but her back had ached for three days. She could not tell much about the world above, but that the well was not the whole world both she and her children knew. The old mother toad could have told them something about it, but she never answered any of the questions anyone asked her, which made the frogs tired of talking to her, but not about her.

"Fat and ugly, and ugly and fat, she is," they said. "And her children will be just as ugly as she is."

THE TOAD

"It may be true," grumbled the old toad. "But one of them has a precious stone — a gem — in his head; or maybe I have it."

The young frogs heard her and stared at her but, not liking what they saw, they dived back down into the deep water. But the young toads stretched their back legs in pride and kept their heads perfectly still. After a while, when they had got tired of that, they asked their mother what it was they were proud of and what it meant to have a "precious stone" in one's head.

"It is something so valuable, so costly," said their mother, "that I cannot even describe it. One has it for one's own pleasure, and everybody envies one for having it. But don't ask any more questions, for I am not going to answer them."

"I am sure I don't have any precious stone in my head," said the smallest of the toads, who was particularly ugly. "Such splendor is not for me. And if it made everyone envy me, then it wouldn't give me any pleasure. I just wish that I could get up to the top of the well and look out, just once. That must be delightful!"

"You stay where you are," croaked old mother toad. "You know the well, and what is familiar is best. Be careful of the bucket, so you don't get hit by it. And if you should get caught inside it, jump! Though not everyone can be as lucky as I was and make such a great leap without breaking one of my legs or losing my eggs!"

"Croak," said the little toad; and that in human language means, "Oh!"

Still its longing for the green world above did not cease, and the next morning, when the full bucket paused for a moment right near the stone that the little toad was sitting on, he jumped in and lay still at the bottom of the bucket.

"Pooh! What an ugly fellow!" said the young man who had drawn the water. "That is the most repulsive thing I have ever seen." Then he poured the water out on the ground and tried to kick the little toad with his wooden shoes, but the little creature escaped among the nettles.

It looked at the stalks of the nettles and up above at the leaves; they were transparent and the sunlight sifted through them. For the little toad it was the same experience as we have when we come to a great forest and see the sunlight playing on the branches and leaves of very tall trees.

"It is much prettier here than it was in the well! I think I could stay here all my life!" said the little toad, and lay down in the nettle forest. It lay there for an hour, it lay for two. But then it started thinking, "I wonder what is beyond here. Since I have gotten this far, I might as well go on."

He crept out of the nettles and onto a road. The sun baked down upon him and the dry dust of the road powdered his little body white. "This is really dry land, almost too much of a good thing. It makes my back itch," the toad said to himself as he marched across the road. In the ditch on the other side, forget-me-nots and meadowsweet were in bloom; and on the bank of the ditch grew elderberry and hawthorn bushes; bindweed twined itself around their branches.

Here were colors to look at! A little butterfly flew up and the toad thought that it was a flower who had decided to fly out and see the world just as he had — and that was not an altogether stupid thought.

"If only one could fly like that flower," said the little toad. "Croak! Oh, how beautiful it is here!"

The toad stayed for eight days and eight nights in the ditch and didn't eat a thing during all that time. On the ninth day he thought, "I must go on," though how anything could be more beautiful than the ditch was hard for him to imagine, unless it were toads or some frogs. The night before, the wind had blown, and he had heard his cousins' voices.

"It is wonderful to live," he said to himself. "It is wonderful to have come out of the well, to have lain in the nettle forest and to have crawled across the dusty road, and to have rested in the damp ditch; but I must go on! I must find another toad or at least a frog, one cannot do without company. Nature is not enough!" And right then and there he set out on another journey.

He wandered across a great field until he came to a lake surrounded by a forest of reeds.

"It may be too wet for you here," said the frogs, "but you are welcome. Are you a he or a she? Not that it matters, you are equally welcome whichever you are."

That night he was invited to a concert, a family concert. You know what that kind of affair is like: there's a great deal of enthusiasm with rather feeble voices. There was nothing to eat, but there were free drinks from the lake.

"I think I will move on," said the little toad. He was always seeking something better.

THE TOAD

He saw the stars blinking in the sky, the new moon, and he noticed how the sun rose higher and higher in the heavens. "I am still in a well," he thought. "It is just a bigger one. I must try and get up higher. I feel so restless, there is a strange longing within me!"

Later, when the moon grew full and round, the poor animal thought, "I wonder if that is the bucket they will let down into the well. I will jump into it and rise even higher; or maybe the sun is the great bucket? It is so big and shines so brightly. I am sure there is room enough for all of us to get into it. I must watch for an opportunity. I have so many thoughts in my head; it feels as if a flame were burning there. I am sure it shines brighter than any precious stone. That gem I am sure I don't have; and I won't cry about it either. No, I just want to travel upward, upward to greater beauty and glory. I have faith in myself, and yet I am fearful. It is difficult to take the first step, but I must travel on: forward, straight ahead."

And it took the kind of steps that such a little animal could take, and soon it was on the road again. And then it came to a place where human beings lived. There were both a flower and a vegetable garden; the toad rested under a cabbage.

"How many different creatures there are that I have never seen before. How huge and glorious is the world! One should look around in it and not stay in one place. It is so beautifully green here!"

"I should say it is!" said a caterpillar that was sitting on a cabbage leaf. "My leaf is the biggest in the whole garden; half the world is hidden by it: the half I don't care about."

"Cluck! Cluck!" said a couple of hens who were out for a walk among the cabbages. The foremost of them was farsighted. She spied the caterpillar first, and pecked at the cabbage leaf so that the little creature fell. Once on the ground, the caterpillar twisted himself from one side to the other, while the hen looked at it, first with one eye and then with the other, wondering what it hoped to accomplish by its acrobatics. "I don't think it is doing it for pleasure," thought the hen, while she lifted her head, in readiness for pecking it.

The toad was horrified at what he saw, and hopped over toward the hen.

"So it has auxiliary troops!" exclaimed the hen. "What a horrible crawling thing!" And she backed away and let the caterpillar be. "I really don't care about that little green mouthful, it tickles your throat." The other hen was of the same opinion and both of them left.

"I wiggled away from them!" shouted the caterpillar. "It is important to keep one's presence of mind. But the most difficult problem is left. How do I get up on my cabbage leaf again? Where is it?"

The little toad was very happy that its ugliness had saved the caterpillar and offered his sympathy for its being so defenseless.

"What do you mean?" grumbled the caterpillar. "I twisted myself and managed to wiggle away from the hen. It is true that you are pretty horrible to look at, but I saved myself. I owe nothing to anyone. Where is my cabbage leaf? I smell it. Here is the stalk. There is nothing like one's own property! But I must get up a little higher."

"Yes, higher up!" echoed the little toad as he went away. "Higher up, I bet it feels just as I do. Such a frightful experience would put anyone out of humor. We all want to climb higher." And the little toad looked up as high as it could.

On top of the roof of the farmer's house was a stork's nest. The male stork was chattering with his long bill, and his wife was answering him.

Inside the farmhouse lived two young students: one was a poet, the other a scientist. One sang and wrote joyfully about everything God had created that mirrored itself in his heart. He sang about it in brief powerful verses. The other examined the things themselves — yes, even cut them up at times, if he had to. He looked at God's work as a huge mathematical formula; he added and divided, and wanted to understand everything with his mind — and it was an intelligent mind. He talked of nature with both understanding and appreciation. They were good young people, both of them.

"Look, there is a fine example of a toad. I will catch it and keep it as a specimen in alcohol," said the scientist when he saw the little toad.

"You have two already. Let it live in peace," suggested the poet.

"But that one is so wonderfully ugly," said the scientist regretfully.

THE TOAD

"If we could be sure it had a precious stone in its head, I would help you cut it up myself," laughed the poet.

"Precious stone?" his friend retorted unbelievingly. "I don't think you know any zoology."

"I think that there is a bit of poetry in the old folklore that the toad, the ugliest of all animals, hides inside its head the most precious of all stones. Think of Aesop and Socrates: didn't each of them have a precious jewel in his unhandsome head?"

The toad did not hear any more of the conversation and it only understood half of it. The two friends walked on, and the toad escaped being preserved in alcohol.

"They also talked of precious stones," mumbled the little toad. "How fortunate for me that I do not possess one or I would have been in trouble."

From the top of the roof came the sound of the male stork clattering; he was giving a lecture to his family, but he kept his glance downward, for he was watching the two young men at the same time. "The human being is the most conceited of all the animals," he said. "Listen to them chattering; they should give their bills a rest. They pride themselves on their ability to speak, their linguistic ability! But if they travel as far as we do in a single day, they cannot comprehend one word that is spoken. They cannot understand each other, while we storks talk the same language all over the world, both in Egypt and in Denmark. As for flying, the human beings can't. When they want to move fast from one place to another, they have to use something called a railroad. It is an invention they will break their necks on. The very thought of it makes a chill run up and down my bill. The world can exist without them. We do not need human beings, all we need are frogs and worms."

"That was a great speech," thought the little toad. "The stork is a very important animal and it lives so high up, I have never seen anyone who lives higher!

"And look how it can swim!" the toad exclaimed out loud as the stork spread its wings and flew away through the air.

The female stayed in the nest and told the young ones about Egypt, about the waters of the great River Nile, and about all the remarkable mud to be found in foreign countries. It was all new and wonderful to the little toad.

"I must travel to Egypt," he said aloud. "I wonder if the stork or one of its young ones would take me. I would serve it faithfully all the rest of my days. Yes, I will get to Egypt, I am sure of it, for I am so happy. In me there is a longing and a desire that is sweet, and so much more valuable than any precious stone."

And that was the precious stone; and this was the toad who had it in his head: the eternal longing and desire for rising ever upward. That was the jewel! That was the flame that sparkled and shone with joy and desire.

At that moment the stork came. It had spied the little toad in the grass. Its bill did not grab it gently; it squeezed the toad. He was uncomfortable and frightened, yet he felt the wind blowing around him and knew that his course was upward toward Egypt; and therefore his eyes shone with expectation, as though a spark were flying from them.

"Croak!"

The heart stopped; the body was still, the toad was dead. But the spark that had shone in its eyes, what happened to that? The rays of the sun caught it, caught the gem that the little toad had carried in its head. But where did they take it?

Don't ask the scientist that question, ask the poet. He will tell you the answer, as a fable or a fairy tale. The caterpillar will be in his story, and the family of storks as well: The caterpillar changes itself into a beautiful butterfly. The stork flies over mountains and across oceans to distant Africa, and returns by the shortest route to Denmark — to that particular place, to that particular house where his nest is. That, too, is magic and unexplainable, and yet it happens. You may ask the scientist, he has to admit it; and you yourself know it is true, for you have seen it.

But what about the gem in the toad's head?

Seek it in the sun, see if you can find it there!

No, the light is too intense; we do not yet have eyes that can see all the glory God has created. But maybe someday we will have such eyes. That will be the most wonderful fairy tale of all, for we ourselves will be part of it.

THE RAGS

Outside the paper mill was a whole mountain of rags. Each one had its own history and pleaded its own cause, but we do not have time to listen to them all. The rags had been collected from far and wide: some were natives, others were from foreign countries. Now it happened that a Danish rag lay close to a Norwegian one. Both of them were patriots: the Dane was as Danish as gooseberry porridge, the Norwegian as Norwegian as brown goat cheese; and as any sensible Dane or Norwegian would agree, this was what was amusing about them.

Each spoke his own language and yet they were able to understand each other, though the Norwegian claimed that there was as much difference between Norwegian and Danish as there was between French and Hebrew. "You have to go to Norway to hear the original language, raw and strong as the mountains. Danish is sugar-sweet. It's like a pacifier that has been dipped in syrup: flat and insipid."

That was the way the Norwegian rag talked, for rags are rags in any country, and are of no account except among their equals.

"I am a Norwegian," he continued, "and when I have said that I have said everything. I am tightly woven and as solid as the Archean rock of old Norway, that country which, like the land of liberty, America, has a constitution. It tickles my threads to think who I am and to let my thoughts ring out in granite words."

"But we have a literature," whispered the Danish rag. "Do you understand what that word means?"

HANS CHRISTIAN ANDERSEN

"Understand!" The Norwegian rag repeated the word very loudly. "I ought to take you who have never seen anything but a dull and flat country and deposit you on one of our mountaintops, so that the northern lights could shine through you — rag that you are. In the spring when the Norwegian sun melts the ice in the fjords, old Danish tubs sail up to Norway with butter and cheese which are quite eatable, but as ballast they carry Danish literature. We don't need it. Why drink flat beer when there are clear springs of pure water all around you? In Norway the wells aren't artificially drilled and then filled with European swagger, newspaper notoriety, and authors doing each other favors or telling about their precious experiences in foreign lands. I speak freely, directly from the lungs, and you, Danes, will have to get used to the language of free men. If you want to be Scandinavians, it is the proud, primeval mountains of Norway you will have to cling to."

"A Danish rag would never think of speaking in such a manner," began the Danish rag. "It would be against our nature. I know myself and, as I am, all other Danish rags are. We are good-natured and modest; we undervalue ourselves. Naturally, there's nothing to be gained by it, but I like being that way, it is so utterly charming. Just because I don't talk about it doesn't mean that I don't know how valuable I am: I do! But no one shall accuse me of bragging. I am soft and flexible and can endure anything. I envy no one and speak well of everyone, though hardly anyone deserves it — but that's their problem, not mine. I like to poke fun at everything, even myself, which proves my superior intelligence."

"Don't talk to me in that insipid, guttural, gluelike dialect from that pancake that you call a country. It makes me sick to my stomach." And with these words the Norwegian rag allowed the wind to carry it to another place in the rag pile.

Both rags were made into paper. By chance, the Norwegian rag became a piece of stationery on which a young Norwegian wrote a love letter to a Danish girl. And the Danish rag fared just as strangely. It became a sheet of paper on which a Danish poet composed an ode in praise of the loveliness and strength of Norway.

This shows that something good can come out of rags, as long as they end up in the rag pile and are made into paper, on which truth and beauty are written. Anything that helps our understanding is a blessing.

That was the story of the rags, and only rags need be offended by it.

WHO WAS THE HAPPIEST?

What beautiful roses," said the sunshine. "And all the little buds will soon become as beautiful as they are. They are all my children, I gave them life by kissing them."

"They are my children," said the dew. "Didn't I suckle them with my tears?"

"I should think they are mine," interrupted the rosebush. "You may call yourself godparents. As for your presents, I consider them christening gifts, for which I say thank you."

"My sweet little rose-child!" they all three said at the same time, and wished each rose the greatest happiness in the world. But that was not really possible. Only one rose could be the happiest, as one would also have to be the least happy of all the roses on the bush. But what we want to know is, which would be the happiest?

"I will find that out for you," said the wind. "I travel a great deal and am thin enough to get through the narrowest crack. I know everything inside and out."

Each rose had heard what had been said and every swelling bud sensed it.

Just at that moment a woman dressed in the black clothes of sorrow came walking through the garden. She looked at the roses and then picked one that was not completely unfolded. Just because it was not fully in bloom, she considered it the most beautiful of them all. She carried the flower to the still silent room where

463

only a few days ago her young daughter had played and laughed happily. Now she lay in a black coffin and looked like a marble sculpture of a sleeping figure. The poor mother kissed the dead child and then kissed the rose, before she placed it on the young girl's chest, as if she hoped that the freshness of a rose and a mother's kiss could make the girl's heart beat again.

The petals of the rose shook with happiness. It was as if the whole rose swelled and grew. "I have become more than a rose, for, like a child, I have received a mother's kiss. I have been blessed and will travel into the unknown realm, dreaming on the dead girl's breast. Truly, I am the happiest of us all."

In the garden where the rosebush grew, there worked an old woman; she did the weeding. She had also been admiring the rosebush, but she had especially been observing the only fully unfolded rose among the flowers. One more day of sunshine, one more drop of the pearly dew of night, and its life would be over. Now that it had bloomed for beauty, it might as well end its days being useful, thought the woman. She picked it and put it in an old newspaper with some other flowers she had collected that had, as she said, bloomed their time. When she got home she would mix the rose petals with lavender, sprinkle a little salt over them, and put them in a jar; that was call "making a potpourri."

"I am being embalmed," thought the rose. "That is something that only happens to kings and roses. I have been the most honored. Certainly I am the happiest."

Two young men were out walking in the garden. One of them was an artist, the other a poet. Each of them picked a rose — the one he thought was the most beautiful.

The artist painted a picture of the rose that was so true to life that the rose almost mistook the canvas for a mirror.

"In this way," said the artist, "the rose will live through many, many years, while millions and millions of other roses will have bloomed and died."

The rose heard it and thought, "I am the most highly favored, the happiest."

The poet contemplated his flower and the rose inspired him. It was as if he could read a story on each petal. It was a work of love, a piece of immortal poetry.

"I am immortal!" sighed the rose. "Oh, surely, I am the happiest."

WHO WAS THE HAPPIEST?

Amid all this array of perfect roses there was one little flower that had a defect. It sat by chance — or maybe good luck — hidden behind the others. The petals on one side were not exactly like the petals on the opposite side, and in the middle of the flower a little green leaf grew. This sort of thing can happen among roses.

"Poor child," said the wind, and kissed the little rose on her cheek. The flower thought it was done in homage. She knew that she was a little different from the others and that she had a green leaf growing in the middle of her flower, but she had never considered it a flaw. On the contrary, she had always thought it a sign of distinction.

A butterfly landed on the rose and kissed each of her petals; it was proposing, but the rose let it fly away without an answer. A grasshopper came; true, he landed on another flower, but it was one quite nearby. He rubbed his legs together and that is a sure sign of love among grasshoppers. The rose that the grasshopper had sat on didn't understand this; but the little rose who had been singled out for special merit, she understood it very well. The grasshopper had looked at her and especially at her little green leaf and in his eyes had been written, "I love you so much that I could eat you up." Greater love no one can show, because that means that truly the two become one. But the little rose did not want to be joined quite so firmly to the grasshopper.

The nightingale sang in the star-filled night. "She sings for me, only for me," whispered the rose with the defect or the badge of merit — all as you look at it. "Why is it always I who am singled out for recognition, and not my sisters? Why was I created so exceptional that I had to become happiest of all roses?"

At that moment two gentlemen smoking cigars came walking past the rosebush. They had been discussing roses and tobacco. They had been told that the smoke from a cigar would turn a rose green, and now the experiment had to be tried. They did not want to take one of the more beautiful roses and that is why they decided on the little rose.

"Again I am the chosen one," she cried. "Oh, I am overwhelmed by the honor, I am the happiest!" The little rose turned quite green, both from the smoke and from being so very extraordinary.

One rose was perhaps the loveliest of them all; she was still a bud when the gardener picked her. She was given the place of honor in the bouquet he made of all the most beautiful flowers in the garden. The bouquet was brought to the young gentleman who owned the house and the garden, and he took it along that evening in his carriage. The flower was the symbol of beauty amid beauty, for the young man took the bouquet along to the theater. The audience were dressed in their very best, thousands of lamps burned, and music played.

When the ballet was almost finished and the ballerina, who was the most admired dancer at the theater, came out for her last great dance, bouquets fell down on the stage like a rain of flowers. Among them was the bouquet with the rose in it, and the flower felt an indescribable joy as it flew through the air. As it touched the wooden floor, the bouquet seemed to be dancing too. It jumped and then slid along the stage. But in its final fall the rose broke her stem. The ballerina for whom, as homage, it had been picked was never to hold the rose in her hand. A stagehand picked it up, for it had fallen behind the sets. He smelled it and acknowledged its beauty, but it had no stem so he could not put it in his buttonhole. He did not throw the rose away but slid it into his pocket. Later that night, when he returned home, he filled a little liqueur glass with water and put the flower in it.

In the morning it was placed on the little table that stood beside his grandmother's chair. The old woman, too weak to get outside in the sunshine, looked at the beautiful rose and smelled its fragrance.

"Poor rose, you were meant for the rich and famous young girl and instead you have come to a poor old woman. But to her you would only have been one more flower, to me you are as lovely as a whole rosebush," the old woman said, and gazed at the flower with eyes as happy as a child's. Maybe the freshness of the rose brought back to her memories of her own youth, long ago past.

"The windowpane was broken, so it was easy for me to get in," said the wind. "I noticed the old woman's eyes and it is true they were like a child's: expectant. I saw the rose too, in the liqueur glass on the table beside her. Who was the happiest of all the roses? I know, I could tell you!"

Every rose on the bush had her own story and each of them believed herself to be the happiest; and such faith is a blessing in itself. The last rose left on the bush was certain that it was far happier than any of her sisters could have been.

WHO WAS THE HAPPIEST?

"I have survived them all. I am the last one, the only one left. I am my mother's most beloved, her favorite child."

"I was their mother," said the rosebush.

"No, I was," said the sunshine.

"No, it was I who was their mother," said the dew.

"You all had part in them, and now I shall share the last rose among you." And the wind blew and scattered the petals of the flower over the branches where the dewdrops hung in the morning and where the sun would shine during the day. "I had my part in it, for I collected the stories of the roses and I will tell them to the world. Which one of them was the happiest, can you tell? I won't, I have said enough."

With those words the wind lay down behind the rosebush and the day was still.

THE ADVENTURES
OF A THISTLE

Around the manor house was a lovely garden with very rare and beautiful plants and trees. Guests always expressed their delight and wonder when they saw it. On Sundays, people from the district, and even from the towns, asked for permission to look at the garden, and sometimes classes of school children came with their teachers.

Outside the garden, right up next to the fence, grew a thistle. It was so big, spreading its branches out in all directions, that it could be called a bush. No one noticed it except the donkey who drew the milk wagon. He would stretch his neck toward the thistle and say, "You are so beautiful that I could eat you up." But he couldn't, for the rope with which he was tethered wasn't long enough for him to reach it.

The manor house was filled with guests: members of the most distinguished families in Copenhagen were there. Many of the young girls were beautiful, and among them was an heiress from Scotland. In her homeland she belonged to the very best society, and she was wealthy. "A bride worth winning," whispered many of the young men and their mothers, too.

The young people were meandering on the lawns. Some of them were playing croquet. They walked among the flower beds, and one of the girls picked a flower and gave it to a young man to wear in his buttonhole. And all the other girls did the same. But the

THE ADVENTURES OF A THISTLE

Scottish girl went about for a very long time without being able to decide which flower to choose. None seemed to satisfy her. Then she noticed the thistle bush with its bright reddish-blue flowers, growing on the other side of the fence. She smiled and asked her host's son if he would pluck one of them for her. "It is the national flower of Scotland," she explained. "It is portrayed in our coat of arms. Get one of them for me, please."

The young man climbed over the fence and plucked the most beautiful of the thistle's flowers; and was pricked as properly as though he had picked a rose.

The girl put the flower in his buttonhole, and the young man felt deeply honored. The other young men envied him, and every one of them would gladly have exchanged his lovely garden flower for the thistle given by the Scottish girl. But if the son of the owner of the manor was pleased, how do you think the thistle felt? It was as if dew had fallen upon it in the middle of the day.

"I am more than I thought I was," she mumbled to herself. "I undoubtedly belong on the other side of the fence: inside the garden, not outside it. It is strange, the world we live in, and not everything gets the position it deserves. Now, at least, one of my flowers is on the other side of the fence, and that in a buttonhole."

Every new bud that came and unfolded itself into a flower was told the story, for there is no reason to keep good news a secret. Soon the thistle bush heard — not from the chatter of birds or the voices of human beings, but from the air, which knows all secrets and can penetrate locked doors — that the young man who had been given the thistle flower had also gained the hand of the young Scottish girl. It was a good match.

"I have joined them together," the thistle bush said. She was thinking of the flower that she had supplied for the buttonhole. Now there was still another story to tell her offspring. "I shall probably be planted inside the garden," she thought. "Maybe I'll be put in a flowerpot; you get squeezed a little, but it is glorious." And the thistle bush imagined it all so vividly that soon she was convinced that this was her future. "I know it, I shall be planted in a flowerpot!"

She promised every new flower that it would be potted, or be put in a buttonhole, which was an even greater honor. But none of them ever was placed in either. The thistle drank the air and the sunshine during the day and licked the dew at night. She was visited by bees in search of honey for their dowries, and they took the honey from the flowers and left the flowers themselves behind. "Robbers!" screamed the thistle bush. "I wish I could prick every one of you." But it couldn't.

Old flowers hung their heads, withered, and died; but new ones came, and every one was greeted with the same joy and expectation by the bush. "You have come just at the right moment," she would say to each one. "Any minute now we are moving into the garden."

There were a couple of innocent daisies and a plantain who admired the thistle bush greatly; they heard every word she had said and believed them all.

The old donkey who pulled the milk wagon was standing in the ditch. He glanced at the flowering thistle, but his rope was too short, he could not reach it.

The thistle bush gave so much thought to the thistle from Scotland, whom she felt she must be related to, that at last she believed that she, too, had come from that country; and that her parents were probably the thistles that had grown in the Scottish coat of arms. This was a daring assumption, but a great thistle is capable of great thoughts.

"Sometimes one is descended from so great a family that one hardly dares to think about it," said a nettle that grew nearby. She had once heard that, in olden times, cloth had been woven from nettles, and she had never forgotten it.

Summer passed and fall passed, the leaves fell from the trees, and the few flowers that were left had even brighter colors, but less fragrance. The gardener's apprentice sang while he worked in the garden:

> Uphill and downhill,
> All is God's will.

The young spruce trees down in the forest began to get "Christmas-yearning," although it was only the end of October and there was long to wait.

"Here I stand. No one thinks about me, and yet I was the matchmaker," said the thistle. "First they got engaged and then they were married a week ago. And I am going nowhere because I can't move."

THE ADVENTURES OF A THISTLE

A few weeks went by. The thistle now had only one last flower. It grew on the stem near the root and was particularly large and beautiful. The cold winds blew on it and its color and loveliness faded; finally its pod stood naked: it looked like a silver sunflower.

The young couple were out walking in the garden. They took the path along the fence, and the young woman was looking beyond it.

"The thistle is still there!" she exclaimed. "But now it has no more flowers."

"Yes, it does," her husband laughed. "There is the ghost of one." And he pointed at the silver-colored pod, which had become as beautiful as a flower.

"How lovely it is!" she said. "It should be carved in the frame around our portrait."

Again the young man had to climb the fence and pick a flower from the thistle bush. It pricked him — that was revenge for calling its last flower a ghost. The silver pod was brought into the garden, and from there into the hall of the manor house, where it was placed beside the painting of the young couple. In the bridegroom's buttonhole a thistle flower had been painted. Everyone talked about the flower in the buttonhole and the silver pod whose image was to be carved into the frame. And the air carried the conversation far and wide.

"What adventures I have had!" cried the thistle bush. "My firstborn was put in a buttonhole and my last is going to be in a frame. I wonder what is going to happen to me?"

The donkey who was tethered nearby brayed. "Come over here to me, my sweetheart, and I will show you what could happen to you, if my rope were long enough."

But the thistle bush didn't answer. She grew more and more thoughtful. She thought and thought, and at Christmas her thinking bore a flower: "When your children are inside the fence, then a mother doesn't mind being outside herself."

"What a kind thought," said the sun ray. "You, too, will go far."

"Will I be put in a pot or a frame?" asked the thistle bush.

"You will be put in a fairy tale," answered the sun ray.

And here it is!

A QUESTION
OF IMAGINATION

There was once a young man who was studying to be an author, and he wanted to become one before Easter; then he would marry and live by his pen. It would be easy, if only he could find something to write about, but no ideas ever came to him. He had been born too late; everything had been thought about and written down before he came into the world.

"How fortunate the people were who were born a thousand years ago," he said. "Even those born a hundred years ago were luckier than I am, for then there was still something left to write about. Everything in the world has been written up; no wonder I can't find anything to write down."

He studied and thought so long and so hard that he made himself ill. No doctor could help him, but maybe the old wise woman could. She lived in a little house where the road entered the pastures. She was the gatekeeper; she lifted the latch for carriages and those on horseback. But she knew a great deal more than how to open a gate. Some say that she knew even more than the doctor, even though he drove in his own carriage and had to pay "rank tax," which only the nobility and the very rich must pay.

"I'll visit her," declared the young man.

Though her house was small, it was nice, if a bit ordinary. There wasn't a tree or a flower anywhere near it. Next to the door there was a beehive — very useful! There was a little potato patch —

A QUESTION OF IMAGINATION

very useful! There was a hedge of blackthorn bushes; they had already flowered but their berries would be bitter until after the first frost.

"The very picture of our prosaic times," thought the young man, and that, after all, was a thought: a pearl found in front of the old wise woman's house.

"Write it down," she said. "Crumbs are also bread. I know why you've come, you want to be an author by Easter and you cannot find anything to write about. You have no ideas."

"Everything is already written. Our times are not like the old."

"No," she agreed, "they are not. In the old times they used to burn old wise women like me at the stake, and the poets had empty stomachs as well as empty pockets. These times are not only just right: they are the best! It is you who have poor eyes. You cannot see and I doubt if you can hear either. Have you been saying your prayers before you go to bed? . . . There is enough to write about if you can write. You will find, peeping out of the earth with the first flowers, stories enough for your pen. In the running water of the brook or the still waters of the lake there are poems to be caught like fish. All you have to do is to learn to understand, learn to catch a sun ray and keep it in your hand. Now you can try my glasses and my ear trumpet. Pray to God, and stop thinking about yourself."

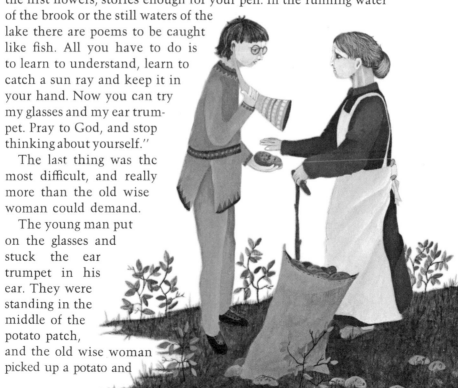

The last thing was the most difficult, and really more than the old wise woman could demand.

The young man put on the glasses and stuck the ear trumpet in his ear. They were standing in the middle of the potato patch, and the old wise woman picked up a potato and gave it to him. It spoke, told its story: the history of the potato, an everyday tale in ten lines.

What did it tell? It talked about itself and its family: how it had come to Europe as an immigrant and had at first been persecuted and condemned because of misunderstanding and ignorance, until finally its true value, which was greater than gold's, was recognized. "By royal messenger, we were distributed to all the town halls in the country, and our importance was proclaimed. But the people didn't believe it, and they did not know how to plant us. One man dug a hole and dumped a whole bushel of us into it. Another planted us here and there in the garden; he expected that we would grow up like trees and that he would be able to shake down the fruit. We grew, flowered, and set fruit, and then we withered and no one thought that below us in the earth lay that blessed wealth, the potato. Yes, we have suffered; that is, our forefathers have. But if you have any family feeling, then you can feel the suffering yourself. We have a most interesting history."

"That's enough," said the old wise woman, and threw the potato back on the ground. "Now take a look at the blackthorn bush."

"We have family abroad, in the home of the potato," said the blackthorn bushes, "but farther north than they grow. The Norsemen came, steering a westerly course, through storms and fogs to an unknown land, and there — beyond the ice and snowbound coast — they found herbs, green grass, and bushes with deep blue berries the color of grapes. Sloeberries are turned into fruit as sweet as grapes by the first frost. The same will happen to our berries. They called that country Vineland, Greenland, Sloenland!"

"That was a very romantic story," said the young man.

"Yes, but come along." The old wise woman had heard the blackthorn bush's story before. She led the young man to the beehive.

He could see right through it. What a busy place it was! In all the corridors stood bees fluttering their wings in order to keep the air fresh in the great factory: that was their job. Bees came streaming in from the outside. They had been born with little baskets on their legs, which they filled with pollen. The baskets were emptied, and the pollen was sorted and made into honey and wax. The bees flew away again. The queen bee wanted to fly too, but wherever she flew, all the other bees would have to follow; and it wasn't the season for changing hives. Still she wanted to fly, so the wings were

A QUESTION OF IMAGINATION

bitten off Her Majesty by the other bees, and then she had to stay where she was.

"Come along," the old wise woman said, and tapped the young man on the shoulder. "Let's go out into the road and look at the travelers."

"What a mass of people!" exclaimed the young man. "And each one of them has a story. It's too much for me, we'd better go back."

"No, go straight ahead, right into the midst of the multitude. Look at them, listen to them, and try to understand them with your heart. Then you will find that you have lots of ideas and plenty to write about. But before you go, give me back my glasses and my ear trumpet." And she took both of them away from the young man.

"I cannot see anything!" he complained. "I can't hear a thing."

"Then you can't become an author by Easter." The old wise woman shook her head.

"What shall I do then?" wailed the young man.

"Neither by Easter nor by Whitsun. Imagination can't be taught."

"But what am I to do? I would love to earn a living by serving the muses."

"That's not difficult, that can be arranged in time for the Mardi Gras. Buy some masks and make faces at the poets. Even when you understand them, don't be impressed, just make a grimace, and you'll get paid well enough to feed a family."

"Isn't that amazing," said the young man, and followed her advice. He became an expert at looking down his nose at poets because he couldn't become one himself.

The old wise woman told me his story, and she has so much imagination that she would give it away, if only one could.

THE DAYS OF THE WEEK

The days of the week wanted to have some time off so they could hold a party. They were so busy the whole year round, and they were never free, all at the same time; but every fourth year is leap year, when an extra day is added to February, to keep accounts straight.

On this day they would have their party, and since it was in February, when Mardi Gras is, they decided to have a masquerade. They were to dress themselves according to whim and taste. They would eat well, drink well, and in a spirit of comradeship give speeches in which they told each other the truth, both pleasant and unpleasant. The old Vikings used to throw at each other bones that they had gnawed on; the days of the week would throw jests and jokes in an innocent carnival mood.

The twenty-ninth of February arrived and so did the days of the week.

Sunday, who is chairman of the week, came dressed in a black suit with a silk cape. Pious human beings believed he was dressed for church, but the worldly ones knew that he was dressed as a domino and ready for a masquerade. The red carnation he wore in his buttonhole was the red lamp that sometimes is lit outside the theater and shouts: "Everything sold out. Have fun, have fun!"

Monday was a young man, closely related to Sunday, and fond of diversions. He always left his work if there was a parade in the street. "I must hear the music of Offenbach," he exclaimed. "It does not affect my brain or my heart, it goes directly into my legs and then I must dance. I had a little too much to drink last night, and my right eye is swollen from a fight, but after a night's sleep I will be ready to work. Remember that I am young!"

Tuesday is strong, the day of the bull, of work. "Yes, I am strong!" Tuesday agreed. "I am used to work. It is I who ties the wings of Mercury to the merchant's boots. I look into the factories to make sure that the wheels are oiled and the machines are working. I watch the tailor at his table and the joiner at his lathe. I keep an eye on everyone, that is why I am dressed in a policeman's uniform. You might call me Policeday." That was meant as a joke, but then policemen are seldom very good at joking.

"Here am I!" said Wednesday. "I am in the middle of the week, the Germans call me Herr Mittwoch. I am the salesman in the store, the flower standing in the middle of all the other honorable days. If we marched in a row, I would have three days in front and three behind me; the others would be my guard of honor. I am sure I am the most important day in the week."

Thursday came dressed as a coppersmith, with a kettle in one hand and a hammer in the other; they were the symbols of his nobility. "I am of the most noble descent," he claimed, "from the heathen gods. In the northern countries I am named after the god Thor, and in the south after Jupiter. Both of them were masters of lightning and thunder, and I am their heir." And then he hit the copper kettle with the hammer.

Friday was a girl. She called herself Freya, or sometimes Venus, depending upon the country she was in. She was quiet and gentle, according to herself. But this particular day she was dressed in her best and looking very gay, for it is the day when women are free. They can even propose, if they want to, such is the tradition on that day, they don't have to sit and wait for a suitor.

Saturday was dressed as an old housekeeper; she had a broom in one hand and a bucket in the other. Her favorite dish was gruel. She didn't demand that the others eat it, just that it be served for herself, and it was.

All the days of the week sat down at the table. I have made a drawing of it. It could be used as an idea for a pantomime, and how amusing it will be depends upon how well you perform it. I have only written it as a February jest, for the only month that sometimes receives an extra day.

THE CANDLES

There once was a big wax candle that knew who it was. "I am made of wax and have been cast, not dipped," it said. "My light is clearer and I burn longer than other candles. I belong in a chandelier or a silver candlestick."

"That must be lovely," said a tallow candle. "I am only made from tallow, but I have been dipped eight times and have a decent-sized waistline; some tallow candles are only dipped twice. I am satisfied! Though I admit it is better to be born in wax than in tallow; but you cannot decide yourself how and where to be born. Wax candles are put in the living room and I have to stay in the kitchen, but that is a good place too, all the food for the whole house is made there."

"There is something more important than food," said the wax candle, "and that is social life. To shine while others shine. There is going to be a ball tonight, any moment they will come for me and my whole family."

Hardly had this been said when the lady of the house came to get the wax candles, but she took the little tallow candle too. She brought it out into the kitchen. There stood a little boy with a basket on his arm; it was filled with potatoes, and a few apples had been put in it, too. All this the kind mistress had given to the poor boy. "Here, my little friend," she said, and she put the tallow candle into his basket. "I know that your mother often works so

478

THE CANDLES

late into the night." Her little daughter, who was standing nearby, smiled when she heard her mother say "so late into the night."

"We are going to have a party, a ball, and my dress has red bows on it, and I will be allowed to be up, so late into the night," she said joyfully. Her eyes sparkled with expectation, she was so happy. No wax candles can shine like the eyes of a child.

"That was a blessed sight," thought the tallow candle. "I shall never forget it, nor am I likely ever to see such happiness again."

The boy went on his way and the tallow candle went with him.

"I wonder where I am going," it thought. "Probably to people so poor that they don't even have a brass candlestick; while the wax candle sits in silver and is in the finest company. Well, it was my lot to be tallow and not wax."

And the tallow candle was brought to a poor home where a widow lived with her three children. From their rooms, with their low ceilings and narrow windows, one could look across the street into the great house.

"God bless her who gave you this," said the boy's mother when she saw the candle. "It will burn late into the night."

And the candle was lit. "Phew!" it said. "Those sulphur matches smell awful. I am sure they don't dare light the wax candle with such things."

In the rich house also the candles were lit. From the windows their light fell out into the street. Coaches rumbled along the cobblestones as they arrived, bringing the elegantly dressed guests, and soon music could be heard.

"Now the ball is starting," thought the tallow candle, and recalled the little rich girl and how her eyes had sparkled even brighter than wax candles. "I shall never see eyes like those again."

The youngest of the poor woman's children was a girl too. She put her arms around her brother and sister and whispered to them, "We are going to have hot potatoes for dinner." Her eyes looked bright and happy too, just as happy as the little girl's across the street had looked when she said, "We are going to have a ball tonight, and my dress has red bows on it."

"I wonder," thought the tallow candle, "whether to get hot potatoes for dinner is as good. The two little ones seem equally pleased." The tallow candle sneezed; that is to say, it sputtered, for a tallow candle can't do much to express itself.

The table was set. The potatoes were eaten. How good they

HANS CHRISTIAN ANDERSEN

tasted! And then there were apples for dessert. The youngest child recited a little verse:

> Dear God, thanks to Your will,
> I once more my stomach did fill.
> Amen.

"Did I say it nicely?" the girl asked her mother.

The mother smiled and shook her head. "That you mustn't ask or think about. What is important is to be thankful to God for what He does for us."

The children were put to bed and each given a kiss, and they fell right to sleep. The mother stayed up and sewed late into the night. She had to earn a living for herself and her children. Over in the house of the rich the candles were still burning and the music played. Above in the sky the stars shone, and they shone as brightly on the poor home as on the rich one.

"That was a nice evening," thought the tallow candle. "I wonder if the wax candle has had a better time in the silver candlesticks? That is a question I would like to have answered before I am burned out." Then it thought of the two equally happy faces: one shining in the light of a wax candle and the other in the light of a tallow one.

Well, that is really the end of the story, there is no more, just as there is no more left of either the wax or the tallow candle.

THE MOST INCREDIBLE

$\mathbb{T}$he one who could accomplish the most incredible was to marry the king's daughter and have half the kingdom.

Everybody tried, not only the young but the old as well. They all exhausted their brains, their sinews, and their muscles trying to do something incredible. Two men ate themselves to death, and a third did the same with drink. That was doing the most unbelievable according to their taste, but it was hardly the right way to go about it. The street urchins practiced spitting on their own backs; that, they thought, was doing the most incredible.

A day had been set when everyone could come forward and show what he considered his most incredible accomplishment. Judges had been appointed. The youngest was three years old, and the oldest over ninety. There was a great exhibition of the strangest things, but all the judges and the people, too, soon agreed that the most incredible was a great clock. It was most cunningly and artfully constructed both inside and out. Every time the clock struck the hour, little figures enacted a story to tell what the time was: twelve performances in all.

"It is quite incredible!" everyone said.

When the clock struck one, Moses came out and wrote down the first commandment: "There is only one God."

When it struck two, you saw the garden of Eden, with both

Adam and Eve as happy as kings, and that without owning so much as a wardrobe, or having need of it.

When the clock struck three, the holy three kings appeared with all their costly gifts. One of them was black.

At four, the seasons of the year came out. Spring carried a cuckoo and a beech branch that had just come into leaf; summer a grasshopper on a straw of wheat ready for harvest; fall held an empty stork's nest — the bird had flown; winter had an old crow who could tell stories in the long cold nights: old memories.

When the clock struck five, the senses came. Sight was an optometrist; hearing, a coppersmith; smell, an old woman selling violets; taste was a cook; and feeling was dressed as an undertaker with black crepe right down to his heels.

At the stroke of six, a gamester came out; he rolled his dice and they showed six!

Then came the seven days of the week or the seven deadly sins, no one was quite sure which they were. But they belong together and you cannot tell them apart.

At eight a choir of monks sang vespers.

At nine the muses came. One had steady employment at an observatory, another worked in the historical archives, the rest were engaged in the theater.

When the clock struck ten, Moses appeared again with the tablets of the law; God's commandments are ten.

Again the clock struck and this time children came out. They played and sang and there were exactly eleven of them.

Now there was only the last performance left, twelve o'clock. The night watchman came, carrying the spiked mace of his office; he sang his midnight song:

> It was near the middle of the night
> That our Saviour, Jesus Christ, was born.

As he sang roses grew, changed, and became the heads of angels with wings that were all the colors of the rainbow.

It was beautiful to look at and lovely to listen to. It was a unique work of art. It was the most incredible; about that everyone agreed. The artist was a young man: goodhearted, as happy as a child, friendly and helpful to everyone, and kind to his poor old parents. He certainly deserved a princess and half a kingdom.

THE MOST INCREDIBLE

The day for announcing the winner of the competition had come. The whole town had been decorated. The princess sat on the throne of state. It had been restuffed with horsehair, but that hadn't made it any more comfortable to sit on. The judges all glanced slyly at the young man and tittered among themselves. He looked happy and had reason to be; after all, he had created "the most incredible."

"No! I will do the most incredible," shouted a tall, gangly, strong man who had just entered the hall. "I am just the man for it." Then he swung the ax he had brought with him and smashed the clock. Crash! There it lay, wheels and springs and figures all broken into tiny bits, completely spoiled!

"Only I could do that!" he said, turning toward the judges. "He could create it, but I could and dared destroy it, that is the most incredible of all!"

"To break such a work of art," the judges all agreed, "that was the most unbelievable deed of all." The people said the same. Now he must have the princess and half the kingdom. The law is the law, even when it is incredible!

From all the towers of the town, the heralds blew their trumpets to announce the marriage. The princess was most unhappy. Still she looked beautiful, dressed in her costly robes. All the candles in the church were lit. It was to be an evening wedding; that is the most fashionable. Young noblewomen escorted the princess, and young noblemen the groom. They sang as they walked up to the altar.

The groom looked about arrogantly. He walked as straight as if his back could never bend.

The singing ceased. The church was so quiet that you could have heard a pin drop. Then the stillness was broken by the great doors of the church being thrown open.

"Boom, boom!" The great clock that the young man had made came marching up the aisle. It stepped between the bride and bridegroom. That the dead do not rise to haunt the living we all know; but a work of art can. The body had been hurt, but the spirit of a work of art no ax can break.

The clock looked exactly as it had before it was destroyed. It began to strike the hours, one after the other, and all the figures came out. First came Moses; he threw the heavy stone tablets of the law at the feet of the bridegroom. He looked so angry that it

HANS CHRISTIAN ANDERSEN

appeared as if flames were darting from his eyes. "I cannot pick them up again, for you have broken my arms," he said, and the bridegroom felt that he could not move, his feet were held by the stone tablets.

Adam and Eve, the holy three kings, and the four seasons now appeared; and all of them told him the truth about himself and cried: "Shame!"

But the bridegroom did not feel any shame.

As the figures appeared, they grew in size until they seemed so large that they filled the church. When the twelve strokes of midnight sounded, the night watchman came forth and everyone stepped aside. He walked straight to the bridegroom and dealt him such a resounding blow with his spiked mace that he fell to the floor.

"Stay there!" the watchman shouted. "And never rise again. We are revenged and so is our master. Now we will be gone."

And the clock disappeared and was never seen again. But the candles in the church formed great flowers of light, and the golden star in the ceiling sparkled as if it were on fire, and the organ began to play by itself. Everybody who was there declared that this was the most incredible thing they had ever seen.

"Now," said the princess, "let me marry the right one. He who created the clock is the one I want as a husband and master."

He was there in the church and the people became his attendants. Everyone was happy, everyone blessed him, and not one person envied him, and that is incredible!

THE GREAT SEA SERPENT

There once was a little fish. He was of good family; his name I have forgotten — if you want to know it, you must ask someone learned in these matters. He had one thousand and eight hundred brothers and sisters, all born at the same time. They did not know their parents and had to take care of themselves. They swam around happily in the sea. They had enough water to drink — all the great oceans of the world. They did not speculate upon where their food would come from, that would come by itself. Each wanted to follow his own inclinations and live his own life; not that they gave much thought to that either.

The sun shone down into the sea and illuminated the water. It was a strange world, filled with the most fantastic creatures; some of them were so big and had such huge jaws that they could have swallowed all eighteen hundred of the little fish at once. But this, too, they did not worry about, for none of them had been eaten yet.

The little fishes swam close together, as herring or mackerel do. They were thinking about nothing except swimming. Suddenly they heard a terrible noise, and from the surface of the sea a great thing was cast among them. There was more and more of it; it was endless and had neither head nor tail. It was heavy and every one of the small fishes that it hit was either stunned and thrown aside or had its back broken.

HANS CHRISTIAN ANDERSEN

The fishes — big and small, the ones who lived up near the waves and those who dwelled in the depths — all fled, while this monstrous serpent grew longer and longer as it sank deeper and deeper, until at last it was hundreds of miles long, and lay at the bottom of the sea, crossing the whole ocean.

All the fishes — yes, even the snails and all the other animals that live in the sea — saw or heard about the strange, gigantic, unknown eel that had descended into the sea from the air above.

What was it? We know that it was the telegraph cable, thousands of miles long, that human beings had laid to connect America and Europe.

All the inhabitants of the sea were frightened of this new huge animal that had come to live among them. The flying fishes leaped up from the sea and into the air; and the gurnard since it knew how, shot up out of the water like a bullet. Others went down into the depths of the ocean so fast that they were there before the telegraph cable. They frightened both the cod and the flounder, who were swimming around peacefully, hunting and eating their fellow creatures.

A couple of sea cucumbers were so petrified that they spat out their own stomachs in fright; but they survived, for they knew how to swallow them again. Lots of lobsters and crabs left their shells in the confusion. During all this, the eighteen hundred little fishes were separated; most of them never saw one another again, nor would they have recognized one another if they had. Only a dozen of them stayed in the same spot, and after they had lain still a couple of hours their worst fright was over and curiosity became stronger than fear.

They looked about, both above and below themselves, and there at the bottom of the sea they thought they saw the monster that had frightened them all. It looked thin, but who knew how big it could make itself or how strong it was. It lay very still, but it might be up to something.

The more timid of the small fish said, "Let it lie where it is, it is no concern of ours." But the tiniest of them were determined to find out what it was. Since the monster had come from above, it was better to seek information about it up there. They swam up to the surface of the ocean. The wind was still and the sea was like a mirror.

They met a dolphin. He is a fellow who likes to jump and to

THE GREAT SEA SERPENT

turn somersaults in the sea. The dolphin has eyes to see with and ought to have seen what happened, and therefore the little fishes approached it. But a dolphin only thinks about himself and his somersaults; he didn't know what to say, so he didn't say anything, but looked very proud.

A seal came swimming by just at that moment, and even though it eats small fishes, it was more polite than the dolphin. Luckily it happened to be full, and it knew more than the jumping fish. "Many a night have I lain on a wet stone — miles and miles away from here — and looked toward land, where live those treacherous creatures who call themselves, in their own language, men. They are always hunting me and my kind, though usually we manage to escape. That is exactly what happened to the great sea serpent that you are asking about — it got away from them. They had had it in their power for ever so long, and kept it up on land. Now men wanted to transport it to another country, across the sea. — Why? you may ask, but I can't answer. — They had a lot of trouble getting it on board the ship. But they finally succeeded; after all, it was weakened from its stay on land. They rolled it up, round and round into a coil. It wiggled and writhed, and what a lot of noise it made! I heard it. When the ship got out to sea, the great eel slipped overboard. They tried to stop it. I saw them, there were dozens of hands holding onto its body. But they couldn't. Now it is lying down at the bottom of the sea, and I guess it will stay there for a while."

"It looks awfully thin," said the tiny fishes.

"They have starved it," explained the seal. "But it will soon get its old figure and strength back. I am sure it is the great sea serpent: the one men are so afraid of that they talk about it all the time. I had not believed it existed, but now I do. And that was it." With a flip of its tail, the seal dived and was gone.

"How much he knew and how well he talked," said one of the little fishes admiringly. "I have never known so much as I do now — I just hope it wasn't all lies."

"We could swim down and look," suggested the tiniest of the tiny fishes. "And on the way down we could hear what the other fishes think."

"We wouldn't move a fin to know anything more," said all the other tiny fishes, turned, and swam away.

"But I will," shouted the tiniest one, and swam down into the

HANS CHRISTIAN ANDERSEN

depths. But he was far away from where the great sea serpent had sunk. The little fish searched in every direction. Never had he realized that the world was so big. Great shoals of herring glided by like silver boats, and behind them came schools of mackerel that were even more splendid and brilliant. There were fishes of all shapes, with all kinds of markings and colors. Jellyfish, looking like transparent plants, floated by, carried by the currents. Down at the bottom of the sea the strangest things grew: tall grasses and palm-shaped trees whose every leaf was covered with crustaceans.

At last the tiny fish spied a long dark line far below it and swam down to it. It was not the giant serpent but the railing of a sunken ship, whose upper and lower decks had been torn in two by the pressure of the water. The little fish entered the great cabin, where the terrified passengers had gathered as the ship went down; they had all drowned and the currents of the sea had carried their bodies away, except for two of them: a young woman who lay on a bench with her babe in her arms. The sea rocked them gently; they looked as though they were sleeping. The little fish grew frightened as he looked at them. What if they were to wake? The cabin was so quiet and so lonely that the tiny fish hurried away again, out into the light, where there were other fishes. It had not swum very far when it met a young whale; it was awfully big.

"Please don't swallow me," pleaded the little fish. "I am so little you could hardly taste me, and I find it such a great pleasure to live."

"What are you doing down here?" grunted the whale. "It is much too deep for your kind." Then the tiny fish told the whale about the great eel — or whatever it could be — that had come from the air and descended into the sea, frightening even the most courageous fishes.

"Ha, ha, ha!" laughed the whale, and swallowed so much water that it had to surface in order to breathe and spout the water out. "Ho-ho . . . ha-ha. That must have been the thing that tickled my back when I was turning over. I thought it was the mast of a ship and was just about to use it as a back scratcher; but it must have been that. It lies farther out. I think I will go and have a look at it; I haven't anything else to do."

The whale swam away and the tiny fish followed it, but not too closely for the great animal left a turbulent wake behind it.

They met a shark and an old sawfish. They, too, had heard about the strange great eel that was so thin and yet longer than any other fish. They hadn't seen it but wanted to.

A catfish joined them. "If that sea serpent is not thicker than an anchor cable, then I will cut it in two, in one bite," he said, and opened his monstrous jaws to show his six rows of teeth. "If I can make a mark in an anchor I guess I can bite a stem like that in two."

"There it is," cried the whale. "Look how it moves, twisting and turning." The whale thought he had better eyesight than the others. As a matter of fact he hadn't; what he had seen was merely an old conger eel, several yards long, that was swimming toward them.

"That fellow has never caused any commotion in the sea before, or frightened any other big fish," said the catfish with disgust. "I have met him often."

They told the conger about the new sea serpent and asked him if he wanted to go with them to discover what it was.

"I wonder if it is longer than I am," said the conger eel, and stretched himself. "If it is, then it will be sorry."

"It certainly will," said the rest of the company. "There are enough of us so we don't have to tolerate it if we don't want to!" they exclaimed, and hurried on.

They saw something that looked like a floating island that was having trouble keeping itself from sinking. It was an old whale. His head was overgrown with seaweed, and on his back were so many mussels and oysters that its black skin looked as if it had white spots.

"Come on, old man," the young whale said. "There is a new fish in the ocean and we won't tolerate it!"

"Oh, let me stay where I am!" grumbled the old whale. "Peace is all I ask, to be left in peace. Ow! Ow! . . . I am very sick, it will be the death of me. My only comfort is to let my back emerge above the water, then the sea gulls scratch it: the sweet birds. That helps a lot as long as they don't dig too deep with their bills and get into the blubber. There's the skeleton of one still sitting on my back. It got stuck and couldn't get loose when I had to submerge. The little fishes picked his bones clean. You can see it. . . . Look at him, and look at me. . . . Oh, I am very sick."

"You are just imagining all that," said the young whale. "I am not sick, no one that lives in the sea is ever sick."

"I am sorry!" said the old whale. "The eels have skin diseases, the carp have smallpox, and we all suffer from worms."

"Nonsense!" shouted the shark, who didn't like to listen to that kind of talk. Neither did the others, so they all swam on.

At last they came to the place where part of the telegraph cable lies, that stretches from Europe to America across sand shoals and high mountains, through endless forests of seaweed and coral. The currents move as the winds do in the heavens above, and through them swim schools of fishes, more numerous than the flocks of migratory birds that fly through the air. There was a noise, a sound, a humming, the ghost of which you hear in the great conch shell when you hold it up to your ear.

"There is the serpent!" shouted the bigger fish and the little fishes too. They had caught sight of some of the telegraph cable but neither the beginning nor the end of it, for they were both lost in the far distance. Sponges, polyps, and gorgonia swayed above it and leaned against it, sometimes hiding it from view. Sea urchins and snails climbed over it; and great crabs, like giant spiders, walked tightrope along it. Deep blue sea cucumbers — or whatever those creatures are called who eat with their whole body — lay next to it; one would think that they were trying to smell it. Flounders and cod kept turning from side to side, in order to be able to listen to what everyone was saying. The starfishes had dug themselves down in the mire; only two of their points were sticking up, but they had eyes on them and were staring at the black snake, hoping to see something come out of it.

The telegraph cable lay perfectly still, as if it were lifeless; but inside, it was filled with life: with thoughts, human thoughts.

"That thing is treacherous," said the whale. "It might hit me in the stomach, and that is my weak point."

"Let's feel our way forward," said one of the polyps. "I have long arms and flexible fingers. I've already touched it, but now I'll take a firmer grasp."

And it stuck out its arms and encircled the cable. "I have felt both its stomach and its back. It is not scaly. I don't think it has any skin either. I don't believe it lays eggs and I don't think it gives birth to live children."

The conger eel lay down beside the cable and stretched itself as far as it could. "It is longer than I am," it admitted. "But length isn't everything. One has to have skin, a good stomach and, above all, suppleness."

THE GREAT SEA SERPENT

The whale — the young strong whale! — bowed more deeply than it ever had before. "Are you a fish or a plant?" he asked. "Or are you a surface creation, one of those who can't live down here?"

The telegraph cable didn't answer, though it was filled with words. Thoughts traveled through it so fast that they took only seconds to move from one end to the other: hundreds of miles away.

"Will you answer or be bitten in two?" asked the ill-mannered shark.

All the other fishes repeated the question: "Answer or be bitten in two?"

The telegraph cable didn't move; it had its own ideas, which isn't surprising for someone so full of thoughts. "Let them bite me in two," it thought. "Then I will be pulled up and repaired. It has happened to lots of my relations, that are not half as long as I am." But it didn't speak, it telegraphed; besides, it found the question impertinent; after all, it was lying there on official business.

Dusk had come. The sun was setting, as men say. It was a fiery red, and the clouds were as brilliant as fire — one more beautiful than the other.

"Now comes the red illumination," said the polyp. "Maybe the thing will be easier to see in that light, though I hardly think it worth looking at."

"Attack it! Attack it!" screamed the catfish, and showed all his teeth.

"Attack it! Attack it!" shouted the whale, the shark, the sword-fish, and the conger eel.

They pushed forward. The catfish was first; but just as it was going to bite the cable the swordfish, who was a little too eager, stuck its sword into the behind of the catfish. It was a mistake, but it kept the catfish from using the full strength of its jaw muscles.

There was a great muddle in the mud. The sea cucumbers, the big fishes, and the small ones swam around in circles; they pushed and shoved and squashed and ate each other up. The crabs and the lobsters fought, and the snails pulled their heads into their houses. The telegraph cable just minded its own business, which is the proper thing for a telegraph cable to do.

Night came to the sky above, but down in the ocean millions and millions of little animals illuminated the water. Crayfish no larger than the head of a pin gave off light. It is incredible and wonderful; and quite true.

HANS CHRISTIAN ANDERSEN

All the animals of the sea looked at the telegraph cable. "If only we knew what it was — or at least what it wasn't," said one of the fishes. And that was a very important question.

An old sea cow — human beings call them mermen and mermaids — came gliding by. This one was a mermaid. She had a tail and short arms for splashing, hanging breasts, and seaweed and parasites on her head — and of these she was very proud. "If you want learning and knowledge," she said, "then I think I am the best equipped to give it to you. But I want free passage on the bottom of the sea for myself and my family. I am a fish like you, and a reptile by training. I am the most intelligent citizen of the ocean. I know about everything under the water and everything above it. The thing that you are worrying about comes from up there; and everything from above is dead and powerless, once it comes down here. So let it lie, it is only a human invention and of no importance."

"I think it may be more than that," said the tiny fish.

"Shut up, mackerel!" said the sea cow.

"Shrimp!" shouted the others, and they meant it as an insult.

The sea cow explained to them that the sea serpent who had frightened them — the cable itself, by the way, didn't make a sound — was not dangerous. It was only an invention of those animals up on dry land called human beings. When she finished talking about the sea serpent, she gave a little lesson in the craftiness and wickedness of men: "They are always trying to catch us. That is the only reason for their existence. They throw down nets, traps, and long fishing lines that have hooks, with bait attached to them, to try and fool us. This is probably another — bigger — fishing line. They are so stupid that they expect us to bite on it. But we aren't as dumb as that. Don't touch that piece of junk. It will unravel, fall apart, and become mud and mire — the whole thing. Let it lie there and rot. Anything that comes from above is worthless; it breaks or creaks; it is no good!"

"No good!" said all the creatures of the sea, accepting the mermaid's opinion in order to have one.

The little tiny fish didn't agree, but it had learned to keep its thoughts to itself. "That enormously long snake may be the most marvelous fish in the sea. I have a feeling that it is."

"Marvelous!" we human beings agree; and we can prove that it is true.

THE GREAT SEA SERPENT

The great sea serpent of the fable has become a fact. It was constructed by human skill, conceived by human intelligence. It stretches from the Eastern Hemisphere to the Western, carrying messages from country to country faster than light travels from the sun down to the earth. Each year the great serpent grows. Soon it will stretch across all the great oceans, under the storm-whipped waves and the glasslike water, through which the skipper can look down as if he were sailing through the air and see the multitude of fish and the fireworks of color.

At the very depths is a *Midgards-worm*, biting its own tail as it circumscribes the world. Fish and reptiles hit their heads against it: it is impossible to understand what it is by looking at it. Human thoughts expressed in all the languages of the world, and yet silent: the snake of knowledge of good and evil. The most wonderful of the wonders of the sea: our time's great sea serpent!

THE GARDENER
AND HIS MASTER

$\mathbb{A}$ few miles from Copenhagen stood an old castle with thick walls, towers, and corbie gables. Here lived, in the summertime, a noble family. This castle was the handsomest of all the castles and farms they owned. It was in such good repair that it looked as if it had been newly built. Inside it was both cozy and comfortable. Over the entrance portal had been cut in stone the coat of arms of the family. Rose vines grew up the wall and made a frame around the shield and the windows. A big lawn that was smooth as a carpet stretched in front of the castle; hawthorn bushes, both red and white, grew in the garden, besides beautiful and rare flowers seldom seen outside the hothouse.

The noble family had an excellent gardener. It was a pleasure to look not only at the flower garden but at the vegetable garden and the fruit orchard as well. Near the orchard a small part of the original garden was still to be seen. It was filled with bushes cut in the shapes of pyramids and crowns. Among these stood two big ancient trees. They had but few leaves on them, even in summer; and if one did not know better, one could have believed that all the branches that had been cut off the bushes had been carried by the wind into the trees. But all the little bunches of twigs had been flown up there: they were birds' nests.

From ancient times, rooks and crows had nested there. The two old trees were a city of birds, and the birds were the proprietors.

THE GARDENER AND HIS MASTER

They were the oldest family in the castle, and they felt that they were the masters. They tolerated the two-legged ones that could not fly but had to stay forever on the ground. But human beings did not interest them, even when they came with their guns and frightened them, so they flew out of their trees, screaming with hoarse voices: "Caw! Caw!"

The gardener had often asked his master for permission to have the old trees cut down; they were half dead as it was, and ugly. If they were gone, the birds would be gone too, and one would be spared listening to their screaming. But the master wanted to get rid of neither trees nor birds. He said they had been there from ancient times, and they belonged to the castle.

"Those trees are the birds' inheritance; let them keep it, my good Larsen," he would say. The gardener's name was Larsen — but that is neither here nor there, as far as my story is concerned. "Haven't you enough land, little Larsen? Why do you need to take the birds? If the park isn't big enough, you have a kitchen garden, the orchard, and the hothouse."

And what the master said was true, the gardener had a large domain that he took great pains to keep. His master and mistress acknowledged it, but at times they could not help informing him that they had seen flowers or eaten fruits at the table of friends that were superior to what he could produce. This made the gardener quite sad, for he always did his very best. He had a simple, loving heart and took great pride in his work.

One day his master called him to the castle and told him, in a most courteous but patronizing way, that while dining with some noble friends the day before they had been served some pears and apples so succulent that they and all the other guests had never before tasted their like. The fruits were not native, of that he felt sure, but they ought to be imported; that is, if they could be made to grow here. They had been bought in the biggest greengrocery in the city, and the master wanted the gardener to ride in immediately and inquire what the names of the fruit were and if shoots for grafting could be sent for.

The gardener knew the greengrocer well, for it was to him that he sold, with his master's permission, the surplus fruit and vegetables from the gardens. He saddled a horse and rode to town and asked the greengrocer where the much-praised apples and pears had come from.

"They are from your own orchard," said the greengrocer, and showed the gardener some of the fruit, which he recognized at once. He hurried back and told his master the good news that the apples and pears he had found so delicious had come from his own garden.

Both the master and mistress refused to believe it. "I don't think it possible, Larsen," said the master. "You will have to get it in writing from the greengrocer before I will believe it."

The gardener rode to town once more, and this time he returned with a testimonial from the greengrocer.

"It is strange, but I guess it must be true," said the master. From then on great bowls filled with pears and apples from their garden stood on the table, and they were proud of them. Crates were sent to all their friends in town, in the country, and even to some in foreign lands. It really was quite exciting, quite an honor; but it had to be remembered that that particular year had been a good year for fruit everywhere.

Some months later the master and the mistress were invited to the king's table. The day after, the gardener was called into the drawing room again. For dessert His Majesty had served some melons, from the royal hothouses, that had been most succulent and tasty.

"You must go to the royal gardener, Larsen, and get some melon seeds so we can grow them ourselves."

"But the royal gardener got his seeds from us," answered the gardener, very pleased.

"In that case, the royal gardener has understood how to grow them. Every one of them was superb," said the master, looking more annoyed than pleased.

"I guess I can be proud of them," said the gardener, "for it will please you to know that the royal gardener had no luck with his melons this year; when he saw ours he asked for three of them for the royal table."

"Larsen! Don't tell me that it was our own melons we ate."

"I am sure they were," said the gardener. "But I will go and ask."

And he did and it was their own melons they had eaten and he got it in writing from the royal gardener.

His master and mistress were both pleased and surprised, and told everyone the story and even showed the testimonial from the royal gardener. Melon seeds were dispatched to their friends, as apples and pears and shoots for grafting had been sent before.

THE GARDENER AND HIS MASTER

Seeds from the new type of melon were exported. They were named after the castle, so now its name could be read in French, German, and English. It was all quite unexpected.

"I hope the gardener won't begin thinking too much of himself," said the master to the mistress.

He didn't; but the fame was a spur, he wanted to be one of the best gardeners in the country. Every year he tried to improve some of the vegetables and fruits, and often he was successful. It was not always appreciated. He would be told that the pears and apples were good but not as good as the ones last year. The melons were excellent but not quite up to the standard of the first ones he had grown.

As for the strawberries, they were fine, but berries as big and juicy were served at other tables. The year the worms ate the radishes, no one seemed to be interested in talking about anything else, even though so many other things had grown well that year. It was as if his master felt relieved at being able to point to a failure.

"The radishes didn't work out this year, little Larsen," they would say, and repeat it. "The radishes didn't work out."

Twice a week the gardener took fresh flowers up to the castle. He arranged them marvelously so each color complemented the others; his bouquets were a delight.

"You have taste, Larsen," his mistress would say. "But remember, taste is a gift from God, not of your own making."

One day he arranged in a crystal bowl a water-lily leaf and a strange blue flower as big as a sunflower.

"It is the lotus flower from Hindustan!" exclaimed the mistress. She had never seen anything so beautiful before. The bowl was put where the sun could shine on it in the daytime, and at night it was illuminated with candles. Everyone who saw it found it lovely and rare, and said they had never seen a flower like it before. The young princess, who was both good and kind, was so delighted with it that she was given the flower to take home with her to her castle.

The next day the master and mistress went down into the garden. They wanted to pick one of the marvelous flowers themselves. They looked everywhere, but they couldn't find it. At last they called the gardener and asked him where the blue lotus flower grew.

"We have looked everywhere," they said, "both in the flower garden and in the hothouse."

"You won't find it either place," answered the gardener. "It is only a humble flower from the kitchen garden. But beautiful it is, like a blue cactus, though it is only an artichoke."

"I wish you had told us that." The master sounded annoyed. "We thought it was a rare foreign flower. How could we have thought anything else? It is most embarrassing. The young princess was so enamored of it that we gave it to her. Although she is very well versed in botany, she did not recognize it; but then I am sure botany has little to do with vegetables. My good Larsen, how could you bring such a flower up into the rooms of the castle? You have made us appear ridiculous."

The beautiful blue flower from the kitchen garden was banished from the elegant rooms of the old castle. It didn't belong there! The master and mistress excused themselves to the princess and explained that the beautiful blue lotus flower was only a common vegetable. Their gardener was the culprit who had been so impertinent; they had reprimanded him severely.

"Oh, what a pity! How unjust!" exclaimed the princess. "He has opened our eyes, showed us a beautiful flower, where we would never have thought of looking for it. I will order the royal gardener to bring me an artichoke flower every day as long as they are in bloom."

And the royal gardener did; and the master and the mistress told Larsen that he, too, could bring a freshly cut artichoke flower to their rooms every day.

"It is really quite a fascinating flower," they said, and complimented the gardener. "Larsen loves praise, he is like a spoiled child," the mistress said, and the master nodded in agreement.

That autumn there was a terrible storm. During the night it grew worse and on the outskirts of the forest great trees fell; their roots were pulled right out of the earth. The two great old trees that housed the colony of birds did not fare better. Down they came, nests and all. Inside the castle one could hear the angry screams of the birds, and some of the servants said that the birds knocked on the windowpanes with their wings. The master said it was an affliction. The gardener said nothing; he was happy to see the old trees gone.

"Now you are contented, Larsen." The master looked at the fallen trees. "The storm has cut them down for you; the birds have departed for the forest, a part of the old times has gone. Soon there will be nothing left to remind us of it. You, this has delighted; me, it has grieved."

The gardener had a plan — it was an old one he had thought of long ago — as to what he would do with the area where the trees had stood. It was a sunny spot and he meant to make it the most beautiful part of the park.

The trees had smashed the bushes in their fall, and they could not be saved. In the cleared plot of land he now planted all the typical common plants of Denmark, gathered from forests and fields. Bushes, trees, and flowers that no other gardener had ever dreamed of introducing into the park of a castle he planted there. Each got the soil, the sun or shade it desired; he nursed them with devotion and the plants grew and flourished.

The juniper from the heath of Jutland thrived. It rose like a miniature Italian cypress. Near it grew the holly, green in winter and summer. And in front of them were ferns of all different types, like dwarf palm trees. The great thistle, the most despised of all weeds, bloomed with flowers so beautiful that they would have enhanced any bouquet. Not far from them, where the soil was a little more moist, the common dock was allowed to flourish, with its big picturesque leaves. From the fields had been brought great mulleins that looked like giant candelabra. Woodruff, primrose, lily of the valley, the calla, and the three-leafed wood sorrel: all were there; none had been forgotten. It was a marvel to look at.

In the direction of the fields the garden was fenced by a row of dwarf pear trees. They had been imported from France but, having been given plenty of sun and careful nursing, they soon bore fruits as big and succulent as in their own country.

Where the two old trees had stood a flagpole was erected and from its top the white and red flag of Denmark flew. Near the flagpole another smaller pole stood, around which the vines of the hops twisted themselves; in the late summer the sweet scent of their flowers could be smelled far away. In the winter a sheaf of oats hung from the pole; it is an old custom to provide a meal in this way for the birds at Christmas.

"Larsen is getting sentimental in his old age," said the master.

"But he is loyal and true," added the mistress.

At New Year's, one of the illustrated papers from Copenhagen carried a picture of the old castle. One could see the flagpole and

HANS CHRISTIAN ANDERSEN

the sheaf of oats for the birds. It was particularly mentioned how pleasing it was to see that such an old tradition was kept alive.

"It does not matter what Larsen does," the master remarked. "The whole world will beat the drums for it. There is a happy man. We must be almost proud of having him."

But they weren't really proud of it. They felt that they were the owners and that they could dismiss Larsen if they wanted to. They didn't, for they were decent people, and there are lots of their kind, which is fortunate for the Larsens.

That was the story of the gardener and his master. I have told it, now why don't you think about it.

THE PROFESSOR
AND THE FLEA

T here once was a balloonist—
that is, a captain of a balloon—who came to a bad end: his
balloon ripped and he fell straight to the ground and was smashed.
His son, who had been along on the trip, had parachuted down two
minutes before the tragedy. That was the young man's good luck.
He landed safe and sound, with invaluable experience in balloon-
ing and a great desire to make use of it; but he didn't have a
balloon or any money to buy one with.

He had to make a living, so he taught himself how to talk with
his stomach; that is called being a ventriloquist. He was young and
handsome, and when he had bought new clothes and grown a
mustache he had such a noble look that he might have been
mistaken for the younger son of a count. All the ladies found him
attractive; and one of them so much so that she ran away from
home to follow him. They traveled to distant towns and foreign
lands, and there he called himself professor, no less would do.

His greatest desire was still to get a balloon and then ascend into
the sky with his wife, but balloons are expensive.

"Our day will come," he declared.

"I hope it will be soon," said his wife.

"We can wait; we are young. Now I am a professor. Crumbs are
not slices, but they are bread," he said, quoting an old proverb.

His wife helped him. She sat at the door and sold tickets, which was no fun in the winter when it was cold. She also took part in the act. She climbed into a chest and then vanished. The chest had a double bottom; it was a matter of agility, and was called an optical illusion.

One evening after the performance, when he opened the false bottom, she wasn't there. He looked everywhere but she was gone. Too much dexterity. She never came back. She had been sorry and now he was sorry. He lost his spirit, couldn't laugh or clown, and then he lost his audience. His earnings went from bad to worse and so did his clothes. At last the only thing he owned was a big flea. He had inherited the animal from his wife and therefore was fond of it. He trained the flea, taught it the art of dexterity: how to present arms and to shoot off a cannon; the latter was very small.

The professor was proud of the flea and the flea was proud of himself. After all, he had human blood in his stomach, if not in his veins. He had visited the grand capitals of Europe and performed before kings and queens, at least that was what was printed in the playbill and the newspapers. He knew he was famous and could support a professor — or a whole family if he had had one.

The flea was proud and famous; and yet, when he and the professor traveled, they always went fourth class — it gets you to your destination just as quickly as first. They had a silent agreement that they would never part; the flea would remain a bachelor and the professor a widower, which amounts to the same thing.

"A place where one has had a great success one should never revisit," said the professor. He knew human nature and that is not the poorest sort of knowledge.

At last they had traveled in all the civilized parts of the world; only the lands of the savages were left. The professor knew that there were cannibals who ate Christian human beings. But he was not a real Christian and the flea not a human being, so he thought that there was no reason not to go there, and he expected it to be a profitable trip.

They traveled by steamer and sailing ship. The flea performed and that paid for their passage.

At last they came to the land of the savages. Here a little princess reigned. She had overthrown her own parents, for though she was only eight years old she had a will of her own and was marvelously charming and naughty.

THE PROFESSOR AND THE FLEA

As soon as she had seen the flea present arms and shoot off his little cannon, she fell wildly in love with him. As love can make a civilized man into a savage, imagine what it can do to one who is already a savage. She screamed, stamped her feet, and said, "It is him or no one!"

"My sweet little sensible girl, we shall have to make him into a human first," said her father.

"You leave that to me, old man," she answered, and that was not a very nice way to speak to her own father, but she was a savage.

The professor put the flea in her little hand.

"Now you are a human being," declared the princess. "You shall reign together with me, but you will have to obey or I shall kill you and eat the professor."

The professor got a room for himself. The walls were made of sugar cane; if he had had a sweet tooth, he could have licked them; but he didn't. He got a hammock for a bed, and lying in that was almost like being in the balloon he still dreamed about.

The flea stayed with the princess, sat on her hand and on her sweet neck. She pulled a long hair out of her head and made the professor tie one end around the leg of the flea; the other end was fastened to her coral earring.

The princess was happy, and she thought that if she was happy, then the flea ought to be happy too. But the one who was not happy was the professor. He was used to traveling, sleeping one night in one town and the next in another. He loved reading in the newspaper about himself, how clever he was at teaching a flea human accomplishments; but there were no newspapers among the savages. Day after day he lay in his hammock, lazy and idle. He was well fed. He was given fresh birds' eggs, stewed elephants' eyes, and roasted leg of giraffe, for the cannibals did not eat human flesh every day, it was a delicacy. "A child's shoulder in a spicy gravy with peppers is the most delicious dish there is," claimed the princess.

The professor was bored. He wanted to leave the land of the savages but he had to take the flea along; it was his protégé and the supplier of his daily bread.

He strained his power of thought as much as he could, and then he jumped out of the hammock and exclaimed, "I've got it!"

He went to the princess' father and said, "Please allow me to

work. I want to introduce your people
to what we, in the great world, call
culture.''

"And what can you teach me?''
asked the father of the princess.

"My greatest accomplish-
ment,'' answered the pro-
fessor, "is a cannon which
when fired makes such
a bang that the earth
trembles and all the birds
in the air fall down roasted
and ready to eat.''

Bring on that cannon,''
said the king.

But the only cannon in the
whole country was the little
one the flea could fire, and that
was much too small.

"I will make a bigger one,'' said.
the professor. "I need lots of silk
material, ropes, strings, needles, and
thread. Besides some oil of camphor,
which is good against airsickness.''

All that he asked for, he got. Not until
he was finished and the balloon was
ready to be filled with hot air and
sent up did he call the people together to see his cannon.

The flea was sitting on the princess' hand, watching the balloon being
blown up. And the balloon stretched
itself and grew fatter and swelled. It
was so wild it was difficult to hold.

"I have to take the cannon
up in the air to cool it

THE PROFESSOR AND THE FLEA

off. Alone, I cannot manage it, I have to have someone who knows something about cannons along to help me, and here only the flea will do."

"I hate giving him permission to go," said the princess as she held out the flea to the professor, who took it on his hand.

"Let go of the ropes, up goes the balloon!" he cried.

The savages thought he said "up goes the cannon," and the balloon rose up into the air above the clouds and flew away from the land of the savages.

The little princess, her father and her mother, and all their people stood and waited. They are waiting still and if you don't believe me you can travel to the land of the savages. Every child there will tell you the story of the flea and the professor. They are expecting him back as soon as the "cannon" has cooled off. But he will never return, he is back home. When he travels on the railroad he always goes first class, not fourth. He has done well for himself, with the help of the balloon, and nobody asks him where or how he got it. The flea and the professor are wealthy and respectable, and that kind of people are never asked embarrassing questions.

THE CRIPPLE

Once upon a time there was a big farm with a manor house. The master and mistress were rich, young, and happy. Fortune had smiled on them and they smiled back; they wanted everyone to be as happy as they were.

On Christmas Eve a large, beautifully decorated Christmas tree stood in the grand hall. A log fire burned in the fireplace and all the old paintings had their frames decorated with spruce branches. Here there were to be dancing and gaiety on the happiest night of the year, for the wealthy couple and their friends.

In the big dining room where the farm hands ate, Christmas was already being celebrated. Here, too, stood a Christmas tree, with red and white candles, tinsel, little Danish flags, and hearts woven from glossy paper which were filled with sweets. All the poor children in the countryside had been invited; they had come with their mothers. The grownups did not look long at the tree, they were more interested in the table where the presents were laid out. There were linen and woolen cloth, from which little girls' dresses and boys' pants could be sewn. Only the little children stretched out their hands toward the candles, flags, and tinsel.

They had all come early in the afternoon and had been served the traditional Christmas dinner, which began with rice porridge and whose main course was roast goose and red cabbage. Afterward the candles on the tree were lit, and when the children had emp-

THE CRIPPLE

tied the little paper baskets of their sweets, the presents were distributed. Finally everyone was given a glass of punch and apple fritters. Then it was time for the guests to go back to their own poor cottages; there the gifts were evaluated once more and the dinner discussed.

"Garden-Kirsten" and "Garden-Ole" — they were called by these names because they did the hoeing and the weeding in the park — were a married couple who had five children. Every year they received their share of gifts.

"Both the master and mistress are generous," they would say. "But they can afford to be; and besides, they enjoy it."

"There are clothes enough for the four children, but haven't they given anything to the cripple? They don't usually forget him even though he can't come to the party."

By the "cripple" Garden-Ole meant his oldest son; his name was Hans. He was a clever boy and once had been very active, but then his legs had suddenly "grown wobbly," as his mother said. For the last five years he had been bedridden.

"Well, I did get something," said his mother. "But it wasn't anything much, only a book he could read."

"He won't get fat from that!" his father remarked.

But the gift made Hans happy. He was a very alert child and loved to read. Not that he didn't work, for even though he was confined to bed he had lots to do: he knitted socks and even bedspreads. The young mistress had praised his work and bought two of the bedspreads. The book was a collection of fairy tales. It was thick; there was much to read and think about.

"It is useless!" said his parents. "But let him read; it helps him pass the time, and he can't always be knitting."

Spring came. The cherries bloomed and flowers came up from the ground; weeds did too, which meant that there was plenty of work in the park, not only for the gardener and his apprentices but for Garden-Ole and Garden-Kirsten as well.

"It is drudgery!" they both complained. "As soon as we have raked the garden paths, the guests come walking on them and spoil our work. The master must be rich to be able to afford to have so many strangers here."

"Yes, the blessings of the world are strangely distributed," said Ole. "The minister said that we are all God's children, but then why do some get everything and so many almost nothing?"

"It is all because of man's fall from grace," replied his wife.

That evening, when they returned to their cottage, they had the same discussion. Hans was lying in his bed reading his book of fairy tales.

Life had not dealt easily with them. Hard work had made not only their hands hard but also their opinions and judgments. Their situation was beyond their own power to change it; they had not been able to get along; life was too difficult. As they talked they grew angrier and more bitter.

"Some people have wealth and happiness and others only poverty. Why should we suffer for Adam's and Eve's disobedience? Had we been in their place we wouldn't have behaved as they did."

"But we would have," exclaimed Cripple-Hans. "It is all written down here in this book."

"What is written down in the book?" asked his father.

Hans read aloud for them the old fairy tale about the woodcutter and his wife. They, too, had been complaining about Adam's and Eve's curiosity being the cause of their misery, and claiming that, had they been in their stead, then the apple would have stayed on the tree. The king, who had been riding past, heard what they said. "Come with me to the palace," he offered, "and you shall live as well as I do. You will be served seven courses at every meal plus dessert; but the tureen that stands in the middle of the table you must never touch, for then your life of leisure will be over."

They followed the king to the castle and the very first day the wife said, "I wonder what is in that tureen."

"That is no concern of ours," replied her husband.

"Oh, I am only curious," exclaimed his wife. "I would just like to know what is inside. . . . If only I dared lift the lid a bit. I am sure it is a great delicacy."

"It may have a mechanical attachment, like a pistol, so that it goes off the moment you touch it, and then everybody in the whole place can hear it," said the woodcutter thoughtfully.

"Ugh!" cried the wife, and she didn't touch the tureen. But she dreamed about it that night. In her dream the lid of the tureen lifted itself and she smelled the loveliest punch, the kind one gets at weddings and funerals. Next to the tureen lay a silver coin and on it was inscribed: "Drink, and you will become the richest person in the world, and all others will become paupers." When she awoke, she told her husband about her dream.

"You shouldn't think so much about the tureen," was his comment.

"We could just lift the lid a little, ever so gently," pleaded the wife.

"Very, very gently," agreed her husband.

And the wife lifted the lid the tiniest bit, and out jumped two little mice and ran away, down into a mousehole.

"That was it!" said the king, who had been watching them. "Now you can go back where you came from, and don't be bitter about Adam and Eve. You have been just as curious and ungrateful as they were."

"I wonder how such a story has become known and printed," said Garden-Ole. "It might have been us! Such a tale is worth thinking about."

The next day they went to work. The sun scorched them and the rain soaked them; and they grumbled. All the disgruntled thoughts they had during the day they chewed on in the evening.

It was still light when they had finished supper and Ole asked his son to read the story of the woodcutter once more.

"But there are many other stories in the book," Hans replied. "Stories you don't know."

"Those I don't care about," said Garden-Ole. "I want to hear the one I know."

And Hans read the story again, and that was not the only evening he had to read it, or that it was discussed.

"It still does not explain everything," Ole said one evening. "Human beings are like milk. Some are churned into sweet butter and some become whey. Why should some always be lucky, be born to a high station, and never experience sorrow or want?"

Cripple-Hans was listening to what his father said and, though his legs were wobbly, his mind wasn't. He read another story from his book of fairy tales, the story of the man who had never known sorrow or want:

The king lay dying and could only be cured by being given the shirt of a man of whom it could truthfully be said that he had never known sorrow or want.

Messengers were sent to all the corners of the world, to all kings and noblemen, who one might suppose were happy; but every one of them had experienced, at some time or other, sorrow and want.

"But I haven't!" said the swineherd who was sitting in the ditch.

"I have been happy all my life." And as if to prove it he both laughed and sang.

"Then give me your shirt," ordered the messenger. "You shall have half the kingdom for it."

But the swineherd did not own a shirt, even though he called himself the happiest person in the world.

"That was a fellow," shouted Ole; and he and his wife laughed as they hadn't for years.

"What are you all so happy about?" asked the schoolteacher, who had just entered the cottage. "Laughter is new with you. Have you won in the lottery?"

"No, nothing like that," explained Ole. "Hans has been reading to us the story of the man who had never known sorrow or want. That fellow was so poor he didn't even have a shirt on his back. When you hear a story like that it is hard not to laugh. Imagine, it is printed in a book of fairy tales. Well, everyone has their load to bear, and hearing about others makes your own lighter."

"Where have you got the book from?" asked the schoolteacher, and smiled.

"Hans got it at Christmastime over a year ago. The mistress gave it to him because he is a cripple and has a liking for reading. Then we would have preferred a new shirt; but the book is strange, it can give answers to the questions you've been thinking about."

The schoolteacher picked up the book and started to leaf through it.

"Let's listen to the same story all over again!" exclaimed Garden-Ole. "And when you've finished that one, we can hear about the woodcutter and his wife." Those two stories remained enough for Ole. They were like two sun rays in the low-ceilinged rooms of the cottage, in the warped, cowed soul of the man.

Hans had read the whole book, not only once, but countless times. The fairy tales carried him where his legs refused to go — out into the world beyond the cottage walls. From that day on the schoolmaster came often during the afternoons, when the cripple lay alone in the house. Such visits were a feast to the boy. The old man told him about the size of the earth and its strange lands; how the sun was almost half a million times as big as the earth, and so far away that it would take a cannon ball twenty-five years to reach it: a journey that the rays of the sun could make in eight minutes. These were things that any school child knew, but to Hans it was

THE CRIPPLE

all new and even more wonderful than the stories in the book of fairy tales.

Once or twice a year the schoolteacher dined at the manor house, and here he told what a blessing the gift of the fairy-tale book had been, not only to the boy but to the whole family. As the schoolteacher was leaving, the mistress gave him a silver mark to give to Hans when next he visited him.

"That my parents can have," said Hans when the schoolmaster gave him the money.

And they were most happy to receive it. "Cripple-Hans can be both a blessing and of use," they commented. It sounded harsh but wasn't meant so.

A few days after the schoolteacher's visit to the manor house, the carriage of the young mistress stopped in front of the cottage. The sweet, tender-hearted woman had come to pay a visit to the boy, because she was so pleased that her Christmas gift had brought so much happiness to both the child and his family. She had a basket with her that contained a fine wheat bread, fruits, and a bottle of black currant juice. But for Hans she had something really amusing: a wire cage, painted gold, in which sat a little black bird that whistled ever so prettily. The cage was put on a chest at a distance from the boy's bed.

Hans could lie in bed and look at it and listen to it. The bird sang so loudly that even the passers-by could hear it.

Garden-Ole and Garden-Kirsten did not get home until long after the lady of the manor had departed. They saw how happy Hans was, but they were not happy; the gift seemed to them nothing but trouble.

"The rich never think about things like that, having servants at their beck and call," they said. "Cripple-Hans can't take care of it, so we'll have to. In the end the cat will get it."

One week went by and then another. The cat had been in the room many times without scaring the bird or harming it. Then one afternoon, while Hans was reading his book of fairy tales, it happened. The boy was reading the story of the fisherman's wife who wished that she was king and then became it; then she desired to be Pope and also that wish was granted; but when she wished that she was God Himself, she was put right back into the muddy ditch where she had come from. From this story no moral can be drawn about the cat and the bird, it just happened by chance to be the one Hans was reading.

HANS CHRISTIAN ANDERSEN

The cage stood on the chest; the cat sat on the floor and looked with its yellow-green eyes up at the bird. The animal's expression said, "You are so beautiful, I would love to eat you." Hans guessed its intentions; he read it on the face of the cat and screamed.

"Go away, cat! Go outside!" The cat tightened its muscles, ready to jump. Hans could not reach it and he had nothing to throw at the animal but his treasure, the book of fairy tales.

He threw it! But the binding was loose. Half of it went one way and half another, and neither hit the cat.

The cat turned and looked at the boy as if to say: "Don't mix in my affairs, little Hans, I can run and leap and you can do neither."

Hans kept staring at the cat. The bird was beginning to be frightened now. There was no one whom Hans could call; he was alone in the house. It was as if the cat knew it. Again it got ready to leap. Hans waved his bedcover and finally threw that at the cat, but the cat didn't mind, it jumped up on a chair and then onto the window sill. Now it was nearer the chest and the cage.

Hans could feel the pulsing of his heart, though he did not give it a thought; all his attention was on his bird and the cat. He could not get out of bed, he could not walk, for his legs could not carry him.

It felt as if a hand were squeezing his heart when the cat leaped from the window sill to the chest, pushing over the cage so it fell on the floor. The bird screeched and flapped its wings against the wires of the cage. With a scream Hans jumped out of bed and ran over to pick up the cage and chase the cat away. He was not aware of what he was doing until he stood with the cage in his hand; then he ran out of the house to the road. Tears streamed down his face and he kept repeating as loudly as he could: "I can walk! I can walk!"

He was no longer a cripple; such things can happen and it did happen to Hans. The schoolmaster lived not far away. Hans entered his room, barefoot, wearing his nightshirt and still carrying the cage with the bird in it. "I can walk!" he sobbed to the old man. "Oh, my God! I can walk!"

That was a happy day in the little cottage. Both Garden-Ole and Garden-Kirsten agreed that it was the happiest day of their lives. Hans was asked to come to the manor, along the path he had not walked for many a year.

It seemed to the boy that the hazelnut bushes and the trees

THE CRIPPLE

nodded to him and said, "Good day, Hans, welcome out here." The sun shone in his face and his heart.

The young squire and his wife looked so happy that one would have thought that Hans was a member of the family. The young woman was the happier of the two, for she had given the child both the book of fairy tales and the little bird that had been the cause of his recovery.

The bird had died of fright, but the book the boy would keep and read, no matter how old he became. Now he would be able to learn a trade; perhaps he could become a bookbinder. "Then I would be able to read all the latest books."

Later that day, his parents were called to the manor house. The young mistress explained to them that she and her husband thought that Hans was a very good and clever boy, who could read well, and understood what he read. "God always blesses a good cause," she added.

That evening Garden-Ole and his wife were really happy, especially Garden-Kirsten. But not a week had passed before their eyes were filled with tears. Hans was a good boy, and he had new clothes, but now he was leaving, traveling across the water to the capital, to go to school, where he would learn such things as Latin. It would be several years before they would see him again.

The book of fairy tales Hans was not allowed to take with him. His parents wanted to keep it, and Ole often read from it, but only the same two stories that he knew.

Letters came from Hans, one happier than the next. The family he lived with were well to do and very kind, but the best of all was the school. There was so much to learn that he wished he could live to be a hundred and become a schoolmaster himself.

"It is so strange that it should happen to us," said his parents, and held each other's hands and looked as solemn as when they went to communion.

"That it should happen to Hans," said Ole, "shows that God also remembers the poor man's child; and his being a cripple makes it sound like one of the stories from Hans's book of fairy tales."

THE SNOW QUEEN

A FAIRY TALE TOLD IN SEVEN STORIES

THE FIRST STORY, WHICH CONCERNS ITSELF WITH A BROKEN
MIRROR AND WHAT HAPPENED TO ITS FRAGMENTS

All right, we will start the story; when we come to the end we shall know more than we do now.

Once upon a time there was a troll, the most evil troll of them all; he was called the devil. One day he was particularly pleased with himself, for he had invented a mirror which had the strange power of being able to make anything good or beautiful that it reflected appear horrid; and all that was evil and worthless seem attractive and worth while. The most beautiful landscape looked like spinach; and the kindest and most honorable people looked repulsive or ridiculous. They might appear standing on their heads, without any stomachs; and their faces would always be so distorted that you couldn't recognize them. A little freckle would spread itself out till it covered half a nose or a whole cheek.

"It is a very amusing mirror," said the devil. But the most amusing part of it all was that if a good or a kind thought passed

THE SNOW QUEEN

through anyone's mind the most horrible grin would appear on the face in the mirror.

It was so entertaining that the devil himself laughed out loud. All the little trolls who went to troll school, where the devil was headmaster, said that a miracle had taken place. Now for the first time one could see what humanity and the world really looked like — at least, so they thought. They ran all over with the mirror, until there wasn't a country or a person in the whole world that had not been reflected and distorted in it.

At last they decided to fly up to heaven to poke fun of the angels and God Himself. All together they carried the mirror, and flew up higher and higher. The nearer they came to heaven, the harder the mirror laughed, so that the trolls could hardly hold onto it; still, they flew higher and higher: upward toward God and the angels, then the mirror shook so violently from laughter that they lost their grasp; it fell and broke into hundreds of millions of billions and some odd pieces. It was then that it really caused trouble, much more than it ever had before. Some of the splinters were as tiny as grains of sand and just as light, so that they were spread by the winds all over the world. When a sliver like that entered someone's eye it stayed there; and the person, forever after, would see the world distorted, and only be able to see the faults, and not the virtues, of everyone around him, since even the tiniest fragment contained all the evil qualities of the whole mirror. If a splinter should enter someone's heart — oh, that was the most terrible of all! — that heart would turn to ice.

Some of the pieces of the mirror were so large that windowpanes could be made of them, although through such a window it was no pleasure to contemplate your friends. Some of the medium-sized pieces became spectacles — but just think of what would happen when you put on such a pair of glasses in order to see better and be able to judge more fairly. That made the devil laugh so hard that it tickled in his stomach, which he found very pleasant.

Some of the tiniest bits of the mirror were still flying about in the air. And now you shall hear about them.

THE SECOND STORY, WHICH IS ABOUT A LITTLE BOY AND A LITTLE GIRL

In a big city, where there live so many people and are so many houses that not every family can have a garden of its own and so must learn to be satisfied with a potted plant, there once lived a poor little girl and a poor little boy who had a garden a little bit larger than a flowerpot. They weren't brother and sister but loved each other as much as if they had been. Their parents lived right across from each other; each family had a little apartment in the garret, but the houses were built so close together that the roofs almost touched. Between the two gutters that hung from the eaves and collected the water when it rained, there was only a very narrow space, and the two families could visit each other by climbing from one gable window to the other.

In front of the windows each family had a wooden box filled with earth, where herbs and other useful plants grew; but in each box there was also a little rose tree. The parents got the idea that, instead of setting the boxes parallel to their windows, they could set them across, so they reached from one window to the other. In that manner, the two gables were connected by a little garden. The peas climbed over the sides and hung down; and the little rose trees grew as tall as the windows and joined together, so that they looked like a green triumphal arch. The sides of the boxes were quite high and since the children could be relied upon not to try to climb over them, they were allowed to take their little wooden stools outside and sit under the rose trees; and there it was pleasant to play.

In winter that was not possible; then the windows were tightly closed and sometimes they would be covered by ice. Then the little children would heat copper coins on the stove and press them against the glass until the roundest of holes would melt in the ice; through each of these peeped the loveliest little eye: one belonged to a little boy and the other to a little girl. His name was Kai and hers was Gerda. In summer they had to take only a few steps to be together; but in the winter they had to run down and up so many stairs and across a yard covered by snowdrifts.

"The white bees are swarming," said the old Grandmother.

"Do they have a queen too?" asked Kai, for he knew that real bees have such a ruler.

"Yes, they have," said the old woman. "She always flies right in the center of the swarm, where the most snowflakes are. She is the biggest of them all, but she never lies down to rest as the other snowflakes do. No, when the wind dies she returns to the black clouds. Many a winter night she flies through the streets of the town and looks in through the windows; then they become covered by ice flowers."

"Yes, I've seen that!" said first one child and then the other; and now they knew that what the Grandmother said was true.

"Could the Snow Queen come inside, right into our room?" asked the little girl.

"Let her come," said Kai." I will put her right on top of the stove and then she will melt."

The Grandmother patted his head and told them another story. But that night, as Kai was getting undressed, he climbed up on the chair by the window and looked out through his peephole. It was snowing gently; one of the flakes fell on the edge of the wooden box and stayed there; other snowflakes followed and they grew until they took the shape of a woman. Her clothes looked like the whitest gauze. It was made of millions of little star-shaped snowflakes. She was beautiful but all made of ice: cold, blindingly glittering ice; and yet she was alive, for her eyes stared at Kai like two stars, but neither rest nor peace was to be found in her gaze. She nodded toward the window and beckoned. The little boy got so frightened that he jumped down from the chair; and at that moment a shadow crossed the window as if a big bird had flown by.

The next day there was frost; but by noon the weather changed and it thawed. Soon it was spring again and the world grew green; the swallows returned to build their nests and the windows were opened. The little children sat in their boxes, above the eaves and high above all the other stories of the houses.

The roses bloomed particularly marvelously that summer. The little girl had learned a psalm in which roses were mentioned in one of the verses; her own roses reminded her of it, and so she sang, and the boy joined her:

> In the valley where the roses be
> There the child Jesus you will see.

The two little children held each other's hands, kissed the flowers, and looked up into the blessed sunshine. Oh, these were lovely summer days, and it was ever so pleasant to sit under the little rose trees that never seemed to stop flowering.

One afternoon as Kai and Gerda sat looking at a picture book

HANS CHRISTIAN ANDERSEN

with animals and flowers in it — it was exactly five o'clock, for the bells in the church tower had just struck the hour — Kai said, "Ouch, ouch! Something pricked my heart!" And then again, "Ouch, something sharp is in my eye."

The little girl put her arms around his neck and looked into his eyes but there was nothing to be seen. Still, it hurt and little Gerda cried out of sympathy.

"I think it is gone now," said Kai. But he was wrong, two of the splinters from the devil's mirror had hit him: one had entered his heart and the other his eyes. You remember the mirror, it was that horrible invention of the devil which made everything good and decent look small and ridiculous, and everything evil and foul appear grand and worthwhile. Poor Kai, soon his heart would turn to ice and his eyes would see nothing but faults in everything. But the pain, that would disappear.

"Why are you crying?" he demanded. "You look ugly when you cry. There is nothing the matter with me. Look!" he shouted. "That rose up there has been gnawed by a worm; and look at that one, it is all crooked. They are ugly roses, as ugly as the boxes they grew in." Then he kicked the sides of the box and tore off the two roses.

"What are you doing, Kai?" cried the little girl, and when Kai saw how frightened she was, he tore off yet another flower; and then climbed through the window into his parents' apartment, leaving Gerda to sit out there all alone.

Later, when she came inside with the picture book, he told her that picture books were for babies. And when Grandmother told stories he would argue with her or — which was much worse — stand behind her chair with a pair of glasses on his nose and imitate her most cruelly. He did it so accurately that people laughed. Soon he learned to mimic everyone in the whole street. He had a good eye for their little peculiarities and knew how to copy them.

Everyone said, "That boy has his head screwed on right!" But it was the splinters of glass that were in his eyes and his heart that made him behave that way; that, too, was why he teased little Gerda all the time — she who loved him with all her heart.

He did not play as he used to; now his games were more grown up. One winter day when snow was falling he brought a magnifying glass and looked at the snowflakes that were falling on his blue coat.

THE SNOW QUEEN

"Look through the glass, Gerda," he said to his little playmate; and she did. Through the magnifying glass each snowflake appeared like a flower or ten-pointed star. They were, indeed, beautiful to see.

"Aren't they marvelous?" asked Kai. "And each of them is quite perfect; they are much nicer than real flowers. They are all flawless as long as they don't melt."

A little bit later he came by, with his sled on his back, and wearing his hat and woolen gloves. He screamed into Gerda's ear as loud as he could, "I have been allowed to go down to the big square and play with the other boys!" And away he went.

Now down in the snow-covered square the most daring of the boys would tie their sleds behind the farmers' wagons. It was good fun and they would get a good ride. While they were playing, a big white sled drove into the square; the driver was clad in a white fur coat and a white fur hat. The sled circled the square twice and Kai managed to attach his little sled onto the back of the big one. He wanted to hitch a ride.

Away he went; the sled turned the corner and was out of the square. It began to go faster and faster, and Kai wanted to untie his sled, but every time he was about to do it, the driver of the big white sled turned and nodded so kindly to him that he didn't. It was as if they knew each other. Soon they were past the city gate; and the snow was falling so heavily that Kai could not see anything. He untied the rope but it made no difference, his little sled moved on as if it were tied to the big one by magic. They traveled along with the speed of the wind. Kai cried out in fear but no one heard him. The snow flew around him as he flew forward. Every so often his little sled would leap across a ditch and Kai had to hold on, in order not to fall off. He wanted to say his prayers, but all he could remember were his multiplication tables.

The snowflakes grew bigger and bigger until they looked like white hens that were running alongside him. At last the big sled stopped and its driver stood up and turned around to look at Kai. The fur hat and the coat were made of snow; the driver was a woman: how tall and straight she stood. She was the Snow Queen!

"We have driven a goodish way," she said, "but you look cold. Come, creep inside my bearskin coat."

Kai got up from his own sled and walked over to the big one, where he sat down next to the Snow Queen. She put her fur coat around him, and it felt as if he lay down in a deep snowdrift.

HANS CHRISTIAN ANDERSEN

"Are you still cold?" she asked, and kissed his forehead. Her kiss was colder than ice. It went right to his heart, which was already half made of ice. He felt as though he were about to die, but it hurt only for a minute, then it was over. Now he seemed stronger and he no longer felt how cold the air was.

"My sled, my sled, don't forget it!" he cried. And one of the white hens put it on her back and flew behind them. The Snow Queen kissed Kai once more, and then all memory of Gerda, the Grandmother, and his home disappeared.

"I shan't give you any more kisses," she said, "or I might kiss you to death."

Kai looked at the Snow Queen; he could not imagine that anyone could have a wiser or a more beautiful face; and she no longer seemed to be made of ice, as she had when he first saw her outside his window, the time she had beckoned to him. In his eyes she now seemed utterly perfect, nor did he feel any fear. He told her that he knew his multiplication tables, could figure in fractions, and knew the area in square miles of every country in Europe, and what its population was.

The Snow Queen smiled, and somehow Kai felt that he did not know enough. He looked out into the great void of the night, for by now they were flying high up in the clouds, above the earth. The storm swept on and sang its old, eternal songs. Above oceans, forests, and lakes they flew; and the cold winter wind whipped the landscape below them. Kai heard the cry of the wolves and the hoarse voice of the crows. The moon came out, and into its large and clear disk Kai stared all through the long winter night. When daytime came he fell asleep at the feet of the Snow Queen.

THE THIRD STORY: THE FLOWER GARDEN OF THE OLD WOMAN WHO KNEW MAGIC

But how did little Gerda feel when Kai did not return? She asked everyone where he had gone and none could answer. The boys who had been in the square could only tell that they had seen him tie his little sled to the back of a big white sled that had driven out of the city gate.

No one knew where he had gone and little Gerda cried long and bitterly. As time passed people began to say that he must have died; probably he had drowned in the deep, dark river that ran close to the city. It was a long and dismal winter.

THE SNOW QUEEN

Finally spring came with warm sunshine.

"Kai is dead and gone!" sighed little Gerda.

"I don't believe that," said the sunbeams.

"No, he is dead and gone," she repeated, and asked the swallows if that were not true.

"We don't believe it either," they answered; and at last little Gerda was convinced that Kai was not dead.

"I will put on my new red shoes, the ones Kai has never seen," she said one day. "And then I will go down to the river and ask it a few questions."

It was very early in the morning; she kissed the old Grandmother, who was still asleep, put on her new red shoes, and walked out through the city gate and down to the river.

"Is it true that you have taken my playmate? I will give you my new red shoes if you will give him back to me."

She thought that the little waves nodded strangely; so she took her treasure, her new red shoes, and threw them out into the river. They struck the water not far from shore, and the little waves carried them back to her. It was as if the river did not want her little shoes since it had not taken Kai. This little Gerda did not realize, she thought that she just hadn't thrown them far enough out; therefore, she climbed into a rowboat that lay among the reeds, stood up in its stern, and threw the shoes out over the water again. The boat had not been moored and, by stepping into the stern, she loosened the bow from the sand and the rowboat started to drift. Although she noticed it at once and turned around, prepared to leap up onto the bank, the boat was already several feet away from shore and she didn't dare jump.

The boat floated faster and faster downstream with the current. Poor Gerda was so frightened that she just sat down and cried. No one heard her except the sparrows and they could not carry her to shore. But they flew alongside the boat, twittering: "We are here! We are here!" to comfort her.

The boat drifted down the river. Gerda sat perfectly still; she was in her stocking feet; the shoes followed the boat but they were far behind. The landscape was beautiful on both sides of the river. Beyond the banks, which were covered with flowers, there were meadows with cows and sheep grazing upon them; but there was not a human being to be seen anywhere.

"Maybe the river will carry me to where Kai is," thought Gerda. And that thought was a great comfort and she felt much happier.

HANS CHRISTIAN ANDERSEN

For hours she sat looking at the green shores; then the boat drifted past a cherry orchard; in the middle of it stood a strange little house with blue and green windows and a straw roof. Before the doors two wooden soldiers kept guard and presented arms when a boat glided by on the river.

Little Gerda, thinking that they were alive, waved and called; but naturally they did not answer. The current of the river carried the boat to the shore, and Gerda started to shout for help as loudly as she could. An old lady came out of the house; she had on a big broad-brimmed hat with the loveliest paintings of flowers on it.

"Poor little child!" she cried when she saw Gerda. "How did you get out there on the river, all alone, and sail so far out into the wide world?" The old lady waded out till she could catch hold of the boat with her shepherd's crook and drew it into shore. Then she lifted Gerda out of the boat. The poor child was happy to be on dry land once again, but she was a little afraid of the old lady.

"Tell me who you are and how you have gotten into such a predicament," the old woman asked.

Gerda told her everything and the old lady shook her head. When Gerda asked whether she had seen little Kai, all the old lady could say was that he hadn't gone by her house but that he probably would arrive there sooner or later. She told little Gerda not to be so sad but to come and eat some of her cherries and look at her flowers. They were prettier than any picture book, and every one of them could tell a story. The old lady took Gerda by the hand, opened the door to her little house, and led her inside.

The windows were placed high up, and the colored glass gave a strange light to the room. On the table stood a bowl filled with the most delicious cherries, and Gerda ate as many of them as she could. While she ate, the old woman combed Gerda's hair with a gold comb and her hair curled prettily around her little rosebud face.

"I have longed so much for a little girl like you," said the old woman. "You just wait and see what good friends we shall become."

While her hair was being combed, Gerda began to forget her playmate Kai more and more. The old lady knew witchcraft; but she was not an evil witch, she just liked to do a little magic for her own pleasure. She wanted little Gerda to stay with her very much;

that was why she went with her shepherd's crook out into the garden and pointed it at all the rosebushes. Immediately, the sweet flowering bushes sank down into the earth and disappeared. One could not even see where they had been. Now she need not fear that when little Gerda saw the roses she would think of Kai and run away.

Then she took Gerda out into the garden and showed it to her. Oh, what a beautiful place it was! All the flowers imaginable were there; and all of them in full bloom, although they belonged to different seasons. Certainly no picture book could be as beautiful as they were. Gerda almost jumped for joy, and she played among them all day until the sun set behind the tall cherry trees. Then she was given the loveliest of beds with a red quilt stuffed with dried violets to cover herself; and there she slept, dreaming sweeter dreams than even a queen on her wedding night.

The next day she played in the warm sunshine with the flowers again; and in this manner many days went by. Gerda, at last, knew every flower in the garden, and though there were so many different kinds, there seemed to be one missing, but she did not know which it was.

One day as she was sitting looking at the old lady's grand hat, with its painted flowers, she saw among them a rose. The old woman had forgotten the one in her hat when she got rid of all the roses — that happens if you are absentminded.

"What!" exclaimed Gerda. "Are there no roses in the garden?" She ran about the garden, looking and searching, but nowhere did she find a rosebush. She felt so sad that she wept and her tears fell on the very plot of earth where a rose tree had grown. Through the earth, moistened by her tears, the tree shot upward again, blooming just as beautifully as when the old woman had made it vanish. Gerda kissed the flowers and thought of the roses at home and of little Kai.

"I have stayed here much too long," she cried. "I must find little Kai. Do you know where he is?" she asked the roses. "Do you think that he is dead?"

"No, he is not dead," answered the roses. "We have been down under the earth, where the dead are, and Kai was not there."

"Thank you," said little Gerda. She asked the other flowers if they knew where Kai was.

Every flower stood in the warm sunshine and dreamed its own

HANS CHRISTIAN ANDERSEN

fairy tale; and that it was willing to tell, but none of them knew anything about Kai.

What story did the tiger lily tell her? Here it is:

"Can you hear the drum: boom . . . boom! It has only two beats: boom . . . boom. Listen to the woman's song of lament; hear the priest chant. The Hindu wife is standing on the funeral pyre, dressed in a long red gown. Soon the flames will devour her and her husband's body. She is thinking of someone who is standing among the mourners; his eyes burn even hotter than the flames that lick her feet, his flaming eyes did burn her heart with greater heat than those flames which soon will turn her body into ashes. Can the fire of a funeral pyre extinguish the flame that burns within the heart?"

"That story I don't understand," said little Gerda.

"Well, it is my fairy tale," answered the tiger lily.

Next Gerda asked the honeysuckle; and this is what it said:

"High up above the narrow mountain road the old castle clings to the steep mountainside. Its ancient walls are covered by green ivy; the vines spread over the balcony where a beautiful young girl stands. No unplucked rose is fresher than she, no apple blossom, plucked and carried by the spring wind, is lighter or dances more daintily than she. Hear how her silk dress rustles. Will he not come soon?"

"Is that Kai you mean?" asked little Gerda.

"I tell only my own story, my own dream," answered the honeysuckle.

Now it was the little daisy's turn:

"Between two trees a swing has been hung. Two sweet little girls, with dresses as white as snow and from whose hats green ribbons hang, lazily swing back and forth. Their brother, who is older than they are, is standing up behind them on the swing. He has his arms around the ropes so that he will not fall. In one hand he has a little bowl; in the other, a clay pipe. He is blowing soap bubbles. The swing glides, and the bubbles with their ever changing colors fly through the air. The last bubble clings to the pipe, then the breeze takes it. A little black dog, which belongs to the children, stands on its hind legs barking at the bubble and it breaks. Such is my song: a swing and a world of foam."

"Your tale may be beautiful but you tell it so sadly, and you didn't mention Kai at all," complained little Gerda. "I think I will ask the hyacinth."

THE SNOW QUEEN

"There were three beautiful sisters; they were so fine and delicate that they were almost transparent. One had on a red dress; the second, a blue; and the third, a white one. They danced, hand in hand, down by the lake; but they were not elves, they were real human children. The air smelled so sweet that the girls wandered into the forest. The sweet fragrance grew stronger. Three coffins appeared; and in them lay the three beautiful sisters. They sailed across the lake, and glowworms flew through the air like little candles. Were the dancing girls asleep or were they dead? The smell of the flowers said they were corpses, the bells at vespers ring for the dead."

"Oh, you make me feel so sad," said little Gerda. "And the fragrance from your flowers is so strong that it makes me think of the poor dead girls. Is Kai dead too? The roses, who have been down under the earth, said that he wasn't."

"Ding! dong!" rang the little hyacinth bells. "We are not tolling for Kai, we do not know him. We are singing our own little song, the only one we know."

Gerda approached a little buttercup that shone so prettily between its green leaves.

"You little sun, tell me, do you know where my playmate is?" she asked.

The buttercup's little shining face looked so trustfully back at her, but it too had only its own song to sing and it was not about Kai.

"Into a little narrow yard," began the buttercup, "God's warm sun was shining; it was the first spring day of the year. The sunbeams reflected against the white walls of the neighbor's house; nearby the first little yellow flower had unfolded itself. It was golden in the sunlight; the old grandmother brought her chair outside to sit in the warm sun. Her grandchild, the poor little servant maid, had come home for a short visit. She kissed her grandmother. There was gold in that kiss: the gold of the heart. Gold in the mouth, gold on the ground, and gold in the blessed sunrise. Now that was my little story," said the buttercup.

"Oh, the poor Grandmother," sighed little Gerda. "She must be longing for me and grieving, as she did when little Kai disappeared. But I will soon go back home and bring little Kai with me. There is no point in asking any of the other flowers, each one only sings its own song."

She tied her long dress up so that she could run fast, and away she went. The narcissus hit her leg smartly when she jumped over it and Gerda stopped. "What, do you know something?" she asked, and bent down toward the flower.

"I can see myself, I can see myself," cried the narcissus. "High up in the garret lives the little ballerina; she stands on tiptoe and kicks at the world, for it is but a mirage. She pours a little water from the kettle on a piece of cloth; it is her corset that she is washing, for cleanliness is next to godliness. Her white dress is hanging in the corner; it has also been washed in the teakettle, then it was hung out on the roof to dry. Now she puts it on, and around her neck she ties a saffron-colored kerchief; it makes the dress seem even whiter. She lifts one leg high in the air. She is bending her stem. I can see myself! I can see myself!"

"I don't care either to see you or to hear about you," said Gerda angrily. "Your story is a silly story," and with those words she ran to the other end of the garden.

The door in the wall was closed; she turned the old rusty handle and it sprang open. Out went little Gerda, in her bare feet, out into the wide world. Three times she turned to look back but no one seemed to have noticed her flight.

At last she could not run any farther, and she sat down on a big stone to rest. She looked at the landscape; summer was long since over, it was late fall. Back in the old lady's garden, you could not notice the change in seasons, for it was always summer and the flowers of every season were in bloom.

"Goodness me, how much time I have wasted," sighed Gerda. "It is already autumn, I do not dare rest any longer," and she got up and walked on. Her little feet hurt and she was tired. The leaves of the willow tree were all yellow, the water from the cold, fall mist dripped from it, as its leaves fell one by one. Only the blackthorn bush bore fruits now, and they are bitter. Oh, how somber and gray seemed the wide world.

THE FOURTH STORY, IN WHICH APPEAR A PRINCE AND A PRINCESS

More and more often did Gerda have to rest. The ground was now covered with snow. A big crow landed near her; the bird sat there a long time, wriggling its head and looking at her. "Caw . . . Caw!" he remarked, which in crow language means "Good day." He was kind, and asked the girl why she was out all alone in the lonely winter world.

The word "alone" Gerda understood only too well; and she told the crow her story and asked him if he had seen little Kai.

The crow nodded most thoughtfully and said, "Maybe, maybe!"

"Oh, he is alive!" screamed little Gerda, and almost squeezed the poor bird to death, while she kissed him.

"Be sensible, be sensible," protested the crow. "It may be little Kai I have seen; but if it is, then I am afraid he has forgotten you for the sake of the princess."

"Does he live with a princess?" asked little Gerda.

"Yes, he does," answered the crow, "but are you sure you don't understand crow language? I much prefer speaking it."

"No, I have never learned it; but Grandmother knows it, I wish now that she had taught it to me."

"Never mind, it can't be helped," said the crow. "I shall do my best, which is a lot more than most people do," and the crow told Gerda all that he knew:

"Now in this kingdom, where we are at present, there lives a princess who is immensely clever; she has read all the newspapers in the whole world and forgotten what was written in them, and that is the part that proves how intelligent she is. A few weeks ago, while she was sitting on the throne — and that, people say, is not such an amusing place to sit — she happened to hum a song which has as its chorus the line 'Why shouldn't I get married?'

" 'Why not, indeed?' thought the princess. 'But if I am to get married it must be to a man who can speak up for himself.' She didn't want anyone who just stood about looking distinguished, for such a fellow is boring. She called all her ladies in waiting and told them of her intention. They clapped their hands, and one of them said, 'Oh, how delightful. I had such an idea myself just the other day.' . . . Believe me, everything I tell you is true," declared the crow. "My fiancée is tame, she has the run of the castle and it is from her I got the story." His fiancée was, naturally, another crow, for birds of a feather flock together.

"The newspapers were printed with a border of hearts and the princess' name on the front page. Inside there was a royal proclamation: any good-looking man, regardless of birth, could come to the castle and speak with the princess, and the one who seemed most at home there and spoke the best, she would marry.

"Believe me," said the crow, and shook his head, "as sure as I am sitting here, that proclamation got people out of their houses. They came thick and fast, you have never seen such a crowd. But neither the first nor the second day did the princess find anyone who pleased her. They could all speak well enough as long as they were standing in the street; but as soon as they had entered the castle gates and saw the royal guards, in their silver uniforms, the young men lost their tongues. They didn't get them back, either, when they had to climb the marble stairs, lined with lackeys dressed in gold; or when they finally arrived in the grand hall with the great chandeliers and had to stand in front of the throne on which the princess sat. All they could do was repeat whatever she said; and that she didn't want to hear once more. One should think every one of them had had his tummy filled with snuff or had fallen into a trance. But as soon as they were down in the streets again they got their tongues back, and all they could do was talk.

"There was a queue, so long that it stretched from beyond the city gate all the way up to the castle. I flew into town to have a look at it. Most of the men got both hungry and thirsty while they waited; the princess didn't even offer them a glass of lukewarm water. Some of the more clever ones had brought sandwiches, but they didn't offer any to their neighbors, for they thought: 'Let him look hungry and the princess won't take him.'"

"But Kai! What about Kai?" asked Gerda. "Did he stand in the queue too?"

"Don't be impatient. We are coming to him. Now the third day a little fellow arrived, he didn't have a carriage nor did he come on horseback. No, he came walking straight up to the castle. He was poorly dressed but had bright shining eyes like yours, and the most beautiful long hair."

"That is Kai!" shouted little Gerda, and clapped her hands in joy.

"He had a little knapsack on his back," continued the crow.

"It wasn't a knapsack," interrupted Gerda. "It was his sled."

"Sled or knapsack, it doesn't matter much," said the crow. "I didn't look too closely at him. But this I know from my fiancée: when he entered the castle and saw the royal guards and all the lackeys, they didn't make him the least bit fainthearted. He nodded kindly to them and said, 'It must be boring to spend your life

THE SNOW QUEEN

waiting on the stairs, I think I will go inside.' The big hall with its lighted candelabra, its servants carrying golden bowls, while courtiers stood around dressed in their very best, was impressive enough to take away the courage of even the bravest — and, on top of all that, the young man's boots squeaked something wicked — but he did not seem to notice either the elegant hall or his noisy boots."

"It must be Kai," said Gerda. "His boots were new and I know they squeaked, I have heard them myself."

"Well, squeak they did," said the crow. "But he walked right up to the princess, who was sitting on a pearl as big as a spinning wheel. Behind her stood all her ladies in waiting with their maids and their maids' maids; and all the gentlemen of the court with their servants and their servants' servants, each of whom, in turn, kept a boy. And the servant's servant's boy, who stood next to the door, always wore slippers and was so proud that one hardly dared look at him!"

"It must have been horrible!" Little Gerda shook her head. "But Kai got the princess anyway?"

"If I hadn't been a crow, I would have taken her and that even though I am engaged. My fiancée tells me that he talks as well as I do when I talk crow language. He said that he hadn't come to propose marriage but only to find out whether she was as clever as everybody said she was. He was satisfied that what he heard was true; and the princess was satisfied with him."

"I am sure it was Kai, for he is so clever, he can figure in fractions. Won't you take me to the castle?"

"That is easier said than done," said the crow, and looked thoughtfully at Gerda. "I will talk to my fiancée about it, she might know how we can do it. For I can tell you, it is not easy for a poor little girl like you to get into the castle."

"But I will get in!" protested Gerda. "As soon as Kai hears that I am here he will come and fetch me himself."

"Wait here by the big stone," commanded the crow, wriggled his head, and flew away.

The crow didn't return before dusk. "Caw! Caw!" he said, and alighted on the stone. "I bring you greetings from my fiancée, she sends you this little piece of bread. She took it in the kitchen where there is bread enough, and you must be hungry. It is quite impossible for you to enter the castle. You have bare feet; the guards in their silver uniforms and the lackeys in their golden ones won't allow it. But don't weep, we will get you in anyway. My fiancée knows where the key is kept to the back stairs, and they lead right up to the royal bedchamber."

They entered the royal garden and watched the lights in the castle being extinguished, one by one. At last the crow led her to a little door in the rear of the castle that was half open. Little Gerda's heart beat both with fear and with longing; she felt as though she were doing something wrong; and yet all she wanted to do was to see whether it was little Kai who had won the princess. She was sure it must be he.

In her mind she saw his lively, clever eyes, his long hair; he was smiling as he did when they sat under the little rose trees at home. He would be happy to see her, and she would tell him of the long journey she had made for his sake. She would tell him, too, how sad everyone had become because he was gone, and how they all had missed him. She felt so happy and so fearful.

They had reached the stairs; a little lamp burned on a chest. In the middle of the floor stood a tame crow, twisting its head about and looking at her quizzically. Gerda curtsied as Grandmother had taught her to do.

"My fiancé has told me so many nice things about you. He has narrated your *vita* as it is called, I have found the story most touching! Will you take the lamp and I shall walk ahead and show the way."

"I think someone is coming," whispered Gerda. There was a whirling, rushing sound; and on the wall were strange shadows of horses with flying manes, dogs and falcons, servants and hunters.

"Oh, they are only dreams," said the crow. "They have come to fetch their royal masters. That is only lucky for us; the easier it will be for you to have a good look at them while they are sleeping. But remember, when you gain honor and position, to be grateful and not forget those who helped you get it."

"That is no way to talk," grumbled the crow from the woods.

Now they entered the first of the great halls. The walls were covered with pink satin and decorated with artificial flowers. The shadows of the dreams reappeared, but they flew past so quickly that Gerda did not even get a chance to see whether Kai was mounted on one of the horses. Each hall they passed through was more magnificent than the one before it. At last they came to the

royal bedchamber. The ceiling looked like the top of a large palm tree with glass leaves; from the center of it eight ropes of pure gold hung down, attached to them were the two little beds that the royal couple slept in. Each bed was shaped like a lily; in the white lily slept the princess, and in the red lily the young man who had won her. Gerda peeped into it and saw a head of long brown hair. "It is Kai!" she shouted in her joy. The dreams returned as fast as the wind and the young boy awoke.

He wasn't little Kai!

It was only the long brown hair they had in common, although he was young and handsome too. From the white lily bed the princess raised her head and asked what the commotion was about. Poor Gerda started to cry; and then between sobs, she told her story and explained how the crows had helped her.

"You poor thing!" said the prince. The princess said the same, and they did not scold the crows, on the contrary they praised them; although they warned them not to do it again. Still, they were to have a reward.

"Would you rather be free," asked the princess, "or receive permanent positions as royal court crows, with permission to eat all leftovers?"

Both the crows curtsied and said they preferred permanent positions. After all, they had to think of their old age. "To be secure is better than to fly," they said.

The prince got out of his bed and let Gerda sleep in it; he could hardly do more. She folded her little hands and thought, "How good all animals and human beings are." Then she closed her eyes and slept. This time the dreams looked like little angels. One of them was drawing a sled behind her; and on it sat little Kai; and he nodded to Gerda. But that was only a dream and it was gone as soon as she awoke.

In the morning Gerda was dressed from head to toe in silk and velvet; and the little prince and princess begged her to stay with them. But she asked only for a little carriage and a horse and some boots, so that she could continue on her journey out in the wide world to find Kai.

She was given not only new boots but a muff as well, and good warm clothes. When she was ready to leave, a fine carriage of the purest gold drove up in front of the castle. The coat of arms of the princess was on the door, and not only was there a coachman to

THE SNOW QUEEN

drive her, but a servant stood on the back of the carriage and two little soldiers rode in front. The prince and the princess themselves helped her into the carriage and wished her luck. Her friend, the crow from the woods, drove with her the first couple of miles. They sat beside each other, for the crow got sick if he had to ride sitting backward. The other crow stood at the gate and flapped her wings; she had had a headache since she had been given a permanent position, and besides, she had overeaten. The carriage was lined with candy, and on the seat across from Gerda was a basket of fruit.

"Good-by, good-by!" shouted the little prince and princess; and Gerda wept, for she had grown fond of them, and the crow wept too. When they had driven a little way the crow said good-by, and that was even harder to bear. He flew up into a tall tree and sat there waving with his black wings until he could no longer see the carriage that glistened as though it were made of sunlight.

THE FIFTH STORY, WHICH IS ABOUT THE ROBBER GIRL

They were driving through a great dark forest, and the golden carriage shone like a flame right in the robbers' eyes, and they couldn't bear it.

"Gold! Gold!" they screamed as they came rushing out of the woods. They grabbed hold of the horses and killed the coachman, the servant, and the soldiers; then they dragged little Gerda out of the carriage.

"She is lovely and fat, I bet she has been fed on nuts," said an old robber woman; she had a beard and eyebrows so big and bushy that they almost hid her eyes. "She will taste as good as a lamb," and the robber woman took a long shining knife from her belt; it was horrible to look at.

"Ouch!" screamed the old hag, for just at that moment she had been bitten in the ear by her own little daughter, whom she carried on her back. The child was such a wild and naughty creature that it was a marvel. "Ouch!" the woman cried again, and missed her chance to kill Gerda.

"The girl is to play with me!" declared the little robber girl. "But she is to give me her muff and her dress and sleep in my bed with me." And just to make certain that her mother had understood her, she bit her again as hard as she could.

The robber woman turned and jumped into the air from the pain; and all the robbers laughed and said, "Look how she dances with her brat."

"I want to drive in the carriage," cried the little robber girl, and she was allowed to, for she was terribly spoiled. She and Gerda sat inside the carriage while it was being driven along little paths that brought it deeper and deeper into the forest. The little robber girl was as tall as Gerda but much stronger, and her skin had been tanned by the sun. Her eyes were almost black and looked sad. She put her arms around Gerda and said, "I won't allow them to kill you, so long as you don't make me angry. You must be a princess?"

"No, I am not," answered Gerda, and then she told her whole story and how much she loved little Kai.

The robber girl looked very seriously at her, nodded her head, and said: "I won't allow them to kill you even if I do get angry at you, I will do it myself." Then she dried Gerda's eyes and put her own hands inside the warm soft muff.

At last the carriage stopped; they had come to the robber castle. The walls were cracked and the windows were broken. Crows and ravens flew in and out of the big holes in the tower. Big dogs ran about in the courtyard; they looked ferocious enough to be able to eat human beings; they sprang up in the air but they didn't bark, that wasn't allowed.

In the middle of the great hall a fire burned. The smoke drifted up among the blackened rafters; how it ever got out was its own business. A big copper kettle filled with soup hung over the fire, and next to it, on spits, hares and rabbits were being roasted.

"You are going to sleep with me, over here among all my little pet animals," said the little robber girl, and dragged Gerda over to a corner of the hall, where there lay some straw and some blankets. Above them, on poles, sat about a hundred doves; they were asleep, but a couple opened their eyes and turned their heads when the little girls came.

"They are all mine," said the girl, and grabbed one of them by its legs. The dove flapped its wings. "Kiss it," demanded the robber girl, and shoved the frightened bird right up into Gerda's face.

"Up there are two wood pigeons," the robber girl explained as she pointed to a recess in the wall, high above them, that had been turned into a cage by a few wooden bars. "They would fly away if they could, but they can't."

"Here is my old sweetheart, bah!" She took hold of the antlers of a reindeer that stood tied near her bed and gave them a hard pull. "One has got to hold onto him too, or he would leap away. Every evening I tickle his throat with my sharp knife, that frightens him." The little girl pulled a knife out from a crack in the wall and let its sharp point glide around the reindeer's neck; the animal backed as far away as it could, in terror. That made the little robber girl laugh; and she pulled Gerda down into her bed.

"Do you sleep with your knife?" asked Gerda, frightened.

"I always sleep with the knife," answered the little robber girl. "One never knows what might happen. But tell me again the story of little Kai and why you have gone out into the wide world." Gerda told her story once more, and the wood pigeons, up in their cage, cooed; the doves were all asleep. The little robber girl put one of her arms around Gerda — in her other hand, she kept her knife — and fell asleep. She snored loudly.

Poor Gerda didn't dare close her eyes; she didn't know whether she was going to live or die. The robbers all sat around the fire and sang while they drank. The little girl's mother was so drunk that she turned a somersault. Oh, it was a pretty sight for a little girl to see!

Suddenly one of the wood pigeons cooed, "We have seen little Kai. A white hen carried his sled. He sat in the Snow Queen's sled when she flew low over the forest. We had just come out of our eggs and she breathed on us; all the other young ones died. We, alone, survived. Coo! Coo!"

"What is it you are saying?" cried Gerda. "Where was the Snow Queen going? Do you know?"

"I suppose she went to Lapland, where there always are snow and ice, but ask the reindeer that stands tied by your bed."

"Oh yes, ice and snow are always there; it is a blessed place," sighed the reindeer. "There one can jump and run about freely in the great, glittering valleys. The Snow Queen keeps a summer tent there, but her castle is far to the north, near the pole, on an island called Spitsbergen."

"Oh, Kai, little Kai!" mumbled Gerda.

"Lie still," commanded the robber girl, "or I will slit open your stomach!"

In the morning Gerda told her what she had heard from the wood pigeons. The little robber girl looked quite solemn, then nodded her head and said, "I am sure it is he, I am sure." Then she turned to the reindeer and asked him if he knew where Lapland was.

"Who should know that better than I?" answered the poor animal. "There I was born, there I have run across the great snow fields." And his eyes gleamed, recollecting what he had lost.

"Listen," whispered the little robber girl to Gerda. "All the men are gone. Only Mama is here and she won't leave; but in a little while she will take a drink from the big bottle and then she will take a nap. And then . . . I will help you!"

She jumped out of bed, ran over and threw her arms around her mother, pulled her beard, and yelled, "Oh, my own sweet billy goat, good morning!"

The mother tweaked her daughter's nose, so that it turned both red and blue, but it was all done out of love.

When the mother had drunk from the big bottle, she lay down for her midmorning nap; then the robber girl spoke to the reindeer: "I would have loved to tickle your throat for many a day yet, for you look so funny when I do it. But never mind, I will let you loose so that you can run back to Lapland; but you are to take the little girl with you and bring her to the Snow Queen's palace where her playmate is. I know you have heard everything she said, for you are always eavesdropping."

The reindeer leaped into the air out of pure joy. The robber's daughter lifted Gerda up on the animal's back and tied her on so she wouldn't fall off; and she even gave her a little pillow to sit on. "I don't really care about your boots, you need them," she said. "It is cold where you are going. But the muff I am keeping, for it is so soft and nice. But you shan't freeze, I will give you my mother's great big mittens; they will keep you warm all the way up to your elbows. Here, put them on! Now your hands look as ugly as my mother's."

Gerda cried from happiness and relief.

"I don't like all your tears," scolded the little robber girl. "You should look happy now. Here are two loaves of bread and a ham, so you won't go hungry," she said as she tied the bread and the ham on the back of the reindeer; then she opened the door and called all the big dogs in. She cut the rope that tethered the reindeer and said in parting, "Run along, but take good care of the little girl!"

Gerda waved good-by with her great big mittens, and away they

THE SNOW QUEEN

went, through the forest and across the great plains, as fast as they could. They heard the wolves howl and the ravens cry; and suddenly the sky was all filled with light.

"There are the old northern lights," said the reindeer. "Look how they shine!"

Still they went on both day and night: farther and farther north.

The bread was eaten and the ham was eaten; and then they were in Lapland.

THE SIXTH STORY: THE LAPP WOMAN AND THE
FINNISH WOMAN

They stopped before a little cottage; it was a wretched little hovel: the roof went all the way down to the ground and the doorway was so low that you had to creep through it on all fours. The only person at home was an old Lapp woman who was busy frying some fish over an oil lamp. The reindeer told her Gerda's story; but first he had told his own, because he thought that was more interesting. Poor Gerda was so cold that she couldn't even talk.

"Oh, you poor things!" said the Lapp woman. "You have far to go yet. It is more than a hundred miles from here to the camp of the Snow Queen. She amuses herself by shooting fireworks off every night. I shall give you an introduction to the Finnish woman who lives up there. She knows more about it all than I do and will be able to help you. Paper I have none of, so I will write on a dried codfish."

When little Gerda had eaten and was warm again, the Lapp woman wrote a few words on a dried codfish and told Gerda not to lose it. Then she tied her on the reindeer's back again and away they ran.

Whish . . . Whish . . . it said up in the sky as the northern lights flickered and flared; they were the Snow Queen's fireworks. At last they came to the Finnish woman's house; they had to knock on the chimney, for the door was so small that they couldn't find it.

Goodness me, it was hot inside! The Finnish woman walked around almost naked. She pulled off both Gerda's boots and her mittens so that the heat would not be unbearable for her. The reindeer got a piece of ice to put on its head. Then the Finnish woman read what was written on the codfish; she read it three times and then she knew it by heart. The fish she put in the pot that was boiling over the fire. It could be eaten, and she never wasted anything. The reindeer told first of his own adventures and then of Gerda's. The Finnish woman squinted her intelligent eyes but didn't utter a word.

"You are so clever," said the reindeer finally. "I know you can tie all the winds of the world into four knots on a single thread. If the sailor loosens the first knot he gets a fair wind; if he loosens the second a strong breeze; but if he loosens the third and the fourth knots, then there's such a storm that the trees in the forest are torn up by the roots. Won't you give this little girl a magic drink so that she gains the strength of twelve men and can conquer the Snow Queen?"

"The strength of twelve men," laughed the Finnish woman. "Yes, I should think that would be enough." Then she walked over to a shelf and took down a roll of skin which she spread out on the table. Strange words were written there, and the Finnish woman read and studied till the perspiration ran down her forehead.

The reindeer begged her again to help little Gerda; and Gerda looked up at her with eyes filled with tears. The Finnish woman winked, then drew the reindeer into a corner, where she whispered to him while she gave him another piece of ice for his head.

"Little Kai is in the Snow Queen's palace and is quite satisfied with being there; he thinks it is the best place in the whole world. This is because he has gotten a sliver of glass in his heart and two grains of the same in his eyes. As long as they are there he will never be human again, and the Snow Queen will keep her power over him."

"But can't you give Gerda some kind of power so that she can take out the glass?" asked the reindeer.

"I can't give her any more power than she already has! Don't you understand how great it is? Don't you see how men and animals must serve her; how else could she have come so far, walking on her bare feet? But she must never learn of her power; it is in her heart, for she is a sweet and innocent child. If she herself cannot get into the Snow Queen's palace and free Kai from the glass splinters in his eyes and his heart, how can we help her? Two miles from here begin the gardens of the Snow Queen. Carry Gerda there and set her down by the bush with the red berries, then come right back here and don't stand about gossiping." The Finnish woman lifted Gerda back on the reindeer's back, and he ran as fast as he could.

THE SNOW QUEEN

"I don't have my boots on, and I forgot the mittens," cried Gerda when she felt the cold making her naked feet smart. But the reindeer did not dare return. He ran on until he came to the bush with the red berries. There he put Gerda down and kissed her on her mouth; two tears ran down the animal's cheeks; then he leaped and ran back to the Finnish woman.

There stood poor Gerda, barefooted and without mittens on, in the intense arctic cold. She entered the Snow Queen's garden and ran in the direction of the palace. A whole regiment of snowflakes advanced against her. They had not fallen from the sky, for that was cloudless and illuminated by northern lights. The snowflakes flew just above the snow-covered earth; and as they came nearer they grew in size. Gerda remembered how they had looked when seen through a magnifying glass, but these were even bigger and horrible to look at. They were the Snow Queen's guard. And what strange creatures they were! Some of them looked like ugly little porcupines, others like bunches of snakes all twisted together, and some like little bears with bristly fur. All of the snowflakes were brilliantly white and terribly alive.

Little Gerda stopped and said her prayers. It was so cold that she could see her own breath; it came like a fine white smoke from her mouth, then it became more and more solid and formed itself into little angels that grew as soon as they touched the ground; all of them had helmets on their heads and shields and spears in their hands. When Gerda had finished saying her prayers a whole legion of little angels stood around her. They threw their spears at the snow monsters, and they splintered into hundreds of pieces. Little Gerda walked on unafraid, and the angels caressed her little feet and hands so she did not feel the cold.

But now we must hear what happened to little Kai. He was not thinking of Gerda — and even if he had been, he could not have imagined that she could be standing right outside the palace.

THE SEVENTH STORY: WHAT HAPPENED IN THE SNOW QUEEN'S PALACE AND AFTERWARD

The walls of the palace were made of snow, and the windows and doors of the sharp winds; it contained more than a hundred halls, and the largest several miles long. All were lighted by the sharp glare of the northern lights; they were huge, empty, and terrifyingly cold. Here no one had ever gathered for a bit of innocent fun;

HANS CHRISTIAN ANDERSEN

not even a dance for polar bears, where they might have walked on their hind legs in the manner of man and the wind could have produced the music. No one had ever been invited in for a little game of cards, with something good to eat and a bit of not too malicious gossip; nor had there ever been a tea party for young white lady foxes. No, empty, vast, and cold was the Snow Queen's palace.

The northern lights burned so precisely that you could tell to the very second when they would be at their highest and their lowest points. In the middle of that enormous snow hall was a frozen lake. It had cracked into thousands of pieces and every one of them was shaped exactly like all the others. In the middle of the lake was the throne of the Snow Queen. Here she sat when she was at home. She called the lake the Mirror of Reason, and declared that it was the finest and only mirror in the world.

Little Kai was blue — indeed, almost black — from the cold; but he did not feel it, for the Snow Queen had kissed all feeling of coldness out of him, and his heart had almost turned into a lump of ice. He sat arranging and rearranging pieces of ice into patterns. He called this the Game of Reason; and because of the splinters in his eyes, he thought that what he was doing was of great importance, although it was no different from playing with wooden blocks, which he had done when he could hardly talk.

He wanted to put the pieces of ice together in such a way that they formed a certain word, but he could not remember exactly what that word was. The word that he could not remember was "eternity." The Snow Queen had told him that if he could place the pieces of ice so that they spelled that word, then he would be his own master and she would give him the whole world and a new pair of skates; but, however much he tried, he couldn't do it.

"I am going to the warm countries," the Snow Queen had announced that morning. "I want to look into the boiling black pots." By "black pots," she meant the volcanoes, Vesuvius and Etna. "I will chalk their peaks a bit. It will do them good to be refreshed; ice is pleasant as a dessert after oranges and lemons."

The Snow Queen flew away and Kai was left alone in the endless hall. He sat pondering his patterns of ice, thinking and thinking; he sat so still one might have believed that he was frozen to death.

Little Gerda entered the castle. The winds began to whip her face, and could have cut it, but she said her prayers and they lay

THE SNOW QUEEN

down to sleep. She came into the vast, empty, cold hall; then she saw Kai!

She recognized him right away, and ran up to him and threw her arms around him, while she exclaimed jubilantly: "Kai, sweet little Kai. At last I have found you."

But Kai sat still and stiff and cold; then little Gerda cried and her tears fell on Kai's breast. The warmth penetrated to his heart and melted both the ice and the glass splinter in it. He looked at her and she sang the psalm they had once sung together:

> Our roses bloom and fade away,
> Our infant Lord abides alway.
> May we be blessed his face to see
> And ever little children be.

Kai burst into tears and wept so much that the grains of glass in his eyes were washed away. Now he remembered her and shouted joyfully: "Gerda! Sweet little Gerda, where have you been so long? And where have I been?" Kai looked about him. "How cold it is, how empty, and how huge!" And he held onto Gerda, who was so happy that she was both laughing and crying at the same time. It was so blessed, so happy a moment that even the pieces of ice felt it and started to dance; and when they grew tired they lay down and formed exactly that word for which the Snow Queen had promised Kai the whole world and a new pair of skates.

Gerda kissed him on his cheeks and the color came back to them. She kissed his eyes and they became like hers. She kissed his hands and feet, and the blue color left them and the blood pulsed again through his veins. He was well and strong. Now the Snow Queen could return, it did not matter, for his right to his freedom was written in brilliant pieces of ice.

They took each other by the hand and walked out of the great palace. They talked of Grandmother, and the roses that bloomed on the roof at home. The winds were still; and as they walked, the sun broke through the clouds. When they reached the bush with the red berries the reindeer was waiting there for them. He had brought another young reindeer with him and her udder was bursting with milk. The two children drank from it and the reindeer kissed them. Then they rode on the backs of the reindeer to the home of the Finnish woman, where they got warm, were given a good meal and instructions for the homeward journey.

HANS CHRISTIAN ANDERSEN

They visited the Lapp woman. She had sewn warm clothes for them and was getting her sled ready.

The two reindeer accompanied them to the border of Lapland. There the green grass started to break through the snow and they could not use the sled any longer. They said good-by to the reindeer and to the Lapp woman. Soon they heard the twitter of the first birds of spring and in the woods the trees were budding.

They met a young girl wearing a red hat and riding a magnificent horse. Gerda recognized the animal, for it was one of the horses that had drawn her golden carriage. The girl had two pistols stuck in her belt; she was the little robber girl, who had got tired of staying at home and now was on her way out into the wide world. She recognized Gerda immediately and the two of them were so happy to see each other.

"You are a fine one," she said to Kai, "running about as you did. I wonder if you are worth going to the end of the world for?" Gerda touched her cheek and asked her if she knew what had happened to the prince and the princess. "They have gone traveling in foreign lands," answered the robber girl.

"And what about the crow?"

"The crow is dead," said the girl. "His tame fiancée has become a widow, she wears a black wool thread around her leg. She thinks mourning becomes her, but it is all nonsense. But tell me what happened to you and how you managed to find him!"

And both Gerda and Kai told her everything that had happened to them.

"Well, the end was as good as the beginning," said the robber girl, and took each of them by the hand and promised that if she ever came through the town where they lived she would come and visit them. Then she rode away out into the world; and Kai and Gerda walked hand in hand homeward.

It was really spring. In the ditches the little wild flowers bloomed. The churchbells were ringing. Now they recognized the towers; they were approaching their own city and the home they had left behind.

Soon they were walking up the worn steps of the staircase to the old Grandmother's apartment. Nothing inside it had changed. The clock said: "Tick-tack . . ." and the wheels moved. But as they stepped through the doorway they realized that they had grown: they were no longer children.

THE SNOW QUEEN

The roses were blooming in the wooden boxes and the window was open. There were the little stools they used to sit on. Still holding each other's hands, they sat down, and all memory of the Snow Queen's palace and its hollow splendor disappeared. The Grandmother sat in the warm sunshine, reading aloud from her Bible: *"Whosoever shall not receive the Kingdom of Heaven as a little child shall not enter therein."*

Kai and Gerda looked into each other's eyes and now they understood the words from the psalm.

> Our roses bloom and fade away,
> Our infant Lord abides alway.
> May we be blessed his face to see
> And ever little children be.

There they sat, the two of them, grownups; and yet in their hearts children, and it was summer: a warm glorious summer day!

FAIRY TALES

HANS CHRISTIAN ANDERSEN

From the limited edition collection,
The Collected Stories of
The World's Greatest Writers

THE FRANKLIN LIBRARY

To our subscribers—

The fairy tales and stories collected here have become so much a part of our lives that we tend to forget that their creator, Hans Christian Andersen, was a real man who died just a century ago. Like Aesop or Rabelais, Andersen seems now like a fictional creation himself, a storyteller whose fabled existence served primarily as a vehicle for his creations.

Because fairy tales strike so deeply to the roots of our unconscious, there is the tendency to see them as something other than works of art, but Andersen's stories have survived precisely because they are consummate works of art, small jewel-like creations that strike universally responsive chords.

The body of work represented in your Franklin Library collection of Hans Christian Andersen's *Fairy Tales* goes beyond the traditionally constructed fairy tale into realms of imagination that are often as unresolved and nightmarish as any of the anxiety-ridden fiction of the last fifty years.

This is a comprehensive collection of tales by one of the great masters of modern literature, as well as a fantastic voyage into the enchanted world of black forests, beautiful princesses, wicked witches, steadfast tin soldiers, talking darning needles and the hauntingly beautiful wild swans.

The Editors

A universal literature to free the imagination

Perhaps there are those who find fairy tales childish, or who insist that the fairy tale is not viable in a modern society, that it is rooted in feudalism and a belief in magic. But the true test of viability is a simple one: if a tale is enjoyed by its readers, then it will live. And no modern author has given more pleasure than the great Hans Christian Andersen.

To read the tales included in this collection—"The Ugly Duckling," "The Red Shoes," "The Snow Queen," "The Wild Swans" to name but just a few—is to recapture the feeling of delight that we first experienced as children when we sat on the laps of our parents or grandparents and encountered the assorted horrors and joys that a fairy tale can stir in the imagination. While there is no arguing the fact that a very specific aspect of a fairy tale is directed at children and has to do with instructing them morally, the greater artistic impact of a fairy tale is on the imagination.

Fairy tales are celebrations of a free imagination. In the tradition of folklore, "fairy" stories are the collective imaginative work of a people, expressing their need for an exemplary hero, for a definition of right and wrong, for a celebration of beauty. Hans Christian Andersen may have been among the first to take the fairy tale as a literary form and to invent new ones. A few of his tales, such as "The Wild Swans" and "The Tinder Box," are reworkings of folk material, but the great majority are products of his incredibly vivid and fertile imagination.

4

Hans Christian Andersen was a talented and original artist as well as a great writer. Besides his pen sketches and paper cutting (the elaborate paper cutting above incorporates many of his familiar themes), he created several works of collage at least fifty years before collage was "discovered" by the cubists as a modernist technique. *Hans Christian Andersen: The Story of his Life and Work*, Phaidon Press.

A very special storyteller

Hans Christian Andersen was marked from the beginning as a special person. The son of humble parents, he was a boy of rare talents and obvious artistic destiny. Like so many gifted people, he was sensitive and often troubled. His special qualities isolated him from other children and made him seem odd, but it was his parents' great strength that they never sought to make Hans Christian conform. At the age of fourteen, he left his native town of Odense for the capital city of Copenhagen, where he was determined to make his name with the Royal Theater. He achieved little success in the performing arts, however, and gradually became totally absorbed with his writing.

His first published works were conventional narratives and it was not until he reached his thirties that he offhandedly became involved with the writing of fairy stories. His first volume of stories, which included "The Tinder Box," "Little Claus and Big Claus," "The Princess and the Pea" and "Little Ida's Flowers," was an auspicious event to many people but not to Andersen himself. In a letter to a friend, he wrote: "I have also written some fairy tales for children, and Ørsted [a world-famous Danish physicist and a great comrade of Andersen's] says that the fairy tales will make me immortal, for they are the most perfect of all my writings; but I myself do not think so."

Six months later, the second volume of fairy tales was published, including "Inchelina" (also known as "Thumbelina"). Although reviewers at the time advised

Andersen to stay away from this foolish stuff and return to "serious" work, it was now becoming apparent to the author that he had found the form of expression for which he had been searching so tirelessly.

The spirit of a nation

By 1837, Andersen had published some of his most famous tales, including "The Emperor's New Clothes" and "The Little Mermaid." The latter was a favorite of the author's, who found it the only one of his works thus far that had affected him while he was writing it. "The Little Mermaid" also became an immediate folk-heroine for the Danish people. It is easy to see why, for this early story contains all the grace, wit and humanity that characterizes Andersen's body of work.

"The Little Mermaid," which like all fairy tales deals essentially with the mortal combat between good and evil, is a creation of amazing clarity. In it, Andersen depicts an undersea world in which status is measured by the number of oyster shells one wears on one's tail. In all of his fairy stories, Andersen uses a technique whose transparency does not in any way make it obvious. The detailed description of unreal, fantastical things renders them real and identifiable: the mer-king's palace has "walls made of coral, and the long pointed windows of the clearest amber; but the roof is made of cockleshells that open and shut with the current." We can see this palace, with its swirling aqueous lines, and we can see Andersen as the architect of the fantastic—planning, measuring and constructing a real and proper environment for his imaginary spirits to inhabit.

7

Although Danes of all classes responded to Andersen's tales with great enthusiasm and affection, as well as national pride (as when they had the famous statue of Andersen's "Little Mermaid" placed in Copenhagen harbor, above), it wasn't until he had gained worldwide attention and acceptance that he was finally appreciated in his homeland as the great writer he was. Culver Pictures.

As exquisitely shaded as it is, "The Little Mermaid" also has a story line that is thoroughly absorbing. Like many of Andersen's stories, it is a Christian tale of goodness, unselfish love, sacrifice and redemption. And it is a tragic yet ultimately hopeful story, a story which so stirred the Danish people that they turned the heroine into their national symbol, erecting the famous statue in the Copenhagen harbor as a tribute to Andersen. One can see why this story spoke so strongly to the Danes with their love of the sea, their roots in Norse mythology and their Christianity; but it is interesting to examine briefly the ways in which fairy tales are designed to speak to all people throughout the world, and how profoundly they affect our behavior and growth.

"The life of the psyche"

W. H. Auden, in an essay on Andersen and the Grimm brothers, wrote: "Broadly speaking, and in most cases, the fairy tale is a dramatic projection in symbolic images of the life of the psyche." Fairy tales, as products of a collective unconscious, cut across the spectrum from high-to-lowbrow in their appeal, and their meanings cannot be exhausted by any one analysis. The fairy tale is also easily translated from one culture to another: thus Cinderella, which was first written down in China during the 9th century, could be reworked by the Grimms in the early 19th century and then turn up again during the 20th century in various popular entertainments, e.g. *Ella Cinders* and even *My Fair Lady* to some extent.

The successful fairy tale survives for two reasons: it answers crucial questions and it delights as a work of art. The questions that children face—how to gain a feeling of selfhood and self-worth, how to relinquish dependencies, how to overcome sibling rivalries and oedipal dilemmas—are the stuff of fairy tales. The distinguished child psychologist Bruno Bettelheim, in his study of fairy tales entitled *The Uses of Enchantment*, writes: "nothing can be as enriching and satisfying to child and adult alike as the folk fairy tale . . . more can be learned from them about the inner problems of human beings, and of the right solutions to their predicament in any society, than from any other type of story within a child's comprehension." Thus, fairy tales deal with the most difficult issues in an often brutally honest way, but with the ultimate message that adversity can be met and conquered by perseverance.

"The whole world and a new pair of skates"

Many of Andersen's fairy tales follow the formula of a hero emerging triumphant after a long struggle (the great Danish author Isak Dinesen has said that she lived more courageously than she would have, had she not read Andersen throughout her life). Perhaps the epitome of Andersen's fairy tales is "The Snow Queen." In this story, which shifts from the natural to the supernatural world with an uncanny ease, the little boy Kai has imbedded in his heart and his eye splinters from the Devil's glass which render him cold and unfeeling. He is taken away to the kingdom of the Snow Queen, where he is kept prisoner. His little playmate Gerda, all innocence and warmth, travels in pursuit of Kai. She is helped by an old woman with magic powers, by a prince and a princess and their royal crows, by a wild robber girl, and by a reindeer who takes Gerda up to Lapland. When Gerda arrives in Lapland, she meets a wise Finnish woman who tells her that although she can give her a potion that would make her strong as twelve men, Gerda's real power lies within herself.

Gerda eventually succeeds in her mission, thus showing that power and success are very much tied up with goodness and trust. "The Snow Queen" is a true fairy tale in that it deals with moral issues, in that its heroes are human, and by virtue of its happy ending. It is also a triumph of style. In the short space of this story, even the minor characters come to life as vividly as they do in the novels of Andersen's good friend Charles Dickens. Furthermore, the story is suffused with the special wit and keen observation that characterizes all of Andersen's work. The royal crows accept "permanent positions" rather than fly freely: they are as fussy and delightful as characters in a Restoration play. And then there is the irony of the hero being promised "the whole world and a new pair of skates" if he can solve the riddle of life; it is this kind of inspired logic that creates a mood of enchantment.

Fairy tales for adults

Andersen's feeling for nature was so strong that many of his tales feature animals, trees and plants as the main characters. Most famous of these tales is, perhaps, "The Ugly Duckling." So utterly has this tale passed into our collective consciousness that it is surprising to discover

Andersen was often invited to read his stories aloud to groups of adults and children, especially for the families of the aristocracy. But he also had a reputation for compassionate visits to those less fortunate in one way or another, as depicted by a French artist in the scene above, where Andersen is comforting a sick child with some of his tales. The Bettmann Archive.

that the story is wholly the inspiration of one man. Although children love the story, "The Ugly Duckling" is really more of a fairy tale for adults. The duckling turning into a swan represents the kind of radical transformation that doubtless appeals more to adults than to children. What makes "The Ugly Duckling" such a delight to both child and adult, however, is Andersen's particularly uncloying way of rendering the animal world as human. One of the ducks in the story is old and aristocratic, with "Spanish blood in her veins." When Mother Duck and her ducklings parade past this queenly fowl, Mother admonishes her brood: "Don't walk, waddle like well brought up ducklings. Keep your legs far apart, just as your mother and father have always done. Bow your head and say, 'Quack!' " The Ugly Duckling, like the animals in "Inchelina" and "It Is Perfectly True!" has a psychological makeup just like that of a human being. It is this that differentiates Andersen's tales from so many less successful attempts at creating moral parables through the use of animal characters.

An affinity for all things large and small

Although it is relatively easy to identify with a charming little duck, Andersen's imagination was so free he could identify with almost anything. Pine trees, tin soldiers and shirt collars were just as much entitled to real, breathing life as animate things were. No better example of free flights of fantasy exists in Andersen's work than "The Darning Needle." This totally persuasive tale has to do with "a darning needle who was really so fine that she fancied she was a sewing needle."

Through a series of mishaps, the darning needle finds herself in the gutter, being washed away with the flotsam and jetsam. Through it all, she keeps her confidence, holding herself proud and straight because she knows who she is and she knows that she will never change. Within the two or three pages that comprise the story, we witness a comedy of manners almost as telling as a Jane Austen novel and often as lively as a Swift satire. And on top of all else it has to offer, the story is truly and remarkably funny.

The darker side

There is nothing more accessible than traditional fairy tales with happy endings, such as "The Wild Swans," "The Snow Queen" and "The Ugly Duckling." As a result of their popularity, however, the more somber stories of Andersen's have been somewhat overlooked. We have all encountered the gay little tale of Inchelina, but what of that other child found on the leaf of a water lily, the bog king's daughter? In this story of a beautiful but evil girl by day, who becomes an ugly but kind-natured toad at night, we have the Beauty and the Beast combined in one. Eventually goodness conquers evil as it does in most fairy stories, but "The Bog King's Daughter" is a dark-hued tale, with the kind of conflicting-selves motif that can also be found in the works of Joseph Conrad and Henry James.

Another unusual tale included in this collection is "Anne Lisbeth." This stark creation has to do with a young woman who abandons her own illegitimate son to become a wet nurse to a royal child. Her own son lives a horribly deprived life. Eventually lost at sea, he comes back to haunt his mother demanding a burial in hallowed ground. This is a radically different subject for Andersen and demonstrates his amazing versatility.

Perhaps the most chilling of Andersen's stories is "The Shadow." In this brilliant tale, a philosopher from the Northern countries goes to the Mediterranean where his shadow breaks off from him to form an independent life. Sometime later, when the philosopher has returned to Scandinavia, the shadow calls on him. Prosperous now and wed to a princess, the shadow offers its onetime host the chance to survive by becoming the shadow's shadow. The philosopher refuses and is killed; the parasite emerges triumphant. This tale of anxiety and loss of identity is reminiscent of some of the great themes of 20th-century literature.

From sunshine to wormwood

In an often-quoted comment on his stories, Andersen said: "They lay in my thoughts like a seed-corn, requiring only a flowing stream, a ray of sunshine, a drop of wormwood, for them to spring forth and burst into bloom." Indeed, his stories do run the gamut from sunshine to wormwood, from joy to bitterness. Similarly, his life was marked by an extreme sensitivity which led his emotions to run this very same gamut. A word that was even slightly unkind could devastate him; a rose handed him in apology could make him weak with joy. In a letter to his friend Henriette Wulff, he wrote: "My soul is a sensitive plant; when attacked by friends it is unable to put up with anything, however small and trivial." This unique sensibility, it has been proposed, might well have been the source for his treasured fairy tale "The Princess and the Pea," which is the ultimate example of sensitivity.

Although his life was profoundly rewarding and, unlike many another artist, he was raised to the status of folk-hero within his own lifetime, Hans Christian Andersen's own story was, in many ways, a profoundly sad one as well. It was, like a fairy tale, a life that encompassed great adversity and great triumph.

In this drawing by J.H.T. Hanck, made in 1839, the house where Andersen spent most of his childhood (the one in the middle) seems almost a fairy tale creation rather than the place of poverty and deprivation it was. Hans Christian Andersen Museum, Odense.

HANS CHRISTIAN ANDERSEN
(1805-1875)

The peasant boy from Odense

Hans Christian Andersen was born in the city of Odense in 1805. His father was a cobbler; his mother, fifteen years her husband's senior, was a washerwoman. From the very beginning an atmosphere of superstition, myth and magic surrounded him. Odense, an ancient city, was said to have been founded by Odin, the Norse god of victory and death. Furthermore, Hans Christian's mother subscribed wholly to superstitious beliefs, and she plied her young son with stories of the Ellefolk (descendants of Adam's first wife Lilith, who more or less resembled poltergeists) and of the Nisses (tiny red-capped men who made their homes in church steeples and who could be helpful as long as you didn't laugh at them).

Although they were poor, the Andersen family was a happy one. Hans Christian's father was determined to let his son freely choose his own path in life, and although his mother wished for her son to apprentice as a tailor, she was similarly tolerant. Indeed, everyone seemed to indulge Hans Christian for, even though he seemed odd in appearance and manner, he had a special capacity for making himself liked.

A charmed life

After his father's death, Hans Christian worked at two factory jobs, but in both instances his rare singing voice was put to use as amusement for the other workers. Still, the rough ways of the laborers were not for the delicate sensibilities of Hans Christian, and at the age of fourteen years he left home for Copenhagen where he hoped to establish himself in the theater.

His experience in Copenhagen is very much representative of what might be called a charmed life. Despite his poverty, his awkward appearance and his untutored ways, Andersen found wealthy and influential men who sought to be his mentor almost as soon as he arrived in the capital city. Although he suffered such disappointments as being rejected from the Royal Theater, he made a number of devoted friends who would influence and help him for the rest of his life.

From 1822 to 1830, he was educated under a royal grant, a superb opportunity that was marred by a pathologically vicious schoolmaster who was to haunt Andersen's dreams right up to his deathbed. The year 1830 was pivotal for Andersen because he suffered an unhappy and unrequited love affair and also journeyed out of Denmark for the first time, travelling to Germany where he could enjoy, and later publish a book on, the Harz Mountains. It was also during this trip that for the first time he read the Grimm brothers' fairy tales.

A traveling man

There was nothing that Andersen loved more than to travel, and for the next few years he devoted his time to journeying through France, Germany, Switzerland and Italy. He made acquaintance with several distinguished authors during this period, notably Victor Hugo and Heinrich Heine.

On his return to Denmark in 1835, Andersen published a novel based on his Italian experiences entitled *The Im-*

One of the many women Andersen loved in vain was the world famous singer Jenny Lind. Known as "The Swedish Nightingale," her affection for the author was always more sisterly than he wanted it to be. The Bettmann Archive.

provisatore. It was a huge success, overshadowing another development of that year: the publication of his first fairy tales. In the next few years, Andersen would become increasingly absorbed with writing for the theater, while devoting a portion of his energies to the fairy stories as well.

Andersen was fond of pointing out how far he had come from his childhood days in his parents' humble home in Odense. Nothing could better illustrate this fact than the surroundings in which he died, at the Villa Rolighed (above). Culver Pictures.

A number of infatuations with young women led to unhappiness for Andersen. He greatly admired women and liked their company, but the women usually formed sisterly attachments to him. Andersen diverted himself from this failure by further travel, going to Turkey and Austria-Hungary. Back in Denmark, he was much sought after by royalty and aristocracy, a development which he delighted in.

And a national hero

By the 1840s, Andersen was convinced that his greatest talent lay in the writing of fairy stories, and he devoted most of his career to their creation. These tales met with enormous popular and critical acclaim, and he became known as Denmark's greatest writer as well as a national hero. He continued with his travels, and his reputation enabled him to meet many of the leading figures of the day, such as Liszt, Dumas, Mendelssohn and Elizabeth Barrett Browning. In his own lifetime monuments were erected to him in his native city of Odense, and numerous honors were granted him by the monarchy. When he died in 1875, as a result of complications involving bronchitis, the whole world mourned his passing.

Today, over a century later, his grave is never without flowers, his home in Odense is constantly visited by admirers, his stories are never out of print, and there is always some lucky child discovering Hans Christian Andersen for the first time.

Accomplished and marvelous

Just as Andersen's stories have a childlike quality in their boundless ease in realizing the marvels of the imagination, but are, at the same time, skillfully structured creations of an artist who is a master at his craft, so too the illustrations in your Franklin Library edition of Hans Christian Andersen's *Fairy Tales*. Artist Robert Lo Grippo has met the challenge of painting scenes from Andersen's tales that illustrate them without being overwhelmed by them, and he has done this by capturing the essence of Andersen's style—a combination of the authority that comes with the maturity of fully developed skills with the innocence of wonder at the marvelous. Lo Grippo's creations not only complement Andersen's art, they are beautiful and amazing works of art in their own right.

To carry the artwork and the text we chose a specially milled 65-pound Smooth White paper. The design incorporates an innovative use of the illustrations with the text, which was set in a 10-point Trump Medieval typeface. The paper itself has been tested and shown to have a life expectancy of well over three centuries, and with added protection of the 22-karat gold shield formed by the gilt edges of the pages when the book is closed, should last even longer. The entire volume is bound in the finest top grain tan cowhide ornamented with a 22-karat gold cover design incorporating one of Andersen's original paper cuttings.

No domain so boundless

Although his art was never self-conscious, Andersen had very real insight into the nature of his work. He wrote:

> In the whole realm of poetry no domain is so boundless as that of the fairy tale. It reaches from the blood-drenched graves of Antiquity to the pious legends of a child's picture-book; it takes in the poetry of the people and the poetry of the artist. To me it represents all poetry, and he who masters it must be able to put into it tragedy, comedy, naive simplicity, and humor; at his service are the lyrical note, the childlike narrative and the language of describing nature. . . .

The fairy tales of Hans Christian Andersen are boundless and are filled with the spirit of life. His works are illuminated by his special vision of the ways of man and of the world in which he lives, and no modern artist has ever made a more enjoyable, accessible, or lasting statement.

The Editors

THE FRANKLIN LIBRARY
Franklin Center, Pennsylvania
1977

The Franklin Library is the publishing division of The Franklin Mint

Hans Christian Andersen